OPERATION FOOLS MATE 48

M.L Baldwin is a former Tank Commander who joined the Second Royal Tank Regiment in 1996 and served with them on operations in Northern Ireland, Kosovo, Iraq and Afghanistan over a 19 year career. He was awarded a Mentioned in Dispatches (MiD) during his last tour of Afghanistan. After leaving the forces he decided to try his hand at becoming an author, which is where you join him now in his journey. Inspired by the likes of Clive Cussler and Tom Clancy, he wrote his debut series of books for Operation Fools Mate back in 2023 which he hopes people will enjoy reading as much as he enjoyed writing them. This book is book two of the series, and follows directly on from the events of the first book Operation Fools Mate 24. Using his own first hand experiences of life on the front line of combat operations, he hopes to bring a level of realism and excitement to his stories that will both shock and excite his readers. After all, the modern battlefield is full of technology but ultimately, it's the human element and a certain degree of luck that play its part the most. His expertise in his field have garnered widespread acclaim and featured interviews on BBC Radio, whilst his articles in leading publications such as The European, NationalWorld, MSN, the Daily Star (UK), The London Economic and others, have helped solidify his reputation as a sought-after authority in the field. Keep watching for more exciting titles. In his own words, "I'm not finished yet, I'm only just getting started."

Also by M.L Baldwin

THE OPERATION FOOLS MATE SERIES

Operation Fools Mate 24

Operation Fools Mate 48

Operation Fools Mate Deadlock

OPERATION FOOLS MATE

48

By M.L Baldwin

www.mlbaldwin.co.uk

Contents

The 75mm main gun is firing. The 37mm secondary gun is firing, but it's traversed the wrong way. The Browning is jammed. I am saying, "Driver advance!" on the A set, but the driver – who can't hear me – is reversing. And as I look over the top of the turret and see 12 enemy tanks 50 yards away – someone hands me a cheese sandwich."
A Tank Commanders Perspective - Lt Ken Giles Second battle of El-Alamein

Dedicated to all the brave men and women of this great country who in their lifetime have ever had to put on a uniform and put the needs of the country before their own selves.
For all the sacrifice, the hard work, the blood, sweat, and tears,
Thank you.
May you all find peace and happiness in whatever life you choose to settle into.

1

Not To Plan

Bovington Camp 6th Division Headquarters

Colonel Golgolvin and Captain Lunyou stood side by side in the General's office, both men staring straight ahead as Colonel General Igor Kuzmin, Commander in Chief of the Southern forces, stared back at them from across the desk, his face betraying his anger. The Commander in Chief South, or CinCS as he was known to his officers and men, had only arrived that morning, coming straight to the camp with the lead elements of his division after landing at Weymouth. His mood was already foul after he'd endured five weeks couped up in the hull of a modified containership with over fifteen hundred of his soldiers and their equipment. It had slowly transited the 13,000 miles from Eastern Russia through to the Port of Weymouth. At first, he had relished the thought of sneaking through the busy shipping lanes, his men and equipment hiding out of sight as they prepared for the invasion to come, but after only one week at sea, and with no view out of the ship, he and his men had become extremely nauseous. He spent another four days trying to combat the effects of sea sickness that seemed to affect everyone. The memories of half-filled buckets of vomit sloshing around below deck and the incessant smell that seemed to cling to his clothes was one he'd rather forget. It wasn't until well into the second week of the journey, that his men had finally found their sea legs and the roll and pitch of the boat was forgotten. To keep his men active, he'd paired them with some of the ship's navy crew to go topside, to learn the ship's systems in case of an emergency or onboard fire, and to give them a chance at some fresh air and sunlight. So long as his troops on deck wore the customary red or orange coveralls over their uniforms, then no onlookers would know who or what they were looking at on deck. He'd ventured up himself a few times, having been invited onto the bridge to chat to the Admiral in charge of the flotilla. He'd remembered how both men had laughed as they slowly navigated the Suez Canal, as the Admiral had informed him that the twelve ships in front of them and the twenty behind, were all theirs, converted freighters, each carrying their own deadly cargos bound for the UK. The General had simply smiled at the onlookers on shore, as they frantically waved back at the great ships, unaware of the destruction and death they were carrying onboard.

General Kuzmin was sat at his desk, silently staring at the two men in thought. Behind them, in the huge offices, they could hear the officers and men of his headquarters setting up the temporary command post. He could feel his body still fighting the urge to constantly roll or pitch, in some imaginary sea as his mind played tricks on him and, he wondered how long the effects of being at sea would last. The thought was quickly lost to him as he focussed on the matter at hand, finally breaking the silence.

"Colonel Golgolvin, I seem to recall your orders were to capture this base and all of its armoured vehicles and tanks. You were about to explain to me how you failed this objective even though you had the benefit of complete surprise and tactical advantage?"

He watched the Colonel swallow, his Adams apple bobbing in his throat as he looked down to him and spoke confidently.

"General, those were my orders; however, the camp was already on high alert and some of the British vehicles were already preparing to leave as my men completed the drop. The light conditions were not favourable and we were seen from the ground by the enemy, eliminating any chance of surprise. When we landed, I met with Captain Lunyou, whose orders were to keep eyes on the camp and secure my drop zone. He informed me that he'd already attacked the camp earlier in the day, alerting the British and forcing his own unit to pull out of the area. When we arrived at the camp, one of the British tanks was already prepared for us and waiting in an ambush position. My Sprut tanks were unsuccessful in destroying it and it delayed us long enough to allow the others to escape. That is why we failed in fulfilling the full objective."

General Kuzmin looked over to the Captain furiously, "Is this true? Did you attack the camp without orders?"

The FSB Captains face shone with sweat as he replied coldly, "No General, we did not attack the camp, we merely defended ourselves, the British attacked us as we were quietly observing the camp."

"They attacked you. How? Were you seen?" he asked suspiciously.

"One of my men was in the process of investigating a phone box, we'd observed a man using it, and wanted to know how it was still working after disrupting the phone systems. My Sergeant was on his way to sabotage it, when the man in question suddenly attacked him."

"A phone box?" General Kuzmin replied, disgusted, his mouth set in a sneer as his voice began to rise. "A PHONE BOX! So, this whole operation was put at risk because of a phone box? Is that why we now find ourselves playing priyatki with the British?"

The Captain said nothing as he continued, his eyes narrowing, "Attacked him with what?"

"Sir?"

"You said your Sergeant was attacked by this stranger, so what was he attacked with? Was the man armed?"

"With his fists," the Captain replied, the tension in his voice clear to hear.

"HIS FISTS?" he shouted back, as he continued unbelievingly, "so how did it escalate to you shooting at the camp?"

"The man had already taken my Sergeant's pistol and was firing indiscriminately into the air," he lied. "Once the sentries on the gate heard the shooting, the guards were alerted and came over carrying weapons. I was forced to take action, otherwise my Sergeant would have been captured. We extracted ourselves and then carried out our orders to secure the drop zone for the Colonel and his men."

"And in doing so, you lost us our eyes on the camp," the General added, "had you been there you would have seen what the British were up to or maybe even attempted to stop them."

He shook his head angrily as he stood up, with both hands planted on the table, his tone accusatory. "Well from the sounds of this Sergeant, you would have been better off letting him get captured if he fights as poorly as that! An unarmed man simply takes one of our FSB operator's pistols and then makes a mockery of you both. To think you were the first of our forces that the British got to fight, a very *poor* example of an FSB officer." The General shook his head with disdain.

Captain Lunyou said nothing, choosing to wisely keep quiet and remained standing to attention.

General Kuzmin's eyes were drawn to a picture frame that had fallen over on the desk as he stood up. He turned it over, seeing a family picture of a man with his wife and two kids. He guessed the photo had belonged to the officer whose office he now inhabited. He reached over to a stack of papers, noting they were addressed to the Colonel of the camp. So, this *was* the Colonel's office, he thought.

He walked over to the open window in the office, picking up the picture frame from the desk, hurling it outside, watching with some satisfaction as it smashed on the floor below. He turned to the Captain his voice acidic, "Captain you're lucky that General Terekhov still needs you, otherwise you and your men, would now be swimming the distance I've just had to sail to get here. For now, you're dismissed, leave us, and I want that fool of a Sergeant dismissed from your unit by the end of the day."

"Yes Sir!" the Captain replied loudly, as he saluted and left the office. The CinCS watched him go, noting the Captain arrogantly left the door wide open. He was about to shout after him but thought better of it. One of the General's staff outside closed the door, allowing both men privacy. The General visibly relaxed resuming his seat behind the desk, removing his hat and throwing it casually onto the desk. The Colonel still stood there, wondering what else the General had to say.

After a moment General Kuzmin sighed and looked up pointing to the chair opposite, his voice calmer. "Ok Yuri, take a seat, we both know where the blame lies in this failure. And it's not with you."

Golgolvin sat down with a questioning look on his face, after the dressing down he'd just received. Seeing the look, Kuzmin answered, "Yuri you've served with me these past five years, your record in Crimea and Ukraine speaks volumes. However, that little bastard's dad is one of the President's closest friends and just so happens to own all the nation's media companies. I guarantee that what we say and do in front of him, will end up back in the ears of his father before the day is out. I couldn't be seen to blame him totally for the failure, he'd simply go and cry to daddy and then they'd blame it all on you. This way, at least he thinks I'm unhappy with you both, and his dad will keep it all buried out of the ears and eyes of the people. By tomorrow, the proud Russian people will be reading all about how little Lunyou saved the day and helped *you* take this camp."

"If that's the case General, then his dad will probably say he parachuted in on his own and took on the camp single handed." his tone sardonic.

"Yes," he replied smirking, "he probably will. But so long as his dad has the ear of the President, you'd be well advised to watch yourself around him. Even your rank won't protect you and if he wanted to, he could make your life difficult." Golgolvin grimaced, as he remembered making the Captain run to the camp last night after relieving him of his 4x4.

Kuzmin leaned back in the chair as he continued, "How many men and vehicles did you lose last night in taking the camp?"

Golgolvin answered immediately, "Twelve men killed and six wounded and we lost one of our Typhoon vehicles. Three of my men died trying to put out the flames in the hangars, they were hoping to save at least one of the enemy tanks from the fire, but they found out too late that the fire reacted to the water." Seeing the confused look on the CinCS he added, "The British had made a sort of napalm using sugar and diesel, the water acted like a catalyst, the more we put on it, the hotter it burned. I think it was based on the Greek fire I learned about in history class at school. We found out from some of the prisoners that their Garrison Sergeant Major was a chemist long before he was a soldier, but he was killed in the fighting. Shame, because I really would have loved to have known how it was made."

"Your men that died, do you wish to recommend any for bravery?"

"No," Golgolvin replied, a look of disdain on his face. "We failed in taking the camp and those tanks. Casualties or not, I do not want to see us rewarding failure, it would set a bad example to our troops."

The General nodded in understanding as he added, "And did you find out why the British were evacuating the camp? Did they know we were coming?"

"I don't know yet General, we've only been able to interrogate their junior soldiers, all their senior officers either escaped in the vehicles, or were killed in the fighting defending the camp. One of the prisoner's did mention however a man being detained after Captain Lunyou's attack on the camp that afternoon who was held and questioned in the guard room. Could it be one of Lunyou's men was captured and talked perhaps?"

"Unlikely," he said dismissively, "the British wouldn't have had the time to glean that information from him, and besides, their interrogation techniques are far more cultured than ours or the Americans. Our FSB operatives would take days, perhaps even weeks to crack, no, there must be something we're missing. For now, I want you to hand those prisoners over to Captain Lunyou and his men, as annoyed as I am, he and his men do have a certain talent for extracting information."

Golgolvin nodded as the General then asked, "Yuri, in your estimation, from what you've seen of the camp and from what you've been told, how many vehicles do you think got away last night?"

He pulled a notebook out of his leg pocket, quickly scanning though the pages as he replied, "We could be looking at eleven of their heavy tanks, some of those could be training tanks though, and between eight to ten warriors, that's the British version of our BMP3. Also, there were some lighter armoured vehicles, mainly equipment that they used previously in Afghanistan, wheeled I think, and some engineer vehicles. There were also four tanks in Lulworth, these had a new prototype gun fitted that the British were trialling for their newer tank. By the time we got our forces across to them, they'd managed to get away in the darkness. I was hoping that we would come across them and destroy them on the way in from Weymouth, but so far, they've vanished without a trace."

Kuzmin rubbed his chin thinking to himself as he replied cautiously, "That's still a lot of enemy armour out there somewhere Yuri, and I don't want it left unchecked."

Golgolvin raised an eyebrow in surprise at the General's caution, replying, "But it's only eleven tanks General, with little ammunition and no support. Our units should be able to dispatch them easily enough, even if we didn't have control of the air. Leave them to the tanks of the 350th General, our T-90's will make mincemeat of them."

The General went silent as he sat thinking, drumming his fingers on the desk. Seeing something was troubling him Golgolvin asked. "What is it General? What's on your mind?"

He looked up, pursing his lips in thought before replying softly. "There are no T-90 tanks."

"What?" Golgolvin replied confused. "But the 350th Tank Regiment? The new brigades? Surely, they'd want them here?"

The CinCS shook his head slowly, "Yuri, the tanks, the new brigades, the regiments we trained with, the whole of the damn 4th Division, all of it has been sent to Ukraine without my knowledge. High command has deemed that to be the new priority."

"New priority?" he blurted out quickly. "But that was our most experienced force, men who'd fought in Ukraine with us, the combat experience alone was worth its weight in gold. We've been training with them for nearly a year! And the tanks, General, we need them to win here. How is it that we're no longer the priority?"

He shrugged his shoulders and replied, "High command's recent intelligence assessment of the British was that its army is weakened and spread too thinly, what with the NATO commitments in Latvia, Estonia and Poland. The people here are ready for a regime change, fed up with the government and its constant bickering. They won't oppose us, not when they suspect they're under attack from their own. They regarded the 4th Division as too good to use here, so have sent it to combat the latest Ukrainian counter offensive. Some elements in Moscow believe that we can finally win by using our best forces there."

"Our best forces?" Golgolvin replied irritated, "and what are we supposed to use? I thought we were the main effort. Which units came over on the ships?"

The General lent back in his chair, "We sailed with a new division, called the 6th shock force, made up of fresh new units recently formed from the mass conscriptions. I only found this out once when we boarded the ships, I was as surprised as you are to hear. By then it was too late, the 4th Division was being sent to Ukraine and the 6th was already loaded up on the ships."

"Conscriptions?" Golgolvin looked puzzled as he continued doubtfully, "I thought the conscriptions were for a home defence force, to defend the country whilst we were away? Surely General, you can't mean to tell me, that this whole operation has now been left to raw recruits? Troops that have never seen combat before. We're expected to pull this operation off, with *green* troops?"

"They're not *all* green troops Yuri," the General countered in defence. "We've seeded some very capable officers within the regiments and made sure that the five weeks on board those ships were spent in constant training."

"But General, training on a ship is nothing like training on the ground, we've trained for months with the 4th Division for this very operation, to pull them out at the last minute, and replace them, it seems like-"

"Be careful Colonel," the General interrupted, "be careful what you say, even in here."

Golgolvin nodded, understanding the implications, the General was warning him that the walls always had ears, and no-one's ears were more tuned in, than those of the FSB.

"Besides Colonel, these are *Russian* troops, they've all been trained to the same standards as us. Regardless of whether we have worked with them or not, they'll know what we expect of them, all will do their duty."

"And their equipment?" Golgolvin replied, "if not the T-90 then what do they have for tanks?"

"The 6th Division has the latest versions of the T-80 and T-72, all re-purposed for the task. Good tanks Yuri, old designs, but good."

Golgolvin said nothing as the General sat smiling confidently at him. Golgolvin had seen for himself how badly these tanks had performed in Ukraine. And the word 're-purposed' to him meant that they were simply given a new lick of paint and a clean bill of health. Surely, he thought, they were not serious, someone must have made a mistake. He remembered during the build-up training, watching on proudly at seeing how effective the T-90 was, its main gun far superior to the western tanks and its Shorny Oriel self defence systems were impressive, able to jam and confuse the most advanced targeting systems known to the west. Now, he thought bitterly, they were gone, gifted to another commander on another battlefield. Now he had to go with what he had. Sensing his doubts the General added, "We have the numbers Yuri, more than enough for what we need to do. Their army is scattered like dust in a breeze, unprepared for us."

"But General, we're not facing an inexperienced foe, this is the British Army, weakened or not, they'll-"

"Pah!" the General interrupted waving his hand, "come Yuri, you don't believe all that NATO propaganda, do you?"

Golgolvin kept quiet, as the General continued, his voice more confident, "Now listen Yuri, we've got to play with the hand we're dealt with, yes, our troops are inexperienced, but within one day on the battlefield they'll learn all they need to learn. How much experience did our great grandfathers have when they went to war to fight against the Nazis?" The General's eyebrows raised to emphasise the point he was trying make as he continued.

"My great grandfather was a farmer one day and a war hero the next, credited with destroying twenty tanks, all with no training and no experience. Our men won't need long until they're bloodied and then the British can prance and march around all they want, telling everyone how great they are.

"But their army is-" Golgolvin tried to interject.

"WE HAVE THE NUMBERS COLONEL!" General Kuzmin's fists thumped on the desk, silencing him as he yelled.

Golgolvin sat in silence, wondering what pressure the General was under. He'd known this man for years and had never seen him dismiss Golgolvins concerns so easily or shout him down.

The General abruptly stood up irritated, walking back over to the window and looking out again at the camp. He shook his head in frustration, he hadn't meant to raise his voice, he trusted the man before him. Of course, he understood the problems they faced, Golgolvin had no idea that he had already sent up the same arguments, had the same thoughts, had tried to argue and reason with Moscow, but eventually the answer that had come back was the same to all the Generals concerns. "Do the job, with what you have, or we'll find someone who can."

After a few moments he looked back over to Golgolvin, his voice softer. "Look, Yuri, we've been ordered to remain in place for now and finish offloading the division's equipment and troops, it's taking more time than we first planned to get everything off loaded. I'm expecting a delay of around sixteen hours."

Golgolvin tried to keep his voice low as he exclaimed, "Sixteen hours! But General, I thought speed was essential? Surely the ships are loaded with the regiments ready to go? Wasn't that part of the plan all along? The logistics were supposed to be ready to go so that we could be on the move almost immediately."

The General held up his hand to calm him as he continued, "Yes, Yuri, that's what was *supposed* to happen; however, it looks like the ships were not loaded according to the plan. All the logistical officers responsible for loading the ships and equipment belonged to the 4th Division, remember? The last-minute changes meant people were rushed into position without the proper planning. Now I've got the 6th Division regiments and battalions split over multiple ships, some carrying vehicles, others carrying crews. I've got ships docked in Poole carrying soldiers, whose equipment is in Portland. It's a bloody mess Yuri, and we need those sixteen hours to sort it out."

"But General," he stammered, "surely Moscow needs to be told of this, someone needs to be accountable. How could this happen?"

The General shrugged, sitting back down at the desk. "Sure, I could send back reports blaming people, of course, but no-one cares Yuri. I'm in charge, the blame would come back to me. So why complain? Better to get on with it, we're here now and that's all that matters."

Golgolvin looked on confused as the General asked, "What's the condition of your own airborne brigade?"

Thinking quickly he replied, "I've got 568 men and the first six of our twenty-four Havoc gunships from the ships in dock. But I've only received five of my transport helicopters, my lift capacity will be limited. I was expecting to have had the other thirty Hind helicopters off loaded, armed and ready to fly before the end of the day, but after what you've just told me…"

"Forget your missing helicopters for now," the General interrupted, "if you had to go with just the ones you have now, then, how soon can you leave?"

"We can be ready to go within the hour General, but my men are still in charge of the security of this camp, we'd need to handover to someone else."

"Okay Yuri, I want you to hand over control of camp security to the 344th Infantry and then get your unit ready to move."

"Where are we going?"

"The tanks that were allowed to get away, were to have been destroyed or captured already. Now thanks to that young imbecile Lunyou, we don't know where they are or what they're up to. I can't just simply ignore them and now you know the state of our forces, you can understand the importance of knowing our flanks are secure. I want you to take whatever helicopters you have ready to find and pursue the enemy. Give them no time to re-group Yuri. Our offensive resumes sixteen hours from now and I want the enemy on the run for all that time, not waiting in defensive positions for us."

Golgolvin stood up to attention, his face fierce with determination, keen to make amends for last night's failure.

"I will see to it General, you have my word."

The CinCS nodded in response, looking up at him. "Good luck Colonel."

Golgolvin saluted and left the room quickly, his head full of the many hundreds of things he now needed to get organised. He looked at his watch, knowing his men would be already enjoying their breakfast. Smiling to himself, he knew, as much as they'd grumble about missing the meal, they'd be more than happy at the thought of hunting the enemy again. He walked out into the bright rays of the morning sun, seeing the flag of Tumat flapping in the breeze outside the newly appointed headquarters building. He watched it for a few seconds, wondering if anyone really paid any attention to it, an alien flag of a foreign country that none of them felt any affinity to. Leaving those thoughts for now, he walked briskly across the camp, towards the cookhouse. It was time to go and get his men, it was time to go hunting...

2

Sam

The Farm

It took them just fifteen minutes to get the vehicles into the giant barn, which Mike reckoned was big enough to have accommodated another four tanks, as finally, the last vehicle was manoeuvred into position. The tank was left till last, being reversed in, its long barrel pointing outwards, but still hidden from view in the giant barn. As the vehicle engine's shut down, the exhausted soldiers fell from the vehicles, the tiredness plain to see in the slow lethargic way they shuffled about, their eyes dull and red rimmed. Mike was stood by the barn door, still chatting to the farmer, when the two Corporals came over to join them. "Guys, this is Sam, he's offered us a bed for the day, we can stay here till nightfall and leave tonight."

Both soldiers shook the farmer's hands, grateful for the roof now above their heads.

"Thank you, Sam, for letting us stay."

Sam merely waved his hands, obviously uncomfortable with the compliments.

Turning to them both, Mike said, "Look I'm not telling you how to do your jobs, I know everyone's tired and we all want to get our heads down. But, before we do can I recommend we get a roving sentry, armed and ready to go, but keep them out of sight from outside. Also, we'll need someone on the radio, listening out, someone may still be trying to raise us. Doubtful, but you never know."

Both men nodded, Patty replying, "If you're happy writing out the list for the ground sentry Spider, I'll sort out the radio list?"

"Yeah mate," Spider replied as Mike continued, "I'd also recommend we use the back of one of your vehicles for the radio stag. Not Two-One-Alpha though, we need somewhere to put Private Jackson before we do that, agreed?"

"Yeah agreed," both men nodded glumly.

Watching them both walk away, Mike felt the eyes of the farmer staring at him with curious amusement as he asked.

"Say, that's a strange relationship for a soldier, you recommend this, and you agree with that? The army seems to be a bit more diplomatic and softer than I remember."

Looking back at him he smiled, "I'm not army Sam, at least not anymore, I'm civilian, got swept up in all this yesterday. Now I'm kind of an advisor, helping this lot to get where they're going."

"And where are they going?"

Guffawing Mike replied, "I don't know! I thought I did, but now, I really don't know. For now, we're here, and this is as good as it gets, tomorrow, who knows. We'll cross that bridge when we get to it."

"Unless some fucker's already blown that bridge!" Sam replied jokingly.

"Yeah, well if that's the case then we'll bloody swim across it, now, how about you tell me how you knew all about cam and concealment back there by the woods, you ex-army yourself?"

Laughing loudly, the farmer exclaimed, "Am I bollocks! I'm ex-navy son, 45 Commando, retired now for oooh best part of thirty years. Been running this farm ever since it was left to me and my wife."

"Commando?" Mike joked, "when the hell were you guys learning how to hide in woods? I thought all you lot spent your time on the water? Tanning yourselves on the decks of boats, and scaring away the ladies?"

The eyes of the farmer seemed to take on a distant look as he replied, "The Falklands, 1982, the battle of Two Sisters. Sat on an exposed hilltop, with the enemy on higher ground firing rifles and mortars at you all day and night. You sit there long enough, take enough casualties, and you quickly learn all you need to about cam and concealment."

Mike hadn't meant to upset or insult the former Commando, especially with all the kindness he'd offered. He quickly replied, "Shit, I'm sorry Sam, I didn't mean to be disrespectful."

The farmer snapped back out of his thoughts, his eyes focusing on Mike as he playfully slapped his arm, "What? Don't be daft army, I'm thicker skinned than that!"

Mike smiled more out of relief than humour. Looking back towards the vehicles he could see some of the soldiers were removing jackets and body armour, attempting to get themselves comfortable around the barn areas to snatch whatever sleep they could.

Mike was tired, he wanted to sleep, but before he could, he knew there was one more thing to do. He turned back to the farmer.

Sam, do you have a waterproof cover? Something like a tarpaulin that I can have."

Thinking quickly the farmer replied, "Sure, there's one at the back of the barn, I'll go get it now if you follow me. "

Both men walked past the vehicles and bodies now sleeping and headed towards the back of the barn. On the floor, covered in hay sat a blue tarpaulin, Sam picked it up, shaking it off and stating, "It's a bit dirty, but it should do for what you want."

Nodding in thanks and seeing it was more than large enough Mike picked it up, walked over to the back of Two-One-Alpha and opened the door, leaving the farmer at the back of the barn. Looking inside the vehicle, Mike felt annoyed and guilty. He'd left her looking peacefully at rest, now with her body being unstrapped, it had rolled around the floor of the vehicle during the journey. Now she was lying face down, looking macabre and undignified, rigor mortis making her arms look unnatural. The blood had pooled and covered her face and matted her hair. Climbing inside and cursing himself for not tying her down, he began laying the tarpaulin on the floor, the plan being to roll the body into it, saving the others from having to see her body again. Death was never pretty, Mike thought, and the young soldiers did not need reminding just yet of such things. He stopped suddenly, as he saw the farmer by the vehicle door, the look of shock on his face as he took in the picture before him.

"Sam, sorry I didn't mean for you to see this."

"But...when you said you wanted a tarpaulin...I never thought you meant..." before he could say anything further, the farmer reached in, snatching the tarpaulin away. Mike thought at first, he was angry at getting the tarp covered in blood, but then the farmer continued, his voice softer than before, "I'll not let you wrap the poor lass in this, its covered in muck, sheep shit and straw. She deserves better than that. Give me a moment, I'll be right back." The farmer disappeared for a few minutes before returning with a larger black heavy-duty bag with zip. Handing it to Mike he explained, "It's a body bag for the cows, in case we lose one, after foot and mouth we went and brought a load. Its new, waterproof, clean and dignified, and better than a tarpaulin." The farmer stepped inside and unzipped it, laying it out alongside the dead soldier and between them both, they carefully picked up the body, making sure her arms were inside and the blonde hair clear of the heavy zip as the bag was closed. The farmer quickly tied up the straps, adjusting the size so the excess fabric was wrapped around her body tightly. Mike saw a tear streak down the farmer's cheek, quickly wiped away as he asked, "Sam, you okay? I'm sorry, I didn't expect you to help me with this."

"Oh, I'm okay army, don't you worry about me, it's not the first time I've had to put people into bags. It's just...been a while since, and I'd forgotten just how young they looked," his voice quiet.

"Do you have somewhere we could put her body? Somewhere cool perhaps? With the heat of the day, I don't want-"

"Reefer." Sam quickly interrupted, "I've got a refrigerated container behind the barn, its packed full of meat, but I'll clear some room."

The farmer stepped out and went off to the back of the barn, picking up a trolley as he went. After five minutes he came back, quieter than before, the empty trolley in tow.

"Right, I've made room for the young lady, the company's going to be poor, but I don't think she'll complain."

Carefully and with little effort, they loaded her onto the cart, wheeling her out of the back door towards the huge walk-in freezer. Feeling the icy blast as the door opened, Mike shivered as both men stepped across the floor to the area the farmer had cleared, setting the black body bag on the floor. As Mike walked away, he looked back to see the farmer kneeling, straightening out the bag, making sure it was all perfect. Mike sighed; he hoped after what the farmer had seen already in his life, he hadn't awakened the demons of old. Finally satisfied, the farmer stood and walked outside, closing the door behind them, a welcome respite from the cold. Both men stood there quietly watching, as the first rays of the sun started to appear over the woods.

"Sam, do you have a bucket and some water I can use? Also, some soap if you can spare it?"

Grunting in acknowledgment, the farmer walked off, Mike following, back to the outside of the barn area, where an assortment of brushes, buckets, a hosepipe and industrial detergent was stored.

"There's water there, cold only and a mop. When you've finished with it all, don't put it back there with the others, throw it over there on the burn pile at the other end of yard."

"Thanks Sam," Mike replied, watching as the farmer walked over to the big green tractor parked in the yard, opening it up and starting the engine. Without another word or looking over, he simply drove out of the yard and up to the woodland, the plough already beginning the work of hiding the tank tracks, before someone came looking.

Leaving him to it, and deciding there were no more words to say, Mike took the buckets and brushes inside.

An hour later, he stood admiring his handiwork, he'd tried his best with the light he had in the barn, but even so, most of the blood was now gone from the back of the vehicle. The only sign now of something ever being wrong was the two buckets full of used mop heads, the blood drying to them already and the black bag full of old rags that he'd used to clean up. He quickly checked over the back of the wagon to check he hadn't left anything behind and was about to leave when out of the corner of his eye he saw a bag jammed into the far corner. Thinking it was rubbish he pulled on the bag, its edge catching on the seat, as the bag slipped out of his wet hands and spilled its contents on the floor. Looking down in surprise he saw a large sum of money spill out, the notes crumpled and dog eared. Who did this belong to, he thought. He quickly scooped the money back up, trying not to get it wet as he re-tied the bag and put it back where he found it. He didn't know who it belonged to, but knew it was none of his business and was too tired to care. Hopefully no-one would know he'd touched it. He left the vehicle and walked out of the barn, towards the burn pile, throwing the used items carefully onto the pile, then seeing in the light of day his blood-stained arms, went back to use the hosepipe to clean himself up. Ten minutes later he staggered towards the tank, the snores coming from those around him already asleep. Climbing back onboard, his foot slipped on the turret, hitting the smoke grenade dischargers, the metal gashing his leg, the pain dull and easily forgotten as in a daze, with eyes burning from fatigue, he made his way onto the engine decks. Settling down from memory on what he deemed to be the most comfortable part of the back deck, and feeling the warmth from the engine decks still seeping through, he closed his eyes and fell into a deep sleep.

Mike was standing on a beach, the sun shining, as Kate was laughing waist deep in the water, splashing around and calling to him. He couldn't hear what she was saying, so he walked closer towards the water, watching as it receded, as if the tide was going out and Kate moving with it. What was she saying? He struggled to hear her, cocking his head and straining to listen, but the noise of the waves crashing against the beach was too loud. He shouted back, calling her to come to him, to move closer but she just kept laughing, beckoning for him to join her. He walked closer again, expecting to feel the cool water on his legs, but the tide again moved backwards, just out of reach, taking Kate with it. What was going on, he thought as he began to walk faster, breaking into a jog, but still, the sea kept moving faster and further away from him, Kate still moving with it, why didn't she come to him, he thought angrily. He started yelling to her, she was moving further away, more distant this time, now he panicked, beginning to run, faster and faster, suddenly he was sprinting, as fast as he could, shouting at the top of his voice, Kate was now a dot in the distance, still waving and laughing. Suddenly he tripped and fell over onto the hot sand, feeling the warmth on his body. Lying there he tried to get up, suddenly a hand appeared out of the sand, it looked decayed and old, the flesh rotten and the fingernails long and sharp, grabbing him roughly, shaking him, then another hand appeared, and another, suddenly there were hands everywhere, grabbing Mike, pulling him, shaking him, shoving him. He tried to fight back, to use his training, but he couldn't remember anything, he didn't have the strength. In the distance he heard another voice getting louder and louder until suddenly realising, he shot up, awake, his eyes open. He'd been dreaming. He still had his jacket pulled up over his face, he'd placed it there to block out the light from the sun as he felt rough hands shaking him again. "For fuck's sake mate, wake up will you, you're on stag!" the owner of the voice sounded frustrated.

Removing the jacket and sitting up, Mike looked up at the sentry standing above him. Recognising the soldier, Mike tried to remember his name. Was it Fusilier Kerr, didn't they call him Jo? Recognising the word 'stag' that soldiers used to describe sentry duty, Mike guessed the Corporals had put him on one of the guard duties, not that he minded, he was more than happy to pull his weight.

"I'm awake," Mike replied, as he saw the soldier about to shake him again. "What stag am I on?"

"Oh shit, sorry *Sir*, I didn't know it was you, sorry I'm after your driver. It's for ground stag *Sir*." Mike noticed the tone was sarcastic, and the young Fusilier kept overemphasising the use of the word 'Sir'. As his sleep addled brain began to kick in, he suddenly thought, of course, this was Jonah's driver, no doubt the gift was still giving. Leaning over the side of the vehicle, he pointed to the figure lying prone and snoring away happily. "There you go Fusilier, there's my driver, he was right in front of you all along. You must have walked past him to get to me," Mike's tone accusing.

Smirking, the soldier stepped back over Mike and made his way down to wake up his relief. Mike got up, rolling up his jacket and stowing it behind the commander's hatch, watching as the sentry walked to the backdoor of one of the Warriors. He saw Jonah sat inside, wearing a radio headset, with one leg lazily dangling out of the open door and swinging idly, a look of amusement on his face as he stared back at him. Mike stared back, clapping his hands quietly in silent acknowledgement, noting the age-old trick he had seen played out before on annoying officers. Waking up the wrong person for a duty, could, and did, happen by mistake; but sometimes people would do it out of spite, Mike had seen some soldiers be woken three or four times at night, ruining what little sleep they could get by angry junior soldiers. He hoped that this would stop, because he really didn't want to be playing these spiteful games with everything that was going on. Happily, he watched as Jonah, reacting to Mike's silent clapping, angrily disappeared from view into the back of the vehicle. Knowing he wouldn't be able to sleep anymore, Mike turned, stepping down off the tank and walking over to the barn door, leaning against it, stretching off his aching arms and legs and stifling a yawn as he listened to the sounds of the farm. In the distance, he could see Sam, on his tractor, still ploughing the fields, removing all evidence that the tracked vehicles had ever been in that area of the woods that bordered his farm. He watched as the farmer's wife walked towards him across the farm courtyard, carrying a tray of assorted cups of all shapes and sizes, smiling to him as she approached. Already the sun was up and shining, the rays pouring through the cracks in the barn roof, creating circles of light on the floor. He looked at his watch, it was 09:57. He'd been asleep for four hours. It had only felt like five minutes. He wasn't sure whether it was the sun shining in his eyes, his neck hurting from lying on the tank's back decks or the need to be awake and alert that stopped him from getting back to sleep, but with the sounds of snoring still coming from the vehicles parked from view in the barn, he knew it was worthless to try. Clearly others were not struggling to sleep.

He smiled as the farmer's wife approached him, her face warm and welcoming.

"I thought you could all do with some tea," she said, "I've got more cups in the house, I'm just waiting for the kettle to boil. When everyone wakes up, I'll start to cook some bacon sandwiches for you all."

Mike smiled gratefully, "Look, Mrs Collins, this is really generous of you. Please don't go to any bother though, I don't want you to be put out."

Carefully placing the tray down besides Mike, she looked up grinning, "Now don't you go being daft, from the looks of you all this morning you could do with some food and it's the least we can do for you. Besides I'm happy for the company, sometimes Sam can be a grumpy old sod! And none of this Mrs Collins either, its Mary to you."

Mike happily accepted the mug of tea, as she asked, "So bacon sarnies, how many of you are there?"

"Sixteen..." then realising quickly he added regretfully, "no, sorry Mary I mean fifteen, there's fifteen of us."

Seeing the shadow cross his face, Mary wisely decided not to push the issue. Had the farmer spoken to his wife already, Mike thought. She put an arm on his shoulder giving him a little squeeze before picking up the tray and walking in amongst the sleeping mass of bodies. Mike heard some of the guys immediately waken at the thought of hot food and drink, hearing the voice of Corporal Patterson waking them up. "Lads, Mrs Collins has brought hot drinks if you want it and there's bacon sarnies on the way."

Cupping his mug, he looked out to the fields, thinking back to the previous night, seeming a lifetime ago; had it only been last night, he thought, as the past hours events played out in his mind. He watched the farmer, sat alone in the cab, ploughing methodically through the fields, almost all the military tracks gone, removing any trace they were there.

Enjoying the tea, his belly began to grumble, the thought of the bacon sandwiches beginning to really make him hungry. It also made him realise, that they had nothing with them, sure they had some weapons, and the vehicles, but usually they'd have sleeping bags, food, water, torches, the army always prided itself on being self-sufficient. In their current state they were no more than beggars, it was only down to the charity of Sam and Mary that they had somewhere relatively safe to stay now.

Quickly realising their predicament, he realised something would have to be done. But not right now, first there was the matter of the bacon sandwich, that would have to come first. He'd wait until the soldiers had some more rest and some food in them before he talked through the plans for the day.

Twenty minutes later and Mary was the most popular person in the barn, as along with Sam, they came back over carrying trays piled high with bacon sandwiches. Mike nodded in thanks as he took one of the doorstop sized wedges, his mouth aching in anticipation as he hungrily tucked in. The trays were being passed down the line of hungry soldiers and for once, it was quiet in the barn, no-one spoke as the only sound was munching and the smacking of lips as the sandwiches were devoured. Mike looked over to see Rachel, the big Fijian, Changa standing protectively by her side, she was still quiet, but at least she was eating, a good sign, Mike thought. Everyone was smiling, the tensions from the previous night seeming to ease slightly thanks to a bit of sleep and some food. Mike waited until he was sure the two Corporals had finished eating, before walking over to sit opposite them on a hay bale, away from the ears of the others.

"Hey guys."

They both looked up and smiled as Spider replied, "Morning Mike. I have to say, top marks on finding this place, breakfast in bed doesn't get any better than this."

"I've got to be honest it was more luck than judgement, besides Sam's the one we should thank. Without him, we'd be up on that hill, I looked out at it earlier, he was right, even if we had cam nets, in daylight, we'd be visible from the ground and the air. Coming in here was a good move."

They both agreed, nodding as Mike continued, "Look, I think we'll all agree that none of us were prepared for this, I haven't even got a clue what we've got on the tank, let alone what kit you've got in the stowage bins of your own vehicles."

Patty looked behind him to the troops sat about as he replied, "You thinking it would be a good idea to get the lads and lass on the wagons, go through them, and see what we have kit wise?"

"I do," Mike replied, "we don't know when, or if, we might need tow ropes or towing gear to get a bogged vehicle out, we don't know what tools we have, if there's any food on board, any water, not to mention personal gear. Do any of you guys have any because I don't? I need a sleeping bag, warm gear and after last night's little bit of fun, I could certainly do with a torch."

Patty nodded, "Mike, I don't think anyone has any of that gear and if we don't have it, what do you suggest? I don't see any QM's stores local to here."

"Let's find out what we do have first, let's check the vehicles like you said and get the guys to tell us what kit they do have. Also regards the weapons, let's make sure the ammo is dished out evenly, each vehicle should have one personal weapon, then if a vehicle gets split from the others going forward, we're not all totally defenceless."

"Okay," replied Spider, "that's not a bad idea. At least a kit check will keep everyone's minds focused on something, I suppose the last thing we want is them to be bored and start thinking too much. We'll get them all on it after we've finished chatting."

The men stopped talking as Fusilier Kerr walked over, seeing Mike with the Corporals, he looked awkwardly at the floor, his actions that morning still fresh in Mike's mind.

"What's up Jo?" Patty asked, looking up at him.

"Err Jonah's told me to come over, to tell you that girl's body that was in the back of our wagon, it gone. Someone's taken it."

"What do you mean taken it, taken it where?" Spider stood up abruptly, staring angrily at the Fusilier.

"I removed her body last night, me and the farmer," Mike said leaning back, playing with a piece of hay that he plucked from the bale he sat on. As all three looked back at him he continued, "Last night when we got in, I got the farmer to help me, he's got a refrigerated container out the back. We wrapped her up in a body bag and carried her out to the freezer. In a heat like this, you wouldn't want her still laying in the back of that wagon. I got a bucket and some water and cleaned up the mess that was left in the wagon, it's not perfect and could probably do with going over again, but it'll do for now and saves your guys the job."

"Why would you do that yourself?" Spider asked incredulous.

"Because I've done it before, it's not nice, especially for the younger guys to have to mop all that up. Besides the guys needed the sleep more than I did." As Mike said that last part, he stared directly at Jo, to emphasise the point. The Fusilier gulped and looked to the floor, feeling more uncomfortable now, as he realised the man he had messed with earlier had just done him a favour, saving him a job he would no doubt be doing now.

Looking at Jo and then at Mike, Patty sensed there was more to it. Deciding not to ask, he quickly replied, "Okay Jo, looks like the mystery has been solved, you can run back to Lance Corporal Jones and tell him he now owes Mr Faulkes here. I'm sure he's going to love that."

Mike watched as the Fusilier looked back at him, his face almost apologetic as he imperceivably nodded in thanks, before turning to walk away.

Spider sat back down, looking to Mike, "You shouldn't have done that, that was Jonah's cross to bear, he should have been the one cleaning out his wagon."

"Oh, come on Spider, we both know he doesn't give a shit. He wouldn't be there cleaning up after himself, he'd leave it to Reaper and Jo there. His mind's elsewhere at the moment, another reason why I was happy to do it. Now speaking of blood..."

Both men leaned forward as Mike continued, "Can we get everyone's names, ranks, and blood groups written out, include their zap numbers and get a copy into every vehicle. That way we all know who's on what vehicle and if it gets hit, how many people we need to get off."

"Jonah can do that," Patty replied, seeing Mike's doubtful look he added, "Don't worry though, I'll check it through myself, make sure he does it properly."

"Alright," Mike nodded satisfied. "Regards to water, for drinking and washing, there's a hose and tap out the back, I'd go straight from the tap though, we're on a working farm after all, and I'm not wanting to guess what that hose pipe could have been stuck up," Mike was happy to see the two men laugh as he continued.

"With regards to the fuel problem, I'm going to speak to Sam, see if he has a fuel tank here, hopefully he's got some red diesel for us to borrow. If not, we can refuel your vehicles using the tank, she's got a refuel, defuel pump, we should be able to get away with giving you all 100 litres of diesel each, it's not much but it's enough to bounce us across to another farm. If we must, we can keep doing this until we get somewhere where the good guys are. Unless you both have any better plan?"

Both soldiers looked at each other shaking their heads as Spider replied, "Nope, that plan sounds all fine to me."

Standing up Mike added, "Okay, I think for now, we've got enough to be getting on with, let's get everyone on it and I'll go speak to Sam about that fuel."

Leaving them there, Mike walked outside to the farmyard and over to the other outbuilding where he'd last seen Sam earlier, loading up feed for the cows into a large tractor trailer. He stopped outside the open door, not wanting to just bowl in uninvited. He was after all just a temporary guest. "Sam, you in there?"

"That you army?" the voice echoed off the large open barn. "Come on in, I won't bite."

Mike walked in, his eyes adjusting to the darkened interior. At the far end, Sam was working on a piece of farm machinery, beside him on the floor was an old rusty toolbox, with a collection of spanners and hammers lying in a pile.

Mike walked over, the farmer announcing loudly, "This bloody thing spends more time breaking down, than working. Another two hours of wasted work, while I sit on my ass and try to fix it.

"I've no idea what it does, so doubt I could be of any help." Mike said. Looking up, Sam smiled as he answered, pointing with a spanner, "This thing here is what I call my Politician."

"Politician?" Mike looked on confused.

"Yep Politician," Sam continued smiling, "it's my muck spreader, its sole job in life is to spread the shit far and wide, covering everything it gets near."

Mike laughed as Sam looked over to the toolbox, "Could you pass me a 12mm spanner please, and that there bloody big hammer."

Mike gave him the tools, hearing the bangs and heaves as Sam worked on part of the machine. After a few moments his hand shot back, "Now could I have that 16mm spanner and the pliers."

Mike passed over the tools, saying nothing as again the bangs and grunts followed. Suddenly with a loud clang something heavy hit the floor, the farmer shouting in triumph, "Whay that got the little bugger!" Looking triumphant, the farmer stood up, wiping his oily hands on a rag, as he looked over to Mike. "So, army, what brings you in here?"

"Sam, this morning when we came in, I mentioned that if we did any damage to your fields you'd be well paid by the government. The same holds true for anything we use or take. Therefore, do you happen to have any fuel that we can buy off you, any red diesel at all?"

The farmer stood there thinking to himself before asking inquisitively, "How much fuel would you boys be needing?"

Doing the quick calculations in his head, Mike replied, "About a thousand litres, that should get us to where we need to go."

Mike saw the farmer purse his lips together, his head slowly nodding as he thought. "Okay army, I can get you that, but I don't have that here now, I can get it brought here later tonight though. Would that do?"

"That would definitely do!" Mike grinned triumphantly; he hadn't expected to get any. Then thinking about another problem they had, he asked, "Sam do you have a vehicle we could borrow? We'll pay to rent it of course; I need to get into Dorchester for a few hours."

Looking confused the farmer asked, "Why do you want to go back there? I thought that's where you'd come from, you were wanting to go north?"

"I do, and we will, but we don't have the kit we need to get there. Our guys are still missing gear, and I know where to go to get it. If I can borrow a truck or 4x4 I can go into town and get what we need, then come straight back. If you're happy with that?"

"Give me thirty minutes, and I'll get something ready for you. Now before you go, can you give me a hand moving the Politician here outside?"

Smiling and rubbing his hands together Mike replied beaming, "Of course."

3

Beggars and Thieves

Sams Farm

Thirty-five minutes later and Mike was at the front of the barn next to the 4x4 with Patty, Doc and Reaper. Sam had managed to rustle up a battered looking red Toyota pickup, the panels dented, paint faded. The car perfectly matched the guys attire, to blend in Mike had asked Sam for some clothes for the other soldiers and now all three were wearing a mixture of loose blue coveralls, wellies, checked jackets and Patty had a flat cap. Mike laughed as he saw them stood there, although his own clothes were dirty, they at least looked normal, the other three looked like they were the types about to park a caravan on some council land and live there. All they were missing now was the dog. Spider walked over to the group, cracking a smile as he saw them. "Christ boys, you going to read my fortune or tell me my drive needs a new layer of tarmac?"

Only Reaper didn't smile. Mike was aware that he took great pride in his appearance and seeing how he looked in the reflection of a window and hearing Spider's comments only annoyed him further. "Fucking hell, it's bad enough we're stuck here, but now I've got to go out looking like this. What if someone I know sees me?"

"Then you blow them a kiss and say you're off to a fancy-dress party." Patty replied smiling. "Anyway, stop moaning, we need the items on those lists."

Each soldier carried a shopping list of essential items they needed for their vehicles and crews. Mike had spoken to Smudge and Bill and luckily thanks to the guys at ATDU, the tank had all its equipment and tools onboard, ready to go. So, it was mainly personal kit that they needed. With fifteen soldiers, they knew they needed fifteen of everything, so it should be pretty straight forward, albeit a pretty big shopping order.

Mike stood looking up at the sun, it was going to be another warm day, he thought, and the guys were not exactly dressed for it. He looked over to Patty, "Patty is anyone armed? does anyone have a weapon with them?"

As if in response, Patty and Reaper pulled two Glock 17 pistols from beneath their coveralls, both had magazines fitted.

"We've got these, afraid they're empty though, can't risk taking a rifle in with us, too bloody big to hide on us."

"Okay, but I'd rather we take a rifle with us, let's keep it in the vehicle, someone can stay with it when we go in. I'd rather have the ability to shoot back if we have to."

Spider walked off, returning a moment later with one of the rifles, and a magazine in hand. Doc checked the weapon was safe before fitting the fully loaded magazine. Opening the rear passenger door, he placed it on the back seat, pulling a tatty old tartan rug across it, to hide it from view before closing the door. All four men followed Mike towards the front of the vehicle as he quickly explained the plan, one foot resting on the bumper.

"Right guys, just so everyone is happy, all we're doing today is a bit of shopping, the plan is to go in, get what we need, then get the hell out, nothing else.

They all looked on as he outlined the plan.

"I'm going to be driving, I'll take us into Dorchester using the back roads, I'm happy with how to get us there, unless someone else wants to drive?" Looking up, seeing no objections he continued, "I'll get us to the auto parts store first, they'll have the toolboxes and all the camping gear we need. A few shops across from there, is the supermarket, that's where we'll get the food and water. I appreciate how we look but we'll try to blend in as best we can. Now we don't know what the situation in Dorchester is, when I spoke to the police last night, they told me there was enemy armour coming up from Weymouth. Where it is now, I don't know, but we haven't heard any vehicles drive past us yet, so let's assume that for the moment Dorchester is enemy held and they've stopped there. If we drive in and we see signs of any enemy, we turn around and head back. Agree?" All four men agreed in unison. Taking a breath Mike continued, "Now if anything goes wrong, if we come under fire or get separated, or for whatever reason we have to ditch the vehicle and get away quickly, on the inside of your coverall sleeves in permanent marker I've written the address of the village down the road from here, to give you somewhere to head to. When you get to the village you take the first immediate right, which brings you onto the track we're going to drive down. It's another mile down the track and then you're at the farm gates. You'll know where you are then. We're no more than five miles north of Dorchester, so if you had to you can run the distance to here." Mike saw Reaper and Doc grimace jokingly, clearly running the five miles in the heat didn't appeal to them. He continued, "If however, you can't run the distance..."

Mike paused as he took out his wallet, producing three £20 notes and giving one each to the three men going with him. "Now this is the last of my cash, so don't go hitting the bars just yet, but if you have to, you can use it for a taxi to get to the village. Don't get the driver to drop you off here at the farm though. Remember Sam and Mary are taking a big risk helping us and when we go tonight, they'll be left behind. If anyone suspects they've helped us, it could drop them in the shit in the future with whoever may be coming. Until we're up and running properly again everyone we meet who helps us is at risk. Remember that what we do now, what you all do now, has consequences. If anyone needs reminding of that, I'm happy to show them again what's in the reefer."

Seeing the serious faces staring back at him, Mike knew he'd hit the right note. Looking around the soldiers individually, one last time, he asked, "Questions? Patty? Doc? Reaper? Spider?"

Seeing there were none, he nodded, "Okay guys, let's go get some shopping."

All four men got into the 4x4, Patty in the passenger side, as Doc and Reaper took the back seat and Mike climbed into the driver's seat, settling himself in and getting comfortable, checking the mirrors were all okay. As he did so, Spider came over to lean through the open window looking across to Patty. "Take it easy mate, go careful won't you." Despite the banter between the two of them, Mike could see he was genuinely worried about being left alone. Looking at Mike he said, "Bring them back will you," his face betraying his concern. Mike smiled, hoping to lighten the mood replying, "If I can survive shopping with my wife, then this is a walk in the park. We'll see you when we see you." With that, the 4x4 drove away in a cloud of dust, leaving Spider stood alone listening to the chatter in the barn. Fuck, he thought, you better come back, because I really don't want to be doing this on my own. Taking a deep breath he walked into the barn, ready to face the ever-constant questions and ready to give the never known answers.

Mike tried his best to avoid the potholes as the vehicle bounced along the track, forgetting how good the tank's suspension had been, he didn't remember the track being as bad when they drove down it last night. The vehicle lacked air conditioning, so all four of the windows were rolled down, allowing the dust to occasionally come through, coating the men inside. Mike noted they were all quiet, the usual banter having stopped, so reaching down he turned on the radio, besides it would be nice to know what was going on in the world. The radio was basic, and after a few attempts Mike was able to get one of the regional stations playing. Expecting to hear some kind of news, he was confused when all he heard was the music blasting out, playing the usual summer tunes. He looked at his watch, it was 11:47, the news was always played on the hour, so settling in, with the tunes playing, he turned off the farm track and onto the B-road, leading them to the village. Passing through the village, Mike saw another old red phone box, he slowed, hoping to find the phone still in place, however his excitement was short lived, it had since been converted to a community defibrillator, the big green cross now clear. Disappointed, he continued past, driving through the village and continuing to head south on the smaller B-road, one of many that would take them through the quieter roads into Dorchester. As they whizzed along Patty looked at the hedges whipping past, mere centimetres from the wing mirror and exclaimed, "I'm glad you know where you're going, because I'm lost already."

Keeping his eyes on the road, Mike merely smiled, "The perks of living down here, great summers driving my cars on some good roads. It wasn't always like this though, there's been many a mistake that's cost me a wing mirror."

Patty was about to reply, when Doc quickly interrupted, leaning forward from the back seat to turn up the radio. "Hang on guys, the news is on, let's find out what's going on."

"And I'm Gregory Kiln and these are the top stories this hour. The Prime Minister has announced that in preparation for the UK's new trade deal with India, he and the foreign secretary will be flying to Delhi to meet the Indian delegation personally this week. The leaders are expected to discuss business matters along with both leader's love of the fine arts-"

"Hang on, didn't he do that last week?" Patty asked confused.

Ignoring him everyone continued to listen, the next news item was about to start.

"In other news, the convicted bank robber, Jeremy Diggs is expected to hear the results of his appeal later this week, the convict was sentenced to life imprisonment back in 2018 for his part in the robbery of one of London's most prestigious banks. However, recently his legal team have been attempting to get him released on compassionate grounds, citing ill health. It's believed that the 73-year-old bank robber has only months to live and lawyers are arguing he should-"

Mike reached down and muted the radio, "This doesn't make any sense, I remember this story from last week, he gets his appeal and was released on Saturday, four days ago, this is old news, why play it now? Nothing about London, or the attack on the camp last night."

Patty looked over, "Shit, you don't think someone's simply replaying old, recorded radio stations, are they?"

Keeping one eye on the road, and reaching down, Mike scanned through to one of the BBC radio stations, at this time of the day he knew there would normally be a chat show talking about the topics of the day, with people phoning in. He found the station and the chat shows voice cut through the car.

"Okay, so Syliva has just been in touch to say, I think it's extremely outrageous that we should be made to pay for this, the government should instead be offering to help and stepping in. Okay so that's Sylvia's views, let's hear what you think, please get in contact with us at the studio, either by phone or email. Speaking of which, we've got Dan on the line, Dan what do you think? Should we pay other countries for our own border security?"

Mike lowered the volume before everyone could hear Dan's views, his mouth open in shock. He glanced at Patty, "I think you're right, these are last week's radio transmissions being played back. Think about it, no one's phones are working and the internet is still down. So how are people ringing or emailing the station?"

"They're not." Reaper replied, leaning forward, "it's all a load of bullshit, all of it, someone's hiding what's really going on down here. But to be able to replay the radio stations, that's big, I mean really big! Just who the hell is doing this to us?"

Patty nodded in agreement, looking out the window, "Let's just get in, get what we need and get the fuck out, because the sooner we can get back to finding our own side, the happier I'll be."

"Amen to that." Doc said tapping the back of Patty's seat, "amen to that..."

Continuing down the B-roads, Mike noted the lack of traffic, even these roads would usually have one or two cars coming the other way, he thought. As if to confirm this, Doc announced ominously, "Is it me or is there a distinct lack of people driving down here?"

No one spoke as the road began to open more, leading onto a larger A road, then at last they saw the roundabout he wanted. Off to the left of them, situated on the outskirts of Dorchester was a shopping complex, a large open sprawling concrete metropolis, with various fast-food outlets, coffee shops and more importantly the large supermarket and auto parts store. Now at last they began to see vehicles, thankfully civilian and not military. The car park was not as busy as it should be for a weekday but at least they could see people. Parking near the supermarket, they could see the shoppers coming out, witnessing their panicked faces and overloaded trolleys, Mike realised he was beginning to see the early signs of panic buying. He could feel something was off, soon he was sure a tsunami of people would arrive as word got out. Looking to the guys in the back he replied, "I think we should go for the food first, looking at what people are doing here, it won't be long before the masses arrive and when that happens, I think everything will go to shit." Patty looked around him at the cars and saw the same thing as Mike. "Yeah, it reminds me of the days before Covid, everyone panicking and getting toilet rolls. They all know something's wrong; they just don't know what yet, you can almost feel it's about to kick off." He turned to Reaper in the back seat, "Give me your list Reaper, we'll go in, you stay with the vehicle, make sure no-one tries to steal it."

Reaper looked back shocked as he handed the note over, asking, "Patty you think it's going to get that bad?"

Looking around him, at the people loading up the cars he replied sadly, "Yes mate I do. Keep that rifle close to you, just in case."

As Mike got out, he leaned back in to say, "Reaper, I'll leave the keys in the ignition, okay."

Nodding in reply the Fusilier sat alone on the back seat, as he watched the three men close the doors and walk towards the supermarket. Usually with the clothes they were wearing, people would have stared at them. But Reaper noticed that no-one even gave them a second look, so pre-occupied were they in loading up their own cars. He looked over at the tartan rug, lifting the cover, seeing the assault rifle was still hidden beneath it. He knew it was there but did it more to re-assure himself. He looked over to the driver's seat and saw the keys in the ignition, merrily jangling away. He leant forwards and snatched them out, another temptation gone, he thought, as he pocketed them.

After five minutes of sitting in the vehicle, the heat had become too much, even with the windows open, so pulling the rifle and rug closer to the door he stood up, thankful of the small breeze as he now stood leaning against the open door. He watched the cars coming into the car park, most were family cars, SUV's and 4x4's, all coming to load up with supplies. He could start to see it now himself, everyone leaving the supermarket was quiet, looking at the floor, nervous, scared. What had happened here? What did they all know that he didn't? He watched as one lady came out with an overloaded trolley full of cat food and tampons. She glanced over to Reaper as she fought with the trolley, wanting to go one way, and the trolley going the other. Out of old habits, he was about to walk forward to offer to help, but realising the weapon was on the back seat and his job was to keep an eye on the truck, he stayed firmly where he was. Finally, after a few minutes and with a lot of struggling, he watched her get to the back of her blue people carrier emblazoned with stickers. As she opened the boot, she looked back over, an angrier sweaty look now on her face, as she said loudly, "Thanks for the help, nice to see people have still got manners." Reaper awkwardly looked away, looking back to the main road, watching for anything out of the ordinary. Shit, he suddenly thought, what would he do if he did see an enemy vehicle? Mr Faulkes hadn't talked about that? Would he run in to warn them? Should he sound the horn? No, he'd wait, he'd wait by the vehicle, so long as he didn't look or act out of the ordinary, no-one would react to him.

How long had he been there? He looked at his smart watch to check the time, annoyed that the battery had finally died. He'd left the charger back at the camp, how would he charge it now? Even his phone battery was almost dead, sure, he had the cable to charge it, but no way of doing so, the Warrior he was driving wasn't like a modern car, it didn't come with USB points to charge your items. When he got back to the farm, he'd see if he could find a power point there to use. Not that it mattered, he thought, as he pulled the phone out his overalls to check. Still no network and no messages. He'd hoped his girlfriend was okay, the last time they'd spoken it had been an argument, something trivial and petty now. Why did it always end with an argument, he thought moodily.

His thoughts were interrupted, as he heard a car horn, long and loud behind him. He looked up to the junction, seeing one of the cars leaving the supermarket had just collided with a trolley, scattering items all over the ground. The driver was already out and arguing with the trolley owner, he could hear the shouts over the distance. He could feel the tension in the air, it was electric, Mike and Patty had been right, it just all felt off, like when you can tell a thunderstorm is on the way by the feel of the static in the air. For the fourth time he looked under the blanket, checking the weapon was there. It felt strange to be stood here, no uniform, no helmet, and his weapon hidden away. He felt naked.

He kept watching as the cars continued to arrive, people walking more briskly towards the supermarket entrance, the fear of missing out playing its part. It was always human nature not wanting to be left behind, Reaper had felt that only last night as the armoured vehicles had begun to leave around them. Without meaning to, he began to replay in his mind the events of the previous evening at the fuel point. They'd all been queuing to fuel up the vehicles and waiting for their orders. Patty and Spider had stayed to get the wagons filled up, whilst he and Jonah had been told to go up to the offices and pick up the officer, some Captain, who was to lead them out. The Captain had the maps and the plans and knew where they were to go next, they were told. But, they hadn't gone to the headquarters, instead, Jonah had ordered he follow him back to the accommodation block, to his room, to stand watch as he went inside, rummaging through his lockers, pulling out three carrier bags, and quickly hiding them into a stuff sack. Then he went to another room in the block, clearly not his own, as he used the rifle to shoot out the lock. He was in there a full five minutes, the time dragging by, as Reaper had shouted, almost pleaded with him to hurry up. They could hear the vehicles leaving the fuel point, and he'd been so scared of being left behind. Jonah had emerged from the room laughing, almost mocking him, as he grabbed him by the shoulders and threatened him. He wasn't to tell anyone where they had been, if he did, he'd kill him. Then suddenly they could hear shots being fired, someone was firing at the camp! This was real, not an exercise like Jonah had said. They'd ran as fast as they could to get back to the vehicles, Jonah had told him they still had time, they could get the bag onto the vehicle and then go back for the officer. But they hadn't. As soon as they got back, they saw the enemy Paratroopers already at the camp fences, and he was scared. Patty was shouting at him, "Where was the Captain?" and before he could say anything Jonah had jumped in shouting, "He's already gone, we should go!" Had they left the Captain to die? Was it his fault?

"Reaper!"

He quickly turned around, snapped from his thoughts. Patty was stood in front of him holding a fully loaded trolley, "You okay?"

"Yeah, sorry Patty, I was miles away."

"Right, well get your head out of your arse, you're supposed to be watching the vehicle. Now how about you give us a hand loading this lot. Its fucking chaos in there."

With a sense of urgency, they both set about loading the pickup, as Mike and Doc now struggled over, each pushing their own trolleys, heavily loaded with supplies. Sweating, they all helped to load up the truck, making sure they left enough room for the other items. Patty took the three trolleys and simply pushed them into the car park, watching as they rattled to a halt in the middle of the space.

"Shouldn't you take them back?" Reaper asked naively.

Patty looked annoyed as he shot back, "Reaper, what the fuck's got into you? Since when did you care about taking trolleys back?" Pointing over his shoulder with his thumb he continued, "Have you seen the fucking chaos going on in there? There's people fighting in the aisles over toilet paper and baby food, I don't think anyone is going to give two fucks about the trolleys."

Mike looked around, seeing the car park was really starting to fill up now, people were now running to the supermarket and angry car horns began to blare out, as drivers began losing patience with slower drivers. It was all starting to go downhill.

He quickly pulled the tarpaulin over the flat bed, hiding the food and water from view. After seeing Reaper was not himself, he made the decision, "Right, okay Doc you've got what you need, now I want you to stay watching the car and our supplies. The rest of us let's get going."

Leaving Doc with the car keys and rifle, Reaper joined the others as they briskly walked towards the auto part store. Mike had expected it to be crammed with people, but was surprised when, on walking in, there was no-one there. Looking around confused he grabbed one of the trolleys and started to walk past the tills, when a large security guard stood in front of him, blocking his way. The others behind him all walking with trolleys looked up.

"What's up? Is there a problem?" he asked, the mountain of a man looked up towards a tall wiry man with glasses approaching them.

"No problem, gentlemen, it's all good," he said, in a screechy annoying voice. "The store's currently closed though to all walk-in trade, today it's now members only." He pinched his face together and said mockingly, "And you don't look like members."

"Members?" Mike replied confused, "since when does bloody auto parts have a membership?"

The guy walked over to the window, watching the chaos outside, as he replied sardonically, "Well, since everything started going to pot, the world's not what it used to be, is it Oleg?"

The gorilla in a security uniform grunted in acknowledgement. As the shop owner continued more jovially, "Now you three are in luck, because today, we have a special new members discount, for you three, membership will only cost £50 each."

Patty interrupted, "50 quid each, just to be able to shop in the store, you're taking the piss mate, that's illegal!"

The shopkeeper merely stood smiling and shrugged his shoulders, "Well you see what was illegal yesterday, is legal today, I mean where are the police? Where's anyone now? Have you tried to call them recently? Everything's going downhill and everyone will want what we have here. And I'm afraid if you want to shop here, you're going to have to pay. So now its three people, wanting to be members, that's £300."

"Hang on!" exclaimed Mike, "you just said it was £50 per person, that's £150, not £300."

"I've changed it to £100 each, on account of I don't like your friend there." he replied, nodding in the direction of Patty.

Patty was about to speak, when Mike quickly stepped in front of him, shaking his head. "Patty let me deal with this."

Seeing Patty's face flashing red with anger, Mike turned to face the shopkeeper, "I suppose the prices in here have all been raised to reflect the situation as well?"

Nodding as he spoke, the shopkeeper replied sarcastically, "They have I'm afraid, it's inflation, overheads, staff costs, prices just keep going up."

"Just so I know how much budget I have, a sleeping bag that would usually cost me £40, what does that cost now? I just want to make sure I can afford the membership and the items."

Patty interrupted, "Mike you can't pay that, we're being ripped off!"

Holding his hand up to silence him, he looked at the shop owner, waiting on an answer. Smiling and holding his hands together the wiry man said, "Well I'm not that greedy, so let's say the sleeping bag that was £40, would today be..hmmm £80. I think that's a fair increase."

"THAT'S DOUBLE THE PRICE!" Patty exploded. The security guard walked towards him, about to get physical, as Mike, sensing trouble, quickly stepped between them trying to defuse the situation shouting, "OK WE'LL PAY! We'll pay." The huge guard stopped to look over. At least he was well trained, Mike thought, as he quickly continued, "Look if you want us to pay your prices, we will, But I'm guessing it's cash only?"

"Of course, cash is king," the man smiled, the greed plain to see in his eyes. Mike had no idea how many others these two had conned, but it was clear he planned to rinse Mike of any remaining money he had left. There was no way they had enough money, Mike had already put the shopping on his debit card and knew attempting to buy the rest of the items, he'd run out of money. With the mountain of a man for a security guard stood next to him, Mike was powerless to argue and now he wished they'd brought Changa with them. At least it would be on more equal terms.

"Okay, we'll go back out to the cash point, get some more money and then come back okay."

The man motioned to the door, the same thin annoying smile, "Of course Sir, we shall look forward to seeing you shortly."

I'll bet you will, Mike thought. Leaving the trolleys by the automatic door, Mike stepped outside, the others following as they all finally noticed the angry faces of people in the cars outside. Obviously others had tried to get in to buy things and they'd had the same cold response. Now they were probably wondering if it would be worth becoming a member. Mike knew it wouldn't be long, soon the urge to get the items would overwhelm them and they'd go pouring in, money in hand and the horrible wiry man and his gorilla guard would make tens of thousands of pounds in one day, maybe more as people became desperate. He'd seen profiteering before in other war-torn countries, but never in the UK and never on such a brazen scale as this. But like the shop owner had said, there was no-one there to stop him.

As they walked back to the car, Patty finally exploded. "What the fuck Mike, you can't be seriously thinking about paying that? The guys a fucking maggot, he's going to rip us off, we should have fucking punched his lights out."

Letting him rage, Mike ran over and grabbed one of the empty trolleys in the car park, walking it back over before replying, "Look, calm down okay. I understand your anger, I wanted to smash him in the face as well, but without Changa here with us, I don't fancy taking on that security guard. His arms were bigger than my legs for Christ's sake."

"Right, so what do we do? Do we just give up? Drive away empty handed?" Patty replied, sarcastically.

Mike tried to calm himself down, to cool his own temper. Reaching under the tarpaulin, he pulled out four bottles of water, offering one to each of them. Taking a long pull on the bottle, he smacked his lips, watching the others do the same, after a moment he replied, calmer now.

"Look Patty, we need that gear, the others need that gear, they're relying on us. I've got no intention of just walking away, and I'm certainly not paying what he wants for it."

"Okay," he replied nodding and looking at the others, "so what's the plan?"

Taking a deep breath, he smiled and replied, "Did I ever tell you about when I saw the fall of Basra?..."

The shopkeeper was standing by the doors, watching gleefully as the fools all ran around outside like headless chickens. It was always the way, he thought chuckling. Today they'd run around throwing money about like water and tomorrow everything would calm down and be back to normal. He'd seen the same thing when Covid had hit the country back in 2020, he'd managed to make money back then, when everyone became obsessed with toilet rolls and antibacterial wipes, selling his own brand of antibacterial online at far higher prices and with far less of the alcohol required. Sighing to himself and looking forward to the money he would earn that day, he watched as the three farmers now came back towards his shop. Ahh they were bringing their own trolley, far larger than the ones in the shop. Good, that meant they were going to buy more items! Farmers always carried cash, he grinned. Looking outside he saw the other fools in their cars, deciding whether they should pay the fee to enter. Already he'd had people come in, some giving sob stories, pleading with him to let them buy the goods on his shelves. But he didn't have a heart, he had a head, a good head for business. What a master stroke, he thought, to have set up the membership fee, all totally legal and even if it wasn't, who would stop him? Before long, his store would be packed, his shelves empty, and his pockets full of more money than he would know what to do with. For now, let's deal with these three fools, let's see just how much juice I can squeeze out of the oranges. Smiling as the automatic doors opened, he walked over to them.

Mike walked through the double doors, sensing they were being keenly observed by the people in the cars, all watching the events unfolding, as he pushed the trolley before him. In the trolley, covered by the tartan blanket sat the SA-80. He'd told the others not to interfere, leave him to do the talking and to say nothing. They had left one of the empty pistols with Doc, still watching the car and Patty carried the other, hidden from view under his checked jacket.

Mike smiled as the shopkeeper walked towards him, theatrically opening his arms. "Gentlemen, how nice to see you again so soon, now let's arrange your membership shall we." Walking over to the checkout counter, he ushered them over, no doubt already thinking of the money to come. Mike watched behind him, making sure the oaf of a security guard was close by. Smiling, he reached down, quickly flicking off the blanket and picking up the assault rifle. The smile on the face of the shop keeper was quickly replaced by confusion, then fear, as he found himself looking down the barrel of the weapon. As predicted, the oaf began to move forward, Patty quickly pulling his pistol, pointing it close enough for a perfect chest shot, but far enough that he was out of reach if the man tried anything. The security guard looked down at the barrel, first a look of anger then resignation. His muscles wouldn't help him now.

"I have money," the man stammered, "I can get the till open and give you money."

"Are you here alone, is it just you and your thug here?" Mike asked coldly.

"Yes!" the man stammered.

Mike stepped closer, his voice raised, "Are you sure? ARE YOU FUCKING LYING TO ME?"

"Yes, yes, just us, I've sent the others home this morning, I didn't want anyone else to share the money." He shouted quickly, his voice reaching a higher pitch than before.

Without saying a word, Reaper ran off into the store to check there was no-one else, quickly returning with two large rolls of industrial sized gaffer tape and some tow rope. Patty motioned for the security guard to lie down, his hands behind his back and legs bent backwards. Without making a sound, the large man quietly lay down as Reaper taped his hands together at the wrists, then his legs together at the ankles, using more tape than usual, seeing as the man was larger than most. After tying his wrists and ankles he then tied his legs together at the knees, and his arms at the biceps. They really didn't want this man to get loose. Finally happy he was secure, they tied his wrists and ankles together with the rope, wrapping it around his neck, hog tying him, making any movement impossible. If he struggled with his bonds, he'd be at risk of choking himself, the message being lie there, don't move and you'll be fine. Without saying a word, the guard watched with hate filled eyes as they taped over his mouth, checking he could breathe out of his nose. Despite how they felt about the man, no-one wanted him to suffocate to death.

The shopkeeper stood silently watching on, his eyes wide with shock as he watched his protection meekly give up and surrender. As the seconds went by, Mike saw his confidence grow slightly, his eyes lowered as he quickly thought a way out. He was smart, Mike could see, greedy but smart.

"Gentleman if it's money you want, I can get you lots of money, there's people outside willing to pay a fortune for what I have, for what we have in here. If you help me sell it, we can split the proceeds say fifty-fifty?"

Finishing on the security guard, Reaper turned to the shopkeeper, grabbing him and turning him around, taping his hands together in front of his body, before pulling out the wheeled chair from behind the cashier desk. He turned it over, snapping the wheels off and throwing them into the store, before placing it down and forcing the shopkeeper to sit. Then he tied his feet together and taped his legs, arms and chest to the chair, ignoring the whinging as the man pleaded, "Please, that's too tight, you're hurting me." He was going nowhere.

Happy the man was bound, Reaper and Patty stood next to Mike. Mike spoke calmly and quietly, "We're not here to rob you, nor help you steal money off the people outside. What you're doing is illegal, it's called profiteering. You're making money off other people's misery, they're trying to get away, to protect themselves and people like you, leeches like you, feed off that." Mike could feel his anger rise, conscious of the fact his finger was near the trigger. Calm yourself Mike, he thought, this isn't what you're here for.

Looking at the other two, he quickly replied, "You've got the lists, let's go start shopping."

Grabbing a trolley each, the three of them began quickly going through the items on the list, rapidly filling up trolley after trolley, before long there were five large, overloaded trolleys next to the door. Mike looked over the lists, checking they had everything on it, and then some. Satisfied he finally nodded, Reaper ran outside, waving over to Doc driving the 4x4, which came and parked right up next to the doors, reversing in to allow them to load up the gear. Doc jumped out to help as they quickly loaded everything into the truck, the suspension creaking in protest as the flat bed sunk closer and closer to the wheels. The final items they had to cram into the back seat, as Doc looked back outside and turned to the others, "I'm fucking glad you're finished, it's getting crazy out there now, people are fighting in the car park. I've already had to threaten two people with the pistol who tried to get the tarp off the truck. As he spoke, they heard shouting, as people now began to crowd outside the store, the ones in their cars now getting out to join the mob. With a crack, they heard the shop front windows of the store being smashed, as people now tired of waiting began to smash at them in desperation, to get at the items inside.

Realising time was running out, Mike handed the rifle to Doc, "Here you go Doc, keep them back for a little longer, use warning shots if you have to."

Doc ran out, staring people down, seeing the rifle in his hands people hesitated, turning to go after easier pickings. He looked out amongst the cars, it was chaos, in only a matter of minutes, people were now walking out of broken shop fronts with TV's, shop fittings, some even taking the mannequins without any clothes on. You could never understand the human mind, he thought.

Standing by the door, Mike looked at Patty and Reaper, "What do you think, anything else we've forgotten?"

"No way," replied Reaper, "we've got everything they wanted and then some. Let's get the fuck out of here."

Outside a car alarm was going off, Mike turned and walked over to the shopkeeper, watched on by the other two. He was tempted to release him, but then something stopped him, instead he knelt, bringing his face close to the man.

"You brought this on yourself, you made this happen. When you sit here, watching your shop being ransacked by those people out there, I want you to think about the people you profited from, perhaps then you can understand the misery and suffering people like you inflict on desperate people."

"You can't leave me like this! Those people outside will tear me apart! At least release me!" the voice rising in terror.

"When they come in here, you'll be the last thing on their minds, they'll want what's on your shelves. Besides you've got him down there to protect you." Mike stated, pointing to the tied-up guard. "Perhaps if you pay them enough, one of them will release you, maybe you can strike a deal with them," Mike suggested, raising his eyebrows. He stood and began to walk away, the shopkeeper behind him now pleading, "Wait, come back! PLEASE, COME BACK!"

Stepping outside with the others, they saw one of the cars had been broken into, its doors ripped open, and the owner trying desperately to stop the people that were stealing the items from within. Mike was tempted to help, but quickly stopped himself, it was futile, for every person you tried to stop another two would come in behind you. Ignoring the chaos, he quickly shouted, "Okay get in, we need to go!" He slid into the driver's seat, Doc being the last person to get in, still brandishing the assault rifle menacingly, holding some of the people back. Mike engaged first gear and went to pull away, the car juddering before rolling back, the engine stalled. Fuck, you idiot, he thought, all the weight in the car and he didn't give it enough gas. With the engine revving loudly, he moved forward slowly, trying to gently nudge people out of the way with the cars bumper. Some people tried to grab at the tarpaulin on the back as the car passed, but Doc had already opened the sunroof and was stood half out of it, shouting in warning as he waved the rifle menacingly, forcing them back. In the rear-view mirror

Mike watched on as at least twenty people ran into the auto parts store. It wouldn't be long before, like a horde of locusts, they'd picked it clean. He was glad they came when they did, another twenty minutes and it would have been too late. Navigating past cars, abandoned trolleys and people running through the car park, he made his way out of the chaos and back onto the main road, relaxing slightly as he felt the car pick up speed. Knowing that they were clear of the mob, he tapped Doc on the legs, "Best sit down now Doc, we're clear, keep a low profile remember."

Doc carefully settled himself back down, looking at the others in disbelief. All four of them looked at each other, not knowing what to say at the chaos they had just witnessed. At least they had the goods, thought Mike. Turning off the main road, Mike carefully began to navigate down the country lanes, conscious of the heavy weight in the back as the suspension of the car struggled. They could already smell the clutch burning, and Mike was hoping the 4x4 would make the short distance.

It was Reaper who finally broke the silence. "I've never robbed a store at gunpoint before."

Doc looked up, eyes wide in disbelief, "No, me neither, first time for me."

Patty looked at Mike, "So, what are we now, beggars and thieves?"

Mike shook his head, "We didn't steal anything, its Martial Law now, military law. You're all members of the military. You saw a black marketeer who was illegally profiteering, you confiscated his goods, and turned the rest over to the public. We're not thieves, and don't go thinking otherwise."

Satisfied with what he'd just said, he saw the others visibly relax. It had never been the plan for it to play out like that and Mike had not expected the rioting to happen so quickly. At least now, they had all the gear they would need to keep going. The only thing remaining was fuel and ammo. Feeling happier, Mike reached down and flicked on the radio, the summer tunes filling the car. Last week's radio or not, it didn't matter, it was still music and he fancied listening to it. Smiling at the others, with the dry road dust billowing behind them, he began to sing the lyrics to the girl band song that blasted out. At first the others looked aghast, like he was some alien from another planet, but one by one, they all joined in, the singing helping loosen the mood. Within two minutes the car was bumping down the road, the sounds of four voices wildly out of tune, bouncing off the countryside.

4

Any Good News?

Wonderland Operations Centre (WOC)

Jeffery sat watching the second hand of the clock slowly counting down, as everyone chatted around him, the order and structure of previous meetings gone, as more people wanting to be heard began to talk over each other. It was 06:20, he'd called everyone in early that morning at 01:00, they'd been at it all night, had time really flown past so quickly, he thought. There were supposed to only be ten people in the room, but instead he counted over twenty people, all crammed around the conference table, the more senior people sat around the desk, the others were sitting or standing where they could, all trying to speak over each other. Only Sir Charles was missing, the Chief of Defence Intelligence (CDI) having been pulled out an hour before, to compile the latest intelligence on what the enemy were doing. He rubbed his forehead with his hand, massaging the headache that had lingered there these past twelve hours. No amount of paracetamol seemed to shift it and the incessant arguing wasn't helping, the conference rooms walls seemed to help bounce the voices loudly back at him. He looked up to see his aide Sonya arguing with the Permanent Undersecretary across the table who had arrived during the past few hours straight from London. Both had been at loggerheads since they had first met, the cat and mouse game of politics being played out for all to see. At the far end of the room, he saw the Chief of the Defence Staff (CDS) and the Chief of Police animatedly talking to each other, discussing the ramifications of what was happening. All around him, people were locked in their own battles with each other as the fragmented reports coming in from all over the country were not painting a good picture. Everyone at the table had been up all night trying to come up with the answers to the questions that seemed to be coming at them thick and fast. His stomach grumbled for food, as he quickly tried to shake off the thought of breakfast.

Deciding he'd heard enough, he stood up, the conversations lowering in volume then stopping altogether as everyone looked up at him.

"Okay everyone, while we're waiting for Sir Charles, let's all just take a breath and think this through logically. The public will be scared and wanting re-assurance and calm. They'll expect there still to be a government in charge and this emergency to be under control. At the moment that's not what we're doing here."

Sonya looked up, "Sir, I think we should start telling the public about the attack on Chequers, and what's going on. If we don't, we'll run the risk of being behind this, and not ahead of it. I know the CDS wants us to keep quiet about the PM, but even so, rumours will spread, and people are already scared."

The CDS shook his head, "I'm sorry Sonya but I disagree with you, the less the public know the better, if we start announcing what we know is to come on the news, then we'll see panic and rioting on the streets. We're still waiting to get confirmation from the Met Chief of Police that the King and Queen are safely out of the Capital. If we announce this before they're safely out, then we may end up trapping them in there. There's almost nine million people in London, if they all take to the streets at once, then our own units will be trapped in the melee. Let's at least wait until we get confirmation that they're safely out of the area."

The Minister's Chief Aide looked back at him, a thin smile on her lips, "General, with all due respect-"

"With all due respect is usually followed by an insult Sonya, so just say it as it is." the CDS interrupted, also flashing a tight-lipped smile.

She nodded, her face grim, as she continued, "Very well General, how about you consider the public opinion of how we will be perceived. Hours after an attack on the Capital, whilst the rescue efforts are still underway, we divert essential resources needed in that rescue to help evacuate the King and Queen, whilst leaving those nine million people you mention in the dark about what's really going on. Won't it look like one rule for one and another for everyone else?"

The CDS nodded, "It will Sonya, and I agree with what you're saying, but I'm afraid we can't help that, this is just too big a threat to ignore and worry more about public opinion. For now, we need to just get the Royals out of there."

"What's the situation on the ground at the missile strike locations, London, Swanwick and Chequers at the moment?" the Defence Minister asked.

The Police Chief looked up to one of his own aides who handed him a piece of paper.

"Sir, firstly the NATS centre at Swanwick, the rescuers are still combing through the wreckage, but we think that three missiles were targeted there, however only two hit, we've no idea where the third came down. As for the casualties so far, its reported 120 killed, 248 wounded and another 28 people missing. The more serious casualties are being treated at Southampton General, the rest are being transferred to Hampshire and Portsmouth."

"Do they require any additional help?"

"Yes, they do, I've already managed to get additional rescue services coming from Somerset and Wiltshire to assist them.

"That's good." the Minister said impressed, "and how is London looking?"

"Sir, the Gold commander on scene has the incident site now locked down and she's already evacuated everyone from within a two-mile radius of the attack. Rescuers are still searching through the rubble, but it's a huge task and with multiple attack sites it will take some time to locate everyone both alive and dead. So far, the numbers are 196 confirmed dead, with almost 400 wounded and another 247 people missing. Most of the missing are either those working in the Houses of Parliament or passengers that were on the Millennium Wheel. The Police can't begin the underwater recovery of any of the bodies just yet, as they're still waiting for the wreckage to be cleared. All the London Hospitals have activated their critical incident protocols and are treating casualties as they come in, all the local hotels have now been emptied to make way for those now homeless from the cordon. She's asked for additional manpower and already we've got troops from the Household Division, Buckingham Palace and Horse Guards to assist, but if we can spare any more officers or troops, I'd recommend that they go there."

"Very well Chief," the Minister nodded, "London gets the priority. What about Chequers, any further news?"

The Police Chief paused looking across to Sir Charles's empty seat. "I believe Sir Charles will be better placed to discuss Chequers as he was dealing with that."

The CDS looked up, interjecting, "Sir Charles informed me before he left, apart from our previous report, it's still looking like only seven survivors. I'll try and get more information when we finish here."

Nodding, the Minister asked, "Do we still not have any further news from the police units that were sent to get the Royal Family out?" He looked back to the Police Chief waiting for an answer.

"No Minister, we're struggling with radio communications, the same as everyone else. I've had periodic communications with New Scotland Yard, the last message I received at 01:30am was that my counterpart in the Met, had sent units to extract the King and Queen from Buckingham Palace."

"At 01:30?" he interrupted, "we gave that order out at 9pm, why the delay, what took so long?"

"I'm not sure Sir, like I say, we've had outages in the communications between ourselves and New Scotland Yard, perhaps that was a factor. Either way, the police units are there already and along with the Royal Protection Officers they should by now be safely on their way out of the capital."

"Okay, what about the Prince of Wales and his family, where are they now?"

The CDS now intervened, "Sir, The Prince of Wales and his family have been safely extracted from Adelaide Cottage and are now within Windsor Castle along with a Squadron from the Household Cavalry and a Company of Welsh Guards to protect them. They're at least out of immediate danger."

"Air Cover?" he asked knowing that air cover had been powerless to stop the attack on London.

"We have a squadron of F35's now operational out of Heathrow, with three aircraft on constant overwatch of both the capital and Windsor castle. I'm assured by the CAS that there should be no more Kinzhal attacks, we'd have had them by now. We're doing all we can to defend London against any further attacks from the air."

The Minister looked down at the pile of papers in front of him, already knowing the answer. "CDS any news from NATO?"

"Not yet Defence Minister, the aircraft we sent across last night, returned an hour ago carrying the latest NATO reports and a letter addressed to myself from the SACEUR, (Supreme Allied Commander Europe) General Davidson. He's ordered NATO's alert status to be raised and has called a meeting today for 11am to discuss matters."

"11am? To discuss matters?" The Minister's tone was unbelieving as he continued, "They do realise that we are under attack? And that one of their most senior partners is requesting help? And they can't do it any earlier than 11am? Am I missing something General, are we disturbing their breakfast or is this just simply a matter of inconvenient timing for them?"

The CDS looked up regretfully as he replied, "Sir, we shouldn't be surprised by this, SACEUR needs authorisation from the NATO General Secretary and other heads of government before he can move. It will take time, and even then, we may not have them onside. Remember that this operation calls for them to be indecisive. We might not receive any help at all."

Jeffery rubbed his nose with his fingers in irritation, knowing the CDS was correct. This fucking plan, he thought to himself, and all thought up by one of our own bloody officers! He felt a spike of pain shooting up his head again as his eyes ached for some sleep, rubbing them to bring life to them, he looked up around the people at the table, seeing Peter watching on from the back.

Jeffery looked at him curiously and was about to ask his thoughts on the matter, when the Undersecretary stood up, all eyes on him. Clearly, he had something he wanted to discuss and had decided it couldn't wait any longer.

"What is it Undersecretary? What's on your mind that can't wait?" he asked testily.

"Defence Minister, I know there is a lot going on at present, but we really need to discuss the matter of the designated survivor clause. At present we strongly believe that the PM and all other cabinet ministers to be dead or incapacitated and are no longer able to carry out their duties. Therefore, we *must* have a PM, and we *must* have government. I urge you to reconsider your position, the country needs a Prime Minister."

Jeffery looked around the table, some nodding in agreement, his own aide included. Up to now, any hint of him accepting the title or role had been rebuked, he wasn't too sure of the legalities of it for a start, nothing on this scale had ever happened before. He didn't want to jump in with both feet, claim the title and then discover that someone more senior had survived or worse still what was left of his own party had voted him out. He looked over to his aide.

"Sonya where do we stand in this, do I have a legal claim to me PM, with no Cabinet left?"

Sonya quickly thought it through, before replying confidently, "The Civil Contingencies Act 2004 gives the reigning monarch the powers required to make emergency decisions in the event of there being no government in place. At present due to the King not being available, then that power falls to one of the remaining Cabinet Ministers, in order of seniority. As there are no longer any Cabinet Ministers left then the most senior person is you. Therefore, you are now the caretaker Prime Minister until the King either endorses you, or our Party meet and nominate a new leader, who the King must then meet himself and endorse."

Damn, he thought, replying, "So it looks like whether I want it or not, I'm now the one making the decisions." He looked up to everyone there, "However with the current events ongoing now, I can't rightfully claim the title of Prime Minister, not yet. For the time being, until we get confirmation on the death of the PM and the other cabinet members, I'd like to keep things as they are. For now, please still think of me as the Defence Secretary."

A few mutterings were heard, quickly getting louder until eventually the Undersecretary stood up wanting to be heard again. Jeffery raised his eyebrows.

"Yes, Undersecretary?"

The Undersecretary smiled, replying, "My apologies Secretary for State, but sometimes you must tell people what they need to hear and not what they may want to hear.

He cocked his head curiously, where was he going with this, he thought, as unperturbed the Undersecretary continued.

"You can't simply shrug off the role of Prime Minister, as much as it pains you to hear it, it's not your right to simply turn the role down. The country must have a Prime Minister, as it must have a head of state. When the King dies, the heir to the throne does not get to pick and choose if they want it, they must accept it and the crown continues, this is the heavy weight that people of power must bear, which is much the same for all levels of Government. You chose the role of a cabinet minister; you chose to be a member of the Government. Like it or not, you're now next in line for PM. Either accept it and become the Prime Minister, or I must ask that you resign immediately and leave office. Either way that is *legally* the only course of action that you now have open to you."

Jeffery sat there, slightly taken aback at what had just been said. Had the room just become hotter, he thought, as he felt himself begin to sweat slightly. The CDS stood up, weighing in himself.

"I have to agree with him Minister, it would make things a lot easier to manage, and NATO would respond better to a world leader rather than a-"

"Lowly Defence Minister?" Jeffery interrupted, noticing the CDS shift uncomfortably as he said it.

He looked around the room, his eyes finally resting over to his aide, his eyebrows raised. "What do you think Sonya? Think you can handle being the PM's Chief of Staff?"

She smiled before adding, "Either shit or get off the pot."

He smiled at hearing the phrase she'd used before whenever he was having doubts. Suddenly the pain in his head seemed to ease slightly and he didn't feel quite so tired.

His lips pursed in thought, finally he made his decision as standing, he planted his hands on the desk, addressing the room.

"Fine, let's make it happen, what do I need to do?"

The Undersecretary walked towards him, a serious look on his face and bible in hand. "First I need you to place your left hand on the bible."

Twenty minutes later and he sat back down, the people in the room all shaking his hand and congratulating him. Although he'd dreamed of this day, he'd never imagined it in such sombre circumstances, sensing the looks on the faces and the mood of the room, he quickly added, "Okay, people, thank you for the congratulations, but this is not a time to celebrate, we've got lots still to do. Now, let's concentrate on getting this country of ours back in the game." He waited as everyone resumed their seats, looking to Sonya. "Sonya, your first job as my Chief of Staff, I need you to find me a new cabinet, start with Defence Secretary, Home Secretary and Foreign Secretary. Let's get those three positions filled first, and we'll worry about the rest later."

She quickly wrote the details down before leaving the room, as all eyes turned to Sir Charles who entered the room in haste, his arms full of paperwork. Everyone crammed around the tables made room for him, as he handed out the paperwork to those nearest to pass around, and then walked up to the main screen, flicking it on and connecting his laptop, nodding to the CDS that he was ready.

The PM sat there for a few moments, watching and waiting, eventually clearing his throat to announce. "CDS, before we get the latest update from Sir Charles, can you just bring everyone else up to speed at last night's event please."

The CDS was huddled together with the First Sea Lord and the CAS, discussing the latest intelligent reports. He looked up as the PM spoke to him, his glasses resting on the end of his nose. "Prime Minister, there's a lot to go through, so I'll try to keep it as brief as I can. At sea, we've got most of the home fleet trapped in Portsmouth, the Queen Elizabeth, along with our entire fleet of Type 45 destroyers and two type 23 frigates. The good news is that Sir Tony was able to get two Type 43 frigates out of Devonport, the HMS London and HMS Argyll, and one of our new Astute class Subs, HMS Archer. All of which are off the coast of Plymouth currently awaiting your orders."

The PM nodded to Sir Tony, as the CDS stood up, walking over to a large map of the UK that was displayed onscreen. Using the digital marker pen, he could draw onscreen without fear of damaging the display.

"Now, onto the air, and CAS please jump in if you feel I miss anything out." she nodded in response as the CDS continued.

"We've had reports of cruise missile attacks at our bases in Lossiemouth, Kinloss, Boulmer, Swanwick, Conningsby, Brize Norton and Waddington. Along with further attacks on 24 of our radar sites all along the UK. Now, these attacks on our radar sites, along with the loss of Swanwick ATC, and RAF Boulmer, mean that for the moment, we're blind to what's going on in the air. The attack on Waddington took out three of our AWACS (Airborne Warning And Control System) aircraft along with four of their air refuelling tankers and the attack in Lossiemouth took out our entire squadron of Poseidon AWACS aircraft. The CAS is currently working on getting other aircraft in from Cyprus, but that might not be for another ten hours or so.

The PM continued listening, writing notes as the CDS took a sip of water and continued.

"The attacks on our airbases have put them all out of action, however, we did manage to get some of our aircraft into the air, with most of those surviving aircraft now being relocated into smaller, regional airfields and airports."

"Losses?" the PM simply asked, as the CDS looked over to the CAS, who seeing the prompt stood up.

"We're looking at losses of 50 to 60 percent of our UK fighter strength Prime Minister and 70 percent of our AWACS, tankers and support fleet." A collective gasp rose across the room as the figures were relayed, only the PM quietly looked on, he'd already been briefed earlier, and when he'd been told, the shock had been the same for him. He nodded to the CAS as she sat back down and the CDS continued, drawing two distinct red lines across the map of the UK. One just South of London and one just North of Newcastle.

"With our air losses and little to no coverage of the UK radar picture, I'm recommending that for now, we keep all air operations limited to between these two lines, any attempt to go north or south of them and we could be looking at more significant losses."

"Hang on CDS, are you suggesting that we've lost control of the airspace around the UK already?" the Undersecretary shot out unbelievingly.

The CDS looked back over to him. "That's exactly what I'm saying. For now, we're limited as to what we can do, until we can replenish our losses and get eyes back in the sky."

"Good God!" the Undersecretary muttered, as the CDS continued.

"I'm afraid it's not much better on the ground." he began to draw red circles around the areas he spoke about.

"We have reports of enemy paratroopers landing here in Ringwood, Verwood and here in Chichester, all small towns with major routes in and out of them. We think the Russians are capturing these key areas, preparing for their advance northwards. Also, we have three amphibious landings underway along the south coast, here at Bognor Regis, here in Worthing, and here in Rustington."

"But we've no reports of landing craft in the channel..." the PM interjected, as the CDS paused, looking over to Sir Charles.

"Sir Charles, I believe you have the latest intelligence on these landing sites..."

The CDS sat back down as everyone stood to see the screen, as the video footage came through, shot using a high-powered lens as Sir Charles began to narrate. "If you remember back to last night's meeting, we all wondered what those ramps being retrofitted to the cargo ships were for..."

The camera panned out showing a shingle beach, it was evening, the sun beginning to set behind the cameraman. In the distance in the dim light four large cargo ships sat offshore, each fitted with a huge ramp that projected from the side of each ship, lowered into the water. Out of each ramp came a large hovercraft, similar to the one that everyone had seen in the past crossing the channel, except these were painted battleship grey, and even from that distance, everyone watching could see the size of them, each one bristling with guns. Hearing the murmurs, Sir Charles continued, "What you're all looking at are four Zubr class hovercraft, each weighing 550 tonnes, with the same firepower as one of our type 23 Frigates. Each, able to carry three main battle tanks or ten armoured vehicles and one hundred and forty troops."

Everyone craned forwards to see, as the footage was fast forwarded another twenty minutes, and although the light had faded, the four leviathans had skidded up the beach, disgorging the tanks and infantry before turning back to sea, to pick up more men and armoured vehicles.

The PM sat open mouthed as Sir Tony shook his head frustratedly. The Russians had made themselves an amphibious fighting force using civilian ships!

The screen went blank, as the CDS stood back up to continue.

"We're looking at the possibility of these landings being a feint, to draw our forces south out of Aldershot, as they haven't advanced too far from their beach heads yet.

However, for now, we're monitoring them. Meanwhile, the main enemy landings are taking place in the south at Portland and Poole, and in the north at Newcastle. In the north we've counted twelve cargo ships in the dockyard, with possibly more inbound. We estimate the numbers there to be at least four Russian Guards divisions, with approximately sixty thousand soldiers and around five hundred tanks and armoured vehicles."

The PM shook his head slowly at hearing the numbers, as he asked apprehensively, "Okay, and what about in the south?"

"We believe another six divisions are being landed, split across the areas of Portland harbour and Poole harbour, including these three landing sites at Bognor Regis, Worthing and Rustington. Numbers are vague, but we could possibly be looking at anywhere in the region of sixty to eighty thousand troops, and perhaps eight hundred tanks and armoured vehicles."

The PM jotted the figures down, his eyes being drawn to the numbers arrayed against them. Taking a deep breath, he asked, "Anything else?" all the while hoping that was the end of it.

The CDS pursed his lips together before replying, "Catterick, Tidworth, and Warminster all came under heavy cruise missile attack last night, with most of the camps' facilities destroyed. Thankfully losses of troops were light, most of the units were stood down with troops away on leave, however the hangars at Catterick were full of vehicles. I'm still waiting on confirmation of numbers, but we could be looking at having lost substantial amounts of armour and equipment."

More mutterings broke out amongst those gathered, as the PM spoke up.

"Settle down people, come on, we knew it was going to be bad, let the CDS finish."

The murmurs and chatter died away, the CDS nodding in thanks as the PM asked.

"What about the tanks at Bovington, did they get away last night?" the PM looked over hopefully, noting that the CDS had not even mentioned them.

The CDS looked back at the report in his hand, reading the lines again before looking up. "I'm afraid to report PM that the camp was attacked by Paratroopers as the tanks were trying to get away. They used a glider club to the north of the camp as their drop zone. I'm still trying to get more information from the area, but the Russians have been very effective in jamming our communications in those areas. Some of the local radio stations have been put out of action already and I believe the civilian population may not even know what is truly going on down there.

"But did the Colonel manage to get his unit away in time?" the PM asked again.

The CDS shook his head slowly, glancing over to Peter as he spoke, "I'm sorry Sir, I don't have any further details."

The PM looked down, then asked, "What happened to the enemy aircraft that were involved in the attacks, have they left our airspace?"

"No Sir," the CDS continued, "I haven't briefed you on this yet, but we've just found out early this morning that Bournemouth Airport was seized by enemy paratroopers last night, it's being converted now into an airbase, giving the enemy somewhere to launch fighter support from."

The PM looked surprised, "Christ, they've already got an active airport? Why Bournemouth?"

"The runway length is more than long enough to accommodate every aircraft they have. And location wise it's perfect to help cover the southwest. All the aircraft involved in last night's attacks on the capital are believed to have landed there afterwards. One of the NATO reports we received, mentions that at around 03:00 the Norwegians were tracking two squadrons of SU57 fighters flying down the eastern side of the UK before soviet jamming blocked them. We believe one squadron has landed at Bournemouth and the other is somewhere in Scotland. We have yet to see them in the air. So far, the soviets are keeping their air assets firmly in the areas they control, and apart from limited sorties with helicopters we think they're waiting for their land forces to be ready."

"Helicopters?" the PM asked, "where the hell did they come from?"

"A small force were flown off the cargo ships just before nightfall, we believe they're assisting the land forces in the Southwest only, we've yet to receive reports of any in the North.

As if on cue the CDS nodded over to Sir Charles who took over the briefing.

"Prime Minister, our latest intelligence reports are showing that in all those areas that the CDS just mentioned, the enemy seem to have halted their advance. We think it's to gather and unload their forces, get them all set before striking forwards.

"How long?" the PM enquired, seeing the confused look on Sir Charles, he repeated, "how long can we expect them to halt for?"

"Ahh, we believe we may have a window of opportunity of between 12 to 24 hours.

"12 to 24 hours?" Sonya exclaimed, the CDS looking over to her, replying.

"Small mercies Sonya, small mercies. I wasn't counting on them halting at all."

The Prime Minister looked over to his Head of Intelligence, "Sir Charles, what news have we got from GCHQ? Any more news on the phones or internet? We could really do with the ability to talk to one another again." his voice hopeful.

The General quickly scanned a piece of paper, as he read aloud, "Sir, GCHQ have confirmed that the computer virus did not destroy our phone networks as we first thought. Instead, it seems to have simply erased all of the mobile providers stored phone data. Every phones sim card needs to be registered within its network for it to ping off a tower to take and accept calls, the data bases holding those numbers had been erased, which is why no one has been able to use a mobile phone. They think they might be able to regain access to the systems by the end of the day, but then peoples phone numbers will need to be manually entered again into the system. With nearly 30 million phone numbers to input, not everyone will be able to talk straight away, it will take months to input. But working with the providers we can at least get our key personnel chatting again."

"Okay well that's a start," the CDS replied.

Sir Charles continued, "There is another thing, GCHQ have also been monitoring cell tower activity from specific numbers, as the virus was programmed to leave some numbers active, GCHQ believe these phone numbers will belong to hostile agents working against us, which has now worked in our favour."

"How so?" the PM asked questioningly.

"UK communication traffic is heavy, at any one given moment there are normally two to three million phone calls in the UK being taken at any one time. Trying to monitor and geolocate a hostile call in amongst those calls is a huge task, but now with there being NO phone traffic, GCHQ can monitor the 200 to 300 calls being made daily. We can now identify those numbers and are now able to track them. Whoever is using these phones clearly has no idea we could do this, otherwise they'd change the numbers and sim cards after every call."

"So, we may have the ability to listen in to those calls soon?"

"No," he replied sadly, "I'm afraid the phones are believed to be encrypted, but we will have the ability to track the locations, to find out where the people are when they're using them."

"Right, well that's a start, what about the internet? Any luck in getting the country back online?"

Sir Charles sounded cautious as he continued, "That's going to be more of an issue for us, as firstly we think that some, if not all of the pipelines that carried our data cables from the UK to Europe, have now been cut, restricting our data access by about ninety-seven percent."

"Cut? how did they manage that?" The PM asked surprised, "I thought we were dealing with a computer virus? Aren't those cables deep underwater?"

Sir Tony quickly interjected, "Submarines Sir," He looked over as the First Sea Lord continued. "The Russians have six subs all designed for this exact task, deep underwater sabotage. For them, sabotaging pipelines, offshore wind farms, and data cables wouldn't be too difficult. We use our own SBS for the same tasks."

"Well," He replied, "can they be repaired?"

Sir Charles now continued, "I'm afraid not in the timeframe that we need them for Sir, no, for now they'll have to remain out of use. However, we still believe that even with the cables cut we can get limited services back online. People within the UK will be able to access UK systems, send emails and video calls to others in the UK. We just need to find a way to defeat the virus. GCHQ have got our very best minds on it, rest assured as soon as we have any further news, I'll let you know."

The PM raised his eyebrows and asked, "Sir Charles, how is it that you're able to get information on what the enemy are doing? If we're experiencing all these communication problems, how are you getting information in and out so quickly? Some of those areas you've mentioned aren't connected here and as we already know VHF communications are being jammed. So how are you doing it?"

Sir Charles looked over to the CDS who nodded in answer, before tapping away on the laptop. Onscreen a list of numbers and locations now began to scroll across as the CDS turned to him, seeing his questioning look.

"I had these compiled earlier PM, it's the telephone numbers and locations of all the red phone boxes still in service, all 179 of them."

He looked, watching as the list was scrolled through alphabetically, the names of small parishes and towns never heard of before. As it scrolled through, the CDS continued to explain.

"I figured that if Mr Faulkes and Brigadier Rawlinson could use the phone boxes to talk, then so could we. So far, we've managed to get communications established into 58 small villages and towns up and down the country. We're getting the message out to people, the trouble we're finding is making sure that we're telling the right people."

The CDS went silent, deciding not to mention already the five times that he'd been chatting to someone, only to find out that they were either too drunk or too high to care. With the lack of use of the phone boxes in the digital age, people were finding more creative ways to use them, and drug dens and public urinals seemed to be the most popular choice.

"God how did it all come to this?" the PM remarked, his head in his hands, before adding, "our whole country's communications network, now relies on phone boxes and runners. It's like the 1940's all over again."

Realising how negative he sounded, he looked back up, forcing a smile, knowing he was now the one supposed to be setting the example.

"Okay, thank you CDI, good work, now CDS, we've all heard how bad this is, and what the enemy's doing, now, what can we do? How can we stop this, and what do you need?"

The CDS looked back at him, his face set and serious.

"Well firstly Sir, we need to implement Section 52 of the Reserve Forces Act, let's get our reserves mobilised and into the fight."

"Of course." the PM replied, as the CDS quickly turned to his aide, his voice low. "Get that out now on all channels, quick as you can please."

They watched the Major leave the room, as the CDS took a breath and removed his glasses rubbing the lenses with a piece of cloth as he continued.

"At the moment we've got most of our army, navy and air force deployed overseas meeting our other NATO commitments. With your permission PM I'd like to issue the orders for the immediate recall of all our forces. If NATO can't or won't help us then to hell with the commitments."

"You have my permission CDS, let's make that happen."

The CDS nodded as another aide left to carry out the orders. He finished polishing the lenses and put the glasses back on before continuing.

"Now, even if these Brigades left today, it's going to take us at least a week to get the heavy equipment back here. We need to buy ourselves the time we need to get our forces back and get our reserve forces armed and ready. So, this is what I'm proposing.

For the next twenty minutes all tiredness and fatigue had gone as the room listened intently to what the CDS proposed. When he'd finished talking all eyes rested on the PM, waiting for the final decision, as he stared back at the map board, looking at the red and blue lines now scrawled on it. The huge weight of responsibility really bore into him and he couldn't help but think about all the men and women who would suffer at what he was about to order. Finally, he nodded.

"Ok CDS, let's get it done, whatever you feel is necessary."

The General nodded, pleased that the PM was decisive as he glanced over to the Chief of Police, both sharing a look before the CDS asked,

"Sir, can I also recommend that for now, we implement Martial Law in the areas of Dorset and Newcastle, until this state of emergency is resolved?"

"Now hang on General," This time the Undersecretary stood up, his palms flat on the table, "may I ask why you feel the need to do that? I've seen no reason to indicate why we'd need to implement Martial Law.

The CDS looked across at the Chief of Police, who replied.

"Undersecretary, we've not yet had any further contact with any of our police forces in those areas and given what we're facing, I cannot see how we can effectively police these areas anyway. As the CDS so eloquently put it earlier, our police forces are not trained to take on an army, our role is to police by consent, to be used to keep the peace. However, we're already receiving requests from other forces such as Hampshire and Northumberland for more officers. Now I've spoken to the CDS and I have to agree I think Martial Law in those areas allows me to pull my own officers back and help police the areas that we do own."

The Undersecretary looked aghast as the PM reluctantly agreed. "Very well, Martial Law is now implemented in the counties of Dorset and Newcastle. Chief, you have my permission to do what you can in those areas."

He watched as the Police Chief nodded to one of his team and both quickly left the room to get the message sent. Even with the communications blackout, the message could be passed to patrol cars by radio from the neighbouring counties, where word would eventually filter through to the officers on the ground.

The PM stood up, with his stomach still grumbling, if he was hungry then surely others were too. He was about to see if he could get some breakfast sent in, when one of Sir Charles team appeared in the doorway, his face sombre. He stepped inside the room, closing the door behind him and walked over to the CDI, handing him the report before quickly leaving the room. The CDI stood for a few moments, reading the report before looking first to the PM and then to the CDS, his face solemn. "I'm sorry to bring more bad news, but just as we feared, the rescue services have found the body of the Prime

Minister in the rubble, they've confirmed it's him, he's dead. I'd better go and check on what else is being reported."

Sir Charles turned to leave the room, when the Undersecretary asked, "Is there any further news on survivors?"

"No, apart from the seven they pulled out last night, there's been no one else found alive."

"Thank you, Sir Charles," his words echoed behind him as the door closed.

Everyone in the room was quiet, as the PM stood up, and said quietly, "Can everyone please stand and join me in a minute's silence out of respect for the former PM and all those who lost their lives yesterday."

Everyone stood, heads bowed, to observe the silence, when Sir Charles burst back in through the door red faced. The CDS looked up angrily. "What the hell Sir Charles, we're trying to observe a-"

"I thought we weren't doing a news conference?" he interrupted, as he pushed past the seats to get to the TV remote. Quickly he turned it on, the feed from one of the larger main screens now bursting through to the conference room.

Everyone in the room looked on confused as the PM asked Sonya, "We're not, not yet anyhow, are we?" She merely shrugged in surprise, not knowing what was going on as they saw the now familiar news reader appear onscreen. Across the bottom of the screen the words *'UK Government to hold press conference at 08:00'* flashed before their eyes as in disbelief everyone looked around the table, murmurs turning to raised voices as everyone tried to guess who this alluded to.

The PM looked up at the clock, it was 07:20, they had forty minutes to find out who had called the conference.

Sonya quickly stood up and walked to the door, yanking it open and shouted over to one of her civilian operatives, "I want confirmation on who survived Chequers, did any member of the Cabinet survive? Who's called this bloody press conference?"

Sir Charles quickly scanned through his notes, "The seven survivors from Chequers were all from the house staff, two were outside on a break and five were found in the cars, no-one from the Cabinet survived." He pointed over to the PM, "The only Cabinet member still alive is you Sir."

Sonya turned back to the TV, confusion all over her face, "Who the hell has called this then?" she muttered.

The Police Chief returned, his face red with rage. "Prime Minister, it looks like we have a serious problem. Something's going on in London, I've just been informed that the Chief Constable for the Met has been arrested and replaced by her deputy. He's now the new Met Chief of Police and as the *new* Chief of Police he's ordered me to stand down immediately and report to London."

The PM looked confused, "New Chief of Police? Who the hell gave him the authority to do that? What did he say exactly?"

"He's informed me that subject to further investigations and criminal proceedings, Chief Superintendent Jennings has been arrested and I'm to return immediately to London to face a disciplinary hearing myself. Apparently, this has been ordered by the Prime Minister this morning?"

"Hang on!" the CDS leapt to his feet, "the Prime Minister is dead, we all know that. So, who the bloody hell is behind this?"

The CDS reached down and pressed the button to activate the intercom, allowing him to chat to any of the stations outside. "Patch us through to New Scotland Yard immediately please, get us the person who thinks he's the new Chief of Police on the line NOW!"

After only a few seconds one of the operators responded, "Sir, it would appear that someone from London is already requesting a video call with us, it's from the...what the?.. apparently Sir, it's from the *Prime Minister?*" The tone confirming the confusion.

"What?" this time it was the Undersecretary's turn to be surprised. A murmur erupted around the room as this new piece of news was digested.

Everyone turned to look at the screen as the image switched over, showing a large oak desk, two union flags hanging in the background and a man behind the desk in a light blue suit. His cropped blonde hair was slicked back and he sneered arrogantly at the camera.

"Well, I'll be God damned!" muttered Jeffery. Behind the desk, facing them all on the big screen sat the smirking face of the Secretary of State for Science Innovation and Technology Samuel Hewitt.

Jeffery watched the figure on screen, who was urgently scanning the people assembled in the conference room. His smile vanishing immediately as his eyes settled on Jeffery. There was a flash of something there, was it surprise or annoyance? Jeffery couldn't tell. Samuel Hewitt quickly regained his composure, the thin smile returning, his cold blue eyes staring at them.

"Jeffery? You're alive? What on earth are you doing there? Why were you not at Chequers? I was led to believe that everyone in the Cabinet had perished at the PM's function?" He noted that as Samuel spoke, he kept glancing over to someone behind the camera, who was he looking at? Was that a look of annoyance? Jeffery wondered.

"No Samuel, as you can see, I'm fine and still breathing, I was held up in a meeting, hence lucky enough to miss the party. I am confused though; how is it you weren't at the party? You were supposed to be there?"

Someone off camera muttered something, they could all see Samuel look over, as if seeking direction, before he confidently replied, "The PM wanted me here in London as the designated survivor, I was supposed to be in Downing Street when it was destroyed, but luckily for me I was attending an interview at New Scotland Yard."

"That's strange," Jeffery replied suspiciously, "I spoke to Yvette last night on a video call about twenty minutes before the attacks started, she was also in Downing Street and she told me that she was the designated survivor and that the PM had specifically asked for her. She was there signing paperwork; we were on a videocall talking when the red phone was activated. Why would he also ask for you? I thought there was to be only one designated survivor?"

Samuel's face pinched in confusion as he simply said, "You must be mistaken Jefferey, I'm the designated survivor, perhaps you misunderstood her?"

The CDS quickly scribbled something on paper and handed it to one of his officers stood nearby who left the room quickly. Then he wrote in big letters on another piece of paper the words, *'Don't divulge anything yet!'* showing it to the PM.

Jeffery simply nodded in response to the General before replying, "No I don't think I was mistaken, she was in London, and the Foreign Secretary wouldn't lie about that. So again, why were you not at the party?"

"Jeffery I'm not going to try to second guess what the PM was thinking, but here we are, the last two surviving members of the Cabinet." his voice dismissive.

Jeffery looked on puzzled replying, "We haven't had anything confirmed yet Samuel, we still may yet find someone alive. You thought until a short time ago that I was dead, yet here I am."

"Yet there you are, a very unexpected surprise I might add. As for finding anyone else alive, I think we both know the chances of that are extremely slim. What are you doing there anyway? It looks like some kind of briefing room." Samuel peered closer to the screen, scrutinising the figures there, as he continued, "There are lots of people there, ahh I do see some faces I recognise though, there's Sonya, and there's the Chief of Defence, hello General and, ahh, William the Undersecretary, and is that Sir Charles I see hiding in the background?"

"Samuel, no-one's hiding, they're all here working with me," he replied testily, "now look, we're extremely busy working on our current problem, I don't know how much you do know, but we're up against it here and could do with your help to answer some questions."

"Speaking of there, where are you? I don't recognise that background, are you still in London?"

Remembering what the CDS had written he simply replied, "I'm somewhere safe for now, you?"

Samuel smiled back, his tone guarded, "I'm somewhere safe in London."

"Okay," he replied, pedantically, "so we're both nice and safe. Now what the hell's going on Samuel? Do you mind telling me why someone in London is playing at being the PM? And who's called this press conference at eight o' clock?"

Samuel smiled, answering the questions with more questions. "Are you the one who's responsible for all the orders coming into London, are you the one issuing orders to the Metropolitan Police? Was it your idea to try to help the King escape?"

"Try to escape? What do you mean by that?" he answered confused. "I'm responding to the on-going crisis, and yes, I'm the one issuing the orders, and yes, I'm the one who's trying to get the King and Queen out of London safely. Can I ask what you're doing there? From the looks of it, not much."

The officer whom the General had sent off with the note, now returned, whispering in the General's ear. He quickly scribbled a note before passing it to the PM. He looked down seeing the words, "He's lying, just confirmed Foreign Secretary, was Desig Surv." Jeffery looked up, now tired of the lies and games. Whatever Samuel was trying to do, it was beginning to grate on him. Realising Samuel was lying, suddenly gave him a thought. He stared at him, his voice hostile,

"Okay Samuel, enough games, what's going on? Are you the one playing at being the Prime Minister? Have you had one too many sips on the power coffee and it's going to your head? Come on enough games now, for once be honest."

Samuel nodded then his face turned hostile, as if a switch had been flicked inside. His demeanour changed in an instant, gone was the smile and courteous look, as his jaw hardened, his face looking more sinister.

"Very well Jeffery, as you wish." His eyes flicked over to the CDS, "General, I'm ordering you to immediately stand down all of our Armed Forces and rescind the alert status you've been sending out. I want every plane to be landed, every ship to be returned to port and every soldier to be ordered back to barracks. I understand that you're all encountering communications difficulties, so I'll give you until 11:00 to get these orders carried out."

Leaving the CDS open mouthed, Samuel looked over to the Police Commissioner, "Chief, I understand you've been ordered back to London immediately by your superior? I'll expect you here by the end of the day, any later and I'll order an immediate arrest warrant in your name, please don't be late."

Finally turning to Jefferey he said, "And as for you, I'll expect you and your team back in London later today. We need you here to help me sort out all this mess. Seeing as I have no idea where you are, I'll give you until 16:00 to get here, that should you give you enough time don't you think?"

Everyone sat motionless, looks of confusion and anger on their faces at the dismissive attitude of the MP speaking to them. Finally after a few stunned moments it was Jeffery who spoke. "Samuel, who the hell do you think you are to be dishing out orders like that? You're a junior member of the Cabinet and I have seniority, also I'd like to add that I've already been sworn in as PM, now whatever your thinking or scheming, I'm ordering you now to stop it. Stand down."

Samuel smiled and leaned closer to the Camera. "Jeffery, I am the Prime Minister."

"Impossible!" the Undersecretary jumped out of his chair, as people began to shout at the screen with voices raised. It was Sonya who yelled for quiet. The smiling figure on the TV sat quietly, almost revelling at the scene playing out before him. Eventually as calm returned, it was the CDS who spoke, "Ok, if you say you're the Prime Minister, do you mind explaining to me just how that came to be?"

"It's simple, early this morning, the surviving party members held an emergency session where they voted to elect a new party leader. Because at the time I was believed to be the only Cabinet Minister left alive and given what I knew of the crisis so far and the PM's plans for the future, I was elected. At the time you were presumed dead, which is irrelevant now as I'm already sworn in, at 05:40 this morning the King confirmed me as the new PM. I'm now the elected and confirmed Prime Minister of the UK."

The Undersecretary intervened, "Now hang on, Samuel, firstly that vote should never have happened as the Defence Minister at that time was still alive, you can't just presume someone is dead, and simply vote without them, so the vote is nullified. Secondly for the King to confirm your appointment, you need to have an audience with him in person. He's currently on his way out of London. There's no way you've managed to get within five miles of him."

Forcing a smile Samuel retorted, "Undersecretary, from now on you will address me as either Prime Minister or Sir, and the King is not on his way out of London. The King is currently in Buckingham Palace under house arrest, I should know, as I signed his arrest warrant this morning."

Jeffery was thinking quietly, tapping a pen against his mouth watching Samuel on screen as a thought occurred to him. "You just said the King was arrested this morning? You mean that after he endorsed you, you placed him under arrest?"

"I did Jeffery, that's correct, his was the first of many arrest warrants that I've signed today," he exclaimed proudly. "Today begins a new dawn for all of us and a new dawn for our country, think of it as a more republican way of life. You can either embrace it or become its enemy, either way this country of ours is moving forward with or without you."

Shouts of fury erupted around the room, as the CDS smiled thinly and stated loudly, "May I remind you that any detention of the King is illegal and by doing so you've now overplayed your hand. If as you say he is under house arrest, then that opens you up immediately to treason. That's a powerful word to have against you. Is that what you want? Is playing at being the PM worth that? Because that's still a capital punishment in this country."

"General, from your tone and from what you've just said am I to assume that you won't be carrying out my orders to stand down our military forces?"

The CDS stared back intently as he replied, "Oh please don't assume anything from me. In case I've left you in any doubt as to my intentions, I can categorically state that we won't be standing anything down and I won't be following any orders from a self-made tyrant. In fact, I think I can say that on behalf of all the armed forces of this country, you can go and fuck yourself!"

Some of the military personnel in the room smiled and clapped, clearly the CDS had said the right words. Samuel's face flushed red as he countered, "So be it General, it's clear to me now whose side you're on. What about the rest of you? Police Chief, are you coming back to London? Will you follow the orders of your PM?"

The Police Chief looked on smiling, "Of course I will, I'll happily follow the orders of my elected leaders."

The smile of triumph on Samuel's face was short lived however, as the Chief turned to look at Jeffery, "So *Prime Minister*, what would you like me to do?" The CDS clapped him on the back enthusiastically.

Samuel glared back from the screen as he spat out, "Fine, play it your way Police Chief, what about you Jeffery? There's still room in my Cabinet for a good mind, I've always liked the way you've conducted yourself. Do you want a senior role in the future of our country?"

Jeffery looked around the room, before smiling and turning to the camera, "You're right, I do have a role to play in the future of my country, but that role is not with you. Samuel, we've never seen eye to eye before and we're certainly not going to now. Good luck with your plan though, I look forward to seeing you behind bars."

Samuel looked up furiously to the person behind the camera, saying something unintelligible, as the screen went blank as the feed was cut, The PM quickly walked up to the TV and confirmed it was indeed off. Once happy, he looked back at the people assembled there. His anger simmering at the tone and manner of the junior minister. Something about the way that the MP had casually ordered them all about, had rankled him. He looked towards the CDS.

"He was asking about our location, is there any chance he would know where we are now?"

The CDS shook his head, "Not a chance Sir, the first and only Minister to ever know of its existence is you and the people in this room. And even then, when you all flew in here, you didn't see exactly where you landed. Sure you know where my residence is, but we're miles away from that now. One piece of countryside looks like the next. I bet if I dropped you off a few miles from here you'd all never remember how to get back, let alone find Wonderland on the map."

Jeffery leant back against one of the side tables, his face pinched in thought. "Samuel's never been like this before, in all the cabinet meetings I've seen him at he's quiet, unassuming, but highly intelligent. That's why he was made the Science and Technology Minister. What the hell has got into him? I didn't recognise the man we saw then."

Sonya spoke out, "But absolute power can corrupt anyone."

"Yes, but so quickly? From junior minister to PM overnight?" He replied puzzled, "I mean could he be the Prime Minster instead of me? Is he correct, does he have the legal power now?"

The Undersecretary shook his head, "Absolutely not Sir, he's correct in the fact that the Party can elect a new leader, but not in the middle of a crisis, especially when there's a more senior serving Cabinet minister still in government. He's bet on the wrong horse, and with you still alive, the party will simply rescind the decision, revoking his right to be PM. And as for the King endorsing it, if he's had him arrested, then by doing so, his Majesty's decision would be deemed null and void as it could be claimed to have been made under duress. There's no legal basis or standing for Samuel to claim to be the Prime Minister, it's a fantasy, a pipe dream of his."

"The trouble is though Undersecretary," the CDS countered, "It doesn't matter if he has legal precedence or not, if he has always been part of this all along, then he has nearly one hundred and twenty thousand fully armed troops landing here, ready to go soon. I don't care how much we argue the point, with that many soldiers ready to go, we're on the back foot already."

"Do you think he's part of this CDS? Really?" the PM asked reluctantly, "One of our own simply going along with this? I remember the Brigadier saying they'd need someone on the inside for this to work, but that high up in government? I mean, I was fully expecting it to be an aide at best, but one of the Cabinet? Him? I just don't know if I can believe that."

"You heard him yourself Sir," The CDS replied, "He's trying to get us to order all our forces to stand down, even after everything that's gone before, you don't stand down, you *never* stand down, you stand *up*, you escalate and prepare. I believe he wasn't at the PM's party because he knew what was going to happen. Regardless of what we think, we need to seriously consider London as compromised. He's already got the Metropolitan Police Chief listening to him, following orders. I can't imagine what the hell is going on over there now. To order the arrest of the King? And then for someone to carry it out." his voice trailed off in disbelief at the news.

Sonya looked up, "But what about the King's own guard? The Household Division. They're nearby, would they really allow the Police to simply arrest him? Wouldn't they intervene to protect him?"

The Police Chief shook his head as he answered, "Almost all of his Majesty's troops in London are all out on the ground, helping the emergency services with the rescue efforts in Westminster. The only people left guarding the King were his own Royal Protection Officers, and a few soldiers. SO14 belongs to the Met, so if they were going after him, they could have captured him when the shifts changed over."

"It's that simple?" the PM asked incredulously.

The Police Chief nodded slowly, "I'm afraid so Sir."

"Can't we order the Kings troops back into the Palace to simply break him out?" Sonya countered.

"And then what?" the PM intervened, "We've got our troops and armed police fighting each other on the streets of London, in full view of the world's press. Not exactly good for our credibility, is it? No, that's what all this was about, don't forget, someone wants us to do that. I'm not ordering our troops and police forces to lock horns and start battling it out in the capital."

He looked up, slowly nodding his head deep in thought as he began to formulate what to do. He began to tell those around him what he wanted.

"Right, let's start first by confirming what Samuel said. Sir Charles, use whatever intelligence and means you can to find out if the King is under lock and key. If he is being held then find out where. CDS, I want you to get the message out to all our forces, we are the ones they are to take orders from, not this phantom PM, and then I want you to work on our options. Can we mount any kind of rescue operation to get the King out now? Undersecretary, I need you to find out about this vote from the party, has it happened, and if so, how many votes and can we get through to them to reverse or stop the decision? If the King's being held by this quisling PM, then how can he claim to not be under duress when he allegedly endorsed the man? Sonya, I need you to obtain information on this press conference, it's not for another thirty minutes, try to find out where, who's in attendance, and what they'll be speaking about. If necessary, let's see if we can get one of our own to join it and ask some hard questions. Then let's start to get my face out there, show people I'm alive, I'm now the PM and there's still a government in charge, hopefully then people can make their own decisions on what's really happening and who to believe."

Jeffery turned to the Chief of Police, "Chief, get word out to the other police forces, there's an imposter in London illegally pretending to be the PM. They're to only follow guidance or orders from our government, namely us and certainly not from the Met or anyone in London. Once you've confirmed that, then I'd like you to find out through your sources who can we trust in London, do you have any old friends or colleagues in the Met who will see this for what it is? Let's find out if we have any friends left there."

He stood up, invigorated, feeling alive and for the first time in his career, feeling like he knew what he needed to do. The others all stood up determined and focussed as they filed out the door, with a new purpose and energy. The CDS smiled as everyone left the room to carry out their tasks. Finally, he thought to himself, now we have a leader, I just hope it didn't come at the cost of a King.

5

The False God

Wonderland Operations Centre (WOC)

Thirty minutes later and the news conference was displayed on one of the big screens of the ops room. Below the screens, people were still busy working, as they ate their breakfast quickly, the tea and bacon rolls being brought up from the canteen one floor below providing welcome respite. The news being displayed on the TV showed two familiar media presenters sat opposite each other, deep in discussion about the latest breaking news, stating that a new Prime Minister had been sworn in, while they waited for the conference to start. They were animatedly chatting about what this could mean, is the outgoing Prime Minister incapacitated or worse, and were the rumours true about foreign troops landing in the UK? If so, what would the new PM do? Mid-sentence, one of the news readers stopped, the picture changed and was replaced with the familiar lectern, the government crest emblazoned on the front and the flags of the UK in the background. It appeared to be the press conference room in Downing Street, but as Downing Street was now nothing more than a smoke-filled ruin, this had to be some-where else. Jeffery wondered where they were now, as he saw figures emerge through the doorway.

On screen, all those at the conference quietened down, voices hushed, as they saw the newly appointed Metropolitan Chief emerge, a forthright look on his face carrying a pile of folders. He walked over to the side of the lectern waiting for the Phoney PM to join him.

"What the hell does he think he's bloody doing?" the Police Chief muttered.

The flash and click of cameras increased as Samuel Hewitt, the self-proclaimed Prime Minister now emerged into the limelight, a stern and focussed look on his face as he walked to the lectern, his hands resting either side of it as his eyes worked the room.

"Good morning," he began, his tone solemn, "thank you all for being here today, firstly I must share with you all some very sad and grave news and that is that at 06:00 this morning, it was confirmed by rescuers on site, that our beloved Prime Minister was killed yesterday, along with all of his Cabinet Ministers and staff at his country residence in Chequers." He paused as the reporters gasped in shock, some had heard rumours of an attack, but to hear it now confirmed in front of them still hit them like a hammer. Some began shouting questions out, demanding more information, but Samuel simply stood there, raising his hand to silence them. "Please everyone, I'll answer questions at the end, but for now please let me finish."

"All his Cabinet?" the CDS muttered, "Samuel only spoke to you less than thirty minutes ago. He knows you're alive, what is he playing at I wonder?"

Jeffery took a sip of his tea as he whispered back, "I have no idea General, but if people do find out that I'm alive, then they'll question the legality of Samuel's position. You can't have two leaders. If people still think I'm dead, it gives him the time he needs to try and solidify his own position."

Both men resumed their focus on the screen, wondering what Samuel would say next. They heard the voices of the assembled press turn to murmurs, as on TV, he looked around the press room and continued. "Last night, as our capital was attacked relentlessly and as our government offices and Parliament were being bombed, we found out that the Prime Minister's residence had also been attacked. This attack resulted in the destruction of Chequers, killing almost everyone there. The reports we have received have confirmed that there was only one survivor, who is currently undergoing medical treatment here in London."

Everyone in the Ops room turned to the Chief of Intelligence as the CDS asked, "Sir Charles, I thought you said there were seven survivors?"

Sir Charles glanced down at the report in his hands, his own face betraying surprise. "I'm sorry CDS but that's correct. I have it confirmed by the teams on the ground, seven survivors, all on their way to hospital."

The PM turned to the Police Chief speaking quietly he said, "Find out which hospital they're being treated in. If their injuries allow it, let's see if we can't get them sent somewhere *safer* other than a London hospital, I don't like the sound of that."

"Of course Sir," he replied, walking off to carry out the orders as Jeffery turned back to the screen as the Phoney PM continued, "Now I appreciate the severity of the news that I have just given you, and that usually you would have time to process this, however

I'm afraid that what I have to say next will come as even more of a shock." He paused again, as the reporters looked on. Taking a deep breath he continued, "It has been no secret that our Prime Minister had become good friends with the President of Tumat. President Iylanovitch and our Prime Minister both shared a vision, a future of prosperity and peace, a future of trade deals, shared interests and even a future of shared military alliances. The Prime Minister had worked hard to get Tumat recognised at the United Nations and to get them recognised as a member of NATO. This has not gone unnoticed by the people of Tumat."

The CDS whispered to the PM, "He's building up to it."

He turned back to listen. On screen Samuel's voice remained steady and calm. "Our Prime Minister and his Cabinet had made no secret about the fact he wanted the Monarchy abolished. He had always said that the establishment was outdated, out of touch and unnecessary. The finances required to run the establishment, not to mention it's recent scandals and embarrassments had already proven his words to be true. He'd been discussing with the Cabinet in private, his plan next year to put it to the people and have a people's vote on the future of the Monarchy. Let them decide for themselves, he had said."

He paused to sip on a glass of water as Jeffery shook his head in disgust, keeping his voice low and quickly adding, "The PM did *not* say that. He had already agreed with the King to lower the sovereign grant. They were to announce it next week. This is nothing but a big pack of lies."

They remained watching as he continued to speak.

"One month ago, thanks to the shared interests between our countries, the intelligence services of Tumat shared with our government a file, a report that was so unbelievable, so unthinkable that at first, our PM believed it to be untrue. They had asked that we keep the report limited within certain circles of government, therefore only six ministers had seen it or indeed knew of its existence. I was one of those ministers." He paused, allowing the suspense to build as his eyes darted around the room, drawing a breath he carried on.

"The report detailed an upcoming plot by our own Royal Family, who had already been secretly briefed on the PM's plans for a people's vote, to overthrow our government and to replace it with one more Monarchy friendly, to keep the establishment in power." Shouts now erupted again from the reporters, some were openly questioning, others shouting in disbelief. The Phoney PM held his hand up as he tried to quieten them down, but this time they had heard enough. Some were openly mocking his claim, until eventually the Chief of Police intervened, shouting, "QUIET! CALM YOURSELVES NOW! This is supposed to be a press conference. Let the Prime Minister finish the briefing, save your questions till the end." Samuel waited for the silence to return, nodding in thanks to the Police Chief as he continued. "We had been urged by the leaders of Tumat to keep the report hidden away from our own intelligence services, in fear of them having to choose between two masters. As you all know, our armed forces swear their allegiances to the Monarchy first and then to the government. If the report were to be believed, then the PM did not want to run the risk that we could no longer trust our own forces, whose loyalties lie with those who sought to usurp us. So how could the government defend itself, or its people, from an oppressive regime heavily armed with its own army? He had spoken at great length to President Iylanovitch about the problem and between the two leaders, they came up with a defensive alliance, a pact that would see the forces of Tumat come to assist our government if this attempt at a coup were ever to be attempted. Despite warnings from his own senior MP's, the Prime Minster refused to act on the intelligence of the report, opting instead to wait for further evidence to present itself. Despite calls to keep the report hidden, he trusted certain members of his Cabinet, members whose loyalties lay not with the elected people's government, but within the establishment. That is how the establishment came to learn of the plan and that's why last night, they attacked their own government, hoping to quickly destabilise and destroy this government before using the Civil Contingencies Act 2004 to grant the King powers that would allow him to install his own Royal friendly government, a puppet government. To reiterate, last night's attacks were conducted by UK military forces loyal to the Royal Family. Therefore as Prime Minister, I have now given authorisation for Tumat to begin landing its peacekeeping forces to help protect us and to stop any further attacks. Now, time is brief, but I will answer a few questions."

He looked around the room, nodding to someone at the back.

"Prime Minister, are you seriously telling us, that last night's attacks were conducted by our own forces, our own military, under orders from the King, some type of coup d'etat? Is that what you're asking us to believe?" the voice was disbelieving.

He looked directly at him as he said forcibly, "Yes, as horrible as it may sound, that's exactly what I'm saying, you must understand that when you threaten to take away power from these people, power that they've had for centuries they'll fight back. Don't forget that this is nothing new, Lord Mountbatten discussed doing the very same thing to the government in 1968."

A barrage of questions were thrown back as he nodded to an individual at the front. The noises died down as the microphone was passed to them.

"Prime Minister, firstly, the plot involving Mountbatten in 1968 that you talk of was nothing but rumour and conjecture, there was no evidence ever found of a plot. Now with regards to last night's attacks, where is the evidence? Where is this report from Tumat that you mentioned? We need to see it, if it's the smoking gun you claim it is then produce it now, and secondly if I may Prime Minster, where are the Royal Family, you mention the Kings role in this, is he under arrest? Is he in handcuffs? Where is he?"

"The report and all copies were being held in the Downing Street archives, which as you all know was destroyed last night. The five other Ministers who read the report are all missing presumed dead, I'm the only person left alive who saw it and can vouch for its existence. I shall be contacting our friends in Tumat to see if we can get another report sent over, but I have to be honest, these are not the sort of files you make numerous copies of and then leave lying around. As for the King and Queen, they are being held under house arrest at Buckingham Palace, to face charges of treason against the UK government and its people."

Yet more shouted questions were fired forwards as another reporter was chosen to speak.

"Prime Minister, you mentioned earlier that someone had leaked the report to the Royal Family, and were working with the military, do you know, or can you say who that person is? Were they also killed at Chequers? Are there still arrests ongoing? Do you have everyone involved in this suggested plot?"

Samuel looked over at the Police Chief and nodded as the Chief now cleared his throat and began to speak. "I can't comment on an ongoing Police investigation, however what I can confirm, is that we are currently looking at another possible eight suspects at this time, all with close links to both the military and the Royal Family."

Jeffery heard the CDS take a deep breath as if expecting the blow to come as the Police Chief read out the names of suspects.

"Those suspects we wish to talk to further are the former Minister for Defence, Jeffery Dickinson, and the senior members of his defence council, General James Catmur, Admiral Sir Tony Phillips, General William Boswell, Air Chief Marshal Penny Moore, General Sir Charles Lynwood and General Tony Kew."

"Clever boy!" Sir Charles exclaimed, "after seeing us all here earlier on the video call, he's now painting us out to be the bad guys, and girls of course." he added smiling as the CAS raised her eyebrows.

The Phoney PM now intervened at the conference, holding his hand up to silence the murmurs as he spoke. "These seven people are believed to have been the masterminds behind the attacks last night. I've spoken with my own legal team and can confirm that as of this moment they are all no longer serving members of the armed forces, they are to be stripped of all ranks and powers and anyone who knows of their whereabouts is to inform the authorities immediately."

The people working in the ops room all stopped working and looked to the direction of the Prime Minister and the CDS, their shock and confusion clear to see. Sensing the mood in the ops room, the CDS said loudly, "Relax now everyone, this is all part of his little plan. He has no authority and what you're listening to is the enemy speaking. That man holds no authority over us. You're all working for the *real* government of the United Kingdom. I promise that when this is all over no-one's going to jail, now concentrate on your own tasks at hand please."

An uneasy silence descended over the room as everyone settled back down as the drama on the TV played out.

At the press conference there were more shouted questions, one louder than the others, "Prime Minister, is the Defence Minister still alive then? We thought you said all the cabinet were killed? If he's still alive, then doesn't he outrank you? Can you really call yourself the PM in that case? Wouldn't he be the next in line to be the legal PM?"

Jeffery looked over to Sonya questioningly who leaned in closer, whispering. "David Jones, from the Independent. He owes me a favour or two."

"But how did you get the message out to him in thirty minutes?" he asked amazed.

She lowered her eyebrows, smirking. "Ask no questions, get no lies," before stepping back to continue watching. Shaking his head in amazement he focused on what was now being said, the Phoney PM had gripped the rostrum, his knuckles were white, clearly the question had barbed him.

Samuel was forced to raise his voice above the growing noise as he forcefully said, "I can assure everyone now, that me being sworn in as Prime Minister was done correctly and followed the letter of the law. As for this criminal outranking me, that is irrelevant, he and his fellow conspirators have broken the law and committed treason against the state. I'll be seeking to get him removed officially from office as soon as we can assemble what's left of our government, and yes, they're all still alive, he was the only Minister who didn't appear at Chequers, because he knew of the impending attacks. It's only a matter of time before we apprehend him and his team. Now, next question please."

He scanned the room, his face settling on another reporter seated at the front.

"Prime Minister, what about these reports of troops landings in Newcastle and in the southwest? Can you confirm these reports? Who are they? And what do they want?"

"As I've mentioned earlier, those soldiers were sent from Tumat, one of our NATO partners, to help us in this time of crisis. People are not to be scared or fearful, they're here to help at the request of the UK government under an arrangement that was agreed two weeks ago. People are to ignore them and go about their daily lives as best they can."

Samuel looked away, forcing a smile, to answer another question, but unperturbed the reporter clung onto the microphone his voice rising as he quickly replied, "But Prime Minister, I've been speaking to families that have driven all night to get here to London from Newcastle to stay with loved ones here. I've seen their mobile phone footage. It doesn't show troops here to help, I saw with my own eyes the evidence of troops shooting at our police officers in their cars, families being arrested and marched away, men in the streets being shot, I watched the cold-blooded execution of three unarmed border force guards whose hands were tied behind their backs. Would you call that helping? What is going on, what are you not telling us?"

The other reporters remained silent, shocked at what the reporter had just said. Realising he was going to have to answer, Samuel looked back at him, his eyes narrowed.

"I'm sorry, but I appreciate that stories of fear and suffering sell papers, or make great straplines for the press, but that's not the case here. I simply will not believe those rumours, any more than I would the tooth fairy or Santa Claus. Those troops are answerable to the UK government and NATO, and, as such, have to abide by the Laws of Armed Conflict, they can't simply execute people as they see fit. Unlike I might add, those forces loyal to the Crown. I'll say it again for the benefit of those hard of hearing, those troops are NATO troops, here at the request of the UK government. They are here to help us keep law and order and to assist us while we find out which branches of our military we can trust and which we must replace. It's that simple. As for the footage of troops shooting civilians, how do you know what you're seeing? One military uniform looks much like another and at night even more so. For all you know these witnesses of yours could have been watching forces loyal to the Crown trying to seize power there. Now onto another question please."

He turned to choose another, but the reporter was adamant, still he clung onto the microphone refusing to let go, this time almost shouting out, "But I'm not interested in straplines or headlines either! I'm interested in facts, something you're clearly not. The footage showed Russian issue clothing and weapons. Do you really expect us to believe that our own forces, troops that have defended us for centuries would simply murder civilians, and on such a grand scale? And that we're to simply roll over and allow another country's troops in? And where's the other NATO countries in all of this, why no American troops, German troops, Canadian, Dutch, why just Tumat? You're asking us to choose between our own army and a foreign one. Come on Prime Minister...or should I call you the TOOTH FAIRY?"

The room erupted into shouts and jeers, the press had smelt blood and were not buying what he was selling, clearly becoming more frustrated at losing the room, Samuel looked around as the questions now came thick and fast.

"Where did the missiles come from that struck the capital? How do you explain that? Are you saying they were launched by our own navy?"

He was forced to raise his own voice to be heard over the shouting as he struggled to answer. "We believe the missiles were cruise missiles launched from a Royal Navy submarine stationed somewhere in the North Sea. Details are vague though, as the first target struck was the UK's Radar monitoring network in Southampton. Once that had been destroyed, we lost our ability to track the missiles, so cannot pinpoint with any accuracy where the Submarine came from."

"What about these reports of attacks on the RAF bases up and down the country? Or the attacks on military bases? Why are we seeing fighter jets over the capital, if we're not to trust the military?"

Even with the microphone, Samuel had to shout to be heard, "I'm not aware of any attacks on RAF bases, I'll have to confirm that and get back to you. As for the fighters overhead, I'll shortly be issuing orders for all our military to stand down immediately. We cannot trust them at this time of great sensitivity and must be assured of their loyalties before we call them to arms again."

"What do you mean when you say we can't trust the military? My daughter's serving, are you saying I shouldn't trust my own daughter? Will you have her arrested too?"

"Who gave you authority to arrest the King, where's the proof?"

"Is the King in handcuffs? Will he be going to prison? What of the Queen?"

"Why are the phones still not working, and why no internet? Has Britain just become a police state?"

"What do you mean when you say friendly troops, who's really giving them the orders? What does America say about all this?"

"Are you even the real PM? How do we know you're not behind all of this?"

Deciding he had heard enough, they all watched as he simply turned and walked away, closely followed by the new Met Police Chief. Back in the ops room, Jeffery was happy to see the press hadn't simply just lapped it up and that they'd given him a hard time. Now at least he could see not everyone would believe the lies. The public were not as stupid as Samuel and whoever was pulling his strings had thought.

The sound was muted as the Undersecretary looked around him. "Well, I don't know about anyone else, but to me that looked just as good a car crash as any I've ever seen. The public are not going to believe any of that rubbish. If the press were hostile, then I'd love to see what the public make of it."

Sonya nodded, "I agree, I think if we get a press conference organised for 2pm, get you out there, explaining the facts, then we may already win the public over."

Sir Charles, overhearing them, walked over and joined in, his voice cautious.

"Sorry to have to be the one who rains on your little PR campaign Prime Minister, but that little show there, was not meant for the public, or for us, it was all for the benefit of NATO."

"What do you mean?" Sonya asked, "It's always all about the public."

The PM sighed as the realisation hit him. "Of course, NATO are meeting today at 11:00, after watching that press conference, they'll think our country's elected leader has now stood down the military and has endorsed those soldiers being here on UK soil. The General's letter will be discredited now as he's now been labelled a criminal and with no way for us to call them, they'll all stand down and go back to sleep. The Russians just brought themselves time. It was always about the time, not the public opinion."

Jeffery sat back in the chair rubbing his eyes. Time, he thought to himself, it was always about the bloody time, and time for them was quickly running out fast.

He was snapped out of his thoughts as the CDS and Sir Tony approached him, the CDS handing him a small red folder. Looking up in surprise he asked, "What is it CDS?"

Both men wore serious expressions as the CDS replied, "Sir Tony, may have an idea on how to slow down the troops landing in the South."

He quickly read through the file, his hands thumbing through the pages before looking up, his eyebrows raised. "Can this be done Sir Tony?"

"It can, and it will, with your permission PM, we already have the units standing by, ready for the go."

"Losses?" he asked, his head cocked.

The CDS interjected. "I don't think we can think about losses PM, not with what we could gain versus what we risk losing. Losses or not, we must roll the dice on this one."

"Thank you CDS, even so, it'll be on my order that these troops would be risking their lives. I'd like to know how much the butchers bill could cost us, before I give that order.

The CDS nodded solemnly and kept quiet as Sir Tony continued. "There could be some losses PM, yes, no operation is without it's risks, but I would also add, that this is their back yard, these troops have trained there for years. No one knows these waters better than they do, and this is their speciality. Besides, let's do to them what they've now done to us."

The Prime Minister scratched his chin thoughtfully, running through the options. They were both right, here he was moaning about the time running out and this operation, if it worked, could buy them just that. He opened the folder, taking the pen from the CDS and began to sign the orders...

6

One Of Their Own

All four were singing loudly, the adrenalin now beginning to wear off after the past hour's events, as the 4x4 bounced along the small ruts in the roads, the hedges and trees passing close by. Mike had been driving slower than usual, conscious of the precious cargo they were carrying on board, and not wanting it to all come falling out along the road. The tarp they had fitted had helped to secure the load, but even so he still found himself checking his wing mirrors more than usual, expecting to see sleeping bags or cans of food rolling down the road behind them. Sometimes when they hit a bump, they could hear the suspension ground out, with all four men grimacing at the sound. They were out of the wooded areas now and driving past open farm fields, only three miles away from the farm. Not long now he thought. He was looking forward to seeing the looks on everyone's faces when they saw the goods they'd brought back with them. He was imagining even Jonah forcing a smile. He'd really smashed the last of his credit cards, he'd hoped that Kate would understand, after all, it was her that managed the finances. He didn't fancy having to explain to her how he'd casually waxed nearly £3,000 on food and water and hoped that somehow, some form of government office would re-imburse him. Not that the money mattered, right now, he'd give any amount of money just to know where Chris and the other tanks had got to.

"Oh SHIT!" the voice of Patty snapped him from his daydream.

"What is it?" Doc asked from the back seat. Mike instinctively began to slow down further, as Patty quickly replied, "Mike don't slow down, it'll look too suspicious, keep driving, we're being watched."

Patty reached down to turn off the stereo, once the music had stopped, Mike could hear the heavy turbine whine of a helicopter, he'd missed it over the music. Keeping his eyes on the road, he tried to see what Patty was looking at, but with the angle he couldn't look up enough.

"Patty what is it?" he asked, as a large dark shadow slowly cut over them and the road, the down draft blowing the car in its wake. He looked to his right out of the driver's window and had to struggle to keep himself from swearing, as flying alongside them, at a height of no more than forty feet and matching their slow speed, was a Russian Hind attack helicopter. Mike had seen them before when working in Iraq and Kosovo, but they were always destroyed or damaged and never in the air. Now here they were in the middle of the Dorset countryside and one was flying next to them. The missile racks and gun pylons were fully loaded, and he could see just how big it truly was, as it now flew close enough to clearly see the pilot and gunner coldly watching the 4x4. Sat in the troop compartment, he could see another three faces were staring at them, pointing and no doubt deciding if it would be worth stopping their vehicle.

As if to point out the obvious Reaper exclaimed, "Oh shit! If they stop us and see the goods in the back, or find the weapons, we're fucking dead."

"Oh great," exclaimed Doc, "and if they just follow us back to the farm then what?"

"Relax guys," Mike replied, trying his best to look casual, "if they were going to shoot us, they would have done so already, they're just checking us out, now everyone be cool ok, we're just farmers at work, think like that, look like that and be cool."

Staring straight ahead and trying to ignore the helicopter, Patty replied, "Be cool?" That's a fucking flying tank right there, I don't mind admitting that right now I'm pissing in my pants."

Mike glanced at him, a thought jumping into his head as he replied, "What a great idea. Well done, Patty."

Patty looked back in blank surprise, as Mike pulled over to the side of the road and stopped the car in a cloud of dust. The three other men looked on at Mike like he'd lost his marbles, as he got out, walked over to the hedgerow and began to calmly unzip his flies and began to urinate on the hedges. The helicopter had banked around, the car stopping suddenly had caught the pilot by surprise as the helicopter came in low and loud, hovering a mere twenty feet from the 4x4, its guns trained on Mike.

The three men in the 4x4 sat dumbfounded, as Mike stood there taking a piss, now looked up to the pilots and gave them the middle finger as he continued to pee, the massive downdraft of the helicopter causing him to piss over himself covering him with urine.

"What the fuck Mike? You're going to get us shot!" shouted Patty.

They looked on in disbelief, as they saw the pilot and the gunner sat in the nose both laughing at the sight, clearly, they were enjoying themselves seeing Mike pee over himself and unbelievably the helicopter now turned sideways so the three in the back could see, clearly enjoying the show. Mike turned, making a big dramatic gesture of pointing at his trousers and gesticulating wildly in the helicopter's direction, clearly blaming them for his misfortune and his now, wet trousers.

On board the helicopter Colonel Yuri Golovin sat watching the dumb Englishman with amusement. There was always one, he thought, every village or town back home had one, and here, it was this guy. The pilot's voice crackled over the intercom, "Sir, looks like someone forgot to teach this durak to never piss into the wind."

"Yes, I agree," he said smiling, his eyes closely watching the vehicle and its occupants as the pilot continued, "What do you think, we could set down nearby and check them out, see what's in the vehicle?"

Golgolvin watched on as the man zipped up his trousers and walked to the car, the way he was pointing up at the helicopter and his clothes left them in no doubt what he was saying.

After a few moments Golgolvin decided he'd seen enough, "No, these clowns look more like farmers to me, they're rough and ready, I can't imagine anyone else stupid enough to go pissing in the wind and give us the finger. If they're anything like our farmers back home, they're probably still drunk from the night before." His thoughts drifted to home as he quickly decided, "We've wasted enough time here, let's go check out some of the farms in the area."

He sat back into his seat, as the helicopter shot up and forwards to gain speed and altitude, the airframe shuddering as the engines powered up. The helicopter continued slowly on its way as the men sat in the back resumed searching for any signs of any of the armoured vehicles that had escaped last night. After receiving his orders from the CinCS, he'd taken his six MI-28 Havoc attack helicopters and five Hind helicopters along with one hundred of his men and fanned out from Bovington, following the tell-tale tracks of the armour to find and hunt them down. Along with helicopters, he was also using the technological superiority of another unit, designated simply as 'Unit 163'. It was highly secretive, whose capabilities were only understood by the most senior officers in the division. It had been at the General's recommendation that Golgolvin had been told to use them and so far they'd helped him to find and destroy two scattered units of vehicles. One had been a mixture of lightly armed wheeled vehicles, still painted in their desert colours, easy to see from the air and trying to hide in woodland, and the other, two armoured Warrior vehicles, that made no attempt to hide and were parked in open fields. Now, they were onto the scent of another unit, already they had followed the tracks this far, but occasionally the tracks would stop, indicating where the armoured vehicles had taken to the road. When that happened, all the Colonel could do was search the immediate area, like a bloodhound losing the scent, sometimes he would be rewarded with more tracks appearing on the horizon, other times like now, they would simply disappear. He now sat back with the map and binoculars on his lap, judging where they could have gone to. The questioning of the prisoners last night had produced mixed results, some had said a few vehicles had escaped heading east, others said lots of vehicles had absconded and were heading north. Either way, somewhere down there in the calm peaceful looking countryside sat an enemy and every hour they wasted was another hour they would get further away. Knowing he could do nothing now but keep up the hunt he picked up the bino's and began to scan again.

Mike brushed himself off as best he could as he climbed back into the driver's seat, the wet jeans now clinging to his legs, uncomfortable and clammy. He looked over to the three shocked faces staring back and it was Patty who broke the silence, an angry look on his face. "And what the fuck was that all about?" he asked incredulously. "Mind explaining why you felt the need to put on that little show?"

"Simple," explained Mike, "you'd be surprised how often a smile and wave will get you through the trickiest of situations, me going out there and acting the class clown, meant they didn't see us as a threat. If I hadn't had done that, they would have followed us back to the farm, and I couldn't allow that. Besides the tarp back there was getting blown to buggery, another few minutes of that helicopter flying alongside, and it would have lifted off, revealing all the gear in the back, then they would have become suspicious. And I don't think anything that we would have said or done would have stopped them from detaining us. Now if you don't mind, let's get back, I've got some fresh clothes in the back and I'm already beginning to stink."

Seeing the futility in arguing further, Patty simply looked out the window, as Mike pulled the truck off the verge and back onto the track. After only a minute it was Reaper who spoke.

"Shit I ain't never seen anything like that, a full blown Russian gunship and you just go out, take a piss and then flip them the bird! Man, oh man. You got balls of steel there Mr Faulkes, I can tell you that. Balls of steel!"

Doc looked out the window as he replied, "And did you see the size of that fucking gun? it was pointed right at you. A two second burst of that and there'd be nothing left of you."

Seeing Patty was still annoyed and wanting to lighten the mood, Mike looked at Reaper through the rear-view mirror as he replied, "Well I was trying my best to look as big as I could as I got it out, I held it with three fingers, but still managed to piss on two!"

He saw the thin trace of a smile appear on Patty's face, who shook his head slightly before looking at him. "I saw the gunner on the Hind struggle to lock on, it must have been a really *small* target," his voice now more mischievous.

"Yeah, yeah, yeah," Mike replied in mock indignation, humour was always a good leveller, and he was secretly relieved himself it had worked. He always used the analogy of a swan when describing his own actions, calm and graceful on the surface, but underneath the water, out of sight, his legs were flapping like hell. He didn't want to admit it, but secretly he'd been absolutely bricking it. He grinned as everyone laughed again, the tension of the close escape evaporating as all four men relaxed again.

Within ten minutes they were back at the barn, carefully reversing the vehicle through the large doors and into the waiting throng of people who had gathered. All were keen to hear what had happened and to also see what supplies had been brought back."

Spider had already organised the work party and anyone not doing anything important gladly came over to help as the 4x4 was unloaded, the food and equipment laid out in piles, ready for the crews to take away after it had been checked off the list. Mike stood next to Spider, watching on, as Patty brought him up to speed on what had happened on the resupply run. Occasionally he'd look over at Mike, his eyes looking down to the damp patches on his trousers in disbelief, not quite believing what he was hearing. Finally, as Patty finished speaking, he turned to face Mike, shaking his head in disbelief, his voice jovial, "You just couldn't make this shit up could you. Well, you're all back now, and at least you've got the gear and food."

Spider stepped forward and knelt down, looking at the items, happy to see they had managed to bring everything on the list and more. He saw a pile of watches that he recognised, he'd seen them advertised before on the TV. They were the latest in outdoor extreme design, waterproof, shock proof and durable. He leaned over and picked one up, looking over to Mike quizzically. As if to answer, Mike looked over to Reaper who was animatedly telling a story to three of the guys around him. "Reaper, can you just come over here for a second please?" The young soldier smiled and walked over.

"Everything okay Mr Faulkes?"

"Sure, everything's fine," he said calmly, "I just need you to tell me the time please. It's not a trick question, I promise."

Without understanding why, the soldier instinctively looked at his watch hand, seeing the dead face of the smart watch looking back, suddenly realising from earlier it had run out of battery. "Err I'm sorry Mr Faulkes, my watch has died, I don't think I can charge it up either."

Smiling Mike leaned over, picking one of the new watches up, throwing it to Reaper who caught it quickly.

"There you go," he said, "now you don't need to worry about not knowing the time."

Smiling with thanks, the Fusilier eagerly began to break open the packaging as he walked back to the others to continue the story.

Mike looked back to Spider, "I noticed this morning, everyone was too reliant on their phones and smart watches, but with no way to charge them, after today we'd lose the ability to tell the time. Well now with these, everyone gets at least a watch and a torch, so no need to use their phones."

Patty then added, "We've also got everyone a rucksack with a washbowl, towel, fresh socks toothbrush and paste. At least if we get killed tonight we won't be smelling as bad as Mike here."

Spider nodded in understanding, smiling.

Changa and Sid walked over and began to pick up their vehicle's new tools when they both looked up at Mike. Changa with his nostrils flaring asked, "What's that smell? Can you smell that?"

Mike realised he had pushed his luck, he was beginning to stink worse than the barn, which was saying something. "That will be me, I think it's about time I got changed."

Changa looked closer seeing Mike's trousers were damp, "What the...Mr Faulkes have you pissed yourself?"

Ignoring the question, Mike carefully navigated through the new piles of kit, looking for what he wanted, quickly spotting the large rucksack that he had packed himself earlier in the store, marked with orange tape that he had placed on the handle. Picking it up, he checked the contents inside. A wash bowl, toothbrush, shower gel, fresh pair of socks, towel and some fresh clothes. He'd managed to get a pair of decent hiking boots, some cargo trousers which were drab green, a t-shirt, warm pullover and a hunter's goretex jacket which had a multi terrain pattern on. It was different to the uniform of the soldiers around him, but at least it was better than the clothes he was wearing now. They were torn, covered in blood, sweat and now urine and he knew even a washing machine wouldn't fix it, they were certainly destined for the bin when he changed. Happy with what he'd seen, he closed over the rucksack and hefted it over his shoulder before turning to reply to Changa.

"That happened when the gunship turned up."

"Gunship?" Changa exclaimed puzzled, as Sid asked, "What gunship? What on earth happened out there?"

Overhearing the exchange, Doc came over, his voice animated. "Mr Faulkes thought it a good idea to stare down a gunship, and all while taking a piss."

"I wouldn't say it quite like that, but yes I was taking the piss," Mike replied.

Changa's face was the perfect mask of confusion, "What happened out there?"

Mike smiled, "I'll let the Doc tell you both. Meantime if anyone needs me, I'm out the back getting cleaned up." With that he left them chatting as he walked from the barn to where the water tap was located. Quickly filling the bowl with cold water, he went back inside to find himself a quiet part of the barn, away from the others and spent the next ten minutes giving himself a cold strip wash, standing in the bowl to keep his feet clean as he scrubbed the past 24 hours off him. It was only after towelling himself dry and putting on new clothes did he feel finally clean again. The fresh socks were a god send and he smiled as his feet slid into the new boots, they were a little tight, but he knew they would stretch, happy to have something more suitable for being on the tank. He looked at his soft fabric shoes, already torn and discoloured, far from ideal for what they were planning to do over the coming days.

He left the pullover and the jacket in the bag, settling instead for one of the two drab olive t-shirts. It was too hot to wear anything else, the sun was relentlessly beating down on the metal roof of the barn and already the temperature must have been in the high twenties inside. Checking the rest of his gear was stowed in the rucksack, he quickly brushed his teeth using one of the bottled waters, rinsing his toothbrush clean as he packed it away. He grabbed his dirty old clothes into a bundle, wrapped them up and walked back outside to the burn pile he'd used earlier, throwing the dirty clothes there. At some point Sam would no doubt burn it all, he thought. A lot happier now and smelling clean and feeling refreshed, he walked back into the barn through the parked vehicles, watching as the soldiers around him all began to look through their own rucksacks, some were already walking to the tap, bowl in hand happy to at least get freshened up. Seeing the smiles around him Mike felt a sense of achievement, somehow more confident now. Last night, he had been an unknown entity, someone who had just turned up giving out advice, but now at least he hoped the soldiers would realise he knew what he was talking about and hopefully that would count for something. Because he knew this was probably as easy it would get. From now on, things would get harder, much harder and he needed them to trust him implicitly for what was to come next. He walked over to the pile of gear, picking up two of the watches and two of the Maglite torches. The torches each came with two filters, a yellow one and a red one which would be invaluable for working at night, nothing gave away a hidden position at night easier than white light. He walked around the back of the tank to the other side, shielded from view of the others and saw Bill and Smudge sat on the floor chatting animatedly as they both went through their own rucksacks, looking like kids at Christmas as they checked the contents. Walking up to them he passed each a torch and watch, both nodded in thanks as he sat his own rucksack down and looked over the side of the tank again, marvelling at the scrapes and cuts in the armour packs. For the first time in a while, he began to appreciate what having a large, armoured vehicle on the battlefield meant, whilst also quickly realising that protection came at a cost. Tanks were good, but only so long as you looked after them. With this in mind he asked, "Bill have you done your checks on the wagon? Checked the engine levels, running gear and all the tools?"

The driver looked up, thinking for a second before replying.

"I have Mr Faulkes, she's taken a bit of beating, but apart from some loose bolts I found nothing wrong, we're good."

"Okay, and have you checked all the bins, checked you've got all the tools? And then put the tools where you need them? If anything goes wrong, you need to know where every tool is, even in the dark. There's nothing worse than trying to find something in a hurry and not knowing where it is, especially when you're being shot at."

He saw the driver look at the vehicle, thinking before replying, "I think so, errm."

Mike smiled, as he realised, he'd forgotten they were both new to the game, one hadn't yet got to his regiment and the other hadn't yet fired a tank. The things he took for granted about being on the tank came from experience and he'd managed that by accepting help when he was a young fresh-faced Trooper from more senior people in his regiment. Now, it was time to pass that knowledge on, he'd better show them himself.

"Right guys, just stop what you're doing for the moment and follow me."

He climbed on top of the turret, sitting beside the commander's cupola and the Remote Weapon's Station, patiently waiting for the two Troopers to follow him up. Once they were settled, he began, "I apologise guys, today I've been so busy racing around and doing other things with the others that I forgot that both of you have only recently qualified to be on the tank. I keep expecting you to both do things that you might not know how to do. Usually, we'd have an operator with us, a mother hen as we call them, to help and look after the crew. But as it is right now, it's just us three, and when I get off the tank it'll be just you two. So, let's go through a few things about the realities of living on the tank, talk about where your tools will go, tips to make your life easier and general things so that once we get somewhere, I can leave you guys to crack on and get the work done yourselves. Happy with that?"

Bill simply nodded as Smudge replied, "Yes, happy with that."

"Right," Mike continued, "no doubt you've seen that the tank we're on is different from the ones you've trained on. This one is called Megatron, she's what they call TES or Theatre Entry Specific and has all the goodies and toys that a warfighting tank would have. There's a number of differences between this model and the normal tank, and I'll run you through them all."

"Why do they call her Megatron?" Bill asked.

Mike laughed, "That Bill is a good question, and if I ever see my friend again I'll ask him, but for now, I don't know the answer to that."

Mike saw them both looking over at the RWS interestedly, as he said, "But, I do know all about that so, let's get started…"

At the back of their Warrior, Changa and Ping were quietly going through their new vehicle tools and supplies. Changa was ripping off the labels and tags, as Ping stowed the tools in the toolbox. Doc was on the roof, stowing the bottles of water, tinned foods and sleeping gear in the bins, trying to use as little space as possible. All three were quiet, concentrating on the work when Jonah came over.

"You alright guys?" he asked, as all three looked up.

It was Doc who spoke first, "Hey Jonah, you done your wagon already?"

Laughing he replied, "No, that's why I have a crew, Reaper and Jo can do all that shit."

Saying nothing, Doc carried on working as Jonah continued, "So what happened out there Doc? Everyone seems to be chatting about how our new friend got scared at the sight of a helicopter, apparently, he pissed his pants. That true?"

The Doc stopped what he was doing and looked down at him shaking his head. "He didn't piss his pants at the sight of the helicopter, you weren't there Jonah, so don't start spreading that bullshit, I was there, I saw what really happened. And don't start saying that everyone's chatting about it, because they ain't. The only one chatting about it is you."

Jonah showed mock concern as he replied sarcastically, "Wow fuck me! I had no idea the fan club extended this far. Don't keep your tongue in his ass for too long though Doc, make sure you save some for Patty and Spider."

Doc shook his head as he replied, "Why don't you cut him some slack. I've only been with Mr Faulkes for a few hours today, and from what I've seen so far, he knows his business. When you're enjoying your food later or getting into that nice warm comfy sleeping bag tonight, just remember that's because of him."

Jonah pulled a mocking face in answer before turning to Changa, playfully tapping his shoulder. "Hey, where's that lovely lady friend of yours gone to? I was hoping to be able to chat to her, maybe see if she needs a little shoulder to cry on. What do you think Changa, fancy going twos up in the back of the wagon?"

"Jonah for fucks sake," Ping interjected, "she's just lost her mate, I doubt she'd want anything from you."

Jonah looked over in surprise at the tone of the Fusilier. "OOOH listen to young Ping here, suddenly got some balls now have you? What is it, you got a little crush on her yourself, think she'd go for you, do you?" He walked over and stood over the Fusilier who wisely ignored him and continued to check through the tools.

Seeing he was being ignored, Jonah tried to goad him, "You'd be surprised at what people want from me, you little cunt," he spat out. Seeing no reaction, Jonah knocked into him with his knees, pushing the young Fusilier over and knocking the tools over in the process.

"Come on then, nothing to say now?" he demanded. "Where's those little balls you just had?"

Ping just looked up at him, he wasn't stupid. Jonah relished these little moments, he had a reputation back at the Battalion for intimidation and bullying. Ping knew he'd never beat him in a fair fight, and even if he could, Jonah would always rely on the fact he'd outrank him. It wouldn't be the first time he'd used his rank to get out of trouble.

Changa however, had no such problem and stood up, a threatening look on his face, the tone clear. Jonah turned to face him, "And what do you want Fusilier? You forgotten I'm a fucking Corporal?"

Changa wasn't intimidated, he'd pushed past bigger men than Jonah to get into a fight, and although the NCO's eyes were full of malice, Changa also clocked the nervous way that Jonah was standing.

Doc had heard enough, he jumped from the roof and put himself between them, trying to defuse the situation. Glaring furiously at Jonah he shot back, "Jonah, I'm also a fucking Corporal and I'm telling you now, do yourself a favour and fuck off back to your vehicle, you're not welcome here, now piss off."

Staring at Doc his face broke into a sneer, "Oh well look at this, Changa gets involved and now *you've* got balls too. Someone on this crew must be dishing out the bravery pills." He turned to look at Changa, "Don't worry Changa, I won't forget this, first chance I get, you're on shit jobs for a week."

Jonah smirked as he walked past, trying to shoulder barge the big Fijian and failing, like a small wave trying to move a tanker. He may as well have tried to shoulder barge the Warrior vehicle for all the good it would do. Changa reached down to help Ping to his feet who muttered his thanks, as they all watched the angry NCO storm off. It was Changa who spoke, making a clicking noise with his tongue.

"Man, oh man, what is it with him, so full of hate?"

"You get them wherever you go mate," Doc replied, "I had one guy in my old company, name of Leanor, a Lance Corporal, always angry, always bullying the younger lads. He'd spend hours telling everyone how tough he was, how much he'd look forward to deploying on the ground, getting involved in a war. Everyone called him 'Leanor, man of war' he was so keen in green. We all thought that if you were to cut him in half, he'd bleed green and black or so we thought."

"What happened to him?" asked Ping dusting straw and dust off himself.

"The Battalion was put on standby to go to Sudan, in case they needed us to help evacuate the Embassy staff. That morning we'd had briefing after briefing by our officers. What we could expect there, how many casualties we could expect, with the possibility of having to fight in and then fight out. It was supposed to be pretty kinetic and in case anything happened, everyone was told to check we all had life insurance and that all our bills were all paid. We were given the afternoon off, told to go home, be with our families and then parade the next morning at 05:00 to get on the coaches to take us to the airport. The following morning the Battalion assembles, everyone was there, all except Leanor. We all thought he'd catch up, perhaps he was just running late, but even as the coaches drove out the camp, there was no sign of him. We flew into Italy, where we did nothing but wait in a holding area for a week before being sent home. We hadn't been needed after all. After we got back, he turned up to the camp gate with a black eye, and then tried to pull some bullshit story about how he'd spent a night with a woman who had kidnapped him and held him hostage all week."

"What? No way! Bullshit!" replied Changa smirking as Doc continued, laughing at the story, "Honest to God Changa, that's what he claimed! Said the woman had tied him up to the bed, wanting to go all kinky with him and then refused to let him go, never gave a reason why, just wanted him tied up." All three laughed as Doc carried on telling the story, "Of course, no one believed him, apart from the black eye there were no cuts or welts from any restraints. His reputation in the Battalion was shot, and the next time he tried to bully or intimidate anyone the young lads would gang up on him. About a month later the RMP's turned up to arrest him, they'd found CCTV evidence, showing him living at his mums for the week, they'd interviewed her and the neighbours and she admitted he turned up at her doorstep out of the blue, blubbering like a baby and begging her not to let him go. The man who bragged for a fight, who prayed to go to war, he gets the opportunity and his fear gets the better of him. What was she going to do? Of course, she was going to help him. She hid him until it was all over and then he'd punched himself in the face, to give the story more weight."

Ping laughed, now happier as Doc put an arm on his shoulder, "Now Ping the next time that twat does anything stupid to you, I want you to think about that story and imagine Jonah blubbering like a baby."

"Amen to that!" replied Changa, as laughing, they all went back to what they were doing.

Mike had spent the last three hours with the two young tank soldiers, talking and running through everything he'd learned from working on a tank. Watching as they took in what he was saying, occasionally he'd stop and ask one of them a question, just to confirm they were listening. He showed Smudge the best place to stow his gunnery tools, and some tips on keeping the gun-kit, sights and thermal systems in perfect working order. He demonstrated to them how to remove the L7 Machine gun from the RWS and how to remount it quickly, Mike benefitting in a refresher on how to do it. He told Bill about the disadvantages with the add-on armour, how it made changing a road wheel twice as hard as it covered the running gear, then he told him about the little trick his own driver had used in Iraq, of digging a hole, and reversing the tank so that the wheel would sink into the hole and lower itself enough to be removed. By the time he'd finished, he felt satisfied the two soldiers would now be more confident in their abilities and hoped that some of the things he'd said had sunk in. He wasn't kidding himself, but with things going on, they had to be ready, not perfect, just ready.

After they had finished, the two soldiers went back to repacking their gear as Mike removed the General Purpose Machine Gun, or 'Gimpy' as it was called by the soldiers, from the RWS. He knew they didn't have the ammo for it, but he wanted to clean it anyway, more of a test to himself that he could still remember how to do it. He sat beside the tank, the two Troopers watching on in amusement as he began to slowly and methodically take the weapon apart, careful to lay the parts on a clean piece of rag laid out on the floor, keeping them in the order they were removed. With a certain amount of self-satisfaction, he smiled to himself as finally the last parts were separated. The springs, clips and pieces of odd shaped metal now looking nothing like a machine gun.

"You made that look easy." Smudge said looking over.

"Well, it was anything but and I still have to put it all back together," he countered, smiling as Smudge leant over to help, picking up a piece of the weapon and began cleaning.

Bill finished repacking his kit and climbed aboard the tank stowing the rucksack into the driver's compartment the way Mike had showed him. He jumped down and sat cross legged near the other two watching with curiosity at the Gimpy parts laid out. Mike reached down and picked up part of the gun body, handing it over to him, with some cleaning rag the soldier happily accepted and all three sat there in silence cleaning the weapon. After a few minutes, it was Smudge who spoke first, squinting as the late afternoon sunlight began to shine through a small hole in the roof.

"Mr Faulkes, why is this happening?"

Taking a breath, Mike looked across at him, "Smudge, that's a question I'd like to know myself. If I could stop it all right now, I would."

After a pause the young Trooper continued, "Do you think my parents will be alright?" the voice full of hope.

Mike remembered that Smudge had been with the GSM and the dead girl as he asked, "Where do your parents live? Where's home?"

"Knutsford, place called Bexton."

Thinking of the geography of the UK, Mike quickly asked, "That anywhere near Southport?"

Smudge smiled, happy that Mike knew where it was. "Yes, not far from there," his voice low as he continued, "I used to play football for Stockport, my dad would take me, every Sunday morning, he'd get up early and drive me there, my mum would pack us some beef sandwiches and a thermos flask of tea and after every game we'd sit there and chat, about football, cars and women." He smiled to himself as he said the last part. "I don't think he ever did it for the football, I think he did it just to be away with me, it was the only time we were ever alone. I miss those Sundays." He sighed as he picked up another piece of machine gun to clean.

"I'm sure your parents are just fine Smudge."

Mike looked over at Bill.

"What about you Bill, how are you doing so far?"

Bill glanced at Smudge, then back at Mike, an awkward look on his face. Mike instantly knew something had been discussed between these two, he could see from the body language.

"Bill what is it?" his eyebrows raised.

The young Trooper paused from the cleaning as he asked, "Mr Faulkes, when all of this is over will we go to jail?"

Mike looked on confused, "What? What would make you think that? Jail for what?"

"When you were gone getting the supplies, some of the others, some of the infantry, came over to chat to us."

"Okay," he replied trying to keep his thoughts hidden as he continued, "and what did they say?"

"They didn't say anything, but they were asking us loads of questions about you, they wanted to know if we had worked with you before, who you were and what you had done. I told them I'd only met you last night and Smudge told them you're friends with the CO and about your encounter with one of the terrorists who had attacked the camp. I'd heard about it in the cookhouse but had no idea that was you."

"Well, I'm not friends with the Colonel." Mike looked at Smudge to clarify as he continued, "I only met him yesterday, my friend is the OC of the ATDU. He was the person I was visiting yesterday. He's the reason I was down at the camp."

"Ahh okay," Bill replied. He looked down uncomfortably and continued to scrub the gun part, seeing his awkwardness Mike pressed the issue, "Bill what it is? Spit it out, what's on your mind?"

Bill looked up, swallowing nervously as he said, "The infantry, the guys speaking to us, they told us that you're not an officer, that you're not even in the army and that we're not supposed to be listening to you. They told us, ordered us, that we're not to follow your orders and that we should leave you here. If we don't then I'm going to be arrested when we finally meet up with the rest of the army. I'm sorry Sir, but is that true? Are you in the army? Are you an officer? Because the things you say, the things you know about the tank, are they wrong? Are you telling us the wrong things? I thought last night it was strange how you weren't in uniform, you sounded like you knew what to do, I did as you asked, am I going to get into trouble for doing that?"

Seeing the young lad twisting himself in knots made Mike angry, he had a good idea who was behind this, the fact Bill had said someone had ordered him, meant it was someone of rank, and the only other people of rank in the group, not on the supply run were Spider and Jonah. Mike knew that Spider wouldn't have tried to undermine him like that, so that left just one person, Lance Corporal fucking Jones! But he knew for once the anger he felt wouldn't help, instead he had to think back to the soothing words of wisdom his wife would say. She'd seen the anger and the turmoil he'd been through when he left the army, the road rage, the sudden bursts of temper. It had been her patience and comfort that had calmed him down. Now this required wisdom and he calmed his mind as he thought through his plan of action. First things first though, he needed to calm Bill down.

Reaching out he put his hand on Bill's shoulder, looking him squarely in the eyes, "Bill listen to me now, you've done nothing wrong okay. I'm the one who told you to get in and drive that tank, and I'll be the one who is responsible for taking it. There's no blame on you whatsoever. You were left behind by accident, these things happen, and if you didn't leave when you did, then both you and the tank would have been captured. Don't forget that. You helped me to save that tank. You also helped me to save those soldiers through there. Now you're right, I'm not in the army anymore, but I used to be, I know what I'm doing and I'm experienced. And that's why I'd like you to listen to me from now on. Not because you have to, but because you trust me enough to do so."

He saw Bill's demeanour lighten as the words began to strike home, as Mike continued smiling, "Also one other thing and this is one for the record books, I don't know of any other tank driver in the history of armoured warfare who has been credited with an armoured vehicle kill by driving over the enemy. You're the first I've heard of, even our gunner hasn't fired at another tank yet, so put that in your pipe and smoke it."

Bill smiled, looking over to Smudge, as Mike felt the tension evaporating between the three of them. Clearly relieved, Bill nodded and carried on helping clean the gun.

Mike looked up jovially, "Right come on, let's see if I can remember how to put this bloody thing back together."

After five minutes all three stood admiring their handiwork, as the Gimpy, now oiled and cleaned, glistened in the sunlight.

"Your turn now Smudge, let's see if you can remember how to refit it into the RWS."

They all climbed onboard, Mike sat back observing as between the two of them Bill and Smudge worked together, proudly smiling as the GPMG sat back in the mount. Smudge had a small cut to his finger to show for his efforts as the heavy gun had nipped him as it had been placed in the mount. He stood there smiling, the cut finger in his mouth quickly forgotten as he stopped the blood.

Satisfied with what he'd seen, Mike said, "Good, now that's all done, you'd both best get over to the where the food and water have all been dumped, it's already been broken down into vehicle piles, just ask the Fusilier guarding it, which is ours and bring it back, stow it all in this bin here," he said pointing to one of the larger back bins. "And make sure you bring one of the camping stoves back with you."

Bill turned to go, but Smudge stayed where he was. "Mr Faulkes, do you mind if I have a chat in private? There's something I need to tell you about last night."

Bill stopped and turned, waiting for Smudge as Mike replied, "Sure," before looking over, "Bill do you mind just giving us five minutes? Smudge will come along to help shortly." Nodding, they watched Bill jump off as Mike pointed to the loaders hatch, "Why, step into my office young man."

Both men settled themselves into the turret, Mike sat in the commander's station and Smudge settled himself in the loaders side, staring over.

"Right Smudge, what do you want to tell me?"

After ten minutes both men emerged from the turret, the sweat visible on Mike's t-shirt as the heat from the day had cooked them, thankful for the cool breeze as he stepped off onto the floor.

"Right guys, I'll leave you to sort out the food, I'll be back over shortly."

Both nodding in acknowledgment, he left the two tank soldiers as he walked over to find Spider and Patty. Both were with five of their guys by the back of one of the Warriors, chatting away as they packed away the food onto the vehicles. Jonah was glaring at Mike as he approached, Mike ignored him as he quietly said, "Patty, Spider can I have a word in private please?"

Both men looked up seeing the serious look in Mike's eyes. Whatever he wanted to talk about was important. Mike walked them over to the far side of the barn, away from listening ears. It was Patty who spoke first.

"What is it Mike, you look pissed off?"

"Right, you guys have a problem, we have a problem. Firstly, good old Lance Corporal Jones has been visiting my crew when I'm not around, telling them they're not to listen to me anymore and that they're looking at prison time for following my orders. They're only recruits, easily led and influenced and he's taking great pleasure in undermining me. I can't run that tank if they start to question or doubt me. If that happens, and they start to ignore me, then it's all over."

"All right all right," Spider remonstrated, "I'll have a word with him, we'll tell him to lay off, to stay away from them."

"It's not that simple," Mike replied, trying his best to keep his voice low, "I can deal with Jonah myself, but there's something else about him, something that you both need to hear and know about. I just found this out five minutes ago."

"What is it?" Patty asked.

Mike explained all about what he had found that morning, when cleaning out the back of the Warrior and with what Smudge had just told him, how it had all clicked into place. With a growing anger, both men listened to Mike. When he'd finished it was Patty who spoke first, his tone questioning.

"So, after all that happened, it was his fault? He went back to get the money and drugs? And left the Captain behind?"

"Correct," Mike replied, "he thought he had time to do both, I'm guessing he went to his own room, picked up his own stash, then realising the other dealer wouldn't be coming back, went and robbed him as well. Then when the gunfire started, he panicked and ran back to the wagons. Your Captains most likely been killed or captured waiting for a lift that never came."

Spider shook his head disbelievingly, "I've known Jonah for five years, I've never once seen him dealing in drugs. Are you certain of this?"

"Smudge told me a moment ago, he'd recognised Jonah before, selling to the recruits at the barracks. He'd been too scared to say anything before, but last night after what he heard in the back of the Warrior and realising Jonah was to blame, he decided enough was enough. Quite brave for a young lad. I've assured him that this won't get back to him."

Both Corporal's nodded at the implication of what Mike had just said, Patty replying with, "We'll need proof Mike, more than this lad's word. I can't just accuse him of something like this, he's an NCO for Christ's sake. If we're wrong about this, then the lads will lynch us."

"I know," Mike interrupted, "but it just so happens I've got a plan to flush him out. I recommend we do it now before we go any further. I'm not happy with how this looks and if you do nothing it will only get worse."

"What do you recommend?" Spider asked.

"Can you get Jonah and his crew off their wagon, get them over to yours, say it's for a briefing or something?"

"Yeah, I can do that. Then what?"

"Then give me twenty minutes and call everyone together, get them all assembled here. Then we'll see who's who."

"Okay," he replied curiously, as Patty asked, "Do you mind telling us what you've got planned?"

Mike looked on grimly, as he began to explain the plan...

7

A Farmer's Boy

Sam's Farm

Thirty minutes later, and without knowing why, everyone was told to come into the centre of the barn, the haybales had been arranged into a semicircle, inside the vehicles and everyone was sitting on them, talking amongst themselves, trying to guess what was going on. Only Patty was missing, having volunteered to sit on the radio, not wanting to be anywhere near Jonah, for fear of what he would do to him. Mike was sat at the end with Spider, who quickly counted heads, confirming that everyone was accounted for. He looked over to Mike, his head close and whispered, "Are you certain you want to do this, there's no other way?" Mike shook his head, checking no-one was overhearing, "No, of course I don't want to do this, but what choice do we have, these people need to trust me, *you* need to trust me and if this elephant in the room doesn't get addressed soon, then when things get hard, you'll wake-up to find Jonah has taken half the troops with him. You and Patty are new to this, please trust me Spider, this is for the best." Nodding, Spider stood up into the centre of the room, the hushed voices going quiet.

"Okay lads, and lass," he acknowledged the room, looking over to Private Nock, before continuing, "'I've got you all gathered because Mr Faulkes wants to have a word with you all. Mike watched as Spider looked directly at Jonah, sitting with his own crew around him, looking around them, wondering what he meant.

"Mr Faulkes, if you will please." Spider pointed to the centre of the group.

Mike stood and walked to the centre of the hay bales, maintaining eye contact with everyone he could, most of those looking back did so with a smile, some simply watched on with curious amusement.

"Right everybody, I've requested that you be called together this afternoon, because going forward, there's an elephant in this room that needs addressing. Something that we can't leave any longer, someone in here has a secret and now's the time to tell."

He watched the room take notice, people sat up and leant forward inquisitively, wondering what he was going to say, he could see them thinking.

Reaper looked at Jonah and then at Mike, his own face portraying his emotions, there was conflict there, Mike saw he looked unsure of what to do, torn between the loyalty to his commander and correcting the truth.

Suddenly and unexpectedly the Signaller called Rachel stood up. Immediately everyone looked over to her. Mike had forgotten about her; she'd not spoken at all since last night and he'd only seen her briefly throughout the day. Mike was happy to see there were none of the signs of shock he'd seen last night. He quickly thought back to her name, "Yes, Signaller Nock, isn't it?"

"No, it's not," she replied, her voice different now, more controlled, this was not the same woman he had seen last night. "My name's Corporal Nock."

"I'm sorry, I thought you were a Signaller," his voice tried to hide his surprise as he looked over to Smudge.

Seeing him looking at Smudge, she replied with, "It's not his fault, he didn't know. We told him we were Clerks, we didn't want him to know who we were or where we'd come from in case we were captured."

As if to confirm her story, she pulled a Corporal's rank slide from her pocket and placed it on her shirt. Well, this day was full of surprises, Mike thought, as she took a deep breath and continued, her voice loud.

"I want to first take this chance to apologise to everyone about my conduct last night, I wasn't myself, a very good colleague of mine had just died in my arms and well, If I'm being honest, I don't remember much about it. I'm sorry for shooting at you all though." she finished looking over at Mike.

"That's fine," he replied, "though I am curious why you chose *now* to tell us?"

Her face took on a confused look, "Because of what you just said about having a secret a minute ago. I thought you were talking about me and were going to out me in front of everyone. I'd rather it came from my own lips."

He held his hands up in understanding as he replied, "Ahh, no. I'm sorry Corporal Nock if that's the impression I gave, but that's not the secret I'm talking about. Thank you though for telling us, may I ask, how did you end up in the back of the Warrior though?"

"We flew in with Major T-P, we were sent straight in from the General's headquarters. Our orders were to fly in, update the Colonel on what we knew, help set up the vehicle's radio's and then fly out and head back, but our helicopter failed to return. We were on the tank park with you when the Paratroopers arrived."

"Now I remember," Mike replied, adding, "You left with the GSM in his Land Rover. That's how you all managed to get onboard Corporal Webbs convoy."

Rachel looked sadly at the floor as her eyes welled up, clearly her friend's death was still raw and fresh in her mind. He was about to tell her not to worry and to sit back down when she looked back up, taking a deep breath, determined to speak.

"You're the reason the camp was on high alert when they came, aren't you?"

Mike said nothing as the others looked on in mute awe as she continued, "When I was at the General's headquarters, there was a man there named Brigadier Rawlinson, the General was listening to him, they mentioned you by name. You know him, don't you?"

Mike noted it was posed more as a statement than a question, as he replied, "I do know him yes, he's a friend and an old colleague of mine."

"Well, he spoke highly of you, he told everyone in HQ that you were trying to warn them in Bovington, to get them out in time. If you hadn't have done that, all of us, all of this, wouldn't be here now." She waved her hand over the assembled troops and vehicles as she spoke, Mike cringing uncomfortably at the high praise, as she continued. "I'm standing now, to also say thank you, for that, and for what you've done for my friend. I've heard what you did for Sharon, saw what you did for her. Sam the farmer let me say my goodbyes to her earlier." her voice trailed off as she sat back down.

There was an awkward silence for a moment as Mike didn't know how to respond. Everyone else looked on admirably at Mike at the revelation, only Jonah was still sneering, muttering something to Jo, who merely grimaced uncomfortably in response. Mike nodded at Rachel in thanks, before quickly thinking what he would say next.

"Well, it was all thanks to your friend, Sharon, that I was able to find what we are here to discuss now."

She looked over the assembled faces, some showing surprise and some confusion as they wondered what Mike was talking about. After a few moments he carried on.

"Last night, when cleaning out the back of Two-One-Alpha, I found a stuff sack, it had been hastily thrown into the back of the vehicle. It had rolled loose, most likely when we went cross country, Sharon's body had hit it, dislodging it." Mike walked over to the side of one of the hay bales, where he had earlier stashed the bag before the meeting. Spider had kept Jonah and his crew distracted whilst he went to reclaim it from its hiding place in the back of the vehicle. Now he picked it up and held it aloft for all to see. "When I opened it up, I found this." He upended the bag, four large plastic bags containing pills of every colour and white powder spilled out, and another containing rolled up money fell out onto the concrete floor at his feet. Mike had not seen the drugs last night or how much money was inside, but seeing it now clearly strewn on the floor, he could see it was a small fortune.

"Now at the time, I couldn't be sure who the bag belonged to, there were many people on the vehicle, and rather than throw wild accusations, I simply restowed the bag and kept my findings to myself."

Mike looked around the room, watching the faces staring back, he focused on Jonah's vehicle crew, all three looked back at him, two in shock horror, one with pure hate on his face.

"So, someone here owns this bag, but is anyone going to own up to it?"

He waited as everyone's eyes were drawn to the money. Mike knew the money wasn't where the real value was. He'd seen enough shows on TV to know the street value of the drugs would be triple what the money was worth. He looked up again, his voice questioning.

"Well...is anyone going to come forward and claim these drugs?"

"Maybe it belonged to the dead woman." Jonah shouted out angrily.

"Absolutely not! Sharon never touched drugs!" Corporal Nock stood up glaring at Jonah.

Ahh, always easy to blame the dead, Mike thought to himself. He shrugged his shoulders as he replied nonchalantly, "Well if it does belong to the dead woman then she won't mind me doing this." He reached over behind the hay bale and pulled out a small fuel jerry can and lighter. Everyone watched on open mouthed as he calmly unscrewed the can and began to pour the contents out over the pile, ensuring the liquid covered the bags and the notes. Smiling, he picked up the lighter, some of the people there were watching in mute amusement, others in disbelief. Would he really burn that amount of money?

He stepped back a few paces, checking that the only thing that would catch alight would be the pile of drugs and money. He'd already moved the hay away from the small area earlier. He turned to look at the group again. "Last chance, does anyone want to own up to it? Or it's gone forever."

Changa jokingly shouted out, "I'll happily keep the money Mr Faulkes!"

Some of them laughed and hollered as he stood there, enjoying the show, he ignored them all, his eyes concentrating only on Jonah. Would he take the bait, he wondered. He turned his back to the crowd, sparked up the lighter, watching the flame dancing merrily away. He was about to drop it when he heard a warning shout from behind, someone was rushing him and fast. He dropped the lighter and deftly side stepped to the left, his right elbow arching out on instinct at waist level. Mike felt his elbow connect with the target, a perfect hit in the mid-section, answered by a yell of pain as he felt the air rush past, as his assailant collapsed to his right, the momentum carrying him over the bales and collapsing on the floor. Mike turned quickly, ready to face the threat. Jonah was already up on his feet, chest heaving and face red with rage as he fought to get his breath back, wheezing and coughing.

"So, it is yours then?" Mike replied matter of fact, his eyes locking with Jonah's.

After a moment he recovered enough to say, "So fucking what if its mine? It's none of your business. You had no right to take it from my wagon and I'm not just going to let you burn it. Do you have any fucking idea how much that gear's worth?"

"But I wasn't going to burn it," Mike smirked, picking up the jerrycan and making a big show of pouring the contents of the fuel can over his hand, then attempting to light it. The flame was doused immediately as he explained to the surprised faces, "Water, it looks like gasoline, but the effects are very different."

Jonah looked down in anger realising he'd been fooled into action. "Motherfucker!" he spat between clenched teeth.

The laughter had stopped, as those on the bales stood in stunned silence. Spider could not believe it. He shook his head as he shouted across. "Jonah, what the fuck mate? Why? I thought you were one of us?"

Ignoring Mike, Jonah looked over to the soldiers, his arms opened wide.

"Spider, I still *am* one of you, what does it fucking matter? So what, if I sell drugs, chemists sell drugs all the time, no one judges them?"

"Look guys it's still me," he continued pleading, "I'm still Jonah, what does it matter if I do a little bit of extra work on the side? Besides, I only sell to those who want it, if it wasn't me then they'd be buying the gear from someone else. Someone who would cut the gear, they'd mix it with paint thinners, rat poison, you'd be surprised at how many amateurs are out there. At least with me the gear's safe and cut clean. Now come on, lets fucking move on from this shall we?"

Mike looked over to the crowd, whilst keeping a watchful eye on Jonah, as he added, his voice sarcastic.

"Move on from it, he says, let's just all simply forget the fact that he's been selling this shit to the recruits as they come through the camp. Does anyone here have any mates back home addicted to this shit, have you seen what it does to families? To friends? Imagine what it will do to people you're supposed to trust. But that's not the end of it though is it?" he exclaimed loudly, "Corporal Webb, when you were waiting to fuel up, you were told that there was an officer waiting to lead you, a Captain, and that he was in the Colonel's office getting orders for you, is that correct?"

Spider walked over to join him in the centre, "Yeah that's correct, I was told to wait there and go collect him, he had our maps, our orders, everything we needed to get out of there."

"And who did you send to go and get him?" Mike cocked his head questioningly.

Jonah quickly interrupted, "What is this? What is this? You know we went to find him; we got there and were told he'd left already. I've told you this Spider, why the fuck are you listening to him? Why are we dragging all this up again?"

Ignoring him Spider continued, "I'd decided to wait with Corporal Patterson with the vehicles to refuel, there was a large backlog of vehicles and we didn't want someone pulling rank to push in. I'd sent Lance Corporal Jones and Fusilier Grimm to the Colonel's office to get the Captain. It should have only taken them twenty minutes."

"And how long were you waiting for?"

"Almost thirty minutes, they both came back about the same time as the shooting started, we'd already seen the paratroopers landing and the other vehicles start to leave. The fuel point had already run out of fuel, so we were just waiting for the Captain and these two."

"So, had they only been twenty minutes, it's safe to say, you would all have been on your way, with your officer leading you and with the other vehicles? And you wouldn't have come under fire, as the enemy vehicles didn't turn up until later. You'd also still have your fourth vehicle. Would you say that's correct?"

Mike looked over at Jonah, seeing his look of rage replaced with a clear head as Spider replied. "Yeah, I'd say that's correct, if we hadn't had to have waited for them, we'd all have been out of there pretty easily."

Doc stood up questioningly, looking over to Jonah. "Sorry to interrupt, but do you mind me asking what difference this makes on anything? We wouldn't have left our guys behind, so why is it relevant what happened? Surely you can't blame them for it, they were, after all trying to find the Captain. It wasn't their fault he'd gone missing. I wouldn't have left them behind, I'd have waited too, in fact I think everyone here would."

Mike saw some of the faces nodding and heard the low murmur as they agreed with Doc. He saw the triumphant grin on Jonah as Mike replied, "It matters Doc, because they didn't go looking for the Captain, they never even tried. Instead they went back to the accommodation block, to Lance Corporal Jones room to retrieve his stash of money and drugs, this stash." He kicked the pile with his feet, watching with satisfaction as Jonah flinched, before continuing.

"But then, not content with simply taking his own stash, Jonah got greedy and went to another soldier's room, another dealer known to him on the camp, and spent valuable time ransacking his room, knowing the soldier wasn't coming back. That's why they took thirty minutes instead of twenty. They didn't go looking for the Captain at all, he went to collect his drugs and money and as a result you all left him behind, you all left your own officer behind. Mike stared at them, wanting them all to feel the shame of it, before shooting his arm out accusingly at Jonah and raising his voice. "All because this twat put his own selfish needs first!"

The barn exploded into raised voices and jeers as everyone stood to look over at Jonah, who stood glaring back at Mike. Spider had to shout to calm everyone as Mike waited for the accusations to die down. Shouts of "You Bastard!" and "Is this fucking true!" shot out as Jonah stood there. Once everyone had calmed down, Mike looked over to Jonah, his tone accusing.

"You going to tell us why you did it? Or are you just going to stand there quietly?"

Jonah spat on the floor, before looking up and addressing the crowd, his face breaking into a sneer. "I'll admit to the drugs, fair one, but none of this shit and fantasy. You have any proof of this? No, because it's a load of bollocks. We went looking for the Captain and he wasn't there. Simple. Maybe he didn't fancy your fucking company." Nodding in Mike's direction he continued, "I'd already loaded my gear onto the wagon, so, fuck you!"

Mike stood there shaking his head slowly, "No Jonah, yet more lies, and more bullshit. I'm afraid your crew have already confessed to us and told us what you did." He looked around at everyone as he continued, his tone solemn. "In the back of your vehicles, you all have a loudspeaker fitted, it allows the infantry in the back to hear what's being said over the radios and what's being said over the crew intercom. When you stopped to chat to me for the first time, when you got off your vehicle, unbeknown to you, your driver Fusilier Kerr and your Gunner Fusilier Grimm began to talk to each other over the crew intercom. You see Fusilier Grimm wasn't part of your plan, he had no idea what you were planning to do, he thought you were both searching for the Captain. So I can only imagine his horror when he found out about your little side line. You told him that you had time, that you'd go and get the Captain afterwards as you stole from the other soldier's room, but you didn't. You ran out of time and then ran back to the vehicles. When Corporal Patterson had asked you where the Captain was, you simply replied that you couldn't find him, as you stashed your money and your drugs in the vehicle. But unknown to you all, as you were rushing to get back onboard your vehicle, the GSM had opened the back door, getting three people in the back. It was these three people who now, sitting in the back, heard the conversation between Fusilier's Grimm and Kerr, talking about what you had done and what they should do about it. Little did they realise there were five, listening into a conversation meant only for two."

Mike looked over to Jo and Reaper who looked at each other and then at him in shock. Their looks confirming what he had just revealed. So, Smudge had been telling the truth. Looking over to Reaper, Mike asked, "What about it Reaper, do you still feel some kind of misplaced loyalty to this person, or are you going to tell us the truth, tell *them* the truth?"

Reaper's head followed as Mike waved his hand over the assembled crowd.

Reaper looked at them all, then at Jonah, finally shaking his head he decided enough was enough.

"It's true, it's all true!" he exclaimed, the words tumbling out of him as he continued, "I'm so sorry guys, he made me do it, he threatened that if I spoke out, he'd plant the drugs on me and tell you all they were mine." The young Fusilier sat back, his shoulders drooping as he unburdened himself.

Jonah lost his composure again as he exploded forward, trying to get at the Fusilier.

"You fucking turncoat! Fucking rat! I'm going to fucking-"

Jonah's face went from fury, to surprise, as Mike's fist exploded out, lightning fast, hammering him in the gut, causing him to double forward. He collapsed for the second time to his knees as the others came rushing in shouting and grabbing him, his arms being pinned behind him as he fell to the ground. He began to shout, to kick out in rage, trying to get free, then Changa stepped forward, grabbing him by the throat and picking him up, his huge arms locking around his. Whatever Jonah was planning, he had no way of doing it now, as Changa looked over at Mike, Jonah held securely in an arm lock. "You okay Mr Faulkes?" Mike nodded, "Thank you Changa, yes I'm fine," as Doc stepped forwards carrying a large roll of tape. Changa turned Jonah around and within seconds he was bound, hands and feet, with a piece of tape placed over his mouth.

Changa looked over at Spider, "What do you want me to do with this Bakola?" Spider looked over to Mike who merely replied with a shrug of the shoulders, "It's an army matter, I have no authority over him, he's yours to deal with as you see fit." Spider pointed to his vehicle, "Put him in the back for now, I want someone watching him though," Jonah's muffled cries and shouts disappeared as Changa and Doc led him away.

Mike walked over to the drugs and money, placing it all back in the bag, he stood up giving the bag to Spider. "Here you go, it's yours to deal with."

His face creased as he replied, "Mike, what the fuck am I supposed to do with that? Invite some strippers in and have a party? I don't know what to do with it. Let's just throw it away, people died for this shit, its cursed."

Mike shook his head, "I wouldn't go doing that just yet, depending on what you do with Jonah, you may want it as evidence. Why don't you hide the drugs where only you know where it is but keep the money. Cash is handy to have around, especially as my credit cards are now maxed out. You never know when we may need to pay for something, especially as we still have the fuel to pay for later."

"Thats a fair one, I'll get it hidden now, I only hope my bloody crew don't think its sugar and put it in my coffee."

"Well, if they do, you won't struggle to keep awake, will you?" Mike smiled as he walked away from the mass of people, wanting to be alone, climbing the front of the tank he sat himself on the front of the turret, slowly drinking his water, trying to calm his thoughts. His heart was still pounding as he tried to relax and stared out the barn into the farmyard. He hadn't seen Sam or Mary all day, since getting back from the supply run, the 4x4 was still parked in the farm courtyard, where Mike had left it covered over with two of the tarpaulins from the barn, hiding it from prying eyes. Mike was certain it would need a new clutch the way he had driven it. He'd square it away though; he'd make sure when they departed that night, that they left some of the money as thanks and to cover the cost of the damage. He sat for a few moments, until finally his breathing began to slow down and his mind cleared. He looked at his watch, it was 16:38, soon he'd want to be thinking about chatting to the others, to discuss the next move, hopefully the fuel that Sam had promised would arrive, giving them enough range to get further north. Suddenly he was aware of Jo and Reaper at the front of the tank, looking sheepishly up at him. He looked down at them not wanting to move, he had just got comfortable, then quickly realising how rude it would look, he sighed to himself and slid forwards off the tank and stood next to them. "What's up guys? What's on your minds?"

It was Jo who spoke first. "Mr Faulkes, we just wanted to apologise for the way we've been, we're sorry for how we were earlier, I'm sure you know already but me waking you up, it wasn't an accident. Our attitudes towards you, our conduct, it's...well it's not on. And for that I can speak for Reaper here, sorry Fusilier Grimm here too, when I say we're both sorry. Jonah-"

Mike cut him off, "Guys, let me save you both the time, apologies accepted. But I'm not the one you should be apologising to, the people you work with, the ones who trust you, they're the ones you need to be working on. I'm the newcomer here, so let's just keep it easy, wipe the slate clean and start afresh, shall we?"

They both smiled in reply as he continued, "Good, now you'd best be off and chatting to the others, they'll be wary at first, perhaps even hostile, but give them time. It's been a long afternoon."

He watched them both walk away as Bill now came rushing over, "Mr Faulkes, you're wanted over at the radio wagon, it's urgent."

"Okay," he said, following quickly, he saw four people crowding round the back of the wagon and two people inside, one wearing the headset. The radio was being broadcast out of the loudspeaker and he saw Rachel stood by, listening in. As he approached, he saw Spider excitedly turn around, "We're picking people up on the radio, its garbled but they're there!"

Mike listened intently as everyone went quiet, the sounds of the radio static hissing over the speaker. Suddenly a voice came through, it was distorted and hard to hear, but you could hear someone was talking. Then a few moments later another voice came through. A bit clearer this time, but still distorted. Somehow the transmissions were improving.

Then they heard it, a clear crisp voice over the radio, "Any callsign, any callsign this is Golf Two-Zero, we need urgent assistance." Ping who was in the back of the vehicle wearing the headset looked on confused as everyone else turned to stare at Spider. It was Spider's own voice being played back that they could hear.

"That's part of the message I sent out last night," Spider confirmed, "what the hell's going on here?"

"They're fishing," Rachel replied knowingly. Everyone looked to her as she explained, "They're trying to find our units, throwing out these radio messages in the hope of someone replying. Every time someone transmits on the radio if it's not encrypted and set to multi-burst transmission, then the enemy can find them, using DF."

Mike looked as confused as everyone else, "Okay, I think now we can guess that you're not just merely a Signaller."

"No, I'm not, I'm an EWIS officer, Electronic Warfare and Intelligence Specialist, one of my jobs is doing exactly what you're all hearing here."

Sid looked across, "Excuse me Corporal, but what's DF?"

Mike smiled as he nodded towards him, "Like he said, mind explaining what DF is all about?"

She looked up, pointing to the vehicle's radio antennas, "When you transmit, these send out powerful signals on a frequency, the longer you use them or the more you keep chatting, the easier it is for someone with the right equipment to find you. Imagine having a compass that instead of pointing north, pointed to the direction of where the transmission was coming from. Now imagine having two compasses, each separated from the other by a few miles. Each would point in their own direction to the same signal source. You take the bearing, look at a map, draw the two lines on there and where the two lines meet, is where you'll find the person using the radio. Simple, now you have the location. Of course, that's the basic method, nowadays with the equipment people have, it's much more precise. Unfortunately for us, the Russians are the masters at it, which is why we're hearing this radio play now."

"Well at least it's better than listening to the Archers," Mike said amusedly, before continuing, "this multi..what was it?"

"Multi-burst transmission," she added,

"Right this multi-burst transmission, can our own radios do that? Can we prevent them from using this DF against us?"

"Yes, but I'll need to jump on each vehicle to setup. It might take me about thirty minutes per vehicle, but it can be done. Bear in mind though, if I do, we'll only be able to talk to ourselves and on low power only. We'd have a range of nothing more than a kilometre, perhaps two at best. We would be able to listen to others, we just wouldn't be able to reply to them."

Mike looked across to Patty and Spider, "What do you think guys, worth the risk?"

The nods in reply confirmed it was. "Okay Rachel can you get that set up for us, ready for tonight's move?"

She was about to answer, when they felt the roof above them vibrate and rattle, as if a typhoon was approaching.

"What the fuck?" Spider exclaimed looking up.

Shit, thought Mike, as the whine of the helicopter's engines now thundered through, followed by the unmistakable gut thumping sound of a heavy rotor beating through the air.

Mike looked to the others, "Fuck, it's the Hind! Our friends must have found us here."

Patty shouted to everyone, "Take cover! Quickly hide from view, take cover! Get ready to move!"

People began to run towards the vehicles, grabbing kit and chucking everything away preparing to make a hasty exit. Mike crouched carefully and made his way gingerly over to the barn doors, expecting to see a convoy of Russian vehicles coming down the track. He knelt down, peering out trying to locate the helicopter. It looked like it was directly above them, how the hell they hadn't heard it coming in again he had no idea. He looked over to where the 4x4 was parked, the maelstrom of wind from the helicopter's downdraft was flapping at one of the corners of the tarp. Oh no, he thought, he'd covered the car from view, but hadn't expected a helicopter to be hovering mere feet above it. With his heart in his mouth, he watched as the edge of the tarp began to flap, each pull revealing more of the car, until with a huge whoosh the tarp ripped off and flew off down the yard, coming to rest against the far wall - Shit! Now the 4x4 was in full view! He turned around at hearing one of the heavy engines of the Warriors fire up, the drivers expecting to have to drive out right away. He ran over to the driver shouting, "NO! SHUT IT DOWN!" the engine dying immediately. Spider came back over, "What is it?" he asked.

"They don't know we're here, let's just stay low and quiet for now, you can't outrun an attack helicopter, it'll kill us all before we even got a hundred metres from here. So long as it's flying it can't see us."

Spider looked around the barn, Mike was right, with the walls and roof as they were the helicopter would have to fly under the roof to see them.

"But what if it lands in the fields and dismounts troops? They can carry six soldiers on board."

"If it looks like it's going to land, I'll charge out in the tank and ram it before it takes off again, buy you all time to get out of here."

"That's it?" Spider asked incredulously, "that's your plan? Ram a helicopter, just like that?"

Mike shrugged, "Best I can think of with no rounds for the main armament, normally I could shoot him down, but now it's fix bayonets."

Spider shook his head in disbelief. "How the fuck has it come to this!" he moaned as he walked back over telling the drivers to be ready to move, but not to start the engines.

Mike looked over to the tank, Bill was sitting in the driver's hatch, and Smudge was in the open cupola. Seeing their nervous looks he gave them a thumbs up and a smile, satisfied as they both did the same. They were ready if he needed them. He crept back over, watching overhead for any sign of the helicopter, praying if it did land, it would be close enough for his half-arsed plan to work.

Fifty feet above them in the Hind, Colonel Golgolvin looked down below at the barn, he saw the livestock in the fields running in all directions, the helicopter's engines scaring them. But that wasn't what had got his attention. He was staring out over to the fields just to the north, below the wooded area. A noise burst through his headset, "Colonel what are you thinking? You looking over at the woods?"

He turned to look at Major Lenosky, next to him, replying, "Yes Sasha, but it's not the woods that interest me. How many fields and farms have we flown over today?"

Smiling, the Major pulled a hip flask, offering it first to Golgolvin who accepted, taking a long pull at the drink, as he answered "Too many! What is so important about this one?"

Golgolvin handed the flask back as the Major now took a long swig. "Sasha when I was a boy, my father taught me just two things, how to hunt and how to farm. The first came in handy for when I joined the army, the second I had no use for, until that is, today."

Lenosky laughed as he moved forwards, not understanding what the Colonel was saying and wanting to see for himself. "Colonel my apologies, I never was a farmer's boy, you'll have to explain to me what you mean."

Both men peered out of the open side door, the down draught from the rotors whipping around them.

"Look Sasha, all of the fields and farms that we have flown over today, all planted and seeded with crops."

The Major nodded, still not understanding what his Colonel was alluding to. They'd been in the air for most of the day, only landing to refuel once, his stomach grumbled and the thought of some food and the company of a fine woman cheered him up.

"Now look over here, to this large field, recently ploughed, I'd say no later than this morning, and look, it leads all the way from the woodland, down to the barn below us. Now why would a farmer leave a huge field like that empty and plough it today? It should either be full of crops or empty, but not ploughed. There must be another reason. Is he trying to hide something perhaps?"

Golgolvin spoke to the pilot, as the huge helicopter now began to slowly orbit the farm, looking for anything out of the ordinary. The Major pointed below to a 4x4, the same tatty 4x4 they had seen earlier. "So, it looks like we've found where our village idiot lives. And look, they attempted to cover it up. What did they have to hide I wonder?"

"What do you think Colonel? should we call in the other helicopters and investigate?" This time it was the voice of the pilot cutting in, he'd been listening to the conversation.

Thinking it quickly through he replied, "Yes, let's land over there, in the field with the stone wall. Get me as close to the barn as you can then take off and provide overwatch." He took his headset off, reaching over to his AK12 stowed in the weapons rack on the fuselage. It had been a long day, a boring day, he thought, and it wouldn't hurt for them to stretch their legs. He heard the whine of the tricycle landing gear coming down and waited for the pilot to land.

Mike was watching the helicopter, careful not to be seen. He'd seen them orbiting the farm and wondered what had piqued their curiosity. Was it the barn? No, it must be the 4x4, they recognised it from earlier. Oh fuck! They should have put the tarp on better. That was stupid, he thought to himself. He heard the engine pitch change and looked up to see the helicopter now slow down and the landing gear deploy. Oh no, he thought, they were landing! He quickly checked where they would land, he needed to be absolutely sure, if his plan were to work, he needed to see the exact landing location.

It was a long shot, one that he felt would buy them minutes only, but right now minutes were all they had. Suddenly he heard the engine pitch change as the pilot applied power. What was going on, he thought, as he watched it race away over the treetops, the landing gear retracting into the belly.

Back onboard Golgolvin held onto his rifle, waiting for the helicopter to settle, before stowing the rifle back away. He had no idea what was going on, one minute he thought they were landing then Sasha was shouting something he couldn't hear and the helicopter was gaining altitude.

He struggled with the headset, finally getting them back on. "What is it?" he demanded angrily, "Why aren't we landing?"

The pilot's voice came through, "Colonel we've had another hit from unit 163, they're sending us the co-ordinates of someone who's transmitting. It's twelve miles west of here, I'm taking us there now."

Smiling, Golgolvin sat back, at last, he thought, another lamb to slaughter.

Back in the barn there was confusion as Mike ran back to the vehicles, unable to explain what just happened. Had they seen him? He saw Spider stood by the back of his vehicle waving him over. His headset was half on his head, allowing him to hear the people around him and stay connected to the radios, with the loudspeaker blaring.

"What is it Spider? What have you got? Why did they just leave?"

Spider shook his head sadly, "I think they just caught a fish, listen."

He reached over, increasing the volume on the loudspeaker as the scratchy voice boomed over the barn.

"Hello, Golf Two-Zero, Golf Two-Zero, this is Hotel Three-Two-Bravo, we can hear you, can you send us your position. Over?"

The other crews all sat with their headsets on in the vehicles, hearing it playing out.

"Any callsign, any callsign, this is Golf Two-Zero, we need urgent assistance."

There was a pause, this time another voice, a more senior voice came over the radio speaking slowly and clearly. "Hello, Golf, Two-Zero, this is Hotel Three-Two-Bravo, we can hear you, what assistance do you require? And what is your location. Over."

"Fucking hell guys, stop speaking!" Spider said desperately. Mike saw Rachel sat in the back of Spiders wagon, "Rachel is there no way we can warn them, no way to send a message? They're going to be sitting ducks."

She looked sadly back, "I'm sorry Mike but no, if you transmit now, you'll give away our own position and they'll know we're here."

Staring at the loudspeaker in mute hope, everyone listened as the drama played out and they were faced with the paralysing fear of being powerless to stop it.

Onboard the Hind

Five minutes later and Colonel Golgolvin felt a tap on his arm, as one of his Captain's pointed excitedly at the wood block off to their right. Raising his binoculars he looked to the area the man was pointing to. The wood was heavy and thick, situated in the low ground of a valley, already he could see the tell-tale track marks carved into the terrain, something big had gone into the woods, and with only one set of tracks going in, it meant it had not yet exited. The helicopter began to circle the woodland, three pairs of eyes looking out of the side door, hoping to see some sign of the enemy lurking below.

"You're certain of our position? These are the co-ordinates you were given," he asked the pilot.

"Yes Colonel, the transmission's originated from within those woods, unit 163 have confirmed that last transmission was no more than three minutes ago."

As if to confirm something was down there, the sparks of incoming rounds hit the side of the cockpit window, causing the pilot to jolt with surprise, as he jinked the helicopter sideways to throw off the enemies aim, almost causing the passengers in the back to fall. They quickly reached out to steady themselves, shouting curses to the pilot as they regained their footing.

"Sir, we're receiving small arms fire from the woodland," he quickly replied as if to explain the sudden manoeuvre.

"Okay." Golgolvin replied, sitting himself down and holding onto the handhold above his head.

Golgolvin knew that the Hind was fully armoured and was known as the 'Flying Tank' for very good reason. The 5.56mm rounds being fired at it, may as well have been snowballs for all the effect it was having. Apart from scratching the paint and giving away their position he failed to see why the enemy had even bothered to fire at the helicopter.

"Okay, we've seen enough, lets pull back and get our Havocs in here."

The helicopter turned away, retreating a safe distance as the pilot radioed in to the two MI-28 Havoc gunships that were loitering five miles to the south. Coming in low and fast, this was what the Havocs had been designed to do, the Russian version of the Apache, similar in size and design, with the pilot and gunner sat in a tandem style cockpit. The Havoc's pilots knew the threat in the woodline was low, already the British had been too late in deploying their anti-air capabilities and if the vehicles below were from Bovington then they knew the chances were slim that they would even have any form of air defence at all. Watching through binoculars, Golgolvin looked on as the helicopters came in from the southeast, keeping themselves out of sight of the woodline and using the terrain to hide their approach. As one, they both slowed to a hover, the elevated position of Golgolvin in the helicopter giving him a grandstand view, as both helicopters slowly rose to firing positions. Whatever they had seen, they were ready to engage as both helicopters fired two Ataka air to ground missiles. The missiles flashed brightly as the rocket motors engaged, streaking away across the ground towards their targets. Golgolvin blinked, as both missiles impacted the edge of the thick treeline, the trees stopping the missiles from hitting whatever was in there.

Damn, he thought, the woodland was too thick. He was about to send orders over the radio, when, as if realising themselves, the two Havocs gained altitude and came in high and fast, coming in above the targets, switching to the smaller S8 rockets. Each helicopter had two pods of forty rockets each, unguided and fired dumb, they were simply point and shoot, but with a high explosive warhead they could smash through the trees. And that's exactly what they did, as the rockets were fired in one quick salvo, twenty of them hitting the centre of the woodland. A column of flame shot up as each rocket hit the ground, some ignited the dry trees and grassland starting fires, others simply exploded in the canopies of the trees, blasting the leaves and branches off and carving huge smoking holes into the green canopy. Finishing their attack run, the helicopters turned for a second run, when they saw smaller, more powerful explosions from within the trees, Secondary explosions, thought Golgolvin, that meant they had hit something other than wood and earth. Thick black smoke began to rise through the canopy and suddenly like some prehistoric dinosaur darting out of the woodland, a tracked vehicle burst out, it's side on fire, no doubt covered in fuel from another vehicle exploding close by. Golgolvin looked closely, identifying it as some kind of engineering vehicle, with a strange bucket on the back and a dozer blade on the front. The crew must have panicked, he thought, and decided their odds were greater in the open, rather than sitting waiting for death from above and were now trying to escape from the Havocs. As if sensing the easy prey, the two attack helicopters flew close by, shadowing the vehicle, toying with it, as it drove in flames through the open field. Realising their predicament, he watched as the vehicle ground to a halt, the hatches opening and the three crew inside quickly jumping out. One rolled along the floor as his arm caught alight as he jumped through the flames. All ran a safe distance from the armoured vehicle, expecting it to explode and knelt on the floor, their arms on their heads, looking up dejectedly as the two Havocs circled like vultures. Smiling he turned to his Major, "I want Wolfs One to Four up here immediately, have them land south of the woodline then clear through it. Find out what else is in there and flush them out."

Pointing down to the enemy soldiers in the open next to their burning vehicle Major Lenosky asked, "What do you want doing with those?"

Looking out he smiled as he reached for his AK12. "Set us down nearby," he said to the pilot as he looked at the other two in the cabin. "It's been a long day Sasha, we need to step out to stretch our legs, besides I could do with practising my English."

Bovington Camp 6th Division Headquarters

It was 17:50 by the time the Colonel's helicopters came back into Bovington camp to refuel, landing near to the tank hangars, now all reappropriated for the use of his helicopters. Already the ground crews were working on another two of his Hinds, getting them ready for combat, reloading the rocket pods, whilst another crew came out dragging the heavy fuel hoses for his gunships. He jumped out of the helicopter, bending low as he ran from under the giant rotor wash, watching as the fuel hoses were connected up. He became aware of a jeep driving quickly towards him, looking up he recognised the officer as one of the CinCS staff. The jeep pulled up next to him, the officer urging him in.

"Comrade Colonel, your presence is requested by the Commander in Chief."

Golgolvin looked at his watch, then back at the helicopters, knowing he had another twenty minutes to wait before they'd all be ready to fly again. He'd been hoping to get out for another run, perhaps fly back to the farm where he saw that ploughed field. Knowing he was powerless to override the orders, he waved over to Major Lenosky, who ran over.

"What's up?" he yelled, over the sound of the helicopter's engines, looking over at the officer in jeep.

"We've been summoned by the General, Sasha! You're coming with me."

Both wore blank expressions, as they climbed in, the officer driving them back the short distance to the headquarters building, the journey silent as no-one spoke. As they pulled up to the building, Golgolvin could see a hive of activity, soldiers running in and out of the building, some jumping into jeeps and driving away, others waiting by armoured cars for their officers to come out. Clearly something was happening, he thought. The jeep was left parked outside the doors, as Golgolvin and his second stepped out and into the chaos, shouts and hurried orders were being issued to and fro. Exchanging a curious glance, both of them walked inside and up the stairs, standing to attention outside the General's office.

Five minutes later and Golgolvin was stood in the office of the CinCS, with Major Lenosky being left to wait outside. The General was behind the desk, looking serious as he read a report. Finally finished, he placed the report down, looking up and acknowledging the Colonel.

"Ahh Yuri, how did the hunting go? Did you manage to find any of those vehicles?"

Golgolvin nodded, "We managed to find some of the lighter armour Comrade General, but no heavy tanks as of yet. I'm planning on going out again, once refuelled, after you've finished with us here, I've got some more tracks to follow up on."

The CinCS looked up in thought, nodding his head slowly before looking back to the report on the desk, Golgolvin wondered what it was that had distracted the General as the CinCS finally said.

"We've been given our orders Colonel; the offensive begins in two hours. I need you and your unit to be ready to push north towards Yeovil."

"But Sir, I'm still waiting on the rest of my brigade's helicopters from the ships. I thought they'd be-"

The CinCS interrupted him, silencing him with a raised hand. "Colonel, I need you to forget about your helicopters for now, instead, I want you take command of one of our Battalion Tactical Groups, the 344th. You'll use them as you see fit, it seems their own Commanding Officer has had an accident and is currently indisposed."

Accident, the CinCS thought to himself sarcastically, the bloody fool had got into a drunken fight that afternoon with another of his soldiers. Now he was in the hospital, shot through the chest and the young private guilty of the crime, was in the cells awaiting his fate.

Golgolvin looked on confused, "But Comrade General, surely the 334th has its own officers ready to step up?"

"No, it does not, they're a green unit that needs someone more experienced to lead them, hence I'm attaching you and your VDV brigade to them. I need you ready to move and as you've already said, your helicopters are still stuck on the ships. It's a perfect match Colonel, they need the experience and you need their vehicles. Have your men get amongst their troops and teach them from that huge vault of knowledge you all carry around on top of your shoulders."

Golgolvin watched on open mouthed, as the General now picked up a piece of paper, writing quickly on it as he spoke.

"Colonel, your orders are to take your new brigade and continue north, your limit of exploitation is the town of Yeovil, I want you to stay south of it. Under no circumstances are you to enter the town yet. The 344th are now placed under your command, you're their new CO. That's thirty T80 tanks plus fifty BMP's. With these new additions, plus your own troops, you should have all you need to secure our western flank.

The CinCS held out the orders for Golgolvin to take, who instead stared back, not fully comprehending what he was being asked to do. Shaking his head slightly he countered,

"But Comrade General, I'm better prepared to do this with my own Brigade and my helicopters, We won't need the men from the 344th. If they're as green and as inexperienced as you say, then they'll only hinder us. Plus, I've no experience at commanding armoured formations, I'm a Colonel of the VDV, surely, we'd be better waiting for my helicopters to be unloaded?"

The General ignored his complaint, his face impassive as his outstretched hand holding the orders pushed towards him again. "You'll do just fine Colonel with what you have, now take your orders."

Golgolvin looked back, his mouth open in disbelief. He'd only been inside an armoured vehicle a few times, let alone command one. Confused he again began to counter, "General, surely there are far better suited officers out there," he pointed outside towards the window.

The General closed his eyes, his voice firmer this time. "Colonel-"

But Golgolvin wouldn't be stopped, he continued arguing, "My Brigade's spent years together training with their helicopters, each soldier knows the other, trusts the other, surely you can't expect me too simply-"

"You're an officer of the Russian Forces!" the General snapped back, hearing enough, cutting Golgolvin off as he shot up out of the chair, both hands planted firmly on the desk as he leaned towards Golgolvin, his face turning red. "You'll do as you're bloody well told! You will take these men and you will use them Colonel. If you say they're green, then teach them, lead them. A poor officer will always blame the troops he has

113

under him, but that's just a true reflection of the officer. Now, take your orders and get out!"

Golgolvin stood slowly up to attention, ramrod straight and looking ahead as the General's words flowed through him. He knew the man and knew the words would not be personal, he could see he was under immense strain and was merely venting his frustration. He did what any professional soldier would have done in that situation, he wisely kept his thoughts to himself and stared ahead. Sensing there was nothing more to be said Golgolvin reached over, picking up the now crumpled paper and reading through it quickly. Before handing the paper back to the General, his face blank.

"What?" the CinCS demanded irritated.

"I need these orders signed Comrade General, before I can legally carry them out."

Slowly the General picked up the pen, signing and dating them, before handing them back to him. Golgolvin scanned the signature and satisfied, he folded the orders up and placed them inside his smock, before standing back to attention.

The General sat back down angrily, busying himself with a pile of papers as he waved his hand to dismiss him without looking up. Golgolvin saluted, turned and opened the door, walking out of the room. As he left the office, he nodded to Major Lenosky who fell into step with him at his side and followed him outside.

"What now Colonel?" Lenosky asked, surprised to have heard shouting from inside the office.

"Now Sasha, we go to work, but I'm afraid my friend, it's going to be far harder than we first thought."

"Really?" Lenosky asked, looking back inquisitively as Golgolvin questioned him.

"What do you remember most about your time working with armoured vehicles?"

Lenosky sneered in disgust, thinking back to a time before he joined the VDV, when he was an infantryman, replying, "Hot, sweaty, claustrophobic bullet magnets, always breaking down and always making me sick. That's the reason I left and joined the VDV. Why?"

Golgolvin laughed at his friend's response, before remarking, "Because from today, Sasha, that's what we're going to be working with."

From behind his desk, General Kuzmin watched the two VDV officers leave, regretting the words he'd used. He knew Yuri was probably the most capable commander he had with him and had secretly agreed with everything he'd said. But the trouble he faced was that with the limited experience in the other officers, he was now forced to ask more of those he trusted. Already on the elongated journey by ship, he'd grudgingly promoted Captains to Majors, and Majors to Colonels to expect greater things from them, until the lesser experienced men began to take shape. When he'd first seen the reports showing the combat readiness of the units, it had shocked him, some of the more junior units had been sent onboard having only just completed their basic training, with some soldiers never even having fired a rifle before!

He had the same reservations as Golgolvin, but that was the trouble with being at the top, the complaints would always go up, never down. And seeing how he was the head of the landing forces in the south, there was no-one to talk to. Instead, he had to face the fact that he had to keep his mouth shut and just get on with it. His frustrations at the lack of experience and training of troops were matched only by the disaster with the logistics of the ports. With no way of knowing what was loaded onto what ship, he already had units crying out for vehicles, supplies, weaponry, even the air force was currently lacking in arms and munitions. Its entire complement of missiles and ammo were loaded somewhere out there, in the bowels of one of the ships, still waiting to be found. Until they had all of them unloaded, it was a waiting game as to what could be brought ashore. That's why he couldn't promise the Colonel his helicopters, for now, they had no way of knowing where the hell they were. So far, he'd only managed to land one third of their total forces, whilst in the north, having only one landing zone, the northern forces were already all ashore, making the most of Newcastle's huge dockyards and industrious might, to unload far faster than he could. Kuzmin had tried to request more time to sort out the mess, another twelve hours was all that was needed, but no, the orders coming back had been to move now, already the northern thrust was straining at the leash to go.

Not wanting to dwell on it further, he looked up at the clock, their offensive would begin in two hours and there was still much to do, still so much to do…

8

Dipping Your Toe In

Sam's Farm

The mood had now changed, gone was the laughter and banter of before, now everyone seemed more concentrated, focussed on getting their tasks done. The helicopter appearing overhead and the ambush that had played out on the radio had shaken them all, especially as the unit under attack had begged Golf Two-Zero for help, little realising they were talking to their attackers. But the worse part, had been feeling powerless to fight back or help them and Mike had seen and heard the rage from the soldiers around him. "Where the fuck is the air force?" he'd heard Ping demand and Whippet shout across to Patty, "When do we get to fight back? How much running we gotta do?" He understood their anger, but for now, they all had to play it smart. At this moment, all they could do was survive. Rachel had already spent the rest of the afternoon setting up the vehicle radios so the same deceptive trick could not be played on them, all they had to do now was find the others. But where the hell were they? Mike mused.

Mike watched as the vehicle crews of the Warriors fought with the thick rubber fuel hoses, dragging them across the barn floor as they began to fill up the vehicles. Sam had delivered on his promise and another local called Doug, from the neighbouring farm, had turned up in the early evening with a tractor towing a fuel bowser. Mike had asked for a thousand litres, and Doug proudly showed him the full fifteen-hundred litre bowser. He nodded his head in thanks, as the farmer helped the crews fuel up, whilst Sam came and stood by the front of the tank with him.

"So, army, now you've got your fuel, what's next?"

Mike looked out of the barn at the fading light, the sun was already below the treeline, its rays casting a golden hue to all it touched.

"Now, we wait for the light to fade and finally get out of your hair."

He turned to face the farmer, extending his hand, "Sam, I just want to say thank you again, you've already done more than you should have. I just hope we haven't put you all in danger here. Perhaps you should consider taking Mary and stay with friends for a few days, I'm worried that helicopter might come back with troops next time."

Taking his hand and shaking it, the farmer simply replied, "If it does, then it does, I knew the risks when I let you use the barn. Don't you worry about us." Something about the farmer's carefree attitude alarmed Mike.

"Sam please, I'm being serious, your animals can manage without you for a few days can't they? Surely, you'd want Mary to be kept safe? These people won't mess about, you've seen that already, is this place worth dying over?"

The farmer looked back at Mike, his eyes narrowing as he simply said, "Follow me, I want to show you something."

Mike followed the farmer outside towards the back of the farmhouse, where a plot of land was fenced off from the rest of the fields. At the far end of the plot sat a huge oak tree, and Mike followed as the farmer walked over to it. Underneath one of the large branches he saw the gravestone, how had he missed that, he thought. Mike silently read the words on the gravestone. *'Nicola Collins, Born- 19th July 1984 Died – 18th July 2006.'* He looked over as Sam knelt and lovingly placed his hand on the headstone before smiling. "Our daughter Nicola, she was so full of life, so bubbly and happy, she absolutely loved this place, growing up I used to watch her chase the chickens around the yard back there." He nodded in the direction of the house. "And over there, in those fields you drove through earlier, that's where I taught her to drive for the first time, she was only twelve and whilst most kids her age were still learning to ride a bike, she already knew how to drive a tractor." Mike could see the pride in the farmer's face as he continued.

"Growing up, we'd hoped she'd want to stay on the farm. Mary had always tried to make it more exciting for her, but she was young, adventurous, with big dreams, too full of life for this little place to hold her. She wanted to see the world and she wanted adventure, and that's exactly what the army offered her when she walked into the recruitment centre."

Oh, shit, thought Mike, he guessed where the story was going.

"When we found out, we tried to talk her out of it, I tried explaining to her that it wasn't like they say in the brochures and that real war is not for the feint hearted, it's messy, horrible, disgusting, barbaric and it's...inhuman. But she'd always smile that beautiful smile of hers and say, 'but dad, you used to tell me all about your time in the forces, your stories sounded so adventurous, so rewarding, so much fun.' And you know what, Mike? She was right, I had. She'd grown up hearing all about the travel to exotic places, all the fun times, the friends, the experiences. But you see I'd kept the darker stuff to myself. That was my fault. Maybe I should have warned her about the other side, the cost of all that fun and adventure. Not every story has a happy ever after."

Sam looked sadly on, as he picked at the grass around the headstone.

"What did she join in the end?"

The farmer looked over, shaken from his thoughts, "She joined the Intelligence Corps, as an officer, Second Lieutenant Collins. Of course, we were both proud, seeing her passing out parade at Sandhurst was one of the best and worst days, of my life. Within six months she was deployed to Iraq, I'd assured Mary that she wouldn't see any action, her job would keep her safely in the rear. I said she'd spend most of her time looking at reports or writing intelligence assessments. I never thought she'd go out on the ground... But this is Nicola we're talking about and sure enough, she volunteered to go out. She wouldn't tell us at the time, probably didn't want us to worry, but we found out afterwards. She'd get to go out on the ground in the back of the Warriors with the infantry lads. They had no women in the infantry back then and needed female soldiers to handle female detainees, or so they told me." His face took on a frustrated look as he continued, his voice bitter. "I mean, just how bloody stupid is that? They stop women joining the infantry so they don't have to fight on the front line and then realising that they need them there, they pluck them from their jobs, when they're the least experienced. Bloody stupidity, she shouldn't have been out there, not like that."

Sam shook his head to clear his thoughts as he stood up, "The day before her 22nd birthday, she went back out on the ground again. Another search op in the same area. The unit commander had become lazy and had used the same route into the area for the past three search ops, it was no surprise that her vehicle hit an IED by a bridge. There were five people in the back of it." the farmer stopped to wipe a tear away as he tried to compose himself.

"When they came to tell us at the farm, they pulled me aside and asked quietly if she had left any of her items here, toothbrushes, hairbrushes, we gave them what we had. Mary asked me why they wanted them, I just said some rubbish about her friends wanting some of her personal items to put in a memory box, to remember her by. I knew the real reason though."

"DNA." Mike replied quietly.

Sam looked up, "Exactly, DNA! Tells you everything you need to know about the state of my daughter's body. It had been that mashed up, that unrecognisable, our beautiful daughter..."

Mike kept quiet as he saw the anger on Sam's face, he'd seen it before with his own friends, so he wisely kept quiet, letting the farmer vent his feelings.

Through clenched teeth he continued. "I should have told her all about what it's really like, to be so scared to raise your head from a rock you're hiding behind, that you'd rather shit and piss yourself and lie in it, than come out of cover. Or, that when your friend's lying there in the open, screaming at you for help, you're too scared to crawl out to get him, because you know that's what the bastards are waiting for. Or maybe I should have told her what it was like afterwards, when you're picking up parts of your mates that you recognise, these were people you laughed with, people you lived with, now nothing more than meat in a bag. Or how years later, you'd feel guilty about still living, why wasn't it me who died? Why did I get to live? If I'd have told her about that part of the military life, perhaps she'd still be alive."

"Perhaps," replied Mike nodding, his voice soft, "or perhaps she'd have ignored your warnings and joined anyway, perhaps she would have stayed here on the farm, maybe she would have died in a road traffic accident on one of the roads here, or maybe she would have ended up getting some cruel illness like cancer."

Sam looked at him confused, "What? What are you getting at?"

Mike continued softly, "What I'm getting at Sam, is that we all die of something at some point in our lives, and you can't be held responsible for everything that would have come for your daughter. From what you've just told me, she lived life her way and nothing you could have said or tried to do would have stopped that."

For a few moments the farmer said nothing as he looked at Mike, his jaw hardened and then with an explosion of air he breathed out. "Anyone tell you that your bedside manner is fucking appalling?"

Mike smiled softly as the tension evaporated. "You wouldn't be the first to tell me, my wife is always saying the same thing. But getting back to your daughter, it sounds to me like she was always going to do what she wanted to, regardless of the cotton wool you wanted to wrap her in." Mike reasoned.

The farmer wiped his eyes on his sleeve, nodding, "Yeah...fair one, guess that was always the danger of raising such a fireball."

He laughed as the happy thoughts of his daughter came flooding back as Mike asked, his eyebrows raised, "Sam, why did you bring me here?"

"I've brought you here to show you that this isn't just a farm to us, it's not just somewhere we work, it's our home. It's where my family was raised, where my child grew up and where our happiest memories were made. And now, it's where our daughter finally lies at peace. We don't care about the risks or what the consequences are, Mary and I won't be scared away from our home. We won't simply leave our daughter here alone and run away. We're both going to die here on this land anyway and if that's today, tomorrow or in thirty years, we don't care. Can you understand that?"

Mike could see the passion burning in his eyes as he stared back at him. "I understand Sam, I get it now."

The farmer nodded thankfully, "Good, because there's also another reason I've brought you here."

Mike cocked his head inquisitively as the farmer continued, "I want to ask you what you intend to do about the body of the girl in my reefer. Surely you can't be thinking of taking her with you, are you?"

Oh shit, thought Mike, he suddenly felt guilty that he'd forgotten to think about what to do. They could take her with them, but for how much longer? And what if they didn't find what they were looking for tonight, would they keep her in the vehicle with the heat?

Sam could see the conflict in Mike's face as he replied, "Look, I might be able to help you, how about I bury the lass here next to my daughter, she can stay here until things settle down and then when its safe enough, the army can come back and exhume her body. Send her home to be with her parents. Would that work? Besides, it would be nice for Nicola to have the company."

"But if something happens to you and Mary-"

Sam interrupted him, "She'll still be buried here, you know she's here, no-one will disturb her. She'll be left at peace, until her family want her back."

Mike thought for a moment, "I'll need to check with her friend who was with her, but for now, if it's okay with her and you, then I can think of no better place or company to be with. Thank you."

The farmer smiled proudly at the compliment as he asked, "if it's alright with you, I've met Rachel already, I'll ask her myself, you've got more important things to be getting on with, like keeping the others out of the ground."

Mike nodded as both men turned and walked back over to the barn.

Leaving the crews still working on the vehicles, Mike called Patty, Spider, Doc and Rachel over to the side of the barn, away from all the noise and action. In his hands he carried four of the road maps that he'd liberated from the autoparts store. He gave one each to the three vehicle commanders who nodded in thanks. Doc was there, as he was now replacing Jonah as the commander on Two-One-Alpha, the decision being made by Spider earlier in the day. Mike unfolded his map showing the whole of the southern part of the UK and placed it on a bale of hay, for all to see.

"I know it's not military mapping, but it's the best we have for now. Whilst everyone else is getting the wagons ready, I thought we'd all get together and talk through our next leg and discuss where we think we should head to, otherwise we'd be out all night like the blind leading the blind." Everyone nodded in agreement as he continued, "Spider, before we start, if you're in agreement I'd like to recommend we change all your vehicle callsigns from Golf to Tango."

"Why?"

"Think about it," he replied, "if others heard what we heard earlier playing out over the radio, and then we're using the same callsign's later, people will think that we were responsible."

"Fuck yeah of course," Spider replied, "right, Tango Two-Zero it is."

Mike looked over to Rachel, "I've called you here because you were at the headquarters last night and might be able to give us an insight into what was being planned. I'd like to know if we were heading in the right direction to begin with."

She nodded, replying, "From what I heard, the Generals' were discussing evacuating what was left at Tidworth and pushing them northeast towards Aldershot."

"Hmm okay," replied Mike looking at the map. Pointing to Tidworth he replied, "If they're discussing that, they must already be expecting the Russians to push towards them in that direction. Perhaps if we keep heading north, we could put some distance between us and Dorchester and then swing east, try to stay ahead of the enemy."

He looked up to the three Fusilier Corporals, "What's your thoughts guys? You're all from Tidworth, that's where your unit's based, do you want to try and head east for Tidworth? See if we can get you back to your unit?"

Patty shook his head glumly, "Mike there's no-one at Tidworth to meet up with, all our Regiment and vehicles are in Estonia, they've been there since April. If we head that way, we're heading back to nothing more than a families officer and about thirty soldiers on rear party. And if they are moving them further east, we could still miss them."

Doc interjected, "What if we just head east now, forget going north and sacrifice the mileage for time?"

Mikes eyebrows creased in thought, "I think that's going to be a nonstarter for us Doc, if we head east from here, we'll be running alongside the enemy for the best part of thirty miles. We already know they have control of the air and with no ammo for the vehicles we'd be sitting ducks."

The others nodded in agreement, as Patty asked, "What if we headed for Blandford, that's north east of here, gives us a bit of distance, and gets us back with friendly troops?"

"Yeah we could do." Mike rubbed his chin thinking, "My concern though Patty is it's mainly a signals camp. I don't think that we'd gain anything by going there. They wouldn't have anything we could use for the vehicles, no ammo, no spares, plus if they're evacuating Tidworth, they must be evacuating Blandford, it's only eight miles from here, and I can't see the enemy just bypassing it."

"Ok," replied Patty, "fuck it, forget going east, let's just head north, and get ourselves up to Yeovil, there's a fleet air arm base there, I remember going there as a kid to the museum."

Spider's face creased into a grin as he replied, "Mate, what the hell are we going to do with a museum? You fancy taking a biplane out for a spin?"

"No, you berk, it's still an active Navy base, it's where the Carrier planes go when they're not at sea, I bet there's some of our F35's there, if it's air cover we want, let's at least get up there. Maybe that's where everyone else as bugged out to."

"Who knew you were a secret plane spotter." Spider replied humorously as Patty shook his head.

Mike looked on the map, reaching down to the floor he picked up a piece of straw and used it to mark on the map where they were. Tracing the route to Yeovil he replied, "Okay well we're here, on this farm just outside of Nether Cerne. Yeovil looks to be about seventeen miles as the crow flies." He pursed his lips, thinking aloud as he continued, "Now with the fuel that Sam and his mate have given us, we could get there with what we have, the trouble is we won't be able to just hop onto the A37 and drive up there. We'd be spotted for sure, either from the air or the ground and we don't yet know how far north the enemy have gone. I'd have eyes on that road if it were me, it's a main route into Dorchester. This morning it looked like no-one was in Dorchester, but that could have changed since we've been here."

"So, what do you suggest?" Patty asked.

"From memory the terrain up there is hilly, with rivers, steep banks and valleys. It'll be hell on the vehicles and bad for our fuel states, but I think we'd stand more chance of staying in the low ground to the east and away from prying eyes. We don't yet know where everyone is on the ground and I think we'd be better off assuming we're behind enemy lines. So, if we stay off the high ground as much as we can and if everything falls in place, then we might stand a chance of getting to Yeovil by the morning."

"That's provided the enemy aren't there already," Rachel warned.

Mike rubbed his nose in thought before replying, "I don't see them pushing that far yet, besides the focus seems to be on them heading northeast. Unless something changes, I think Yeovil will be our best bet."

Everyone nodded in agreement as Spider replied, "So we're all agreed, Yeovil it is then?"

Happy now with their destination, they spent the next hour planning how they would get there, what route they would take, and their 'Actions on' drills. These were what the military called scenarios for what they would do if they came under contact, or what would happen if a vehicle broke down, or any other scenarios they could think of. By the time they'd finished, every vehicle commander knew the plan, and what to do if they became separated or worse, the lead vehicle was destroyed. After returning to their vehicles, they'd brief their crews on the plan, so by the time everyone was ready to go, everyone, from the lowest rank to the highest knew what was expected of them.

Standing up and stretching his back, Mike looked at everyone in turn as he asked. "So, I think that covers everything, does anyone have any questions. Spider?"

"No."

"Patty?"

"Yes, what's the plan with Jonah? Do we keep him under arrest or what?"

Everyone looked across to Mike, expecting him to answer.

Mike shook his head apologetically, "I'm sorry guys, but that's not my department, he's a soldier and as such is under military law, so he's your problem. But, if you release him, I think there's a strong chance he'll take the first opportunity he gets to run. And knowing what he knows about this place, and how Sam and Mary helped us, if the other side pick him up and he talks, then Sam and Mary are as good as dead."

Spider pinched his lips in thought as Patty replied, "Well look, why don't we just keep him detained for now and then the first sign of the MP's and we'll hand him over." Patty looked over to Spider for confirmation as both men thought over the problem. Eventually Spider nodded in agreement, replying with, "Okay Patty, okay."

Seeing the problem resolved for now, Mike continued, looking over to Doc, "Doc, you happy? Any questions?"

"No."

"Rachel?"

"No Mike, thanks for including me though, was nice to know the plan."

He smiled in response, "Well I recommend we leave at last light, which should be about 21:20 judging by last night, that gives us three hours from now. Let's just synchronise all our watches so we're all showing the same time.

Everyone checked their shiny new watches, courtesy of the earlier shopping trip, even Patty and Spider had swapped their own for the better models, Mike noted smiling.

"Right, I make it 18:21 in five, four, three, two, one, mark!" Everyone checked their watches were all showing the same time to the second as Mike continued, "One final thing guys, we've all been living in a bit of a bubble here since this morning and have no idea what's going on out there on the ground. The roads and countryside could be full of enemy troops, friendly troops or just people trying to get away from it all. Now a lot of our guys are going to be jumpy, angry and quick to pull the trigger. Let's just make sure that if we do open fire, we're 100 percent on what we're shooting at."

"Amen to that," replied Patty as everyone nodded in agreement.

Mike finished off, "Right, let's get to it, thanks everyone," and then turned, leaving the others to chat amongst themselves as he walked back to the tank. Spider quickly ran up behind him, "Mike! Sorry I almost forgot."

He turned as Spider held out one of the SA80's. Seeing the confused look on Mike's face he quickly added, "You said you wanted a weapon on every vehicle, we've all got a rifle each, this was Jonah's, now we want you to have it."

"Thanks Spider, but my gunner has his rifle with him, we've already got one on the tank, why don't you save it for one of the others."

"We don't want the others to have it, we want you to have it. Besides we'd all feel a little better knowing you've got the means to defend yourself. You've got the greenest crew out of all of us, and the last thing we need is your gunner shooting your bollocks off, as he's trying to pass his rifle up to you..." As if to emphasise the point, Spider now pushed the rifle into Mike's hands.

"But I'm a civilian Spider-"

"Who's riding around on top of a bloody great tank!" Spider interrupted, "Do you think the guys on the other side won't shoot at you? Besides it didn't stop you earlier when you were waving it about at the store."

Mike had to admit he did have a point, quickly replying, "I hadn't shot at anyone then Spider, besides it's been a while since I passed a weapons handling test, I doubt the army would like me firing that without the necessary paperwork. You know how much the army loves its paperwork."

Spider smiled, "Well it's just as well then that I'm a Small Arms Instructor." He placed his map down on the floor and took the rifle back from Mike who watched on with curious amusement as Spider removed the full magazine and replaced it with an empty one from his pocket.

"Come on then, let's get your weapon handling test done." He placed the rifle on the floor before looking at Mike and adopting the serious face and tone of an instructor.

"Right then, upon entering the room, you come across this weapon lying there. I'd like you to now pick up the weapon in a safe and controlled manner please."

Smiling, Mike put his own map on the floor, "Okay Spider, if you insist." he picked up the weapon and began to play along.

Ten minutes later and Spider was clapping him on the back. "There you see! Nothing to it, you hadn't forgotten anything. It's just like riding a bike, you never forget. I'm proud to say you've just passed your weapon handling test and are now legally authorised to carry a rifle." Mike fitted the full magazine that Spider handed to him and slung the SA-80 over his shoulder smiling, as Spider said jokingly, "And where do you think you're going? We haven't finished just yet."

Mike said nothing but looked on with interest as Spider now produced one of the black pistols from his smock pocket.

"Glock 17, Gen 4, now these will be new to you, as we only got these three years ago, however I'm guessing you're familiar with the Sig Sauer?"

Mike nodded and stepped closer; his interest piqued. "Yes, the P226, we used them in Afghan."

"Good, well these babies are similar. Same similar types of action, holds seventeen rounds of 9mm ammunition in the magazine and can be carried with a round in the chamber." Mike watched as Spider ejected the empty magazine and expertly stripped the pistol in under ten seconds, then quickly re-assembled it. He handed the pistol over to Mike, who began to strip it the same as he would the Sig Sauer, as Spider continued, "The hammer won't fire unless the trigger is squeezed, which stops it going off if dropped. The trigger can't be squeezed unless your finger's fully on it, which stops it snagging on clothing and going off. And the hammer is rounded off, which stops it snagging on your clothing." Mike remembered his earlier fight with the Russian, his own pistol had snagged on his clothing as he tried to pull it out of his jacket. Had the Russian had a Glock then the outcome might have been different. As Spider finished talking, Mike finished re-assembling the pistol, much to Spider's delight.

"See, similar to the Sig." he confirmed proudly as he took the pistol from Mike and refitted the magazine. Then placing it on the floor he started all over again with, "So, upon entering the room, you find the weapon on the floor. I'd like you to pick up the weapon in a safe and controlled manner."

This time the test took only five minutes, as Spider proudly proclaimed, "See, again, never doubted you."

Mike was about to hand the pistol back when Spider shook his head, "Nope that's yours now, all vehicle commanders are to have a pistol and rifle each, that's on my orders."

Mike placed the pistol in his pocket as Spider added, "I know we don't have the rounds for the pistols yet, but at least you're qualified now. You've got a full mag on the SA-80 and I'll get the paperwork all drawn up the next time we're in a barracks. Happy?"

"As a pig in shit." Mike grinned. "Is there anything else? Unless perhaps you've also got a grenade in your pocket to practise me with?"

Spider took on a look of mock horror, "Woah! Now steady on Mike, you're a tankie, I can't have you knowing how to play with all of our infantry toys now can I?"

Both men chuckled as they turned and made their way back to their vehicles.

The three hours until last light dragged by, as Mike sat on the front deck of the tank, watching the sun slowly setting behind the trees. He'd always hated the waiting in the army and no matter how much he willed it, the sun wouldn't go down any quicker. He'd already spent the time briefing his crew and after checking and double checking that all his gear was packed away, he now sat on the front with Smudge and Bill. They had managed to doze off and both were softly snoring, much to Mikes amusement. He watched Rachel leave the barn with Sam, no doubt to discuss what to do with Sharon's body, and ten minutes later saw her return, looking happy with the decision. Mike wondered if Sam had showed her his own daughter's grave. He checked his watch, it was 21:10, ten minutes to go. He stood up and stretched off, nudging his crew gently with his foot to wake them, watching as the other vehicle crews began to do the same. Smudge rubbed the sleep out of his eyes as Bill settled himself into the driver's cab.

"Bill, get the engine and GUE started and online please and then Smudge get the turret and radios all up and running."

Both soldiers acknowledged, as Mike stepped down off the tank for one final chat to Sam and Mary who now came to see them off by the barn entrance. Patty and Spider also walked over to join them. Behind them the heavy diesel engines of the vehicles began to cough into life, the exhausts reverberating around the barn and thick black smoke belching out before quickly dissipating as the engines warmed up.

Sam held Mary around the waist as his voice boomed out to be heard over the vehicles engines. "We just wanted to see you all off and wish you the best of luck."

Mike stepped forward and leaned closer to be heard, "Sam, Mary, I just want to extend again our deepest thanks and gratitude for your hospitality. Without your help today I don't think we'd have made It through the afternoon." Patty and Spider nodded in agreement as they both stepped forward to say goodbye, shaking the hand of the farmer and giving Mary a loving hug of thanks.

Sam said nothing, simply smiling in response, as Mary pulled Mike closer and gave him a big peck on the cheek, adding, "You're most welcome love, now you all just make sure you get these lovely lads and lasses to where they need to be and safely too I might add."

Mike replied, "We'll do our very best Mary, but I'm afraid that in the end it's not up to us."

"Well, you just-"

"Mary, for Pete's sake love," Sam interrupted lovingly, "they've got enough to be thinking about already without you chastising them, they know what they're about love, they'll be just fine."

Leaning closer to them Sam added, his eyes blazing, "You just make sure that when you do get into the fight, you make those bastards pay."

Mike could see the intensity in the farmer's eyes and had a glimpse of the former Commando. All three nodded and then as one they turned to mount their vehicles. Mike gave Patty and Spider a wink of encouragement as he climbed onboard the tank, checking that Bill's hatch was closed securely before climbing into the turret. He settled himself into the commander's seat, and from memory quickly ran through the checklist in his head, checking the sights were on and all the switches were as they should be. After checking the commander's station, he leant over the breech of the gun to the loader's side to check the switches there. After a quick check and happy the radios were on and all switches were correct, he sat back in his seat and put his headset and helmet on, checking his freshly acquired goggles, were sitting comfortably on the helmet.

"Okay guys, on comms. Bill, can you hear me?"

"Got you boss, loud and clear."

"Good, Smudge can you hear me?"

"Yep all good boss." Mike saw the gunner reach behind and give the thumbs up.

"Right, Smudge gun kit live?"

Mike heard the distinct click as his gunner pulled the grip switch, and the faint whine as the electrical motors came to life, feeling the small subtle movements of the fifteen-tonne turret.

"All on and live boss, good to go."

Mike stood up to check the tank sides were clear before reporting, "Bill you know the drill, same as before, I want you to tension both tracks, please."

Copying the same procedure he had done the night before, the engine revs lowered as the tank pirouetted gently to the right, as Bill tensioned the left track before repeating the procedure for the right. After a short time, he reported back, "Okay boss, HTT done and we're ready to move."

Mike closed his eyes, mentally going through the procedures that at one time were second nature to him. Looking behind his commander's seat, he saw the SA-80 tucked away securely in the gap. He checked his jacket pocket, feeling the pistol.

"Right, one final thing before we move, Smudge, confirm you've got your rifle with you.

"Yep got it down here with me."

Good, thought Mike, he stood up on the seat, his head and shoulders now above the cupola. Looking behind him he saw the three other Warriors ready to go, their own commanders looking over, ready for him to give the signal. He'd already spoken to them about using the radios, they'd agreed they'd wait till they were two miles from the farm before checking them, that way if Rachel's fix didn't work and the Russians could DF them, they'd be far enough away from the barn that Sam and Mary wouldn't be suspects and they'd be on the move, so getting a fix would be harder on them. Mike gave the signal, the good old thumbs up, watching as the other three acknowledged with the same signal. Happy, he looked back to Sam and Mary, giving them one final wave as he ordered, "Bill, keep the speed down and the revs low, and let's get out of here, stay on the track until I tell you to."

With a simple, "Roger," the driver acknowledged and with a clunk, the handbrake released and slowly the tank crept forward out of the barn. The antennas caught on the door and bowed backwards before twanging free as the tank disappeared into the darkness. Mike flicked the interior lights to red and adjusted the brightness, again the demonic glow was back. Then he turned to watch behind him as the third vehicle finally cleared the barn, satisfied that they were all clear, he pulled his goggles over his eyes and left the safety of the farm behind them.

Right, he thought, let's see what happens now...

9

The Blind Leading The Blind

An hour later Mike was leaning forward and standing out of the cupola, as he guided the tank up the steep sides of the valley towards the hilltop. He'd left the three Warriors hidden in the darkness of the forested valley behind them and was driving the tank up to the crest of the hill on its own.

"Okay guys, we're going to use this as practise for getting into a fire position," he briefed the crew. "Smudge, I want you to take control of the gun and using the thermal sight tell us when you can see over the hill."

"Okay."

"Bill, I want you to keep creeping slowly forward until Smudge says he can see over the hill and then you're going to stop the tank and hold us on the brakes. "

"Roger boss."

Mike stood watching, as the top of the hill came into view and the tank hauled itself up and over the crest slowly, as Smudge now gave a running commentary.

"Okay nearly there, little bit more, little bit more Bill and...ON!"

Mike felt the tank rock on its suspension as Bill stood on the brake pedal. The tank was now positioned on the reverse slope of the hill with almost all of it's hull hidden from view, with just the top of the turret and gun poking over the edge. It's what the crews would call the 'hull down' position. It meant the 120mm gun and sights could be used to spot and engage targets whilst keeping the largest part of the tank, the hull hidden safely from sight.

Mike was about to say something when he heard the driver exclaim, "Fucking hell!" and instinctively braced himself in the cupola as the tank suddenly began to roll backwards quickly gathering speed as Smudge exclaimed, "Bill! what the hell you doing?"

Quickly interrupting, Mike shot back, "Bill don't try and pull any sticks, just let her roll back down the valley, you're clear behind."

Bracing himself in the turret Mike could only hold on and watch open mouthed as the valley floor raced up to meet them out of the darkness, the wind whistling past as the tank rolled back down the way it came, bouncing along the valley floor, its tracks clattering away, before coming to a stop, leaving all three crew members with racing hearts after their unexpected trip.

"Everyone okay?" Mike asked quickly, his own pulse racing.

"What the hell happened there?" Smudge demanded angrily.

Ignoring him Mike asked again, "Bill? You alright down there?"

"I'm sorry guys, I...I couldn't hold the footbrake." Bill stammered in shock. He hadn't expected the tank to do that.

"You took the tank out of gear without having both feet on the brake pedal." Mike explained, "You're trying to hold nearly 74 tonnes of metal with just your left foot on a steep hill, unless you've got thighs like a rugby player, you won't be used to doing it yet."

"I'm sorry." Bill apologised.

Over the radio they heard Spider's voice break in concerned. "Tango One-One, Tango Two-Zero, you guys ok over there?"

Mike looked out of the cupola towards the darkened shapes of the Warriors. Knowing they could see him on their own thermal sights he realised they'd watched the whole thing. He quickly replied, the relief plain to hear in his voice. "Tango One-One, yeah we're all good here. Over."

"Tango Two-Zero, roger, next time we'll have the score cards ready for you. Out." Mike could almost hear the laughter in Spider's voice.

"Oh everyone saw it, for fucks sake, they're going to take the piss out of me now!" Bill said dejectedly.

"Bill listen to me," Mike quickly replied, trying to calm his driver down. "That happens a lot more than you think, it catches a lot of new drivers out the first time they're on a hill like this. Next time we stop on a hill like that, either brace yourself against the seat with both feet on the brake pedal, which you should be able to hold for a few minutes or if we're going to be there longer, then crank your handbrake on okay?"

"Okay, I'm sorry."

"It's alright, no harm done, we got away with that one. If it ever happens again though, if we roll away on a hill, whatever you do, *do not* try to pull the sticks and turn the tank. Never try to turn a tank going at speed downhill."

"But what if there's something in the way?" Smudge asked.

"Then we hit it," Mike replied dryly.

"But why hit it? Why not try to turn?" Smudge asked.

"Because Smudge, if you try to turn a tank that's going downhill out of control at speed, there's a bloody good chance it will roll over. And that's something you never want to be inside."

"Oh," the gunner replied, shocked.

"Right guys, let's all put on a fresh pair of panties and try that again, shall we?"

A few minutes later, and the tank began to crest the hill once more, with Smudge and Bill talking to each other.

"Okay Bill, keep going, keep going and ON!"

Again, Mike felt the tank rock gently backwards and forwards, but this time the tank stayed where it was.

"Bill, let's get the handbrake on please."

He heard the handbrake ratchet on as he began to slowly scan the area to their front, the turret turning smoothly as the electric motors whined softly. The A37 was about one mile away on the high ground and he quickly put Smudge to work. Using his own controls Mike showed the gunner the areas he wanted him to look at.

"Smudge, it's time to shine, I want you to scan the area of the road, here. That's your left of arc, identify."

"Identified." Smudge replied, using the words he'd been taught.

"Good, and your right of arc is this Woodline here, Identify."

"Identified." he reported back.

"Now, we're looking for anything military or anything unusual, doesn't matter how trivial you think it looks, you just tell me if you're not happy with it, ok?"

"Yes boss."

"Now Bill, rather than have you fall asleep down there, I want you from now on at night to select your reverse camera, you're watching our rear now, anyone approaches us from behind then you let us know about it, I don't care what it is, even if you think they're friendly then tell us."

Mike could hear the pride in his driver's voice, now that he felt he was doing something worthwhile to help protect the tank.

Mike stood with his shoulders out of the cupola, checking the assault rifle was to hand, as he surveyed the A37 through his binoculars. He was originally going to use the tank's thermal sights to pierce the darkness, but upon seeing the amount of light and chaos there, he realised he wouldn't have to. He looked through the binos, seeing the road was blocked on both sides with the traffic all heading north, the headlights stretching off into the distance. Looking through his bino's he could see that some drivers either through panic or incompetence, had tried to drive around the jam and now found themselves either bogged in on the side of the carriageways, or stuck in the numerous ditches and deep tracks, their cars now stuck at crazy angles with their headlights pointing upwards and lighting the night sky. Some of the owners were illuminated by the lights, pleading with others for a tow, whilst others were pushing vehicles, trying to get themselves out of the mess. Mike felt genuine sorrow for them, as taking the bino's from his eyes he looked back into the dark valley behind him, knowing that one of the Warriors could easily help to pull the vehicles free, but knowing that to do so, could invite their own destruction. Somewhere out there was the enemy, perhaps even watching the same road as they were, waiting for a kind gesture such as that. He shook the thought from his head, they weren't here for that. For now, as much as it hurt him to think it, these people were on their own. His job was to get the soldiers back to their own lines and that meant staying out of view.

"Smudge, anything out of the ordinary? Anything look like it doesn't belong?"

"Well apart from the hundreds of cars blocking the roads, boss, no, nothing at all."

Okay, Mike thought, let's try something else.

"Bill, shut down the main engine and GUE for a moment please."

He stood atop the turret, with his headset slightly off his ear as both the tanks main engine and its Generator Unit Engine shut down, the sounds dying off into the night. He was hoping to hear the distinct sound of a Challenger tank's engines in the distance as noise carried further at night. But the only noise that drifted across to him was the sound of the angry horns blaring, as people fought to get away from the south.. As he kept searching, Smudge's voice crackled through his headset.

"What can you hear boss?"

"Desperate people Smudge, desperate people, all heading the way we're going." Mike replied.

"Why do they bother?" his gunner replied, "I mean, why race away from your home to end up stuck at night on the bloody roads in the middle of nowhere? And what are they going to do when they get where they're going? They'll have no home, no food-"

"But they'll be alive Smudge," Bill interrupted, "and to some people that's worth more than food."

"I know that!" Smudge replied, "obviously, but I mean, is it that bad to stay where you are? Couldn't they simply stay at home and wait for us to come back?"

"They could Smudge," Mike replied still scanning the horizon, "but how long would they be waiting for? Would you be happy living with a foreign army telling you what to do? How long would you live under an army of occupation for?"

"It won't be that long before we come back, will it? I mean, all we need is to meet up with other tanks, get some ammo and come back and kick some ass."

If only it would be that easy, Mike thought, as he replied, "Might be a little longer than you think Smudge, anyway I've seen and heard enough for now, Okay Bill, start her up."

The engine roared to life as Mike climbed back into the cupola, checking they were clear behind he said, "Bill, nice and slowly, back down the hill, you're clear behind."

Leaving the chaos in front of them, the huge tank sunk slowly back into the darkness, disappearing from view, as Mike carefully looked over to the loaders side at the RWS display, having spun the weapon system to the rear, it afforded him a unique thermal view of behind the vehicle. He knew Bill was using his camera, but still liked to have a second pair of eyes watching.

"Smudge, when we're reversing off a position, I want you to get used to scanning our front, from now on, every time we leave a fire position it's your job to keep an eye out for any threats to our front."

"Yes boss, will do." his gunner replied enthusiastically. Mike smiled, compared to where they were last night, they'd come on in leaps and bounds, for a totally green crew missing a loader they were doing well. Now all they had to do was practice firing back, he though amusedly.

The tank made it's way back to the valley floor for the second time, but in a more controlled manner as the three Warriors came out of the darkness to join it. With the tank leading, the small convoy continued making its way slowly north out of the valley, keeping in the low ground and skirting round the hills rather than going over them. Mike kept the speed of the tank down, hoping the less the engine had to rev the better.

Sound carried at night and he hoped the low revs and high banked terrain would help mask the sounds of the convoy as it crept forward. The tactic was the same, the Warriors would hang back as the tank moved forward slowly, getting eyes on the terrain to their front, the crew using their thermal sights to check the ground ahead for any threats or signs of enemy activity. Once they were happy it was clear, then Mike would choose their next position before moving, judging the terrain and best route to it. They would jockey off the position, reversing off the slope hidden from view and moving off slightly to the left or right of their original position. Then they would come back over the slope slowly, but from a different position to the one they had been in. If anyone was watching and waiting to shoot, then this simple manoeuvre would cause the enemy to waste time having to readjust onto a moving target in a different position to the one they were seen in. Once the tank was clear of the hill or spur, they would advance forward to their next fire position. Only when the tank was in position and ready, did the Warriors following behind then advance, taking up the previous position that the tank had just occupied. In military terms it was called 'bounding forward' and by keeping the vehicles moving this way it meant they could cover ground as safely and quietly as possible. Even though the tank carried no ammo, it was good practise for the crew and Mike made sure that every bound they came to, they treated it with the same level of threat as if a whole company of T-90 tanks were waiting for them. Sometimes they would have to navigate through villages, it couldn't be avoided, and Mike could only wonder what people in bed would be thinking as the tanks tracks rattled through, no doubt shaking houses on their foundations. Thankfully with phones still not working, no one could be give away their location.

Mike looked down to check their position on the map, against the GPS on the radio. It wasn't ideal, as all military maps came with contour lines, showing the topographical features of the ground ahead. He was having to make do with a road map and his own local knowledge and as far as he could see, the only helpful information that the map gave him, was four miles to the east of them, was an American Diner that had a family two-for-one deal. Another problem was that the military used grid co-ordinates that were marked on their mapping and with the road map having no such markings, he couldn't know for sure exactly which valley they were in. He looked over with frustration to the empty bracket where the commander's computer would usually sit, now empty with bare wires hanging out. The 16-inch computer, when fitted, was linked to the tank's radios and GPS and would be loaded with military mapping, giving the commander the position of the tank on the ground, a perfect sat nav system. With it missing, Mike's job became significantly harder. He estimated they were in the area of Minterne Magna and that they'd travelled half the distance to Yeovil. Progress was far slower than he had hoped, as rather than just drive down the roads, he'd kept everyone away from the towns and villages as much as possible, being forced to pick routes that followed the forestry blocks and skirted the fields edges. Sometimes he'd been forced to drive over the fences and through the fields and felt sure that when the farmers woke in the morning they'd be raging at the damage. It couldn't be helped though and so far, they hadn't run across anyone, so it was working. Checking his watch, he saw the time was 00:20. Good, they still had another four hours until sunrise.

He saw the tank was approaching the edge of a treeline they had been following. He felt the vehicle slow as Smudge and Bill worked together to get the turret peering around the corner of the trees without revealing their position. He was about to use the radio when Smudge quickly said, "Boss, I think I've got vehicle tracks to our front."

Mike looked across in surprise to the Relaxed Viewing Monitor, seeing the display for himself and picking out the mass of darkened black shapes on the green tinge of the display.

"Bill, stop!"

The tank rolled to a halt, as Mike leant forwards and looked through his sight, taking control of the gun with his controls he began to scan the ground ahead of them, careful of how close the barrel was to the trees. He wasn't looking at just one set of tracks, there were dozens, and all caused by heavy tracked vehicles. The fact that they were showing up clearly on the thermal sight meant that whatever had caused them had only come through this way a few hours before and could only have been made by tracked vehicles. Looking ahead at the terrain he could see they were on the edge of a small valley, running east to west, to their front with the ground dipping away to the east and disappearing around a spur before heading north. The problem for Mike was, he couldn't tell which direction the tracks were moving in. Were the vehicles going east or west? Could these be from their own tanks, could this be Chris's missing squadron? he wondered.

He looked across the valley, to the other side, further east of them it flattened out, with trees on the northern side. If they could get there, it would offer them cover from the valley and they could continue north, safely out of sight.

He reached for his Pressel.

"Tango Two-Zero, Tango One-One, move your callsign up to us, we need a face-to-face."

He heard Spider acknowledge on the radio as the three Warriors closed up and parked one behind the other. Mike quickly jumped off, making sure to take his assault rifle and ran over to Spider's vehicle. He climbed up the front decks and onto the turret, kneeling next to the commander's cupola. Spider pulled one of his earpieces away enough to be able to hear Mike.

"What's up?"

Mike pointed towards the valley ahead of them. "We've got to cross this valley, but we've vehicle tracks to our front, lots of them and recent, moving left to right, I'd say no more than about three hours ago."

"Are they friendlies?" Spider asked hopefully.

"Not sure, but I can't tell if they're going east or west."

"Why does that matter?"

"Because we have to keep following the valley and I don't want to blunder into the back of something hostile."

"You don't think that they've made it this far already do you?"

Mike shrugged, "We were stuck in that barn a while."

"Ok, so what shall we do? We can't just sit here all night." Spider replied worriedly.

"Look, there's a woodline about 900 metres east of us on the other side, we can drive down the valley, follow the tracks a short while and break off back into the woodline, then carry on. We'll only be out in the open for a few minutes."

"There's no other way around?" Spider asked hopefully.

"Afraid not, this valley cuts right back to the A37 and if we follow it east the ground opens up, we'll be visible for miles. If we don't cross here, we'll have to back track another 3 kilometres and cross somewhere else and we don't have the time to do that."

Mike watched as Spider shook his head in resignation, "Okay Mike, okay, let's just get it done. Should we go across individually?"

"What's the point? Without ammo we can't even cover each other and then there's four times the risk with four vehicles doing it separately. Let's stay as we are, keep everyone closed up and get across as a oner."

Mike flashed a smile of confidence as Spider's look in reply told him he was far from happy. Realising he'd said all he could, Mike jumped down and ran back to the tank, climbing back on board and settling quickly into the cupola, leaving his rifle hanging off the commander's hatch, ready for action if needed.

"Back on now guys," he replied letting the crew know he was on the headset, as he keyed the radio.

"Charlie Charlie Tango callsigns, Tango One-One, we're going to stay closed up to cross this open ground to our front, follow my lead and stay in our tracks. Tango Two-One-Alpha acknowledge."

The Charlie Charlie call was a codeword, meaning the message was meant for all callsigns within Mike's convoy. Rather than get everyone to acknowledge, Mike had simply asked for one callsign, the rear vehicle of Doc's Warrior to call back.

"Tango Two-One-Alpha, roger."

Mike checked behind him, in the darkness he could just see the silhouette of the rear vehicle.

"Bill, when you're ready nice and slowly, take us down into the valley, you'll see the tracks appear on your thermal sight. When you see them, I want you to follow them off to the right ok?"

"Yes boss, happy we go now?"

"Yep, off we go please."

With a gentle nudge the tank moved forwards, Mike checked behind to make sure the others were following, "Smudge, I want you to keep eyes on the valley, let me know if you see anything."

"Will do."

Silently hoping that nothing was in the valley watching, Mike held his breath and waited...

The Russian Sergeant was in a foul mood, his driver could see that, as they bounced along the track. First, he cursed at the engineers and technicians who had made the useless set of Night Vision Goggles that now sat bouncing around on the floor. Then he'd cursed the mechanics, who had made the truck's engine, that had refused to restart after they last stopped. Then he cursed the drivers he was supposed to be following, who had all sped off and left them behind. Then he cursed the map makers of the map he was attempting to read and now, finally he was cursing the British. Thanks to them here he was, at 25 years of age, bouncing around the cab of this fucking truck, in the middle of the night, fighting to read the map and chasing to re-join their units.

He threw the map to the floor in disgust, he'd never been good with them and had always relied on the others to lead. Angry with it all, he moodily lit his fourteenth cigarette that night, cursing loudly when the truck hit a pothole and he smashed himself in the nose with the lighter. He leaned over and cuffed the driver round the head. "Idiot!" he snarled, "turn on the bloody lights if you can't see where you're going!"

"But what about the enemy?" the young driver stammered.

"But what about the enemy!" the Sergeant mocked him, "Let me tell you about the enemy, since landing here do you know how many of *the enemy* I've seen?"

The driver glanced across as the Sergeant held up a thumb and fore finger, the international sign for zero.

"That's how many of them we've come across. So, stop shitting your pants and turn the bloody lights on. Besides, in case you haven't noticed we're behind the lines, the only people ahead of us will be our own troops."

Against his better judgment the driver reached down and turned on the lights, suddenly bathing the valley in front of them with light. For the next two minutes the driver made a better job of avoiding the ruts while the Sergeant smoked, a smug, triumphant look on his face.

"Hello, what have we here?" the Sergeant replied, quicky reaching over and turning off the lights.

He saw the dark shapes of the armoured vehicles on the track in front of them, moving slowly forward, the dust being kicked up causing the driver to back off slightly as they closed up to them. The driver looked across nervously, but the Sergeant smiled back confidently, "Relax, they're ours, don't you recognise a BMP 3? We've finally caught up with our guys again. Follow them, they'll lead us to our units."

The Sergeant sat back, relaxing, as he put his feet up on the dashboard, perhaps tonight wasn't so bad after all.

Mike was concentrating on looking ahead when suddenly Doc's voice came through over the radio.

"Tango One-One, Tango Two-One-Alpha, we've got a vehicle with its lights on, coming up behind us. What do you want us to do?"

Oh shit, thought Mike, who the hell was this? He looked backwards and through the dust cloud could make out the lights bouncing down the tracks behind them. They were still another 800 meters away from the turn off and the vehicle was too close. Even if he got Bill to floor it, the vehicle behind would catch them before they made the turn.

"Tango Two-One-Alpha, can you get eyes on with your sights? See if it's on its own and what type of vehicle?"

"Roger, wait one," Doc replied. After a few tense moments he came back, "Tango One-One, It's a military truck, six wheeled and on his own, and it doesn't look like one of ours."

Why would he be out here on his own, Mike thought, as Doc continued, "Tango Two-One-Alpha continuing, he's seen us and has joined the back of our convoy, he's turned his lights off and is tagging along, I think he thinks we're friendlies."

Mike couldn't believe their luck, here they were trying to keep a low profile and now one of the enemy's trucks was happily following behind.

"Tango Two-One-Alpha, he probably thinks you're a BMP3, you do look similar. Put your gun front and play nice but keep eyes on him. If he turns away quickly or you think he's made you, then you're clear to pursue and ram him."

Mike knew the Warrior would easily outrun the truck if it attempted to flee.

"Bill, I want you to slow us down for now."

"Okay boss," he heard in reply as Spiders voice burst through the headset, "Tango One-One, Tango Two-Zero, what are we doing?"

Mike smiled to himself as he began to tell the others the plan...

The truck driver had noticed that the vehicles having already slowed to a crawl, were now slowly increasing speed. At first, they were easy to follow but now he was struggling to see the track as the armoured vehicles suddenly increased speed further, almost shooting off, throwing up a large dust cloud that surrounded the truck, filling the cab. Coughing, the driver looked over to the Sergeant who cried out in alarm as the back of the BMP suddenly loomed out of the darkness and dust. The truck driver slammed on the brakes and skidding, stopped mere feet from the vehicle.

"I wish these fucking BMP drivers would make their minds up!" the driver raged out of shock, "one minute they're charging off, then they're slowing down. Why can't they make their minds up?"

The Sergeant picked his cigarette from the floor as the dust settled, and calmly put it back in his mouth, his tone sardonic. "These convoys are always the bloody same, we start, we stop, we hurry up, we wait. Fucking army!"

The driver angrily slammed the truck into gear as the armoured vehicles began to move again, this time though keeping the BMP a respectable distance in front of them.

After a few minutes, the driver heard a noise from behind and looking in his mirror could see the dark shadow of another BMP behind him.

"Looks like someone else was lost."

He smirked as the Sergeant looked behind and then shot him a knowing look, "*We* were not lost, I knew exactly where *we* were. Now shut up and concentrate on following these vehicles." The driver's smile vanished as he focused on keeping the six wheeled truck out of the worst of the ruts.

Five minutes later and the driver noticed they were leaving the main tracks and turning to go uphill, the truck going down through the gears as the terrain rose steeply through a wooded track. He watched as the main tracks disappeared off into the darkness and saw the fresh ones the vehicles were making. He looked over to the Sergeant who just looked out of the window calmly. Sensing his driver's mood, he turned back, pointing to the vehicles in front and behind. "They know where they're going, our orders were to follow them, so we follow them."

The driver smiled nervously, keeping his eyes on the track, he'd felt sure they were to follow the valley, unlike the Sergeant he *did* know how to read a map and had paid attention to their Captain when, during their orders, he had told them the route. Still, he was only a Private he reasoned, and the Sergeant had given him orders. So, ignoring the nagging feeling in his stomach he settled in and concentrated on following the shadow in front of them.

"All callsigns, Tango One-One, good job everyone, looks like we have them. Tango Two-One you set?"

"Tango Two-One, ready."

Good, thought Mike, if this worked then they might just be able to bag their first Russians without having to fire a shot.

Unbeknown to the Russians in the truck, Mike had counted on them being lazy, not paying attention to where they were heading, instead just happy to play follow the leader. He'd seen it before countless times in the past, when on long road moves, it was only ever the lead callsign who would be checking the maps, concerned about what direction to take. Those at the back of the convoy would usually get their head down and go to sleep, telling their drivers to simply follow the vehicle in front. That all worked well until you lost sight of the vehicles you were following, in which case, you had better have your wits and map ready, or as in the case of the truck, you'd be following the wrong vehicles. Mike had got his vehicles to speed up to increase the dust cloud, hoping to confuse and blind the Russians long enough, so that they wouldn't notice Spider and Patty's Warriors leave the track. Now Spider's vehicle was behind following the truck and Patty had raced away back the way they had come, to check for any other vehicles and to prepare the ambush sight. Thanks to the amount of dust being kicked up, the Russians hadn't noticed that not only had Mike turned them a complete one-eighty, and they were heading back up the valley from where they'd just come, but now they were heading south, off their tracks and back over Mikes earlier route. He wanted to get them as far away from prying eyes as he could, the last thing he needed was another lone vehicle stumbling upon them. He'd already seen the area he wanted to use; it was a track running through a forestry block that they'd passed through earlier. It was perfect, and it was there Patty was now waiting, his men deployed in the trees waiting to strike. Mike watched as the darkness seemed to close in on them as the trees towered over them, hemming them in. He scanned ahead, trying to pierce through the darkness as he saw the shadow of the Warrior in front of them, blocking the path. He knew Patty and his men were waiting either side of the track. He waited until the tank was nearly on top of the Warrior before saying, "Okay Bill, hold it there."

As the tank slowed and stopped, he jumped off, grabbing his assault rifle, cocking it, making it ready to fire, as he ran back along the convoy, keeping out of the way as Doc's Warrior pulled up. He reached into his smock pocket and pulled out the flashlight, ready to use. Using the Warrior as cover he kept himself hidden and waited.

"What now?" moaned the Sergeant, as the vehicles again stopped. "I was hoping to be in bed by now," he complained, as he reached into his smock pocket for another cigarette. They watched in the truck's side mirrors as they heard the engines of the vehicle behind louder than before as the vehicle seemed to accelerate and pull up very close to the rear of the truck. That's far too close, the Sergeant thought, and was tempted to go out to speak to the BMP driver, as suddenly everything around them seemed to explode into noise. The door was yanked open, and he yelled in surprise. dropping his lighter and trying to reach for his rifle as two pairs of large hands seemed to explode out of the darkness and reach for him. He tried to fight back, wanted to fight back, but fear took hold and instead he found himself on the ground, lying next to the truck wheel, looking up into the faces of the men. These were Russians, weren't they? His confused mind played out what had happened, perhaps he reasoned they were Russian and they'd mistook him for the enemy. Of course, that's what happened. He began to get up, to talk in Russian, to explain what had happened, when he felt a boot to his chest, it took him down quickly. Through gritted teeth he looked up at one of the men towering over him, His face was black, covered in cam cream and the man snarled, almost spat the words out to him. He couldn't understand what he was saying, but he understood the barrel of the assault rifle poking his chest. He looked over to the driver's side, the driver was also on the ground, on his belly, another two soldiers quickly tying him up. The same look of disbelief and shock on his face too. The Sergeant felt his hands roughly pulled backwards and the zip ties clicking into place, as both soldiers pulled him to his feet. One stood back covering him with a rifle, whilst the other quickly pulled open his pouches, emptying him of his six AK12 mags and then reaching across to his holster, removing his sidearm and spare magazines. He looked down, not knowing what to say or do. After they had finished, one of the soldiers led him to the front of the truck, motioning for him to kneel. Ignoring the stones tearing into his knees he slowly collapsed, watching as one of the soldiers climbed up into the cab, and after a few moments came back out carrying both their AK12 rifles, proudly showing them off to the others. He closed his eyes in fear, he'd heard what the British would do to them, he knew they'd kill them. For now, all he could do was pray.

Mike helped Ping tie up the driver, keeping him covered as the soldier applied the zip ties. Once he was happy the POW wouldn't be running off into the night, they stood him up, Mike stood back, keeping his weapon pointed at the POW as Ping searched him, removing anything that they thought could be used as a weapon. Once he'd been searched, they led him over to the front of the truck, making him kneel next to the other POW. Mike climbed up into the cab, using the torch to check the handbrake was on. He was tempted to turn the engine off, but couldn't read the cyrilic writing on the controls, so thought better of it, besides they might want to use the truck. Using the torch to check the cab, he quickly found two AK12 rifles and proudly held them aloft for Patty and Sid to see as he climbed out. Once on the ground he slung his own rifle behind his back and made both weapons safe, removing the full magazines and cocking the working parts to the rear. Both weapons were loaded and the glint of brass flew past them as the live rounds ejected into the darkness. Mike was well trained on the use of the AK family of weapons, he'd used them in Iraq and Afghanistan when teaching the local forces.

Mike picked up one of the Russian pistol magazines and quickly emptied it of rounds, pulling his own Glock 17 out, ejecting the empty magazine and refilling it with the Russian rounds. Thankfully both pistols were 9mm, so the ammunition could be used, however the magazines couldn't, the Grach's magazine wouldn't fit in the Glock. He picked up the other three pistol magazines and put them in his pockets for use later.

Mike looked up, "Patty do you know how to handle the AK12?"

Patty was so focussed on the POW's, he almost had to tear his gaze away from them as the adrenalin still coursed through him. This was the first time they'd seen the enemy face to face. His eyes blazed white against the darkness of the cam cream.

"What? Sorry, what?"

Mike smiled understandingly, "AK12, are you familiar with how they work?"

"Er yeah, sorry Mike, yep we were taught all about the AK family on our small arms instructors."

"Ok well, let's give Sid and Ping our weapons and use these."

Nodding, Patty unslung his weapon and handed it to Ping, as Mike did the same to Sid. Both men had done the take down unarmed, thanks to the lack of weapons. Hopefully that would be the last time they'd have to do that, Mike thought.

"Sid, she's loaded and made ready," he said as Sid nodded in understanding taking the rifle, before resuming his guard over the POW's.

Keeping one for himself, Mike handed the other AK12 over to Patty along with six of the magazines. Patty nodded his thanks as he placed the magazines into his assault vest. Then both men proceeded to check the actions of the rifles, pulling the bolts backwards with the triggers pressed. Once they were both satisfied everything was all working as it should, they fired off the empty rifles into the trees, checking before they did that the safety catches worked. Hearing nothing but the clicks of the firing pins hitting empty chambers, they both loaded the magazines back onto the rifles before cocking them again to make ready.

Mike was conscious that the POW's could see them and he made a big show of it, showing them they were more than familiar with how their weapons worked. He picked up the remaining six magazines for himself and placed them in his pockets before saying, "Right let's see what's in the back shall we?"

Picking the two POW's up, Sid and Ping frogmarched the Russians towards the back of the vehicle, the diesel fumes stinking as the exhaust belched out into the sky. Spider's Warrior had pulled right up to the back of the truck, preventing anyone inside from trying to open the tailgate and jumping down. The canvas cover was pulled tight, and no one could see in even without the darkness. The Warrior's 30mm cannon was pointing menacingly inside the truck and Spider was sat in the perfect fire position, covered by his hatch, with his rifle pointing into the trucks rear. The message to anyone in the back was clear, no one would be getting out of this truck alive.

Mike turned to the Sergeant, identifying him as the person in charge by the way he acted, seeing his stripes.

He poked him with the rifle barrel.

"Do you speak English?"

The blank stare told him he didn't.

"What about you? English?"

The driver merely stared at the ground, refusing to look up, defeat etched all over his face.

Mike resorted to what most English people did when abroad, speaking slowly and gesticulating he pointed to the rear of the truck,

"What's inside the truck? What are you carrying inside?"

Both men remained silent.

"Answer him!" Sid exclaimed loudly, pushing one with his rifle barrel.

"Mike!" Spider hissed from atop the turret. Getting his attention, Mike climbed up.

"What's up?"

"Rachel's in the back listening in, she speaks Russian, want her to come out to help?"

"Yes, fucking please!" Mike answered happily, that was the best bit of news he'd heard all night.

He climbed down as Rachel and Changa came out of the fighting compartment in the back. Changa walked over, staring at the two men intensely, something about the big Fijian unnerved them and Mike saw their eyes widen in shock.

Rachel walked over to Mike.

"What would you like me to ask?"

"Ask these two what's in the back of the truck."

Without a pause she broke into Russian. Mike recognised the dialect from his time in Kosovo. He knew a few words himself, but apart from the very basic swear words most his vocabulary was useless, unless he wanted to know where the supermarket was, which to be fair wouldn't help tonight.

The two Russians looked up in shock at hearing their native tongue being spoken. The driver remained tight lipped, but the Sergeant became animated and began to talk quickly back, occasionally Rachel would stop him and say something, before allowing him to continue.

Finally, after he had finished Rachel replied, "He says that they don't know what's in the back as it was loaded up by another unit. All they were told this evening was jump in and drive the truck. He says they were forbidden to look in the back."

"What a load of bollocks," replied Patty, "who doesn't know what's in the back of their truck?"

Ignoring him Mike said, "Ask them where they were going, why were they on that track?"

Rachel began chattering away, stopping quickly as the Russian replied. She looked a little shocked.

"Apparently, they were following a military police unit. Why would there be military police ahead of us?"

"Because now *we're* behind the front lines." Mike said angrily as he realised what this meant. "We spent too long in the barn, the enemy had already overtaken us!"

He realised the truck's heavy engine was still running and the POW's were sat kneeling by the exhaust. Mike was tempted to leave them there slowly breathing in the noxious fumes, but quickly thought better of it. He looked over to Rachel.

"Can you read Russian as well as speak it?"

"Of course," she replied confidently.

He looked to Changa, "Take Rachel with you, find out how to shut the truck down, and how to re-start it back up. Then switch it off for now."

Changa nodded as Mike walked up to the back of the truck, he slung the AK12 over his back and pulled his pistol. Climbing up onto the tailgate of the truck he began undoing the clasps for the cover with his free hand. Once he had enough of them undone, he looked over to Spider who waved back whilst holding the rifle, ready to cover Mike if he needed it. Taking a deep breath and holding the pistol in front of him, he slowly pulled up on the heavy canvas, not knowing what to expect. The first thing to hit him was the stench of unwashed bodies, and he crinkled his nose at the smell as he pushed his body into the tight space. Realising the cargo area was far darker than his eyes would see, he let go of the canopy and reached for his torch and almost jumped back in surprise as the light beamed out and reflected off the black boot mere inches from his face. Calming himself, he shone the torch slowly round the cargo bay, his early excitement dissipating as he counted twelve bodies in the back, all were lying next to each other, all were tied up wearing black hoods and none were moving.

"What do you see?" Patty asked quietly, he was stood by the tailgate looking up and Mike saw him gag and reach for his nose as the smell reached him.

"We've got a truck full of people, all tied up and wearing hoods." He replied trying to hide his surprise. "I can't see anyone moving though."

Mike carefully crawled through into the truck, reaching down he gently pulled the hood from one of the nearest bodies. It was a woman, her face was bruised and bloodied, but her skin was hot to the touch, at least she wasn't dead, thought Mike.

"Hey, can you hear me?" he asked softly, seeing no response he pinched her ear, to see if she responded to the pain. Nothing. She was out cold.

He looked back out, "Patty, I've got some of them alive in here, get Doc up here, and bring plenty of water."

Within a minute Doc was climbing aboard, with his medical bergan, Spider and Patty in tow. Mike had already removed the hoods and was using his pocketknife to carefully cut the zip ties from their hands and legs.

"Woah, someone needs a shower," Spider said as he climbed aboard. The words dying on his lips in regret as he saw the state of the people inside. "What the hell!" he exclaimed.

"Quickly, help me cut their ties," Mike urged, reaching out for a bottle of water and pouring a little on the head of the young man lying at his feet. He saw some small movements, some eye flickers, but not much, but it was better than none at all. He began cutting the bonds of another man, this one was wearing a police officer's uniform, again his face battered and bruised and was unresponsive. A quick splash of water on the mouth and then onto the next. They closed the canvas flap over the tailgate to hide the white light as Doc wedged a torch into the truck's metal frame, allowing him to work in better light.

Ten minutes later, all the people were lying free of their bonds, some they had placed in the recovery position, others had to lie on their backs as Doc had inserted cannulas, to get fluid quickly into them.

Patty broke the silence as they surveyed the scene. "Who the hell are they? And what did those bastards do to them?"

Mike tried to make sense of it, he quickly looked over at the bodies, counting three in military uniform, five in police uniform and the remaining four in civilian clothing. He was interrupted from his thoughts as Doc said, "Well I've done all I can now, apart from their visible injuries, it looks like they're all suffering from dehydration and some kind of sedative. All we can do now is wait for it to wear off."

"Sedative?" Asked Patty, "Why?"

Doc shrugged his shoulders, "Who knows, maybe they didn't want these people to see where they were going?"

"Then why bother with the hoods?" replied Mike curiously, "be interesting to hear what they say when they wake."

Doc looked uncomfortable as he replied, "About that, there's something else you guys need to see."

Patty took the light and shone it over to where Doc was pointing at two of the sleeping bodies. They were both women and Mike guessed their ages to be late twenties to early thirties. One of them looked vaguely familiar, even though her face was heavily bruised, and her lips swollen, Mike was sure he had seen her somewhere before. He shrugged off the thought as Doc pointed at the clothing. One was wearing jeans and a short-sleeved polo shirt and the other who Mike thought looked familiar had a long, red, patterned summer dress.

Doc sighed before saying, "I'm not jumping to conclusions, but there's a strong possibility these two were sexually assaulted, either before or after they were sedated."

Patty's mouth dropped open as Mike replied, "What makes you say that, Doc?"

Taking the torch from Patty, Doc shone the light on the area he wanted them to see. "Both of these women look to have been redressed whilst asleep, the one in the red dress has her underwear on backwards, her blouse buttons are torn and the other girl's jeans are not buttoned up correctly and her bra under her top is undone at the back. It's as if they've been redressed clumsily whilst still asleep."

"For fucks sake." Patty said softly.

Mike kept his anger hidden, remaining quiet as he carefully lifted up each of the sleeping girl's hands, looking carefully under the fingernails. Nodding to himself with what he saw, he placed them back down and asked. "Doc, how long until this sedative wears off?"

"Hard to say, could be soon, could be hours."

"And if we left them here? Would they be okay in the back of the truck?"

Doc shook his head, "No, they need someone here to monitor them until they wake, they're dehydrated and there's still a risk they could swallow their tongue and choke, plus imagine waking here in the middle of nowhere in the back of the truck. Someone will need to be here when they start to wake up. And before you ask no we shouldn't move them either. My opinion, we should at least stay till they wake up."

Mike looked at his watch, shit was it 2am already?

Spider was thinking the same as he said with the growing frustration in his voice, "So if we do decide to wait, we won't be getting to Yeovil just yet then."

Sensing the frustration in Spider's voice, Mike ushered them back out of the truck, Doc needed space to work. And Mike wanted to chat in private. Before he climbed out, he looked back over as Doc was busy checking the pulse of another prone body.

"Doc, we'll get you some more help, how many bodies do you need?"

Without looking up he replied, "It's a bit cramped in here, but another person wouldn't go amiss."

Nodding in acknowledgment Mike jumped down, looking over to Sid. "Leave Ping to guard those two for now, go tell all the drivers to switch the engines off, and then get yourself back here and into the back of the truck to help Doc. The Fusilier nodded and disappeared into the night as Mike walked back over to join Patty and Spider. He could hear the anger in Spider's voice as he joined them.

"Looks like you seem to have made your mind up already about us staying."

Mike looked at him slowly shaking his head. "Spider, I'm sorry but I was wrong, we should have taken a different route. We were never going to get to Yeovil going the way we were going, not now we know what's ahead of us. We were lucky to get as far as we did, those soldiers we captured proved that. Up ahead, perhaps another two or three miles somewhere is the front line, we're not going to get through that, not without ammo. We need to think this through again, let's wait up here in this forestry block, same as we did yesterday, give the Doc time to get these people fit to travel, and then we can move on."

"Can we wait here another day?" Patty asked.

Mike thought it through as he replied, "Well we're off the beaten track, not far from Cerne Abbas, and the woods here are thick enough to hide us from the air, we've just got one way in and one way out of here. The track looked like it hadn't been used in a while. So, I'm thinking that if we close off the tracks at either end with camouflage netting to hide us from view, then we should be okay in here.

"Camouflage netting? And where are you going to rustle up that from?" Spider asked disbelieving.

"We've got some on the tank and I saw a full-sized cam net rolled up on the roof of truck. We use each one and stretch it across the track both sides. Anyone looking in will see nothing more than an overgrown track that stops suddenly. It won't be perfect, but it'll do for sure. I recommend keeping the vehicles as we are, the truck in the middle as a makeshift ambulance with the Warriors on the outside."

Patty nodded as Spider shook his head, his frustration beginning to show.

"Mike all this sitting and waiting...The guys are feeling... No, I'm feeling like all we're doing right now is just driving around the fucking countryside on a bloody jolly. You heard what happened to those women in the truck. It's our job to protect them and right now we're not doing that. We've got all this bloody firepower and no way to help. What's the fucking use of us getting it back if we can't use it? How much longer before we can get in the fight? I feel like a fucking amateur about now and all we're doing is watching and waiting."

Mike leaned over, putting his hand on his shoulder reassuringly, "Spider, we're still here, we're still alive and still in the fight. And we're better off now than we were yesterday, now we've got more fuel, weapons and now we've got a truck and uniforms to use if we want to."

Spider looked up replying angrily, shrugging off Mike's hand. "Great! So, all we need now is another week of combat camping and we'd have picked up enough waifs and strays and weapons to make up a battlegroup! Is that what you're after? Would that do for you? Your own private little army? Perhaps that's what you wanted all along, perhaps you don't want us to get back?"

Mike said nothing, letting the Corporal vent his anger, as a few moments later he saw his shoulders sag, as quickly Spider realised what he'd just said. Taking a deep breath Spider replied, "Shit, I'm sorry Mike, I didn't mean that, I'm just...angry."

"What do you want to do Spider?"

"What?"

Mike repeated the question, his voice softer.

"I said, what do you want to do?"

"I don't understand?" Spider cocked his head as he looked back.

"Moving around in the daytime with these vehicles is suicidal," Mike explained, "we all know that, especially with no air cover for us. But we also know that the Russians night-time capabilities are terrible. Tonight's proved that, if that was our lot out there looking for us, they'd have seen us already. So, our best option is to move at night and use the terrain as best we can. We know this area, we know the terrain, so the advantage is ours. We've managed to get this far through perseverance and luck mainly, but we're here, still undetected and alive. So, if you stay with the vehicles, you keep your protection and mobility, but you can only move at night and you're a big target. Every day that we're out here, increases the risk of us being spotted..."

Spider looked on as Mike continued, "Now, if you're not happy with that, then you could simply ditch the vehicles and continue on foot, now you can move more quietly and are less of a target to spot. If you wanted to, you could also move in the daytime, you wouldn't stick out quite so badly, and the risk would be lower, less noise, less footprint on the ground and easier to hide. But, the distance you'd walk in three days on foot, you could cover in one night with your vehicle. That's three more days in enemy territory on foot, for every one night's drive in the vehicle. But you're now having to carry all your gear and you've lost your protection, your radios, your ability to communicate, your sighting systems. You'd simply be twelve people, lightly armed, behind enemy lines sneaking through. And today the front line could be four miles away, tomorrow it could be eight, the next day twelve, so your two- or three-day planned extraction now turns into five days, then eight days, then who knows how long. Without the vehicles you could end up spending most of your time walking around Dorset. So, its risk versus reward, do you want to take the risk and stay with the vehicles or do you feel safer going on foot?"

Patty looked on confused, "Mike you said twelve, but there's fifteen of us."

"Nope, there'll be twelve of you, If you decide to leave the vehicles and go on foot then I'm not going with you, neither will Bill or Smudge. I'd need them to help me get that tank back, I know how important it is, besides I'm an ex tankie, we don't do walking."

Mike saw Patty smile at what he'd just said but Spider stayed silent. He could see the infantryman weighing up the pro's and cons in his head. Eventually Spider nodded his head slowly.

"Look I know how important these vehicles are, I get it..."

Spider looked around at the woods, seeing the sky was already beginning to lighten he looked back over to Mike sighing as he continued, "You're right. Let's stay here for today, get these people back on their feet and then see where we can go tomorrow night."

"What should we tell the lads about what's in the truck?" Patty asked.

"Tell them the truth, they've all helped to save some people tonight, plus it'll make them feel like the night wasn't wasted." Mike replied.

"And what about the women, should we mention that?" Patty sounded unsure as he asked.

"I'd keep that between us for now, especially as we don't know what happened. I don't think those women would want us to know, and the last thing we need is someone taking it out on the prisoners."

"The mood I'm in right now, that could be me." Patty fumed as dark thoughts began to fill his head.

"Yes, but we don't know if these men had anything to do with it. We can question them about it later, but one thing I would say, did you see the state of those girls' hands?"

"No, why?" Patty asked.

"Both girls had fingernails that were broken and human skin under those that weren't. Whatever happened to them, they were awake at the time, and put up one hell of a fight. Our two POWs haven't got a scratch on their faces."

"So that's what you were looking for." Spider replied.

Mike nodded, not wanting to dwell on it anymore he tried to lighten the mood. "Well, you both look like you need cheering up, so I come bearing gifts.

Reaching into his pocket he pulled out the three loaded pistol mags.

"Here you go, one each for both of you and give one to Doc when he's finished. Now we all have rounds for our pistols at least."

"Where did you find those little babies?" Patty asked. Both men took the mags as Mike replied, "Found them in the Russians gear, now come on, let's get to work, we've got a lot to do."

Patty turned to leave remarking, "I'll brief the lads and get the sentries posted."

Spider put his hand out to stop him, "No Patty, I'll do it, it'll do me good to clear my head." Turning again he looked over to Mike, "You really think we can get ourselves out of this?"

Mike looked confidently back at him, "I do, and you want to know something else Spider? You said you feel like an amateur?" Spider looked over questioningly as Mike pointed to the POW's and continued, "How do you think they feel now? Because they're the bloody amateur

10

Worse Than We Thought

Rawlinson Family Farm

The drive from Wonderland back to Peter's farm was uneventful, the traffic light, the roads seemingly empty. Peter was in the back seat of one of the General's Range Rovers, usually Patch would have been driving him, instead he was slumped asleep in the passenger seat, his head against the headrest, mouth open, blissfully snoring. Driving them was a Corporal from the Military Police as the CDS had seen fit to give him an armed escort for their journey back. They'd spent the past few hours at Wonderland observing the Russian invasion, until it finally dawned on Peter that his home and the workshops of Aurora, stood right in the path of one of the enemy's main thrusts. The CDS had granted him leave to head back as quickly as he could, with two police motorcycles up ahead, blue lights flashing brightly, cutting through the darkness and illuminating the countryside as they raced homeward.

As they neared Peter's home, he leant forwards, nudging Patch's seat gently. Without any fuss Patch woke immediately, looking back and nodded in thanks to Peter.

Peter didn't want to startle his wife, so he asked the Corporal to instruct the out riders to switch off their blues and twos, plunging them all back into darkness again, as the convoy turned into his driveway, stopping by the farm gate that was closed and locked.

"What now Sir?" the driver asked, looking at him in the rear-view mirror.

He was about to reply when he saw a torchlight cutting through the night, the owner walking towards them from the fields. Suddenly another torch was shining through the passenger side of the Range Rover, blinding the occupants, causing Patch to wince and hold up his hand to his good eye, as the voice of Alan cut through the night.

"State your business." he demanded, quickly softening his tone and lowering the raised shotgun as he recognised Patch and the Brigadier.

"Oh, it's you boss! Sorry, we weren't expecting you back yet." Flicking the torch off, he quickly walked up to the gate, unlocking the thick chain, sliding it through to open the gate and waving the convoy in. Within minutes they were pulling up to the farmhouse, ablaze with lights, no doubt his wife having been wakened by the commotion at the gate, had come to see what was happening.

Peter climbed out of the car, looking up to the front door as it opened. Elizabeth stood silhouetted in the doorway in her dressing gown, her sleep filled eyes widening as she recognised her husband.

"Peter!" she exclaimed in surprise as he walked quickly towards her, a huge smile on his face, arms held wide, embracing her in a powerful hug, holding her close, almost squeezing the air out of her lungs.

She was startled at his response, he'd always been a romantic, certainly affectionate, but always behind closed doors and never with an audience. With her face still buried in his shoulder, she looked embarrassedly back at the others, all now watching on with curious amusement.

"Peter!" she remarked, her mouth muffled against his chest, "what's got into you?"

He held her there, feeling the love radiating off his wife, as if simply being in her arms would somehow reset the past 24 hours. Seeing the destruction of London and all the terrible events that had unfolded at Wonderland had really hit him hard. He'd never have said anything to the CDS or to anyone else, but his wife knew all of his secrets, she was his soul mate. She knew the pain and the heartache he'd carried and could name every one of his demons. It was true what they said of being a soldier, behind every great soldier, was an even greater partner, ready to help carry the load. She was his rock and right now, just having her there in his arms felt like the world was the right side up again.

He gently pulled his wife's head towards his, ignoring the looks of the others, nor caring as he gave her a big kiss on the lips, before replying. "I love you darling; did I ever tell you that? I love you more than words can ever say."

She looked on confused at his sudden show of affection, before smiling, no longer caring why he was did it, just happy that he was.

She smiled, her own eyes lighting up as she replied, "Well, I love you too Peter, and at the risk of sounding a prude, do you mind me asking what's got into you? And why you're back so soon?"

"Does a husband need an excuse to tell his wife he loves her?" he simply said, enjoying the moment, as she looked adoringly back at him, the look slowly changing to one of sad realisation as she suddenly exclaimed, keeping her voice hushed.

"Oh God! London, and the attack on the PM, was that-"

"Yes," he cut her off, his eyes almost welling up as the images from last night began to play out again in front of him.

"Oh Peter, all those people," she said sorrowfully, seeing the look of happiness quickly replaced by one of immense sadness. He refocussed his thoughts, shaking away the darkness that threatened to overwhelm him, quickly thinking to the task at hand.

"Listen darling, this isn't why I'm here, we don't have long, we need to be quick."

She looked back at him, resigned as the realisation hit her.

"That's why you've had me pack our bags, we're leaving our home?"

He said nothing, his lips closed tight as he simply nodded, as she finally asked.

"How bad is it?"

He'd promised never to hide anything from his wife again and trying to keep it simple, he replied. "It's bad. Perhaps worse than we thought. The Russians are now pushing further north than I'd originally thought. At the rate they're going, they'll be here in less than three hours. We've got probably less than thirty minutes before the people around us realise that, and then there'll be panic and chaos as everyone tries to leave. The roads could be jammed if we wait too long, which is why James saw fit to give us a police escort. We're being relocated somewhere safer."

She looked around her at the home they'd built together, shaking her head in sorrow, not knowing what they'd find when they returned. Suddenly her eyes opened wide as she looked over to the stables.

"But what about the horses? We can't just leave them! Ajax and –"

He took her by the arms, lowering his head to look directly into her eyes, speaking softly to comfort her.

"Darling, the horses are all going to be just fine, before we leave, I'll get Alan to turn them loose, he'll lock the barn doors open and they'll roam free around the farm's fields, with enough grass, feed and water to survive for months."

She bit her lip worriedly at the thought, finally relenting, she nodded in understanding as he now walked her back inside the house.

"Now darling, I need you to go upstairs and get dressed, don't worry about the bags, Patch will take care of them and get them into the car. And make sure you get all the family jewellery from the safe, leave nothing in there, because I can't guarantee it will be there when we get back."

"We are coming back?" she asked, more of a statement of fact than a question.

He smiled, nodding in reply, holding her closer and hugging her again.

She nodded silently, taking it all in as the realisation finally hit her, they were leaving their home. He smiled warmly, watching her go upstairs, waiting until she had disappeared before turning to run over to the police outriders. Both officers were still on their motorbikes, engines running, helmet visors lifted and waiting for their orders. Peter quickly pulled out the two letters he'd written on the way down, on each was a list of people and their addresses, all of whom worked for Aurora.

"Okay gentlemen, as quick as you can please, I need you to stop at all the addresses below and show them this letter. Once you've been to all of them, your orders are to return to headquarters. Please be careful and watch out for any military units that you don't recognise. Questions?"

Both officers shook their heads, busily glancing at the list and typing in the first address into their bike's sat navs mounted on the handlebars. Only once they'd both finished did they look up at the Brigadier, their faces serious as one replied, his voice muffled in the helmet.

"Don't worry Sir, we'll make sure they all get the message."

Peter warmly rested a hand on each of their shoulders.

"Thank you both for doing this and good luck."

With a nod of the head, both men flicked down their visors and rode away, the blue lights back on, stopping briefly, brake lights illuminating in the distance as they waited for Alan to unlock the gate again. Then they were gone, swallowed up by the night, the sounds of their motorbike engines screaming off into the distance, long after the lights had disappeared from view.

Peter watched them go, hopeful that they could at least get to half of the people on the list. He turned, knowing there was much to do and so little time. Racing inside the house, he ran to his office to gather some of his personal possessions.

Twenty minutes later and he was outside again, waiting. His eyes wandered over to the dark shapes moving across the fields, the darkness keeping them hidden. It was only the snorting of Ajax and sound of hooves thundering over the ground that gave the horses away. At least they'd be happy, Peter had made sure Tony and Alan had turned out every hay bale into the fields, so long as the horses didn't gorge themselves, they should all be fine. He looked back to the front door as Elizabeth appeared dressed, ready to go. Peter was happy to see she'd been smart enough to wear an oversized green jacket, it would keep her warm during the cold snap, but more importantly, its deep pockets were filled with the family heirlooms, some handed down from generations before and too valuable to leave behind. He waved her over to the Range Rover, it's engine was running, and Tony and the Corporal were stood waiting beside it, the rear door already open.

She looked over, seeing their own blue Range Rover parked behind it. It's engine was running, with Patch and Alan in the front waiting to go, she frowned as she approached him.

"You're not coming with me, are you?" it was a statement rather than a question, Peter looked away guiltily, his wife had always been sharp.

"Our bags are already loaded up in this one, you're going to go ahead with Tony and the Corporal here and get yourself to our new home."

"You're off to Aurora, aren't you?" she asked, cocking her head inquisitively, already confident of his answer.

Seeing the look of concern on her face he stepped forwards, holding her hands in his. "Darling, you know how important that work is to us, to me. I've got to try to save what we can, it's years of research and work that I think we can use in the future. Some of those projects could really turn the tide for us. Please, let me do this, I'm partly responsible for what's happened, at least let me have a chance in trying to help fix it."

She smiled forgivingly, her hands resting on her husbands' cheeks, something about her husband's vulnerability was so endearing. She kissed him lightly on the forehead, whispering softly into his ear.

"Peter, you're not to blame for this, please don't carry the burden for it. Forget London, forget the attacks, forget what's going on around here. You're a loving husband, a fantastic father, with a family who love you. Remember that always. First and foremost."

She looked into his eyes as the words hit home, he smiled, closing his eyes and nodding, feeling a little of the weight lift from him as she added. "Now go and save what you can, but please don't stay too long, I need my husband back."

Smiling, he kissed her again, pulling her close in an embrace as they both stood and turned, looking around the house and the grounds, one last time. Saying a final goodbye to their home.

"Boss, I'm sorry but we need to be going."

It was Tony who interrupted them, sensing the time ticking away, as already they could see the lights coming on in the distant houses around them, as people began to wake up to the noises of Peter and his family evacuating.

He nodded in understanding and slowly uncoiling her arms from his, he gently ushered her into the back seat, tears welling up in her eyes as the reality began to dawn on her. He'd hated saying goodbye, but this was different, instead of him leaving, tonight they were both leaving. He slowly shut the door, the privacy glass blocking her from view as he turned to face the others, his focus returning.

"Ok, Corporal, you both best be leaving, don't stop for anything until you're at the rendezvous. You happy with where you're going?"

The Corporal looked back, with fierce determination as he replied. "I'm happy where we're going Sir, I'll make sure Mrs Rawlinson gets to where she needs to be."

Peter smiled at the soldier's enthusiasm, as he watched him climb into the driver's side, before turning to Tony, still carrying one of the farm's shotguns.

"Tony, thank you for everything you've done. I can't tell you how much-"

He was cut off mid-sentence, as without warning the big man stepped forwards, his face saddened, embracing the Brigadier, his free arm wrapping around him in a bear hug, almost choking him.

Peter said nothing, simply waiting as the big man held him for a few moments before releasing him, his eyes red as he spoke, the voice choked with emotion.

"Boss, if anyone's thanking anyone, it should be me thanking you. You saved me, more than you know. Now you'd best be off, I don't want Alan or Patch seeing me like this."

Peter smiled warmly, he'd never known Tony to be emotional about anything, but they were all feeling it, they all knew deep down the farm would never be the same again. This was perhaps, goodbye.

Without wanting to get emotional again, he smiled and waved as Tony opened the door, stowing the shotgun and climbing into the passenger side, the Range Rover leaning over as his giant frame squeezed into it.

Peter watched, as with all four wheels spinning, the Range Rover sped away into the darkness, their headlights illuminating the fields, giving him one final glimpse of the horses. Peter could briefly see two of them enjoying a roll in the grass, whilst Ajax was already munching at the hay, oblivious to what was going on around them. With one final look, he waved goodbye to his wife, watching as the Range Rover slowed for the gate, now locked open, before turning onto the road and disappearing into the night.

After a moment he turned, jogging towards the open rear door, climbing inside and settling in, his eyes adjusting to the vehicle interior. Patch was looking at him through the rear-view mirror.

"You ready Boss?"

He reached over, his hands resting on the shoulders of the two men.

"Thank you, you two."

They both nodded in acknowledgement, no words were needed. His gaze fell back to the front door, his thoughts and emotions threatening to rise again, shaking his head he firmed his resolve. He needed to be elsewhere.

"Okay Patch, Let's go, let's get the hell out of here."

Aurora Headquarters and Factory

Twenty minutes later, they were at the company headquarters of Aurora, Patch navigating the Range Rover through the large double gates that lead to the complex. The hangar building was part of an old civilian airfield, long since shut down, perfect for what Peter had in mind for Aurora. The airfield was in the middle of nowhere, away from prying eyes. Peter had discovered it not long after moving to their home, whilst he and Elizabeth were walking their dog. A few years later and he'd seen it was up for sale, conveniently at around the same time as Aurora were looking for bigger premises. A handshake and a fair price paid and it was his, lock stock and barrel. He'd kept most of it deliberately looking ramshackle, already the grass runways were overgrown, livestock and cattle were now its only users, and what remained of the control tower had fallen in on itself, a relic of the past. The only new addition had been the brand-new double link fence, built to stop ramblers and trophy hunters from wandering into the hangars, and the newly laid car park, built to house the fifty or so employees that worked here. Peter had purposely kept the airfield looking dishevelled and dis-used, not wanting to draw attention to its value, hoping the mere sight of it would detract people from venturing any further. To aid in its camouflage, he had the new car park hidden behind the building. To anyone walking by, the old car park would look empty and disused, meanwhile on the other side of the building out of sight, workers could safely park, knowing their cars would be unseen, not drawing suspicion to the true nature of the building. Patch drove around the outside of the hangar, already light from inside was spilling out from under the doorway, indicating someone at least was in there. Peter estimated it would take about an hour for the motorcycle officers to get around everyone on the list, then perhaps another hour before they arrived. Maybe even another hour to get what they could away, whilst destroying anything they couldn't. He knew they were pushing it for time, but what other choice was there? He simply couldn't allow all their hard work and research to just be handed over, not when the stakes were so high. His thoughts were distracted as he heard Patch exclaim from the driver's seat. "Boss...What the hell?"

He looked over, curious as to what his driver had seen, when his eyes opened wide with surprise. They'd all been expecting to see an empty car park, instead nearly all the spaces were full, most of the cars they recognised, some they didn't. All three looked at each other as Patch pulled up next to the hangar doors, exiting the car at once, Peter quickly reminding them to leave the shotguns out of sight in the car. He didn't want to alarm anyone with the sight of armed men walking around. He stopped at the main door, already hearing the frenetic noise of people working inside. What the hell was going on, he thought curiously, with a heave he pulled open the smaller door, his eyes blinking at the sudden brightness pouring out at him. It was as if he'd entered another world, coming from the quiet, empty space outside into a bustling, hectic one. For a second, he stood, watching in mute awe, as if an audience member were watching a stage production, as people moved purposefully around the hangar, concentration etched on their faces. Some were shouting across the hangars to each other, others silently boxing up items, but everyone was working. His eyes were drawn to two figures in the middle of the cavernous hangar, chatting amongst themselves, clipboards in hand. They both looked up, smiling in recognition at him and waving him over. One was David Jones, an ex RAF pilot and Aurora's senior flight controller and the other was Kyle Howard, senior programmer and computer engineer. He walked over to them, a mixture of curiosity and admiration on his face. As he neared, he smiled, waving around the warehouse.

"Guys, what the hell? How did you manage this?"

Kyle looked over to David who answered for them both.

"Well, this morning, we all woke up to see all the TV and Radio stations were either off the air or playing last week's programmes. After what transpired in London, and rumours of what was going on in the south started to filter up to us, we realised whatever it was, it was big. So, I drove over to your house to see what you wanted us to do. You weren't in, but Alan let me in to speak to Elizabeth, she'd couldn't say much, except that you had been called away urgently. I figured whatever it was, it had to involve us at some point. So, I drove around, gathered everyone in, and we've been here since. At first, I thought we might just be getting some of the kit ready to deploy, but the more we've heard of what's going on, the more we thought that unlikely. We talked it through with the rest of the team and decided it would be best if we got ready to go, just in case. So, we've packed everything up. It just seemed the right thing to do."

Peter smiled appreciatively at the initiative of the ex-Officer, thanks to him, they'd now saved themselves hours of work, and better still, it looked like almost the entire hangar was packed away. His joy was short lived as he thought guiltily of the two police riders that he'd sent away, now racing around the countryside for no purpose. Hopefully one of the families staying behind would get the message to them. If not, they'd be cursing him for sending them on a fool's errand.

Seeing his faraway look, it was Kyle who stepped forward, reading off the list.

"Peter, we're nearly done with the loading of the heavy equipment, we've even loaded up the lame ducks, just in case we manage somehow to get the parts to fly them."

Peter nodded, recognising the term used for the drones they'd not yet managed to get airborne. Some were awaiting critical spares, others just needed software updates. Either way they were coming with them. Worse case, if they needed to, they could cannibalise them for spare parts. He continued listening, as Kyle added.

"We're still backing up all our data from the computers, that's what's taking us the most time, with the files so large and the computers so heavy, we can't simply take them with us. We've got ten portable hard drives being downloaded now. They should be ready to go in an hour."

Peter looked down at the suitcase sized laptop next to Kyle, recognising it as one that he'd custom built some months ago.

"I'm assuming by the way you're looking after that laptop, that's Wendi?"

Kyle nodded, looking down as he replied.

"I didn't want her programming to be chopped up and put on the hard drives, the risk of corruption was too large. Instead, I've downloaded her core programming onto here, and her mainframes are packed away with all the gear. The battery and hardware in it are good enough that she should be okay for the trip. When we get to where we're going, I'll get her computers back online and upload her back in. She did say before we closed her down, she was looking forward to trying somewhere new."

Peter smiled at the programmer, ever since bringing him on board to the Wendi Project, Kyle had almost doted after the Artificial Intelligence program that they'd created. It was almost as if he and some of the team believed she was real. It had begun as a simple programme to be used to control drones in a swarm attack, the idea being to overload an enemy's defences by overwhelming them with small fast drones. Peter had got the idea from a picnic he'd tried to have on one of the long summer days of the past. He'd remembered feeling annoyed by the wasps as they'd landed all over their food, at first, he'd managed to hold them off, but then, in greater numbers they'd kept coming, eventually forcing him and Elizabeth to abandon the food and flee to the safety of the car. He'd remembered sitting there, watching through the car windows, fuming, as they landed on the food, frustrated at how something so small could cause them so much trouble. But, as annoying as it was, it also gave him the idea.

He'd come into work the next day, outlining what he wanted and set the team to work. What had once been a simple drone development programme had begun to grow, as the complexities of managing hundreds of tiny drones began to take shape, the programmers adding more and more levels of coding. The project was officially to have been called the Weapons Engineered Nanobyte Developing Intelligence project, which was quickly shortened to Programme WENDI by the developers. Then one day in 2020, with the country in lockdown, and everyone forced to stay at home, Kyle had taken the WENDI programme home to work on, his own customised home computer more than adequate to the task. With nothing to distract him, Kyle had worked for nearly four months with no break, re-writing the code, constantly evolving it, until one day he had what he'd called his Eureka moment. One day, without knowing exactly how he did it, he'd awakened Wendi. Peter had been sceptical at first, hearing his chief programmer animatedly talking about this new form of Artificial Intelligence as if it was alive, and how it could revolutionise the way humans thought of the world around them, but his doubts were short lived. As soon as they'd uploaded Wendi into their advanced computer systems, he'd instantly seen the potential that the AI could bring to Aurora. As smart as his team were, some of their greatest advancements thus far had come from what Wendi had helped them to design, from the cutting-edge engines that their drones used, to the revolutionary new fusion reactor, small enough to fit inside a suitcase, powerful enough to run a house for years. But for all its success, Peter had his doubts, unable to shake the fear of the threat that AI could pose, so he made sure although the computers of Aurora were state of the art to help Wendi grow, they were also limited into what they could access, with no connections to the outside world. Peter had explained it to Kyle, likening it to a cage, whereby the bars were covered in velvet and the view spectacular. Kyle had complained at first, urging Peter to re-consider, how could Wendi evolve or grow, without suitable outside interaction, he'd argue, and what would Wendi say about it if she found out? Peter didn't care how it was perceived by the AI, the last thing he wanted was someone to hack into their system to expose the programme or worse Wendi to upload herself to the wider world and disappear off into the ether. Already other countries were secretly developing their own weaponised versions of Wendi, and Peter knew, at some point, there could be an information war, and what better way to fight AI, than to have your own version of it, ready to go. At least that's how he and the CDS had thought about it. Ever since being introduced, James Catmur had been a regular visitor to the facility, always interested in seeing the innovations that Peter and his company were coming up with. He'd taken a keen interest in Wendi, and the drone programme, and it was with James's input that Aurora had secured the MoD funding. Peter had been very careful in what he'd accepted and signed for, he knew that as good as the investment from the MoD could be, there was no such thing as free money. And the last thing he needed was for his company to be taken out from underneath him and turned over to the MoD. Despite James's protests, he'd made sure the funding was for the drone development only, keeping the Wendi programme on a short leash and out of reach of the MoD. Already they'd spoken privately about using Wendi to combat the virus that was crippling the nations computer and phone networks. Peter had been forced to lie, stating Wendi wasn't ready yet, and that to use the AI against something already evolved and firmly integrated could corrupt it, destroying it for good. Secretly Peter knew Wendi was more than ready, he just wasn't ready to release it. Once it was out, any element of control they had over it could also be gone. He'd seen enough Science Fiction films and read enough novels, to know what the potential outcome, good or bad could be. After all, this was his genie in the bottle, and he'd decide *when* and *if* to release it on the world.

He looked over again as David cleared his throat to speak.

"Peter, about the computers, like Kyle said, if we can't take them with us and they're too fragile and heavy to make the trip, we were wondering if-"

"Destroy them," he simply replied, interrupting David.

Both men looked at each other as if they'd already been discussing that very same thing. David seemed to be smiling, but Kyle looked regretfully at the floor.

The computers were all state of the art, able to handle the most complex of algorithms and manage terabytes of data within seconds. But all that performance came at a price, the processors ran at such high temperatures, they were super cooled by an advanced liquid cooled nitrogen system that was integral to the building. So, as fantastic as the system was, its achilles heel was that it couldn't be moved, it would have to stay behind with the building. At a cost of over £200,000 per computer, and the building having ten of them, it was a huge waste of money and equipment to simply destroy. Peter could see from the look on Kyle's face, as someone who lived and breathed computers, it seemed as if he'd just sentenced them to death, but from Peter's perspective, computers could be replaced, people could not. Peter thought to himself, that sometimes he'd wished Kyle would spend more time around people, and less time around computers. Not wanting to dwell on it further, he simply asked,

"Anything else Kyle?"

Kyle quickly composed himself, aware his boss was watching, as he ticked the job off his list, reporting back, "Peter another problem we have, is that we haven't yet been able to secure enough transport. We've got hold of a few vans but-"

He was cut short as Peter walked forwards, clapping a hand on his shoulder, happy to now be the one to surprise them.

"Kyle, David, you both worry about packing it all up and leave that part to me."

Both men exchanged looks of surprise as Peter walked off into the centre of the hangar, closely followed by Patch and Alan. Once they were all out of earshot it was David who spoke first.

"I don't' know where he's been or what he's been up to, but I can't tell you how glad I am to see him here."

David smiled as he said. "Told you we should kill the computers. That's £10 you owe me."

Kyle grimaced, pulling out one of his empty pockets and shrugging.

"Guess I'll have to owe you that."

David laughed knowingly; Kyle never seemed to have any money when he lost. Ignoring the bet for now he nodded up to the offices. "Come on, let's see how they're getting on up there; besides I want to be the first to say I've smashed up a £200,000 computer and all with the boss's blessing."

Kyle shook his head sadly, his shoulder slumping. "What a waste! I can't believe we're doing this, all that hardware." He lifted the laptop, adding, "I just hope Wendi forgives me."

David smirked, ignoring the comment about the AI, as he replied, "That's nothing, wait till you fly for the RAF, there you can get away with crashing a 50-million-pound aircraft, and if you do the job properly, they may even promote you!"

He saw the trace of a smile on the programmer's face, the tension of the past few hours finally dissolving, as they walked off towards the offices...

Ninety minutes later and still they were waiting. Peter looked at his watch, for probably the fifth time in as many minutes, trying not to think about the options if no-one arrived. James had promised to send him the trucks he needed to get them out of there, but what if something had gone wrong on the way? There were hundreds of scenarios to explain why the trucks wouldn't come for them. He silently cursed himself for the reliance he now had placed on someone else's shoulders. Aurora was his responsibility; he should have planned this better. Sensing the tension in the air, he turned to look at the small workforce sitting on the crates and around the equipment. Some smiled back at him, others were oblivious to what was happening, chatting amongst themselves excitedly. They'd finally finished getting the equipment ready to go almost an hour ago, now, only a skeleton workforce remained behind. Peter hadn't seen the sense in keeping everyone there, not when he knew they all had families of their own to evacuate, and especially not when he knew his own wife was already safely on her way. Without a moment's hesitation, he'd sent most of them home, giving them all his best wishes for their chances to get away, hoping to see them again, but holding them to no promises. They were not in the military, there were no orders to follow, no military laws to keep them there, they were free to do as they wish. All he could do, was give them the rough area he'd relocate the company to, if they made it there afterwards, then fine, if not, then they went with his blessing and his hopes.

Of the ten people who had volunteered to stay behind, all were either single, or had partners' that lived far enough away to not warrant evacuation. David and Kyle were part of the group, and Peter watched them both as Kyle animatedly explained the latest Sci-fi TV show to David. David appeared to be doing his very best not to look bored, Peter knowing that he rarely watched the TV, focusing instead on more of a sporty, outdoor lifestyle. He smiled, pleased with the team he had with him, proud of what they'd all achieved. Looking at the boxes, pallets and crates, he realised it didn't look like much, but he knew, that what they contained could level the battlefield, he was sure of it, so much so, that he was willing, like everyone else there that night, to risk capture to get it to safety.

He heard a noise in the distance, recognising it as machine gun fire, followed by a large explosion. It was far enough away, but close enough to cause concern. He exchanged looks with Patch and Alan and as if able to see what they were thinking, Peter responded.

"Guys, I think now might be a good time to go and get the shotguns from the car."

Both men needed no encouragement and were almost out of the door before Peter had finished speaking, coming back moments later, weapons loaded, barrels closed, safety catches on, ready to go. Each man carried a leather belt on their waist, with twenty-five cartridges each. Not enough to win a war, but certainly enough to buy them time should they need it.

The remaining conversations and laughter died away, as the others heard the gunfire, finally understanding the seriousness of what they were facing.

More heavy gunfire was heard in the distance, this time though it was answered by smaller calibre weapons, Peter estimated it was someway off to the east of them. Whoever it was, at least someone was fighting back.

Peter walked over to the hangar doors intending to open them, having them closed and not seeing what was going on outside was beginning to unnerve him. If something were to arrive, it was better that they see it coming, he reasoned.

Suddenly everyone turned towards the doors, in the distance they could hear it, getting closer, and louder, the sounds of heavy diesel engines, followed by the squeal of brakes. Something was coming towards them. Peter opened the smaller door and looked out just as the heavy diesel engines pulled up outside the hangars. There were more than a few nervous looks as no one knew what to expect was outside waiting for them. Peter held up a re-assuring hand, attempting to calm the frayed nerves as he walked over to the hangar door controls, his confidence relaxing them all. With a flourish he and Alan pulled on the levers opening the doors, the cold air blasting though as the doors slowly slid open, the bright headlights of the trucks waiting outside in the dark causing them to shield their eyes from the glare.

Peter waved them in encouragingly, a big smile on his face as he counted them in, there were eight of them, all drab green military trucks with cargo bodies, on huge, all terrain wheels. James had delivered on his promise. Peter noticed as they came in, they were all spattered with mud, showing the signs of anything but an uneventful journey. He wondered where they'd come from to be looking like that as they pulled past him. In the back he saw the faces of the soldiers looking back at him, faces painted green and black, all serious, all quiet. Whatever they'd witnessed, it was enough to kill the usual light-hearted banter he'd been expecting.

The lead vehicle was guided inside the hangar, stopping close to the far set of doors as the others pulled up close behind it. As one, the engines were switched off as soldiers dismounted from the rear of the trucks, some lowered the tailgates with a crash, others lifted up the canvas sides, already pre-empting that forklifts were to be used. Without wasting time, David with his clip board still in hand, began to bark out orders, people around him springing to life.

"Right, let's move people. Jamie, Bob, jump in the forklifts, let's get these pallets loaded onto truck one, those pallets and crates over there onto truck two, anyone else not doing anything pick something up, put it in a truck. Let's go, let's go!"

The group split up, some of them raced away, jumping into the forklifts, others began to manhandle the crates towards the trucks, all of them familiar with the military routine that Peter had instilled in the company. The soldiers jumped in to help where they could, feeling instantly at ease with the way David was instructing them. David was keen to impress upon them the cargo was precious and was to be treated with great care.

One of the soldier's stood looking around the group ignoring the movements of others around him, his eyes searching for someone. Suddenly they locked onto Peter and he briskly walked towards him, something about Peter made him automatically stand to attention, the movement making Alan and Patch look on amusedly. The soldier ignored their amused gaze, asking,

"Sir, are you Brigadier Rawlinson?"

Peter looked him up and down, recognising the Sergeant's rank and the unit badge, 143 Wessex Regiment. He smiled appreciatively, wondering if the man knew Peter had helped to create the unit.

"That's me Sergeant, how can I help?"

"Sir, I've been ordered to help you extract your equipment and your staff, I believe you know where we're going?"

Peter's eyebrows pinched together in confusion as he replied.

"My staff? No, I think you've made a mistake there Sergeant, it's equipment only, my staff have their own cars and will be making their own way to where we're going."

The Sergeant shook his head.

"Sir, I'm afraid that's just not going to be possible."

Peter smiled forcibly, not wanting to argue.

"Sergeant, we don't have the time to argue about this, my people are going in their own cars, whether you like it or not."

Peter saw the Sergeant blink in confusion and look away, as if he was trying to think of what to say next. Instead, he decided to walk towards the giant hangar door, pointing out to the car park.

"Sir, are those the cars that your staff are going to be using?"

Peter walked out, looking out at the assembly of cars, confused as to where the Sergeant was going with this. One was a camper van, two were sports cars, the rest were a mixture of typical family saloons. He nodded his head, confirming.

"Yes Sergeant, may I ask why that's so important?"

The soldier nodded glumly, looking away into the night before steeling himself to answer. Clearly, he wasn't accustomed to saying no to a Brigadier.

"Sir, I'm afraid to have to tell you this, but if your staff try to get away in those vehicles, they won't get very far. The roads are in absolute chaos at the moment, traffic's snarled up in every direction for miles. The reason we're late is because for the last three miles we were forced to travel cross country."

Peter nodded in understanding, realising that's why the convoy was spattered in mud, as the Sergeant continued.

"If anyone tries to follow us in anything less than a 4x4, then they'll get stuck, and I don't have the time to keep stopping my convoy to pull them out. We've already come close to a few Russian units, thankfully, the traffic's slowing them down as well, but that won't last long, not now they're shooting anything in their way. So, if you want your equipment *and* your staff to make it out of here tonight, then I strongly suggest they load up with my men into the trucks."

Peter looked thoughtfully at the soldier, thinking through what he'd just said. The Sergeant stood back to attention, looking occasionally out to the darkness, clearly wanting to be away from the complex as quickly as possible as Peter remained thinking. Not quite the simple journey he'd probably volunteered for, Peter remarked to himself.

He looked outside again at the cars, then back to the trucks. It would be a squeeze and uncomfortable as hell, but he knew it would be the only way. The Sergeant was right.

He saw the Sergeant breathe easier, as he made his decision.

"Ok, Sergeant, I'll take your word for it as to how bad it is out there, my staff will go with you. But, they'll need to take some of their belongings with them from the cars."

The Sergeant looked relieved, he'd been expecting the Brigadier to argue with him, costing them more wasted time, instead, this one had listened to him! He looked on respectfully at him, happy to have been heard, as he agreed.

"Fine Sir, I'll have my lads help them load it all up."

Peter dismissed him as he ran off towards the trucks, shouting out orders to his troops. Peter turned to Patch, pointing over to their Range Rover.

"Reckon you can follow them in the Rangie? Or should we start loading our gear into one of the trucks?"

Patch feigned mock horror, looking at the Brigadier in almost disbelief at the question of his driving ability, causing Peter and Alan to both laugh in response as he replied.

"Boss, my days of being thrown around in the back of one of those shit boxes, freezing my arse off and smelling farts for hours ended a long time ago. If you don't mind, I'll stick with the Rangie."

Peter laughed appreciatively, patting him on the shoulder, he knew better than anyone how good Patch was behind the wheel, he'd just wanted to lighten the mood. Still smiling he added.

"Patch, go clear us some more room though in the car, we'll take Kyle and David with us, it'll be a squeeze, but we should be able to get all their gear in."

Patch replied, adding his own light tone.

"Kyle? Boss, have you ever travelled long distance with him? Remember what I just said about smelling farts for hours? Times that by two when he's in the car!"

Peter smiled, ignoring the light-hearted comments and leaving them both to it as he walked back into the hangar, his focus now on loading the equipment, not that it was needed as between the soldiers and his own team, they were already halfway through.

He found David at the back of one of the trucks, slowly guiding the operator of the forklift into position, the heavy crate slowly disappearing inside the truck. He waited until the forklift was out of the way before pulling him aside, repeating the conversation with the Sergeant. David looked up, listening intently, waiting for Peter to finish, remarking.

"Fair enough, I don't fancy getting my shoes muddy, besides my camper's seen better days, I doubt the clutch would survive all that punishment."

Peter nodded, looking around him at the others,

"I'm off to tell the others, I'd better remind them to take only the essentials, it'll be a squeeze."

David merely gave the thumbs up to acknowledge, quickly distracted as another pallet of equipment began to get loaded into the truck, awaiting his guidance. Leaving him to it, Peter sought out the others.

Ten minutes later they were finally finished, the convoy of trucks were loaded with all that remained of the staff and their belongings, the soldiers and all the equipment they needed at their new premises. The Sergeant was in the lead truck, waiting and watching, as Peter climbed up onto the truck's foot plate.

"Sergeant, take your convoy outside and wait for me, I'll only be another five minutes."

The Sergeant's mouth opened in surprise at the order, as he remonstrated.

"Sir, maybe I didn't make myself clear before, but we need to move now! We-"

"Sergeant!" Peter said calmly but forcibly, interrupting the soldier midsentence, who sat stone faced and silent in reply.

Keeping his voice calm, he continued. "I appreciate the need for urgency, however, we're still leaving behind a lot of valuable items that I do *not* want to simply gift to the enemy. Now give me the five minutes I need to get it done."

The Sergeant took a deep breath, looking at his driver, before relenting, the urge to leave being subdued.

"Ok Sir, *five* minutes."

Peter jumped down, stepping back as in a belch of smoke the heavy diesel rumbled to life, the truck jolting forwards out of the hangar, quickly followed by the others. He watched as they lined up, all facing away from the building, the drivers looking in their rearview mirrors at him, the looks saying it all. They all wanted out of there.

Peter left them to it, making his way upstairs to the offices, the noise of the truck engines dying away as the dividing door closed with a creak behind him. His office overlooked the hangar floor, he stood in the doorway, looking in one last time. Reminiscing at the days gone by where he'd sat with a drink overlooking the team, as they designed and manufactured their wares. It had been a great place to work, but as with all good things it had now all come to an end. Quickly reminding himself what he'd gone there for, he cut short his trip down memory lane, walking into the area where all the computers were kept. He could see the damage already done recently by David and a sledgehammer, the hard drives were all smashed up, broken in bits on the floor, with wiring and circuit boards from the computers lying all around. But despite their best efforts, he knew it wouldn't be enough. He walked over to where the computers cooling systems were located, pulling out the set of keys quickly finding the one he needed to open the security door. He unlocked and opened the door, stepping inside as a blast of cold air hit him immediately. He shivered in response, flicking on the lights and walking up to the control panel, flicking switches, turning dials, disabling all safety protocols, watching as the gauges all began slowly sliding into the red, and a red alarm light blinked furiously as overhead a klaxon began to alarm. He ignored it, taking one final look around, satisfied at what he'd done as he quickly walked back outside, happy to be in the warmer air. He wedged the security door open with one of the chairs, then walked briskly away, making sure to keep the doors to the computer room and his office open, before running back down and pulling out the set of keys again. He found the one he needed, as he stopped by the door marked 'Armoury'.

With a clang, he threw back the bolt, opening the heavy steel door, walking inside a corridor lined with doors, all were open, and each room looking as if a tornado had hit it, most were empty, with boxes discarded on the floor, as his staff had already emptied them of anything worth taking. He walked past them all to the final door, this one much larger than the others, resembling a large safe door. Finding the keys he needed, he unlocked the two bolts, giving a huge heave as the door swung slowly outwards, revealing a large windowless room, with racks and shelving that lay wall to ceiling. Normally the room was filled with all the machine guns and heavy weapons that the drones used, but now it was empty, the weapons already boxed up and loaded on the trucks. One of the advantages about working with the MoD was that Aurora systems were one of the few companies in the UK to be granted a Class 5 Armoury, meaning any weapon, regardless of size could be stored there, provided of course that they could fit through the steel doors and Peter had someone qualified to operate them. Peter walked up to the counter, his eyes quickly laying onto the Milkor 40mm Multiple Grenade Launcher (MGL) that he'd had David get ready, the six High Explosive grenades beside it in the box, ready to go. The Milkor resembled an oversized revolver, with the circular six round magazine jutting out of the matte black body, but unlike a revolver, it also had an extra hand grip under the barrel, and this one was fitted with the latest Collimator sight, very easy to use, pointing the relevant aiming mark where you needed the grenade to hit, and letting physics do the rest. When Aurora had applied to use the 40mm MGL, he'd been the first to jump at the chance to get qualified on the weapon and had spent hours on the ranges in Lulworth with the infantry, learning to fire it. He knew he'd never be a marksman, but he'd reasoned, it was a grenade launcher, you didn't exactly need to be precise.

Picking it up, he quickly unlatched the pistol grip, levering it away, allowing him access to the magazine and began loading the grenades into the six-round drum magazine, before latching the pistol grip back on, throwing the empty box onto the floor. His head scanned the room for anything else that might be left behind of value. Seeing nothing of worth, he ran from the room, slinging the MGL over his shoulder and running back out into the corridor and outside into the empty hangar. Patch and Alan were both there, already cutting open the fuel tanks of the five cars they'd just driven into the centre of the building, the owners grudgingly agreeing as Peter had to promise to buy them new cars when it was over. As the two of them worked, Peter closed the huge hangar doors, hoping to add to the destruction they were about to unleash, as one by one, the cars began to leak the flammable liquid over the concrete floor, the fuel quickly spreading into the offices and open doorways. Peter waited in the open doorway, as the two men finally finished, running back towards him, faces set in grim fascination at what was about to happen. Satisfied he was ready; he ran back up to the lead truck.

"Right Sergeant now you can get going, we'll be following behind in the Range Rover. Make sure that any roadblocks you encounter, you tell them that we're with you. I don't want to have to watch you disappear into the distance as I'm held back explaining myself."

The Sergeant's eyes opened wide, as he looked in awe at the MGL Peter was carrying, unsure of where he'd just produced it from.

"Sir, where the hell did you get *that?*"

"Never mind about that Sergeant, did you just hear what I said?"

The Sergeant's eyes snapped back to Peter as he looked up, nodding.

"Yes Sir, any roadblocks, tell them that you're with us and wait for you to make it through."

Nodding in satisfaction, Peter ran back down the line of vehicles, the MGL banging against his back, towards the Range Rover. Patch and Alan were waiting by the car doors, as inside, Kyle and David were already bunched up on the rear seat, Kyle still holding the laptop protectively. Unslinging the MGL and making sure his finger was away from the trigger, he climbed into the passenger seat, the others following as the engine started.

"Get us to the end of the road Patch, I'll do it from there."

Patch nodded as the car reversed away and turned, quickly following the convoy out of the complex, the faces in the rear truck looking out curiously as to what was about to happen. Peter was watching in the rear-view mirror as the building began to get smaller, deciding finally that they were far enough away, banging on the roof of the car.

"Okay Patch, this'll do."

The vehicle skidded to a halt, Peter's door already open before it came to a rest. He walked forwards ten paces; certain he was clear enough of the car. Patch and Alan were leaning out of the open doors, as David and Kyle watched through the rear window.

Peter checked the stock was extended, the sight was on, and the safety off, lining up the aiming point of the collimator sight onto the building. He'd estimated they were 300 metres away and lined up that part of the sight on the huge hangar roof, knowing the target was so big he'd certainly hit.

Taking a breath, he calmly pulled the trigger, the soft thunk of the grenade launching, sounding far quieter than on the ranges, as the magazine spun through, ready to fire the next round. He fired the second round, then a third in rapid succession, before lowering the weapon to see the results.

He couldn't see the arc of the grenades in the night sky but, saw the flash a few seconds later, as the first one tore through the thin roof, followed quickly by the other two, exploding inside amongst the cars. He heard the explosions, the solid boom echoing through the night, then with a flash the night was lit up as the hangar door's exploded off, the three tonne doors ripping off their hinges, crashing to the ground, as the explosive pressure blew them outwards. The interior lights blinked off, briefly plunging the inside into darkness as the fuel ignited, the flames quickly spread outwards towards the armoury and the offices, casting a yellow glow over everything. Peter watched in mute fascination, waiting as flames began to spread out and rise as the fire took hold, car tyres exploding in the heat, sounding like gunshots, as the flames poured forwards like water, towards the stairs and the computer rooms.

It didn't take long, perhaps thirty seconds, before the hollow explosion rang out from the area of the offices as finally the building's huge liquid nitrogen tanks exploded. The building's outer wall crumbled as the upper floors collapsed in on themselves, pulling the steel support beams of the roof down with them. With one side of support gone, the roof finally gave way to gravity, as it collapsed, crashing down into the flames, which began to increase in intensity as the car's fuel tanks began to explode. Sparks and flames shot out through the debris and rubble, as secondary explosions began to sound off from within the pile, as the explosive ordnance left behind in the armoury began to cook off.

Peter turned to see everyone looking at him confused, only he knew the reason for the building's collapse. Just like the building's armoury, when he'd planned on having the liquid nitrogen tanks installed, Aurora had to have trained technicians on site to safely handle the liquid. With Peter being the CEO, he was told he'd have to know some of the aspects of it. He'd nearly fallen asleep reading the 60-page Health and Safety booklet on storing the chemical, but the one thing he did remember was what happened when it got warm. Liquid nitrogen needed to be kept at extremely low temperatures, usually -200 Celsius to store and kept as a liquid, otherwise with a boiling point of -196 Celsius, any sudden increase in temperature and it would turn to a gas, and with a ratio of 700 to 1, it meant that when turning to gas, for every 1 litre of liquid nitrogen you stored, it would expand to 700 times its size. Therefore, any container trying to store it would rapidly expand within milliseconds with enough explosive force to go off like a bomb. Aurora kept 100 litres of the liquid in the specially made Dewar tanks, which meant that because Peter had kept the doors to the offices opened, turned off the cooling system and disabled all the pressure relief valves, it was only a matter of time before it had blown as the temperatures of the stored nitrogen had climbed, with enough force equivalent to a seven tonne bomb going off. That's why all of them were now gaping at the destruction of Aurora.

Patch, Alan, Kyle and David stood in awe at the spectacle, as Peter ran towards them shouting,

"Come on guys, no time to stand admiring the work, let's get after the convoy."

Already the convoy's lights were only visible in the distance as a faint glow, the Sergeant clearly not hanging around to wait for them.

Peter applied the safety catch as he stowed the MGL in the footwell, keeping it close in case it was needed again as he climbed in, looking about at the others as they settled in for the bumpy ride.

"Everyone ready?"

The looks in response told him they were, as Patch fully focussed on his job, engaged first gear and shot off, chasing the convoy. Within minutes they were closing up behind the rear vehicle, the Rangie slowing down as Patch settled himself into what he knew would be a long, and possibly eventful drive. Peter watched the inferno in his wing mirror as it was slowly swallowed up by the darkness, soon no more than an orange glow on the horizon. As he witnessed it disappear, he began reflecting on what had just happened, so intent was he on getting everyone away and getting the building destroyed, he hadn't had time to fully think about it all. Now they were on the road, he finally had the space to ponder and a wave of sadness suddenly hit him as he realised what he'd just destroyed. He'd spent years getting Aurora built up from nothing and now in the blink of an eye had been destroyed. He began to wonder about the future, what would become of them and all their effort and hard work? Would this be the end of them? Would they get to where they were going only to find nothing there, or worse be moved on again? His gloomy thoughts were disturbed as the sound of snoring came from the back. Sharing a look with Patch, he looked to the back seat, all three men were asleep, wasting no time, their heads rolling sideways with the vehicle's movements.

Looking ahead at the truck, he could see another two of his engineers sat hunched by the tailgate, coats pulled up, collars upturned, attempting to sleep, being jostled as the truck bounced down the track, not nearly as comfortable as the guys in the car's the back seat.

Peter realised as he looked up at them, Aurora wasn't just about a fancy building, or the computers it contained, it wasn't even about what was in the crates on the trucks. Aurora was about the people Peter had brought together. It was a team of people, bonded by ideas, dreams and beliefs, with the technical knowledge and ability to turn those ideas into reality. The regrets and sorrow he felt quickly disappeared, replaced by a sense of fierce pride as he thought about his team, the sacrifices they were all willing to make to keep Aurora going, to prove once and for all that all those long nights away, all the thousands of hours of painstaking work and risk were worth it, especially now that the country needed them. Thinking of the team, his mind cast back to Mike, trying to shake the feeling of guilt that he suddenly felt, it had been his idea for Mike to stay in Bovington to try to convince them all. Before he'd left Wonderland, he'd tried to get an update from James, but it was still the same details as before, no updates on the garrison, except for the fact that Russian Paratroopers had landed, and the base was now under enemy control. Peter just hoped that whatever had happened down there, Mike was still alive and had made it out in time. Not wanting to dwell anymore on events beyond his control, he turned his mind to events he could control. He sat back, his mind racing through all the details, questions and problems they could face when they got to the new home, knowing sleep wouldn't come easy, not now. Peter felt energised with renewed purpose, people were relying on him, he'd done it before, he could do it again. Now it was time for Aurora to rise like a phoenix from its ashes.

11

Calendar Boys

Two hours into their journey and Peter felt the convoy slowing down, looking ahead as Patch slowed to a stop.

"Fucks sake, what is it now?" he heard Patch exclaim in frustration.

Peter kept quiet, letting his driver vent his annoyance. He had to admit, he had wrongly thought that once the trucks had been loaded and enroute, the hardest part had been done, but he was mistaken. The journey they were on, could usually have been completed in a couple of hours, instead they'd already been travelling for that amount of time, and had only covered ten miles, with still another thirty to go. It had been slow going, with the roads jammed as they were, and with the constant threat of attack from the air, the convoy had been forced to drive almost the whole distance across fields and tracks, most of it with their lights off. Peter had been right to listen to the Sergeant's warning about taking their cars, already the convoy had passed dozens of vehicles that were stranded in the rough terrain, the occupants desperately trying to stop the convoy for help. At first, despite his reservations, the Sergeant had relented and stopped to offer help, his soldiers managing to make short work of pulling a few cars out of ditches, with the families singing their praises. However, no sooner had they freed them, than the drivers, not being used to driving cross country with overloaded cars, beached them again further down the tracks, or slid them into water filled ditches, impossible to get out again without help. Peter remembered how the looks of praise and thanks had quickly turned to looks of anger as they realised the convoy was not stopping again, but instead, continued past.

Peter opened his window as the Sergeant ran down the convoy, approaching their car, leaning in, he reported.

"Sir, looks like the bridge ahead is jammed up with traffic all waiting to cross it, but they're being held up by what looks like a vehicle checkpoint, someone manning it has a vehicle placed across the road."

"Police or military?"

The Sergeant shook his head.

"Neither Sir, looks to me like a load of civvies are manning it, but they're armed, some have firearms others have bats and the like."

Dammit, Peter thought, they had no choice but to cross it, being the only bridge in the area for miles and the river was too deep for the trucks to cross safely.

He looked behind him, quickly shaking Alan awake.

"What is it?" he murmured sleepily.

"Alan, get your game face on, I need you with me."

Peter stepped out of the vehicle, looking over at the trucks.

"Sergeant go and get two of your guys please, they'll come across the bridge with me and Alan, let's find out what all this is about."

The Sergeant looked at him hesitantly, sensing something was wrong, Peter quickly asked, his eyebrows raised.

"What is it, Sergeant?"

Looking embarrassed, the Sergeant replied, the words dragging out of him.

"Sir, the lads, they've got the weapons for show, but we've not got any ammo. We didn't have the time to get any before we were sent to you. If it kicks off down there, we've got nothing to shoot back with."

This night gets better and better, Peter thought, he'd assumed that the unit was fully armed, he'd seen the weapons, but hadn't even asked if they had any ammunition. He looked back at Alan as he climbed out, glancing down at the shotgun, it wouldn't be enough. And even if they did have the weapons, the last thing he wanted was a shootout on the bridge. As he stood there thinking, his eyes settled on the MGL sat in the Range Rover's footwell. Suddenly a thought flashed into his mind, something that he'd seen done in the past. Smiling he turned back to the Sergeant.

"Right, never mind about that Sergeant, go get them anyway and tell them to make sure they have a magazine fitted. Ammunition or not, I want it to look like they're fully armed."

"Sir, are you sure about this, wouldn't you rather me to go down there instead Sir? Or perhaps take more men to come with you?"

The Sergeant's voice was more of a warning, clearly he felt uncomfortable with the Brigadier going down there.

"No, you stay here with the convoy and start pushing your way through the traffic, besides I don't want to go down there looking too intimidating from the outset, otherwise whoever they are, they might be tempted to open fire first, ask questions later."

Looking on doubtfully the Sergeant simply nodded, hastening off to get everything organised.

Peter leaned back into the car.

"David, if you please, I'd like a quick word. Oh, and bring the MGL with you, there's a good chap."

Five minutes later, Peter and his small group were making their way through the line of cars, squeezing themselves through the gaps, thankful not to have been the Sergeant as they saw the task awaiting them in getting the trucks through. He'd passed lots of angry people, some standing by their cars, others sitting inside, some honking their horns as he drew closer to the bridge. He stopped, his eyes drawn to a group of people off to the side, all queuing up to chat to two people sitting behind a table. Two burly men were listening uninterestedly as a woman was leaning over the table, crying and pleading with them to let her cross. One of the men appeared to be the leader, Peter could see he'd placed a pistol on the table, to add dramatic effect whilst the second man seemed to be intent on rifling through the woman's handbag, upending it, scattering the contents on the table. Another thug stood behind them, menacingly brandishing an assault rifle glaring back at her, in a blatant effort of intimidation. Across the far side of the empty bridge they'd placed a transit van, rusty and faded blue, it was clearly how they controlled the traffic flow. Not that it was needed to stop anything, as seven heavy set men stood brandishing bats and machetes and were more than enough of a deterrent.

Peter turned to face the others, Alan had the look of menace about him, not fazed by what was about to happen, but the other two young Privates looked apprehensively at him, as if he was about to make them walk across broken glass barefoot. Seeing the uneasy looks on their faces he quickly shot out,

"Right listen up gents, if you all want to survive the next ten minutes, then I need you to just follow my lead and say nothing. Whatever I do, whatever I say, just keep your mouths shut and *say nothing*. As far as you're concerned, you're to act as if your weapons are loaded. Do you understand?"

Their eyes shot sideways at the bridge, taking in the scene, before nervously nodding.

"All you have to do is play it cool, do as I say, follow my lead and we'll be alright." Peter added reassuringly, as he walked onto the bridge, the others following close behind.

As they approached, he saw the leader's look of arrogance turn to surprise as the heavily armed group approached the table. He stood up from the chair, surprise quickly returning to arrogance when he looked around him, drawing comfort from his ten gang mates, no doubt feeling secure in safety in numbers. Ignoring the people waiting, he picked up the pistol and nodded to the other two, both following as he pushed past the crowd, the gang all closing in towards Peters group, like a pack of dogs drawing direction from their leader. He strutted towards Peter, his chest jutting out, his arm holding the pistol out in front of him, as he proclaimed.

"And where the fuck do you lot think you're going? Trying to cross without paying the fee?"

Peter said nothing, instead looking behind the gang, seeing already from the large pile of valuables behind the table, that they'd had a great night. With the lack of police, Peter had guessed these were just chancers, trying their luck until someone stopped them. He looked around the group, thankful the only firearms they seemed to possess were the pistol and assault rifle, everyone else had baseball bats or machetes, hand weapons only. Peter recognized the pistol as a Glock 17 and the rifle looked to be a HK53, he guessed the gang had somehow stolen them or acquired them from one of the Police Armed Response Units. The way both men held the weapons filled him with confidence, clearly, they'd seen too many movies and had no time on a weapons range.

All the group were men, some had vast beer bellies, far outstripping their waistlines, others looked gaunt, the total opposite of the others. The gang leader looked to be mid-thirties, with a scar over one cheek that seemed to give him a constant sneer.

Peter's silence had the intended effect, unnerving the leader as he shouted back, stepping closer, clicking his fingers irritably.

"Oi! You listening old man? You hear me? I said this is *our* bridge, you think you and your soldier boys get to cross for free? You pay like anyone else!"

"Perhaps they think they don't have to pay!" a skinny man jeered, stepping forward, buoyed by the courage of his leader. His piggy eyes darted to the weapons they carried as he taunted them, looking back at the group, his voice rising.

"Ooh look they've got guns! But hang on...so have we!"

The group began laughing as he danced about drunkenly, mimicking someone crying and wiping their eyes out of feigned pity.

The leader laughed along with them, his voice taunting them as he demanded,

"So, let's talk about payment."

The gang leader's gaze was suddenly distracted, as he looked over their shoulders behind them, hearing the commotion and shouts in the distance, as the military convoy began to slowly weave its way through the crowds, his eyes lit up with greed as smirking he asked,

"What's in the trucks, grandad?"

Peter could see Alan slowly stiffen at the taunts, but knew he'd remain where he was, ever the professional. He knew he couldn't reason with the group, and he certainly wasn't going to pay.

Peter continued to ignore him, as he looked back over to the van, the rest of the gang were all nearby with no one else near to it. Silently thinking, he judged the distances of the shrapnel, working out the safety distances. Happy with the numbers, he decided he'd seen enough, now it was time for a show of force.

He spoke confidently, allowing his voice to carry an air of arrogant authority. It all hinged on what happened next.

"My name is Brigadier Rawlinson and as a member of His Majesty's Forces, I order that you cease this illegal gathering immediately and allow these people to pass. I must impress upon you all that I have the full and absolute authority of the British government, to use lethal force if necessary."

"OOOH!" a few of the gang taunted back in response to the threat, buoyed up by the leader's confidence and their numbers.

"He sounds dead posh, bet he's got money on him."

"String 'im up by his balls, see what falls out of his pockets, bet he won't be so fucking cocky then, the toffee-nosed twat."

"And what the fuck do you think you're going to do us grandad?" the leader taunted him, smiling at the jeers as he aimed the pistol squarely at Peter's chest.

Peter could feel Alan tense next to him, the shotgun barrel slowly beginning to rise. With the most subtle of hand gestures, he waved his hand sideways knowing only the ex-soldier would understand it. The message was simple. "Stand down."

He saw the shotgun barrel dip slightly as Alan relaxed, not fully understanding what the Brigadier was planning, but trusting his judgment.

Peter nodded imperceivably at him, the movement lost on the gang as they continued laughing and taunting them, the threats growing louder.

Peter ignored them, eyeballing them as he continued, his voice confident and loud, booming over them.

"I have two Apache gunships on standby, who have you all in their sights. If anything happens to me or my men, you'll be immediately engaged with 30-millimetre cannons."

Peter could see some of the group had stopped laughing and were looking upwards at the night sky, as if trying to seek out the new threat. As if to hammer the fact home he added,

"Now for the final time, drop your weapons, disperse and allow these people to cross, or I'll be forced to have you all killed."

Some of the group looked over at the leader nervously, others continued to laugh, but not with quite the same confidence as before. Something about Peter's confidence and arrogance was unnerving them. Seeing them waver, the leader looked angrily at them, trying to re-shift the balance of power.

"Bullshit! Fucking bullshit old man, I bet there ain't no gunships out there, you're trying to bluff your way across. I bet I could shoot you all dead right now and no-one would shed a tear!"

Peter lifted his hand to his wrist, as if talking into a hidden microphone, causing the leader to blink in surprise.

"Valkrye Six-Two, prepare for show of force on the bridge."

As if to emphasise what he'd just said, Peter held his hand to his ear, as if listening to a reply, nodding his head as if in a conversation with someone in his ear and ignoring the strange looks the two soldiers and Alan were giving him.

"Yes, that's correct Valkrye Six-Two...No, there's no need to fire on the hostiles just yet. Show of force only, target the van fifty metres south of us, I want you to use one Hellfire rocket. That's correct you're cleared to go weapons hot...Want me to point it out for you? Okay, watch for my signal..."

Peter ignored the curious gazes of his men, as he looked up extending his arm out to the van sat fifty metres away. Some of the gang now lowered their weapons, fascinated, staring open mouthed by what they had just heard, watching where the Brigadier was pointing. Only a few of the gang still looked on jeering, including the leader, whose patience was running out.

He stepped forward, his anger simmering over.

"Right enough of the fucking about old man, there ain't no helicopters and you ain't getting over this bridge without-"

He was cut off mid-sentence, as the van exploded. Everyone on the bridge, all except Peter's group yelled and dived for cover. The van's metal sides peeled open as if it were a giant banana, the windscreen sailing out over the bridge landing in the water. Within a second the fuel tank exploded, flames and debris shooting into the night sky as the van tore into two. The front section was flung forwards, hanging precariously over the edge of the bridge, teetering as if it would fall any moment, whilst the rear section remained where it lay, the wheels splayed out and burning furiously. Fragments began to rain down around them, causing Peter to look back apologetically to the others, who all grimaced as they finally took cover, waiting the few moments it took for the lighter debris to finish raining down around them. When finally they stood up, the gang were all lying on the floor, weapons thrown down, some having placed their hands over their ears, the noise and violence of the blast wave shocking them into submission. Unlike the soldiers who were used to loud explosions, the gang had never experienced anything like it before.

Within minutes it was all over. Peter had them all disarmed and kneeling, with their hands on their heads, being covered by Alan, now holding the fully loaded HK53 and with a face showing he meant business. He'd relieved it from the previous owner, along with the two spare magazines in his pockets with a condescending pat on the head, the taunts from earlier being gratefully paid back. However, unlike its previous owner, Alan knew only too well how to use it, the weapon was raised and finger lightly resting on the trigger. They all looked fearfully at him, even the gang leader had lost his cockiness, his pistol now being held by Peter.

Peter could still see some of them looking nervously skywards, as if they could somehow hear gunships circling overhead. Good, he thought, let them fear what they can't see. As if to add to the drama he lifted his wrist and spoke to the imaginary pilots, all the while the nervous looks of the gang following his every move.

"Valkrye Six-Two, good hit, good hit, stay on station, remain in overwatch. Out."

Knowing the threat of the gunships would keep them in check, and with the bridge still empty, Peter turned to the soldiers.

"Right, one of you keep everyone off the bridge until the convoy gets here, the other get back and tell the Sergeant to push onto the bridge now." Leaving them to it, he calmly walked up to the gang leader remembering the cockiness and arrogance of before as the man began to plead.

"Look mate, you've got the bridge, just let us go, we'll disappear off it."

Peter looked down at the man, thinking. He didn't have the time or the resources to arrest them, but he certainly wasn't going to let them all just walk off. He knew they were dangerous, the way they'd taken over the bridge had told him that. If he let them go, they'd probably go and do the same thing somewhere else. He needed to shock them, but first he had a question. Kneeling, he drew eye level with the leader, pulling the pistol out of his waist band and showing it to him.

"Where did you get this from?"

"What?" he replied, his eyes flashing over to Alan then back at him.

"The weapons." Peter replied, speaking slowly. "Where did you get them from?"

For a few seconds he saw the leader thinking, his head darting back to his other gang members, all of them sharing a look of defiance that Peter recognised.

"No comment." the leader said arrogantly, some of the cockiness now returning. Peter smiled back at him, sharing the look of amusement, seeing the smile on the face of the leader disappear, as he replied. "Oh, but you're not under police arrest and this isn't a police cell. You're under *military* arrest, and that's a different ball game entirely."

Peter stood back up.

"Do you all know what martial law is?" he asked, his voice loudly carrying across the group.

"Marshal who?" the leader spat back, nervous laughter coming from the group as he retorted, "I've heard of Marshal Wyatt Earp, does that count?"

The laughter died away quickly as Peter stepped forwards, placing the pistol against their leader's head, the steel barrel cold and unforgiving.

Peter continued, his voice menacing. "*Martial* law is where the military take over from the police, freeing them up to go elsewhere, except military laws are different to civilian laws. All the laws, all the rules, that you and your little gang have been used to flouting and breaking in the past, are all now no longer relevant. Now it's the military that get to keep the peace and now it's the military that *enforce* it. Except, we don't have the time or resources to drag vermin like you through the courts, so we have the power to be judge, jury...and executioner."

He saw them all look nervously about as he said that last part. Peter wasn't being totally truthful though, but he doubted there would be any human rights lawyers in the gang, he just needed to scare them enough.

Now he had their full attention.

"Did you know that Martial Law has been called in Dorset? And that as a *senior* army officer, I can sentence people for crimes as I see fit and that what you've been doing here tonight, on this bridge is punishable by death?"

"What? No!" One of the gang members shouted out as it finally began to sink into them how serious things were. His voice became high pitched as he urged. "We didn't mean any harm to no-one; we've only been taking from people who had plenty. No-ones been hurt, I swear! We only scared them a little."

Ignoring his pleas, Peter carried on, his voice slow and steady, as if educating a child. Knowing some of what he was saying was true, some of it not, so he just wanted the warning to sink in.

"I'm legally allowed to hang your dead bodies from this bridge by your neck as a warning to others about profiteering and looting. Should I do that? Should I make an example of you all?"

"Look, please, PLEASE! we get it, you won't see us again!" another shouted out, others began to plead, to remonstrate and make their case.

"It wasn't my idea, I never wanted to be part of this."

"Shut up Bobby!"

Peter said nothing, letting them all argue amongst one another, apportioning the blame, creating division amongst them as their final shreds of defiance melted away. They went silent as the lead truck pulled up next to them, the passenger window down and the Sergeant yelling across, a concerned look on his face.

"Sir, is everything okay?"

Without looking up and still looking at the gang Peter replied.

"Everything's fine Sergeant, make your way across the bridge if you please."

The truck rumbled across followed by the next, as the convoy slowly ambled past them.

"You really are going to kill us, just over this?" the leader replied dejectedly, the defeat and despair clear to hear in his voice as the realisation kicked in about what was about to happen.

Peter kept the pistol at his head, staring intently down at him, prolonging the silence, using it as if a weapon. He could see the nerves playing on the leader, his chest rising heavily as he sucked in great lungs full of oxygen, his fears playing out in his mind.

Finally, Peter asked.

"Now, I'll ask you one more time, no playing around, no jokes. Where did you get these weapons from?"

The leader swallowed nervously; his voice softer than before.

"We came across a police car on its roof about four miles from here, it was all shot up and shit."

"What about the police officers? Did you kill them?" Peter asked suspiciously, his eyes narrowing.

"No! No! No!" the leader pleaded, his eyes opening wide. "They weren't there I swear it, just a load of blood all over the floor. We found the guns lying in the car."

Peter stood silently thinking it through, as the man added.

"We're not killers, honest! Yes, we've fucked people over, but we're just trying to make some money is all. Please..."

Peter looked at the others, seeing them all looking at the floor, all trace of their anger and arrogance gone. Even the skinny one was quiet, Peter having broken any trace of defiance.

Making his decision he stood back, lowering the pistol.

"Right, all of you...STRIP!"

The gang all exchanged looks of confusion, the leader stammering.

"What?"

Peter continued, his voice louder than before.

"I said strip! Take off all your clothes, underwear and socks too. I want you all stood in front of me as fresh as the day you were born!"

Some of them began stripping away their clothes, others seemed to linger, muttering curses as if expecting Peter to stop them at any moment, as if it were some sort of joke. Seeing them dithering Peter waved the pistol at them again.

"Come on! We don't have all bloody night! Get those clothes off or would you rather we go back to the plan to shoot you?"

It took them a minute or two before finally they were all stood naked, shivering in the night air. Something about seeing them naked was disarming, as if they were no longer a threat. Peter had to hide a smile at two of them, it was a cold night, but not that cold.

As if sensing his thoughts, they embarrassedly covered their manhood with their hands, trying to salvage some dignity. He paused, letting the awkwardness of the moment drag on, remembering all the misery they'd inflicted on others.

"Right move over there." he demanded, pointing over with the pistol where he wanted them to move to. The gang members looked angrily at him as a crowd now began to advance onto the bridge, following the military convoy. Wolf whistles and cat calls were being shouted at them.

With Alan still covering them, Peter turned and began to fling all their clothes, shoes and hand weapons over the bridge into the fast-flowing river below. He watched, satisfied to see it all disappear into the depths or float away. He was finishing just as the Range Rover pulled up, the amused glances from the occupants clear to see. Patch called out from the driver's seat humorously.

"I count only ten of them Boss, you'll need twelve if you're thinking of doing a calendar."

Peter ignored the remark, the crowd was already closing in and he didn't have much time. Already the gang were looking over nervously, something about being naked and unarmed added to their feeling of helplessness, which is exactly what Peter intended. Now instead of causing trouble, they'd be thinking of just getting away and finding clothes, to hide their embarrassment.

"Right, I'll keep this brief, if you go that way, through the crowd of angry people that you've spent all night robbing, and *if* you manage to make it through them, then you'll encounter the enemy. Perhaps they'll welcome people like you with open arms, perhaps they won't.

They all looked over to where Peter was pointing, the crowd of people and cars were now waiting behind the 4x4 to come onto the bridge, already their stash of valuables were being plundered, with people taking back what was rightfully theirs and what was rightfully not.

Peter pointed towards the trucks.

"But, if you go this way, the direction we're going, then you'd better improve your attitudes gentlemen, because that's the way I'm going. These soldiers you tried to stop earlier are fighting for our country. Think about that. By pulling stunts like this, you're helping the enemy. Is that what you want? Now gentlemen, I bid you all a fond farewell and hope you enjoy your walk under the stars as nature intended."

187

Leaving them standing there shivering, he turned with a flourish and jumped into the 4x4, Alan finally breaking into a grin, as he lowered his weapon, picking up the shotgun still lying by his feet and climbing into the 4x4. As he closed the door, he couldn't resist a little taunt, leaning out the window, winking suggestively and waggling his little finger at them all, the gesture not lost on them.

"Bastard!" one of them shouted angrily in response, flicking him the finger as the 4x4 shot off after the convoy, the occupants laughing loudly.

In the 4x4, the tension of the past ten minutes finally dissipated as everyone began to laugh, eventually it was Alan who broke the laughter.

"Boss, what the hell was all that about with the Apache's?"

Peter smiled, turning to look at him and pointing to David, the MGL still sat on his lap. David had also been trained in its use.

"Simple, I had David follow us down watching from the riverbank, he was to shoot at the van with the MGL after I gave him the signal. I wanted to check the van was empty, and it was far enough away not to do us any damage."

"Ahh okay," Alan replied thoughtfully, then adding. "And the signal was you pointing over to it, which was why you made the pantomime with the fake gunships?"

"Exactly. I had to bank on the fact that none of those idiots knew what calling in an airstrike would entail, hence the radio play. If they thought they were all lined up ready to be shot, it would give us the advantage. People always fear the unknown, more than they fear what's in front of them."

Alan nodded thoughtfully, then thinking of something else he added, "but what if the van did have people sat in it? Or that gang had opened fire on us before you got the chance to play it out. What then?"

Peter was thinking about how best to reply when Patch beat him to it, looking at him through the rear-view mirror and adding jovially.

"That's easy Alan, that's the reason why the Boss took you with him, and not me?"

"Really? Why's that Patch?" he enquired suspiciously, "because I'm more of a fighter in tight spots, or perhaps it's because I'm calmer and more dependable under pressure than you?"

Patch laughed, shaking his head keeping his focus on the road.

"No mate, nothing so grand, I'm afraid, it's because you're expendable."

Everyone chuckled, Alan flicking him the middle finger in the window. Peter was going to keep quiet, but something about how the night had been so far made him add,

"Patch that's not fair, and I'd never call Alan expendable."

Patch glanced sideways at him, unsure of where Peter was going next with this as Alan looked on admirably at him, smiling at the compliment. The smile dying on his face as Peter added beaming,

"Replaceable perhaps, but never expendable."

Alan sat back smirking, shaking his head in mock disgust as they all broke into laughter again. It had been a long night and as the slivers of dawn began to appear, Peter couldn't help but wonder, what sort of day would this turn out to be..?

12

Salt In Their Blood

Portland Harbour

The sentry took another long hard drag of the cigarette, inhaling deeply, as the smoke filled his lungs, closing his eyes for the briefest of moments before exhaling a long-drawn-out breath, watching as the smoke was carried away into the night sky. Here at least was peace, as he looked down into the inky blackness of the sea. He'd walked to the end of the sea wall, protruding about a mile outside of the port. A huge ring of steel and concrete that created an outer harbour, which had been designed and built during the second world war to protect the allied shipping using the port, it still stood now after all this time, a testament to its engineers and builders. Now though, instead of protecting the defenders, it was being used by the invaders, as behind its thick fortified walls sat the huge flotilla of cargo ships, all rolling gently in the swell at anchor, waiting to unload into the busy Portland dockyard. There were only two entrances through these walls, and both were now being blocked and guarded by two huge tugboats, each one attached to a floating boom and steel net that had sunk all the way to the sea floor. Nothing was going to be coming into the harbour, either above or below the water. The sentry's gaze looked over the bay, thankful to have been one of the first of the soldiers off his ship, even if it had meant his unit were now pulling port guard. He'd rather be out here in the fresh air on sentry duty, than spend one more second sat on one of those lumbering beasts. Even now he still found the need to fight the urge to throw up. Shuddering at the thought and, with the cool breeze that had picked up, he turned his collar up on his tunic to protect against the cold. Even in the summer, the night air of this country seemed chill, he mused. Behind him the shouts and noises of the port were carried away into the night, as the crews worked frantically to get the ships unloaded. He adjusted his rifle on his shoulder, his arm going numb as the sling bit into it uncomfortably. Fucking rifle, he thought angrily, as he looked out to sea as the moon hung in the night sky. The uncomfortable feeling in his arm was quickly forgotten as he saw how beautiful it all looked, as the moon's reflection bounced back at him off the surface of the sea. For the briefest of moments, he forgot all about where he was and what he was there to do, and just marvelled at the beauty of it all. "Peaceful." he muttered, when suddenly behind him he heard a shout, disturbing his thoughts. He turned to see the distant figure of his Sergeant shouting for him. He looked at his watch, it was nearly midnight, he was late for the shift change.

Shit, he thought, he'd get into trouble now, he wasn't even supposed to be out here, and his Sergeant wasn't the sort of person you left waiting.

He took one long last drag of the cigarette and threw it over the sea wall, watching it disappear into the sea.

"All quiet here," he said to himself smirking, "just me, the moon and the empty sea," before setting off at a jog, his rifle clumsily bashing into his back as the Sergeant's shouts became louder.

Below the sea wall, where the sentry had been looking, hidden in ten metres of water, four dark figures, members of the UK's elite Special Boat Squadron slid silently along in the depths, unaware of the sentry and hidden from his view in the inky blackness.

Each diver was dressed identically, wearing a jet-black wetsuit, rebreather system, full face helmet, each being propelled along by a Deep Submergence Vehicle, or DSV, holding onto the grab handles, similar in design to a motorbikes handlebars. The equipment they carried was state of the art, some of it classified. The rebreather system strapped to their chest and backs, was smaller than any you'd find in the civilian market, lightweight and using a refiltration system, it allowed the divers to re-use the carbon dioxide being emitted from their lungs, which also meant eliminating any exhaust bubbles so as not to give away their position to anyone on the surface, not that it mattered much in the dark. Each diver's head was encased in a full-face helmet, allowing their eyes and ears to be dry and allowing the men to talk under water if needed. The helmets comprised of a two-way underwater radio of limited range and a Heads-Up Display, or HUD, linked to the dive combat computer attached to their right-hand wrists. The dive computer and HUDs display emitted a dull red glow, visible only to the divers, giving them a topographical map of the seabed floor and directions to where they were going. Not that they needed it, each man had dived in these waters for years, Portland being used extensively in peacetime for the SBS to train in. Even so, ever the professionals, they had still committed to memory the routes in and out, as well as the locations of the ERV or Emergency Rendezvous. The HUD's soft red display meant it would be harder to spot on the surface, and more importantly, if the divers had to remove the masks, it wouldn't interfere with their night vision. The DSV's they were being pulled along by were called Dolphins, small black streamlined minisubs, shaped like a torpedo and measuring five feet in length. Each diver was tethered to their DSV via a quick release harness and umbilical cable, allowing them to be pulled along comfortably without the need to hang on, keeping their arms free to use their equipment, but, if necessary, able to quickly cut free. A simple carbon fibre handlebar extended from the controls at the rear, with two twist grips. The controls on the left made the sub dive and climb, and the right, made the sub go backwards and forwards. To turn the sub, the divers would turn the handlebar, much the same as they would a road bike. There was a small bullet shaped screen to protect the divers when moving at higher speeds, pushing the water over the diver's head and body and away from them. The Dolphin had no gauges or displays, just one small display at the bottom left of the control area, showing the diver the vehicle battery level. The divers preferred instead to rely on their own HUD's and dive computers to give them their speed and heading. Easy to control and highly manoeuvrable, the Dolphin had been designed to sneak them in underwater but could also push them to speeds of up to forty knots if needed, thanks to its experimental motor. The motor used a process called super cavitation, to create tiny bubbles in front of the Dolphin, creating less water resistance and drag on the vehicle. At slower speeds the battery could last for over six hours and with the ability to take them to depths of well over two-hundred metres, it wasn't hard to see why the divers loved using the vehicle. On the front of the Dolphin sat a powerful pair of sensors, using lasers and quantum dots to paint an accurate picture of what was ahead of them, displaying what it saw on the helmets HUD system via the umbilical. If the seas were right, then the system could work out to well over one-hundred metres, however tonight, with being so close to the harbour wall, the visibility was poor, as the sea was dragging years of sediment from it, limiting their systems to only forty metres. Not that it mattered, being able to see forty metres in the dead of night underwater was still one hell of an advantage. For weapons, each diver carried a HK P11 pistol on their right leg, in a specially made holster, a funny looking pistol that could fire 7.62mm darts electrically underwater. The pistol carried five darts and was designed for underwater silent close kills, deadly to any diver out to fifteen metres underwater and could even be fired above water, out to thirty metres and quietly, with no noise. Its only downside was that it couldn't be reloaded, once the firer had fired all five barrels, that was it, ammunition expended. Strapped to each of their left legs was a canvas bag, containing a MILA magnetic limpet mine and timer, and attached to the dolphin's frame was a waterproof bag, into which the frogmen had placed their silenced HKmp5 sub machine guns and spare magazines. However armed they were though, this mission was about stealth and although they had the weapons, if things went to plan, they shouldn't be needing them.

The lead figure, Sergeant Fletcher or 'Fletch' as his mates called him, checked the data being shown on his HUD with what he had committed to memory. He knew never to rely solely on the tech.

The insertion plan had called for them to stay close to the wall, helping to mask their sonar signatures, just in case the Russians were using sonar. They continued forwards, keeping the speeds of the dolphins below three knots, slow but quiet. At these speeds the motors had been designed to be barely audible. He knew that they had the tide going in with them, it was running in at two knots and helping to push them along, helping them to conserve battery power. This had all been part of the planning, the tide would be changing direction in three hours, more than enough time for them to conduct their mission and be swept back out with the outgoing tide towards their ride home. Five miles to their south, in deeper waters, sat the Astute class submarine, HMS Archer waiting to pick them up.

After five minutes of gliding along, his HUD began to make out the darkened silhouette of the tugboats hull looming out of the darkness above them, the red tinge of his night vision display making it easier to spot than with the naked eye. He continued under it, following the shape of the floating boom, until he came upon the steel net, blocking the harbour. Designed to stop enemy submarines from making it through, the steel weaved net would be formidable. Cutting through it would be difficult and some of the nets could be fitted with sensors, alerting the tugboat crew that something or someone was touching it. Fletch didn't yet know if this net was fitted with such a feature, he'd have to have a closer look. If it was, it would be a problem, but not a problem they couldn't fix. He'd spent years practising for just such a mission and was an expert in overcoming these obstacles.

Checking behind him to make sure the three others were still with him, he used hand signals to indicate they were going deeper. They had the radios, but the noise could be carried underwater and they were only to be used in an emergency. They would stay silent as long as they could. Fletch began to increase his depth, closely watching that he didn't stray too close to the net, having to reverse the Dolphin against the tide, as now it began to work against him, pushing him towards the netting. The other team members all followed closely behind as they began sinking deeper, carefully watching the depth gauges as they sank below fifteen metres. Not much longer and they'd start to see the seabed, he thought, as already its picture was displaying in his HUD.

Suddenly the netting seemed to stop and disappear above them. He stopped descending and checked his depth gauge, it read 15.5 metres. The seabed was still another four metres below them and out of sight to the naked eye. He turned to look at the others, who, in the dim lights of his display could see his face through the helmet. They could see him smiling, all of them knew what had happened. The Russian tugboat crew had been lazy.

The net was designed to reach to the sea floor, leaving no room to squeeze under, even for a diver, however as the tide would cause the sea level to rise and fall, the boom and its netting would need to be adjusted to make sure the net would continue to reach the seabed. For whatever reason, the crew of the tugboat had not monitored the nets depth and now they had a net paid out to fifteen metres in seas of nearly nineteen metres. Until the tide dropped again, which he knew would be two hours from now, the gap would stay open, allowing Fletch and his team easy entry to the ships beyond. He looked around him at the team, tapping his head shoulder and thigh, the indication for a final equipment check. Each diver now began the series of checks that they always carried out before going into a mission. Fletch looked over his gear, checking his oxygen levels were good, there were no kinks or damage to his air hoses, the battery levels for the equipment were all good, his pistol was still holstered and hadn't fallen out and finally the limpet mine was still securely in the bag and strapped to his leg. Once finished, he looked up at the team, giving the okay sign with thumb and forefinger, waiting patiently while they completed their own checks. As soon as the last man had finished, all four divers were giving the okay sign. Fletch nodded in acknowledgement, before giving them the thumbs up sign, then tapping his watch, holding up one finger and pointing to the seabed. They all knew what this meant. Now they were on the clock, the team would now split into two diver teams, each diving pair having a specific target, and in one hour, they'd meet back here at the net, which would now be the final ERV. If anything went wrong, this was where everyone would meet back at.

Fletch waved off the first pair, watching them quickly disappear into the darkness, then turning to his partner and nodding, he pressed the thumb throttle on his controls as both divers smoothly accelerated away to carry out their own mission.

Two hours later and fletch was still waiting back at the ERV, looking at his watch. The other team were now thirty minutes overdue. Where the hell where they, he fumed. The tide had turned and was now beginning to accelerate out of the harbour at about four knots, forcing both of them to keep using the precious battery power of the Dolphins, just to stay in position. He checked the battery gauge, he still had over fifty-six percent of battery, but that wasn't what concerned him, he'd been watching the steel net over the past hour slowly sink lower and lower, as the tide fell, until now it was hanging no more than one metre from the seabed. Another twenty minutes and the second team would be trapped in the harbour. He checked his watch again, running the times through his head. The timers for the mines were set to go off in fifty minutes. when they did, the Russians would know they were there. And they needed at least thirty minutes of travel time to make the rendezvous with the mother ship, so unless they left in the next thirty minutes, they'd miss the ride home. And, if the net did come down, it would take them the best part of forty minutes to cut through, too late to escape the patrols and even if they did make it out, they'd miss the rendezvous as the sub wouldn't wait for them. He quickly looked over to his partner, tapping his helmet where his ear was. He wanted to use the radio. It was risky, but he had no choice, he didn't want to leave them behind.

After the silence it felt strange to be talking again as Bug's voice came through his headset quietly and distorted, the sound being masked by the water.

"What you thinking Fletch?"

"I'm thinking they've got a problem; I'm going back in to see if I can find them. You stay here in case they come back."

"They're big boys Fletch, leave them to it."

"I can't."

"We don't have the time Fletch, shops closing in about twenty minutes." he saw Bug pointing over to the net.

Fletch looked down, quickly keying in a twenty-minute timer into his watch and setting it running before replying, "Then it looks like I'd better move my arse."

Leaving him there, Fletch powered up the Dolphin, choosing speed over stealth as he throttled up to ten knots, heading out on the teams last known bearing. He knew what the other team's target was, he'd head there and see what he could see, but even so the chances of finding them would be slim. He keyed the underwater radio, knowing the range would be limited, but then so was their time.

"Dolphin Two, Dolphin One, check."

He checked his depth, watching as the seabed began to slowly rise to meet him, adjusting his depth so he didn't plough into it. His HUD was giving him a decent view ahead of him, but even so at ten knots it seemed strange to see things flashing past out of the darkness after crawling along at three knots. Narrowly avoiding hitting a large fish, he slowed the Dolphin as now he began to now pick out the dark shape of a hull looming ahead, checking his hand-held computer he could see he was still 3/4 of a mile out from the dock. This was one of the ships at anchor, still waiting to unload. He slowed down and glided beneath it, marvelling at the size of the hull as he travelled its length. As he headed towards the bow, he was careful to keep away from the huge anchor chain as it disappeared into the darkness. He wanted to speed up, but caution stayed his hand, even though it was pitch black up top, he couldn't risk a crewman on deck looking down and seeing the disturbance in the water as he shot through. After a few moments he was clear of the dark mass of the hull, and throttled up, increasing his speed now to fifteen knots, glancing at his watch and conscious of the time. He had about seventeen minutes of time left. Where the fuck were they, he thought angrily. He knew he'd never get to the docks in time travelling at fifteen knots, so he cranked the power up, the Dolphin shot forward, easily accelerating up to twenty-five knots, at this speed his HUD was having to work overtime to keep the picture clear, the sensors and computers frantically trying to update what the display could show. He felt the pull on his body as the water flowed quickly around him. The harness tightening around him as the small craft shot forward. His heart skipped a beat when the picture in his helmet froze, for a few seconds he was blind as the software recalibrated, he was about to throttle back when thankfully the display updated, and he quickly resumed his dash.

It took him seven minutes to cover the distance, throttling back as he saw the lights of the dockyards above him. He had to be careful, with the light pollution spilling above him helping to illuminate the water, and the water being as clear as it was, he could be spotted. Perhaps that's what had caught the other team, he thought. Not wanting to get any closer he quickly tried the radio again, trying to remember back to the kit brief, how far underwater could the radio transmit, he asked himself.

"Dolphin Two, Dolphin One, check"

Suddenly the voice of Grub came faintly over the earpiece, the sound tinny as the sound struggled underwater.

"Dolphin Two, check ok, we need a little help over here."

Fletch breathed a sigh of relief, thankful to be talking to them, before asking.

"Roger, send location."

There was a pause of a few moments, before Grub came back on, "We're towards the stern of Target Two, under the pier. And we're not alone."

Fletch narrowed his eyes, before looking at his watch. He had less than seven minutes remaining, leaving him no time to go back and get Bug to help. Fuck it, he thought, looks like I'm the cavalry.

"Okay Dolphin Two, what have you got there?"

"Three Tangos, all armed, working near the rudder. Looks like they're guarding a diver."

"Are they looking for you? Are they aware?"

"Negative, they're just on guard, but we can't break free whilst they're watching, we'll be compromised."

He quickly turned the Dolphin around, diving as deep as he could, and running along the seabed, amazed at the amount of light that still spilled down from above. He was counting on everyone topside being blinded by the lights and not able to make out the shape of him as he tried to rescue his troops. After a few moments he could see the shape of target two's hull, it was huge, sitting only six metres above the sea floor. How the hell had it managed to get into the docks on a low tide, he thought. He slowly inched towards the stern, his eyes being drawn to a faint glow and bright flash of light through the darkness. He stopped thirty metres short, keeping himself in the darkest part of the water, allowing his forward sensor to paint the picture ahead. It looked like one of the divers was working underwater, using a welding torch to cut away something wrapped around the huge rudder. He was wearing a large and bulky dive suit, that had thick cables disappearing topside, and the work area was illuminated by three powerful arc lights that cut through the darkness, bathing everything in a milky white glow. Behind the diver, about ten metres away floated three navy divers, all looking outwards into the light. The suits they wore looked cumbersome and immense when compared to the gear that Fletch's team wore, but each diver was carrying a weapon, Fletch couldn't make out the details, but he guessed it was the Russian APS, an underwater assault rifle. It fired steel bolts, carried thirty in the magazine and was deadly out to twenty metres. Unlike his pistol it could also be reloaded and that put him at a disadvantage. He could just make out the shapes of Grub and Jonesy, the two other team members, hiding under the dock's overhanging concrete structure behind a large pillar. He immediately saw the problem they faced, the guards were in direct line of sight to them and perfectly placed, with the lights illuminating the work area, so that if they tried to break for cover they'd be seen and shot before going less than ten metres. Plus, they'd alert the dock, and there was still time for the mines to be discovered. Fletch checked his watch, they had five minutes remaining. Looking upwards he knew that with the powerful underwater lights creating a pool of light, anything they did could be seen from above. Whatever he was going to do, He'd have to be quick.

He tried to shield his eyes from the glare as the welder began to ignite the torch again, even at this range it was blinding him. He realised that where the divers were positioned and where they were looking, the welder must be seriously screwing with their own night vision, maybe even blinding them. Knowing time was against him he acted quickly.

"Dolphin Two, be ready to move in thirty seconds."

"Roger."

He gunned the throttle, turning away from the welder and shooting out at an angle of ninety degrees from the guards, he was still too far away for them to see him. He began to silently countdown from ten in his head, on the count of one he abruptly pulled the Dolphin around, turning 180 degrees and heading on a course taking him between the welder whose back was now to him and the enemy divers. He accelerated the dolphin up to twenty knots, the distance closing rapidly. He couldn't be too quick, he needed just enough momentum for the plan to work. The light began to make the water look milky as he passed through it. Just as he thought, the enemy divers' eyes were whited out, they should have seen him by now, but couldn't and wouldn't see him approach, until it was too late. He was nearly upon them, then in one swift action he cut the power to the Dolphin, releasing the quick release harness and pushing off the vehicle in one smooth action. He relaxed his body, letting the momentum take him up and away as he drifted quickly up and over the top of the divers, pulling his pistol out from holster. The Dolphin continued drifting towards them, still carrying a lot of the speed, as the divers began to finally see and react to it as it came out of the darkness, the diversion that Fletch had planned it to be. The closest diver began to point his weapon at the vehicle, his movements slow and laborious, as above him Fletch already had the pistol pointing towards his head. He fired once, the gun making no noise as the water seemed to part, as the projectile jetted out towards the diver. The dart smashed though the top of his head, bubbles of crimson pouring out of the wound as his body began to spasm, dropping the rifle as his arms and legs began to shake uncontrollably. Ignoring the macabre dance, Fletch shifted his gaze to the second target. The second diver was still looking over at the Dolphin as Fletch drifted towards him, firing as he approached. The first round hit his arm, the shot was poor and Fletch hadn't compensated for his drifting motion, as he fired again, this time hitting the diver's chest, who folded up in slow motion, but still wasn't dead. Fletch could see him struggling to aim his weapon towards him, the pain etched on his face. Fletch fired a third time, this time hitting the face plate. It exploded with a crack as an explosion of bubbles burst out, alerting the third diver. Fletch turned to aim, pleased to see the Russian diver was struggling to bring his weapon to bear, the huge magazine of the weapon making it slow and clumsy to turn in the water. Fletch fired his last round, cursing, as he saw the round jet harmlessly past the man's shoulder, he'd fired his five rounds, now his pistol was empty. Dropping the pistol, he began to power stroke towards the diver, pulling out his dive knife and desperately trying to close the distance. It was all he could do; his rifle was still stowed away in the Dolphin. Fletch was nearly on him, kicking and pulling himself through the water, as hard as his legs and arms would allow him, but the enemy diver was faster, his rifle had only centimetres to go before he could fire, Fletch could see the man grinning through the mask, he was going to enjoy this.

Two dark shapes loomed up behind the diver, too late he realised the danger he was in, Fletch saw his eyes go wide in shock as a hand reached out from behind him carrying a knife. The knife was drawn across his regulators air pipe, cutting it in two, the bubbles pouring out, as Fletch came at him from the front, one hand grabbing the diver's weapon, the other grasping his shoulders, as he watched the panic on the diver's face as cold water began to pour into his breathing system. His arms flailed and his legs kicked out, trying to surface, but behind him the strong arms of Grub and Jonesy held him down as Fletch watched on as the man began to drown. After a few seconds he'd seen enough, drowning was never a nice way to go and Fletch wasn't the sort to relish what he'd done. He stabbed his knife into the man's heart, killing him instantly and ending his suffering.

All three divers released their hold on the body, watching as it slowly drifted away from them. Jonesy and Grub both turned to look at the welder, he still had his back to them, working away and oblivious to the butchery that had gone on behind him. Grub indicated with his knife, nodding towards the man, but Fletch shook his head, instead indicating for silence with his finger to his lips. Sheathing his own knife and still carrying the APS, he power stroked over to where the Dolphin lay, floating upside down as the current began to pull at it. He turned it over, checking it wasn't damaged, before quickly attaching the harness and umbilical again, then holding onto the controls, he checked his watch, cursing. They were almost out of time. Stowing the APS and keying his radio, he quickly shot out.

"Right, we're out of time, back to the ERV, grab a body and drag it out with you."

"What about Mr Lucky here, shouldn't we take care of him?" Jonesy replied, looking over at the welder, oblivious to the danger."

"Leave him, let him report the men missing. It doesn't matter anyway, the timers all go off in thirty minutes. Now, fucking move!"

Fletch rode up to the first body of the diver, the one he'd shot in the head, grabbing his leg he quickly attached it to the cargo strap of the Dolphin, looking behind him to check the others were doing the same. Once they all had their grisly cargo attached, they hit the throttles, the Dolphins more sluggish to respond as they carried the extra weight and drag. He looked at his watch, they had less than a minute to go before the netting was down. Angrily he looked at the speed, he was barely doing fifteen knots. After a few moments the water got deeper and darker as the light from the docks began to recede as they extended the distance. He dived down, noticing the diver's body was now trying to float back away, pulling them back up.

"Right, that's far enough, let's ditch the bodies."

All three men pulled their dive knives and began to slash and hack at the air hoses and compensators of the divers, the air escaping in huge bubbles. After a few seconds Fletch felt the body get heavier, as the diver's gear began to lose buoyancy. He pushed it away, watching with satisfaction as it began to sink towards the sea floor.

"Sorry chum, better you than me," he remarked drily as he watched the others do the same. As the last body disappeared, he looked back, the others all held their thumbs up, indicating they were good to go. With the emergency over, it was back to radio silence and hand signals again. He nodded then pressed down hard on the thumb throttle, the Dolphin, now lighter again accelerated away, quickly climbing up to thirty knots, then forty. His HUD began to flicker again and struggle to keep up with the speed, but Fletch didn't care, not now, he'd dived these waters before, he knew there was nothing now between him and the entrance, except the net, and that was likely to be on the sea bed by now. They'd have to cut through it, he was sure of it, and that would take time. He only hoped that the sub would wait for them. If it didn't then they'd all have a bloody long swim. He checked the battery level of the Dragon, twenty-six percent, damn this speed was draining it, he thought.

Four minutes later and he began to slow down, diving to the sea floor as the tug's hull appeared overhead against the darkness. The others closed up next to him as they stopped near the net, the heavy steel lattice structure looming large in front of them. It seemed bigger this time, Fletch thought to himself, as disappointingly he could see the net was now resting on the sea bed.

He was about to get the cutting tools out when he sighted Bug, drifting through on the other side, frantically waving to get his attention. Looking over he could see the diver pointing over to the right-hand edge of the netting.

Fletch manoeuvred the Dragon over to where Bug was pointing. His face broke into a grin as he looked down under the netting. With the seafloor being mostly sand, Bug had somehow managed to dig a trench large enough for them to slide under. It would be a squeeze, but it was damn quicker than cutting the net.

Ten minutes of heavy breathing later and all four men and their Dolphins were the right side of the netting. Fletch watched as Bug drew up near him, his eyes looking admiringly at the APS before giving a thumbs up.

Fletch smiled back, patting the operator on the back and pointing towards the trench, who merely shrugged his shoulders in response. The message was clear, all in a day's work.

The rest of the team drew near, and they all began to religiously check their gear again, making sure nothing was left behind in the mad dash for the net. Fletch had ditched his pistol, but given what had happened, he felt the loss was justified, besides, he thought to himself, I've got an APS now, that will look good in the Squadron bar. Finally satisfied that everything was accounted for, the final thing was for Fletch to confirm if the second team had been successful. He looked over to Grub, reaching into his dive bag and producing the two arming pins from the limpet mines, proof that they were attached and armed. He saw Grub smile behind the mask as he also pulled two pins from his own dive bag and handed them to him, giving him four. That meant all four mines were attached and armed, now all they had to do was wait and see if they detonated. He looked at his watch, the mines were set to go off in twenty-six minutes, now it all rested on the other two teams currently raiding Poole Harbour. He could only hope they'd also had a successful night of it and were already on their way home. Nodding his head triumphantly, he patted Grub on the shoulder, before pointing out to deeper water. It was time to go home.

Taking his lead, one by one, they slowly slipped away into the darkness, their mission completed. And just like that...they were gone.

13

World On Fire

Portland Harbour

The Captain looked up, irritated at the intrusion of the Sergeant disturbing him as he stood in the doorway. Rubbing the sleep from his eyes he sat up on the side of the bed, reaching over and pulling his boots off the floor, he began to put them on, tying them up quickly as he waited for the man to report.

"Well, what is it?" he demanded angrily.

The Sergeant stood to attention, "Sir, we've got men missing from the docks."

"What do you mean missing?" he replied testily, looking at his watch. It was 02:55, he'd only managed to get an hour of sleep. The soldiers were probably in town drinking again, not missing, he thought moodily. That's where I should be, not babysitting these bloody docks. He stood up quickly, picking up his smock and pistol belt from the back of the chair, his brain still shaking off the tiredness. So much for an easy guard duty, he thought, as he looked back at the figure in the doorway.

"Sergeant!" he snapped, the man looking at him, "I said what do you mean by missing?"

"Divers Sir, we've got three divers missing."

"Divers?" he exclaimed confused. "What were they doing in the water?"

"I don't know Sir; I was just told to come and wake the duty officer as soon as I could."

Shaking his head in frustration he hurriedly buttoned up the smock, throwing his pistol belt over his shoulder, he could dress himself as he walked. Grabbing his peaked cap from behind the door, he signalled for the Sergeant to lead the way. No-one ever told him anything, he thought moodily, as he walked out the guard building and into the darkness of the night sky.

203

Both quickly crossed the harbour towards the far dock, where one of the largest of their container ships, the MV Rasputin was being unloaded. Lined up in neat rows under the glare of the dock's giant arc lights, were a company's worth of BMP3's and two companies of T-80 tanks. Already they were halfway through unloading the ship, hoping to have the rest of the equipment off before morning, then the crews could come ashore and be re-united with their vehicles. Until then, the vehicles remained, cold and unmoving.

They shielded their eyes from the powerful glare of an arc welder, the sparks bouncing across the concrete floor, as they walked across the pier and headed towards the stern of the ship. Twice they had to avoid being squashed, as armoured vehicles were lowered to the dock side from above, with no care taken as to those below. The flurry of activity increased as they neared the stern. Dock workers brought over from Russia on the ships were operating the heavy dockside cranes, using specially adapted sleds to lift the tanks out of the hold of the cavernous ship, but it was taking far too long to accomplish. Originally the ships had been fitted with giant ramps, which could lower along the side of the ship and drive off the vehicles, like a car ferry. Unfortunately, the Russian designers had failed to consider the rise and fall of the spring tides and the sheer size of their ships. Now, on anything other than the lowest of tides, the ramps would come to a stop some ten metres above the dock. The weight of the heavy vehicles on the ramp would cause it to fail, dropping the vehicles to the floor. Already three smashed hulls of T-80 tanks sat at the far end of the dock, their only use now to be cannibalised for spare parts.

As they arrived at the stern, the Sergeant lead the Captain over to where a group of dock workers and soldiers stood clustered at the water's edge, looking down and murmuring excitedly. On a crate, with a blanket wrapped around him sat a diver, smoking a cigarette and shaking, his face white, but the Captain couldn't be sure if it was from shock or from the cold water. A Lieutenant, dressed in the uniform of the Russian Navy stood over the diver, quickly writing down what the man was saying. He looked up as the Captain approached, quickly saluting as the Captain demanded,

"Well, what is it? Why have you woken me? The Sergeant informs me we have men missing, *divers* missing? Care to explain?"

The Lieutenant pointed to the giant ship, "Sir, the Rasputin's rudder was damaged earlier this evening when she was brought into the dock. We need it repaired to be able to get her out again after unloading." The Captain looked over at the ship towering above them, then back at the diver as the young Lieutenant continued, "This man was part of my team that we sent down to fix the rudder, along with a guard detail of three of our Spetznaz divers. His shift finished twenty minutes ago, he resurfaced, but they didn't."

"Why was I not informed of this before you put them in the water?" the Captain demanded; his eyes boring into the young officer.

The Lieutenants eyes darted about nervously as he replied, "I'm sorry Sir, but this was a naval matter, not an army matter, onboard a ship belonging to the navy."

"I'm the duty officer in charge of the base's security, Lieutenant. That covers anything above and *below* the water, it's not a question of navy or army, this is a *military* matter."

He ignored the stares of the Lieutenant as he turned and looked at the diver who was taking a long pull on a hip flask, trying to coax some warmth into his body. The Captain grabbed the hip flask from him, holding it aloft as the man looked on, eyes wide and trembling.

"What did you see? Tell me in your own words."

He shrugged his shoulders, his eyes following the hip flask. "There's not much to say, I was working on the rudder and occasionally I'd look back and see them. One minute they were all there, the next, they'd vanished."

"And you didn't think that was strange?" the Captain demanded his eyes narrowing, "That they all just vanished into thin air?"

The man raised his arms in mock surrender, his voice louder, "I'm not in the navy, I didn't know what they were doing, as far as I was concerned, they could have swum away on a patrol or something."

"So, you just stayed down there and continued working?"

"What was I supposed to do? If I had come up complaining the guards were missing, I'd have been the laughing stock of the dock. I never asked for them to go down with me, I had a job to do, to fix the rudder, so I stayed. Besides, I thought the guards were going to surface with me. It was only after I'd surfaced that we noticed they were missing."

The diver held out his hand for the hip flask, ignoring him, the Captain walked over to the water's edge, under the giant stern of the ship, looking down into the dark waters, trying to work out what had happened. Next to him the group of dock workers and soldiers were all muttering, trying to make sense of it themselves. Two of the dock workers began muttering about an old village tale of sea monsters with salt for blood, that preyed on unwary sailors with no respect of the sea, whilst one soldier was heard animatedly suggesting it could be sharks. The Captain shot him a disapproving look. Already the rumour mill was starting. There were no sharks or sea monsters in these waters, he thought angrily, besides, the divers had all been Spetsnaz and fully armed. No, this wasn't anything that nature or the occult had sent.

He looked over to the far side of the dock, where the other ship was also being unloaded, and without turning he asked.

"Lieutenant, what's the name of that ship?"

"That's the Nikita Sir."

"And how long has she been in dock?"

"She arrived four hours ago, they've had some problems with the cranes, it's delayed unloading her."

He turned back to the diver, "How long ago was it that you last saw your guards?"

The diver closed his eyes to think. "I was over halfway through my shift, so I'd say about forty minutes ago."

He turned back to the Lieutenant, "And you say this man came out of the water thirty minutes ago?"

"Yes Sir, we've searched all around the docks hoping to see them surface elsewhere, but as soon as I realised that they were missing I sent the Sergeant to come get you."

"And their orders were to stay with the diver, not go on any other taskings around the dock?"

"No Sir," The officer replied, his face stern. "I gave them the orders myself; I was very specific."

The Captain looked over to the diver, his eyes searching for something, anything.

"How much time can they spend in the water?" he shot back. Seeing the Lieutenant look confused he quickly added, "How much *air* would they have?"

The Lieutenant looked at his watch as he answered, "With their reserves, they should have enough air for another ten minutes."

He quickly looked up at the ship again and then back out into the darkness, to where the sea wall stood. Thinking it through, shaking his head he turned to the Lieutenant, his arm shooting out.

"I want new divers suited up and in the water immediately! Have them check every inch of hull of the Rasputin and the Nikita."

"What about our Spetznaz divers?" the Lieutenant asked, a look of confusion on his face.

"The ship, and the docks are the priority Lieutenant, your men knew the risks when they went into the water."

The young officer looked like he was about to argue, then seeing the cold stare of the Captain staring back he kept quiet, standing straighter and enquiring, "What are they looking for on the ships?"

Throwing him a look of disdain at his stupidity, the Captain shot back, "You're Spetsnaz! Surely you should know! Have them look for anything out of the ordinary, anything that's attached to the hull that has no business being there. And do it quickly, we may not have much time."

The Lieutenant turned to walk away, when something made him stop. He looked back at the Captain, who could hear it too. The workers on the docks all stopped working as one, everyone hearing the noise. Somewhere below their feet they heard a soft rumbling sound, followed by a series of popping noises and then, suddenly, two huge geysers of water fountained up from alongside the ship, throwing huge columns of water hundreds of feet up into the air. The Captain and all those around him were drenched as the water rained down on them. Ignoring the shock of the cold water soaking him, he ran over to the far side of the dock, looking over at the ships side in the dark water which had begun to boil and froth. After a few moments, the water began to settle back down, the waves receding as the water began to calm again, a strange eerie calm descended over the dock. Peering over, he could see the water besides the ship was beginning to bubble and an oily mass was beginning to settle on the surface of the water. He looked across to the other dock, to where the Nikita was moored, as another two explosions sounded out, far quieter than he would have imagined, watching as another two fountains rained skywards. His mouth opened in surprise, quickly closing as he realised what was happening. He turned to the Lieutenant whose own face wore a mask of shock, snapping him from his malaise.

"Quickly man! Sound the alert! Get the tugs, get these ships out of here, clear the docks, we're under attack!"

"But... they're not ready yet, we need to finish unloading them." was all he could stammer. Unaware of what was happening. The Captain ran to him, grabbing him by the shoulders, and pointing to the frothing water, shaking him to action as he shouted back.

"Can't you see man? They're sinking! Now clear the docks before they sink here!"

The Lieutenant came alive as it finally dawned on him what was going on. He un-clipped the radio from his belt and began to speak rapidly into it as all around them the sirens and alarms began to blare out, alerting the guard force and shaking people into action. Over the next few minutes, the dock came alive as half-dressed soldiers ran out from buildings and formed up into groups, waiting for orders, but not knowing exactly what to do. The Captain looked over to where the tugs were moored, watching as the crews raced down the gangway, the tug lights coming on as they fought to start them up quickly. "Too slow," he muttered, "too damn slow!"

Someone on the bridge of the Rasputin had activated the ships alarm system, as a series of powerful long blasts began to sound, drowning out the noise of the docks alarm.

He found himself watching, transfixed, knowing he was powerless to stop it from happening, as slowly the giant ship began to settle deeper into the water and began to lean away from the dock, tilting over to port. Roused from their sleep by the ship's alarm, sailors and soldiers were appearing on deck, some with sleep filled faces, not sure what was happening, was this a drill, some must have thought. Within seconds they could feel the deck shifting beneath their feet, awakening immediately, sensing the danger they were in. Some began leaping from the superstructure into the water, others tried to leap across from the deck onto the dock, at the ever-expanding chasm. Some were lucky, others not, it was sickening to hear the thud and yells as people landed on the concrete. Some tried to roll with the fall, others fell in heaps, groaning as they landed, legs and arms breaking. The ships list increased quickly, surprising the Captain at how quickly everything was happening. He watched as the mooring ropes began to groan, getting ever tighter as the ship leaned further away from the dock. He jolted with shock as, with a crack like thunder, the heavy ten tonne bollards snapped as if made of matchwood, the ropes skittering away across the docks like angry snakes as they slammed into the people watching, dragging them screaming across the dock and into the water. Dock workers and military personnel, who at first were planted in surprise, now began to run away from the dock as they saw the danger. The ship's cranes that were still loaded with tanks, began to sway dangerously, as the ship tilted further, setting of a deadly pendulum motion that nothing could stop, each swing becoming further and faster from the ship, until the chains holding the vehicles to the sleds began to snap, hurling the forty tonne vehicles out, like medieval catapults.

A T-80 tank begin to swing dangerously close to the Captain, he was tempted to run, but he was now stuck at the far end of the dock. If he ran now, it would mean a gauntlet of death, trying to run the length of the ship. He decided to stay where he was, watching the tank and ready to leap clear if he had to. The tank swayed overhead, the steel wires beginning to fray and snap as they began to give under the stress. The tanks motion stopped and it swung back towards the ship, the final wires parting as the tank sailed through the air. People at the railings yelled in terror, as it came crashing into the superstructure and tearing through it, as if it were nothing more than paper, taking more people with it into the depths of the decks below.

He saw motion off to his left and turned to see one of the tugboats had now left its mooring and was heading at full speed towards the docks. He looked over to see the second ship, the Nikita, at the far end of the docks, was already tilted over at a 45-degree angle, towards the docks, its cargo raining down and smashing into the dockyard. It was already too late to tow it away. He watched, grimacing, as the tugboat Captain came in fast and careless towards the stern of the Rasputin, the boat hitting the people swimming in the water. The boat's Captain ignored the shouts of those in the water, as he focussed on the stern, which was now towering over his little vessel. On the bow of the tugboat, a crew member was shouting up to the people on the stern using a bull horn. At first it looked like he was telling them to jump onto the tug, then the Captain quickly realised, he was telling the soldiers to throw down the heavy ship's lines. Some of the men ignored him, choosing to run away towards the bow of the vessel as they now fought against the tilt of the deck. But some didn't and he watched, as, ignoring the danger, a group of twenty of them began to try to manhandle the heavy, greasy ropes over the stern railings, which dropped onto the deck of the tug, the man with the bullhorn quickly stepping aside to avoid them. With shouts of triumph the men on the deck cheered the small success, as the tugs crews ran forward to secure the lines to the tugboat's powerful winches. After a few moments he could see the powerful winches begin to pay out more line as the steel cable from the tug began to go forward, the tug beginning to move backwards away from the ship, as it sought the room to turn around. The tug turned 180 degrees, facing away from the Rasputin as the lines began to stretch taught, until the movement of the little tug stopped, anchored in place by the huge ship. The water around the stern of the tug began to froth angrily as the powerful engines and propellors began to beat into the water. The Captain watched on, convinced the tug wouldn't be able to move the huge ship, but urging it on anyway.

"Come on, COME ON!" he shouted, willing it on. Slowly, almost imperceivably, he began to see the small movement of the tug. His eyes darted between the tug and the ship, ignoring the chaos as people continued jumping from it, instead he was looking to see if the ship was moving. Was it, he thought, yes it was! It was working! The tug was pulling it clear! The men at the stern gave another cheer, waving at the tug's crew as the propellers began to now bite at the water and the tug began to make way. He looked over at the Rasputin, all her lights were ablaze, illuminating the ship in a clean white light, showing there were still hundreds of soldiers and sailors aboard. Some had donned orange lifejackets and looked to the stern of the ship and pointing, wondering why the ship seemed to be moving backwards. Others were beginning to assemble around the large orange lifeboats, the sailors shouting and trying to maintain order as they pushed and cajoled people into them. Smoke and flames began to leap from the gaping torn hole where the tank had disappeared, as small explosions sounded below within the belly of the ship. No doubt the tank ammunition had caught fire and was cooking off.

The Captain looked on, hopeful, as now almost half of the ship was clear of the docks, the cheering from the sailors had stopped as they realised the tug was pulling them into the deeper darker waters and away from the safety and light of the docks. Now men began to jump in earnest, into the cold dark water, the light from the dock providing a false bastion of safety as they sought to stay near it. Already there were hundreds of men in the water, all shouting for help as more joined them. A patrol boat quickly cast off its lines and began to try to help, plucking up the survivors, its decks soon awash with oil drenched men.

The Captain looked back to the Rasputin, noting the list to port had seemed to slow. Perhaps the flooding had been contained, he thought, perhaps the damage control teams on board were getting the upper hand. He was suddenly optimistic, they were going to clear the dock after all, perhaps they may even be able to save the ship. He made a note to recommend the tug's Captain for a decoration, his bravery had helped to keep the dock open. He looked back at the other side of the dock, the Nikita had rolled fully over onto its side, the blue hull sticking out of the water and bubbles frothing around the hull. The superstructure had buried itself into the concrete of the dock, as smoke and steam escaped away into the night. On the ship's hull, clung hundreds of sailors and soldiers, looking like ants as they shouted and fought to keep out of the water and oil. They'd lost one dock, at least they still had the other. He blinked in surprise as suddenly a huge explosion rocked the Rasputin, the blast hurling him to the floor and blowing his cap away. Something inside the ship had detonated.

For a split second, the night turned as if it were day, the flash of the explosion illuminating the whole bay, casting a ghostly picture of the ships at anchor before darkness returned. Yellow flames burst out of the superstructure, as the white bridge and crew quarters disintegrated, tossing soldiers and sailors alike, into the water, as the blast wave shot outwards. The stern of the ship was lifted out of the water as the hull of the ship was torn apart under the superstructure, where the hole had been. The forces of the explosion burst out, peeling the steel hull apart as if it were made of paper, down to the keel, as the ship was split into two, the water pouring quickly into the open hull. The little tugboat stood no chance as it was hit by the blast wave that shot out. As the tug was thrown forwards the bridge was flattened, killing everyone instantly as the men on its bow were tossed into the water like skittles. The steel ropes became taught, the winches being torn from their mountings as they endured pressures far greater than they were designed for, before finally snapping as if made of cotton thread. The hull was swept away and rolled sideways, taken away from the ship by the huge tidal wave that formed from the blast, rolling over and capsizing, the tugs props still spinning as the engines still ran on full power. As the Rasputin's hull began to settle again in the water, the giant tidal wave rolled into the harbour, washing over the upturned hull of the Nikitta and tearing the people away from its safety, slamming the survivors into the water and against the docks. The patrol boat was picked up by the colossal wave as if nothing more than a bath toy and slammed against the concrete pilings, disintegrating into a cloud of fibreglass, machinery and flesh as its fuel tanks ruptured, erupting into a fire ball that shot skywards, burning those left alive in the water. The burning fuel, floating on the surface of the water, set alight the oil and diesel that had leaked from the Rasputin. A slow steady fire began to spread out across the dockside, like larva, it slowly rolled forward, the flames licking out and igniting all that it touched. The Captain staggered to his feet, trembling, as he heard the blood curdling screams from those in the water being burned alive. He turned in shock and disbelief and what had just happened and at the change in fortune. Looking out to the ship, his heart sank as he watched the Rasputin, now broken into two, begin to roll over and sink. The stern had gone dark, the deck lights flickering off as it slowly sank, shadows danced in the light as the darkened figures still alive onboard began to climb up and away, as the water crept closer. The forward section of the boat was still floating, rolling lazily in the swell, illuminated by lights, painting a macabre scene as it continued to lurch over to port, the hull sinking down into the water as it settled on the seabed. More explosions, smaller than the first, rumbled from underwater, as finally the ships lights blinked once, then out, plunging the scene into darkness. The flames from the dock spread into the night and began to lick at the torn hull, screams echoing all around. He turned to see the Naval Lieutenant stood next to him, he'd lost his cap and was clutching a broken arm, the glow from the fires raging around them reflecting off his eyes, full of tears.

Not knowing what to say to the other, both men simply stood and watched, in mute shock, ignoring their own injuries as all around them, the world seemed to be on fire.

14

A Merry Dance

Nine miles south of Yeovil

Colonel Golgolvin cursed, as, for the twentieth time that night, he smashed his ribs into the cupola side.

"For fucks sake driver, will you look where you're going!"

"Sorry sir, I didn't see that rock." the driver replied apologetically.

The Colonel fumed to himself, he hated the claustrophobic feeling of being inside the armoured vehicle as the driver changed down the gears, the vehicle rocking on its suspension as it began to negotiate another of the steep valleys. Where the hell were the enemy, he raged, he was a paratrooper, not a fucking tanker he fumed.

For now, he was concentrating the bulk of his forces in chasing down the enemy tanks that had created the heavy, large tracks they were following. He'd received reports of the enemy tanks heading north from his forward elements, you didn't have to be an expert tracker to follow them, the tanks left such a distinct trail that there was no way the British could hope to hide their progress and these tracks were fresh, so the tanks that had made them had only passed through recently. He hoped to stop them before they could get to the safety of Yeovil, he had no idea what lay in wait for him and didn't want to get embroiled in a street fight in the town. He'd tried at first to get his units to use the main roads but had to quickly abandon the idea as the flood of refugees streaming north had choked most of them. The cars and trucks were lined up nose to tail on both sides, forcing his units to sometimes crush the cars to get across. One of his lead vehicles had excitedly reported on finding an empty piece of road, and before he could warn them, had begun to drive along it, going no more than a hundred metres before an anti-tank mine buried there had detonated, flinging the vehicle onto its side. The lesson had been clear enough, if the refugees were not using parts of the road, then

213

neither should they. Now, he'd had to rely on the eyes of his lead units to follow the tracks whilst still navigating the terrain.

"Hang on Sir," the driver warned, shaking him from his thoughts as he braced his elbows against the sight and hatch, wincing in anticipation of the jolt to come.

The vehicle lurched up and crashed down, sparks flying off the tracks as yet another rock gouged into the vehicle hull. Cursing to himself he quickly sat down in the seat, struggling with the map to identify where they were and where they were going. Fuck this, he thought to himself.

"Driver! Halt!"

He waited for the vehicle to finish lurching to a halt before he keyed his radio to the frequency of the lead elements of the BTG, frustration clear in his voice.

"Hyena, this is Wolf, give me your position."

After a few seconds the young voice of the Captain in charge of the Reconnaissance patrol came back.

"Wolf, this is Hyena, our lead elements are now passing Katya. Terrain is poor and we're going slowly."

Terrain is poor, he thought to himself, that's an understatement if ever there was one.

"Do you still have sight of vehicle tracks?" he barked out.

Golgolvin smiled to himself as the Captain began to send his reply, then quickly cursed mid-sentence, no doubt he was finding the route hard as well. Good then it wasn't just him struggling tonight. Although they'd all practised trying to manoeuvre at night in vehicles, the reality was it was always harder when doing it for real and already he'd had to bawl out four of the commanders for turning on their headlights. The cold reality was that their own night vision equipment was outdated and poor and still reliant on the ambient light from the night sky. They should have had the newer thermal imaging units, but these had been sent with the 4th Division to Ukraine. Some units had been sent the newer Chinese thermal sights but these were few and far between and he certainly didn't have any in his BTG. He cursed the planners, the Russian army *should* be prepared to fight at night, the British certainly were. He was snapped out of his anger at the situation, as the voice came back through the radio.

"Yes, we are still following the tracks, they are still heading northeast." the Captain replied.

Staring down at the map, Golgolvin found the waypoint called Katya that the Captain had mentioned.

Good, he thought, that meant they were only six miles south of Yeovil. His orders had been to stay south of the town, and at this rate they would be at the town's outskirts before dawn.

He scanned the map, trying to think like the enemy, looking for possible ambush points or areas where he would launch a counter-attack. So far, his ground units had reported minimal enemy contact. Two of his T-80 tanks had engaged a small group of enemy infantry manning a road block on the A37, and one of his BMP's had destroyed a green Land Rover racing away from them, probably a forward observer trying to report their position to the enemy. Where were the rest of them? Why wouldn't they stand and fight? Where had the enemy disappeared to? He cursed as he looked again at the town of Yeovil on the map, he was tempted to send his units in, but the General's orders were still fresh in his ears.

Shaking his head, he folded his map and stood back up, ignoring the pain in his ribs as he braced himself for yet another hour of being smashed about.

God grant me a helicopter, he muttered, as the dark shape of a T-80 slowly meandered past them into the darkness, its turbine engine whining loudly, as he looked back, seeing a big enough gap for his command vehicle to slot into the convoy he spat out,

"Okay, driver let's go."

With a look of determination set on his face he grimaced as the vehicle jolted forward into the darkness.

Wonderland Operations Centre (WOC)

The Chief of the Defence Staff stood alone in the briefing room, glaring at the map on the screen as he held the latest report in his hand. The Russians, or Tumats, or whatever the hell they were calling themselves, were on the move, he angrily thought to himself. He looked at the map as the latest intel was loaded onto to it, friendly units and positions were coloured in blue, the enemy units were coloured in red. Depressingly he noted the lack of blue on the map. They still needed time to get the country on a war footing. It was like playing a game of chess with all your key pieces missing before you had even started the game, whilst your opponent had the luxury of two of every major piece. The large red arrows striking out from the south coast heading north showed him a sizeable force was moving further inland, whilst in the north, more red arrows scythed west out of Newcastle, heading for Carlisle, threatening to cut the country in two across its narrowest point. He'd managed to plug some of the gaps. Already General Boswell, was in the north, doing what he could with the limited resources he had and in the south General Kew had been dispatched to try to salvage what he could from the Tidworth garrison, but the CDS knew, the real fight for them, would be time. With luck, the mission tonight would buy them at least that.

He was disturbed as the PM walked into the room, wearing pyjamas and dressing gown and carrying two cups of coffee. The CDS smiled and raised an eyebrow at his attire, remembering their earlier exchange when he'd arrived at the initial briefing and the CDS was out of uniform. He was tempted to say something, but wisely kept quiet, this was now the most powerful person in Government, the days of joking were long gone.

"Can't sleep Sir?" he asked, as the PM stood next to him, handing one of the steaming cups over.

"No, I can't CDS, could you?"

He was amazed at the change in the man since assuming the role, gone was the indecision and constant seeking of approval of the past, now he seemed to stand taller, focussed, and more driven.

He nodded his thanks as he accepted the coffee, agreeing as he replied, "No Sir, I couldn't either."

The PM looked up at the clock on the wall, noting the time and deep in thought, before finally asking, "What time are they due back?"

"They should all be rendezvousing with HMS Archer anytime now Sir."

The PM cradled his cup as he sipped the coffee, his eyes remaining firmly on the second hand of the clock before asking. "And when will we find out, if it's a been a success or not?"

"HMS Archer will maintain radio silence until they've cleared into deeper waters. Once she's safely away, she'll send the code word if it's mission success."

The PM nodded, taking another sip as he asked, "And remind me again please CDS what is the codeword?"

The CDS tasted his own coffee, remarking how good it was to himself as he replied. "Leveller Sir, the codeword is leveller."

The PM simply nodded, alone with his thoughts before turning to face his CDS.

"Is it always like this?"

The CDS nodded, "Yes."

"And does it ever get easier CDS, the waiting I mean?"

The CDS smiled back, shaking his head. "No Prime Minister, it never gets easier."

Nodding in reply and pursing his lips, the PM resumed the clock watching, silent and alone in his thoughts as the second hand ticked away, seemingly louder now in the quiet of the room.

The Forestry Block, 1 mile west of Cerne Abbas

Mike walked along the dark line of vehicles until he came to the tank, seeing the silhouettes of Bill and Smudge standing to the side. He walked up to them keeping his voice low.

"Bill, anything to report on the vehicle? How's the running gear looking?"

"She's all good boss, lost some more rubber on a few of the road wheels and some track pads are missing but she's still good."

"And fuel state?"

"We're still showing 3/4 full."

The fuel we took onboard back at the farm had really helped, thought Mike. Thank you Sam.

Satisfied that the vehicle was fine, he then concentrated on the crew.

"Bill, Smudge, I take it that this is your first time actually out on the ground on a tank?"

Even in the dim light he could see both nodding as he continued, "Okay, I've got to go and get a few important jobs done, once I've done them, I'll come back and explain a few things to you. In the meantime, I want you both to keep your noise and light discipline to a minimum. It's red light only, I don't want to see any white light. Make sure the periscopes and sights are all closed on the tank, you'll be surprised how much light can escape. Then once you've done that stay here by the tank. You're not to move from the tank until I come back. You both understand?"

Both nodded quietly, Mike was about to turn when he noticed something.

"Smudge, where's your rifle?"

"It's in the turret, It's safe and secure Sir."

Mike closed his eyes and took a deep breath. Remember these are new recruits, he thought to himself.

"Right," he replied, "if an enemy soldier walked through that treeline and pointed his rifle at you or one of our prisoners managed to escape and began to run up here to attack you, what would you do? How would you defend yourself?"

"Err, I'd climb aboard and get my rifle Sir."

"No Smudge, you'd be dead. Plain and simple. This isn't training anymore guys, now it's winner takes all, first person to fire usually wins. So, from now on, I want you to keep that rifle loaded and within arm's reach at all times. Never leave the vehicle without it. Even if you're only popping off for a quick piss, that rifle stays with you. Clear?"

"Yes Sir."

"Good, now go get your weapon and get those jobs done. I'll see you shortly."

A short while later and Mike stood admiring his handiwork, looking at the cam netting stretched across the track. Granted, it would never pass a close-up inspection, but its job was to keep people from walking up the track to begin with, so long as it kept people away, then it should work.

He stood with Changa and Sid, both nodding in appreciation, both being the first of the roaming sentries. Their job was to walk amongst the vehicles quietly looking out for any signs of trouble coming their way and being the first line of defence if it did. Mike looked at Changa, wearing his helmet and body armour noting the Fijian looked colossal and Mike pitied the fool who had to face him down. He smiled and patted Changa on the back leaving them to it, walking back towards the centre of their new home for the next day. He had a quick check on the cam net at the other end and satisfied that it would do its job, walked back to the centre of the vehicles knowing they'd now done all they could. The tank was in the centre and he quietly walked up to the shadow of figures he could see sitting by the tracks. His crew were still where he had left them.

Placing his newly acquired AK12 against the tank he slowly sat back down to join them.

"That you, Mr Faulkes?" he heard Bill whisper.

"Yes, it's me Bill. That Smudge with you?"

"I'm here Sir," the gunner answered.

"Good," he replied, "so, we're here for the day now until tonight, it's dark now but expect it to be sunrise in the next hour or so."

As he spoke, they could already start to see the grey slivers of dawn approaching from the east.

"Now the vehicles are all parked one behind the other and we're the second callsign in. In front of us, you've got Corporal Patterson's Warrior, then us, then it's Lance Corporal Martin's Warrior, then the truck we captured and finally the last vehicle is Corporal Webb's. The radio sentry's going to be done out of the back of Lance Corporal Martin's vehicle."

He paused to check they were listening. "Bill, which vehicle has the radio sentry in?"

"Lance Corporal Martin's."

"And which vehicle is it on the track?"

"It's the one behind us now Sir."

"Good, now we've got two roaming sentries out instead of the one, leave them alone and don't talk to them or distract them. Same goes for you both when you're on sentry, don't get distracted and don't go wandering around for a chat. It's a boring but very important job when you're on sentry duty, the people here will be relying on you for their security. It's not like being back at the barn. Out here in the woods, people could just wander in from any direction. Usually we'd have dug in sentry positions, but because we're all one behind the other on a single track we can't do that."

They both nodded, Mike didn't want to sound like he was talking down to them or teaching them something they already knew, but the way they kept nodding intensely told him they were paying attention.

"Now I've asked that Corporal Webb put us all on sentry together as a crew, I'll be the radio operator and you'll both be the roaming sentries. When we've finished here, I want you both to go and tell the radio operator where you're sleeping, he'll make a note of it, otherwise the sentry will wake up the wrong people when he's looking for you both."

Mike paused again to let the information sink in before finally replying, "Right, final thing now guys, I know it's a lot to take on board, trying to remember all of this, especially as you're both fresh out of training, and we're a man down, but the more we do this, the more you'll remember and the better you'll get, until eventually it'll be second nature. So, keep your chins up guys, and we'll get through this. Now any questions?"

Smudge kept quiet but Bill asked, "Mr Faulkes, Smudge has a rifle and you've told him to not leave the tank without it. What about me? When do I get a weapon?"

Damn he had me there, Mike thought. In an ideal world everyone one would have been armed.

"Are you trained on the Glock 17?"

"We both are Mr Faulkes, they taught us in training." Smudge replied, answering for them both.

Quickly thinking he replied, "Tell you what then Bill, for now, take my pistol, it's got a full magazine."

He reached inside his smock and pulled out the pistol, making the weapon safe, using his finger to check inside that the chamber was clear as it was still too dark to see properly. Upon handing it over, Bill expertly checked it was clear before refitting the magazine and placing the pistol in his chest rig. Mike saw the faint glimpse of a smile on the drivers face. Who could blame him, with all this time of being unarmed, having a weapon might have been the bit of comfort he needed.

"Anything else?" Mike queried.

"No, I'm good, thanks boss, I don't feel quite so naked now."

"Right then, I'll leave you both to get sorted."

Mike was about to leave when Smudge asked, "Boss, the people we found in the back of the truck, any news on how they are?"

"Not yet Smudge, Doc did say though that it would take time for them all to come round."

"Why were they in there? And why where they all asleep?" Smudge asked again.

The pictures flashed through Mikes mind of the two women and what had happened to them. He wisely kept quiet.

"Perhaps those two Russians can tell us," Bill answered hopefully.

"Perhaps they can Bill, perhaps they can." Mike muttered, as leaving them he walked back to the truck, his thoughts becoming darker, just as the sky became lighter.

Wonderland Operations Centre (WOC)

The CDS and PM were on their third cup of coffee, still in the briefing room, except they'd stopped watching the clock, both realising that it wasn't going to get them their codeword any quicker. Now they were chatting about possible future operations, or ways to help the country recover from the mess it was in. They stopped, as Sir Tony came running into the room, laptop in hand and a look of relief on his face.

"Leveller! We have confirmation PM, Leveller!"

The PM smiled, the smile quickly disappearing as he looked up again.

"Losses Sir Tony?"

"None Sir!" he exclaimed happily.

Hearing this news, both men stood up, the PM breaking into a triumphant grin and reaching over to shake the hands of the CDS as Sir Tony continued.

"HMS Archer confirmed it moments ago, mission success, all three teams back in. Her sonar confirmed the detonation of twelve limpet mines, followed by the sounds of ships breaking apart."

"Do we have eyes in any of the ports, can we conduct a BDA?" the CDS shot back quickly.

"BDA?" the PM looked over; eyebrows raised.

The CDS quickly replied "Battle Damage Assessment Sir, tells us how badly we've hit the bastards."

Sir Tony added, "Archer launched two UAVs' before leaving the area, both were shot down, but not before they managed to send us some footage via data-link." He put the laptop on the desk, pressing a key, as the video began to play. It was a high-resolution video taken at altitude, but they could see the flames around the dockyard, the sea seemed to be on fire. The image zoomed in on the area of the docks and at the altitude the ships looked like toys in a bathtub. One was on its side against the docks, its mass blocking any further attempts to dock a ship there. The second dock looked empty and for a moment they thought they had failed, but then as the camera zoomed out, they saw the glowing wreck of the Rasputin, still burning, flames licking out from the hulk and going skyward. The CDS peered closer, as suddenly the picture stopped.

Sir Tony quickly began, "That's all we managed to get, but I've had some stills made."

He tapped again and the image that the CDS was trying to look at came back on. He reached over and picked up his glasses to get a better look, then stared at the wreck of the Rasputin. "She looks like she's broken in two," he exclaimed. "How big were the mines our team used?"

Sir Tony shook his head, "Not that big CDS, the mission was to sink the ships, not cut them in two. Archer reported hearing a louder explosion about six minutes after the limpets went off. She was carrying ammunition, perhaps it went off and destroyed her."

The PM looked on as Sir Tony selected a different video file, this time the view was of a different dockyard, with a large island visible in the distance.

"Poole Harbour, taken ten minutes after the attack." Sir Tony added, as the feed zoomed in, two of the huge container ships were lying on their sides alongside the dock-yard, half submerged, limiting access to the quayside. Smaller fires were seen burning on the quayside, as people, looking more like ants, scurried around to try to fight the fires. The feed was cut abruptly, replaced by another image of the scene, magnified on the ships.

They looked up at each other, as the PM asked, "Well, CDS? What's your assessment? Did we do it? Can they use the docks?"

Smiling, he removed his glasses, looking at them both. "I think we've done it PM, look at the way they're sunk, blocking the access to both docks, they won't be getting anything in or out of there anytime soon."

The PM smiled as the CDS continued, "For the first time since this all started Sir, I think we've just brought ourselves half a chance."

3 Miles south of Yeovil

Golgolvin watched as the sun begin to rise in the east, the light beginning to filter into the valley. The blacks and greys of the night beginning to merge into shades of orange and red as the sun's rays began to appear. In the distance he could see the outskirts of Yeovil begin to form, his lead callsign's last report mentioned that they were only three miles from it. He was tempted to send them in, to see what sort of defences the British had placed there, but thought better of it. He was torn from his thoughts of what to do next when the Captain's excited voice burst through over the radio headset.

"Wolf this is Hyena, we have a visual on the enemy tanks."

At last, he thought. He waited for the Captain to give him their positions. Growing impatient he quickly keyed the radio.

"Hyena, Wolf, report their positions."

"Wolf, Hyena we are engaging them now."

No don't engage them, he thought angrily, I've got the tanks for that!

He keyed the pressel, hoping he wasn't yet too late. "Hyena *do not* engage, give me their positions."

With his foot he tapped the Signals Sergeant who was sat below in the fighting compartment, monitoring the other company radios. He looked up as the Colonel shouted over the noise of the engine, "Get all units awake and moving to that position as soon as we have it!"

The Sergeant nodded furiously, happy that after all these hours of bouncing about in the dark they were finally about to get their prey.

Golgolvin looked up, as the units around him now began to come alive and push out into their battle formations, the BMP's raced off to the flanks as the tank commanders began to lower themselves in the hatches, preparing themselves and their crews for the fight to come. He still hadn't heard from his Recce platoon and began to curse them, when at last the Captain replied.

"Wolf this is Hyena, two enemy tanks, position grid square Mike 38, bottom of the valley orientated northeast."

He checked the position against his map, that was only one km away from his forward tank unit in another valley. He had them! His own tanks could stay on the high ground and fire down into the valley. He quickly passed over his orders to the tanks, watching satisfied as the T-80's nearest him raced away, keen to join their comrades up ahead. After so long searching, finally they had them.

"Driver, see those tanks up ahead, can you follow them at that speed?"

"Not if the Colonel wishes to keep all his teeth I can't."

Ignoring the comment he barked, "To hell with my teeth, stick to their arses like glue, and I'll have a bottle of good vodka ready for you when we get back. I need to see this for myself."

"Everyone in the back best hang on tight," the driver exclaimed as Golgolvin felt the vehicle lurch down a gear and accelerate off in pursuit. And for the first time that night, he forgot all about the aches and pains in his arms and ribs and smiled...

The ground was cold and hard as the young Lance Corporal remained hidden from view, keeping himself low as he watched the valley below him for any signs of the enemy. He shifted his weight slowly, trying to ease the aches, as he fought to steady his breathing and bring it under control. His clothes were damp with sweat and already he could feel the cold morning air beginning to cool his body down. It had been a hard climb out of the valley, even at his young age of 24 and aided by the adrenalin coursing through his veins. Now as he lay there watching, he looked up at the sun, looking forward to its warmth, but also regretting the fact it would make his escape much harder.

He looked back down at the two vehicles in the valley floor, sad to be leaving them, they'd done well to get this far, with the remaining fuel he'd had, he'd coaxed every single mile he could out of them, leading the Russians on a merry dance around the countryside, until eventually the engine had coughed and spluttered as it ran out of fuel. He thought back to the previous night, it had been the OC's idea to do it. After they had evacuated from the camp the ATDU Tanks had met up with the Colonel and the other armoured vehicles, including two of the Driver Training Tanks. Major Richards had suggested to the CO a plan to lure the Russians away, by giving them a hare to chase, but it meant sacrificing the DTT's. One tank wouldn't do it, they'd need two, to make it look like a convoy of vehicles. So, with that in mind they'd hitched them together with the towing gear and the REME had managed to rig a fuel pipe between the vehicles so that the lead DTT could now run off the rear DTT's fuel supply. Instead of two drivers, they'd only need one to drive the decoy and he'd jumped at the chance. He knew the dangers, but he'd been willing to take the risk for his friends to get to safety. He'd left them early on the first night, driving north of Dorchester and meandering around as many of the fields as he could, making sure to leave as many breadcrumbs as he could. Sometimes he'd come across his own tracks and laughed to himself, drunk with the fear of the fact he could die at any second. Perhaps they would think they were crop circles he'd chuckled as he kept up the ruse. Sometimes he'd see in the distance the flash of explosions or tracer fire arcing up to the sky, letting him know someone was in the fight. He could only hope that whoever it was they were giving it good to the enemy. Eventually he'd seen the first rays of the sun begin to appear and realised that he'd have to find somewhere to hide. He couldn't just drive around in the daylight, he'd be a sitting duck for sure and even though his mission was crazy, he didn't want to give up just yet. He'd chanced upon the cement factory in the middle of a large open area of countryside and had driven the vehicles through the gates and along its dusty track, as the cement dust blew up in a cloud coating everything and making him cough as he'd parked both vehicles next to the giant grey hopper. He'd jumped off, hoping to stay hidden out of sight for the day and continue that night. He was thankful that no-one showed up for work that day, perhaps the site was closed, he had thought, as he'd explored the area, finding a water hose, which he used to top up his water bottle. At least he wouldn't be thirsty as his belly grumbled with hunger. For the rest of the day, he'd stayed there quietly expecting at any moment to be discovered, but no one came. He heard and saw the helicopters flying overhead, but no one seemed to take the slightest interest in the stationary DTT's. He'd looked over and realised that with the grey dust coating them, instead of the usual green, they were now a dull grey, and blended in perfectly with the hopper. Anyone looking at them would think they were looking at part of the giant machine, the perfect camouflage. He'd laughed again, not believing his luck, despite his hunger, at least he was alive to be hungry, he'd reasoned. As well as the helicopters he'd heard more explosions and gunfire, all south of him and hoped his unit hadn't been discovered yet. No, they couldn't be, he'd justified to himself. His unit would be away to the west by now and certainly nowhere south of him.

As the sun finally dipped below the horizon, he'd climbed back into the driver's cab and restarted the engine. He'd wondered whether to carry on or simply leave the vehicles now. After a few moments he had shaken the thoughts from his head, come on Baz, get a grip. You volunteered to do this, so let's see it through. He sang a tune to himself as he engaged first gear, making his way out on the same route he had come in. Off in the distance he could remember seeing hundreds of headlights, not moving, perhaps that was the traffic on the A37. Without a map, he already decided he'd follow the road north, and see how far the fuel would take him, perhaps he'd make it to Yeovil he mused. On the second night, he'd periodically stop and switch the engine off, hearing the engines in the distance of the pursuing vehicles chasing him. So, they were following him, he'd laugh to himself. I wonder how many I've drawn away, he'd think, as he'd restart the engine and keep going. But with only four miles to go from Yeovil, eventually his luck had run out and that's how he now found himself finally out of fuel and stuck in the bottom of the valley. He'd planned to try to fire the vehicles, to destroy them and prevent them falling into enemy hands, but with the fuel tanks dry and nothing explosive on board, he knew he wouldn't have time. Leaving them there, he simply jumped out and ran as fast as he could, not daring to look backwards as he climbed the 600 metres up the hill. He could hear the vehicles getting closer and fear began to take hold as, at any second, he expected to hear the gunfire and feel the rounds tearing through him. His adrenalin had kicked in and ignoring the pain in his chest, he pumped his arms furiously, his legs burning and powering him upwards, as the crest finally came into view. Suddenly he'd done it, he'd made it, and threw himself to the ground, angry with leaving the vehicles intact, but he'd done his job. And now, the Russians were foolishly following him, whilst the remainder of the Bovington Garrison evacuated to the safety of the west.

He smiled to himself as his thoughts came back to the here and now, as he heard the engines in the distance getting louder.

"That's it you bastards, keep coming, keep on coming." he said loudly to himself.

He looked up at the sky, certain to hear at any moment the sounds of the helicopters in the distance coming in. But apart from the vehicles, it remained quiet. Where are they? he wondered to himself.

He thought through what to do next. He hadn't counted on making it this far and now here he was, no weapon, no supplies and no plan.

Should he risk it? Make a run for it? He looked to the south; the only route left open to him. He couldn't go north, not now the enemy were so close, the terrain was open and he'd be spotted for miles and going to the west or east meant he'd come across one of the Russian units tracking him. To the south the ground was heavily wooded and full of valleys, providing him cover and at least he'd be offered protection from the sun, he thought, which wouldn't be too long before it rose. His thoughts quickly turned to food as his belly rumbled again. Could he trap something perhaps, could he set a snare to catch an animal? He'd seen them do it on the TV, how hard could it be? His thoughts were interrupted as he saw movement off to his left on the far side of the valley.

He could see the antennas of the enemy vehicle slowly sticking up on the opposite ridge as it crawled up the slope. I can see you, he muttered to himself. If only he had an anti-tank rocket.

Deciding he'd stayed there long enough he made his mind up to go south, he'd keep hidden in the woods and valleys and then after a few miles he'd head west. If his luck held out, he reasoned, he'd come across some friendly units at some point. He took a final look at the vehicles and slowly crawled back down from the edge of the lip, only when he felt certain that he wouldn't be seen from the opposite ridge did he dare to stand up, before breaking into a jog, heading for the woodline. He'd done what he needed to for his friends, now it was time to do what was needed to keep himself alive.

Golgolvin hung onto the periscopes of the hatch tightly, as the vehicle smashed along at breakneck speed. He'd spent most of the night slowly meandering along in the convoy, feeling every bump and jolt, but now realised the secret to travelling in these vehicles was in their speed. Now, instead of hitting every ridge or bump slowly, the BMP floated over them at speed, as its suspension did its job expertly, cushioning and dampening the blows. Over the radio he listened in as the company commander of the tanks began to co-ordinate with the forward units.

"Hyena, this is Tiger, any change on enemy vehicles?"

"Tiger, no change, they're in the valley looking to the northeast. We're still watching them."

"Hyena, roger that, then we'll approach from the southwest. Out."

The driver did a great job and within minutes they were closing up to the rear of the of tank company's formation as its company commander skirted round the valley, keeping the T-80's safely hidden from view to the enemy tanks below.

Not wanting to get too close he quickly spoke to the driver.

"Okay that's close enough, you've earned that bottle. Now keep us back about 200 metres from that ridge."

He heard the driver acknowledge as the BMP slowed to a crawl, the driver using the terrain to partially cover the vehicle as it dipped into some low ground.

Satisfied with the position the driver had placed them in, Golgolvin stood tall, watching the T-80's as finally they were in position to attack. He could see their commander had arrayed five of his tanks looking out, providing overwatch to the far distance, it always paid to have eyes looking out, as the other five were readied to begin their attack. Flicking over to the company frequency he listened to the attack as it unfolded.

"All Tigers, this is Tiger Command, Tigers Two, Three, and Five will begin the attack first, followed by Eight and Nine. Report when ready."

"Tiger Two ready."

"Tiger Three ready."

"Tiger Five ready."

"Tiger Eight ready."

"Tiger Nine ready."

Golgolvin knew that even though outnumbered, the enemy tanks in the valley would put up a huge fight. He could see that the company commander had been smart with his plan and had chosen to overwhelm them with five of his tanks, three of them popping up to fire one round each, then disappearing back behind the ridge, as another two popped up to do the same. He'd seen the crews practise this tactic on the ranges before, hearing them call it the 'Tank Carousel.' He knew the tactic was to confuse the enemy gunners enough to be able to get the tanks destroyed without getting shot at in return.

He watched in fascination as the radio squawked, "All Tigers, commence!"

He could see three of the tanks rumble slowly forward, clearing the crest of the ridge and watching as their turrets turned quickly, the guns pointing down. Within seconds he saw the first flash of the tanks gun fire, the report of the gun sending a shock through his own vehicle, quickly followed by the flash and explosion of the second tank and the third. He looked on as the three tanks reversed back into cover, the auto loaders already loading the next rounds as the next two tanks pulled forward, the turrets quickly finding their targets and the barrels pointing down into the valley. Another two explosions and another two rounds fired, as they pulled back to be replaced by the three again, ready to fire. Because of his position he couldn't see down into the valley at what they were firing at and instead had to wait for the reports to be sent, relying on the tank commanders to relay what they were shooting at.

He watched the tanks as they continued the choreographed routine twice more, patiently waiting for the report to say they were under fire, expecting to hear incoming rounds from the tanks below or at least hear explosions as their own rounds penetrated the enemy vehicles. After the third such manoeuvre and realising that they'd now shot fifteen tank rounds at the unseen enemy, he lost his patience coming on to the company net.

"Tiger Command this is Wolf Command, send me an engagement report."

After a few moments the company commander's voice came over the net, irritated at the interruption.

"Wolf Command, Tiger Command, we are currently engaging two enemy tanks, wait out for further updates."

Golgolvin shook his head angrily, something was wrong. Why no incoming enemy fire? And he knew the armour on the Challenger was good, but to survive fifteen of their own tank rounds? He needed to see this for himself.

"Driver, see the gap between those two tanks up ahead, take us through it and up to the edge of the valley, I want to see what they're shooting at."

The drivers voice betrayed his concern.

"Begging the Colonel's pardon Sir, but just so I'm clear, you want us to stick our heads over the valley, even though there's two enemy tanks down there."

"Just do it!" he snapped; he was in no mood to be explaining himself to a mere driver.

"Very well," the driver replied, "It's *your* head Sir!"

He was about to reply to the driver's insubordination, when he was jolted back into the hatch as the BMP lurched into gear. He angrily looked down towards the driver's hatch, certain the driver had done it on purpose. It could wait, he thought, as his attention was now focussed on the ridge edge.

The vehicle sped between the tanks, slowing down and then crawling slowly forward, as the tanks began yet another firing cycle, The Colonel looked over to the company commander's tank, how long was he intending to allow this to go on for, he thought. That was now twenty rounds fired at the enemy tanks, surely they'd be destroyed by now?

"Driver, HALT!"

The vehicle slowly rolled to a halt as the valley bottom came into view, he quickly raised his binoculars, the dim morning light allowing him to see better than his night-sight could, as his eyes were drawn straight away to the dark shapes of the two enemy vehicles about 700 metres in the valley floor. They were facing away from them, and one had a small fire burning from within its engine decks. He looked again, confused as he took in the scene. Something looked wrong. Was one towing the other? And where were the turrets? Had they been knocked off already? He scanned the ground around the enemy tanks looking for any signs of the destroyed turrets as suddenly the realisation dawned on him. They were training tanks!

The T-80's were moving forward for another attack run, he quickly keyed the radio, the anger clear in his voice.

"ALL TIGERS! CEASE FIRE!"

Two of the tanks stopped immediately but the third, the company commander's tank continued forward, the gun lowering and firing almost immediately, ignoring the order.

He watched as the anti-tank round sparked off the back of the tank on fire, sending more flames into the sky as the debris tore off into the air, visible at this distance.

Again he ordered, "Tiger Command, *this is Wolf Command*, I repeat, cease fire immediately, acknowledge!"

The company commander came back almost immediately, "Wolf Command, Tiger Command, those tanks are not destroyed yet, recommend you leave us to continue engaging until destroyed."

He couldn't believe this, was the man blind?

"Tiger Command, OPEN YOUR FUCKING EYES! Those are *not* gun tanks, you're engaging training tanks! Acknowledge!"

Suddenly there was silence, as the Major realised his mistake. He'd been so focussed on trying to destroy them, he'd not actually looked at what he was firing at. Now as he stopped firing and took a breath, he could see the distinct shape of the turretless tanks, the turret being replaced by the large angular shaped passenger compartment.

After a few moments his voice came back over the air, more reserved than before as he now realised his mistake.

"Wolf, this is Tiger, roger your last, all Tigers cease fire now."

Golgolvin looked angrily around him at the tanks, silently cursing them as their commanders stayed low in the turrets, none dared look in his direction.

It hadn't just been the tanks though; even his reconnaissance platoon had reported the enemy vehicles as main battle tanks.

He looked down to the Sergeant in the back, visibly angry.

"I want you to get a message out, all unit commanders are to report to me when we stop. Clearly, they do not know what the enemy look like!"

Leaving him to pass the message on, he turned back to the radio, changing the channel to talk to his recce platoon.

"Hyena, Wolf! Get back to your original tasking and make sure you know what you're bloody looking at next time!"

The voice of the Captain was quiet as he acknowledged.

He looked at his watch, the offensive had been underway now for seven hours and the only thing his unit had fought so far were training tanks. Where were they, he fumed to himself. The enemy had to be somewhere.

He was angry, angry with his own tanks, angry with his own recce forces, angry with his driver, but more so, angry with himself. He'd been fooled, he'd just been sent on a wild goose chase and knew it. But more so he was angry with the fact that now he'd have to send the report. Now, he'd have to explain to the General about yet another failure, and that was something he wasn't looking forward to doing.

15

A New Dawn

The Forestry Block 1 Mile west of Cerne Abbas

The sun was fully up and beaming through the treetops when Mike felt himself being gently shaken awake.

"Sir, Mr Faulkes, you awake yet?"

He opened his eyes immediately and sat up, the dark piece of rag covering his eyes to block out the sun, falling away. He squinted against the glare as his eyes slowly focussed on the figure before him. It was Whippet, one of the roaming sentries.

"I'm awake Whippet, what is it?"

"Sir, sorry to wake you but Doc told me to come get you, the people in the truck, they're beginning to wake up."

Mike stood up, nodding his thanks as he picked up his rifle, slinging it over his shoulder, and making his way off the back deck of the tank, careful not to step on the sleeping figures of Smudge and Bill, both having found themselves spots on the turret to sleep. He smiled to himself, it was surprising the places you could sleep when you were tired, he thought, as he dropped to the ground and began to walk down the line of vehicles. He glanced at his watch, it was 11:15, at least he'd managed to get another three hours sleep after coming off his two-hour guard shift. As he approached the truck he saw the two Russian prisoners, sat back-to-back with the hoods over their heads leaning against one of the huge wheels. He doubted they'd be getting any sleep. Earlier, before everyone had settled into the routine of the day Patty had made sure that both prisoners were gagged and hooded, and in case they could understand English, Patty had found two sets of ear defenders and taped them to the Russians heads, preventing them from hearing any conversations around them. Jonah was sat slightly off from them, also tied up, but unlike the others, his mouth and face were uncovered. He wasn't stupid, he knew his own safety lay in playing along, and he looked at Mike, his eyes following his progress as he passed by saying nothing. Ping was guarding them all, the young Fusilier nodded to him respectfully as he went by. Mike approached the rear of the truck, hearing new voices from the back and smiled to himself. Fingers crossed that everyone had made it. He approached the tailgate, the canvas now pulled up, allowing the fresh air and daylight into the back.

Spider was in the back, helping Doc, as they quietly passed bottles of water to people who were now sitting upright, a mixture of fear, bewilderment and shock on all their faces.

Spider stuck his head out of the back and quietly said, "Morning Mike, everyone just started waking up about fifteen minutes ago. I sent for you as soon as I found out myself."

Mike nodded as he replied, "Morning Spider, is Patty aware?"

"Yeah, he knows, he's on radio stag at the moment. Could you pass us up a few more bottles?"

Mike reached down, picking up another four bottles from the pile on the ground before climbing up into the cargo area and handing them to the outstretched hands. Some people lacked the strength to undo them, so quickly taking them back, he twisted the lids off, before returning them.

"Sip, don't gulp it," Doc kept repeating over and over as he handed out the bottles to eager hands.

Mike looked over to the two women he'd seen earlier, both were awake but slumped against the trucks side, the exhaustion of their ordeal clear to see on them. Did they remember what happened, he thought. Best not to mention anything whilst everyone was here. He saw the woman in the red dress instinctively pull it further down, trying to cover her legs further from the eyes of everyone there. She knew, he thought to himself, regretfully.

Trying his best to ignore her plight, he looked around the truck asking, "So, do you mind us asking, but could someone explain how you all came to be in the back of the truck?"

"Who are you? How did we get here?" a voice croaked back in response.

He turned to look at the speaker, it was the female police officer he'd seen last night, her face was bloodied and bruised and her uniform blouse was no longer white, but instead dirty and torn. He saw the rank on her shoulder tabs and guessed she must have held a senior position, perhaps even a police Chief.

Doc and Spider said nothing, looking at Mike. Clearly, they wanted him to answer.

"We're the British Army," Mike began, "we captured this truck last night, it was only when we got it back here and looked inside that we found all of you."

Some of the faces looked relieved, whatever hell they had just been through, at least for now they were safe.

He saw her eyes look suspiciously over his rag tag uniform taken from the Auto parts store and his AK12 slung over his shoulder, then to Doc and Spider.

"So, you're British Army then?" her tone questioning, "and what rank do you hold? What unit are you with?"

"I'm no longer in the army, I'm more of what you might call a civilian advisor." Mike deflected.

"Civilian advisor?" her tone was abrasive, "So who is in charge here then?"

Mike looked over to Spider and replied, "That would be Corporal Webb."

She looked over, "Corporal Webb? A Corporal in charge of a unit like this?" Mike detected her sarcastic tone, something was amiss, she didn't believe what he was saying. To be fair, it was kind of farfetched, even he had to admit that.

"I'm sorry but I don't think so, you're not the British Army," she continued. Spider looked on opened mouthed as she turned to the others and said, "Don't believe a word of it, these people are the enemy, posing as friendlies to get us to talk, it's another of their tricks, keep quiet and say nothing."

Spider quickly replied, "Er excuse me lady, but I can tell you now we're not the bloody Russians, can't you see the uniform I'm wearing, it says *British Army* on it, and why can't I be in charge, there's nothing wrong with being a Corporal you know."

Mike had to turn his face to hide the smile as he heard her reply.

"Who knows, maybe you got the uniform from one of our dead soldiers, or maybe you bought it. The uniform doesn't make the soldier, it's the person inside it that does. And from what I'm seeing, you don't look like much!"

She folded her arms in defiance, glaring back at Spider. Mike was impressed at that the way she'd gone from being tired and shocked, in to attack mode so quickly. Was she playing at being tired and weak all along? She did have a point though, as rescue efforts go, this was a pretty poor show.

Doc was about to say something when Mike quickly intervened, "Okay, if you're all feeling up to it, I'd like you all to carefully and slowly step out of the back of the truck, I'll tell you all about us and how we got here, but not in here!"

"Sir!" Doc warned, "these people are weak, they need to rest."

He looked over to Doc, his own tone reassuring, "It's alright, fresh air and sunlight will do them good, doctors' orders, besides I'm sure they're all sick of being in the back of this bloody truck. I know I am."

Doc looked back, nodding slowly then added, "Alright, but make sure you all take it slowly, your limbs will be stiff and will need to be warmed up, and keep drinking slowly."

Mike jumped down from the truck, looking up as the face of the police Chief appeared. She looked down as if expecting Mike to pull a trick at any moment. What had happened to her, he wondered. Seeing there was no trap waiting, she slowly climbed down, her legs protesting as she used them again. After ten minutes, everyone had been helped out of the truck, breathing in the fresh air and taking in their new surroundings of the woods.

Mike could see clearly now, three of them were in military uniform, five were Police officers and four were civilians. All of them were showing signs of the rough treatment they'd received from their captors. Why were they all in the truck? he wondered. As Doc jumped down, Mike quickly said, "Doc, leave them to us now, go get yourself away and get some rest, you've done more than enough."

Mike could see he was about to protest when Spider walked over to him and said something into his ear, he couldn't hear what was said, but could see the Doc nodding in understanding. Eventually he looked over at the group, then at Mike and conceding with what had been said, he turned and walked away. Keeping his voice low, Mike walked over to Spider, and curiously asked.

"What did you say to him?"

Spider looked back, his face serious, "Simple, I just told him that he'd spent all his time looking after these people and the one patient he was neglecting was himself. Besides, given what these people had just been through, he was exhausted and almost looked like one of them. That seemed to do the trick. He'll be okay after a few hours of shut eye."

Mike looked at the group, all were staring back, waiting for an explanation. Taking a deep breath he started from the beginning, how he'd ended up in Bovington, how they'd only just managed to escape the attack on the camp, how they'd found Spider and Patty and how their rag tag unit had been formed. He mentioned finding the barn but kept Sam, Mary and the farm's location out of the story. He'd mentioned last night, how they were trying to make their way north to re-join the British units they thought had gone there, how they'd stumbled on the truck and how they captured it. And how they now found themselves in the woods behind the enemy's front lines. He mentioned that because there had been no time to prepare they now found themselves low on weapons and ammo and that was why he was carrying a Russian weapon. He pointed over to the Russian prisoners as if to add credence to the story, some of the group were muttering to themselves, no doubt already planning acts of vengeance in their head. Mike chose to ignore the threats for now. If the POWs were under guard they were protected, regardless of what they had done. After he'd finished there was silence, as the group stood, some rubbing arms and legs, nursing them back to life as they took in what he had told them.

The police Chief looked over at Jonah, seeing his uniform she asked, "He's British, what did he do wrong? Why have you got him detained?"

Not wanting to explain too much, Mike simply shrugged his shoulders and replied, "He's under military arrest, that's for the army to decide."

She pursed her lips together in thought, before deciding not to push the matter further.

There was silence amongst the group, some were looking at the vehicles around them, others just stood there, eyes closed enjoying the warmth of the sun, thankful to be alive. Eventually it was one of the soldiers, an Engineer Corporal who broke the silence. His voice was low and croaky.

"We were captured at the camp, early on the first night, trying to get one of our vehicles ready to go, there were five of us at the beginning..." His voice trailed off for a moment as his thoughts came back to him. The two other soldiers looked up as he continued, "I'm Corporal Fletcher, lads call me Fletch, these other two are Sappers Wright and Manfred." Both soldiers smiled in introduction as they were named, as Fletch continued, "We tried to make a run for it, but those bastards chased us down in their vehicles. After capturing us, they made us sit and watch as they dragged our colleagues' bodies out for us to see..." His voice trailed off again as his thoughts almost overwhelmed him. He closed his eyes briefly to calm himself, as he continued, his voice lower this time. "We were all taken back into the camp, beaten and interrogated, questioned over and over, always the same questions, where are the other units? What was our destination? Where did the tanks go? We couldn't answer, not because we were being brave, but because we really didn't know, they'd already killed our Staff Sergeant, he was the only one who knew where we were going and hadn't had the time to brief us yet. Being dead, he wasn't going to tell them what they wanted to hear, so they went to town on us. The beatings I could manage, it was when they started pulling my fingernails that I realised they weren't going to stop, not unless we gave them something. So that's what I did." He looked down at his bent and broken fingers, as if to justify what he said next. "I told them a lie, that we were heading to Yeovil. I didn't know you were also heading that way, I'm so sorry."

Mike could see how much the Corporal was beating himself up as he replied, "This wasn't your fault, you did what you had to survive, no-one can judge you for that. Besides for all we know they might have always been heading this way."

The Corporal looked up slowly nodding as he continued, "Not long after I told them, the beatings stopped. A bag was placed over my head, and I felt a sharp pain in my neck, I remember hearing laughter, someone was laughing, then nothing. I blacked out and woke up in the truck with you all staring at me."

Mike was about to reply, when one of the police officers spoke up, a police Sergeant. "I was the duty Sergeant in Weymouth police station. We'd just sent out our units to the docks, there were people running into the station, reporting all manner of things going on over there. Illegals landing there and ships turning up to the port unannounced. We could hear gunfire and explosions in the area, we tried to call it up to get support, but no one was answering the radios. We tried getting hold of Poole, Dorchester, Police HQ, but no-one was listening." He looked over to the police Chief angrily as he said that last part.

"All your radios were being jammed; no-one would have heard you outside of Weymouth." Mike replied, trying to ease the tension.

He looked over to Mike in understanding as he continued. "One of our patrol cars eventually came back, shot to shit, the P.C was just sat inside, white with shock. I'd ran out to ask him where his partner was, all he kept saying was they'd ran over her with a tank. I couldn't get any more sense out of him, he just clammed up. We took him inside and tried to get him to talk, who had done this? What tank? Who was he talking about? But before we knew it, they were already outside. Three big wheeled armoured vehicles and one tank. One of the DCI's went out to talk to them, to find out what they were doing here. He thought perhaps the army may have been training and hadn't informed us. He got no more than three feet outside the door before they opened fire. There were no warnings, no ultimatums, they just opened fire on him, an unarmed man. We didn't have any weapons, certainly none to take out those vehicles, so the rest of us surrendered and were bundled from the building, I don't remember much after that, except being interrogated in a large room. They were asking us what we had seen? Who were we? Would we be willing to work with them? After seeing what they had just done to the DCI, I told them to shove it up their arse. I wouldn't be helping them. I was given a beating for my outburst and a bag placed over my head and then driven somewhere else. I don't remember much about the journey, except the smell of cheap cigarettes and sweat. I think it was a warehouse, the floor felt like concrete, there were others in there, I couldn't be sure about the numbers, but I could hear them, some were crying, some were moaning in pain, some were just breathing heavily. Every time I tried to speak out, someone would kick me, so they must have had guards in there. At the far end of the building there was a door, I remember it would bang against the frame when it opened. Sometimes I'd hear the door crash open and then they'd take someone away, you could hear the screams or the cries from another part of the building, and sometimes they'd bring them back, a lot quieter than before."

Mike could tell from the look on the police Sergeant's face he'd been through a traumatic couple of days. He looked over to the two women, wondering if they had been held in the same place.

The police Sergeant's tone changed, as he continued speaking, glancing over to the Russian prisoners. "After several hours, it began to get more quieter, I wondered if perhaps they were letting people go. Perhaps it would be my turn soon. Well soon enough it was my turn, I heard the door open, felt someone stand over me, I think I said something to them, I can't remember, but I felt a sharp pin prick to my neck, and then just like that, the lights went out. I woke up here in the truck, with one hell of a headache."

"I think I was held there; I remember that fucking door banging." One of the other police Constable's chimed in, as all eyes now turned to him.

Over the next thirty minutes, Mike listened as the rest of the group began to explain how they were captured. The PC that had just spoken was called Arnie, who continued to explain how he was on his way to Bovington with a fire engine and two ambulances when the convoy was ambushed two miles from the camp. After a brief firefight, they were all captured, and had watched horrified as the female paramedics were dragged away from the others and into the woods by some of the soldiers. Arnie's eyes filled with tears as he described the helplessness at hearing their screams. He'd been beaten along with the firefighters and all of them were taken to the same facility, where they were hooded and beaten again until he to felt the cold stab of a needle in his neck. Two of the civilians were tourists, both looked to have had been coming out of separate bars in Weymouth and walking back to their hotels, simply in the wrong place at the wrong time. One, called Colin, had been caught filming the Russian vehicles travelling out of the port as they ran over a police officer and was accused of spying. The other called Tim, had been witness to three Russians executing a police officer on a bridge. Next to speak was the police Chief, she told them her name was Catherine Stokes and she was a Chief Superintendent. She then proceeded to say how herself and the younger PC had both been captured at their headquarters after refusing to help the Russians. They'd both been dragged out of there and placed in the holding facility with everyone else. The other two civilian women were reporters for the local news, which explained why Mike recognised the one in the dress, her name was Joanna Fulman, he'd seen her on the local TV, doing her daily news reports. The other reporter was called Linda Harding, and she calmly explained their story, as Joanna remained quiet. They'd both been rushed to the area by their bosses to do a report on the phone outages, instead they'd hit reporter gold, they stumbled upon the invasion early on and were filming it when they were captured. The Russians had killed the rest of their news team and sent the two women back to the holding area. Mike and Spider could guess the rest. No matter where they had been found or how they had been captured, all of them had the same ending, all had been held at this facility, and all of them remembered the door.

After the final person had finished speaking, Mike stood looking at the ground and sipping from one of the bottles of water. Finally, after a few moments of silence he looked up.

"Right, well now we know how you all ended up together, whatever your circumstances, it would all appear to have something to do with this holding facility you mentioned."

"So, what happens now?" the Chief Super asked?"

Spider and Mike shared a quick look before Mike replied.

"For now, we need you all to sit tight and wait here with us, we can give you food and water, and let you regain some strength, then tonight when we leave, you can all walk into the town that's close by and make your own way to safety."

"But what if we want to leave now?" Colin demanded. "My family are going to want to know where I am and that I'm safe."

The others nodded in agreement and within seconds Mike had some of them demanding to go. The three Engineer soldiers kept quiet, as if understanding the predicament, they were in. They knew they'd be staying with the unit regardless. One of the reporters, Linda, spoke loudly, "Look I don't think you understand the seriousness of this. I need to report back in, the stuff I've seen, *we've seen*, needs to be told, we're talking war crimes here. People need to be made aware. If we don't get this story out and quick, someone else will!"

Wow, Mike thought to himself, after everything she's been through, all she wants to do is be the first to get the story out. Her colleague remained quiet, clearly, she didn't feel the same way.

Mike held his hands up as their voices began to get louder, alerting one of the sentries who walked back into the group and stood next to them. "Keep your voices down people, we're trying to stay hidden remember." Mike warned.

Suddenly realising their predicament, everyone quietened down, as Mike began to explain. "Firstly, excuse the pun, but you're not out of the woods just yet, we're still behind enemy lines remember, which are not far from here and you're still in a lot of danger. Secondly, it's not a case of simply walking out of here in the daytime, people will see you and for now we need to keep our location secret, and that means you all need to play along with us and stay hidden. Thirdly, some of you are weak, dehydrated and need to limber up, the last thing you need to be doing is walking around in the heat of the sun, drawing attention to yourself."

Linda was still arguing, her finger pointing accusingly at Mike. "Now listen here Mister, I've reported on the war in the Sudan and I've reported from Ukraine, I know all about danger, so don't patronise me on the risk, and as for my fitness, I run marathons in my spare time, so I could probably run rings around you lot. For the sake of this story, I'm willing to take the risks. So, give me some water, point me in the direction of that town you spoke about and I'll make sure you get a mention in this story."

"I'm sorry Linda, but I can't allow that, you can't leave just yet."

She looked back forcefully, "You can't make me stay here, I'm *not* in the army remember!"

Mike was about to reply when the Chief Superintendent stepped forward trying to calm things down. "He can't make you stay, but I can. Look he's right, we can't leave here just yet, the risks are too great, calm down and think it through."

"Or what?" the reporter replied testily, putting her hands on her hips.

The police Chief nodded towards the other police officers, "Or I'll have you detained by my officers and held for the rest of the day. I don't want to do that, not after everything we've all just been through." Her tone softened as she looked over to the soldiers, "Don't forget Linda, these people just rescued us, at least you owe them for that and I don't think waiting until tonight is too much to ask, do you?"

Mike could see the reporter think it through in her head before her tone softened, as she replied, "Alright fine, I'll wait, it's not like anyone can phone through the story anyway."

She walked over to join her colleague adding, "But tonight, no matter what, Joanna and I will be leaving you."

"Fair enough." Mike agreed. He looked over at the others, as finally, he could see by the looks on their faces that their predicament was slowly dawning on them. They may have been saved for now, but they were not out of danger yet. They would all have to sit tight and wait for the darkness to return.

Mike saw Joanna shift uncomfortably, neither of the women had tried to explain away their torn clothing, almost as if they thought if they ignored it, then perhaps it didn't happen. Mike remembered what he'd seen in the truck's cab, quickly he looked over to Spider.

"Spider, would you mind explaining the rules for our new guests while they stay with us, explain where they can and can't go, please."

Spider looked up, "Sure thing."

"Also, let's see if we can get some food rustled up for them, I'm sure by now they're hungry."

Mike saw some of their faces brighten at the mention of food. He left them listening to Spider as he walked back past the prisoners to the front cab. He noticed Jonah wasn't glaring at him anymore, instead he was looking apologetic. Ignoring him, he climbed up into the cab, quickly rummaging around the trucks equipment, until he found the soldiers personal items. He upended the bergens, the contents spilling out, until he found spare sets of clothing. He picked up two sets of trousers, checking they were clean and then picked up four t-shirts and two green jumpers. It wouldn't be fashion week for the women, but it was better than what they were wearing now. He quickly bundled the clothes back into one of the bergens, then returned to the group, where Rachel and Changa were passing out cans of all day breakfasts. Nobody cared that it was cold, Mike had forbidden everyone from starting the vehicle's engines to use the onboard cookers, or Boiling Vessels, for fear of being heard and discovered. For now, they were all on what the military would call 'hard routine' which meant no fires, no vehicle noise and no ability to get hot food or drink. It increased their chances of remaining hidden for the day but meant everything would be cold. A small discomfort, but worth it to keep them all alive.

Hearing Spider finish his briefing, Mike then added, "If I were you guys, seeing as we're limited in space, why don't you use the back of truck as your admin area, take it in turns to go up and get yourselves cleaned up, in privacy. We can spare a jerry can of water for you to wash with. With the canopy down, no-one will see in."

Leaving them to it, he walked over to the two reporters, as they quickly gulped down the cold breakfasts. They both had surprised faces as he deposited the bergen at their feet. Speaking quietly so as the others wouldn't hear, he said to them both, "There's spare clothes in here, if you want them." Joanna looked at the floor as her colleague simply nodded in thanks. Knowing he'd already said too much, he turned and walked away, Mike wished he could somehow summon the words to console them both, but he couldn't. Suppressing the anger inside him he walked past the prisoners back to his tank, followed by Spider.

"Mike, mind me asking what you're thinking?"

He stopped, checking no-one else was within earshot as he replied, "I'm thinking about that truck, and why they were all drugged and put in it. If the Russians were going to execute them, then why not just shoot them and get it over with? Why put them in a truck and drive around with them? None of that makes any sense to me."

"Execute them? You think that was why they were all in there? Why would they choose the kill them?"

"Why not? You heard them, all of them had heard or seen the Russians commit war crimes. Why leave them alive to report back what they had seen? Remember the early years of the Ukraine war? All that footage leaking out showing the Russian army killing civilians. If they're trying to justify this invasion, then all of these stories would have to disappear. And that means making the witnesses disappear."

"But that's murder!" Spider spat out. "That's outright fucking murder. Is this what we can expect now for anyone left behind?"

"Spider, we're not fighting the boy scouts, their army is mostly conscripts, with no more than three years training at the most. These aren't professionals by any standards, they don't abide by the same laws and standards that we do, these are bullies, outlaws and thugs with guns."

"What about those two by the truck?" Why are we keeping them alive?" Spiders tone was menacing.

"You know why Spider," Mike looked at him forcefully. "We're not sinking to their level, trust me that's a dark path that few come back from."

Mike clapped him on the back, "Come on, lead by example, I can't have you being a grumpy sod all the time and thinking of executing everyone we capture."

"What do you mean by that?" Spider asked surprised.

Mike smiled, "I mean, these past few days you've been turning yourself into Mr grumpy. I don't know you that well, but some of your guys are noticing, and they know you better than me. So, if they're saying it and seeing it, then so am I."

"I'm not fucking grumpy-" Spider began, stopping suddenly as Mike pulled a face, mimicking him looking grumpy and silently saying the same thing. His face broke into a grin as he realised how he'd sounded, as both of them began to quietly laugh.

"There you go," said Mike, "and that ladies and gentlemen is what we call a smile."

Spider stood there chuckling, something about Mikes laughter was infectious and without knowing why, he kept laughing, perhaps it was the stress of it all, perhaps he was going crazy. He didn't understand it and he didn't care. All he knew was that nothing seemed to faze this guy and he was happy they found him, or was it the other way round. He had found them. Either way the stress of the past forty-eight hours melted away, and for next few moments, both just giggled away like kids.

They were aware of someone behind them, turning to see Rachel. She'd volunteered herself to do one of the roaming sentry guards and hearing the laughter, had come to investigate.

"Something funny?" she asked inquisitively.

"No, just relieving some tension is all." Mike replied, the laughter dying off.

"Does that work? Laughing it off?"

"Sometimes, Rachel, sometimes. Now what can we do for you?"

"I was chatting earlier to your gunner, Trooper Smith, I think you call him Smudge?"

"Smudge, yes that's correct, what about him?"

"He told me that you'd used a red phone box to call us back at WOC, is that true? Is that how you were able to call us? Do the red phone boxes still work?"

Mikes brows pinched together in curiosity as he replied, "That's true, why do you ask?"

"Cerne Abbas is where they have that huge carving of a giant in the hill, the one with the big er..."

"Penis?" Mike added, his eyebrows raised, seeing her discomfort.

Spider chuckled as he said it.

Ignoring Spider, Mike quickly replied, "Yes that's right, Cerne Abbas, we're in the woods overlooking it, Rachel, what are you getting at?"

"I was only there two weeks ago, my girlfriend took me as a surprise, I remember it because we were joking about two lesbian women getting a photo taken next to the largest...penis in the country and not being interested in it."

"Okay," Mike replied curiously, wondering what on earth the Corporal was getting at.

"Well, I thought you'd like to know, when we were there, another thing we noticed and got a photo of, was this..."

She walked forward handing her phone to Mike, who broke into a big smile. Spider looked on confused, as Mike handed him the phone to see for himself. There in all its glory was a picture of Rachel and her girlfriend, both wearing silly grins enjoying the moment, and both were holding the telephone receiver and standing in the open doorway of a beautiful big red shiny phone box.

16

Change of Plans

Portland Harbour

Colonel General Kuzmin stood watching on as the huge cleanup operation of the docks was underway. He watched the patrol boats moving slowly through the oily rubbish strewn waters as the crews worked with the hooks and poles to carefully pull floating bodies onboard. Some were blackened beyond recognition, twisted into un-recognisable shapes, each body telling a story of misery that loved ones back home would struggle to understand. It sickened him to see the waste of it all, his eyes drawn back to the dockyard at the ever-increasing pile of filled body bags that was laid out. It had only been six hours since the attack, turning the once functioning dockyard into a slaughterhouse of butchery and death. He'd had been awakened in the early hours by the noise of the attack as the Rasputin had exploded and remembered staring out of the window of the manor house he occupied, in shock at seeing the dull orange glow on the horizon almost five miles away. By the time his aides had arrived to report the attack to him, he was already dressed and issuing orders to his helicopter crew. He'd visited Poole harbour, seeing for himself the destruction before coming here. He looked on at the wreck of the Rasputin, it was still smoking, its upper decks burned and twisted as it lay near the dockyard. So far and yet so close, he thought. He listened in on the reports from the Admiral on how the navy came so close to getting her out. The Admiral continued speaking, as now, Kuzmin cast his eye over to the southern dock, where on it's side, lay the 120,000-tonne cargo ship the Nikita. She at least hadn't caught fire, and already navy and salvage divers were checking the hull to see if she could be patched and re-floated. The early reports had said the Rasputin had taken three-thousand soldiers and sailors down with her, along with twenty tanks, but the Nikita had gone down quicker, trapping nearly five-thousand men below decks. Still, the rescue teams were pulling the lucky ones still alive trapped in air pockets up from her decks. On board she still had almost an entire regiment's worth of equipment and ammunition. But the worst of the news hadn't been the loss of the ships, or the loss of the men, it had been what they were carrying that had caused him to look so vexed. On board the Nikita, were their entire complement of MI 28 Havoc attack helicopters and MI-24 Hinds. Colonel Golgolvin's airborne brigade would be now airborne in name only, the few helicopters they'd managed to get ashore early in the operation, would be all they would have to use for now, until replacements could be sent from home. But the Rasputin's loss was far worse, she had been carrying their entire weapons complement for all their fighters and bombers in the south. Packed full of rockets, incendiary bombs and high explosive rounds, it had been no wonder she had exploded as she did. Already their aircraft had empty weapons pylons, awaiting re-armament, with an ever-expanding list of targets and missions waiting to be carried out. Without the weaponry, the planes would be useless and without the planes how could they claim air superiority over the front lines? When you added up the loss of life and the war material lost, it was a devastating loss. He shook his head angrily as the Admiral finished reading the cargo manifest, walking up to him and snatching the clipboard from him.

After a few seconds of scanning the pages, he looked up, his eyes burning with anger.

"Where did you get this?" he hissed.

The Admiral frowned in confusion, at the sudden show of aggression.

"I asked you, where did you get this?" the General repeated loudly, adding, "I have been demanding to know where our helicopters and munitions for the planes were, for the past 24 hours. Only to be told that NOBODY knew their location. I was told that the ships were loaded in no specific order, and yet here you stand, with a LIST showing in great detail what each and every one is loaded with! Is this done deliberately? Are the navy trying to sabotage this operation?"

The Admiral continued to look back at him confused, before finally replying.

"But Comrade General, these lists came from *your* own office, Colonel General Terekhov sent them to us personally, to assist in the unloading of his unit."

"His unit?" Kuzmin replied confused, looking down at the loading manifest. On it was written all of the ships unloaded so far, and when they were unloaded. He scanned the pages as the Admiral continued.

"Yes, Comrade General, *his* unit. He told me that he was to take priority in unloading, that's why they were the second ship unloaded."

Kuzmin's eyes scanned the manifest, seeing for himself, orders signed by Terekhov, all part of something called 'Project Houdini.' He had no idea what they were for and had never heard of this Houdini, and he was supposed to be the commander in the south! What the hell was Terekhov playing at, he thought angrily, as the Admiral now questioned.

"Sir, my apologies, but I was led to believe that you were made aware of this, and that you'd already seen the manifest for the ships?"

Dammit, he thought, he needed to speak to Terekhov about this, but not with half his officers knowing! The last thing he needed was to look weak in front of the others, deciding for now to defuse the situation he merely grunted in reply, tearing off the manifest and tucking it into his pocket before adding, "It looks like there's been an oversight Admiral, between my headquarters and the navy. Rest assured I'll get to the bottom of it. For now, we concentrate on fixing this bloody mess!"

His hands swept around the port again as one of the naval officers stepped forward to speak.

"Sir, I think we may have to suspend unloading operations, for the time being, until we can clear the wreckage."

"Impossible!" one of the army Colonel's shot back, "our timeframe dictates we're unloaded and ready for operations now! We're already behind schedule, almost half of our combat power is still at sea scratching their arses. Every minute we delay, allows the British more time.

"But the docks are closed!" the naval officer shot back, "until we can reopen them it will be impossible to get the ships in."

"The men are already talking about these phantom figures in the sea, I've got salvage divers already refusing to go into the water, even with a close protection team." another voice added.

"Enough!" the voice of the General cut through, stopping everyone.

He turned to the group of officers, his voice demanding.

"Why do we still have men left aboard the ships? Why aren't they ashore yet?"

The officers all looked at each other for answers as finally the port operations officer began.

"Sir, you're talking about nearly 100,000 troops, we don't have the logistics set up to deal with them all yet, not to mention the room to put them all ashore. The hotels, the guest houses in the area are full already."

"Hotels? Guesthouses?" he shot back venomously. "These are soldiers of the Russian Forces! They don't need guest houses and hotels! They'll sleep in fields covered in cow shit if they have to! I don't care where they go, just get them off those damn ships! I'll not have our troops sat there like cows waiting at the slaughterhouse! get them all off!"

"Dammit! Must I think of everything?" he raged, continuing, their silence annoying him as in response, some of the more junior officers looked to the ground. "You're supposed to be officers of the Russian Military, and instead you stand there like scolded children!"

He stood scowling at them as he tried to compose his thoughts. Quickly realising that belittling them would get him nowhere. He looked at the Admiral who hadn't looked away. His tone accusing.

"So, Admiral, how did this happen? Where were the navy in all of this?"

The Admirals face went red, as he shot back defensively. "Comrade General, the port has been closed to all sea traffic since we landed, with our submarine nets blocking the only routes in or out, the attack must have come from either the land or the air. *That* security is the responsibility of the army!

Ahh, thought Kuzmin, the shift of responsibility begins. He turned to the army Colonel.

"Colonel? Care to elaborate? Your regiment was tasked with the port's security; how was this attack allowed to happen?"

The Colonel swallowed nervously, before firing back, "General, we believe the attack came from the sea, not the air or ground. The navy had divers in the water that we were not aware of. These men were reported missing, far too late for us to have the time to react. By the time we were made aware that the men were missing, the attack was already underway."

The Admiral shot a murderous look at the Colonel. He was about to answer when they were interrupted by a pair of new figures walking towards them, one exclaiming loudly.

"Perhaps the nets were not as effective as the Admiral thought!"

"Who are you?" the Admiral asked arrogantly, his eyes narrowing at the Major who had dared to interrupt him.

Seeing the confused looks, the General introduced them, "This is Colonel Olensky, regional FSB commander for the area and his deputy, Major Tchesky," noting how the Admiral stiffened slightly now he knew who the men worked for. The FSB were feared throughout the military, their ruthlessness and absolute power knew no boundaries, even for an Admiral.

Everyone turned to the new arrivals as the Admiral spat out defensively. "Impossible! Those nets are made of carbon weaved coated steel and sink to the seabed. We've already checked them, there's not a cut or mark on them. Whoever did this *Major* did not come by the sea!" Everyone noted the Admiral had sneered at the man's rank, clearly rankled at having been spoken to in such as a way by a mere Major.

General Kuzmin continued, "Since my arrival, I've had the Colonel and his men carry out his own investigation." He turned to the Major, "Please Major, continue with your report."

The Major nodded, looking at the Admiral he continued, "Admiral, you're correct in your report, the tugs and booms do indeed guard the harbour entrances, however, were you aware that the tidal range at this time of year is over seven metres?"

"Yes, every sailor here is aware of the tide, Major."

Unperturbed the Major continued, "that means that every six hours the depth of the harbour entrance drops or raises by seven metres."

"I know how the tides work! I was a sailor long before I became a senior member of the navy *Major!*" The Admiral shot back, his tone scalding. Clearly, he was getting annoyed at the way he was being spoken to.

"Then may I ask why your crews in charge of the boom did not take this into account?"

All eyes turned to the Admiral as he quickly countered, "They do, I've issued orders that the boom and nets be raised and lowered every hour with the tide."

The Major smiled thinly, the tone venomous. "No Admiral they do not. I've just come back from visiting one of the boats, and the crew reported that the nets are adjusted every six hours. That means that for every five of those six hours that the tide is rising and falling, both entrances are open, sometimes by as much as seven metres, more than enough for a dive team or a mini submarine to get through."

The group of officers all began to curse loudly at the news, as they realised, the whole attack could have been preventable, but for the lazy crews on the tugs.

The Admiral looked on furiously as Colonel Olensky began to speak.

"Comrade General, I've already sent out orders for both tugboat Captains and crews to be arrested immediately and charged with dereliction of duty and failure to carry out orders."

Kuzmin nodded, his own face a mask of rage as he looked out again at the devastation, shaking his head, he felt his jaw harden and his thoughts turn murderous. He was distracted when two officers nearby began to argue. Looking up, he watched as they continued the argument, oblivious to the senior group of men standing nearby, both animatedly discussing the contents of a clipboard whilst pointing out toward the Rasputin. One looked to be an airforce Captain, the other from the navy who wore the rank of Lieutenant. Both men carried on, unaware they were being watched by the General, until finally, his patience wore thin as he snapped out.

"WHAT IS IT?"

Both officers looked over wide eyed, seeing the command group staring. Both slammed to attention, instantly stung to silence.

Kuzmin walked over, taking the clipboard from the naval officer and glancing at it, before raising an eyebrow at them both, his eyes appraising them.

"Well, I asked, what is it? What's important enough to get you arguing amongst yourselves in front of my command group?"

The naval officer swallowed nervously, his eyes darting about, but the Captain merely looked back, confidently reporting.

"Sir, I'm Captain Sakharov, Air Captain to the 146th Air wing. I've been sent down by Colonel Bresavik from Bournemouth Airport to chase down our ammunition resupply."

The General nodded in response, angrily turning and pointing out to sea at the devastation in front of him.

"Well Captain, you see the ships in the distance pulling bodies aboard, next to the black hulk of what was once a ship?"

The Captain's eyes narrowed, as he looked to where the General was pointing.

"Yes, Sir, I see it." he announced, smiling triumphantly, the smile quickly disappearing as the General shot back.

"Well, that's what's left of the ship that was carrying your missiles! If you hold your breath long enough you might be able to salvage one or two."

The Captain wore a look of disbelief at the revelation, as ignoring him, the General turned back to his command group, rage clear to hear in his voice.

"I want the crew's court martials to be completed by the end of the day Colonel. We don't have the time to string this out, I want all of them to be found guilty and then I want the punishment to be swift and merciless."

"Will jailtime be enough?" Colonel Olensky asked, eyebrows raised.

Kuzmin shook his head, his tone poisonous as pointing out to towards the devastation at the pile of bodies on the dockside he replied.

"No, they deserved better, they expected better and I'm going to give it to them. This Division has a laziness ingrained into it and I intend to cut it out like a surgeon would a cancer. I want all ranks, regardless of position to understand, there is no excuse for dereliction of duty. The crews will be sentenced to death, and I want the executions carried out this evening.

Some of the group looked horrified, only the two FSB officers seemed to be unfazed.

The Admiral began to protest, stepping forward. "But Sir, I understand the need to punish those responsible, but are we really going to execute our *own* men? Is that what we're doing now? What kind of message does that send to our forces?"

The General held up his hand to silence him.

"Admiral, you said yourself earlier, dock security is an army matter, well *discipline* decisions are mine." The Admiral wisely kept quiet as the General continued, trying to hide the anger in his voice. "Already I have lists waiting back on my desk with hundreds of names on for men refusing to fight, criminal conduct, rape, murder, desertion, yes that's right DESERTION! And we've only been here forty-eight hours! Now, I need a military that fears its commanders, *fears me*, more than it fears the enemy. Now, seeing as we've already paid the price for this...failure, I intend to collect on that. By making an example of these men I will show our forces that their actions now have responsibilities, that can and will, result in their own death. And if by executing a few useless men that message is clear, well, then that's a price I will happily pay. Now, just be thankful *Admiral* that I do not have the Colonel add your name to the list."

The Admiral's mouth opened in shock at the veiled threat, as ignoring him the General looked around to the assembled officers, pointing out to the ships moored at sea, continuing, "I want every soldier off those ships and on the shore within the next twelve hours and every piece of equipment, every tank, armoured vehicle, helicopter, rifle, grenade, bayonet and bullet on shore within the next twenty-four."

A naval Colonel stepped forward, a resigned look on his face. "Sir, what you're asking, with the docks here and in Poole out of action, we'll need that time just to clear the docks."

Kuzmin stared back impassively. "I don't care how you do it, beach the ships on the shore if you have to, drive the tanks off the beaches, I want it done. We've got troops fighting on the front lines waiting for resupply and reinforcements, I won't let your excuses stop that."

He turned to walk back to his helicopter, when as an afterthought he turned back to the Admiral.

"Oh, and Admiral, I expect no more...mistakes like this again. From now on, you are personally responsible for the dockside security. Do *not* fail me."

The group split up, the Admiral walking back towards the docks, followed by his staff, as the General walked away in the opposite direction with the FSB officers following. The helicopter's engines were already beginning to spool up and the giant rotors slowly turning, as the crew could see the General was finished for now.

Kuzmin stopped short of the helicopter, holding out his arm to stop both men, as shouting above the noise of the engines as he turned to the FSB officers.

"No, you both stay here, manage the court martials, see that they run smoothly."

The Colonel looked like he was about to argue, quickly sharing a look with the FSB Major, but seeing the look on the General's face he thought better of it. He simply nodded and saluted, as both men watched him continue alone towards the helicopter, Kuzmin ducking his head upon instinct as he stepped into the fighting compartment of the Hind. He quickly settled into the cargo netted seating and lit a cigarette, removing his cap and resting it on his lap, watching as the crew chief jumped aboard and manned the side door machine gun. Outside he watched the ground slowly disappear, the two FSB officers trying to salute, but quickly holding onto their caps as the downdraft of the helicopter began buffeting them. He smirked to himself, fucking FSB, he thought, always there watching, recording everything that's said, reporting back to Moscow. He closed his eyes, inhaling deeply at the cigarette. He'd tried to quit twice already, but with this operation being as it was, he knew he wouldn't be quitting anytime soon. Instead, he sat silently, thankful for a few moments alone, his mind racing through the problems that faced him. He hadn't been over exaggerating with the Admiral when he'd mentioned the discipline problems, the fledgling army he commanded was made up of mostly conscripts, some with less than twelve weeks training. To have kept so many couped up on the ships, then let them loose on the English countryside, would always be fraught with problems. He'd been given strict orders to keep any unwanted attention out of the public eye, they were here as saviours, not conquerors. But the men, his men, just couldn't help themselves. Like the wolves let loose amongst the sheep, he'd had endless discipline problems, hopefully the executions would curb the fire in them. How many names of soldiers facing discipline issues did he have on his desk already awaiting his signature? Too many. Shaking his head in frustration, he sat watching the British countryside flashing past in shades of green and yellow, watching the crew chief, alert and scanning with his 12.7 DHSK machine gun, his eyes hidden behind the darkened visor. At least for him, life was simple, Kuzmin thought moodily.

Bovington Camp 6th Div Headquarters

The flight back to the base took less than six minutes, and the General knew they were landing when he felt the thump of the landing gear coming down. He quickly savoured the last drag of the cigarette, throwing the butt out of the side door, as he watched the now familiar buildings of Bovington camp come into view. His mood soured further as he thought how it was now seconded as his headquarters, he hadn't thought to have been here now, instead his army was supposed to have been already on the march towards Tidworth. But without the fresher troops off the ships, he had no way to reinforce the ever-expanding front lines and with the danger of stretching his forces too thinly, he'd resorted to slowing their lightening advance to a trickle, covering only twenty miles now, instead of the planned forty. Now, he was stuck here, a prisoner of his own making, waiting yet again for logistics. He knew he should go straight to the operations room, to find out the latest progress on their advances but in his pocket, he could feel the crumpled manifest from the ships, taunting him. He had to speak to Terekhov. He waited until he felt the helicopter touch down, the heavy aircraft settling on the ground as he pushed past the crew chief and jumped out, the helicopters engines already beginning to whine down behind him as he raced over to the headquarters building. Without pausing, he sprinted up the stairs, his anger beginning to rise again, as he made his way along the corridor towards the FSB offices, not pausing to wait, he crashed through the double doors and into the office of Colonel General Terekhov. Terekhov was at his desk, watching a video on a laptop, with two others standing nearby, all of them looked up as he burst through.

Of the other two, Kuzmin recognised immediately Captain Lunyou, looking over at the second man, he was a big burly stocky man, and his face was set into a natural sneer. The man's neck was huge and his face was marked with bruising, and a broken nose. His inspection of the man's face was brought to a halt as both men saluted and stood to attention. Kuzmin returned the salute and looked over at Terekhov, who, seeing the anger on his face, forced a smile before ordering.

"Leave us! I believe the CinCS has something he wishes to discus with me in private?"

Kuzmin waited until both had left, and the door was closed before stepping forwards, angrily holding out the docking manifest.

"You knew what was loaded on the bloody ships all along!"

Terekhovs eyes narrowed as he stood up, taking the crumpled paper and making a show of uncrumpling it on the table and smoothing it out, trying to read what was written. Angry at the display, Kuzmin shot back, reciting what he'd already read.

"Let me save you the bother, August 30th, 21:40, fifty trucks and armoured vehicles given priority one unloading clearance, Project Houdini, as per orders from Colonel General Terekhov. *Colonel General Kuzmin Commander in Chief South approved.*"

Terekhov looked up, smiling thinly as Kuzmin continued.

"I gave no such approval. What the hell is Houdini? And more importantly why the hell did you keep the manifest to yourself? Do you have any idea of the problems we're facing thanks to this?"

"Comrade General Kuzmin, please, sit." Terekhov replied, pointing to the empty seat opposite.

"I DON'T WANT TO SIT! I WANT TO KNOW!" he yelled, thumping the desk angrily.

The FSB officer looked back, his own face reddening at the outburst, not accustomed to being yelled at, especially in his own office. Both wore the same rank, but regardless, it was the CinCS who was in command, Terekhov had to concede that fact.

Seeing as he couldn't simply excuse the man, he sat back down, folding his arms as he began.

"Project Houdini is an internal FSB matter, that need not concern you at this time-"

"Bullshit!" Kuzmin shot back interrupting him, "I want to know what it is!"

Terekhov remained defiant, shaking his head sorrowfully. "I'm sorry Comrade General, but without official clearance from Moscow I cannot and will not speak about it."

Kuzmin looked on open mouthed, thinking to himself, so Terekhov wasn't acting alone, Moscow had planned whatever this thing was, but then hadn't felt the need to trust him with it? What else were they keeping from him?

Seeing Kuzmin's shock Terekhov continued, "Regarding the shipping manifests, I naturally assumed that being the senior commander, your headquarters would have been given a copy. Perhaps the fault lies within your own staff?"

Shit, Kuzmin thought, perhaps he was right. What if, after barging in and making a scene, the fault was his? What if the report was sat buried under the mountains of reports in his headquarters? After all, how did Terekhov have it? But then what if all along Terekhov was playing games?

Terekhov leaned forwards in his chair, seeing the CinCS anger begin to fade, as he spun the laptop on his desk around to face him.

"Anyway, instead of us attacking each other, perhaps we should work together, I have something of interest to show you..."

Hill 254 on the outskirts of Yeovil

Golgolvin watched from the turret as, all around him, the command post was setup with an ease and efficiency that told him the crews knew what they were about. Two of the BMP's had reversed together until their back doors were almost touching, allowing the operators of both vehicles to talk across to each other. Whilst the remaining three BMP's of the command group were all arranged in a semi-circle, covering the first two, facing outwards with the rear of the vehicles almost touching each other. The turrets all pointing menacingly to ward off any threat from the area of the town. Between the two command vehicles, map boards were now setup, and chairs arranged allowing the Colonel to sit and brief soldiers and plan future operations with his chain of command. He watched as the setup took no more than ten minutes to complete, where once was a treelined field, now stood a fully operational command post. The spot they'd chosen was at the edge of a woodline, in dead ground to the town, but giving them a good view of the town if they needed it by standing on top of their turrets, whilst also providing good cover from enemy fire should any be directed at them. At this range they knew they were safe from small arms fire and anti-tank weapons, the only real threat being from either tanks, air or artillery. But even with the protection the woods and the terrain gave them, the crew still quickly pegged out the camouflage netting, hiding the entire operation from view, a lesson some of the more experienced units had learned the hard way in Ukraine. Nodding in appreciation, he gratefully accepted the cup of coffee handed up to him by his second in command as he turned to scan the town again.

They were overlooking the town about two miles away, the town disappearing as it dropped into a valley beyond them. From where they were positioned, they could make out the streets and houses on its outskirts, but the town looked devoid of life, except for the occasional vehicle driving quickly through the streets he could see nothing that told him the town was awake. He checked his watch, it was 07:40, surely by now there would be signs of life down there? Placing his coffee down, he picked up his Bino's and began to slowly search the area, looking for anything out of the ordinary, any signs of military activity. Nothing, was anyone even there?

Without taking the Bino's away from his eyes he said.

"I don't like the look of this Sasha, it's too damn quiet."

The Major said nothing, blowing on his own cup of coffee as he turned to see a soldier walking towards them. It was a young Lieutenant, one of the command operators. He stood to attention, saluting the two men and was about to say something, when Golgolvin quickly interrupted him, dropping the binos, his voice firm.

"Do *not* salute us when in the field Lieutenant. If an enemy observer were watching now, they would identify us as officers. Do you wish to get us killed this early on by a sniper?"

The Lieutenant stammered, standing awkwardly as he lowered his hand and tried to look normal, his eyes glancing across the landscape, trying to see if anyone was watching. "Sorry Sir, I wasn't thinking."

Both men smiled to themselves, seeing the man's awkwardness was a welcome relief from last night's journey. Clearly the Lieutenant was new to this, he thought, as stifling a yawn he picked up the coffee and enjoyed the drink as he raised an eyebrow patiently, waiting for the soldier to report.

Looking up to the turret, the Lieutenant had to shield his eyes from the early morning sun's rays as he squinted, "Sir, the CP (Command Post) is now setup, all units are reporting they are now in forward positions overlooking the town. All unit commanders are enroute here as per your orders."

"Good," he replied, as he climbed out of the turret and jumped to the floor, standing tall and stretching his back, hearing the crack of the bones as they clicked back into place. Shaking his legs and coaxing them back to life, he turned and playfully punched the Major, who smiled back. For the first time since yesterday evening, he was free of the confines of the vehicle. He turned and walked back over to the CP, ducking under the cam net as both men followed. Walking over to the maps, he began to look at the area they were operating in. Looking at the mapping of the town he raised an eyebrow, comparing it to what he had just seen. The map was dated 1983, and showed a vast blob of a town, with a few streets, nothing compared to what he had seen through the binoculars. He looked at the Lieutenant and said nothing, pointing to the date. The Lieutenant nodding apologetically as he replied, "All we have for the town Sir, we've requested more mapping but-"

"You've been ordered to go with what you've got?" he interrupted, the Lieutenant nodding as Golgolvin continued.

"Very well, then let's wait for the unit commanders."

The Lieutenant smiled, and was about to salute again, when thinking back to what had just been said, he quickly stopped himself, instead, turning and disappearing into the back of one of the command vehicles.

Golgolvin looked at the Major, silently shaking his head as he whispered, "I'll tell you Sasha, you'd think command were almost wanting us to fail in this, maps from 1983! I'd get better mapping from a bloody mobile phone!"

Twenty minutes later and they were all there, thirty heads watching him with interest as he stood in front of them, every commander of every unit that he now had under his command. The early arrivals were lucky enough to have bagged a chair, the others, resorted to sitting on their body armour. Most were officers but some were senior Sergeants. Some of the faces he recognised, his own Brigade being split amongst the BTG, but most were new, young and apart from the route march last night, had never worked with him before. He could tell from the stares and the way they looked at him, having a VDV officer in charge of an armoured unit was not something they appreciated. He was tempted at first to go softly on them, until he had proven his worth, thinking perhaps to tread carefully. But then something fired up inside him. He *was* a Colonel of the VDV and he *was* experienced, he didn't have to earn their respect, his men knew what he could do. Fuck the rest of them, they'd either fall in line or he'd kick their arses into line.

He pushed his concerns aside as he began, the disdain in his voice clear to hear.

"Last night was a complete fuck up, I don't know what your units have been used to in the past, or who's commanded you before and I don't care."

He saw them sit straighter, as his words hit them like rocks, as he continued, his finger pointed out to the faces of those looking at him, emphasising his words as he spoke.

"You've not worked with me or my men before, perhaps, for some of you this is the first time working with paratroopers, but I can tell you this. From now on, I expect your best, I demand your best. You and your men represent me, everything they do, everything you do, now reflects on me, I am *your* commander."

"When can we expect to assault the town?"

He looked up to the voice that interrupted him, recognising the commander of one of the tank companies, a chubby faced Major called Lebedev, still angry at having been dressed down earlier over the radio.

Seeing the look on Lebedev's face and the way he'd just spoken out annoyed him. Golgolvin was tempted to belittle the man, but that wouldn't help, it would make him look spiteful, a weakness in a commander. He needed them all onside. Keeping his voice calm and firm he merely replied.

"When I tell you *Major*. For now, your orders are to wait here."

Unperturbed, Lebedev continued, the condescending tone barely hidden in his voice.

"Sir, we've come all this way, the town's just there, no more than two miles away, undefended. Let's go in now, find those tanks and quickly put an end to it. By tonight we can be in Yeovil toasting our success."

The Colonel looked at him almost sympathetically, he knew the Major had some experience and success in Ukraine, the man had constantly been heard bragging about it, but he also knew that most of the units under his new command were fresh out of training, lacking the combat experience for what was to come. Last night had proven that. He kept his concerns to himself as he merely replied.

"Our orders are to wait Major, that comes directly from Commander in Chief South, who gives those orders to me, your commanding officer, who finally gives them to you. For now, we wait."

"But Sir, how long are we to wait here? I've not seen any sign of the enemy. Are they even down there?"

Some of the men looked to each other, sharing quick glances or muttered comments that agreed with the Major. His own men looked angrily at them in response as the Major now stood up and shot back, buoyed on by the comments of those around him.

"Sir, if it's because you're not used to working with the armour, I can happily lead the attack in..."

Some of the group were nodding in agreement as the two men stood there, both staring at the other with Golgolvin wondering what Lebedev hoped to gain from the encounter. Lebedev must have realised he'd overstepped the mark as he looked around, seeing the murderous stares of the Colonels' paratroopers sat amongst them. Lebedev smiled and sat back down, the resignation clear in his voice. "My apologies Sir, of course it's your command, your decision to take."

Golgolvin's eyes narrowed as he tried to gauge the man, trying to work out his angle. To try to undermine him in front of the others, what would he gain? He shook his head slowly as he forced a smile, pointing over to the direction of the town.

"Major Lebedev, have you seen how quiet the town looks? Does that not surprise you given what we've been told to expect from the British? Does that not concern you?"

"Not really Colonel, we've got them against the ropes, their army's finished before it can even get started. We've all heard how good they are, but now we're proving how good we are. We're in their back yard and they don't know what to do. They're ours for the taking."

The Major leaned back on the chair, folding his arms across his chest triumphantly, as he turned to face the others, the other armoured officers all nodding and smiling sharing his enthusiasm for battle. The Colonel's own men remained stern faced and tight lipped, not enjoying seeing their Commanding Officer being openly confronted. Golgolvin decided this had gone on long enough, it was time for the Major to be brought down a peg or two.

"Major, when you were in Ukraine, did you ever face a Challenger 2? Did you ever see one in combat?"

Lebedev smiled as he unfolded his arms, leaning forward he shook his head unconcerned.

"No, why would that matter? I've come up against countless enemy tanks before. I'm still here to talk about it, they, on the over hand, are not. When we do come across them, we'll take them out easily enough."

"Easily enough." Golgolvin replied quietly, smirking to himself before adding.

"And yet, last night, your Company struggled to identify two of their training tanks. Did you destroy those easily enough?"

The Major's smile vanished, replaced by a look of anger as the Colonel continued, ignoring the man and addressing the group, his voice rising.

"My men encountered a Challenger 2 when we fought to take the camp, I watched with my own eyes how it was hit by three, THREE, tank rounds! And still it sat there firing at us, only to escape away into the night. Do not believe what we have been told at home, this enemy is not to be underestimated!"

He watched as Lebedev leant over to talk to a Captain next to him, muttering something in his ear. Both men smiled, clearly the joke was about him.

Annoyed, he continued, "For now, we wait. If those tanks are in that town waiting, then I have no intention of sending our forces down there to be ambushed, even you Major!"

Ignoring the look of disgust on the Major's face, he turned to the artillery Captain.

"Start to collate a target package, find buildings that you think could conceal ambush positions, then begin to soften them up with bombardments, let's see if we can get them to fire back and identify their positions."

The officer nodded, quickly scribbling into the notebook, as he turned to look at the reconnaissance commander, who was keen to impress again, after last night's disappointment.

"I want our recon forces to begin probing operations, work with the artillery and start getting eyes into those streets, I want to know what we're looking at before the end of the day. Take your time, I don't want anyone rushing headlong in there."

The recon commander nodded, leaning over to chat to the artillery officer, both men already formulating plans.

Satisfied, he looked up, about to issue his orders, when a blast wave of air seemed to shake the net above them, a tornado of noise, followed by the roar of a helicopter overhead, the thud of the rotors causing the men to look up fearfully, all quickly breathing a sigh of relief as they recognised it as one of their own, a Hind.

He stepped out and watched curiously as the helicopter landed behind them, in open fields, the pilot was careful not to get too close, conscious of the downdraft and the damage it could do the maps and tables laid out near the command post.

Now his commanders and officers were all looking up from their maps curiously, their gaze following the helicopter as the side door slid open and a lone figure jumped out, running towards them, fighting against the down draft as the massive rotors continued to turn, the pilots choosing to leave the engines spooled up. Golgolvin felt a spike of anger as he realised the Hind was his own helicopter.

He turned irritably to his second in command who merely shrugged his shoulders. Who the hell was this, he thought, and why the fuck is he flying in my helicopter. He stepped away from the group, quickly closing the distance as he approached the lone figure, recognising him from earlier, as the Captain belonging to the CinCS staff.

"What is it?" he demanded, still angry at the thought of the Captain using his helicopter as a taxi.

"Comrade Colonel, you're to accompany me immediately back to Headquarters."

He blinked in surprise, before quickly recovering, "Why?"

"Colonel, I haven't a clue, all I know is that CinCS and some FSB officers wants to see you immediately."

"What about my men here? I'm in the field in command?" he questioned, pointing to the assembled men.

The Captain shook his head, "Not for now Colonel, the General has ordered that you're to hand command over to Major Lebedev and accompany me."

Golgolvin turned, looking over to the group, his brain racing. Why the hell would the General and the FSB be recalling me? And why was Lebedev now in command? Have I made a mistake, he thought. A knot of fear began to form in his stomach, could he be about to be replaced? Had Lunyou managed to convince his dad back home that the mistake at the camp was his all along?

Seeing his hesitancy the Captain pointed towards the helicopter, his tone more forced. "We need to be going Sir, the General was very clear, he wanted to see you right away."

Shaking his head in frustration Golgolvin quickly ran over to the command vehicle, picking up his assault vest and weapon, before turning to look at the company commander.

"Major Lebedev, you're in command until I get back, make sure those orders are carried out, keep everyone on their toes and stay away from that town. Repeat that order."

Lebedev looked up surprised, as those around him looked at the helicopter then back at him, wondering what had happened. Lebedev's mouth showed the smallest of grins as he repeated. "Of course Sir, I'm now in command, I'll get those orders carried out."

Golgolvin stepped forward, his tone forceful as he reiterated, "And you will stay away from the town, under no circumstances are you to attack the town. Repeat it!"

Lebedev's mouth curled up in irritation at the Colonel's curt tone, as he repeated.

"I'm not to attack the town...Sir!"

Golgolvin remained staring at Lebedev, unsure of whether to trust him or not. Unfortunately, his hands were tied, the General had named him as his second and only the General knew why.

As he walked out of the CP he quickly pulled his second in command close, leaning in and whispering, "Sasha, I don't trust him, keep an eye on him, make sure things stay as they are until I get back."

Sasha looked over at Lebedev, who was now laughing and animatedly chatting to the men around him. Clearly he was popular with the men of the 344th.

"How long until you get back?" Sasha asked, the concern in his voice.

Golgolvin shrugged his shoulders, keeping his fears to himself as he grimaced. "I don't know, but I'll get back as quickly as I can."

Sasha tried to sound optimistic as he replied, "You never know, perhaps it's not bad news, perhaps the Division has our helicopters ready?"

Both men shared a look, knowing the truth, it was rare for a commander to be pulled in off the ground, anything worth saying could be said over the radio. He embraced his colleague, not sure of when, or if, he'd see him again as he replied jokingly.

"Keep the men busy, it'll keep their minds occupied. And stay away from my vodka!"

He waved his goodbyes as he ran after the Captain who was already jogging back to the helicopter, curious as to what could be so important, praying and hoping it wasn't the news he dreaded.

17

Damsels and Demons

Bovington Camp, 6th Div Headquarters

Golgolvin was out of his seat before the helicopter had even touched the ground, keen to find out what was going on, he pushed past the Captain who had travelled back with him, the downdraft of the helicopter tearing at him as he bent over to fight it. Like an invisible arm pulling at him, it suddenly stopped, as free of the rotor wash, he stood up and jogged to the figure waiting for him.

"What the hell is going on?" he demanded; his face red with anger. The flight had done nothing to calm his nerves, his mind was already playing through all the scenarios and he'd imagined everything from a firing squad to hard labour in a Siberian prison camp. The fear had made him angry and he was in no mood to mess about.

A Captain from the General staff met him, saluting, his face impassive as he said coldly, "Apologies Colonel, but the General wants to see you right away."

"I know that!" he spat back, "but why?"

The Captain said nothing, instead, ignoring the Colonel he turned and strode towards the offices, leaving Golgolvin standing red faced. He was tempted to attack the man, but quickly held his temper, he was tired, he was hungry and now he was uncertain. He closed his eyes for a second, clenching his fists and calming himself, it might be nothing, he thought, as taking a deep breath to steady himself he followed the Captain.

He entered the offices, now fully converted into the headquarters and operations room of the 6th Division. The room was a maelstrom of activity, maps showing the south coast of England were pinned to the walls, large red markers showing units placed onto it, whilst soldiers, sailors and airmen, jostled around each other, each person lost in their own part of the giant Russian war machine as it began its stranglehold on the county. He was escorted to the door to the General's office, noting that now, flanking the door, were two armed soldiers, assault rifles held besides them, ready to act. They turned to look at him, quickly looking down to the assault rifle he carried, watching him as he approached for any threat. He stared back, not wanting to look away, until, after a moment they finally saw his rank and both slammed to attention, one of the men reporting loudly.

"Sir, please leave your weapons and body armour outside before entering the General's office."

Slowly and with great care, he placed his combat rig and weapons over to where the sentry indicated, before standing upright and adjusting his crumpled tunic. The sentries resumed their cold gaze back towards the room, as he knocked on the door and waited.

"Come!" he heard the General shout, as he opened the door, stepping into the room, walking up to the General's desk and slamming to attention, his salute crisp and quick. His eyes quickly took in the room, even though his head hadn't moved a centimetre, his paratrooper instincts kicked in, as he felt the presence of the people behind him.

The General looked up from his desk, saluting casually and offering the Colonel to sit. Golgolvin remained standing, turning to look behind him, trying to hide the surprise on his face as he recognised the men from the night of the drop zone, Captain Lunyou, and his Sergeant.

"Colonel, please sit." the General urged, pointing to the seat.

Golgolvin made a show of turning the seat sideways, something about having the two men behind him, made him defensive, which was a feeling he didn't like, especially with his own weapons left uselessly outside of the room. Uncomfortably he saw that both men were still carrying their weapons, he noticed the Sergeant smile at the gesture, no doubt aware of the effect they were having on him, hovering menacingly at the back of the room.

Seeing his discomfort, the General snapped out, "Captain Lunyou, enough of the bloody games! We don't have time to play them, now get yourself over here and dismiss the Sergeant, he can wait outside."

Captain Lunyou nodded, as the Sergeant saluted the General and marched loudly out of the room, closing the door heavily, any attempt at grace or poise lost on the big man.

Golgolvin nodded towards the door, "I thought you were told to get rid of that oaf?"

Lunyou forced a smile out of courtesy as he took a seat next to him, before replying, "Sergeant Feodor has proved useful to me, granted he's not known for his tact or manners, but then we're not in the business of grace and manners, are we? Besides, it's thanks to Sergeant Feodor that we're here now."

Ignoring the Captain Golgolvin quickly looked over to the General.

"Sir, may I ask as to why I've been replaced in the field and why I've been pulled away from my men? Am I to be placed under arrest?"

The General held his hand up to interrupt, smiling as he replied, "Colonel, you have not been replaced, nor are you under arrest. When we've finished here, I will expect you to return to your units."

Confused Golgolvin looked quizically to the General. "Sir?"

"I've requested that you come back, because you may have information regarding the location of the enemy tanks..."

"Information?" Golgolvin tried to hide the surprise on his face.

"However, before we begin, there's something I need to tell you." the General said sternly, standing up and punching the table lightly, his knuckles rapping on the desk, looking frustrated as he continued.

"There's no easy way for me to say this...The rest of the helicopters for your Brigade are gone, they went down with the Nikita in last night's attack."

Golgolvin froze, open mouthed as he took in the news. The CinCS continued to tell him about last night's attack on the ports, the reason it had happened, who they suspected, the loss of the ships and how the whole Division was behind on its unloading of troops and equipment. The General was careful not to add too much of what he really thought, occasionally looking over to Lunyou, conscious that what he was saying would no doubt be reported back in Moscow.

A silence descended over the room as the CinCS finished, watching him, almost waiting for him to say something.

After a few moments of silence, the General, almost anticipating the question to follow, quickly added.

"Of course, Colonel Golgolvin, this now means that the few helicopters we do have, must now be considered of extreme value. Therefore, I'm afraid they will be pulled from your command and placed centrally under the sole command of headquarters, just for the time being. Once we have replacements sent over from the homeland, we can then think about getting them back to you."

So that was why the Captain was using his helicopter as a taxi, Golgolvin thought, frustrated as the news sunk in.

"Do we know when we can expect the replacements?" he asked, already knowing what the answer would be.

The General shook his head as he replied, his voice solemn. "Given where we are, I can't promise anything quickly. Perhaps six to eight weeks...perhaps."

He bit his lip in frustration, his whole Brigade had been designed and trained to be quickly deployable. Now without the helicopters what were they? Merely infantry? The thought of bouncing about with the armoured vehicles didn't exactly appeal to him. How would his men react to the news? He pushed the thoughts from his mind as he looked over again at Lunyou, who simply sat there watching, an amused expression on his face.

Sensing the tension between the two of them, the General now changed the subject.

"Colonel, you still have a Battalion Tactical Group under your command, I'll see to it that you get the extra vehicles needed to transport your men. For now, consider your wings clipped. Speaking of your new command, are there any updates since your last report?"

He shook his head, "No Sir, as per commands orders we've halted our advance for now, I've kept our units away from the town, we've set up overwatch positions to the south, but the town looked quiet, suspiciously quiet."

"Do you think the British are waiting in ambush for us?"

"Perhaps, but with your permission I'd like to send one of our helicopters in to get eyes on the area, to see what's going on."

The General shook his head, "Permission denied, I can't risk losing any more helicopters for now, they'll be needed elsewhere."

Needed elsewhere, Golgolvin thought sarcastically, like taking Captains and their new girlfriends for trips around the harbour? He wisely kept his angry thoughts to himself, instead replying with.

"Okay, well can I at least get permission to get ground units in there, let's see if they are waiting for us, and in what strength?"

The General pursed his lips together in thought and rubbed his chin. After a few moments he shook his head.

"No Colonel, I've pushed you as far north as I dare for now. I don't want us to overextend our positions, not while we're still establishing ourselves here. Besides, Yeovil was never going to be the main effort. For now, keep your forces in their current positions. If the British try anything, I want you ready to defend your position."

He nodded his head, knowing to argue or suggest otherwise, especially with a lesser rank in the room would undermine the General. Not having anything else to say on the matter he now changed the subject himself as he asked curiously,

"General what is this information you brought me here to talk about?"

The CinCS grunted in acknowledgement, happy that Golgolvin seemed to take the news well, as he now slid a laptop over to him.

"Colonel, I want you to press play and watch the following video."

With a curious gaze he looked at the screen, as Captain Lunyou added, "Sergeant Feodor found this being watched last night in the crew room of your pilots. Its footage taken from a gun camera of one of your Hinds, it had them all in fits of laughter to see what the locals are like."

Still none the wiser as to what was so important, he pressed the play button, watching as the grainy image of a man came into view, the focus was out and the picture blurry, then suddenly it snapped into focus, the picture becoming clear. He blinked in surprise; he'd seen this before; he was sure of it. He continued watching the image as the man was stood, trying to urinate, struggling against some unseen force, as an invisible wind seemed to blow at him. Suddenly it came to him, he looked up at them irritably.

"I remember this, it was taken during our hunt for the enemy yesterday. May I ask what it is that's so urgent about an idiot pissing on himself to call me back here?"

"Keep watching." Captain Lunyou replied, as he stared back at the screen, not sure of what he was meant to be looking at, he'd seen this all before. The camera view changed as it zoomed in, focusing on the face of the man, who now looked angry and gestured to the pilots. Captain Lunyou reached over, pausing the video, the man's face now spread on the screen.

He looked closely, seeing the man had a black eye and bruising to his head, as the Captain continued.

"Colonel, this man that you're looking at, is play acting for the camera and is no farmer. He was the one who disarmed my Sergeant at the phone box, and who caused us to attack the camp early on."

"Impossible!" he shot back loudly, "your Sergeant must be mistaken."

"No Colonel, he's not, neither am I, that *is* the man we saw."

He looked up at the General shaking his head in disbelief as Captain Lunyou continued, "We showed this picture to the prisoners here, two of them have already confirmed that this is the man who met with the camp's commander. We believe he is the reason the camp had already been placed on alert when you landed."

He leant back over to the screen, studying the face, could this be him? Had he really been that close to finding the missing units? Unsure, he pressed the play button again, something was niggling at him, as the General now demanded.

"Colonel the question I have is, if that man was here, in this camp and he had the ear of the commander, could he be with the tanks? Could that be how he survived the attack?"

He ignored the question as his attention was drawn to the video again, watching as it panned out, showing the battered truck. Inside he could see the three figures inside and the back of the truck was covered with a tarp. Where had he seen that truck?

"Colonel?" the General asked again, curious as to why he hadn't replied.

Suddenly it hit him. His eyes narrowed as he looked up smiling.

"I know where to find them!" he exclaimed triumphantly, causing the Captain to jolt back in surprise.

"Really?" the General asked hopefully.

He stood up, a thin smile on his face as he simply replied. "I've seen this truck before at a farm..."

B3142 outside Piddle Hinton

Sam sat patiently waiting, humming an old tune to himself, waiting for the road to clear ahead. From his vantage point, high in the tractor, he could already see the problem, it looked like a Russian military truck, driving on the wrong side of the road had crashed head on into a couple of cars, and as the drivers were out pointing and gesticulating wildly at their damaged cars, the driver of the truck merely sat in the cab, shouting from the open window down to them, refusing to get out. His truck was stuck though, it had ridden up onto the bonnet of one of the cars, and every now and then a belch of diesel fumes would bellow from the exhaust and the tyres scrabble for grip as he tried to free himself, which would warrant more shouts and curses from the car drivers as the heavy truck bounced on its springs, going nowhere.

The traffic had built up enough that Sam couldn't turn around, so instead he sat there, watching the drama ahead, silently urging the cars drivers to walk away. Why didn't they realise the danger they were in, he thought. What did they expect? The

Russian to exchange insurance details? His thoughts were interrupted as a police car came alongside, its blues and twos flashing.

Sam stiffened in his seat, were the police already working with the Russians now?

He watched with piqued interest as the two police officers got out of the car, quickly running up to the truck and chatting to the driver. Sam could see from the body language they were almost pleading with him, before finally the truck driver stopped the engine and got out, arrogantly pointing to the drivers and lighting a cigarette as he stood by the side of the road.

Sam shook his head in disbelief, the police *were* working with the Russians. He spat out of the open window, watching as at last, the police now began to control the traffic, directing the cars around the wreckage. Sam sidled by slowly, sad to see a body trapped in one of the cars, that's why the drivers had been desperate to stop the truck. The Russian was young, perhaps no more than twenty years old, and was squatting indifferently at the side of the road, oblivious and without a care. He glared at Sam as they made eye contact, almost daring him to stop. Sam looked away, the world was different now, he thought moodily, as anger rose inside him, quickly extinguished as he thought of the farm, his wife and his dead daughter. No this wasn't his fight anymore, now he was retired from all of that, now it was just him, the farm and his wife. He thought back to the soldiers from last night, hoping they'd made it back safely to their units.

He stifled a yawn, already looking forward to a late lunch with Mary, as his stomach began to grumble. It had been a busy morning, he'd just spent it helping out at his friend's farm to crop spray his fields, whose own tractor was in for repair. He'd been promising to do it for nearly a week now, and after everything that had gone on yesterday, found himself suddenly welcoming the distraction. He glanced at his watch, it was nearly 3pm. Mary wouldn't be happy, he'd promised he'd be back by mid-day.

He kept humming the same tune, over and over as he bounced along the all too familiar roads, not long now and he'd see the farm track leading home. He watched as another two police cars came hurtling up the road, quickly overtaking the stream of cars and racing away over the hill into the distance. What was it now, he thought, another crash? One of the police cars quickly screeched to a halt, its tyres smoking as the driver jammed on the brakes, turning and racing back, screeching to a halt in front of Sams tractor, blocking his way. He stopped the tractor, wondering what on earth he'd done to warrant such a manouvere.

The cars behind were waved past as the two officers jumped out wearing hi-vis vests, quickly followed by a third person who'd been in the back seat.

Sam looked confused, as he recognised his friend Doug was the one now climbing out of the back seat. All three ran up to the cab, Sam quickly recognising one of the police officers was Little Jimmy, Doug's son.

Doug had a look of relief on him, quickly tinged with a look of sadness.

"Sam! Thank God, we found you!" he exclaimed as he pointed to one of the police officers, adding. "You remember my son Jim?"

Sam looked down open mouthed, unsure of what was going on. He looked at the police officer his friend was pointing to. "Of course, I know Jim, now what's going on? Why'd you stop me?"

Jim stepped forward, one hand resting on the tractors side.

"Mr Collins, Sir, can I get you to switch off the vehicle, apply the parking brake and step down out of the cab."

Sam quickly did as he was told, climbing down using the tractors large tyres to lean on, wiping his sweaty hands on a piece of rag, before looking at his friend.

"Right, Doug, what's going on?"

"Sam, this is going to sound strange, but I need you to trust us, I need you to trust me. I need you to get in that car right away, no questions asked, please..."

Sam looked over to the open door of the police car, his jaw hung open in confusion. Looking back at Jim he asked, "Am I under arrest?"

The officer shook his head slowly as Sam countered.

"Well if I'm not under arrest, then I'm not going anywhere with you, now what's going on?"

"Sam please!" Doug urged. Sam could see the tension in his friend's face, but there was something else there, was it sorrow, he thought.

Sam looked at them all quickly, his face firm and jaw hardening as his patience began to wane.

"Look Doug, I don't know what you're playing at, but I don't have the time to be fucking about right now, have you seen what's going on out there?" He pointed behind him before continuing, "Mary's waiting for me back at the farm, I'm already late, and I don't have time for fucking games."

He turned and was about to climb the tractor when Doug blurted out, "For fucks sake Sam! The farms gone! Marys GONE!"

The words hit him like a hammer blow as he froze. Turning quickly, he shot back. "What do you mean gone?"

Doug said nothing but looked sympathetically, as Sam moved forward his hands clenched, eyes narrowing, shouting, "DOUG, WHAT DO YOU MEAN GONE?"

He saw his friends' eyes begin well up and his lips trembled, as if the words wouldn't come. He looked to the police officer then back at his friend as Doug began to speak softly.

"Jim heard it over the police radio, the Russians had information about you and were going to the farm to arrest you. He came and told me, and we were on our way to the farm to warn you..."

"AND?" Sam urged his friend to continue, needing him to say the words.

Jim could see his dad struggling to say the words and was about to continue when his dad waved his hand, stopping him. "No son, he has to hear this from me, I owe him that." Doug's eyes focussed again as Sam stared back at him, taking a breath, as he continued to speak more calmly.

"The Russians got to the farm before we could, but you weren't there. They arrested Mary instead and began to question her about you, something happened..."

"No..." Was all Sam could muster as his eyes began to well, as his friend kept going.

"She managed to get hold of a shotgun..."

"No-"

"She began shooting at them. They-"

"NO!" he shouted, pushing past the men and looking over to the horizon. Now noticing the thick black smoke rising above the treetops. The farm was on fire, his home was on fire. Sam could picture what had happened, his wife had always believed he'd be there for her by her side ready to protect her. He'd been with her throughout some of their toughest times, helping each other along, each one being the rock the other needed. Now in her moment of greatest need, when she needed protecting the most, where had he been? Spraying a fucking field! She must have been absolutely terrified, alone with enemy soldiers in the house. He knew what monsters' men could become, he'd been that monster once. He'd always kept two shotguns loaded and hidden around the farmhouse, just in case the monsters came calling, because as he'd always told his wife, "You never know darling."

She must have got hold of one, tried to fight her way out. The fear she must have felt to have made her do that. Sam shook his head, tears flowing and his hands trembling as his mind began to race, the thoughts replaying over and over again what could have happened to her. But she might not be dead, he reasoned. He hadn't seen her body, what if Doug was wrong. What if they were all wrong. What if she was alive, or worse wounded, waiting for him, crying out for him! Suddenly the fear and sorrow turned to rage and hope. He had to get to her, he had to see her for himself.

The two officers held onto his arms, struggling to keep him there as with tear-streaked face he began to yell and fight back.

"Let me go, she needs me!"

"Mr Collins, she's dead!" One of the police officers tried to reason with him, but Sam was beyond listening and reason, He began to angrily shout and kick out, cursing the officers as they pinned his arms behind him.

"LET ME GO! MARY MIGHT BE HURT! YOU DON'T KNOW SHE'S DEAD! LET ME GO!"

Doug quickly grabbed his friends head with both arms, pulling his face closer to his, staring into his eyes.

"Sam! Listen to me, if you go there, if you go home, they'll kill you, they're waiting for you now. The police are under orders to arrest you on sight. This is what they want."

"FINE! I'll fucking give them what they want!" he spat venomously the hurt quickly turning to rage, his face red. "I'll fucking kill them all! The Bastards! LET ME GO!" he yelled screaming at the two officers.

"It's gone Sam, please!" his friend tried to plead, "The farm, the livestock, Mary, there's nothing left there for you there. PLEASE!"

Sam was beyond angry. A deep guttural roar that shook Doug broke out as he vented his fury, his eyes wide and feral. Whatever Doug was trying to say, Sam was far beyond listening.

Sam never felt the needle as it entered his neck, his eyes registered surprise as quickly his legs became like jelly and he fell forward, held up by the strong grip of the two police officers.

Doug quickly returned the tranquiliser to his pocket, careful to refit the rubber bung. Looking at his sleeping friend he kissed him on the forehead.

"I'm sorry my friend, but I'm not going to let you go and kill yourself. You've known so much loss, now find some peace in sleep, we'll talk about this later."

Jim turned to his dad.

"Dad, we need to go, we need to get him away from here, they'll be looking for him."

Doug looked up to his son, nodding as he replied, "Of course son, how long before you're missed?"

Both officers looked at each other, silently nodding as Jim replied, "Another fifteen minutes, then people will ask questions."

"Right, let's get him over to the hunting lodge, they'll not find him there, you can get there and back in fifteen. I've given him enough to sleep for at least eight hours, make sure you put him on his front, I don't want him swallowing his tongue in his sleep."

"What about the tractor?" the other officer nodded in its direction.

Doug quickly looked around at the fields, making his mind up.

"I'll dump it in the fields over there then try to thumb a lift. Quickly now!" he urged as they bundled the unconscious Sam into the police car. "And son..."

Jim turned to look at his father, his eyebrow raised.

"I'm so proud of you...Thank you."

Sam's Farm

Captain Lunyou stared across the farmyard, watching as his men began to smash through the farmhouse, tearing open cupboards and breaking down doors, trying to find any sign of the enemy.

He looked down sneering at the body on the floor, hidden from view by a tarpaulin that had been dragged out from one of the barns. "Crazy bitch," he muttered, spitting at the body. He shifted uncomfortably, the pain in his foot firing up his leg, reminding him of his carelessness.

They'd only been there twenty minutes, A quick search of the farm found no sign of the man, only the woman, who they'd discovered feeding sheep in the fields. She didn't come quietly, but had yelled and screamed until his Sergeant had delivered a brutal punch to her, almost knocking her out. They'd left her tied to a chair in the farmhouse, to be questioned later. What harm could she have done, they had thought. A quick search of the farmyard had turned out some bloody bandages and old clothes and inside the barn on the concrete floor they found track marks, left by the armoured vehicles. The British had been here alright. But the man they were looking for wasn't, so instead they had turned their attention to the woman. They hadn't even had time to take off their jackets and begin questioning her before she was already talking. His Sergeant had looked disappointed as she had begun telling them her husband had died only weeks ago, they'd let her up out of the chair, to take them to his fresh grave, buried next to their daughter. She'd told them that she now lived alone on the farm, doing all the work herself. The British troops had arrived the previous night she'd said, holding her at gunpoint and stealing food and supplies from the farm. She'd spat out about having no choice. She was a lonely old widow with no-one to protect her. She'd said that when the British had left she had no idea where they'd gone to and that she had been kept locked in the farmhouse. He smiled as he'd watched her dance about, a puppet on strings, letting her tell her lies, all the while knowing her husband, a Mr Sam Collins was alive and well. He remembered the look on her face when he told her in perfect English that he didn't believe her and that the police, their police were already helping them in their search. They knew all about her husband and had confirmed he was indeed still breathing and in the land of the living. The look of horror as she stood alone and scared in the kitchen had given him a savage pleasure. Grinning, he'd told her that they'd wait for her husband to come back, and then his Sergeant would take great pleasure in skinning strips of flesh from her legs and arms, as her husband would be forced to watch, until finally they'd get to the truth. People would do anything for love, he'd said smiling coldly.

He had been prepared for her to break down in tears, to shake, scream, cry, as they usually did, anything really, except what she had actually done. The surprise and shock he had felt was complete as she looked calmly at him, quickly reaching up above the kitchen unit and pulling down a double-barrelled shotgun. He'd only just managed to leap through the doorway as the frame splintered into matchwood as she fired almost point blank at him, a pain shooting up his foot as some of the pellets found their mark. He had lay there cursing, as the shotgun had boomed out again, followed by a cry of pain from one of his men. He remembered looking about, his men were now running back to the farmhouse, to see what was happening. Quickly he'd pulled his pistol free from its holster, careful not to expose himself in the doorway as he'd heard the distinct snick of the barrels being snapped shut. She had reloaded the weapon. He'd waved his men around, to get them to go round the back. It was suicide to go through the broken doorway. He could hear her footsteps thudding on the farmhouse floor, the timbers creaking as she'd walked over to the door and walked into the courtyard, the shotgun booming again, gunshots echoing around the courtyard. Just a few bursts of gunfire later, and it was all over. His men had finally cornered her by the tree, she was found lying face down over the graves she'd spoken about earlier. He remembered seeing the look on her face when he'd pulled her over, to examine the body, it was strange, it hadn't been fear, or anger, but a serene calm, almost as if she had been prepared to die. He'd looked at the graves, feeling nothing but anger for the two men she'd just killed, he'd been tempted to dig the bodies up, out of spite. Perhaps he still would, he thought, maybe later.

The pain in his foot brought him back to the present as he stared back down at the tarpaulin again, fluttering in the breeze.

Already a pool of blood was seeping out from under it, he watched transfixed as the crimson liquid slowly edged closer to the group of ants scurrying on the ground. Some of them touched it, quickly running away, others became trapped in it, the liquid picking them up and floating them away on its path. The philosopher inside him began to think of something about how it all reminded him of life, people were the ants and the blood was fate, some could accept their fate and live with it, whilst others let it take them away, to drown in it. He was interrupted when one of his men came running up to him.

"Sir, what about the cattle and livestock?"

"Kill them all." he said without looking up.

The soldier looked about him, unsure of what to say next, until finally the Captain relented, sighing as he looked up, helping the man come to a decision.

"Are you going to come back and feed them? Water them? Check on them? Are you a farmer?"

"Err no Sir." The man stammered, unsure of what the Captain was trying to say, until finally tiring of the man's stupidity he replied. "Then follow a simple order, kill them all, it's the most humane thing to do, otherwise they'll starve."

"Yes Sir!" The man replied gruffly, not wanting to face the Captain's cold gaze a moment longer.

Golgolvin's convoy arrived shortly after, the three armoured vehicles quickly skidding to a halt next to Lunyou, spattering him with mud. He looked down angrily at his muddy trousers as the Colonel stepped out, his eyes taking in the scene, quickly remembering what he'd seen from the air.

"Not flying today, Colonel?" Lunyou sneered, arrogantly looking at the BTR80 armoured vehicle, the pain in his leg making him angry as he added, "Where's your helicopter?"

Golgolvin was about to snap at the man, quickly remembering the General's warning about his connections in Moscow. Ignoring the barb, he merely barked.

"Stand to attention when you address a superior officer!"

Lunyou grimaced, pointing to the blood soaked boot.

"My apologies Colonel, but in the pursuit of our enquiries It would appear I have been wounded in action. The wound prevents me from standing to attention."

Golgolvin looked down, sneering as he replied, "Very well *Captain*, what have you found for me?"

Lunyou smiled thinly and menacingly as he pointed to the barn.

"In the barn we've found tracks consistent with heavy armoured vehicles and signs that a large group of people were in there. We've found bloody bandages, clothing and this."

The Colonel looked at what the Captain was holding in his hand, a single 5.56mm bullet, the brass glinting in the sun. It must have rolled free from one of the soldiers weapons. All of their own weapons were either 7.62mm or 9mm. This must have come from the British.

His gaze fell to the ground, seeing the body. Kneeling down, careful to avoid the blood that was pooling there, he lifted up the sheet, looking down at the woman.

"Who is this?" he demanded, "and why is she dead?"

"That is the late Mrs Collins, husband of Mr Sam Collins, who owns the farm. We believe he's the one who helped the British. When we arrived, Mrs Collins was alone. We tried to interrogate her, but she had access to weapons we hadn't yet found. She killed two of my men and nearly killed me. As you can see, she put up a bit of a fight."

"Not the first time, you've underestimated an opponent, eh Captain?" The Colonel replied venomously. Quickly adding, "We needed prisoners to interrogate, not more dead civilians."

"The husband still lives." Lunyou shot back forcefully.

"Oh really? Is he here? Do you have him?" Golgolvin asked sarcastically, looking around the courtyard.

The Captain sighed, careful to keep his arrogance under control as he replied. "Not yet, but we have his picture out with the police, and our men are looking for him, he won't get far."

Golgolvin covered the body, standing up and brushing the dirt off his hands.

"The police, do not trust them with this, make sure you-"

"Perhaps the Colonel would be better suited concentrating on his own affairs, and not lecturing the FSB how to go about theirs?"

Seeing the murderous look on Golgolvin's face, Captain Lunyou realised he'd pushed too far, quickly adding, "What I meant Colonel, is that we've seeded the local police forces with FSB officers and members of our own military police. The local police forces will soon fall into line."

Golgolvin was about to say something but checked himself. He didn't have the time to get into petty arguments with little power-hungry butchers like Lunyou. Something about the way he proudly stood over the woman's body, as if she was just a trophy to be hung on a wall, annoyed him. He looked down, quietly thinking to himself how brave she'd been. If only she'd been a little quicker on the draw she might have even killed the annoying bastard. He smirked at the thought of the FSB officer being taken out by a little old lady and a shotgun. He looked around at the farm, as the noise of gunshots now rang out, followed by the bellowing and braying of animals. He looked up at the Captain who answered quickly.

"These are enemies of the state, they should be used as a warning to others. Fight against us and lose your homes, your livelihood and your life."

Golgolvin said nothing, thinking quietly to himself how that mantra had always failed in the past, Afghanistan, Vietnam, Ukraine, all of them had instead fought on all the harder, the more you pushed them. However, this was now an FSB matter, he'd found the evidence he needed, now he'd follow the tracks, let's see where they would take them. He whistled over to the commander of the lead BTR, who turned in the cupola, quickly throwing away the cigarette as he kicked the crew into action, the vehicles heavy engines rumbling to life.

"The tracks lead away off into the woods." Lunyou pointed, sensing what Golgolvin was planning to do next. He merely nodded in acknowledgement, before climbing aboard the vehicle, quickly settling into the cramped cupola. Without a backwards glance the three vehicle convoy sped off over the hill, Lunyou watching it disappear from view.

"Fucking idiot!" he spat after them. He looked up to see one of his men had overheard, quickly he snapped out, "What are you doing just standing there? Get some fuel and start burning the buildings. I want everything burned to the ground; nothing is to be left standing. Move it!"

The soldier ran off, as Lunyou looked down, kicking the body angrily with his good foot as the pain shot back. "And don't think you've got away with it, I haven't forgotten about you!" he shouted at the corpse. Grimacing in pain he called over two of his men.

"Drag this bitch into the barn, I want her burning alongside the rest of the animals."

Smiling in satisfaction he limped away to his vehicle, Sergeant Feodor stood ready to open the door.

"Are we finished here?" The Sergeant asked.

"Yes, I think we are Artem," he replied, looking around at the fires beginning to burn around them.

Smiling and ignoring the pain, he clapped the Sergeant on the shoulder. It had been a good day's work.

"Come on, I need to get this foot sorted out, and then let's find you the company of some beautiful women, I'd say you deserved it."

Somewhere in the Dorset Countryside.

Golgolvin's convoy followed the tank tracks for five miles as they wound through the hills and forests of the area, cutting a deep scar that was easy to see in the daylight, still heading north. He wedged his elbows into the cupola, bending his knees slightly, swaying with the vehicle as it rocked and bounced at speed. He'd learned from the previous night and instead of telling the driver or commander to slow down, he kept quiet, letting the crew do their job, as the heavy eight wheeled vehicle bounced through the ruts and ditches, far more comfortably than his previous trip.

The tracks went up and over a hill, and cut through a woodline, the sun's rays scything through like lasers as they drove through, until they emerged from the treeline, coming to a wide-open valley, the ground covered in hundreds of different sets of tracks all heading north. His vehicle slowed and stopped as he raised his goggles to see for himself, sighing angrily and shaking his head. Up ahead, the tracks they were following now merged with others, disappearing. This was the end of the line.

He looked around the valley, recognising on the map that they'd travelled through here the previous night, remarking how different it looked in the daylight. He opened his map, trying to read the terrain, to visualise where they could have gone. Yeovil was only five miles to the north, could they have gone there? To his east, lay the town of Cerne Abbas, he didn't think there was any chance they'd have gone that way, they'd be certain to have run into one of his forward units, and looking out to the west, it was all open fields and flat lands for miles, they'd have been spotted in daylight. No, he was certain, Yeovil it was. He'd been suspicious before, but now with the tracks leading here, he was certain. The General needed to know, the attack on the town should go ahead. He quickly folded his map, turning to the commander.

"Get me tuned into HQ's frequency I want to talk them right away."

He watched the commander's head disappear, as he leant behind him to change the frequency, as Golgolvin picked up his binos and scanned the valley floor, thinking of what to say on the radio. He quietly said to himself, "This time Yuri, we're going to be doing things the right way."

He looked over as the commander's voice came through his headset.

"We're on the frequency Colonel, HQ are listening."

Keeping his face grim, he keyed the radio and began to send his report.

18

Fight Or Flight

Yeovil Town Suburbs

Fergus shifted forward on the plastic chair, his feet resting on the dusty glass strewn floor, looking at the map spread out before him. Somewhere off to his right he could hear a bird singing, he ignored it, not wanting to be distracted as he watched the progress of the enemy units being plotted on the map. The handheld radio he was holding chirped to life as an excited voice called out.

"Sparrow Two reporting, I've got them in sight, eleven vehicles, they look like eight Infantry vehicles and three tanks, still heading along Jackson Street. Should be with Sparrow Three shortly."

He said nothing but continued to listen as Sparrow Three now came on. The voice was young and eager.

"I've got them Sparrow Two, I'll follow them from here. Still have eyes on them."

Fergus looked down at the map, charting the progress as he made out the street names. Next to him was a Sergeant Major from the Reservists, watching the progress for himself. Fergus had met him the previous night, introducing himself as Sergeant Major Macdonald, Fergus immediately took to calling him Mac, which the Sergeant Major had smiled at. Perhaps it was his nickname all along mused Fergus as he'd took an immediate liking to the man.

"Major, that looks like the fourth thrust coming in, you were right, they're using the main routes in, the lazy bastards."

He looked up, nodding in response. It seemed strange for Fergus to be addressed as Major, it was only last night that he was a civilian. But like some of the fighters around him, he'd been recalled to service. Unlike the Sergeant Major who was dressed in full combats and carried an assault rifle, Fergus had to settle with jeans and a combat jacket, the only form of uniform he could muster at such short notice. But uniform or not, Sergeant Major Macdonald was right, the Russians were being lazy, instead of clearing the town sector by sector, and building by building, they were driving up the roads. Sacrificing safety and security for speed on roads that he'd already prepared special welcomes for them.

Fergus keyed the radio, "Okay all callsigns, enemy now reported by Sparrow Three will be now known as Target Four. Sparrow Three acknowledge."

After a few seconds the young voice was back on, "Errr yeah ok command, enemy now known as Target Four."

Fergus smiled to himself, after only ten hours of training, the Sparrows, as they were now affectionately called, were doing very well. All had been either delivery drivers or taxi drivers to some degree or another with infinite knowledge of the town's streets. Now, armed with this knowledge, he'd had them paired up with the drone operators, so they could report on the enemy from the sky, safe from attack, without the use of maps. Some were still out on the ground though, watching through binoculars and Fergus was trying his best not to look worried about these brave men and women, dodging between the rubble, his eyes and ears allowing him to co-ordinate the defenders.

He grimaced as he thought back to yesterday afternoon, when he'd suggested to the Mayor his plan, the look on their faces at the emergency meeting told him they'd thought he'd lost his marbles. He remembered, as he arrived late to the meeting, the shouts, noise and chaos. Not the usual quiet and sleepy town meetings that he'd recalled of the past. The Town Council knew that an enemy were coming for them, the police dispatch rider, covered in mud and muck had only just arrived, telling them about the Russian invasion, under the pretence of another nation's peacekeeping force. With a grim-faced reality, he'd left them to it, heading for the next town and village, trying to get the warning out as more refugees poured in from the south. From the news and stories coming in, they had perhaps no more than eighteen hours to prepare. The shocked faces of the refugees they had spoken to had told them of the murders, rapes and looting, contrary to the illusion of any peacekeeping force. The Mayor at first was tempted to try to evacuate the town, but after hearing the stories, and knowing the consequences to those left behind, she'd decided to stay and try to defend the town. This was after all her home she had countered, besides where would they run to? If they didn't stand and fight here to protect their homes, then where would they? As people nodded and muttered their support she realised she wasn't alone in her thoughts. The regular army was nowhere to be seen, god knows what they were up to, the Police Chief had said dryly, as they came to realise that the town's defence would be left to its small force of army reservists and citizens. Even as hundreds of volunteers had been assembling outside, they knew that the numbers wouldn't be enough to defend the town against the forces coming against them and even if they did have the numbers, they knew they didn't have the weaponry or the training. The army Reservists were the only ones with the training, but these were soldiers who hadn't seen action for years, how would they hold up now against a modern army, with soldiers that were younger and fitter than they were? As for the weapons, some of the Reservists carried their SA-80 assault rifles, but had a woefully short supply of ammunition, whilst others like Fergus were carrying shotguns, but some of the volunteers had never even picked up a weapon, let alone fire one. Fergus had stood at the back of the room watching as the Mayor had been overwhelmed by what was going on. She could only sit and stare as the questions and shouts came thick and fast. It was Fergus whose voice had carried above the others as, hearing enough, he jumped to her defence, his voice booming out across the room. He shouted out that he had a plan, he could help stop the Russians. Suddenly everyone stopped and the room went quiet, the silence deafening as all eyes had turned to him. He'd never imagined a scenario where he'd be telling the Mayor and the council what to do, but now here it was and suddenly he was issuing the orders. They all knew of him, knew he'd served in the army, a veteran of many tours of Afghanistan, serving in the Parachute regiment, he fought proudly for his unit and his country until at the age of fifty, reaching the rank of Major, retirement had beckoned. Not that he had wanted to, he still kept himself fit for his age, and it had been more of a case of forced retirement, rather than willing. Now he ran a garage in the town, servicing the towns taxis, a small and modest income, but more than enough to supplement the army pension that he received. He'd always kept his ear to the ground with the council, turning up to almost every meeting and where necessary adding his public voice to some of the arguments for planning, budgets and how the council was being run. It was because of this that the people in the room both knew of him and knew what he had to say could carry weight. He had taken a deep breath, and told them that with the Reservists, police force and the volunteers, Yeovil now had thrown together a militia force numbering nearly two thousand strong.

"But we're not soldiers Fergus!" someone had shouted back, other voices beginning to rise again, threatening to drown him out as fear had spread like wildfire. He'd shouted louder, raising his hands to calm them, before lowering his voice again as the silence descended as they listened again. They were frightened, they needed a calm reassuring voice, he just hoped that his would do just that.

He'd told them that no one was born to be a soldier, it was something that people learned and they learned quickly. Some of the best soldiers he'd ever worked with had all come from humble beginnings, and that in battle even the smallest grain of sand can tip the scales. He told them that their new militia force may lack the training, but with the Reservists they had some experience, most were veterans themselves and more importantly, there was nothing stronger than a person fighting to protect their home and family. Plus, he'd added, that the attacker would need at least five times the number of troops as the defender, so even though they were only two thousand strong, he strongly believed they could hold off the larger force. The Mayor had asked though, without the weapons, how could they hope to stop the tanks and armoured vehicles? And this was where Fergus's plan came to light. He'd worked with armoured vehicles before, he'd had good friends serve on them, knew their strengths and weaknesses. A tank or armoured vehicle in open fields and countryside was the master of a battlefield, its sights and guns could see and shoot for miles preventing anyone from getting too close to it. But, get them into a city or town in amongst the buildings, tie down the infantry supporting it and you remove those advantages and it could be defeated. As they all listened, he'd suggested draping vast lines of rope, washing line, or twine across the town's streets with cloths, towels, clothes and blankets, in fact any material they could get their hands on attached to the lines. Hanging at intervals of between one and three metres above the ground, the tanks would drive through the lines, the material hanging off them would then snag on the turrets, covering the driver's' periscopes, the gunner's sights and the commander's periscopes until, eventually the vehicle would be forced to stop, as they would be blinded. The same steel and armour that protected them, would now help to blind them, as they would be unable to see outside. To a tank crew, he knew that being blind on the battlefield was their second biggest fear. The Mayor had asked curiously what the first biggest fear on the crew would be. He'd smiled as he'd replied. Fire. You see now the tank would have to stop, and the crew jump out to clear the periscopes and sights. As the hatches were opened people hiding close by would throw petrol bombs at the tank, the fire would pour through the hatches and set fires amongst the ammunition. The crew could be shot at as they tried to fight the fires, the rest would take care of itself he had simply said.

The Mayor was shocked at how easily Fergus had described that last part, some of the people in the meeting held their hands to their mouths in shock at the thought of burning people alive. Seeing them dither, Fergus had quickly countered, "Don't forget, these are not the bloody boy scouts coming on a friendly visit, talk to the people fleeing Dorchester if you need proof of that. Be under no illusion, these soldiers are coming to kill our families and destroy our homes. We have to fight them using any means necessary, and if you can't stomach that fact, I suggest you evacuate now and take your liberal views with you and leave the hard work to those with the will and stomach to fight." The stony set faces looking back told him he'd hit a nerve, but despite the doubts in the room, it was the Mayor who had the final say. She'd begrudgingly agreed, and that's how Fergus had found himself in charge of the defence of the town. Now on every inner street in Yeovil, clothes, flags and fabric of all kinds was hanging onto the deadly bunting, flapping in the breeze as if the town were celebrating some kind of festival, the townspeople had worked through the night to get the job done to help defend their homes.

Whilst the deadly bunting was being constructed, Fergus had been busy using his newly acquired powers to get the town's outer homes and buildings evacuated, with the residents now all relocated in the centre of town to help with the defences. People at first had refused to go, it was only when he'd told them of the danger they were in, that finally, unwillingly, they'd packed what they could into cases and left. In the now empty buildings, he'd had the town's volunteers working hard with sledgehammers and pneumatic drills, recently liberated from the construction companies, to get the dividing walls of the terraced houses knocked through. Large enough for people to run through, these tunnels and mazes between buildings could allow runners and observers to run through without being seen outside on the streets, providing cover from fire. He'd learned of these rat runs, as they were called, from fighting the Taliban in Afghanistan, who themselves had used them to avoid airstrikes and to get into ambush positions quickly. Another lesson he'd learned from the Taliban was the use of murder holes, small fist sized holes cut into walls, where the shooter could quickly poke a barrel of a rifle through and shoot at the enemy without the enemy getting eyes on the firer's position. He'd been on the receiving end of both these tactics, losing friends and soldiers to them, now here he was all these years later, still sorry at the price paid, but thankful for the lesson learnt, as now he was the defender fighting the aggressor invading his home.

Fergus had his doubts that they could get it all done in the time they had but had proudly watched as the last of the work was finished just as the sun begun to rise. He'd had the three hunting shops in the town empty their stores of every shotgun and rifle they had and now at least most of the militia fighters were armed. He had the Reserve troops broken up and divided amongst the militia, now each Reservist had four of the town's militia to quickly train up, each soldier passing on years of knowledge in a few hasty hours. He knew it wouldn't be perfect, but it was better than no training at all. Besides, he had thought glumly, those that survived the first few hours would become experts pretty quickly, the skills of combat were not something you read about in a book but had to experience yourself firsthand.

After the heavy night of preparations, the Mayor had almost had a fit, when finally, Fergus had told her he wanted to be on the front line. She'd argued that others could do it and that she'd left the defence of the town to him, he was supposed to stay back and lead it, not get involved on the front line. He'd quietly took her aside, pointing to the young, scared faces of the townspeople as they worked around them.

"Look at them Mayor, everyone you see here is scared, me included." he added, pointing to his chest before continuing.

"For this to work, we need them to believe in it, and so do I, so what kind of message does it send to everyone if I'm hiding back here safe and them all on the front lines taking the risk?"

"But Fergus, what kind of message does it send if I get my senior commander on the town's defence killed in the first hour. You're what? Fifty-six years old?"

"I'm fifty-seven," he'd replied, smiling before adding, "As well you know. Besides, you just tell them that clearly I wasn't cut out for paperwork, you know me, I'm a more hands on kinda guy."

He remembered that she hadn't laughed as he quickly added his voice becoming serious. "Look, the first battle will be the most important one, it'll be fight or flight, people will either stand and fight, or run away. You don't lead people in combat from the rear, you do it from the front, lead by example. If I leave them to it, they might break and run before a shot is ever fired. Fear is contagious, but so is courage. I want them to see me standing next to them, see me take the same risks, even at my age, to prove that this can work. Once they know it can, once they believe they can do this, once they trust me and my decisions, then I'll come back and together we can keep the town safe. If we can survive today, we might have a chance of stopping them here."

Fergus's argument had won through, and he'd simply winked and smiled at her as he picked up his shotgun and headed to the door.

Now he was here, sitting in the makeshift command post, surrounded by his own troops, looking at the map, deciding, where and when to strike.

Since daybreak, they'd been following the progress of the four armoured thrusts coming into the town. They knew the enemy were south of them, they'd heard them throughout the previous night getting closer. Then just after dawn they'd heard the dull thud of explosions and tanks firing not far from them, until eventually the steady stream of refugees had slowed to a trickle, then stopped completely. Fergus knew what this had meant. The Russian commander was keeping the route clear for his own troops to come in. Now his Sparrows were putting the rat runs to good use as they quickly sprang from street to street, reporting on the enemy's progress over their small handheld radios before jumping on their hidden motorbikes and racing away. Thank god they'd cleared the towns outer buildings, he thought, as the Russians had decided to use small amounts of artillery to probe the streets, trying to get them to reveal their positions or fire back. It wasn't a heavy bombardment, but it was enough that now every one of Yeovil's outer streets showed signs of damage, with windows and doors blasted out and small fires springing up around them. Some of the buildings had collapsed with the rubble now blocking the street. As upsetting as it was to know people had lost homes, at least they were still alive, safely hidden in the basements of the buildings in the towns centre. Fergus was thankful for the rubble, as now it would help to channel where the Russians could go and gave cover for the defenders to use, as well as create choke points where they could ambush the attackers. Without realising it, the Russian artillery had helped them. After the bombardment, his own troops had emerged, unscathed, unbelievably, no-one had been killed. His own troops were safely away from the front lines, awaiting his orders to advance forward.

Fergus had listened to the excited voices on his radio, checking his map, as he saw one of the thrusts, designated Target Two was coming straight towards his position. Good, he thought, they're coming our way, just as we'd hoped. He looked at the information on his notepad, Target Two, consisted of three T-80 tanks and eight BMP 3's. The other three thrusts were all comprised of the same vehicles, infantry vehicles with a platoon of three tanks in support. Normally there would be a reconnaissance screen, sent out ahead of the main force to probe and find the enemy before the main attack started, but for some reason the Russians had neglected to do this. Perhaps they really were thinking there was no threat here. He watched as the map markers were moved closer, looking around him at the troops who were standing silently, looking at him, waiting.

He turned, grinning to the Sergeant Major, the grin was merely for effect, he wanted them all to see he wasn't afraid. In reality, his insides were churning with nerves.

"Right then Sergeant Major, let's get at it. All ambush teams to their forward positions. Let's welcome our new guests."

The Sergeant Major nodded, and began to bark out orders over the radio, as all around him the troops of the militia came alive, picking up their equipment and weapons and quickly disappearing to get into position. He'd done all he could for now and it was now time to see if they'd fight or run. Leaving the command post behind, he stood up with renewed energy, picking up his shotgun and following his team out. It was time to face the Russians.

Looking through his sight in the third tank, Sergeant Popavitch swore loudly as he sweated in the heat. He looked up through the open hatch as the sun bore down on them, it was only ten o'clock but the sun seemed to relentlessly focus through to his back, cooking him under his body armour. His gunner was across from him, on the left-hand side of the cramped turret, his own body armour and helmet thrown to the turret floor to combat the heat. Popavitch rubbed his eyes, damn he was tired, he'd been at this all night, chasing an unseen enemy, hoping to at least have stopped by now to get some rest. But the pursuit had been relentless, they'd only managed to stop for a few hours before his company commander had assumed command of the BTG. Then, suddenly, they were up again and pushing into the outskirts of the town. Now here he was, watching the road ahead, cursing his Lieutenant in the lead tank, who seemed desperate to get himself killed. He'd tried to warn him about blindly following each other in, he'd seen enough action in Ukraine to know what *not* to do in a tank, and playing follow the leader through these narrow streets was almost suicidal. He angrily sucked at the cigarette, ignoring the ammunition stacked around the turret as he looked nervously behind him, seeing the infantry vehicles all closed up, nose to tail through his periscopes. Where the hell was everyone, and what the hell was with all the clothes, he thought. His gunner piped over the intercom, thinking the same.

"Looks like the fascists were going to have a street party Sergeant, and we called in early."

His driver cut in, "Perhaps the party's for us, and we're the guests of honour."

The gunner lewdly replied, "It's about fucking time Mikheal, I could do with getting my hands on some British pussy!"

Both men laughed as the driver began to mimic a woman's voice. "Please my saviours, my Russian heroes, free me from all these dickless British men who spend more time sucking each other off and drinking tea and no time with me!"

"Be quiet!" Popavitch shouted, rubbing the tiredness out of his eyes. He'd been on the tank all night with these two and had enough of their lewd talk and gutter comments. God knows what shit hole of Russia they'd been found in, he thought, but being a Sergeant had its privileges and not having to hear the rank and file was one of them. An awkward silence descended on the tank as he went back to scanning the street, but he had to agree with his gunner, the thought of the company of a woman was one to relish, even with him being as tired as he was. Perhaps when they finished here he could find himself a woman. He remembered seeing some of the attractive women back amongst the refugees earlier, perhaps they'd still be there, waiting on the road behind them. He had food, he had cigarettes, perhaps there could be a deal to be struck with them. His thoughts were interrupted as the voice of Lieutenant Davich in the lead tank barked over the headset.

"Tiger Nine to Tiger Eight, close up! You're lagging behind again!"

Popavitch shook his head angrily, keeping his thoughts to himself as he keyed the radio.

"Tiger Eight to Tiger Nine, I don't like this, it's too quiet and what's with all the clothes hanging across the street? We shouldn't be bunched up like this Lieutenant, I recommend I take the convoy and pull back and provide overwatch, let you scout ahead."

On the lead tank, Lieutenant Davitch swore and shook his head, the Sergeant was trying to make a name for himself, and now here he was questioning him and his tactics over the radio. He couldn't give a fuck about what he'd done in the past in Ukraine, if he was that good, he wouldn't still be a fucking Sergeant would he?

He keyed the radio, his irritation clear to hear.

"Tiger Nine, I don't care about what you like, I care that you follow my orders. Permission to fall back denied. Now shut the fuck up and grow some balls and follow me!"

Angrily the Lieutenant looked down through the turret towards the driver's compartment, his voice snapping on the intercom. "Driver! Pull your finger out and get moving, advance slowly down the street."

The driver said nothing, keeping his own fears hidden, as Davitch felt the tank jerk as it bounced into gear and began to rumble forward.

On the rear tank, Sergeant Popavitch looked across to his gunner, a sneer on his face, "Make sure you're scanning the windows of the buildings and not daydreaming about bloody women."

"Yes Sarge," the gunner replied slowly, looking across to him. Seeing he wasn't being watched, he silently mouthed an insult. These privileged twats from Moscow always think they are better than us, he thought moodily as he lazily put his head back. Of course, there was nothing there, there had been nothing there all fucking morning. The town's people had all ran away, even *he* could see that."

Fergus remained where he was, slowly breathing through his mouth and trying his best to ignore the pain that shot up his leg. His left leg was in agony, twisting it on some rubble as he ran with the younger soldiers. his muscles protesting at the abuse he'd just given them. But he dared not move, such was his effort to remain undetected. Better to be alive and in pain, than dead, he thought, as he peered through the murder hole he was hiding behind, watching the lead T-80 tank no more than two-hundred metres away at the end of the street. He saw the turret slowly scanning around, looking for any signs of a threat. At any moment he expected to hear the gun roar or the machine gun to bark out, but the guns remained quiet. Good, he thought, so far so good. Behind the lead tank the other vehicles of the convoy closed up, their own turret's scanning round, looking like some prehistoric beasts, as they surveyed the street.

Amateurs, he thought to himself, as he watched them bunch up together, lined up one behind the other, perfect targets. If he was in charge of them, he would have had the vehicles flank out into the other streets, each supporting the other, but instead the commander had kept the unit tight together. Clearly, he felt safety in numbers, but in doing so, now they only had one gun to bear, if the vehicles at the rear tried to fire, they'd hit the tanks at the front of the convoy. He said a silent prayer of thanks as he saw that the infantry were all huddled together on the roofs of their armoured vehicles, preferring the ability to dismount quickly, rather than sit inside the armoured box, waiting for an antitank rocket or mine to punch through to them. Unbelievably the tanks all had their commanders hatches open, good for the fresh air, but a cardinal sin as far as protection was concerned. Fergus would help educate them about that.

He looked over to the fighters who were lying next to him, some had blank faces, others looks of shock, eyes wide open, now the battle was nearly upon them. One young fighter close to him, was shaking from nerves, but remained steadfast, looking at Fergus, his eyes full of fire. Fergus smiled and nodded, hoping to calm the youngster as he reminded him. "You remember what to do when the time comes?"

The young man nodded back, holding the petrol bomb in his hands and the lighter in the other. On his back was attached a crate of the deadly cocktails ready to be thrown quickly on the move. Fergus reached out, clasping the shoulder of the volunteer reassuringly.

"It'll all be okay son, not much longer now, you'll do alright."

The volunteer nodded as he fought to smile before looking back to the ground, his thoughts turning to the task at hand. Fergus watched him carefully, sometimes the shakes would come to everyone, it wasn't about not being nervous, it was about how you handled the fear that made the difference. He checked the shotgun again for the fourth time that minute, something to do rather than necessity, he knew the shells were chambered and it was ready to fire, but it just seemed right to check again.

He looked up to the buildings in the street, in every building, small teams of fighters were waiting, ready to launch the assault. He couldn't see them, but he knew they were there, he'd placed them there himself. Off to his right in another building at ground level waited his Sergeant Major, in command of a small assault team, armed with more petrol bombs and assault rifles, his job was to finish off any vehicles or crews if they tried to escape. Fergus looked back up the street, seeing all manner of clothing flapping in the breeze, his eyes drawn to a fluorescent t-shirt that dangled and danced. Something about the scene made him smile and without thinking he began humming the old wartime tune, "We're going to hang up our washing on the Siegfried line." The youngster next to him stared in awe, how could he be calm and singing now? Fergus stopped humming and smiled back, he was as scared as the volunteer, he just had a different way of showing it. He was about to say something when he heard the engine of the lead tank roar, its turbine screaming like a fighter jet and felt the ground shake, as slowly it moved towards them. Looking up he couldn't believe his luck, the convoy was slowly coming towards them, bunched up and in perfect position to be attacked.

If only we had some fucking antitank with us, Fergus thought moodily, he could easily have dispatched most of the convoy in seconds. But he resigned himself to the fact he had to go with what he had.

The noise and sight of the armoured column rumbling towards them was frightening, Fergus could see the dust and smaller parts of the rubble shaking away in front of him, as the ground began to tremble. He'd seen the effect that tanks could have on infantry, it was called tank shock and even though he'd been through it all before, he still had to fight the urge to get up and run away. If he was scared and having to fight the urge to run, then the others must have been absolutely petrified. Sensing the shift in the mood of the fighters he could see the panicked looks staring back at him, a few were crying, some shaking uncontrollably. They knew now how real this was about to get, nothing prepared you for the reality of when you realise you're just a small fleshy blob on the battlefield, with a forty-six-tonne monster bearing down on you, bristling with weapons, ready to tear you to pieces. His heart sank, they were going to run, he knew it. He'd brought them this far, just to have them all butchered as they ran away. He had to do something to fire them up. Out of desperation he tried to think of something to say, something to rouse them, to fire them up but the words wouldn't come to him. Suddenly he had an idea. Remembering back to his days in the paratroopers, his eyes met the eyes of the young fighter next to him.

He punched the young fighter on the arm, shouting at him.

"You, what's your name?"

"Matt, my name's Matt."

"And who are you fighting for Matt?"

"What?" the young man stammered back.

"WHO ARE YOU FIGHTING FOR?" Fergus shouted, asking again, his own voice becoming stronger and louder.

The others in the group all looked at Fergus as if he'd lost his mind, as he shook the man violently.

"COME ON! CALL YOURSELF A MAN! FUCKING SHOUT IT OUT! GET ANGRY! THEY'RE COMING TO KILL YOUR LOVED ONES!"

The man overcame his shock, his mouth opening as he stammered.

"My wife and child"

"SHOUT IT OUT SO EVERYONE CAN HEAR! Fergus demanded, pointing all around him as the fighters looked back curiously, shocking them all as if Fergus had changed into the devil.

"MY WIFE AND CHILD!" the young man shouted back, the tears had stopped and Fergus could see his cheeks flushing as the anger began to surface. Good he thought, better angry than scared. He turned to the others, his own face burning as the blood began to rush through.

"COME ON! SHOUT IT OUT, ALL OF YOU. I WANT TO HEAR YOU SAY IT. WHO ARE YOU FIGHTING FOR? LET ME HEAR IT, LET THEM HEAR IT!" he yelled, pointing towards the direction of the tanks.

The voices were quiet at first, becoming louder as each person began to become buoyed up by those around them. Their blood began to pump and the battle rage began to show as Fergus continued yelling at them, repeating over and over.

"COME ON LOUDER! THEY'RE COMING TO KILL YOUR LOVED ONES, SHOW THEM YOU WON'T LET THEM. SHOUT IT OUT TO THEM, LET *THEM* FEAR *YOU!*"

Their voices began to rise into a crescendo as each fighter began to get angry, faces flushed red and the crying stopped as everyone began to realise what they could lose if they failed.

"MY WIFE!"

"MY CHILDREN!"

"MY PARENTS!"

"MY FUCKING HOME!"

Fergus watched proudly as all around him the faces of fear were replaced by those of anger as the shouts began to get louder and louder as blood began to pump and adrenalin began to flow.

He shouted out to all who could hear him. The veins bulging on his forehead as his voice boomed out.

"REMEMBER WHO YOU'RE FIGHTING FOR! PICTURE YOUR LOVED ONES, YOUR HOMES AND THINK OF THEM NOW. IF YOU RUN, THEN EVERYTHING YOU KNOW AND LOVE WILL BE TURNED TO ASH AND DUST. THESE BASTARDS ARE HERE TO TAKE THEM FROM YOU AND DESTROY EVERYTHING YOU LOVE. ARE YOU GOING TO FUCKING LET THEM?"

"NO!" they all shouted back.

"LOUDER! LET THEM FUCKING HEAR YOU!" Fergus shouted back, the bloodlust rising in him.

"NO!" everyone was now fired up.

"GOOD! NOW LET THEM COME! WE'LL KILL THEM ALL!"

The shouts and yells began to grow as each fighter began to prepare themselves mentally. Some were urging on the tanks, teeth barred, as an almost primeval instinct began to surface. Fergus smiled to himself as he breathed heavily, his throat coarse from shouting. He'd done it, he'd managed to turn their fear to anger, now they wouldn't run. Like predators they were coiled, ready to spring forward to destroy their prey. Just as he had said before to the Mayor, there was nothing more powerful than a person fighting for their loved ones and their home.

The first tank was now approaching the bunting, ignoring it, as it passed through the lines strung across the street. Fergus held his breath, hoping and praying his plan would work as he watched on. The clothes and rope snagged across the commander's machine gun and was swept down and across the turret, as the line went taught then snapped back, leaving the rags and cloth clinging to the tank. some of the clothes remained stubbornly on the line and were snagged by the second tank where the effect was repeated. By the time the third tank reached the line there was only a few garments left, but even these were having an effect. The infantry on the vehicles behind were struggling to get under the lines as they snagged on them, threatening to tear them off the turrets and Fergus began smiling to himself as he watched them desperately pull bayonets and cut them as they passed, distracting them. With their focus on the lines, they wouldn't be watching the streets. The lead tank now snagged the second line, then the third, the clothes beginning to pile up on the front of the tank as it drew closer. The tank was now only twenty metres from them, but the front of the hull and the turret were covered in piles of cloth and rag. He watched as the tank suddenly jolted to a stop, it's engine whining as it became immobile. Fergus risked sticking his head higher, to see the second tank was also covered, and had closed up, but the third had stopped slightly earlier, and was lagging behind, a gap of about thirty metres had now opened up between the two tanks and the rest of the convoy. Not that it mattered, he thought to himself, the whole street was now an ambush point and the rear Russian callsign was still within it. When the attack came, they'd get them all.

He watched as the lead tanks turret began to violently swing left and right, clearly the crew were trying to shake off the clothing.

In the lead tank Lieutenant Davitch shouted to his driver "What the fuck are you doing? Did I say stop?"

"Sir I can't see anything!" the driver retorted, "there's something blocking the sight."

"Same here Sir," the gunner replied laconically, "I can't see shit out of my sights, those fucking clothes have snagged on it."

Angrily he looked up through his periscopes trying to see out, but saw nothing but brightly coloured material, blocking his view.

"Start rotating the turret side to side, see if we can shake this shit off us." he demanded.

As the turret started to violently swing from side to side, he turned in his seat to look behind him through his rear periscope, the only one he could see anything out of. Watching open mouthed as he saw his rear callsigns was having the same problem.

Cursing his luck, he keyed his pressel to talk to the other tanks.

"Tiger Seven, Tiger Nine, this is Tiger Eight. Our sights are covered, I can't go any further until we clear them, can you cover us?"

After a few moments both tanks replied, the voices of the commanders annoyed.

"Tiger Seven, our sights are covered as well, we've had to stop. I need to get out to clear them."

"Yeah, Tiger Nine, same here Lieutenant, our sights are covered as well. At least we know what the rope was for now."

The tone was sarcastic. God, he hated that fucking Sergeant, he fumed to himself.

"Okay, gunner! Keep your eyes open and cover me whilst I get out. I'll have to remove this bloody crap myself."

"But Sir! How can I cover you? I can't see anything out of- "

"JUST KEEP YOUR FUCKING EYES OPEN!" Davitch interrupted him. He was in no mood to have every one of his orders questioned. "Do you think you can at least manage that?"

He glared at the gunner, who wisely decided not to argue further, instead he meekly put his head back to the sight, seeing nothing but coloured fabric. Sensing there were no further arguments to be had from the young soldier, the Lieutenant nodded to himself triumphantly, as he raised himself off the commander's seat.

Cautiously he peered over the rim of the turret, his pistol in hand as he looked around him. Seeing no danger, he slowly climbed out, glancing behind him as the commanders of the tanks behind began to do the same. He watched the commander of one of the infantry vehicles behind who waved over, pointing to the mess of fabric and shrugging his shoulders, as behind him the troops were frantically cutting it all away.

Ignoring him, Davitch began to try to untangle the mess, how the hell had it got this wrapped up, he thought. Holding the pistol was proving difficult, he needed both hands if he was to sort out the mess quickly. Having another quick look around him, satisfied there was no threat he placed the pistol down and began to tear away at the cloth, sweat dripping into his eyes.

Could this day get any worse, he fumed to himself. Unfortunately for him, it could, and it would.

Fergus watched as the lead tank stopped rotating the turret, realising it couldn't shake off the clothing. He keyed his radio, "all units standby...."

He could feel the adrenalin begin to flow through him as time slowed down, the seconds seemed like minutes, as his senses began to sharpen.

Open mouthed, he watched, as the commanders of the first two tanks began to climb out. They were already in the ambush area and should be the easy targets, but the third tank commander was still slow to come out, more cautious than the other two. He'd have to hope the teams at the rear could deal with it. He saw movement above him and to the left, but he dared not take his eye off the lead tank. Slowly he watched the figure of the commander as he cautiously climbed out and begin to angrily try to rip away the clothing. He held a pistol in one hand to ward off any unseen enemies, but the clothing was proving to hard to remove, so he put the pistol down to be able to use both hands. Fergus could not believe his luck. Why was the commander doing it alone? Behind the commander sat a perfectly good DHSK 12.5cm machine gun. Why wasn't he getting his gunner out to tear off the cloth and covering his gunner with the machinegun? Fergus said a silent prayer to whoever was upstairs, thankful to be going against such amateurs. His teams were ready and poised. Now was the time he thought to himself. Taking a breath, he keyed the pressel. "All units standby, standby, GO! GO! GO!"

He jumped out from cover, running towards the tank, bringing his shotgun to bear on the sight of the commander. Something above them caught the commander's eye as he turned to look up, Fergus could see his eyes open wide in shock as he quickly reached for his pistol. The pistol was in his hand and aiming upwards when Fergus fired one of the barrels. He watched in slow motion as the commanders chest exploded in a cloud of smoke and fabric as the 12guage shell impacted it and the man's body seemed to bend inwards. To Fergus's horror, the commander slammed back against the hatch but didn't go down, his body armour having easily protected against the shot. He saw the man snarl in anger and pain and start to bring his pistol up towards him. Fergus was already running towards the tank, trying to lessen the distance, aiming higher, for the headshot. But before he could pull the trigger, a flaming mass began to pour down on the commander as the petrol bombs landed around the turret. He dropped the pistol, screaming and ducked back inside the tank, engulfed in flames, as the young man emerged beside Fergus, yelling in rage as he threw his own Molotov which flew over the turret and exploded onto the tank's engine decks. The tank's turret was on fire, the clothing easily catching alight as the inferno began to burn. Fergus knew though the tank needed to be destroyed from inside. Looking up, he shouted to the faces now emerging in the windows. "Get them into the hatches, burn that fucking thing!"

All around him, his fighters began to emerge from the buildings, as gunfire echoed all along the street. The Russian infantry on the vehicles suffered the most, the surprise overwhelming them as, in the first few moments of the attack, some managed to point weapons upwards, able to shoot only a few rounds before the petrol bombs rained down on them. Those that were quickest rolled off the vehicles, and into cover, the screams of their colleagues ringing in their ears as they burned only feet from them. Like angry ants the fighters began to emerge, screaming and yelling towards the vehicles, a manic rage enveloping them as some managed to climb up, swarming over the heavy beasts, prising open hatches and throwing the petrol bombs and firing inside with shotguns. Fergus ignored the chaos that was going on around him and concentrated on the lead tank, as a manic rage began to envelope him, was he laughing, he thought, as he ran up to the driver's hatch. He heard screams from inside the turret, as smoke now began to pour out of the commander's hatch.

Good, he thought, the first tank was on fire, as the driver's hatch opened suddenly with a clang and the driver's soot covered face began to emerge, coughing, as the smoke poured out around him. Fergus saw he was carrying an AK12, so without waiting for a response Fergus fired the second barrel, close range into the young man's face. The face disappeared into a crimson mist as pieces of brain and skull splashed over the tank's front deck, as he quickly reached down to the near headless body, grasping the AK12 assault rifle. He tried to reach in to get the extra magazines from the drivers assault rig, but the body had fallen deep into the drivers compartment and the heat and smoke was already too intense. He climbed onto the front of the tank and peered over the top of the turret, using the tank as cover, to look up the street. It was chaos, most of the vehicles were burning and gunfire was echoing all around him, the booms of the shotguns being answered by automatic rifle fire of the Russians that were still alive. He watched as one of the infantry vehicles was trying to reverse away up the street, smoke pouring from its front decks as the petrol bomb burned away, its 30mm gun rapidly firing in all directions. Just as Fergus had predicted, most of the 30mm rounds were harmlessly hitting the vehicle in front of it, the smoke from the fires obscuring what the commander could see. Unbeknown to him, he was shooting at his own men, such was the panic to escape. The BMP increased speed, swerving to avoid a burning vehicle as it collided with a house, the rubble falling forward and burying half of it, the vehicle now becoming stuck and blocking the street, as the crew opened hatches and began to bail out. It was as if the armoured vehicle's panicked flight had finally cracked the nerve of the Russians, as the infantry now turned to run, some of the soldiers were frantically urging their comrades to stay and fight, but they were too few, and within seconds the orderly retreat turned into a panic as soldiers began to run, the fear contagious. Fergus smiled to himself as he said aloud, "Fight or flight," the Russians had chosen flight. Some didn't though, scattered pockets remained in the rubble, bravely laying down fire to protect their comrades as they withdrew. He watched as the experience of the Reservists now began to show as they advance forward, pouring suppressing fire onto the enemy until they were in position to flank and assault them. Fergus's eyes were drawn to movement over on the third tank, thinking at first it was his own troops, his heart almost skipped a beat as he saw the commander crouched low and still alive. The third tank was untouched! No one had attacked it, instead everyone had run past and concentrated on the other vehicles! He watched open mouthed, cursing as the commander was quickly tearing at the cloth on the sights, ignoring the destruction around him, within a few seconds he'd have the tank ready to fire. If it were allowed to get back into the fight they could still lose this. He looked across to the Sergeant Major, trying to hide the fear in his voice, pointing to the tank as he shouted.

"MAC! THE THIRD TANK! TARGET THE THIRD TANK!

The Sergeant Major looked over to where Fergus was pointing, nodding silently at the new threat, as he disappeared into one of the buildings with his team, the last person resembling a pack mule as they carried the spare petrol bombs in a backpack. Fergus looked up to the street, shouting to his team.

"TARGET THE THIRD TANK!"

They looked up, quickly seeing the danger, but realising the tank was out of reach to them. Figures disappeared as they began to run through to the next set of buildings, hoping to get above the steel monster before it could begin its own attack.

Trying to buy them the time they needed to reposition, he quickly aimed the AK12 and began to pour fire onto the commander, the sparks flying off the turret as the rounds ricocheted off. He watched the commander duck down and crawl forward, trying to keep out of sight as he began to tear away the cloth. Fergus tried to steady his breathing as sweat dripped into his eyes as he aimed through the rifle's sights, cursing himself as he missed again. "Come on Fergus!" he swore to himself, "you used to do this for a fucking living, now shoot the bastard!"

The acrid, thick, black smoke from the burning tank began to envelope him and effect his aim, as his throat burned. He knew he couldn't stay there much longer, any second now the tank could explode. Cursing, he jumped off the tank, careful to avoid the pools of fire now pouring onto the ground, surprising himself at his agility and the fact his leg wasn't hurting anymore. He looked around him, shouting encouragement to the others.

"COME ON, LETS GET AT THE THIRD ONE, QUICKLY! QUICKLY!"

Everyone around him seemed to be filled with a renewed confidence and energy as they followed their commander, shouting and yelling, the blood lust now peaked as they followed Fergus past the first tank, taking cover behind the second burning hulk. He looked around him, all five of his assault team were still alive and with him. He turned to Matt, the young pack mule carrying the backpack and indicated for him to turn round, opening the backpack. Fergus slung the AK12 over his shoulder and reached over, grabbing one of the petrol bombs from within. With urgency in his voice, he pointed to the others.

"Quickly! We have to take it down now. Take one and light it, get it onto the turret if you can."

They all nodded in understanding as all of them grabbed at the petrol bombs, the young man seemed happy to be relieved of his cargo, as he took the last of them, lighting the wick.

As one, they leapt from behind their cover of the tank and threw them down the street towards the final tank. Fergus had hoped they'd be able to burn the commander, but his heart sank as he realised it was still too far away for the throw to hit. He watched on as the figure now disappeared from view and the hatch closed firmly, the turret now spinning towards them. They'd ran out of time.

Throwing his own bomb quickly, he grabbed the nearest person and dragged them back into cover, just as the tanks machine gun began to chatter, and rounds zipped up the street towards them. Two of his group weren't as quick, one flew backwards, as the rounds tore through his body, whilst the second was hit as she was about to throw the petrol bomb, it exploded in her arm, showering her with the burning fuel and setting her alight as she fell backwards screaming in pain and shock. Fergus was about to rush forward to help her, when instead she stood up and with manic fury ran towards the enemy tank, her upper body ablaze. Fergus wondered if it was bravery or madness from the agony she was in, as the tank watched her run towards it, allowing her to cover half the distance before finally ending her suffering with a bark from its machine gun.

Fergus looked up to the windows above the tank, hoping to see one of the assault teams there.

"Come on, COME ON!" he shouted, as he hunkered down below the hulk of the second burning tank, his remaining troops looking at him for direction. The second tank was now ablaze, the flames licking out from the turret hatches. Fergus knew it wouldn't be long before the tanks ammo and fuel exploded, he'd seen enough from previous wars to know what that looked like. And when it did, he knew their chances of surviving the explosion would be low. But they couldn't run away now, not with the third tank now pinning them down. For now, they were stuck, between a rock and a fiery hard place. He tried to smile at the others, tried to think of what to say next, but his mind wouldn't give him the answers he wanted. Instead, all he could do was remain where he was, pinned down and waiting. Perhaps Mac would have better luck.

In the third tank, Sergeant Popavitch sank into the commander's seat, cursing as he struggled to close and lock the hatch using just one hand. His right hand had been shot, the bullet passing cleanly through the palm. Blood poured freely down his arm, but he ignored the wound, finally getting the hatch locked. He'd watched the destruction of the column open mouthed as the British had seemed to come out of nowhere. At least he'd managed to get some of the cloth off. Using some of the rag he'd torn away, he quickly bound the wound, it would do for now. He leaned over the gun, slapping his gunner on the shoulder.

"Well? Did you get them?"

"I've got two of them, one suicidal bitch ran at us on fire. The others are hiding behind Yuri's tank." the gunner replied breathing heavily.

"Should have let her burn. Fucking witch." the driver replied angrily. He was still blind to what was going on ahead of them, his hatch and sight still covered.

Leaning forward Popavitch peered through his own sight, seeing the thick smoke that was now almost obscuring the street.

"Fire a round into the ass of Yuri's tank, that should smoke them out. Then be ready on the machine gun, I want that bastard that shot me to know how it feels."

"Sarge? You want us to fire on a friendly?"

"Yes, fucking fire at it!" he demanded.

"But you'll be killing Yuri!" the gunner cried out in horror.

Ignoring him he shouted to the driver.

"Driver! Reverse! Give me some damn room to move!"

"My sights are still covered Sarge." the driver warned.

Popavitch shot back, "You don't need the sights to go backwards Mikhail, I'll guide you, now move it before they're on top of us."

He felt the tank begin to lurch backwards as he went to grab the gun controls, shouting in anger as the pain from his injured hand shot up his arm. He realised he wouldn't be able to fire the gun with just one hand.

"I told you to fire!" he said angrily. The look of shock on the gunner's face, told him he hadn't fully understood what had transpired in front of them. Angrily he slapped the man about the face, yelling as he did so.

"Yuri's dead you stupid bastard! They are all dead! Now fire into that fucking tank before we are!"

The gunner blinked quickly in shock as the news sunk in, before quickly putting his head back into the sight. Leaving his gunner to it, Popavitch looked behind him, using his rear periscope to guide his driver.

He felt the gun lower slightly as the gunner took aim, firing quickly, the breech slamming backwards and the tank shaking from the shockwave. Within seconds the auto loader began its mechanical dance, as the long protruding arm began to select another round from the carousel under the gun, extending up from the floor, and reaching towards the now open breech. The round slid forward smoothly, as the second smaller arm came from behind, loading the charge, pushing it clear of the breech, before the breech slammed shut. The gun was ready to fire again, the whole loading sequence having taken less than eight seconds. Popavitch glanced back to his gunsight, expecting to see the tank destroyed, but apart from the smoke and flames coming from the turret, the tank was still intact. He punched the sight angrily; the tank was still providing cover to the enemy troops hiding in front of it. He was about to order his gunner to fire again when suddenly the tank stopped dead, jolting them all in their seats. Cursing, he looked behind him, they'd hit the vehicle behind, the smoke and flames from it were already licking over their engine decks.

The driver quickly replied, "I think we've hit something!"

He ignored him as he saw movement through his left periscope. British troops were beginning to appear from the upper floors of the buildings beside them. How the hell did they get there so quickly? He reassessed the threat.

"Gunner! New target, traverse left, infantry in buildings, first floor, close range, fire!"

He felt the turret spin to the left, the gun was pointing in the right direction, but they couldn't get the elevation they needed to fire, they were too close and the building too high.

"Shit!" the gunner exclaimed, "I can't get the elevation, we're too damn close!"

Out of desperation the gunner selected the coax machine gun and began to fire, the rounds passing harmlessly through the floor below. Green tracer rounds began passing through the brickwork and flying through the air in all directions, but none came close to hitting the troops.

"Dammit!" Popavitch swore, "driver forward! Get us off this fucking street!"

He wasted valuable seconds as he helped manoeuvre the tank forward and then reversed it back around the burning vehicle, keeping the gun facing the enemy, the smoke obscuring his view and making everything twice as hard. Suddenly they were clear of the smoke, he watched through the sight as the range increased. Another twenty meters and they'd have the elevation they needed to fire the gun. The gunner kept firing the coax, not knowing if he hit anything, just trying to keep the enemies' heads down.

Popavitch kept having to look backwards, guiding his driver up the street, trying to navigate the tank between the huge piles of rubble and the roadblocks of burning vehicles that now seemed to hinder them. As he tried to concentrate on what he was doing, he suddenly realised he hadn't sent a report on the radio. Command would need to know what was going on. He was about to transmit his message when he watched open mouthed as faces began to appear in the upper floors of the buildings behind them. All of them were carrying petrol bombs. The fear he fought so desperately to control began to rise again, as he realised, they were now surrounded. He forgot all about the radio as he tried to fight the new threat.

He tried to hide the fear in his voice as he shouted out yet more orders.

"Gunner! New target! Infantry in building, six o'clock of the hull, put the gun rear. Do it NOW!"

"But I've nearly got the elevation Sarge, give me just a few more seconds and I'll have them."

"We don't have a few more seconds!" he barked back.

He felt the turret begin to spin to the left, then a jarring crash as it quickly stopped, the sound of shrieking metal filling the tank.

"What the fuck was that?" the gunner exclaimed loudly.

"Driver, halt!" he shouted as the tank came to a stop.

Popavitch looked out of his periscope, seeing the barrel of the tanks gun now smashed through the walls of a house. He'd become disorientated with everything going on around him and had brought the tank too close to the houses on the left, now the gun was stuck, embedded in the brickwork. He'd have to open his hatch and use the commander's machine gun if he wanted to fire on the British behind them. He looked at the closed hatch, the thought of opening it and the flames burning through to him filled him with fear. No, he wouldn't be doing that again in a hurry.

He looked on in shock, as more troops now began to emerge from the buildings around them into the street, all carrying those fucking petrol bombs. Where the fuck were the infantry? he cursed to himself, was he the only one left? Suddenly a yellow haze began to glow behind him, the sights becoming blackened and hazy. He turned to look out of the rear of the tank, seeing nothing but flame. The turret and back decks of the tank were now bathed in fire. The British were lighting up the tank.

The smell of burning rubber and fuel now began to pour into the turret as the tank's interior seemed to get hotter. He had to do something, his eyes staring over at the ammunition, if that caught alight it would be over. The panicked voices of his crew began to burst over the headset.

"Are we on fire Sarge? What should we do?"

"Do we abandon the tank? fuck it, shall we get out?"

He shook his head, trying to clear his thoughts, he was desperate to get out of the tank himself, but knew if they abandoned the tank and they survived, as commander, he'd be the one likely shot for dereliction of duty. He firmed his jaw, shouting through the intercom, his voice firm.

"We're not going anywhere yet; you leave this tank and you're as good as dead. Now gunner put this fucking turret front so I can get my bearings."

The gun whirred, the metal shrieking in protest, as finally the gun tore itself free of the house and quickly went back to face front, as Popavitch looked through his periscopes. Seeing the buildings flanking them, and the road blocked behind by their own vehicles and the British surrounding both ends of the street, he quickly made up his mind.

"Driver, advance! Take me through those fucking houses on the left, get me off this street!"

"But we're on fire!" the driver exclaimed.

"Then I suggest you hurry!" he shot back angrily.

The tank shot forward, the engine whining in low gear as the driver built up the speed and engine power before the tank turned left, the tracks squealing and screeching on the road, as at first the damaged barrel, then the body of the tank smashed through the brickwork. Popavitch had braced himself for the crash, but was surprised at how easily the house gave way as the weight of the tank smashed into it. The house gave a groan and the tank disappeared into a cloud of dust and glass as the house slowly collapsed onto it. Inside, the crew shuddered involuntarily as the shriek of metal was heard on the turret roof. They all felt the tank slow, and the engine begin to scream, as the weight of the house now collapsed onto them, adding to the engines burden. At first Popavitch thought the tank would get stuck and held his breath, as the driver went down through the gears, and he could feel the tracks scrabbling for grip, until eventually, it emerged into the next street in a shower of dust. Some of his sights were cracked and covered by large pieces of rubble, but Popavitch didn't care, he was out of the ambush area now and free to pick his own ground. He was about to congratulate the driver, when suddenly, they were racing across the next street and ploughing into the next set of houses.

"Driver where the fuck are you going? Stay on the road, don't go through another house!"

He felt a frantic tugging at his arm, looking across confused, he saw the gunner tapping his own headset manically and shouting. He couldn't hear what he was trying to say. The gunner mouthed the words urgently.

"We've lost comms!"

Too late, Popavitch realised that the driver's sight was still covered with the cloth, and the driver was relying on him to guide him, little realising they were through the house already, and not able to hear his commander telling him to stop, the driver had simply kept his foot on the accelerator and kept going. The fear of the fire making him panic.

Popavitch grimaced, and tried to brace himself in the turret, as the walls came down on the tank a second time, the tank crashing up and down as it tore through the rows of houses. The daylight disappeared and shadows danced around the sights. He saw a bathtub appear in the periscope, hitting the turret with a clang before disappearing into the maelstrom of yellow dust as the tank emerged again into the next row of streets, scattering rubble and debris. The commander's machine gun was torn from its mountings, the ammo belt flailing behind like a scarf as he grimly hung on, unable to do anything but wait, as the driver continued his mad panicked dash. They smashed through another three rows of houses, before finally the headset came back to life, whatever had caused it, had fixed itself, as he now shouted to the driver.

"Driver, can you hear me? Fucking stop!"

The driver slammed on the brakes, the huge vehicle beginning to slow, too late to stop it crashing through another house. Popavitch watched as the outside world began to disappear in yet another cloud of fine dust and darkness, as the groans and crashes of the building coming down around them sounded overhead. He heard the turbine engine whine in protest and was expecting at any second to be finally free of the rubble, when suddenly the tank seemed to fall from under them, the gunner screaming in shock as they all seemed to float through the air before crashing down in a heap. Popavitch was thrown forward, smashing his head against the sight, his leather helmet taking the brunt of the impact. He sat for a moment, immobile and stunned, spots dancing before his eyes as he tried to focus on what had just happened.

Eventually as his head began to clear, he could make out the voice of his driver over the headset.

"Sarge, can you hear me back there? I said, we've gone through a cellar, I think we're stuck, the engine's dead and I can't restart it."

"OKAY! Okay, I hear you, no need to shout!" he replied testily, his head throbbing and his hand hurting like hell. He looked across to his gunner, a bare hint of sympathy in his voice.

"You still alive?"

He heard his gunner groan in pain as he looked back. "My arm, I think it's broken."

Popavitch quickly looked down, grimacing at the sight of the bone that protruded from the gunner's wrist. He looked around him, assessing how bad it was, his eyes taking in the chaos of the turret. Some of the ammunition had fallen out of the carousel lockers and lay scattered amongst the turret floor and cables and wires hung loosely, some sparking away. The autoloader was bent out of shape and would need replacing and he could smell fuel coming in from somewhere, so they had a fuel leak, probably some busted fuel lines. It wouldn't be long before the whole thing would go up. The tank was stuck and it would take a crane to get it recovered. Realising time was against them, he merely grunted an order.

"Okay, abandon vehicle, let's get the fuck out."

He sat up to open his hatch, grunting at the effort of using only one hand, but the hatch wouldn't budge, it was locked tight. He tried again, this time more rushed, the panic of being trapped in the steel coffin starting to take hold. He tried a third time, before cursing, as he looked over to the gunner.

"Try your hatch, see if you can get it open."

The gunner reached up with his good arm, trying his own hatch and grunting with the pain and exertion.

Popavitch watched him, silently urging him on.

After a few moments the gunner sat back, defeat etched on his face, holding his broken arm defensively.

"I can't get it open Sarge, it's jammed."

"Fucking thing!" he spat cursing; the rubble of the house must have jammed them shut. He looked down to the driver's position.

"Mikheal is your hatch open?"

"Mikheal," he shouted again; the silence told him all he needed to know. Quickly, he climbed over the breech, dropping his pistol in his haste to get out, as he made his way through to the driver's compartment, grimacing as he tried to keep the weight off his injured hand. He heard the gunner cursing in pain behind him as he too followed with the broken wrist.

Popavitch stuck his head out of the open hatch, gulping in the dusty air as it hit him. Rubble and timber frames covered the turret of the tank, no wonder he couldn't open the hatch he thought when he saw just how much debris was covering it. His driver was uninjured and had climbed the rubble pile to the ground floor, reaching down, he helped pull both men up, the gunner crying out in pain as he caught his injured arm on a piece of metal.

With no time to waste, Popavitch pushed them towards the remains of the back door, constantly looking behind him, expecting to see the British troops pouring through the rubble. He could already hear them shouting in the distance.

He turned to look at the others.

"Weapons?" he asked, already knowing the answer.

The gunner shook his head holding up his broken wrist and the driver looked to the floor sheepishly. Popavitch cursed silently, they'd left everything in the tank. He thought about climbing back through to grab at least a pistol, but the shouts were getting louder and the need to run overwhelmed him. He saw the smoke rising from the tank, certain that at any second it would catch alight.

"Quickly, this way!" he yelled, as he ran out into the back gardens, the others closely following, the gunner holding his injured arm close to his chest. Within seconds they were gone, lost amongst the houses...

19

The Hornets Nest

Fergus followed his troops as they ran through the smashed houses, following the trail of destruction that the tank had left in its wake. His blood was up and his adrenalin flowed at the thrill of the chase. His ears were still ringing from when the tank had shot at them, unbelievably the commander had chosen to shoot at one of his own tanks to get at them. Thankfully the tank they'd taken cover behind had taken the hit, the round passing through and skipping up the street. He still remembered the shocked looks on everyone's faces as the round shot past them in a blur, the air pressure throwing them to the ground. They thought they'd had the tank finally surrounded, and he'd watched in fascination and rage, as the crew had driven through the houses to escape, using the tank's strength and power. He'd ordered his troops not to follow, certain of a trap, but then the Sparrows had reported it had collapsed into a cellar of a house not far from them and was now stuck. Now it was theirs for the taking. It had weapons and ammunition on board, and if he could capture the crew, or even better capture the tank then they'd have their own armour for the town's defence. They came to the final row of houses, his forward troops advancing cautiously, looking through their weapon sights, checking for signs of the crew. Fergus remained in cover as a team went into the rubble, within minutes they were out, waving him over. He trotted forward, climbing through the rubble to the interior of the house. The tank was below them, it's turret buried under a mountain of rubble and its paint blackened, smoke drifting slowly from its engine decks.

One of the soldiers approached him, pointing to the tank.

"She's stuck fast Sir, doubt we'll get her out, but we've put out the fires, as long as we're careful we should be able to get the ammo and weapons stripped off without too much trouble."

Nodding in agreement Fergus looked over to the Corporal who led the assault team. "Crew?"

The Corporal shook his head disappointed.

"I'm sorry Sir, they were gone by the time we got here, but we did find these on board."

The Corporal produced three AK 12 assault rifles, two pistols and three assault vests fully loaded. Smiling, Fergus reached out taking one of the vests, quickly removing the magazine from his own AK12 and replacing it with a fresh one. Crew or not, things were looking up.

He nodded to the Corporal, "Good work, now get those weapons and vests dished out amongst your team, I'd say you'd earned them."

He turned, as Sergeant Major Macdonald ran up breathing heavily, his own team close behind them. The sweat on their faces told him they'd been running flat out.

"You okay Mac? What happened?"

"I'm sorry Sir," the Sergeant Major said between breaths, embarrassedly. "We ran to the end of the street to get ahead of them, only for the bastards to go through the houses. By the time we'd relocated, they were through and away."

Fergus pinched his lips together in thought, looking down at the tank. "Doesn't matter now though Mac, we've stopped them regardless and now we've got a resupply."

The Sergeant Major looked on quizzically as Fergus keyed the handhold radio. "Zero, this is Zero Alpha, get Jerry up here with his team, we're at the junction of Silver street and Orchard street. Be prepared for casualty evac and weapons pickup."

Tuning back to the Sergeant Major he added, "I want the enemy vehicles from that column stripped of anything of that we can use, weapons, radios, assault rigs, you know what to look for Mac."

"Sir!"

Everyone froze and looked around them, as in the distance they heard the muted reports of gunfire and explosions across the town.

The Sergeant Major broke the silence, looking over and saying what everyone was thinking. "The other teams, they've begun to assault their own targets."

After a few moments everyone sprung back to life as Fergus began to issue new orders, pointing to the Corporal.

"Corporal, keep one of your teams here and guard the tank, when Jerry gets up here-" Fergus had to stop himself, he couldn't keep using first names anymore. He quickly corrected himself. "Sorry, I mean when *Sergeant* Mearns gets here, help him to get all our casualties loaded up and the heavy weapons and ammo off this thing and back to HQ. After he's left, you're to report back to the Sergeant Major and help him, and remember stay *off* the streets, and out of sight, use the rat runs if you can."

"Yes sir," the Corporal nodded, as Fergus added, "oh, and Corporal, well done. Your team did well today."

He watched as the fighters around him seemed to stand a little taller, the pride etched in their faces. They'd done it, they'd faced the enemy and they'd won. First blood had been drawn. He recounted the number of people he'd seen fallen, his own team had lost two during the mad dash at the third tank, another team reported in six injured and four dead. For the cost of taking out the whole column, it was a light price, but even so Fergus was sad at the losses. Suddenly the image of the first tanks driver emerging from his hatch, jumped into his mind, the way the face had disintegrated in front of him, made him shudder. He shook the thought from his head, adding it as another bad memory to an already long list of bad memories, that time would hopefully heal. Knowing there was still lots more to do, he turned to the Sergeant Major, his voice sounding energetic and full of fire.

"Right, I'll meet you all back at the CP, let's go and see how the others do."

Phase Line SASHA, somewhere in Yeovil's Suburbs

Major Lebedev looked down at the map resting on his knees, trying to mark the location of his units after their last report. Cursing as he tried to remember the street name and compare it to the map. He looked up from the map at the street around him, nothing seemed to marry up with what he was looking at, the road he was on was supposed to continue straight towards a railway bridge, but it looked like they were in one of the many housing estates that dotted the perimeter of the town. When he'd been looking from the CP it had all looked so different, now in amongst the buildings, with the outdated maps, he was quickly losing his bearings. Already his units were reporting street names that he couldn't see. He pushed his doubts away, it didn't matter, he knew that all they had to do was make it to the town's centre, from there, like the spokes of a wheel he'd push the units out, establishing a perimeter controlling all the entry and exit points to the town, until eventually Yeovil would be his. It had worked in Dorchester; it would work here. Already they were within the town's outskirts and there had been no sign of the enemy. Colonel Golgolvin had been a fool to have wanted to sit back simply and wait for the British to reinforce the town, in war there were risks, but those risks could be rewarded. Now, here he was, about to take the town all on his own. He'd be promoted to Colonel for doing this, he was sure of it, once the General heard, perhaps he may even become the permanent CO of the unit. He looked back confidently at the column, remarking about the firepower he now had at his command, his column, as he thought proudly back to his parents. If they could see him now, a commander of a BTG, a far cry from the early days in Ukraine when he'd been a lowly platoon commander in command of four aging soviet wrecks. Now with the newer T-80, they would level the field. He looked around the turret, smiling, as he looked over to his gunner, punching him on the shoulder playfully as the man looked up from his sight, wondering what had put him in such a good mood. He was brought back to reality as the two tanks in front of him stopped suddenly, causing his own tank to stop, the driver stamping on the brake. Behind him the column began to bunch up. Looking up he keyed the radio.

"Tiger Two, Tiger Command, what is it? Why have we stopped?"

After a few moments the tinny voice of the commander came through.

"Tiger Command, Tiger Two, the road splits off left and right, but my map shows no fork in the road. What direction do you want me to take?"

Trying to hide his irritation at stopping he quickly shot back.

"You choose, both roads lead to the town's centre, I'll leave that decision to you."

He smiled, knowing the young officer in the lead tank would appreciate the gesture, his own decision!

His headset crackled to life as the Infantry commander in the rear vehicle began.

"Tiger Command this is Dragon Command, I've got smoke, lots of it about one km over to the west. Looks to be the area of Tiger Nine."

He stood up and leaned out of the hatch, ignoring the protection it offered, choosing a better view over safety, as picking up the binos he looked west, watching as columns of thick black smoke began to drift upwards. Looking down to his map, he tried to orientate what the map was showing and what he was looking at. That couldn't be where Tiger Nine was, could it, he thought aloud, questioning himself. He keyed the radio.

"Tiger Nine, Tiger Command, send me a report."

Static was his only answer. He was about to try them again when suddenly another voice burst through the net, panic clear to hear.

"They're burning us alive! Send help."

Keeping his own voice calm he responded. "Unknown unit requesting help, send me your callsign and location."

He waited a few moments before trying again, static his only response as the infantry commander now came back on.

"Tiger Command, Dragon Command, I'm now hearing automatic gunfire over to our west, same location as the smoke. What do you want us to do?"

"Who the hell is firing, and why am I not hearing a report!" he cursed loudly to himself, causing his gunner to look up. Suddenly another voice came over the radio.

"Behind us! They're behind us! Fall back, all units fall back!"

He quickly looked about him, the panicked voice sending a spike of fear up his spine. He fought to control it, his fear turning to anger as he demanded over the radio.

"Dammit! Who's under fire? And where? Don't fall back, go forwards! We're assaulting!"

He looked back at his map, should he split his callsign and go and help? Dammit, why didn't he stay with the command vehicle, the tank suddenly felt small and confined as he tried to control the different units.

He keyed the radio, trying to keep his voice calm. "Dragon Command, remain where you are, Tiger Five this is Tiger Command, detach three vehicles from your convoy and get across to support Tiger Nine."

He waited for the response, but none came. Angrily he pressed the pressel, shouting down the radio.

"Tiger Five, this is Tiger Command, WAKE UP!"

How was he supposed to control an assault when people weren't even answering up? He'd be kicking their fucking arses into their throats afterwards, he fumed. He was about to press the pressel again, when the voice of the infantry commander came back on, his voice more urgent.

"Tiger Command LOOK TO THE EAST!

Quickly raising his binoculars, he scanned the area, seeing yet more smoke rising from the roof tops and green tracer round flying into the sky. Someone was firing over there. Had they finally found the enemy? After a few moments he grew impatient, keying the radio again.

"Tiger Five, this is Tiger Command, I can see you're engaged, send me a report. NOW!"

No one answered, the seconds seemed like minutes as frustrated he quickly spoke again.

"Anyone located with Tiger Five, send me a report!"

After a few moments another voice came over the headset, breathing heavily, gunfire sounding in the background.

"Tiger Command this is Dragon Two-Two, all tanks are destroyed, I'm extracting south, we need support NOW!"

He closed his eyes irritably, thinking to himself, there were always some who panicked early on in a battle, the trick was to keep sense of everything. If everyone could just keep calm and report back clearly, he could co-ordinate the attack. Who cared if people were firing at them, that's what they'd been expecting. Did his soldiers really expect not to have come under fire at all?

Trying to keep his frustration hidden, he replied.

"Dragon Two-Two, calm down and report clearly what you're seeing. What's your location? Who's attacking you? And why aren't you attacking them? Where's Tiger Five? Why isn't he reporting up?"

The voice exploded loudly over the headset, causing him to grimace at the noise.

"ARE YOU FUCKING DEAF? TIGERS FIVE, THREE AND TWO ARE GONE, YOU FUCKING IDIOT! THEY'RE ALL BURNING AND ALL MY VEHICLES ARE DESTROYED! THAT'S WHY I'M NOT ATTACKING, WE'RE THE ONES BEING FUCKING ATTACKED! I'M ESCAPING ON FOOT! IS THAT CALM ENOUGH FOR YOU?"

It took a few seconds for the words to sink in, suddenly he looked back over to the west, towards Tiger Nines last known position. Something was attacking them! He'd now become the hunted!

He looked about, suddenly feeling as if the walls and the streets were closing in on them, he'd blundered into a trap, he knew it now. He was about to issue new orders when his gunner cried out a warning.

"IN FRONT OF US!"

He had a few seconds to look, his eyes opening wide with alarm, as figures now began appearing all around them. An object was hurled towards him, instinctively he held his hands up in front of his face, feeling the thud as it impacted his arms, as liquid splashed down his face, getting into his eyes as he fell back into the seat, the pain immense as the smell of petrol hit him. He was covered in fuel! Luckily for him the wick hadn't been lit. He fumbled for the hatch blindly, his hands scrabbling to close around the handle as he closed the heavy hatch, sealing them from the outside world. He tried to wipe his eyes, the petrol stinging and causing him to squint and shout to anyone listening, for a rag to wipe it off as he fumbled around the turret, the map falling to the floor. All around him he could hear the gunfire and explosions as the convoy came under attack.

Trying to see, he squinted over towards the gunner, shouting.

"Dammit! I can't see! What's happening?"

The gunner looked over, trying to help to wipe away the fuel from his eyes with his jacket sleeve as he reported. "Infantry coming out of the buildings! What shall we do?"

"Fire! Fucking fire at them!" he yelled, as the headset burst to life as panicked reports began to fire through. He could hear the infantry commander over the radio, taking charge, trying to organise the defence as abruptly his voice cut short with a scream.

He knew what to do, he'd use the artillery to drive them back. Then he could rally his forces and continue forwards, it wasn't over yet. Quickly he picked up the map, holding it close, as his petrol filled eyes struggled to make out the details. Using his finger, he managed to trace where they were. Confidently he keyed the radio, trying to ignore the pain from his watering eyes.

"Jackal, this is Tiger command, I want you to fire on position Sasha now. High Explosive, sixty round spread, infantry in the buildings!"

The artillery Captain was two miles away with the heavy guns, staring at the map, plotting the positions of troops against the co-ordinates for the fire mission. A look of confusion spread across his face as he reached for the radio telephone, asking.

"Tiger Command, confirm there are no friendlies in that area, over."

The angry voice shot back almost immediately.

"Jackal I don't have time to fuck about! Friendlies are all located in area Arkady, FIRE AT AREA SASHA NOW!"

The artillery Captain looked to his Sergeant who merely shrugged before beginning to bark out the orders to the gun crews. Sat in freshly dug-in positions, the guns began to turn and aim skywards as the crews began the well-rehearsed routine of loading the breeches with High Explosive and inputting the fire co-ordinates. After only thirty seconds they were primed and ready to fire. The Captain was about to confirm the order again, quickly stopping himself. Major Lebedev was on the ground; he knew where he needed the guns to fire. Swallowing nervously and hiding his doubts, he gave the order to fire.

On his tank, Lebedev was trying desperately to organise the chaos around him, his eyes were red shot and rimmed, but at least now he could see again, the fumes of the fuel making him almost dizzy as he shook his head to clear the thoughts. His gunner had started firing on the figures dashing between the vehicles, twice someone had tried to climb up onto the tank, the driver warning them as he quickly drove forwards, throwing them to the floor before crushing them beneath the tracks. Lebedev couldn't tell which vehicle was still in the fight and which was disabled, but he could hear the panic on the radio as his units were screaming for orders. Leaving his gunner to it, he leant over the map as he began to quickly bark out orders, trying to restore calm as they struggled to fight clear.

"All units calm down, Artillery is inbound. Wait for it to begin dropping, then we'll pull back to Arkady, we'll regroup there."

He quickly thought about what he just said. Arkady? I thought that was where we were now. He questioned himself as his eyes could now make out the areas clearly on the map. Sasha! They were at Sasha! He'd just called in the strikes! He had just enough time to register the mistake, to contemplate what he'd done, when he heard the whistle of the rounds incoming. His gunner looked at him, seeing the fear on his face as outside the rounds began to land. Lebedev ducked down in the turret and prayed, the last thing he remembered hearing was the gunner's screams over the intercom.

Hill 254 on the outskirts of Yeovil

Colonel Golgolvin ran to the back of the command vehicle, hoping he wasn't too late. He'd only just got back, seeing the smoke drifting up from the town and watching the green tracer rounds shooting skywards as the dull thuds of explosions drifted up to him. He'd just spent the past two hours getting back from meeting the General, the BTR80's driving far slower than the helicopter he'd left in. He knew what had happened without getting a report. That fucking fool Lebedev! He'd fumed! He reached the CP, the two officers in there with headsets on looked up, the shock at seeing him, quickly replaced with a look of fear as he scowled at them. The looks on their faces told him all that he needed to know as to how the attack was unfolding.

The anger in his voice was plain to hear, as he demanded.

"Where is Major Lebedev?"

"He's leading the assault Sir." the Lieutenant replied apologetically.

"The ASSAULT! Your orders were to stand down!"

Angrily he shot a look around the command post, his eyes looking for his second in command.

"And where the hell is Major Lenosky?"

"He's just left with the reserve force Sir; they're going to assist Major Lebedev."

"How many men did he take?" his eyes narrowing.

"All of them." the controller replied.

"And vehicles? How many vehicles have the VDV taken?"

The controller shook his head, "None Sir, Major Lebedev had the VDV vehicles and two other tank companies push west into defensive positions. He's taken only his tank company and two infantry companies in with him."

"So the VDV are on foot?" Golgolvin gasped open mouthed. "Why the hell would Lebedev do that? And why only take a smaller force?"

The controller shrugged in response as Golgolvin climbed up onto the command vehicle, looking through his bino's at the town. If Sasha had taken the VDV brigade with him, it could work, perhaps they could still win the fight. He tried to make out details of the battle, but with the limited view all he could see was smoke and tracer rounds. He could just see in the distance his men running into the outskirts of the town, but without vehicles they'd be slower to get there. Would they make the difference? Frustrated, he jumped back down, thoughts swirling through his head. Should he reinforce the attack with the other units? Could they still win, or would he just be reinforcing failure?

"What was Major Lebedev's last known position?"

One of the officers pulled the headset off, looking down at the scribbled report.

"Colonel, Tiger Command reported they were passing through waypoint Arkady, and enroute to waypoint Sasha".

Golgolvin looked at the map trace on the wall, cursing its vagueness as his finger traced the position. Cursing he threw the map aside, "Useless! Where the hell is Arkady and Sasha, according to our maps those waypoints cover at least five streets. Why aren't these phase lines more precise? Where exactly were they and where the hell is that smoke coming from?"

The young officer's eyes followed the Colonel's outstretched arm, before looking flustered as he picked quickly through his notes, trying to find further information. This was not the job he imagined it would be, he imagined he'd be in charge of a fighting unit, proudly leading men at the front, not squashed in the cramped, hot, stinking vehicle with an angry Colonel shouting at him. After a few moments of fighting with mapping, more sweat began to break out on his brow, as he looked back at the Colonel apologetically.

"I'm sorry Colonel, I can't find an exact position myself."

"So do we know, is that smoke *our* units attacking or are *we* being attacked?"

The young officer was frozen into silence, not knowing what to say.

Golgolvin grabbed the man, his voice rising as he demanded. "Answer me man! Are we the ones ATTACKING OR BEING ATTACKED?"

The Lieutenant gulped as if unsure of what to say, finally reaching a decision, he reached over and flicked on one of the radio loudspeakers, the sounds of battle bursting through for Golgolvin to hear.

Over the loudspeaker they heard panicked young voices, all requesting help, suddenly one burst loudly through the radio, he recognised it as Lebedev.

"All units calm down, artillery is inbound. Wait for it to begin dropping then pull back to Arkady, we'll regroup there."

As if on cue he heard the booms of the guns firing a mile away, quickly releasing the Lieutenant he climbed back up to the turret, staring mutely at the town, waiting for the artillery strike. If this worked, if Lebedev managed to salvage the mess and continue the attack and if the VDV could reinforce them, then at least it wouldn't be a total loss. He'd still have his balls in a sling for disobeying orders though, that he could be damn sure of.

Twenty seconds later and he heard the distinct crack and whistle overhead, as the rounds began to come down onto target, the explosions throwing debris high and wide as, after every impact, a shock wave reached them seconds later. He picked up his bino's scanning for signs that the artillery strike was a success, as on the loudspeaker Sasha's voice now burst through.

"Command! We're under fire from our own artillery! Stop the guns, stop the guns!"

No! he said softly, quickly adjusting the focus ring as the devastation came into view. He saw the turret of a tank flying through the air above the roofs, landing from view in amongst a small park. More explosions sounded out, the rounds landing amongst them, as he could now see his own troops being flung like rag dolls through the air. That fucking idiot! Lebedev has dropped the artillery on his men!

He jumped down, quickly barking out the orders.

"Stop the guns! Issue the recall, get them all back."

"But Sir, we've only just begun to attack, at least-" the young officer began as Golgolvin reached in and grabbed him by his jacket, barking out, "The attack is over! Issue the recall...Do it now! Get all units back to us while we still can. And stop those fucking guns!"

He let the terrified officer go, listening in as they began to put out the orders over the radio. Some of the units were quick to reply, others were silent.

After a few seconds the guns ceased firing, he was forced to watch on helplessly though, as the rounds still in the air flew down amongst the troops, the final explosion hurling another vehicle turret through the roofs of the buildings.

He walked away from the CP, feeling angry, frustrated and most of all powerless, as rubbing his hands through his hair as he thought through the next plan of action. Lebedev had rushed this, expecting this to be easier than it was. He'd underestimated the enemy and now his units had paid the price. If that fool survives this, he won't survive me, he fumed, his thoughts murderous.

He just hoped they hadn't all just forced his hand into a hornet's nest.

20

Kittens And Tigers

Wonderland Operations Centre (WOC)

"Sir, I think we may have something!"

The CDS looked over to one of the Signals Sergeants who was waving him over to a desk. The Sergeant was speaking to someone on the landline, the phone cradled in his neck as he scribbled down the message being sent. He walked over, followed by the PM who asked curiously. "What is it?"

The Sergeant replaced the receiver before finishing scribbling down the message and looked up, tearing off the paper and handing it to him.

The CDS quickly read the notes, before handing the note to the PM and muttering, "It looks like our Mr Faulkes is back in the game again." Looking at the Sergeant he asked, "Did he give us his location?"

"No Sir, but he left us the telephone number, said it was another red phone box, but he didn't want to tell us the location. I've checked the number against our list and can confirm it's in Cerne Abbas. He said the notes would make sense to the person they were intended for. Once we understand it and we're ready, we're to call him back. I just hope I didn't fuck up the spelling."

The CDS looked up at the map, quickly identifying Cerne Abbas, remarking,

"He's still ten miles behind enemy lines, what the hell is he doing there?"

The PM began to read the note, replying, "He wants us to get Brigadier Rawlinson to listen in on the phone call." Shaking his head as he tried to decipher the last part, "Looks Gealic, perhaps Welsh?" he enquired, as he handed it back to the CDS.

"Looks like," he replied, as taking the note back he looked back at the Sergeant. "Get me Brigadier Peter Rawlinson on the satellite phone, I need to speak to him urgently." He looked around the ops room and raised his voice.

"Corporal Jones? Is there a Corporal Alice Jones here?"

At the far end of the room, the operators' heads all turned as one, to look at the young Corporal who was typing away on a keyboard. A Captain walked over to her and tapped her on the shoulder, saying something into her ear. She stopped typing and looked up to see the CDS staring at her. Slowly she stood up, removing the headset from her head, a look of confusion on her face.

The CDS waved her over, "Corporal Jones, can you just come over here for a second."

Hesitantly, she began to follow the Captain over, what do they want from me, she thought.

The PM watched on as the CDS asked,

"Corporal Jones? Corporal Alice Jones?" he asked again, just to confirm.

She stood in front of them at attention, nodding her head, the strong Welsh accent plain to hear. "Sir, that's me, Corporal Jones."

Seeing her unease, he smiled warmly, causing her to visibly relax as the CDS replied, "Relax Corporal, stand easy, you're not in any trouble, I just need to know if you know a Corporal Nock?"

The Corporal nodded her head slowly, replying, "Yes Sir, she left with Corporal Jackson and Major T-P the other night."

The CDS cocked his head inquisitively, "Left with the Major? You mean they both work here, in the WOC?"

The Captain intervened, pointing over to one of the empty consoles. "Yes General, they all work over there, they're all part of my team."

The CDS frowned, with a staff numbering in the hundreds he didn't pretend to know everyone's jobs. He looked awkwardly at the Captain as he asked, "And remind me again please Captain, what it is your team do?"

Seeing his discomfort, the Captain answered, smiling, "They're all part of our LEWT wing General."

The CDS's eyebrows remained raised, urging the Captain to explain further. Clearing his throat the Captain continued, "LEWT General, Local Electronic Warfare Team, we monitor the enemies radio transmissions, using signals intercepts, we try to ascertain troop numbers, intentions and intelligence estimates and then pass it up the chain."

"And why were these two Corporals sent away with the Major?"

"Sir, they're both top of their game in linguistics, and speak fluent Russian, plus they're experts at using our Bowman communications systems. They both volunteered to go Sir, we were hoping to get them into the Bovington units, help them secure their comms to us, and then get them back with Major T-P before they were missed. Unfortunately, they're all now MIA." (Missing In Action) The Captain was visibly upset as he contemplated the possibility of losing two of his top team.

Seeing his look, the CDS quickly interrupted, "Cheer up Captain, it looks like they're not quite so MIA after all."

"Sir?" the Captain looked up confusedly.

"We've just received a phone call from an asset on the ground reporting that Corporal Nock is with him, and she wants to speak to Corporal Jones. Apparently, the next part of the message was for her, she'd understand it?"

The Captain looked at a loss as Corporal Jones reached over and read aloud the note. "Bydd Kittens bob amser yn clymu wrth draed teigr, ond ni fyddant byth yn dod ag ef i lawr."

"Well?" the CDS asked, "we've guessed it's the Welsh language, so care to enlighten us as to what it means?"

The Corporal was beaming back at him, her happiness clear for all to see. "It's a phrase we both used when we were young, growing up in the valleys. When we joined the army, we were lucky enough to be in the same training intake. Whenever things got us down and we wanted some privacy, one of us would use this phrase and then we would continue chatting in Welsh, so anyone overhearing wouldn't understand us."

The PM now added confused, "So that's it? That's all this is about? Mr Faulkes just wants us to call him back and talk in Welsh? I don't understand?"

"I do," the CDS replied, smiling. The clever bastard, he thought, as he turned to look at the Corporal. "What does it mean, this phrase?"

She lifted her head up and recited from memory, "Kittens will always nip at the feet of a tiger, but they will never bring it down."

Never a truer word said, thought the General, never a truer word.

He was interrupted as the Sergeant approached with the encrypted satellite phone in hand. "Sir, I've got Brigadier Rawlinson holding on the line."

Nodding in thanks the CDS took the phone. "Ahh Peter..."

Cerne Abbas

Mike was outside on one of the empty café chairs, enjoying the sunshine and reading the newspaper he had just brought as he sipped his coffee. He noticed that the café owner had raised an eyebrow and looked him up and down as he paid. When he saw his reflection in the window, he could understand why. He had to admit he'd seen better days, his clothes were ill fitting and dishevelled, recently borrowed from Colin, one of the captured tourists, but they were better than him sitting there in his ad hoc uniform. Across from him was Rachel, who kept fidgeting and moving around looking uncomfortable as she stirred her coffee for the fifteenth time that minute. She'd swapped her uniform for Linda's civilian clothes and it was clear to Mike that she wasn't happy.

He glanced up at her, his voice low. "Rachel, you need to stop fidgeting, you'll draw attention to us."

She looked up from stirring her coffee seemingly irritated.

"That's easy for you to say, you're not the one wearing trousers two sizes too small."

She had a point, at least his clothes were too big, he'd had to use some string as a makeshift belt hidden under the dirty t-shirt. He looked down seeing how high up her legs the jeans were, Linda was quite a bit shorter in the leg than Rachel and it showed. The irony was that neither of them could wear the footwear of their clothes donors, so instead had to settle with their military style boots. Rachel looked more like an anarchist than a tourist. Not wanting to annoy her further, Mike took a sip of the coffee and said in a voice mimicking a fashion designer, "Relax darling, just take it easy, besides, three quarter lengths are all the rage this season."

She raised her eyebrows and leaned forward, "Relax? Is this funny to you? We're sitting here looking like the oddest couple around, you're old enough to be my dad for Christ's sake, and you want me to relax?"

Without looking up from his paper he replied amusedly, "Don't forget to add the fact that you're gay and I'm married. Besides maybe that's just what we are right now, a simple father and daughter on a bonding trip. This was *your* idea to come with me, I was happy to come on my own. Now relax, enjoy your coffee, watch the world go by and chillout."

She pursed her lips together in annoyance, he was right, this was her idea and now she had to stick with it.

Mike looked around the sleepy village, noting it was void of the usual holiday traffic. Usually, the town was bustling with people, but he noticed apart from a few people going about their daily lives, the only visitors were them. He'd heard helicopters overhead in the distance, followed by large explosions, and the road nearby hummed with the sound of military convoys all heading north. He'd wanted to get eyes on the road, but had dared not look up from the paper, recognising the heavy engine noises as those of the Russians. He may have appeared to be reading, but his brain was in overdrive. He glanced over the road at the phone box, how long since they'd called the number? Was it twenty minutes? It seemed like a lifetime ago since Mike had dialled the number on the piece of paper he had kept after Bovington. Rachel had told him what to say and who to ask for and more importantly what she needed for the next part to work. He'd passed over her request and the telephone number of the box. The voice on the other end simply told them to wait, they'd call back within the hour.

Now frustratingly, this was what they were doing, sipping coffee and trying to lay low, trying to look for all intense purposes like tourists. The pistol jabbing Mike in the hip reminding him he was anything but.

He glanced behind him, seeing the cafe owner suspiciously looking over. Quickly thinking he pulled out his phone and checked the battery level, it was showing forty-five percent. He leant over to Rachel who looked on in surprise, as he got close in and snapped a selfie of them both. He was smiling, she was clearly not.

"What the hell are you doing?" she whispered, confused. "Are you taking a selfie now?"

"That's exactly what I'm doing, we're here trying to look like tourists, so let's do what tourists do. Now come on, give us a smile."

"Tourists? We look more like bloody refugees," she mumbled.

It was more of a grimace as he snapped the next picture but, with the camera on, he was using the phone to see what was going on behind him. Keeping the camera there, he watched the shop keeper look over one last time, then finally disappear from view.

He relaxed back in the chair slightly, thinking how strange this had all become, how surreal it was, to be sitting here drinking coffee whilst the others were hidden in the woods a mile to the south of them. He looked over in their direction, seeing if there was anything out of the ordinary, anything to give away their position. There wasn't, all he could see was the same woods as before, and hopefully that's all people would think they were, as they went about their usual daily routines.

Suddenly they heard the shrill ringing of the phone, causing both of their heads to snap round quickly. Leaving the table, they both got up, checking to see if anyone else was reacting to it as they crossed the road. Quickly Rachel opened the door and picked up the phone, with Mike closing up behind her, the door slightly ajar as they both crammed inside.

She started speaking in a language that Mike hadn't heard before, quickly firing back with syllables and a dialect that made no sense whatsoever. Mike merely stood back, listening in, but watching to make sure no one else was watching them. After a few minutes of her chatting on the phone, she cradled the receiver, "Okay, we're in business, so what's the message you want me to send?"

Mike pulled the crumpled piece of paper out of his pocket, with the message that he'd written out earlier, handing it over. She quickly read the message and without understanding what it all meant, began to send it over the phone as he smiled. This had been her idea and it was good. She'd got the idea from watching a documentary about how the Americans had used Native Americans as code talkers during World War Two. Instead of wasting time with complicated codes that could be cracked, the Native Americans could talk plainly on the radio in their own language, safe in the knowledge that even though the Japanese were listening in, they could never understand the language. And whilst she couldn't speak Navaho, she could speak Gaelic Welsh and so could her friend back at the WOC, with whom she was speaking to now. Both had grown up in the Welsh valleys in one of the mining towns. She had told him the name but damned if he could remember it, let alone pronounce it. He smiled to himself, even if somehow, they were that unlucky that the Russians were listening in, by the time they'd cracked the language and deciphered the message it would be too late. This could work, he thought.

He looked around again, checking for signs of anything out of the ordinary. It felt so surreal to him, he'd been on operations before, checking for danger signs, but that was in other countries, here he was in a sleepy Dorset village, surely there would be no danger here? But it had been two days since the Russians had landed and they could take no chances, for all he knew the Russians could have planted people here years ago. Occasionally they'd hear the whine of a helicopter overhead or the noise of a tank in the distance, reminding them they were now the strangers, even at home. He looked back over to the café owner, who was now clearing up their tables. The man looked bored, almost indifferent. To Mike's delight, he finished up and then went back inside without giving them a second glance.

He was pulled from his thoughts as Rachel asked, "Is there anything else you want me to send to them?"

He took the paper from her, quickly checking the message again. No, it was all there, everything they needed. Satisfied, he shook his head and put the paper into his mouth, chewing it up as she carried on chatting for a few moments more to her colleague. She took a pen and notebook from her pocket and quickly wrote down what was being said, before tearing off the paper and handing it over to Mike. Finished she finally placed the receiver back as she turned to face him as both reading through the notes. Suddenly she noticed something.

"Hang on, you've spelled Thumpr wrong, its missing an 'e'?"

"No I didn't," he replied, tucking the paper into his pocket, "come on, I think it's time we headed back, I think we've outstayed our welcome here."

Wonderland Operations Centre (WOC)

A group of people were hovering over Corporal Jones as she began to talk into the telephone.

Included in the group were the CDS, the PM, Sir Tony and some of the other officers from the room, all wanting to hear what the latest development was. This had been the first time they had heard from anyone in the area since before it had all began and everyone wanted to know the fate of the garrison at Bovington.

The phones receiver had been piped through the loudspeaker, so everyone in the WOC could hear the conversation, not that it mattered, there were few people there who could understand the language. The CDS was stood looking over the Corporal's shoulder as she scribbled down the message as it came through, then translating what was being said to Peter who was listening on his own phone some miles away.

After a few minutes of writing, she stopped and looked up, pressing the button that would kill the microphone, only those in the WOC could now hear what was being said. "Sir that's the end of the message, they've asked if Brigadier Rawlinson has anything in reply?"

Still cupping the satellite phone he quietly mouthed, "Wait one," as he continued chatting to Peter.

"Peter, did you get all that, about the Thumprs?"

The phone clicked as the message was encrypted, there was always a slight delay of a second whilst using it, so long as you left time for the recipient to respond, then you wouldn't end up talking over each other.

"Yes, thank you, James, we've received all that. Could you get a response to them please?"

The Colonel next to him stood poised, ready to write the message, as Peter began to talk. The CDS looked over to what the Colonel had written, double checking it was correct before nodding as it was then handed over to Corporal Jones. She quickly clicked on the microphone and sent the message back.

After a few moments she looked up. "Anything else Sir?"

Checking again with Peter on the phone, he shook his head to her, before replying, "Peter, I'm going to have to call you back shortly, would you be a good chap and wait by the phone for me?"

"Not at all James, I'll happily wait," he replied as the CDS ended the call.

The Corporal finished, placing the receiver down as the CDS reached over to take the paper. Quickly he scanned the first few lines, a look of concentration etched on his face as he asked the Signals Corporal,

"Corporal Jones, now you are one-hundred percent certain that was Corporal Nock that you were talking to? One hundred percent?" his eyebrows raised as he asked.

She nodded her head triumphantly. "Absolutely Sir, I asked her before we began to tell me the nickname of our headmaster at school. She told me, and there's no way anyone else would have known that. That's Corporal Nock alright."

Satisfied, he looked up and began to address the group.

"So, it would appear that Mr Faulkes and his group are hiding in the forestry block just south of Cerne Abbas. He's got one tank, three Warrior's and sixteen infantry, along with a truck full of odds and sods and two Russian POWS. He's asking for a re-supply of ammunition, food, water, and maps.

"That's it?" the PM asked, his eyebrows creasing. "Where's the rest of the garrison? Where's the Colonel?"

The CDS removed his glasses, rubbing his eyes as he replied, "They didn't say Sir, I'm still hopeful that the Colonel managed to get out with some of his fighting strength intact. In the meantime, I think we should concentrate on what we do have here.

"They've been busy," Sir Tony muttered as he read the note. Ignoring him the PM replied, "Hang on, isn't he a civilian? Who's in charge there?"

The CDS shook his head, "No, he should be a Captain. The Colonel and the Major at Bovington recommended him after you activated the armed forces reserve act. I wonder why he didn't mention that?"

"And why does he have a truck full of odds and sods with him?" the PM asked, "surely, he's not picking up waifs and strays as he finds them?"

"No," the CDS said thoughtfully. He tapped his fingers on the desk before quickly picking up the phone. "Hello Peter, it's James again, sorry to keep you waiting. Right I think we need to have a serious discussion about Mike Faulkes, he's one of yours isn't he?"

Everyone watched as the CDS walked away from the group, lowering his voice so as not to be heard. After a few minutes he came back placing the phone on the desk, overhearing the other officers discussing the next steps.

"How on earth does he think we're going to get him a resupply?" One of the Colonel's said.

"Well, you can rule out an airdrop, especially for such as small unit." A Major answered.

Interrupting them the CDS declared, "Small or not, this is the only armoured unit we have contact with still in Dorset. Let's not worry about *how* we get things to them, let's see if first we can locate the things they need." He turned to the Colonel. "Colonel, you've served on armour, find out what the bombload is for a Challenger 2 tank and a Warrior, then start to try and get the ammunition they need. I want whatever you can dig up, ready to go at RAF Brize Norton for 16:00 this afternoon. Then talk to the RAF, we'll get a chinook to drop it down to Colerne in time for tonight's replen."

The Colonel nodded in response, jotting down what the CDS had said, quickly walking away as the CDS turned to the Major, "You Major, I need you to find out what mapping we have of the area and start collecting it in. Get an overlay showing what we know about the enemy positions so far, make it as up to date as possible, I want to give them as much chance as we can. Also, find out what comms we can get them, get the codes, get the callsign matrixes and get it over to Brize, again ready for 16:00. Understood?"

"Yes CDS, I'll get right on it."

Leaving his staff to it, he went back to the screen as Mike's unit was plotted onto it. Shaking his head in disbelief, he couldn't believe what he was seeing. With everything going on, and nearly 20,000 Russian soldiers camped around them, somehow, they'd manage to stay hidden behind enemy lines and still with their vehicles. You're a very lucky man Mr Faulkes, the CDS thought to himself, very lucky.

Colerne Airfield, Bath

Peter hung up the satellite phone, a huge smile spreading on his face as he walked to the portacabin door and stepped out into the sun, allowing its warmth to rejuvenate his aching muscles. Mike was alive. He stood there, savouring the moment as he looked around at the airfield that they now called home, reminding himself again of its name. Colerne Airfield. It was a relic of the cold war, long retired, but still kept under the care of the RAF, which was how James had been able to commandeer it. Now it had been re-purposed to house Peter and his staff, already the two huge hangars were being put to good use as their convoy of trucks were parked in both and were being unloaded by the team. Next to the portacabin that doubled as his office, Patch and Alan were strung out, legs in front of them, sleeping in the two polyprop plastic chairs that they'd managed to find on their scavenge that morning. Both were snoring heavily from under the faded thirty-year-old magazines that they'd placed over their faces, in an effort to blot out the sunlight. Both were no doubt exhausted after their long adventure to get here. Leaving them sleeping, Peter walked over to the first large grey hangar, the sounds of people busily at work echoing from inside.

Walking through the large open door, he immediately sought out David, who was stood by a shipping container, now re-purposed as their armoury. David was method- ically checking the weapons serial numbers against his own list, nodding at Peter as he saw him.

Peter could see he was tired, they all were, but no matter where he looked, everyone still managed to smile, the effort and sweat of last night paying off as they managed to make it safely to their new home.

Peter patiently waited for David to finish the checks, seeing him nod to himself obviously satisfied with what they had. He reached over to help him close the heavy doors, both latching the bolt across, as finally David fitted the heavy padlock, giving it a firm tug to ensure it had locked. Now, David would be the only person with the keys, ensuring he'd be the only one with access to the container's deadly cargo.

"Morning boss, did you manage to get any shut eye?"

Peter could already feel the tiredness dragging at his arms and legs, his head felt like it was full of lead and he knew that if he sat down, he'd probably not get up again. But seeing the others all working hard, he knew it would be insulting for him to complain. Instead, he forced a smile and lied.

"I managed to get a few hours in the portacabin. You?"

David looked back outside to the portacabin they were now calling their office. He smiled, his own body screaming for sleep as he replied.

"Not a wink yet, I'll get my head down after we've finished getting ourselves setup."

Peter knew he wouldn't. He'd seen David was as restless as he was, with so much still to do, there just weren't enough hours in the day. Sleep would have to wait. He clapped his hand on Davids's shoulder.

"Mike's alive." he beamed. Davids's face broke into a grin in response. Peter had told him everything that had happened over the past 24 hours during their journey up here. He began with how Mike had called him up, to the events at Wonderland.

"How?" David asked curiously.

"I don't know," was all Peter could say, "but he's managed to somehow get some armour together and is now asking us for help. I've got his co-ordinates written down; he's asked for a re-supply. How many of our team have made it up here?"

David looked around him as people laboured industriously around them. They'd kept the soldiers from the trucks with them, Peter issuing them new orders that they were now attached to Aurora, to provide protection to the staff and more importantly help with the heavy lifting. The Sergeant had initially dug his heels in, quickly conceding when Peter showed him the orders signed by the CDS giving him total authority.

David did the maths in his head, including the soldiers, quickly appraising the numbers.

"With the people that came up last night, plus the Sergeant and his troops, I count forty-two people, but that number is going up all the time."

"Going up, why?" Peter asked, cocking his head.

David pointed outside the hangars towards the grass verge, Peter followed his gaze.

"They've been coming in all morning."

Narrowing his eyes against the morning sun, Peter could see a collection of cars parked next to his 4x4 that he had missed before. He really was tired, he thought, as finally his sleep filled brain registered what he was looking at. They belonged to his staff. The people he'd sent home early last night had made their way to them, even with the roads congested and blocked, they'd risked it all and somehow managed to get there.

He smiled and nodded as David continued,

"Some of them have had quite a rough time of it by all accounts, but they're here all the same. The only problem we're having is finding accommodation for the families."

"I'll get onto that as quick as I can, but first we need to sort out this airdrop to Mike. Can we get five Thumprs ready to deploy for tonight? Also, we'll need to get a beacon and satellite phone out to him for 16:00. What do you recommend? It'll need to have a range of around sixty miles.

"You want to do a drop in the daylight?" David questioned.

"No choice, I need the beacon and phone with him by 16:00. Like I said, what can you recommend?"

David tapped the pencil against his mouth in thought, the cogs and wheels in his brain whirring away as he thought through the numbers. Peter waited quietly, aware of how analytically David thought through a problem. After a few moments he nodded.

"Ok, we can have the Thumprs ready to fly by 21:00. As for the other items, I think we can get away with a cricket, it'll have to be a one-way trip though, we won't get the drone back. And we'll need to have the operation's centre up and running to fly it."

Peter knew the 'cricket' was one of their earlier drone models, using GPS to get to its destination, it was small, fast and with the range and capability to carry the items. It was a good choice and he patted David on the shoulder appreciatively, smiling. It was starting to be a better day already, suddenly he didn't feel so tired. With a wave of renewed energy, he looked about.

"Where's Kyle?"

"In the hangar next door, we're going to use this hangar as assembly and the flight line and next door will be avionics and operations. He's setting up you know who."

Peter laughed in understanding, it was no secret to the rest of them, if their chief programmer could, he'd probably have married their AI programme.

Leaving them to it, Peter walked out of the hangar, already seeing some of the fresher faced team members smiling and nodding to him. With a sense of pride, he bounded into the next hangar, the scene repeated from before. People working all around him, all with a purpose and tired faces smiling at him in return. He walked towards the far corner, seeing Kyle and his team were already re-purposing the old dusty racks, no doubt decades old and relics of the cold war. Kyle had some of his team washing them, before lovingly placing the valuable computer parts on them, methodically checking for damage before connecting the myriad of wires and cables. He looked up as Peter approached, his face a mask of concentration.

"Morning Kyle. How's it looking?"

Without pausing from his work, the programmer replied.

"It would be going a whole lot better if we weren't having to go all Mother Hubbard in here and give everything a spring clean. I mean, who the hell works like this?"

Peter laughed, Kyle was known for being a clean freak, everything always had to have a place and was spotless. Without wanting to put any undue pressure on him he asked,

"How long before we can begin operations?"

"Operations. You serious?"

Kyle stopped working to glance up, seeing the look on Peters face, he knew it was serious.

"Okay," he answered, resuming his work, "we should have operations up and running by the end of the day."

"I need it up and running by 15:00."

Kyle stopped again, staring at Peter. He knew him well enough to know he wouldn't be pushing for 15:00 unless it was important. He slowly nodded his head, smiling wryly.

"Okay boss, 15:00 it is, we'll get it done."

Peter grinned his thanks; he knew Kyle and his team could do it. He glanced over seeing the laptop on the side.

"What's the update with Wendi?"

Kyle stopped and stood up, wiping his hands on his shirt, he opened the laptop, the screen coming to life. He tapped a few keys and then the empty screen displayed a simple cursor flashing in the top right corner.

"She's okay, I've disabled all of her protocols for now, but once we get the mainframe set up we can begin uploading her. Will you need her to run through any simulations today?"

Peter shook his head, "No, not for now, but we may need her later in the week. Concentrate on getting operations set up first though, then afterwards we can get Wendi online."

Kyle nodded as Peter patted him on the shoulder appreciatively and walked away, leaving them to it. He knew what needed to be done and having Peter watching him, would only add to the burden.

Peter walked back outside, his eyes searching across to the group of soldiers, finally settling on the Sergeant.

"Right," he said to himself, clapping his hands together. "Now let's get something done about this bloody accommodation problem."

Cerne Abbas

Mike and Rachel exited the phone box, walking over the street and out of the village, taking the opposite route to the way they'd come in. Mike deciding that just in case they were being watched they would head south in the wrong direction and then double back on themselves crossing fields and woodland. When they were out of sight of the village, they turned right, taking a small track that led them to some fields and hedgerows, before heading back north, using the woodline to shield them from view of the village.

Over the next hour, they began to make their way back to their unit, finding it slow going as instead of walking through the fields, they had to skirt around the edges, using what little cover from the hedgerows they could manage. Rachel had been horrified when Mike had suggested that if they were caught they should pretend to be a couple, taken by the urge to have sex in the fields. It would explain their dirty clothing at least. She'd looked mortified at the suggestion and had jokingly replied, "Why don't we say instead that I was walking alone and you're a dirty pervert who just likes to follow young women? I caught you in the middle of performing an act on yourself and beat you up, at least that would explain your bruised face?"

"The trouble is with that excuse Rachel, is that some men my age actually prefer the beating!" he said back amusedly.

She rolled her eyes and smiled back, at least she was coping, he thought. He had to remind himself that it was only a few nights ago that she had to watch her colleague die in her arms. He knew that at some point she'd have to unpack all that trauma, but for now with everything going on, she was professional enough to keep it hidden. There was a time and place for everything, he thought, and right now was not the time.

As if to have a reason he quickly countered seriously, "Okay how about we're dog walkers, our dog has ran off, and we're trying to find her. We're in this state because we've been tearing through ditches and culverts."

"Okay, where's the dog lead?" she asked.

"The dogs still wearing it, it saw a young deer and took off after it, ripping the lead from my hands."

"Right, and where did we come from?" she continued.

"Simple, Cerne Abbas, we're locals going for a walk, we own the café we've just visited."

"And what sort of dog do we have?"

"Cocker Spaniel, white and brown, called Rocky."

She smiled back again, "I like the sound of the dog, but the name, Rocky? Urggh, not my cup of tea at all."

"Might not be your cup of tea, but I bet you won't forget it now though, will you?"

"No, I suppose I won't," she replied thoughtfully.

They were just approaching another small, wooded copse when in the distance, echoing through the hills, they heard the unmistakable thump of helicopter rotors. Without a moment's hesitation they both ran as fast as they could towards the treeline and as the noise grew louder, Mike was thankful that the copse was as close as it was. He noted that Rachel seemed to breeze ahead, her youth giving her a distinct advantage, as his own legs felt like lead. He grabbed a handful of his oversized trousers to stop them falling down as the pistol weight banged against his hip. Rachel reached the copse first, diving down amongst the grass, as he threw himself down amongst the trees, as the shadows of three Soviet helicopters passed overhead, low and fast, heading west. One was a Hind, similar to the one that had spotted him the previous day, the other two were attack helicopters, MI-28 Havocs. Not the prettiest, but certainly one of the deadliest. He watched them fly low over the trees, the engines roaring as they hugged the countryside. Wherever they were going it wasn't over their woodline and he was thankful for that. They watched as the helicopters disappeared from view, long before the whine of the engines finally died away and silence descended.

Mike sat up onto one knee, slowing his breathing and brushing dirt off. He looked over to Rachel and was about to say something when he heard a faint noise behind him. Something inside him clicked into place and the instincts and sixth sense that he thought had gone after all these years, suddenly fired up again. Someone was watching them. Rachel looked at him blankly as he turned and pulled the Glock pistol from his waistband, immediately bringing it up to the fire position, it was already cocked, so all he had to do was pull the trigger. Without understanding why, she also pulled her pistol, recently borrowed from Patty and took up a firing position off to Mike's right. She was about to speak when without looking up from the pistol he raised a hand, the signal to keep quiet.

She watched on, ready to fire, covering Mike as he slowly crept forward, making sure his foot was well placed on the floor before stepping forward. The last thing he needed right now was to trip over a twig, that would be the worst of amateur hour. He listened as he walked, hearing another noise, there it was again, it was about ten metres in front of them, off slightly to his right in the longer grass, certainly not natural. Keeping the pistol aimed in that direction he glanced around the copse, was it big enough to house a Russian unit? Could they have stumbled upon a Russian Observation Post? Quickly he thought through the options, if it was a Russian OP then they would have fired at him as soon as he pulled the pistol. It could be an animal, perhaps a young deer, hell it could even be a lost dog. Imagine that there they both were talking about Rocky the dog and right now there could be one, hiding in the grass. Another noise, louder this time and he saw the smallest of movement. No, whoever or whatever was making the noise, it wanted to stay hidden.

He spoke with the voice of authority as he boomed, "Whoever you are hiding in the grass, right now you've got two loaded pistols pointed at you. I suggest you slowly stand up with your hands raised. If you understand me then say something."

Silence was the only answer. Mike cursed to himself; he hated the not knowing. What if after all of this it turned out to be something silly? He slowly turned to Rachel, indicating he was moving forward to investigate. Keeping the pistol pointed she nodded in understanding as slowly he crept further forward.

He walked forward another six paces, each footstep felt like a heartbeat, as the closer he got the more he could see and now spotted the shadow of someone hiding there, trying to remain low in the grass. Mike didn't need to get closer; he could tell a person was there. He spoke again, this time much firmer.

"I can see you hiding in the grass, I'll say again, you've got two pistols pointed at you, if you don't stand up right now, with your hands above your head then I'm going to open fire on you."

Mike quickly thought, what if the person didn't speak English. Without looking away he asked, "Rachel can you translate that into Russian in case our peeping tom here doesn't speak English."

She was about to reply when the hidden voice spoke, Mike could hear the London accent booming out.

"Look, I'm not Russian, and I'm certainly not a peeping fucking tom, just hold your fire and I'm going to stand up slowly."

"With your arms raised." Mike added.

"Yep, with my fucking arms raised." the voice replied dejectedly.

As he slowly stood up, Mike could see he was a soldier, wearing the Multi Terrain Pattern of the British Army. He'd concealed himself well, with thick foliage tucked into his uniform to disrupt the shape of his body. His face was the dark green and black of cam cream, causing his eyes and teeth to gleam out. His helmet had tufts of grass stuffed into it to disrupt its pattern and Mike had to admit, if it hadn't been for the fact the soldier was lying in the lighter grass, his uniform being the darker colour, then he doubt he would have seen him so easily. Mike moved off to the side, so that Rachel had a clear line of fire covering him. Lowering the pistol slightly Mike nodded at the piece of wood the soldier still carried in his hand.

"What were you going to do with that?"

The soldier shrugged as if it didn't matter anymore as he dropped the wood, "I was planning on hitting you with it, taking your pistol and doing a runner." his tone sounded almost apologetic.

"Good job for you that I didn't get too close then," Mike replied acidly, adding, "because my friend here would have killed you."

The soldier looked over to Rachel, seeing her pistol still aimed at him and realising Mike was right. He wisely kept his hands held high as Mike now asked, "So who are you? What unit are you with? And how did you get here?"

"I know you." the soldier said simply.

Mike cocked his head in surprise, "Really? I don't know you."

"Can I take off my helmet and show you my face?" the soldier asked. Mike nodded then quickly added, "But slowly, very slowly, any sudden movements and we'll open fire, regardless of the uniform you're wearing."

Rachel spoke up, lowering her pistol, the doubt in her voice clear, "Oh come on, he's one of us, he's clearly in the army."

Without taking his pistol off the soldier, Mike replied slowly and firmly, "He could have taken that uniform from any one of our dead soldiers and then been sent out here to infiltrate other friendly units, remember the trick they played over the radio on us. Until we confirm who he is, and what he's doing here, we treat him as a hostile."

He saw her raise her pistol back up and aim it at the soldier, as slowly he lowered his hands and unclasped his helmet, removing it and letting it fall to the floor. Then with infinite care he moved his hand to one of his pouches on his chest rig, quickly adding, "It's my water bottle pouch, I'm just going to reach inside, pull it out and wash my face."

They both watched him closely as he very slowly pulled out his water bottle and poured some of the water onto his hands and began to clean his face. After a few moments the cam cream began to rub away revealing the face of the young soldier. Mike, at first looked stunned, then he broke into a big grin as he realised where he'd seen him from. This was the lad that had given Mike the cup of tea when he was chatting to Chris in the ATDU hangar. He lowered his pistol, the soldier grinned back as Rachel looked on confused. "Okay, so is he hostile or not?" she demanded, annoyed that she didn't understand what was so funny.

Mike looked over, "It's all good Rachel, he's friendly, this is one of Major Richards lads, I recognise him from the ATDU.

Stepping forward, the soldier offered his hand, a big grin on his face, "Mr Faulkes, Sir, my name's Lance Corporal Barry Logan, the lads call me Baz."

Mike took the outstretched hand, noting the soldier had a good strong grip as he beamed back, "Well Baz, it's damned great to see you, I can't tell you how happy I am to finally find you. Where are the others? How's Major Richard's doing?"

He watched the grin on the soldier disappear, "I'm sorry Sir, I wish I knew myself, but I haven't seen anyone from the ATDU since the night of the attack."

A look of confusion spread across Mikes face, as the young Lance Corporal quickly told him about his own journey in the DTT's, and how, since leaving them, he'd managed to get this far. Mike's face registered surprise and then respect, as he listened to how the young man had managed single handed to lead the Russians on a merry dance. Mike could hear the young man's stomach rumbling and could see from the way he spoke that he was exhausted, as quickly he interrupted him.

"Baz, how long since you last ate or slept?"

Baz's face was pinched in thought as he replied, "I'd say probably thirty-six hours for food and twenty-four hours for sleep."

"Right," Mike replied, making the decision quickly, "let's not waste time here, let's get you back to our unit, get some food in you and you can tell us all about what you did and where you've been. The others will want to hear this. Then I promise you can get some shut eye. You look like you need it."

"Others?" Baz looked back confused. "I thought it was just you two?"

Rachel stepped forward, placing a sympathetic hand on his shoulder, "Come on, you've done enough on your own, let's get you back with your own side."

Smiling with how the day had turned out, Mike turned and led the trio through the copse, back in the direction of their woodline. So far so good, he thought, now all he needed was tonight to go as planned. If it all went well then by midnight tonight, they'd at least have a have a fighting chance.

Wonderland Operations Centre (WOC)

The PM was chatting to his aide Sonya, going through the latest list of cabinet selections, when he became aware of a commotion outside. Looking up curiously he could see a group of officers animatedly chatting to the CDS and pointing up to the main screen excitedly. His curiosity piqued, he stood up, excusing himself and walking out, leaving his aide looking angrily back at him.

"CDS what's going on?"

The officers all went quiet as the PM approached, the General looked over, a deep furrow in his forehead, deep in thought.

"I'm not quite sure yet, Prime Minister. It looks like we're getting early indications that the Russians have been stopped just outside of Yeovil."

"That's great news, isn't it?" the PM asked, unsure as to why the CDS looked uncertain.

"It could be, if only I knew how they managed it. From what we've seen, we've nothing there to fight them," the General replied, looking back up to the main map of the south.

Already he'd organised to have the major road networks blocked and shut down, the M4, M3 and M27 motorways in the south, as well as the M6, and A1 in the north were all now jammed with cars, some done deliberately, others accidentally, as everyone tried to flee from the Russian advance. Penrith, Spennymoor, Bishop Auckland, Horsham, Guildford, Winchester, Andover and Basingstoke were all now rushing to become fortified towns and cities, with hastily made defences and troops being flooded in. The CDS knew he had to somehow slow the Russian advances down long enough to get the defences organised and had already deemed some towns and cities as lost causes, of which Yeovil was one. Now hearing the town of Yeovil had made a success of it, he was beginning to wonder if perhaps it had been the wrong call.

He held his chin in his hand in thought. Looking up at the screen again he asked one of his staff.

"The phone boxes, put the list up on the screen again."

Onscreen the display changed as every phone box still in service was displayed, in alphabetical order, the operator began to scroll down the list, until they came to the letter "Y"

"There! Stop there!" the CDS barked as the number flashed on the screen.

Pulling his glasses down, he read the number out loudly, a young soldier jotting it down as he spoke.

"Good! I thought so, Yeovil's got a phone box." he exclaimed happily, turning to the group of soldiers whose sole job had been to dial up the numbers.

"Right, let's get that number dialled, I want to be chatting to someone in Yeovil as soon as we can."

Leaving them to it, he walked back over to the PM.

"I'll get you the answers soon enough Sir, besides, it looks like you're needed elsewhere.

The PM turned to see what the CDS was looking at, following his gaze he looked back at the conference room, his aide Sonya was standing up, a look of irritation on her face as she tapped her watch and then pointed to the papers in her hands, the hint very obvious. The Cabinet still needed to be chosen. And quickly.

The PM nodded at her in response before turning and raising his eyebrows at the CDS, the message loud and clear for him to see.

"Looks like my time at the coal face has come to an end. Good luck with the number, hopefully we can talk about it more when we get the cabinet convened later."

The CDS watched him go, smiling, then turned back to the team on the phones as one of the operators looked up.

"Sir, the numbers ringing for Yeovil..."

21

Room For Another

Cerne Abbas

It didn't take them to long to cover the short distance, and soon Mike found himself slowly creeping up through the familiar woodline, along the track to the vehicles, his pistol tucked away and his hands were raised, trying his best to look as passive as possible, waiting for the sentry to see them. They were expecting them back, but the last thing he needed was to be shot by a nervous trigger finger. He'd made Rachel and Baz stay back slightly, they were expecting only two to come back and he didn't want the sight of three people to spook anyone. He was happy to see that the cam netting even in the day light was doing a good job, and if he didn't know it was there, he would have thought the track was overgrown. He was stopped suddenly when he heard a voice low but firm to his front call out.

"HALT! Who goes there?" he recognised the voice as Whippet's.

He looked to see if he could see him, but he was well hidden. Mike quietly called out "Friendlies."

"Password, Charlie Romeo," the young Fusilier demanded.

Quickly remembering the response to the password Mike countered, "Alpha Papa."

"Identify yourselves, I count three of you," the soldier replied suspiciously.

"It's Mr Faulkes, and Corporal Nock coming back in and we've picked up a passenger on our travels, he's also a friendly."

He heard the voice soften slightly as he replied, "Okay Mr Faulkes, you know the drill. Advance slowly please, keep your hands raised until I say so."

Mike did exactly that, walking forwards until he could see the sentry lying next to a fallen log, it was the perfect fire position, and it wasn't until the sentry finally recognised him that he lowered the weapon, visibly relieved.

"Welcome back Sir, apologies about the rude reception but we were expecting two of you. It caused quite the stir when we saw three of you walking through."

"Thanks Whippet, mind if I go back and get the others?"

The sentry smiled as he stood up, pointing behind Mike who turned to see where he was pointing.

Back down the track, no more than ten metres from where he'd left Rachel and Baz, stood a heavily camouflaged Fusilier Pong, who up to now had kept himself hidden between the trees and foliage. Mike was impressed, from the moment they had walked up the track the two soldiers had been watching their every move. Mike had to keep reminding himself that these were infantry after all, and this was their bread and butter. He nodded his head in appreciation as Whippet added, "Ping's one of our company sniper's, you'll have to get up early in the day to catch him out."

As they watched, the Fusilier motioned for the others to make their way into the leaguer, checking through his weapon sights that no-one else was following them as he slowly walked them back behind the cover of the cam netting.

Once safely behind the net, the two sentries left them to resume their duties, as Mike ushered Baz to follow him and Rachel. The Lance Corporal's eyes opened wide in amazement as he saw the vehicles arrayed one behind the other. He hadn't expected to see any of this and could only look on at the people staring back at him, the group now recognising another stranger in their midst. As they passed the truck, Mike saw one of the police officers standing guard over the Russian prisoners. The officer nodded at Mike in greeting before his eyes went back to watching the prisoners, the gaze cold and hard. The officer still bore the cuts and bruises of his own harsh treatment under captivity and Mike wondered if secretly the officer wished he could return the favour. Mike kept going towards the back of the Command Warrior, seeing Patty and Spider were both there. They looked up as he arrived.

"Any luck?" Patty asked hopefully.

Mike pulled out the piece of paper which Rachel had scribbled the reply on, his face beaming as he passed it to them. Spider took the message and began reading it aloud, "Songbird16:00, Be ready to sing 22:00, 355250. Thumpr to acknowledge. What the hell does all that mean? And why'd they spell thumper wrong, it's missing a letter."

"It's not missing anything. It does mean though that all being well, after tonight, we won't be on or own."

"Care to elaborate?" Spider asked.

"Not yet, there's still too much that can go wrong. For now, we wait." he replied.

Knowing Mike wouldn't say too much with everyone else listening in, Spider looked over at Baz as Patty began, "So who's this? Bringing in the strays now?"

Mike replied, "Everyone, this is Lance Corporal Baz Logan, we found him hiding in the copse about 500 metres south of here. He was part of the ATDU squadron that took the tanks away." Mike could see Patty was about to say something when he quickly added, "In case there's any doubts about his identity, I've met him before and can vouch for his credentials."

Patty nodded in reply as Rachel interrupted, "Look, if there's nothing else for me right now, can I go and get out of these bloody clothes?"

Mike looked at her, he'd forgotten how uncomfortable she must be wearing small trousers.

Mike nodded, and quickly put a hand on her shoulder, "Rachel well done for today, that was a bloody good idea you had. Thank you."

She nodded back, smiling modestly as she left, as the others all joined Mike in thanking her, before turning their attention back to Baz.

"So, what's your story then?" Spider asked.

Mike saw Baz staring back hungrily at one of the cans of tinned peaches stored in the back of the command wagon. Before Baz could reply, he interrupted.

"Shit, where's my manners? Sorry Baz, Spider, pass us that can of peaches will you. Poor bugger hasn't eaten for nearly two days."

Spider reached in, opening the can and passing it over, as Baz mouthed his thanks. He was about to give him the spoon, when he saw it wasn't necessary, Baz had simply tipped his head back and eaten from the can. He stood there with a look of pure content on his face as his cheeks bulged with the food as he chomped away. He must have been starving, Mike thought.

They patiently waited for him to swallow the first mouthful, as, taking a smaller amount this time, he began to tell them his story.

They all listened as he recounted everything, where the tanks had really gone, his journey across Dorset, how he'd hidden during the day, and finally how he'd ended up marooned and out of fuel. As he'd made his escape, he'd heard the enemy tanks firing on the DTT's and thought they were going to find him, but he'd stayed hidden throughout the day, moving slowly across the countryside, keeping out of sight of anyone he saw. He had come to the copse to rest and had thought he was well hidden and out of sight when, he'd heard and then seen Mike and Rachel walking up. He explained that had the helicopters not flown overhead, he was sure that they wouldn't have stopped there, so in a way he was grateful for that, otherwise they'd have all passed like ships in the night, oblivious to each other's presence.

As he finished, Mike was the first to ask, "After you ditched the tanks, did you see much more in the way of military traffic?"

"I did, mostly re-supply trucks though, with the occasional armoured vehicle acting as an escort. All heading north though."

"And aircraft? Have you seen anything looking like enemy fighters or bombers in the air?"

"No," Baz replied, shaking his head and adding, "I did see a lot of helicopters though, all heading west, and I heard explosions and gunfire over that way."

Mike remembered seeing the same helicopters earlier in the day. None of this made any sense, he thought to himself. Why were the enemy now heading west? What was over that way? He remembered a quote from Sun Tsu's book on the art of war, that read, "Of the four plans of defence that you will employ to stop your enemy, your enemy will always choose the fifth."

Knowing he wouldn't get the answers standing there he quickly added, "Okay Baz, do any of you have any further questions for him?"

Patty looked up questioningly, "So you single-handedly drove an unarmed lightly armoured training tank, with no way at all of fighting back, all the way up here, bringing the Russians with you, knowing you could die at any moment, just so the others could get away?"

Baz had finished the can of peaches and simply nodded as his mouth was still full of food.

"Fair play mate," Patty said admiringly as he clapped his hands quietly, "fair play." He reached past Spider to reach into the wagon, pulling out another two tins of food. "Here you go mate, we're out of beer and medals, but I think you at least deserve these two."

Baz looked embarrassed as he took them gratefully, before looking over to Mike, who simply shrugged his shoulders. "Nothing to do with me Baz, he's right though, you did well."

Seeing he was uncomfortable with all the attention, Mike decided he'd help him out.

"Right if there's nothing else for him, I'm going to put him on my wagon if you don't mind Spider?"

Spider nodded before adding, "Before you go, I'm sure you've seen already but the police wanted to help us after you went, so I've put them on guarding the prisoners and the three Engineer lads have asked to help with the guard rotation. What do you think?"

Mike thought quickly, before replying, keeping his voice low, "It's a good idea, we could use the extra manpower, so long as you think they're up to it, but make sure they're one hundred percent okay with being around the POW's, the last thing we need is anyone seeking revenge. And as for the Engineers, just make sure they know what they're about."

Spider nodded intently, as Patty replied, "No problem Mike, I'll see to that myself."

Satisfied, he turned, motioning for Baz to follow him, who quickly put the two tins of food into his assault vest and followed on, stifling a yawn.

Mike heard Baz exclaim in surprise as they continued walking forward, as he saw the familiar shape of the Challenger 2.

He looked back smiling as Baz exclaimed, "Hang on? Megatron? How the fuck did that get here?"

Mike watched as he ran his fingers over the pock marks and damage from the previous firefight before looking back at him, totally bewildered. Ignoring him Mike walked to the front of the tank pointing to the sleeping crew and putting a finger to his lips, before he waved him on up to the turret, whispering. "I'll tell you all about it, but first let's step into my office." They both climbed up, Mike going into the commander's station and Baz stepping down onto the loader's side. He let the Lance Corporal settle himself on the seat and then quickly told the story of how it now came to be in his possession. When he'd finished, Baz looked horrified.

"We left her behind! I don't understand, how?" he asked, looking round the turret shocked. "I thought all the crews were there. And that young lad, Trooper Hickok, I bet that was Corporal Haley that made him fucking stay, what if he'd been captured? Fucking Hell, that ain't right!" Clearly the thought of leaving the vehicle, and more importantly, one of their own behind for the enemy horrified him. As Baz sat there shaking his head in disbelief, Mike quickly countered, "It doesn't matter how, or why now does it, what matters is *it* is here, and young Bill is *not* captured, he's safe and well. Now, am I right in understanding that you're an operator?"

Looking up Baz quickly composed himself, "Yes that's correct Sir, loader-operator. I can command as well if you need me to."

That's good to know, Mike thought, as he asked, "Can you use the RWS?"

341

"I can," he replied proudly, tapping the display before adding, "I used to go to the county shows with Megatron with the Army Recruiting Team, I'm happy with how it all works."

Mike breathed a sigh of relief, then quickly added, his voice kept low. "My driver and gunner out there are both recruits, and are still a bit wet behind the ears, they've done well so far, but are still learning. I need a decent operator, one who isn't afraid to take charge when I'm not around and show them the ropes. You fancy the job?"

"Is there anyone else?" Baz replied jokingly.

"No, there's not!" Mike replied chuckling, "So the job's yours if you want it."

Mike waited as Baz opened the breech of the gun and looked inside, his trained eyes checking the bore was clear. He looked over the recoil system quickly, checking the accumulator gauge for the high-pressure system was reading correctly. After perhaps a minute of scrutineering, he yanked on the Breech Closing Lever, watching as the breech blocks slid up and the breech closed with a smooth resounding clunk.

Wiping his hands on his uniform he looked over thoughtfully, "I noticed that you're asking me, not ordering me?" The response was more of a question than a statement.

Mike pursed his lips together; he hated this part. "Well, I'm not in the army anymore Baz if that's what you're thinking, I'm more of a civilian now than a soldier, so you're not under any requirement to do what I ask. However, I'm not going to lie, having a three-man crew makes this hard, I need an operator, especially one who knows the tank so well and like you said already there's no-one else here."

Mike watched as the Lance Corporal looked over the turret again, before looking back at him, as if scrutinising him, before finally replying.

"Major Richards told us before we left, that you were going to come with us and command one of the tanks and that you were to be given a field promotion to Captain. The Colonel had recommended it and the General on the phone had agreed. What happened?"

Shit, he thought, so that's why Chris had been so angry back at the hangar. Mike had made him look like a fool, if he'd already told his troops Mike was going with them.

"I've got a family now Baz, it's not as simple as joining back up and going off to fight a war, I've got other people who are dependant on me," Mike countered.

"So why didn't you go home then? Why did you stay and take the tank and its driver, why bother to save all these people?" he asked questionably.

Mike had to admit this young man wasn't afraid to speak his mind. He had a point though, why had Mike bothered? As if to answer him, Baz added, "Because now you've got all these people depending on you as well, to make the right calls and the right choices. I don't know your family Sir, or where they are, but I do know they'll probably want you to be part of a solution rather than sitting back and watching the problem."

Mike was silent as the young soldier's words sunk in. He suddenly felt guilty that he hadn't thought about his family since being out on the ground, he knew Kate was safe in America, but what about her parents? Should he have gone back and tried to get them out? Was Poole as he left it? For all he knew, his house could have been destroyed and they were dead. What would Kate think of him then? He shook the thoughts out of his head, regrets and hindsight were the two things Mike tried never to dwell on, he could only control what was in front of him and right now in front of him was Baz.

"I don't know why I stayed Baz, maybe it was seeing Trooper Hickok all alone, who knows, but I'm here now, and we still need an operator. So, you game?"

A smile spread across the Lance Corporal's face as he nodded, "Of course I'm game Sir, it's what we all trained for, ain't it?"

"And you're happy to take orders from me, even though you know I'm not in the military?" Mike's eyebrows raised expectantly.

Baz's looked up out of the hatch, his eyes squinting against the sunlight now shining through the canopy of trees overhead as he replied. "The way I see it Sir, someone was prepared to offer you the rank of Captain, so they must know what *they're* doing and if it's good enough for them, it's good enough for me. Besides looking around here, you haven't exactly done too bad for yourselves."

"Good," replied Mike, "welcome aboard, now what do you think, could she still fire?"

Baz pinched his lips together then replied, "She's good to fire, of course I've no idea how long it's been since she last fired, or how many rounds the obturators have had through them, ideally first chance we get I'd get a gun fitter to look at them, but for now she's good." Mike remembered from memory the obturators were part of the recoil system, made of part rubber, part high tensile steel, that helped seal the breech when the gun fired, by squashing up and creating an airtight seal. In peace time they were checked after every day of firing to make sure the rubber was still ok. He couldn't remember the exact figure, but he was sure they had a shelf life of 500 rounds. Baz snapped him from his thoughts as he added, "Not that any of it matters anyway."

Mike cocked his head, "Why do you say that?"

"Nothing to shoot," he answered back, waving his hands over to the empty ammunition racks.

"What if I said I'm working on that now, and hopefully tonight we'll have something that goes bang," Mike replied knowingly and smiling, as Baz raised an eyebrow.

"Well, if that's the case and we're getting a delivery, then can I add a pizza onto the order?" Baz replied jokingly before adding, "how you managing that? Helicopter? Wouldn't that be too loud and too dangerous?"

Mike nodded, replying, "Yes it would, and there's no way of confirming if the air crew would see us. Like you say, far too risky."

Baz's eyes narrowed, "So how are you doing it?"

"I'll show you tonight," he replied, as he checked his watch. "In the meantime, we've got a few spare hours, why don't you try to get some sleep, I promise you'll be busy tonight."

Baz laughed shaking his head, "You're kidding aren't you, how can I sleep with all this excitement to come? If you don't mind, I'll familiarise myself with the systems again and strip the breech and check she's all good. Now I know we're getting some pills to fire; I couldn't sleep if I tried!"

Mike laughed, happy with the energy that radiated off the young man, feeling far less tired than he first thought. He was about to leave, before adding, "Give me ten minutes to go get changed and I'll come back and help. I could do with the refresher training myself."

By the time Mike had got changed and swapped the pistol back for his AK12, he could hear voices already coming from inside, curiously he stepped up and peered inside, seeing Bill and Smudge in the turret helping Baz to strip and check over the breech. Baz and Smudge were both kneeling next to the gun, working on it, with Bill sat on the gunner's seat passing the tools as they were required. Mike said nothing but watched, smiling to himself as he saw them working as a crew together. He watched for perhaps a minute before Baz noticed him. "Hi Mr Faulkes, turns out I didn't need your help after all, these two heard me working in here and came up to help. Good lads." he said, admiringly.

"Do you need an extra pair of hands in there anyway?" Mike asked, already knowing what the answer would be.

"No thank you Sir, I think we've got this covered. Give me an hour with these two and everything should be back in order. I'm sure there's other more important things you need to be getting on with."

Mike silently thanked him, at last he had someone who could run the tank when he wasn't there. He looked back down as he addressed the crew. "Bill, Smudge, Lance Corporal Logan is going to be our operator for the foreseeable, therefore when I'm off the tank, he's the boss. Understand?"

They both looked up nodding their heads as Mike finally said, "Anyone needs me I'm going to be over by the truck."

Leaving them to it, Mike smiled as he walked off the tank, at last he finally he had a crew. All he needed to do now was find some ammo. Deep in thought he walked over to the truck. It was nearly 15:00, it was time to brief the others.

The drone arrived bang on 16:00, he heard it, before he saw it, the low buzzing of the rotors echoing off the trees, like an angry hornet. Mike looked up into the sky, shielding his eyes from the sun's glare as the shadow of the small flying object hovered overhead. It landed just in front of him, the motors shutting down as soon as it touched the ground, quickly returning the silence. Mike sprinted out the short distance, picking up the drone and running back to the shelter of the trees. He sat there panting, looking around quickly to see if anyone else had seen him. No one was there. It had been a risk, but it was one he had to take, there had been no other way. He calmed his breathing as he stood and walked back into the woods, joining Spider and Patty who were crouched in wait.

He knelt down as both men watched him as he deftly turned over the drone, unclasping the rubber bungs that held the large cargo pod in place. He removed the pod, handing the drone over to Spider who looked at the flying device in wonder.

"Always used to wonder how these things operated." he said in awe, looking like a kid at Christmas, as Patty jokingly replied, "Yeah, but you were always too busy with beer and women to care for kid's toys."

Spider looked up smiling, "What is it we used to say when back at depot?"

Both men said at the same time, "If you can't fuck it, fire it, or drink it, I ain't interested."

Both men laughed as Mike ignored them, the private joke lost on him as he concentrated on opening the cargo pod. He unclasped the clamps and looked inside. His eyes were drawn to the small orange plastic case, quickly pulling it out he opened the lid to see the satellite phone safely nestled in a bed of styrofoam. He pulled out the phone, seeing it came with a charging cable that could be connected to a military vehicle. He turned over the phone, on the back was written in permanent marker, 'YOUR ARMY NUMBER.' He put the phone and box on the floor and reached further into the cargo pod, pulling out a smaller electronic box, no bigger than a mobile phone, it had a simple on/off switch and a large extendable antenna. He checked that the device was switched off, before putting it in his pocket and picking up the phone.

He quickly powered on the handset, the display blinking to life and requesting an eight-digit code. Of course, he thought, the code was *his* old army number. He keyed in the numbers ingrained in his memory and pressed enter, the display changing immediately. He checked the phones address book, there was one number stored in the phone under 'WOC.'

He turned to the other two, "Come on, we need to make a phone call, and I don't want to talk here. Come with me."

Both men followed Mike as he walked back into the leaguer towards the truck, opening the door he motioned the others to get inside before following them up into the cab. It was a tight squeeze but with Mike in the middle the other two could listen in to what was being said without anyone else hearing. He pulled out a small notepad and pen from his pocket, handing it over to Patty, who looked back, not understanding.

"Scriber," Mike explained, "I need you to write down what they say to us, saves us trying to remember." Patty nodded as Spider replied jokingly, "Forgive him Mike, he's only used to colouring books."

Mike extended the phone's antenna, pointing it skywards and checked the battery was full, waiting a few minutes as the phone began to pick up and lock onto the satellites overhead. The display showed six satellites in range. Good, that would do. He scrolled through to the phone's address book, finding the WOC's number. He hit 'dial' and waited.

The phone was answered on the third ring an officious clipped voice answered.

"Captain Reinhardt speaking."

"Captain Reinhardt this is Mike Faulkes, I've been told to call you on this number."

There was silence as Mike heard the Captain talking to someone in the background before answering, "Okay Mr Faulkes, stay on the line."

The line went silent, Mike was on hold. He smiled to himself, at least he didn't have to listen to any scratchy music.

After a few minutes the line clicked back on.

"Mr Faulkes, it's General Catmur here, CDS." He felt Patty and Spider stiffen in shock next to him, as they realised who they had on the phone. The General continued," I just wanted to say congratulations, you've done a damn fine job Sir, a damn fine job in getting this far. Brigadier Rawlinson's currently away organising your resupply but wanted me to pass on his thanks also. As I'm sure you can appreciate, I'm a bit busy here, so will pass you over to Colonel Stephens and his team who've got some questions for you. Before I go, do you have any questions for me?

Mike had lots, but realised these were not the questions for the CDS to answer. He simply replied.

"None for you Sir and thank you."

"Good man," was the brief reply, and with that the CDS went. Quick, brief and to the point.

The line clicked again, and a new voice was heard.

"Mr Faulkes?"

"I'm here, I can hear you."

"Good, can I call you Mike?"

"You can," Mike replied, as the Colonel continued, "Okay Mike, as the CDS has already said, I'm Colonel Stephens and I've got a few questions for you before we begin, can you tell me are you on your own there? Or do you have anyone else listening in with you?"

Mike turned to look at the other two as he replied, "I've got a Corporal Webb and a Corporal Patterson with me as well Colonel."

"Ahh I see," the Colonel replied before asking, "Corporal's Webb and Patterson, I'd like your full names, numbers and units please."

Mike listened as both reeled them off quickly from memory. He guessed that whoever was with the Colonel would now be checking their details with the army records.

"Thank you, gentlemen, now Mike, I've got you on the loudspeaker, as we've got some other people listening in, we're all interested to hear what you've been up to and what you've seen so far. So, in your own words I'd like you to start from the beginning, and please, leave nothing out.

"Will do Colonel, but before I do, can the Russians track this? Can they use the phone to direction find us?" Mike asked, remembering what Rachel had already told them.

"No, they can't, the phone you're using is encrypted and using a different type of signal, so you can call us whenever you need and talk for as long as the battery lasts."

"How do you know about direction finding Mr Faulkes?" Another voice chimed in, before the Colonel quickly intervened "Ahh Mike, this is Captain Reinhardt, you spoke to him earlier, he's in charge of our LEWT team. He believes you may have two of his soldiers with you, Corporal's Nock and Jackson."

Damn, Mike thought, this was not the sort of thing he wanted to say over the phone. Patty grimaced as Mike replied.

"Corporal Nock's with us, but I'm sorry to tell you Captain that Corporal Jackson was killed when we escaped Bovington."

There were a few moments of silence on the other end, Mike could hear muttered conversations in the background as the news was relayed. Suddenly the Colonel was back on.

"Okay Mike, thank you for passing that on, we'll make sure Corporal Jackson's family are told. Now, can I ask we get back to the past seventy-two hours. So, between the three of you, what's been going on and how is it that you are still alive?"

Over the next hour they told them about the events, starting from how he managed to find the tank left behind, to how they had now found themselves leaguered up in the thick woods with the captured truck. Sometimes the Colonel would stop him to ask a question, or to ask one of the Corporals. The Colonel seemed very interested to know about Sam and the farm, and what enemy vehicles they'd seen so far. Mike told them about the helicopters he'd seen, the trucks and tanks driving past and how the Russians had used the false radio messages to find some of the hidden units. He mentioned the Russian POW's they had and how they'd chanced upon the truck with its cargo of misery.

"And these civilians were all drugged and tied up in the back of the truck with no guards?" the Colonel asked suspiciously.

"That's right," Mike replied before adding, "the only thing that linked them all was that they had either witnessed or been the victims of war crimes."

"How so?" the Colonel asked, "how do you know this?"

Mike relayed what they'd all seen when they were in the back of the truck with Doc, their suspicions and what the survivors had said when they had woken. All had a story of either cold blooded murder, torture or rape.

"Ahh I see," the Colonel replied, his voice taking on a softer tone. They could hear the chatting in the background again, as what they had said was being digested.

"Right," the Colonel replied. "And these two POW's you have, the driver and Sergeant, they're still alive?" The statement was more of a question and Mike understood why he'd asked, especially after what they'd been carrying in the truck.

"They are, we've got them separated from the others and they're bound and hooded."

"Good." the Colonel replied briefly.

Mike guessed the questioning was becoming serious, as the Colonel now switched tact, calling him by his surname.

"Mr Faulkes going back to what you said earlier about when you took the tank, why did you do this?"

Mike's face creased into a frown, "I don't understand the question Colonel, are you suggesting that I should have left it and Trooper Hickock to be captured?"

"No, I'm just trying to ascertain your motives, you're a civilian are you not? Why didn't you leave it for the military to handle?"

"Because the military were all high tailing it out of there, no one was coming for back for him or the tank. I made the decision to get both out of there and in the process came across the other units."

"Yes, about that Mr Faulkes, why did you turn around and go back for them? Why did you put yourself back into danger? You were about to get away, weren't you?"

What was this, thought Mike, are they hinting that he should he have just left everyone to it and driven away. Ignoring his thoughts he replied, "It just seemed the right thing to do at the time, I couldn't just leave them there. I made the decision and turned the tank round."

"And what did Trooper...Hickok have to say about it?" a new voice demanded. "Was he aware that you were a civilian? Did he know that you had no right to ask him? What gave you the right to risk his life? Under whose authority were you acting upon?"

"Trooper Hickok knew the risks and made the decision with me, he's a brave young lad." Mike added.

There was silence again, then muted conversations on the other end as the Colonel's voice came back on.

"Ok Mr Faulkes, going back to the autoparts store, whose idea was it to tie up the owner and help yourself to the items?"

Help myself, what are they implying with that, he wondered, as he replied, trying to keep his voice calm.

"That was my idea, martial law had been called and the military were now in charge. The shop owner was guilty of profiteering." Mike said confidently. "Besides, we needed the equipment more than he did, I considered it operational necessity. I suggested the plan to Corporal Webb and he made the decision for us to go."

"And when you entered the store Mr Faulkes, were you carrying a firearm? Did you threaten him with a firearm?" the Colonel asked. "Was Corporal Webb made aware you were about to threaten a civilian with a firearm?"

Shit, Mike thought, he hadn't thought about that. He *had* been the one carrying an assault rifle.

He was about to answer when Spider intervened, leaning over and snatching the phone from Mike, his voice rising. "Sir, what the hell is going on there? I'm not sure I understand where you're all going with this, but Mr Faulkes has saved our arses on more than one occasion. And now you're questioning why he did it? He's been with us from the beginning, he's been the one out here on the ground making the decisions, taking the risks, it's been his ideas that have managed to get us this far. You're right he is a civilian, he doesn't have to stay here, putting himself in danger, but he has. Don't fucking question why he's done it, just be thankful he fucking has, he's the reason we're here now and he's the reason we're still able to talk now. Instead of criticising him, perhaps you should be fucking promoting him!"

Mike looked on horrified, trying to silently calm Spider down, his finger on his lips urging silence as Patty covered his mouth laughing. Spider looked on, the anger on his face quickly turning to shock as he suddenly realised who he'd just been talking to.

Shit thought Mike, he shouldn't have said that. There were ways to speak to high-ranking officers and one thing you never did, especially as a Corporal was drop the F-bomb to a Colonel.

Another new voice chimed in, the tone acidic. "Corporal Webb, I'm Major Spencer, just who the hell is in charge there? Are you telling us that at present, you're currently following orders from a civilian?"

Spiders mouth opened and closed, suddenly lost for words as he realised what his outburst had suggested. Out of his depth he looked over to Mike for answers as Mike calmly took the phone back.

"Major Spencer, that's *not* what Corporal Webb is suggesting, he's in charge of the unit, I'm merely acting, at his request as a civilian advisor, he asks for my opinion or suggestion and then he makes his own decision based on what I've said. I think you can forgive him that little outburst, I'm sure you can all appreciate the gravity of the situation out on the ground at present. We're all just a little tired out here, feeling a little bit alone and tempers are beginning to fray."

There was silence on the other end and Mike wondered what was being said. Had the line been cut? After a few moments the Colonel's voice came back on, calmer than before. But now it was back to first names again he mused.

"Okay Mike, I think we're done with the questions for now. You're right, you're on the ground and you can see things clearer than we can back here. I believe Brigadier Rawlinson is already putting together a package for you, expect it around 22:00. You have the beacon?"

Mike looked down, feeling the small box in his pocket.

"We have it Colonel, it'll be on and transmitting in time."

"Good, now if you don't mind, I'd like to chat to the two Corporals, *alone*. Could you give us some privacy, we'd like to discuss military matters, out of the ears of civilians."

Spider's eyes were wide, and he mouthed silently, "Oh shit!" Perhaps saying what he said wasn't a good idea after all. Taking the hint, Mike left them to it, climbing out of the truck's cab and jumping to the ground, careful not to let his rifle barrel dig into the ground as he landed. He closed the door quietly and made his way back to the tank. He had a few hours to kill, so decided he'd go back and get some sleep before the busy night they had planned. He'd only walked five metres when he saw Linda at the back of the tank, waiting for him.

"Mike, can I have a word?"

He looked at her curiously, what would she want with him, he thought. He hadn't spoken to her all day, ever since she'd argued about leaving that morning.

He stifled a yawn as she asked, "Was that a satellite phone I just saw you all using in the truck?"

Damn, thought Mike, she'd been watching them. Ignoring her question, he asked, sighing.

"What is it Linda? How can I help?" his eyes narrowing.

"Are you still planning on getting rid of us tonight?"

"Yes, that's the plan, all being well." Mike secretly couldn't wait. He'd never liked having reporters around.

"Well, I've changed my mind, I'd like to stay with you."

What, he thought to himself, earlier they'd been arguing with her on reasons to stay with them, now here she was saying she wanted to stay.

"Linda, I'm a bit confused, I thought after what you said earlier, that you wanted to go. What's changed?"

She looked around pointing at the vehicles, "I've been chatting to the other soldiers, about you, about Corporal Webb and Corporal Patterson, about this unit. It's an interesting story, how you've all survived so far, how you've all came to be here. It's got legs, I think it'll go far, so I'd like to stick around and have a go at telling that story if you don't mind and seeing where it all could end."

"But what about what you said earlier, about wanting to get out and report on the invasion and what's happened so far?" he asked, pointing to the civilians sat around the back of the truck. "What about telling their stories?" he was trying to convince her of reasons to leave.

She chewed her bottom lip awkwardly, and shifted on her feet as she replied, "Well, by now, every news hack and journo in the country will be reporting on the invasion, even if I get away now, it's old news, nothing to report. As for their stories..." she nodded over to the group, "Sad as it is, by the end of the week nearly everyone will have some kind of sad story to tell, people will be sick of hearing about it, they'll want a happier more positive story."

Mike thought to himself, hang on, didn't this happen to you as well?

She cocked her head and looked at him as she carried on, "I just think that there's more of a story to be told here. I think the public would want to know about it, hell I'd want to know about it." Her voice raised excitedly as she put on an air of dramatic flourish, "Are they all going to make it out of here, the heroes of the hour, or are they going to find themselves captured, or worse, blackened, charred, stains in the English countryside?"

Something about her manner just seemed wrong, the way she described death, trying to romanticise it all. He wondered if perhaps as a way of coping she was burying what had happened to her and was putting a theatrical spin on things. He remembered reading about people, who in times of disaster, would constantly record on their phones, believing if they saw it on the phone's screen, then it wouldn't be real. Most of them still died though, never truly understanding the danger they were in until it was too late. And by then, phone screen or not, it wasn't going to save them. He didn't want her to make the same mistake. There was a danger here, and she had to see it for herself.

"You were captured, you tell me what it was like. Did it make a good story? Would it sound as dramatic if you said it aloud?" he hated saying it, but she had to hear it for herself.

She shrugged her shoulders and looked at the ground, replying, "Sometimes to get a story you have to go where the evil is. If you surround yourself with evil, get close to it, see it, smell it, then sometimes that evil touches you back. That's the cost of what I do, most men take what they can normally never have."

"You seem very matter of fact about it all." he stated, eyebrows raised.

"You can break the flesh, but you don't break the mind," her voice lowered slightly as she continued, "like I said, soon everyone will have a sad story to tell."

Mike looked at her, trying to gauge her reaction. He'd expected her to get angry, to be upset, he'd hoped it would put her off the idea. The last thing he wanted was a journalist hanging around. But instead, she seemed to be at ease with what had happened, almost as if it was simply part of the job. He switched tactics.

"You want to know how the story ends Linda?"

She said nothing, pursing her lips in thought as he carried on. "What if I told you this story might not have a happy ending? What if everyone ends up dead. Somewhere out there, lying in a field or hidden in a forest never to be found again. Or charred broken and twisted in the wreck of one of these vehicles, what about then? If that's how we end up, would you still want to stay with us?"

"You don't really believe that's how this will end do you? Otherwise, why would you have stayed?" she asked.

"It doesn't matter what I believe," Mike countered, "life has a habit of doing what you least expect, especially on the battlefield. No one knows how it'll end, least of all you, I'm sorry but the risks to you are too great, it's not a game, you can get hurt staying with us. So, first chance we get tonight, we're putting all of you on that truck and driving you as far away from here as we can. It's for your own good."

She nodded slowly, her eyes narrowing before saying, "Well I know how this will end. I'm sorry Mike, but the decision isn't yours to make for me. That's my decision and I've chosen to stay, I wasn't asking for your permission, I was telling you what I was doing."

"Well, we'll just wait and see what Corporal Webb has to say on the matter." Mike was about to walk away when she quickly retorted, "Corporal Webb agrees with *me.*"

Mike cocked his head, noting the change in the journalist. She knew something, he could tell, the way she'd confidently just said his name told him there was more to come. She stood there a triumphant look on her face, her hands resting on her hips.

"What have you done Linda?"

She looked around her, checking no-one was listening in as she lowered her voice, "I told the Corporal that in all the past conflicts, the military and the media have a history of working together. Bosnia, Kosovo, Iraq, Afghanistan, all of them have been widely covered by the news. Why should this war be any different? I've suggested to him that I be your embedded journalist, and I be allowed to document what you get up to. I'll be the one to tell your stories, to take the pictures. I mean, this is journo gold, to be with a fighting unit, *behind* the enemy's lines, Mike you don't ever get an opportunity like this gifted to you!"

He shook his head slowly as she continued unperturbed. "It's not just about the boots on the ground Mike, there's a war to be fought at home as well. You *must* win that war, because without the people you lose the support, then you lose the war. Look at Vietnam."

"Linda this is different," Mike argued, "Vietnam was an American conflict, fought thousands of miles away from America. Here, those people back home *are* home. That's where this war is going to be fought. Not overseas, but here, in people's gardens, in the streets they grew up on, in their homes, even in their workplaces. There won't be any need to tell them about it or convince them they're doing the right thing, they'll know, they'll be living through it."

She shook her head angrily as she replied, "Well it doesn't matter what you think, you're a civilian and the Corporal's in charge, I've already cleared it with him. He's going to chat to his bosses about it when he gets a chance."

Mike rubbed his eyes, the tiredness suddenly hitting him. He found chatting to Linda exhausting, as if she had the ability to sap the energy from him. What the hell was Spider thinking, he thought, instantly knowing what Spider *was* thinking. The journalist was young, pretty and not used to hearing the word no. He wouldn't have been the first person to have been charmed by the opposite sex to get their own way.

Hearing enough, Mike held up his hands in defeat, "Fine, Linda, from the sounds of it, you've already wrapped it all up between the two of you, so you don't need me. Now if you don't mind, I'd like to get some rest."

Leaving her there, he climbed up onto the back decks of the tank, seeing the rest of the crew already fast asleep on the turret. Careful not to wake them, he removed his rifle and lay it next to him, before removing the body armour and assault rig that he'd taken from the Russians, although poorer in quality, it was far better than using his jacket pockets to store the extra magazines. The sweat that had pooled under the armour in his t-shirt cooled almost immediately in the slight breeze that blew through the woods making him shiver. He removed his combat jacket, rolling it up into a pillow and then settled himself in, the years of working on tanks paying dividends as his body automatically contorted to find the most comfortable place to sleep. Using a piece of rag, he covered his face to help block out the sun and stop the flies from landing on him. Then he closed his eyes and within minutes was fast asleep.

22

Consequences

Headquarters Yeovil Town Centre

Fergus walked down into the headquarters to a hero's welcome, wincing with embarrassment as people came up smiling, patting him on the back and congratulating him. He'd never been good with praise, all he could do was smile back, trying to keep his face serious as he walked over to the command table, placing his shotgun and AK12 assault rifle on the floor and wiping the dust and soot from his face. He looked at the map, quickly marking where the other engagements had just taken place as one of the fighters came over, handing him a bottle of water. He smiled as he took it, not realising how thirsty he was, as he drank slowly, his throat feeling as if he'd just swallowed razor blades. Setting the bottle down carefully, he looked over his notepad at their number of casualties. Twenty-eight defenders killed and forty-five injured, he shook his head regrettably, feeling the loss of each one, knowing that they should have lost a lot more and he should count themselves lucky, but it didn't feel much like luck, and with both elbows resting on the table, he quickly closed his eyes and said a silent prayer for those that hadn't made it back. Most of his casualties had come from the attack on the last column, just as it looked like he was gaining the advantage, the Russians had called artillery on their own troops. A crazy thing to have done, however it had worked as the fighting had to stop as, both his troops and the Russians, could do nothing but take cover as it rained down from above. By the time the artillery had finally stopped, the Russian column, or what was left of it had pulled out of range to the south. All the British could do was watch in anger and frustration at the missed opportunity. Still, it hadn't been such a loss, he looked over to another number that he'd written. Enemy casualties. They'd at least managed to destroy the other three columns; all their vehicles were now smoking ruins and most of the soldiers in them were either dead or wounded, only a few had managed to escape. He'd seen some of the Russian wounded being loaded up with their own, and were no doubt now being treated back at the hospital. He made a quick mental note to get Mac over there, prisoners were prisoners, wounded or not and the intelligence he could get from them might help them over the coming days.

He looked to his left, to where three large TV displays were set up. Each TV had one of his Sparrows, overwatching their drone displays as the young pilots flew them over the town, looking for any further enemy activity. It all looked quiet for now. He was distracted by the noise of a group of people coming down the stairway, looking over as the Mayor and her entourage walked into the headquarters, chatting animatedly. She'd changed into military style trousers, and green blouse, looking almost like one of the fighters now defending the town. The Police Chief was also in uniform, but the others all wore suits, looking strangely out of place in the military surrounding. As she came in, he could see her looking around appreciatively at the transformation of the basement area where they had set up the HQ. Where once a cold dark basement of a department store had stood, was now the Headquarters for the Yeovil Defence Force, a bustling hive of activity-the basement was located two floors underground, safe enough from the artillery strikes that he knew would eventually come. Already with more time to prepare, the town streets were being systematically closed off, with most road junctions and crossroads now having a roadblock of some type on it, guarded by their defence forces. She smiled and walked up to him, extending her hand in jubilation.

"Well done Major! We did it! We stopped them!"

Not wanting to dampen the mood, he smiled back, holding up his hands in resignation as he said,

"Thank you, Mayor, however if you don't mind, I'd like to hold off on the celebrations for the moment."

Ignoring them, he began to trace his finger along the map streets, looking for certain points and writing down the co-ordinates on a piece of paper before handing them to the drone pilots.

"I need eyes on those areas." he simply said, the pilots nodding in response.

"But Fergus!" the Police Chief interrupted him, confused by his downtrodden look. "We've beaten them! You did it, we did it. At least let yourself be happy for that."

Fergus smiled; his face tight lipped as he walked back over to the map, before replying. "I'm sorry to be the party pooper Chief, but all we've done now is buy ourselves time. Granted, it was a victory and although you can't see it in my face, I am happy, but now we need to be prepared, ready for the hard work to begin."

The Mayor smiled awkwardly; her face confused as she asked. "Hard work? But Fergus, surely you can't seriously be thinking they'll be back again? Will they?"

He looked up from the map, as he spoke.

"Mayor, I told you that the first battle would be the most important one and it was. However, I never said it would be the last. The bad news is that right now, the Russian Commanders will be planning a second assault, except this time we've lost the element of surprise, they now know what they're up against. We can't rely on them to make the same mistakes again."

He watched as the smiles disappeared as what he had said sunk in. Not wanting them to get too downbeat he quickly countered.

"However, the good news is that our troops have fought their first action, they did extremely well and now know the Russians can be beaten. Plus, not all the enemy vehicles were destroyed, some were abandoned, we've managed to salvage them and now have quite a large haul of weapons and ammunition. So now we've managed to arm more of the fighters and we've got three armoured vehicles to boot. We've even managed to get our hands on quite a few RPGs."

The Mayor looked at him confused, "RPG?"

"Rocket Propelled Grenades." he explained, seeing she was still none the wiser he added, "it's a small portable anti-tank rocket, looks like a bazooka, it'll be much better than using petrol bombs, we won't have to get so close to attack them now."

She nodded as he continued, "Anyway, luckily for us some of the reservists know how to use these weapons, they'd used them in Iraq and Afghanistan when training their armies. I've got them at the moment training the others. With any luck within a few hours, it'll give our fighters more of an advantage."

The Mayor looked around the room, her eyes watching the Sparrow's drone feed as she asked. "If a second attack were to come, how long do we have? When could they attack?"

Fergus shrugged, also looking over at the drone feed. "It all depends now on the enemy commander, if their cautious and clever, then they'll wait, they'll regroup and re-organise, they'll get everything into position and hit us when they're ready with everything they have."

"And if they're not cautious? If their commander is a hot head?" she asked.

He smiled thinly, replying, "Well then we can expect an attack anytime now."

Her group all looked over to the drone screens in horror, expecting at any moment to see the tanks and vehicles coming back. All they could see where the blackened ruined hulks from the earlier battle and empty streets. Seeing their shocked faces Fergus sought to calm their fears.

"It's all been quiet since the last attack, we've got eyes on the routes in and the choke-points are now being defended by hundreds of heavily armed fighters. Don't worry, they won't be just walking through the door now without a fight. If they do come, we'll know about it and can react. It's all in hand."

The Mayor looked over confidently, showing none of the fear or reservations of the others as nodding in response she replied. "I know Fergus, I know, that's why I gave you the job."

He smiled, about to reply when the radio they'd setup in the room crackled to life, the voice of the Sergeant Major echoing loudly off the large empty space.

"Command, this is Bravo Three-Three- Alpha, I need to speak to Zero-Alpha."

Fergus walked over to the radio set, taking the handset from the operator as he replied.

"Bravo Three-Three-Alpha, this is Zero Alpha, send."

"I'm on the junction of Dillon Street and Mayfair Avenue. I need you to come down here."

Fergus looked at the operator, both of them sharing a look of confusion as he replied.

"Bravo Three-Three- Alpha, say again? You want me to come down to your location, correct?"

"Yes, correct, I need you here now, it's urgent."

What on earth could be so important that Mac would need him down there? He turned to the Mayor, the look on her face told him she was thinking the same.

He found on the map the street junction. It was only half a mile away, he could walk that in less than ten minutes. He looked to his watch, annoyed at seeing the face had cracked, probably during the attack on the column. So much for 'go anywhere' he mused as he saw it was nearly 14:00. Looking up at the screens again one last time he made his mind up.

"Right, I'm leaving HQ for a few minutes, I've got my radio if you need me." he said, as he picked up his rifle from the floor. He glanced at the shotgun, a thought flashing through his mind as smiling to himself, he picked it up, offering it across to the Mayor, who looked at him questioningly.

He handed it towards her insistently, offering it with an amused expression as he said, "For the lady in your life who has everything."

She smiled, as the Police Chief guffawed before replying, "Major! I don't think the Mayor should be seen walking around with a firearm, what kind of message would that send the public? She's not Calamity Jane."

Fergus pursed his mouth in thought before adding, "How about the kind of message that says the Mayor is just as willing as everyone else to get her hands dirty and is not afraid to fight for what she believes in, and unlike some political figures, she's willing to use more than words."

The Police Chief was about to reply when the Mayor interrupted, stepping forward to take the shotgun. "It's okay Chief, I'm much more of a GI Jane girl anyway, besides, I'm no stranger to shotguns." She expertly cracked open the bore, checking both chambers were empty before looking around at her entourage, answering the questioning looks.

"I was once part of the GB team for shooting clays. Thank you Major, this will do just fine."

He smiled, reaching into his pocket and handing over the rest of the shells, a little look shared between him and the Police Chief, as one of the people in the suits said excitedly,

"Just think of the optics in this, a Mayor not afraid to fight! This will be election gold for next year."

Fergus looked at the man, shaking his head slowly as he thought amusedly to himself, some things never change.

It took Fergus twenty minutes to travel the half mile distance, usually he could have done it in five, but he had to keep stopping to check the roads before running across them. He was sure the area was clear, but he still couldn't take the chance of a lone gunman surviving the earlier battle, hiding in one of the buildings, wanting to take the shot.

He arrived at the junction, seeing the Sergeant Major stood in the open, his team spread out in defensive positions, checking the streets and windows.

"What is it?" he asked breathing heavily as the Sergeant Major ushered him over to the phone box, he could see someone inside, holding the phone.

As he followed, the Sergeant Major pointed over to where a group of kids were watching excitedly, as he began. "The kids over there have said that this has been ringing for the past half hour, they ignored it at first, then Charlie here decided to answer it."

"The phone's working?" Fergus asked surprised, "are the mobiles working as well?"

"No," Mac replied, "we tried them whilst waiting for you, still all down. But it's not the fact the phone's working that will amaze you. It's who's on the other end, they want to speak to you."

Fergus looked quizzically as the Sergeant Major took the phone off the kid, patting him on the shoulder.

"Thanks Charlie, you can get back to your mates now and remember to keep your heads down and stay off the streets after dark..."

The child nodded, quickly running off to join the gang, as Mac put the receiver to his ear and began to speak into it, all the while looking at Fergus.

"Hello Sir, you still there...yes...he's here...that's right...thank you, I'll put him on now." the Sergeant Major's face became serious as he held the handset out.

Fergus looked at the phone in amazement, who the hell was on the other end?

Still watching the Sergeant Major, he placed the phone to his ear, his voice suspicious. "Hello?"

"Good afternoon Major Young, I hear congratulations are in order..."

"Who is this?" he asked suspiciously.

There was a pause as the person on the other end took a breath, then with the utmost of seriousness in his voice replied, "This is the CDS...General James Catmur, and I'd like to know what's been going on there..."

Hill 254 on the outskirts of Yeovil

Colonel Golgolvin stood outside the field hospital, as the sorry remnants of the attack began to slowly filter back in. Medics rushed forward to take in the casualties, some of those less injured, were sitting down, others were rushed into the surgeons' tents behind him. Some were simply left where they lay, the medics already deciding that death was not far behind them. Depressingly, he counted the number of vehicles returning in his head, they'd lost an entire company of T-80's and only eight of the BMP3's had survived to come back, each vehicle nearby, offloading stretchers and survivors, their hulls and turrets, blackened and damaged from battle. Some of the soldiers coming in had been forced to run back, their own vehicle's destroyed, some were dragging or carrying injured colleagues. His own men were mixed in with the other units, the difference in the camouflage pattern of the uniforms marking them out from the others. He was ashamed to see two of his own VDV troops walking back in without their weapons, he walked angrily towards them, about to rebuke them, they were VDV, his troops, they should know better! You never leave your weapon behind! As he got closer, he could see their horrifying injuries. Where once there were hands, there were now nothing more than nubs, the flesh melted to the bone, the fingers fused together. Their smocks were in tatters and their upper bodies were exposed, he could see the burns injuries, blisters, red and raw that were seeping a yellow liquid down their chests. He could do nothing but stare silently as they slowly filled past, his rebuke dying on his lips. One of them looked up, recognising the Colonel and nodded, clearly in a lot of pain, but still having the strength to smile, more like a grimace, but still a smile, not wanting to show pain in front of his Commanding Officer.

Golgolvin was suddenly ashamed by his thoughts. Who was he to judge them, he'd left them behind to be commanded by an idiot. These were his men, his responsibility and he should have been leading them, not that fucking fool Lebedev. And where was Major Lenosky? He'd left him to keep a tight rein on that fool. Sasha wasn't the kind of man to have bowed down meekly, why had he gone along with the attack? Overall, it made for a sorry, depressing sight and he looked around at those around him, the moans and cries of the wounded sounded pitiful, growing in volume as more and more injured were brought there. He'd grown accustomed to the sights of battle, to the many ways soldiers could tear living breathing things into chunks of flesh, the gunshots, the shrapnel wounds, even the crushing injuries from blasts and bombs, but the burns, they were the worst, he could never get used to them, no matter how many times he saw or smelt it. To see the disfigured broken things that were once people, lying there made him angry, and the smell of burned flesh, like pork filled his nostrils, almost making him gag. He vowed he'd never eat pork again, but then he'd said that before and he still did. He shook the thought from his head as he looked at the soldiers, all wearing the same looks of shock. The morale would be the worst of it, by nightfall, news of the defeat would be on the lips and ears of every Russian military person in the south. He shook his head; how could he explain this to the General?

His thoughts were interrupted as a young Lieutenant's head now poked out from inside one of the tents.

"Sir, we've located Major Lebedev, he's alive!"

The anger he felt earlier quickly flashed to the surface, as he thought, good! The fool yet lives!

"Where is he?" he barked.

"He's in surgery over at the surgeons area, it's located-"

"I know where it is!" he shot back angrily, striding off.

He marched up to the surgeon's area, his eyes focused on the tent, trying his best to ignore the cries of the dead and dying, waiting to go in. He was about to burst in, when, one of the medical orderly's wearing a surgical gown, quickly stood up from tending to the casualties and stepped in front of him, putting his arm up to bar the way.

"You can't go in there Sir!"

"I'm the CO! I'll go where I fucking well please!" he shot back, about to push past as the man who stubbornly remained steadfast, pushing him back as he replied.

"I'm sorry Sir but you still can't go in. That's the surgeon's tent, it's a sterile area and the surgeon's operating on someone now. If you wait here, I'll tell him you want to see him."

He stopped and looked at the orderly, the anger burning in his eyes, he could push past, barge in, but then how would that look with his men? This man was only doing his job, they all had been doing their job. He looked down at the blood on the orderly's gown, then back up to his face. He looked exhausted. How many more of them were like this, he wondered. His anger began to subside, seeing the man wasn't going to back down and clocking the stares from the wounded waiting to go in. He nodded silently as the orderly took a breath and let his arm fall. Lebedev could wait, he'd wait.

He stood back, about to light a cigarette to calm himself down, when he noticed the looks of fear on the men lying around him as the match was struck, their eyes watching the flame. It took him a few moments to realise, then quickly he threw the cigarette away extinguishing the match, snarling to himself. "Idiot! These men have been burned alive! The last thing they want to see is more flames!"

Frustrated, he sat down amongst the pile of stretchers, unable to look away in morbid fascination at one of the burned bodies. The head looked more akin to a red skull as all of the facial features were missing. The hair, the ears, the nose and lips were gone, burned away by the intense heat of the fire. The teeth were barred manically thanks to the loss of the lips, almost as if in a mocking grin and the cheeks were devoid of all their flesh, allowing him to see through to the tendons and lower jaw. He let his gaze wander lower, to the bare chest of the individual, pockmarked in strips of flesh and what was once the uniform, all melted into one, huge mass. He looked on in shock as he saw the rise and fall of the chest. The poor wretch was still alive! How was that possible? Surely the man couldn't live like this, he questioned. He looked back up at the face, the eyes were now open as the person looked back at him, the sockets gleaming pure white against the blood red of the death mask that he now wore.

He saw the mouth open slowly, hearing the dry rasp and rattle of the windpipe as he tried to talk. The chest heaved quicker, as he attempted to draw breath, the eyes looking around at him. Was he trying to talk to him? He bent closer, going down on one knee as he put his head closer to the mouth.

"What are you trying to say?" he asked softly, looking into the bloodshot eyes, "What is it?"

With a rasp of pain, the body lifted one of its charred arms slowly towards him, the flesh hanging in ribbons, the fingers pointing like broken twigs as it loosely began to tap at his pistol holster. He looked down nodding in understanding, the poor soul wanted him to end his misery.

He shook his head, his voice low. "I can't do that; I won't do that. You're alive. That's all that matters."

The individual tried to speak, the body convulsing in the pain and effort, as again the same raspy noise emitted from it, only this time slightly louder. The tongue and muscles clear to see moving in the mouth, as the eyes opened wider almost pleading with him. Again, he shook his head, the voice firmer.

"No! I haven't come here to kill my own men" he tried to reason, adding, "your friends and officers from your unit will be out there somewhere looking for you. They'll be happy to see you still alive."

He looked down seeing nothing but pity, without thinking, he reached over to his chest rig and pulled out his water bottle, unscrewing the cap a little. The eyes followed him as he upended the bottle, instead of pouring out, the water now dripped slowly.

The head nodded slowly in understanding as he carefully poured drops of water into the mouth, the burned flesh causing him to wince in pain as it tried to drink the water. After only a few sips the water began to dribble out of the cheek bones and down the neck, the water tainted with the blood.

Suddenly the burned claw shot out, grabbing him by the tunic, pulling his head closer, the strength catching him off guard. He turned his head, dropping the water bottle and wincing as spittle flecked with blood shot out as the charred figure tried to speak to him, the hacks and coughs making him gag as the smell of the burned flesh seemed to wrap around him.

"GET OFF ME!" he yelled angrily, his fingers wrapping around the charred wrist, twisting it to break the hold and pulling it roughly away, a large chunk of the forearm coming away in his hand. The wounded figure cried out in pain, his injured arm falling limply by his side as he coughed and wheezed. Golgolvin stood up, picking up the discarded water bottle and grimacing at the sight of the flesh laying on the floor, as he wiped his bloody hand on his tunic, looking down at the pitiful thing whose eyes remained locked on him.

His voice was tinged with sadness as he spoke. "I'm sorry, but I'm not the man to do that. You'll have to wait for someone else."

Unable to feel the man's gaze on him any longer and sickened from hearing the horrible wheezing noise, he walked away, feeling ashamed at leaving him there. He walked along the line of stretchers, searching for any familiar faces. Suddenly he saw a figure being tended by one of the medics, sitting up, waving to him frantically. He smiled in recognition as he saw it was Sasha. Even now, with the bloodstained bandages covering his torso, the man tried to rise proudly as he approached, ignoring the cries of the medic to stay still. He held up his hand to stop him.

"Sasha, Don't! Stay where you are, listen to the medic."

The Major admitted defeat and grimaced in pain, cursing as he shuffled to a more comfortable position. The Medic ignored his protests as he finished wrapping the bandages to his torso, quickly saying to Golgolvin,

"He's lucky to be alive Sir, he's got shrapnel lodged close to his spine, it needs to be removed."

"Acch! stop it with the bad news already! I'm fine! I walked back here, didn't I?" Sasha remonstrated with the medic, who began to pack his gear away, raising an eyebrow as he replied.

"Yes, you did Major, and like the doctors have already told you, any sudden movements and you could be paralysed, permanently. Until we remove it, you're not to move."

Ignoring the Majors stare, the medic looked to Golgolvin.

"Sir, we'll get him into surgery shortly, but he's not to have anything to drink. And try to keep him from moving can you, he seems to ignore everything that I tell him to do."

Both men waited until the medic was out of earshot before Golgolvin began.

"I thought you were dead."

Lenosky looked back painfully, wincing as he spoke, "I thought I was dead!"

Golgolvin smiled in reply, quickly his face took on a more serious tone. Both men couldn't ignore the misery that surrounded them. It had to be said, he had to know.

"What the fuck happened? When I left, I thought I'd told you to keep Lebedev on a short leash."

Lenosky's face looked strained as he replied.

"You did. But then you also went and made him the CO in front of everyone, giving him the authority to outrank me. About an hour after you left, he took two of the tank companies and the VDV's vehicles and sent them over to the west. Meanwhile I was ordered to take the VDV on foot and secure our routes in for the supply convoys. That's about five miles over that way." Lenosky pointed behind them.

"What?" he asked incredulously as Lenosky continued,

"I tried to argue, but Lebedev threatened to have me arrested and our men placed under his command. He genuinely thought you weren't coming back."

"That bastard!" he replied as thinking aloud he continued, "he wanted the VDV out of the way so he could take the town."

Lenosky nodded in agreement as he continued to tell the story.

"He knew the men would follow my orders and he wanted us out of the way. Paratroopers or not, even we couldn't be in two places at once. We'd only marched three miles, when I heard on the radio the attack orders being sent. I knew what he'd done then, so I turned the men around and we power marched as fast as we could, but by the time I got back to the CP the first column was already being attacked. I gave battle orders as we went in, but the maps, the locations, it was a maze down there. And then when we finally made it to them…"

His voice trailed off as Golgolvin finished for him. "You arrived just in time for the artillery to drop around you. And with no vehicles for protection, you were sitting ducks."

Lenosky looked distant as the thoughts came flooding back. His voice angry and bitter as he added.

"Our own artillery! Called in by that fucking idiot! I mean you could fucking see it happening from up here clear as day, why did he want to go down with them? He should have stayed up here and led the attack in!"

Hearing enough, the Colonel placed a hand on his friend's shoulder, careful not to touch the bandages. The blame wasn't his. His friend was right, he'd placed him in an impossible situation. Lebedev had been the fool, he'd taken the only experienced troops he had and sent them on a fool's errand, just so he could have his attack. And now where had it got them?

Quickly, Golgolvin stood up, startling the Major who also began to rise, his arm shooting out to keep him where he was.

"No! You stay there old friend!"

"But Sir, you need me to plan the next attack."

"I do, but I also need you on your feet, not in a wheelchair. You're no good to me injured. Now I'm ordering you to stay there, and get that fucking shrapnel removed."

He lowered his voice as he continued, "I need men I can trust Sasha."

Lenosky sat there proudly looking back, nodding in understanding.

"Very well Colonel, order's received and understood."

He grimaced and turned, looking up to where the medics were working.

"Medic! Get your ass over here, I've got some damn fine Russian metal to get rid of and no time to waste!"

Leaving the Major to tend to his wounds, he turned back to the surgeon's tent. He'd waited long enough. He needed to see Lebedev. The same spike of anger came back, filling him with murderous rage, the more he saw of the misery, the more he needed answers.

He walked back up to the tent, the same medic was still there tending to the injured as they waited their turn for the surgeon. He saw the man look up and sigh in response.

"Sir I've already said-"

"I know what you've said Corporal, but I need to speak to Major Lebedev. I've been told he's in there with the surgeon. Is he alive or not?"

The medic took on a confused look as he repeated, "Major Lebedev?"

Losing his patience, he barked out. "YES! MAJOR LEBEDEV! I want to see him, right now! I don't care if he's in the middle of the surgery, have the surgeon wake him up! Get him here!"

The medics arm pointed out slowly to the pile of wounded, as he replied confused.

"But Sir, you've already spoken to Major Lebedev."

"What?" he stammered confused, looking over to where the man now pointed. He was about to chastise the man for playing sick jokes when suddenly it hit him. The words were lost in his mouth as he took in the picture again of the burned and broken body lying on the floor. It had once been a man; it had once been Major Lebedev.

He followed the medic over, his anger rising as he thought of the small mercy he'd shown him, as he took in the picture again. He looked at the name scribbled hastily on the paper above the stretcher, cursing for not seeing it before. Lebedev, Major, DNT.

The Medic pulled him aside, whispering in his ear.

"Sir, Major Lebedev's crew brought him in, he'd been covered in petrol during the first attack, which luckily hadn't ignited."

"How did he get so burned then?" he asked confused. The Medic sighed, pursed his lips together and replied solemnly, "he was injured in the legs during the artillery strikes, his crew were pulling him back and left him with another unit while they went back to get more casualties. The soldiers they'd left him with thought he could do with a cigarette."

"Ha!" he shot back, causing the medic to blink in surprise as he exclaimed. "So, after all that, they still set fire to him, it looks like cigarettes can be the death of you after all!"

The medic was taken aback, not sure what to say as the Colonel's face took on an almost amused expression. He looked over to the paper. "DNT?"

"Do Not Treat," The medic replied, before adding. "The surgeons don't believe the Major will survive the night, so we're putting him here and making him as comfortable as we can."

"As comfortable as we can?" he repeated sarcastically. Looking around hearing the screams and seeing the devastation that this man had caused.

He made his mind up, quickly looking again at the body.

"Fetch the surgeon, I want this man in with him now, I don't care who you have to kick out, get him in."

"But Sir, his lungs are like tracing paper, he's in immense pain, even breathing will-" the medic began as Golgolvin shouted back.

"THAT'S A FUCKING DIRECT ORDER CORPORAL! You disobey me again, and I'll have you arrested and dragged over there and shot. Do you understand?"

The Medic looked incomprehensibly at the fire raging behind the eyes of the man. He'd watched him earlier show compassion, now like a switch that had been thrown, there was almost a savage pleasure there. He believed what he had just said, he would have him killed. Sensing the futility of arguing he simply replied, "Yes Sir!" and ran off to get the surgeon.

Waiting for the man to disappear he knelt back down, the burned figure was watching him again, those eyes radiating nothing but fear.

Uncaring, Golgolvin lit a match, holding the flame near to his face as he watched him scrabble weakly to get away. After a few seconds he lit the cigarette, inhaling deeply and blowing the smoke into Lebedev's face, causing the weak rasping coughing to begin. He waited until the coughing fit finished before leaning closer, his voice low and full of menace.

"Do you have any idea of the damage you've done? Of the suffering you've caused my men? MY MEN!" The eyes shot around wildly as he shouted the last part, his own face inches from Lebedev's. This time there was no mercy, no revulsion in him, no looking away. Now he was happy to see the mask the man was forced to wear. As if to answer, he quietly spat out, as those eyes looked on fearfully, the voice rasping as it fought to speak.

"You wanted mercy earlier, and you know what, I was almost tempted to give it to you. Imagine that! I could have eased your suffering with one quick pull of the trigger. But when I think now of what you've done, you don't *deserve* mercy!"

Lebedev was becoming agitated, scrabbling weakly at the ground, his mouth opening and closing, as strange noises emanated from within as he continued the verbal attack.

"I wanted you dead earlier, but seeing you like this, this...thing." he said, the disdain pouring out of him.

"No, now I don't want you to die, *I want you to live*, you hear me Lebedev? I want you to live! I want the Surgeon to fix you up, to make you better and give you many more years of life. I want you to go back home a disgrace, to wear this mask and carry these scars with the shame they deserve. I want you to live many years of shame and suffering, because better men have died today, and you don't deserve to die amongst them!"

Lebedev was frantic, his eyes were looking left and right, and his body shuddered and convulsed, as if the Colonels words were acid being poured on him.

"What's going on here?"

He looked up into the eyes of the surgeon, in full operating gown and blood-spattered gloves. Clearly, he'd been pulled out to speak to him.

Standing up he threw away the cigarette, to address him.

"I'm Colonel-"

"Yes, I know who you bloody are, why did you pull me out of surgery? I've got men dying back there that I'm trying to keep alive. This man says you've threatened to have him killed!"

He looked over the Surgeons shoulder, seeing the Medic looking sheepishly at the ground. Smiling wickedly, he pointed to the body at his feet.

"I want this man put into surgery immediately."

The surgeon knelt, quickly checking over the body as the Colonel stood there glaring down. After a few moments he stood up, shaking his head.

"Impossible! I've got to spare our resources for those we can save."

"I said I want him put into surgery! Now stop wasting time and make sure he lives! That's an order!"

The Surgeon looked him up and down as if studying him, his eyes taking in the angry features, before looking back down at the body, taking in the scene in an instant. His head nodded slowly, replying.

"Okay Colonel, well as I see it, you have two problems."

"Really? And what are they?" he asked aggressively.

"One, this man is already dead, I'm not a god, I'm only a doctor, and I can only save those that are still breathing."

Golgolvin looked down bitterly disappointed, as he saw the eyes were now lifeless and the chest still as the surgeon continued.

"Two, you're a Colonel, you can order whoever you like around here...except me and my medics."

Looking up, he watched as the surgeon pulled his apron aside, the bloody handprint leaving a smear as he revealed his uniform underneath, the Colonels rank clear to see. Seeing the confusion on his face he continued.

"Colonel Igor Kapinsky, Commanding Officer of the 63rd field regiment hospital. You're lucky I was in the area, conducting an inspection of my medics, my medics Colonel! Not yours!" His voice rose to a shout, before finishing softly.

"Now, if you've finished with this little act of personal vengeance, I'd like to go back to saving the lives of *your* troops. So, fuck off and take your anger elsewhere and leave us to it!"

He stood there, the anger dying inside him, the words making him feel suddenly ashamed. Had it been vengeance, he asked himself. Was he now that spiteful? He looked down again at the body, shocked at his last words, with what he'd said to the man as he died.

He looked up, about to say something to the surgeon, to justify what he'd done, but the medical Colonel had already walked away...

Cerne Abbas

Mike became aware of someone tugging his arm quickly. "Mike wake up, quick!" the voice hissed. How long had he been sleeping? It felt like minutes, as he sat upright, instantly reaching for the rifle. His eyes adjusted to the light as he focused on Patty kneeling next to him.

"What is it?" he asked, his eyes darting around looking for any threat.

"Come with me, you need to see this."

Without asking any more questions Mike stood up, quickly donning his assault rig as he followed the Corporal off the tank. Others were being woken up quickly and around all the vehicles the same scene was playing out, as with sleep filled eyes the soldiers began to get themselves up and ready without knowing why.

Mike followed Patty, hearing the sound of heavy engines in the distance, getting louder as they walked. Oh no, he thought to himself, what is it now?

Already the sun was starting to go down, rays of golden light breaking through and the shadows already beginning to creep along the track. He checked his watch, it was 19:15, still a few hours of daylight left, he thought.

Both men carefully snuck past the cam net, crouching lower as they approached the edge of the woodline. He saw Spider and Changa lying there already, surveying the scene through their weapon sights. The Fijian looked up and nodded as Mike lay down next to them and began to scan ahead with his bino's, careful not to catch the sun's reflection in its lenses.

About a mile away on the far side of the valley east of them, he could see vehicles moving about like dark green beetles climbing up the hill, the exhaust smoke belching into the sky. Mike adjusted the focus ring, the picture become clearer. They were the enemy, no doubt about it.

As Mike continued to look, Spider began to say in a low voice, "They started arriving about ten minutes ago."

Mike recognised some of the vehicles as being Russian 2S35's self-propelled artillery, similar to the British AS90. He watched as the heavy vehicles smashed through the far treeline, hiding themselves from view before being followed in by the trucks and jeeps. Some of the soldiers had jumped out of the jeeps and were guiding the other vehicles in. He guessed each self-propelled gun would have a crew following in a jeep and the trucks would be carrying their extra ammo. He lowered the glasses and looked over to Spider.

"Looks like an artillery unit and it looks like they're settling in." Mike counted five of the guns had already gone into the woods and another six were waiting to go inside, with a similar number of trucks and jeeps. He hoped the woodline was big enough for them and they didn't decide to come looking over in their direction. If they did, then they were going to be in for a shock.

"What do you think? Any chance they'll see us?" Patty asked.

Mike looked up at the sun again, then back at the enemy position, thinking quickly. "No, we should be okay guys, sun's setting in the west, if they look over here the sun's glare will blind them. We'll be safe until sundown."

"And tonight?" Spider asked, turning his head from the weapons sight.

"Will still go ahead as planned," Mike finished for him. Spider went back to looking through the weapons sight as Mike kept looking at him, wondering what had been said on the phone.

As if to echo his earlier thoughts Patty remarked dryly, "Let's hope they don't decide to come looking over here for more space."

"For all we know there could be another enemy unit already on their way to these woods." Spider added morosely. He looked over to Mike again as if expecting an answer.

Mike shrugged his shoulders, "Not a damn thing we can do about it if they are Spider." he said in a matter-of-fact way. He slowly crawled backwards until he was sure he was out of sight of the enemy and then crept up to one knee, adding, "Look, it'll be sundown in two hours, until then, just as a precaution, let's keep everyone on a short leash and close to the vehicles, ready to move. Then if someone does turn up, best we can do with no ammo is crash out of here, unless of course you have a better idea?"

Mike didn't mean for the bitterness that was heard in his voice, but he was still a little annoyed at how his conversation with Linda had gone. He knew Spider was the man in charge, but even after the past few days, he felt that at least Spider could have discussed it with him. Ignoring the growing resentment, he got up leaving the others and walked back to the leaguer.

Sensing something was wrong, Spider quickly followed.

"Mike is everything okay?"

Mike stopped and turned, keeping his voice low so as not to be overheard.

"You tell me, Spider? You making promises to people without thinking of the consequences?"

"What?" the look of confusion on his face was almost comical. "I don't understand?"

"Linda? Telling her she can stay with us?"

Spider's face registered at last. "Oh that. I said I'd think about it, but only after chatting to you."

"Really? She's under the impression that she's here to stay, apparently, she's told me you've already given her permission and you're speaking to your bosses?"

"What? I never said that! I told her that I'd speak to you first. That cheeky bugger!"

Mike shook his head, like some naughty child that first asks the mum then the dad, she'd tried to play them off against each other.

Suddenly a thought jumped into his head. His eyes quickly looked over Spider, "Hang on, where's the phone?"

"What?" Spider's face looked on in confusion as Mike quickly added,

"The satellite phone! Linda saw us with it earlier, where's the fucking phone?"

Spider instinctively patted his trouser pockets, his mouth opening in shock. "I left it in the truck..." the words died on his lips as he realised what he'd done.

Mike turned and sprinted through the line of vehicles, seeing the truck ahead. He could see the unmistakable shape of Linda in the cab, the phone was in her hands. He vaulted up to the door, raising himself on the footplate, his hands shaking on the door handle. She'd locked it from inside. He tapped on the glass, trying not to raise his voice. "Linda, open the door. Linda!" He hissed. She looked at him glassy eyed, ignoring him and turned to face the other window. She was having a conversation with someone. He quickly jumped down, Spider now joining him as he ran around to the passenger side door. Same result. She'd locked herself inside. Mike could do nothing but watch in mute rage as she continued to chat on the phone. Realising he was running out of options, he took his jacket off, wrapping the cloth around the butt of his rifle to try to mask the noise he was about to make. He was just about to smash the window when he heard the door unlock. With a face like thunder, he yanked the door open, she sat there calmly holding out the phone to him.

"What the fuck are you playing at?" he spat out.

Ignoring his outburst, she simply replied, "They want to speak to you."

"*Who* wants to speak to me?" he demanded through clenched teeth.

She rolled her eyes as if it was all a game and said, "Your operations room, silly." she shimmied past him, leaving him red faced on the footplate as she jumped down oblivious to the glare of Spider, who was seething with anger. She'd just made them both look like fools. Mike put the phone to his ear, uncertain of who was on the other end.

"Hello?"

"Back so soon Mr Faulkes?" the voice replied, "it would appear you've been a little careless with your phone."

Mike recognised Colonels Stephens voice. He glanced down at Spider who said nothing but stared back at him. He closed his eyes and took a deep breath. "I'm sorry about that Colonel, it looks like the young lady was more resourceful than I gave her credit for."

"Yes, it would appear that Miss Harding has been very resourceful." the Colonel replied cheerfully. "Either that, or you're just being careless." Was he enjoying this, Mike thought to himself.

Colonel Stephens continued, "So Mr Faulkes, we've been thinking about what Miss Harding has had to say. And we've given it some thought, and we think that, provided she's aware of the risks, we agree and think that she should be embedded within the unit."

"Hang on," Mike replied confused, "you've given this some thought? When did you get the time to do that?"

The Colonel chuckled, "Mr Faulkes, Miss Harding called us over two hours ago, she's had your phone all this time. Did you really not know?"

Fuck, Mike thought, as he glared down at her again, she stood triumphantly looking back, almost revelling in what was happening. He looked over at Spider and shook his head slowly in silent anger. The look on his face told the Corporal what he was thinking. Spider had just fucked up! Seeing Mike's anger, he looked down with embarrassment

"Okay so what does that mean Colonel?" he asked, not quite sure where they were going with this.

"It's simple, by agreeing to be part of the unit, she agrees to come under military rule. She'll report only on what we tell her to, and everything she sends back will have to be passed through the censors. She'll follow the directions given to her by the soldiers in the unit."

Mike turned and stepped into the cab, closing the door behind him. Already there was an audience outside and he didn't want everyone listening in.

"Colonel, she doesn't listen as it is, what makes you think she'll suddenly step into line now?"

"She'll either follow the directions given to her or she'll be arrested. It's as simple as that. One wrong move, one foot out of line, one report sent that's not been through the censors and her reputation will be in tatters. She knows the risks." The Colonel made it sound so easy, just like that, thought Mike.

Mike sighed heavily, this was a mistake, he knew it. What would Patty and Spider think? He quickly added, "Colonel you'd best brief Corporal Webb on this instead of me, as you all so clearly illustrated earlier, I'm a civilian. He needs to be told if he's to have half a chance in keeping an eye on her."

"Now, now, Mike, come on, there's no need for dramatics, I'm sure Miss Harding will do just fine. As for Corporal Webb, you can tell him after we've finished chatting."

Oh so we're back to first names now are we, thought Mike, as the Colonel continued.

"Now onto our next business of the day. Mike, are you aware of the Armed Forces Reserve Act? In times of Emergency the country can, and will, recall veterans to rejoin the armed forces."

Mike drew a breath; he didn't like where this was going. "I'm aware of it Colonel, let me guess, you're going to tell me that now you've invoked it, I'm recalled to service as a Staff Sergeant." he tried to hide the resentment in his voice.

"Almost Mike, almost." the tone jovial, "no, we've decided your unit needs an officer, the two Corporals couldn't sing your praises enough when we last spoke, and after Corporal Webb's passionate little outburst earlier in defending you, it's clear to us where their loyalties lie. So let me be the first to say congratulations *Captain Faulkes*."

"What? Captain? Hang on Colonel, that doesn't make any sense. Just like that? Can you even do that? I'm a civilian, I'm afraid you've got the wrong man for this." Mike tried to hide his surprise and shock as the Colonel carried on, unperturbed.

"Brigadier Rawlinson had recommended you, Major Richards tried to offer it to you and now I'm *telling* you. It's a done deal, the CDS has already signed off on the paperwork. If you remember back to when you left the army, you had to sign your discharge paperwork?"

"Yes, but I had to sign it, it was the only way I could get my redundancy money." Mike argued.

"But you *did* sign it Captain Faulkes, and when you signed, it quite clearly stated in the small print that if such an Emergency were to arise, you were bound by law and your oath of attestation to come back. I'm afraid, that despite your protests, you're back into the fold, like it or not."

Mike was about to ask about the consequences if he simply refused, when as if reading his mind, the Colonel continued.

"And it's a good job you're not thinking about refusing to soldier, Captain Faulkes, because with the evidence we have compiled against you, I would have hated to have informed the civilian authorities about your criminal conduct as a civilian. Especially now that Miss Harding also has the information and has threatened to publish the story. I mean, come on think about it, a civilian riding around on a bloody tank, thinking he's some kind of white knight charging about. Sorry Captain Faulkes, but that's not the publicity we want.

"Hang on! What criminal conduct?" Mike asked naively.

"Well, we've got unauthorised use of a firearm for starters, then there's threatening behaviour with a firearm, kidnap, unauthorised use of a military vehicle, destruction of public property, destruction of private property, and impersonating an officer, and these are only the charges you've admitted to. I imagine that more could be found, but thankfully because you're now an officer in the military, acting under orders, all of these charges are null and void, if you get my meaning *Captain*."

Fucking hell! Mike fumed; they really were out to get him tonight. His hands gripped the truck's steering wheel, the knuckles turning white. He had to stay calm, the others were still outside looking in. They had him, whether he liked it or not. If he refused the threat was clear, they'd have him arrested the first chance they had, and then what? Labelled a national disgrace for the rest of his life? And even if they didn't throw the book at him, what about the reporter? She'd spent the day chatting to everyone, getting the full story on him. If she published this, there would be no getting out of it. No, that was not how he wanted this to go. He thought about it quickly, it wasn't like being young again, he wouldn't be signing on for another twenty-two years of service. His thoughts cleared as he began to gain control of his anger, sighing as he replied.

"Ok Colonel, I guess when it's put like that, I've never really had a choice. I'll play along.""

"Top man, I expected as much, now getting back to the issue of Miss Harding, for now she stays, but only so long as she plays along. Any problems and now you deal with her. Do you understand?"

"Totally." Mike replied looking out the window at her. She smiled back at him, playfully giving him the thumbs up. Did she know all along this was going to happen?

"Now is there anything else Captain?"

"Yes, Colonel we've got an enemy unit camped nearby, looks like an artillery unit. They're settling in for the night, about one mile east of us in the next wood block."

"Ahh I see, is there any threat to tonight's plan?"

"I don't think so Colonel, they don't know we're here. By the time they realise we're here it'll be too late to do anything."

"Right, we'll make a note of it for now, keep eyes on them if you can, if you see any other units let us know. Anything else?"

"Yes, what about the two POW's we have? Guarding them is becoming a bit of a strain, we could do with getting them out of here."

"Yes, we could do with getting them back here," the Colonel emphasised. "Unfortunately, though Captain no-one will send an airframe to come get them, too risky you see."

"What if I said there was a way?"

"Really?" the Colonel sounded intrigued, "do tell Captain, do tell."

Mike outlined the plan he had in his head, the Colonel patiently listening, occasionally stopping Mike to ask a question.

When Mike had finally finished, the Colonel replied, "Sounds like a good play Captain, I'll brief the Brigadier and we'll make it happen. Right, well if there's nothing else, call back when you've secured the re-supply, and are ready to go. We'll send your orders then. Good luck."

Mike switched off the phone, making sure to power it down. The battery showed only twenty-three percent charge left. He'd have to charge it up when they were back on the tank.

He climbed down out of the cab, Linda playfully punching him on the arm.

"So, Captain, what's next? What's our orders?"

He said nothing but looked at her, his anger still lingering at the stunt she'd pulled. She'd made them all look foolish, and to add insult to injury, the Colonel had bought into her bullshit.

Spider looked back, a look of incomprehension on his face. "Captain?"

Before Mike could say anything, Linda quickly chimed in, "Yes, you heard right, Mike's been made a Captain, now it's official, our story can begin."

"How did you know?" Mike asked testily.

Ignoring the barb she jovially replied, "I suggested that you be made an officer, it would make the story more credible, plus when I'd heard about what you'd been up to by the others I told the Colonel the best way to get all the charges dropped were for you to already be an officer to begin with. They're going to backdate the commission to when you first took the tank."

Seeing his simmering look of anger, she patted him on the shoulder. "Relax Mike, it's all been taken care of, now all you have to do is concentrate on getting us all out of here."

They watched her walk away, saying nothing as Spider felt the tension in the air.

"You okay Mike? You look like you could kill someone," he asked quietly. Mike shook his head slowly, his anger surfacing as his voice was full of scorn.

"It's *Captain* now, remember? And how could you be so fucking foolish with that phone Spider? Leaving it in the cab, I trusted you with that!" he spat out.

Mike saw the Corporal look to the ground with shame. Realising nothing he could say would help Spider merely replied, "Look, I fucked up, I'm sorry about that."

"Well, your fucking apology won't fix this now, will it? You wanted an officer, well now you've got one. The trouble is for me though, is it's just cost me my fucking freedom. I really thought I was out of all this shit!"

Mike stood glaring at him. He was angry, but he knew it shouldn't be directed at the young NCO. Not knowing what to say anymore, he simply nodded and replied, "Dismissed...Corporal!"

Spider turned and walked away, his head down. Mike stood there, his fists clenching as he tried to calm himself. How would Kate take the news? Christ what about her parents? Who'd look after them? With more questions than he had answers for, Mike stormed off moodily back to the tank, standing there wasn't going to help him, hell it wouldn't help anyone. And the mood he felt right now, he didn't want to be anywhere near Linda fucking Harding, especially not carrying a loaded rifle. For now, like it or not, Captain Faulkes was here to stay.

He knew he needed to clear his head and looked around for something to distract him. Of course, he thought, he'd need somewhere out of sight to brief everyone later. He walked back to the tank, ignoring the stares of Bill and Smudge as he climbed up to the turret and searched through one of the turret bins. He found what he was looking for, one of the tanks spare thermal sheets. Taking it out, he dragged the long piece of material over to the trees, using some string, he tied the edges to the branches and wrapped the material around three of the trees, creating a three sided box, tall enough to hide someone standing and large enough that ten people could easily stand in there. He stood admiring his handiwork, it wouldn't win any prizes in a beauty contest, but it would do.

His stomach began to grumble, reminding him of the need for food. Dusting his hands off on his trousers he made his way back to the tank, wondering what cold tinned delight waited him. For now, all he could do was wait and ponder.

23

Ghosts Of The Past

The Phone Box, Yeovil Town Centre

The Mayor stood silently as Fergus finished the report, explaining all about the phone box behind them and his conversation that he'd just had with the Chief of Defence. She glanced over to the Chief of Police who was also stunned into silence. After a few moments she looked to the phone box, her eyes searching for anything that could warrant her uneasy feeling about it.

"This isn't a hoax? This is really them?" she asked apprehensively.

He nodded, adding, "They told me things about me that they could only have read from my military files, not the sort of things you find on google. Plus, I've met the CDS, back when he was a Major, I'd hosted him in 2 Para's officer's mess when he was attached to us."

Fergus had kept the rest of the story quiet, the part where he'd introduced the Major to an airborne tradition of naked bar. He still had to supress a chuckle at the memory of when the lads had stripped him naked, oblivious to his roars and shouts, something the CDS had reminded him of earlier.

"And they want to speak to me?"

"That's right Mayor, the Prime Minister wants to talk to you directly."

One of her advisors looked up, his eyes wide. "The Prime Minister! Mayor, this is amazing! An opportunity like this-"

She looked over, forcing a smile, interrupting him. "Thank you, Kenny, but amazing is not the word I'd use. I'm not really looking at this as a move up the political ladder. Let's not forget our current predicament..."

She hesitantly scanned the phone box, seeing the handset resting on the shelf, knowing the PM waited to speak to her. She swallowed nervously, as Fergus urged her on.

"He seemed keen to talk to you right away Mayor, I've got the line left open, and a scribe nearby ready to write for you. He's got a list of prepared questions for you to ask for if you get time. You ready?

She nodded at Fergus as he added with a smile. "Okay Mayor, let's do this, you'll do fine."

She nodded, burying her reservations as she became focussed, the leader in her stepping forward, the same Mayor that Fergus had seen during the meetings. Proudly he watched her step into the box, and pick up the phone, the door wedged open and the scribe ready to write. She looked to her entourage and smiled as she began.

"Good evening Prime Minister, so glad to hear your voice..."

A whole hour had passed before she finally replaced the phone's receiver and emerged from the box, with the heat of the day making her hair damp and clammy, and sweat soaking her clothes. She walked up to the waiting group and continued past them, walking quickly as they fell into step behind, all exchanging curious looks as they saw the serious look on her face.

"Mayor?" the Police Chief asked curiously. "What was said?"

She looked back, not breaking stride, almost increasing her pace as she replied.

"Chief, I'm sorry, but we need to get the council assembled back at the HQ, I'll discuss it all there."

She looked over to Fergus, firing off quickly, "Major, I need you to keep a runner back at HQ, and put a guard on that phone box. For now, that's the only link we have to the government."

He peeled away from the group to stay back and organise the guard, as she turned and shouted after him.

"And be at the HQ in thirty minutes Major, we've got a lot to talk about."

"Yes Mayor!" he shouted back, as turning he looked at the Sergeant Major, his face full of pride.

"You ever seen such a mobile fireball?"

The man shook his head laughing, as together they walked back to the assembled soldiers and fighters. Fergus thought to himself, she was right though, there was much to discuss.

Thirty minutes later and Fergus was waiting with the rest of the town's council, all looking over at the Mayor who was deep in conversation with one of her aides. She kept looking down at her notes, checking what the scribe had written and adding her own lines where necessary. Fergus thought she looked as if she was writing a speech, when suddenly, satisfied with what was written, she stood up, cleared her throat and addressed them all.

She began by reporting what the PM had told her, bringing them up to speed on what had happened recently, the cyberattacks, the attacks on London and the PM's residence, how the former PM had been killed and the former Defence Secretary was now the PM. Fergus had winced at the news, he never liked the old PM, but to have him assassinated this early on was a bitter blow. He continued to listen, as she mentioned how the invasion wasn't just limited to the south of England but was also happening in the north. But the worst news was yet to come. She continued, telling them that in London a new government had been formed, totally illegitimate and blaming the military and royal family for the attacks, quoting it as an attempted coup. This puppet government had ordered all of the country's military forces to stand down and had arrested the King and Queen as they were trying to evacuate London. Charges had already been made against them and they were now prisoners under house arrest. It was all fabricated of course, but the damage was being done overseas and already NATO members were hesitant to help, the Russian forces being falsely labelled as members of the Tumat military, sent to help an allied NATO member. From what the PM had said, it looked like there would be no help coming from NATO. The United Kingdom, for now, was on its own.

"Good god!"" the Chief of Police exclaimed, as some of the council members held their hands to their mouths in shock.

She looked around the room, watching everyone as she said forcefully.

"So that's why there's been no contact with anyone outside of the town, all the phones are down and all the radio and TV stations have been hijacked. I don't know if you're aware of this, but the Russians are controlling our local TV and radio broadcasts. We're being fed the feeds from a week ago. No-one in the area outside of these four walls has any idea of what's going on around the country.

"Well at least now we know," one of the councillors called Duncan remarked, adding, "now we know there's no help coming, at least we can begin the plans to evacuate."

"Evacuate?" she looked back. "Where? Didn't you hear what I've just said Duncan? This is happening everywhere. Where would you have us run to?"

"All I'm saying is, that there's no point in holding out here if there's no help coming. If NATO aren't going to get involved, then what chance does our army have?"

Fergus scowled at the man as he continued, "Besides, how do we know there isn't a coup underway? How do we know the person you spoke to was even the legitimate PM?"

"How would you evacuate?" the Chief of Police stood up, planting both arms on the table looking over to the councillor.

"Well like the Major said earlier, we've already beaten them once, they won't attack now, not with the daylight fading. They'll be back tomorrow, so we pack everyone up now and leave tonight."

"The whole town, tonight?" the Chief replied, his voice tinged with sarcasm, "and like the Mayor just asked, where would you go to?"

"I don't know! Bristol? Exeter? Anywhere but here."

The Chief's mouth twisted into a sneer as he replied, "Duncan, you'd cut and run and become someone else's problem, leaving those unable or unwilling to leave behind, to fend for themselves?"

"Now LOOK!" Duncan cried out standing up to confront the Chief, "this is not a civilian matter, this is a military matter, and as far as I'm concerned, the military have left us all to it! You heard what the Mayor just said! NO-ONE is coming to help us! We have to help ourselves!"

Fergus stood up, his gaze forcing them both to silence and to sit back down. He looked directly at Duncan, a frustrated look on his face.

"You don't get it, do you?"

"Get what?" the councillor shot back confused.

"The time to have evacuated was yesterday, do you remember? The meeting, the discussions, the panic? That was your time to run. Instead, everyone voted and the vote was to stay and fight. Now it's too late."

"Look, Fergus..."

"Major Young." the Mayor corrected him. "It's Major Young now, not Fergus. Don't forget that, Duncan, you disrespect the man when you disrespect the rank."

Fergus looked over at her, amazed at the rebuke as the councillor nodded at her apologetically.

"Sorry, *Major*," he corrected himself, his tone abrasive as he continued, "As we've already discussed, the Russians are beaten, they've run away, you did your job, bravo, well done, take a pat on the back. Now's the time to make the most of that victory and get the hell away from here, not sit and wait like cows in an abattoir."

Fergus shook his head slowly, smiling sardonically at the man. "What do you think the Russians will do when they see everyone loading their cars and trucks and making a beeline out of the town? When they see hundreds, no thousands, of people suddenly packed in the streets, the panic, the chaos, the jams. All trying to get away. What do you think they'll do?"

The councillor just sat silently, not wanting to answer as Fergus continued.

"Do you think they'll sit and watch us simply run away? After today? After what we've done? Huh? After we've already killed their soldiers, by *burning* them alive. What mercy do you think they'll show us? I'll tell you what mercy they'll show us. NONE! We lay down the rules today when we stopped their attack. We brought ourselves time, but in doing so, we've committed our townspeople to the fight. To collapse our defences now and attempt to flee will just bring about our destruction."

Duncan opened his mouth to reply when Fergus stopped him by adding. "And what message does that send to our people? To the people who lost loved ones today? What would you say to the parents, to the wives, girlfriends, husbands, brothers and sisters who died to protect this town, when you run away, to give it up? What do we tell them? That their loved ones died for nothing?"

Duncan sat there, stunned into silence. Not knowing how to answer, as Fergus sat back down, a look of disappointment on his face. After a few moments of silence, the Mayor stood up, her voice commanding.

"Thank you everyone for your frank and candid views, I appreciate the input, even if I may not agree with all of it myself. But as Major Young has already mentioned, last night we voted to stay, and that's still what I'm advocating now, and that's exactly what I told the PM we were going to do. He's agreed with us 100 percent."

"Well, it's all very well him agreeing, but how about some bloody help!" Duncan muttered, interrupting the Mayor. She looked angrily at him, causing him to sit back meekly and look away as she carried on.

"Like I was saying, the PM agrees and *has* decided to send us some help."

Everyone sat straighter at her words, their eyes looking hopefully up, as she continued.

"Now I don't have the full details, and the PM didn't want to say too much on the phone, but they've got military units nearby. They're going to try to get them to us by tomorrow."

Could it be tanks, armoured vehicles, Fergus thought, they could certainly use those! Why, with those extra units he could seal off the town and attack the Russians camped outside on the hills. Confidently he looked up, the excitement plain to hear on his voice. "Mayor, sorry to interrupt but do you have an idea on numbers? Is it a regiment or a squadron or a company that we're getting?"

She shook her head regretfully. "I'm sorry Major, I have no idea what we're getting. All I was told was that they'll try to get us tomorrow and that was it."

He looked at his watch, there was still time. Looking up, the Mayor could see him standing to get her attention.

"Yes, Major Young?"

"Mayor, with your permission I need to get away with the Sergeant Major now and do another check on the town's defences, see where we're weakest, if we do get these units tomorrow I want to have the positions ready for them to go straight into."

"Of course, of course," she replied nodding as he picked up his rifle and assault vest, before she added. "Major Young, before you go however, there's another quick matter we need to discuss."

He stopped his dash towards the stairs and turned back, quickly walking back towards the meeting.

"Yes Mayor, what is it?"

She stood up and smiled, looking down to her notepad before saying proudly. "Major Young, after informing both the Chief of the Defence Staff and the Prime Minister about your actions today in the organisation, leadership and execution of the towns defence, both have saw fit to promote you to the rank of Colonel, with immediate effect.

Oh shit, Fergus thought to himself, as she walked up to him shaking his hand.

"May I be the first to say, congratulations Colonel Young!" she boomed as the others stood up and clapped. She pulled him close, all smiles and speaking softly in his ear.

"We really need to get you a uniform Fergus."

"What's wrong with what I'm wearing?" he shot back jokingly.

"Jeans? Really? You're a Colonel now. I expect you to at least dress like one."

Keeping her close, he smiled and muttered into her ear. "You've never complained before about what I wear."

She shot back quickly raising her eyebrows, "That's because I never leave you wearing it for long enough!"

Within seconds the exchange was over, she turned and walked back to her seat, the others oblivious to what was said between them. Fergus waited a few moments before turning, blushing as he left the room. As he climbed the stairs, he couldn't help but laugh, they'd kept their relationship hidden for nearly a year now hidden in plain sight. What would another few days matter...

Colerne Airfield, Bath

Peter was by the small hangar door, looking out at the evening sky, watching the sun finally beginning to set. He looked again at his watch, judging the flight time and the wind conditions, then looking back over to the rest of the team standing by the covered drones, waiting on Peter's launch command. Everyone looked to be set, the fatigue and tiredness gone from earlier. All of them were glancing at each other, keeping their doubts and nerves under control, even though the tension hung heavily in the air. They'd gone through this routine in the past, conducting hundreds of launches and landings, but now, this was real. For the first time in Aurora's history, they were about to do a combat drop, behind enemy lines. This was it, every person there knew all their tens of thousands of hours of trials and research would all hang now on what happened tonight, but more than that, real lives were depending on what the drones were carrying.

It had been tight on time, even though the drones were ready, the Chinook bringing the ammo had arrived late, causing a last-minute flap as everyone had struggled to get it unboxed and re-packed into the drones. Peter had forgotten that back in the day as a tank commander, just how much he'd hated unboxing the tank ammunition, and as if to remind him, he now carried the fresh cuts to his hands from the metal lids that seemed to be designed to do just that. But even though late, it wasn't the Chinook's timings that had left him feeling sour, it had been the ammunition they'd sent, and the CDS's insistence that they were not send anything else out in support. Peter had argued with him, the CDS was worried about their latest tech falling into enemy hands, but Peter had countered with the fact that their most senior integration officer, already trained on the equipment and the most experienced in its use, was the one now needing it's help. If Mike were captured and made to talk, then the Russians would have more than enough information on the new capabilities. So why not help him out and give him the best fighting chance they could? Also, why not use the mission as a test bed to see how it all performs. The conversation had almost degenerated into a shouting match, the former friends at logger heads, until eventually the CDS had pulled rank to win the argument. His orders were crystal clear. Under no circumstances was Captain Faulkes to be sent anything other than the ammunition and supplies sent down on the Chinook.

Peter had struggled with the order, knew he had to follow it, but then when the Chinook had landed, and he saw just what it was it carried, a rage burned inside him. So, without any further fuss he'd seen to it that not only were the drones carrying the ammunition re-supply but also a few extra toys that Mike would know how to use. Orders be damned, he'd fumed, If Mike was going to be hung out to dry by the army, then Aurora would look after their own. Besides, Peter had thought, it was his company, it was his equipment and he'd send it to whoever he damn well pleased.

Peter looked up again, burying his dark thoughts and cursing the low light, the sunlight now a faint glimmer on the horizon as he prayed for the darkness. Looking again at his watch, he knew he'd delayed as long as he could, any longer and Mike would think they'd forgotten him. It would have to do, he looked over to David, simply saying.

"Okay David, launch approved."

David nodded, coming to life from where he stood on the hangar floor, turning to the team and speaking over the headsets.

"Right everyone, we have the green light for launch. Let's get ready."

Above them the hangar lights flicked off, plunging them all into semi darkness, preventing anyone outside of the airfield from seeing what was going on inside. Now the team were working under red light conditions, the individual torches all shining dimly, as each person began the choreographed routines they'd practised over and over before. Already the covers were being whipped off the drones, that had shielded them from prying eyes, as the hangar doors began to slowly open to the outside world. Peter grimaced as they began to squeal in protest, making a note to have someone get some WD40 on them for next time.

Quickly and with infinite care, the drones were wheeled outside into the darkness by their teams. Peter could just make out the dark shapes of them, each the size of a medium sized van. Shadows danced over them as the team of engineers and pilots all methodically checked and re-checked that everything was in order. They couldn't afford any mistakes, not tonight, not knowing lives really were depending on this.

Peter waited patiently, knowing that this was the most crucial part, even the smallest thing could bring it all crashing down for them. An insecure cargo, a cable not connected, a strap left flapping to be sucked into an engine. Any one of a thousand things could be missed, which was why now everything had to be checked and double checked.

Peter watched on, as one by one, each team finished their preflight checks, the senior flight engineer for each team then walked over to David, handing him their check lists. Once the last person was in, David had one more quick visual inspection on the check sheets and once finally satisfied he talked into the headset.

"Control, Flight, pre-flight checks completed, launch approved. Launch, launch, launch."

And that was it, no fanfare, no countdown, with the minimum of noise, everyone stood watching, some with fingers crossed, as one by one, the five heavily loaded drones silently rose up into the night sky and disappeared into the night.

Peter hadn't realised he was holding his breath until after the last drone had lifted off, only then did he dare to breathe, turning to the others and hearing some of them quietly congratulate each other. Others kept quiet, not wanting to jinx their good fortune so far. He wisely kept his own thoughts hidden, as did David. They'd both hold off on celebrations until after the drop was complete. Leaving the others there, he quietly followed David into the operations hangar...

Cerne Abbas

It had finally turned dark at around 21:00, but the full moon was still casting too much light, not that there was anything he could do about that now. Mike slowly adjusted his position, checking his watch again by the moonlight, the cam cream causing his eyes to sting slightly as he lay at the edge of the woodline. It was 22:17, they should be here by now. He checked again for the tenth time that the radio beacon lying next to him was on. He could see the small green light flashing dimly and hear the faint humming noise as it sent out a small signal only detectable within a two-mile radius. He thought back to Peter's coded message. "Be ready to sing for 22:00" meant he had to have the beacon on and transmitting by this time. In the distance he could see the torch lights moving around the enemy positions and hear them laughing and calling to each other as they settled in for the night. Clearly, they were not expecting any threats in the area, and, as annoying as it was to see their enemy's contempt for them, he had to be thankful, because if they weren't expecting any attack, then that meant Mike's small force was still undetected. So long as they stayed on the other side of the hill and were not pointing anything at them, they'd be fine.

He looked over to the shadow of the woodline, seeing nothing but darkness, but sensing and knowing that the others were there, all waiting for something to happen. He'd briefed everyone earlier on what to expect, some of them had looked at him with scepticism, others in awe. Now was the time to deliver, he thought. He checked his watch again, it was 22:19.

He checked again around him, looking for signs of anyone approaching in the darkness. Still nothing. Good let's keep it like that, he thought.

Suddenly the radio beacon next to him began to vibrate. It was picking up a signal. He picked it up, looking skywards into the night sky. He knew he wouldn't be able to see or hear the drone yet, it was still too far away but that didn't stop him looking anyway.

His eyes could see something against the night sky, a black object coming slowly closer, blotting out the stars. He looked around again, checking someone wasn't coming out of the darkness to stop them. Breathing harder as excitement grew, he felt the rush of air on his face and the faint noise of the electric motors as the heavy shadow slowly got closer, until out of the night sky a large black flying object appeared, slowly settling down on the ground less than three metres from him. He stood up proudly looking at the flying object in the darkness as it sat there, the quad motors stopping almost immediately. The Thumpr or Transport Heavy Utility Mobile Platform Remote was one of Aurora Systems brainchilds, that Mike had helped to design and build. It looked nothing like the smaller privately owned drones, having a large teardrop shaped body and four wings at each end with a motor and propellor hidden inside a circular housing. The motors didn't house a standard propellor, instead it was rimless, with what looked like circular teeth on the inside edge of the rim, which when spun at high rpm created a vortex of air inside the housing. By channelling this vortex, the motor was able to generate huge amounts of lift, for very little power output. Without the propellors there was no excess noise, allowing the Thumpr to be very quiet. It was far larger than most drones being the size of a medium sized van and weighing in at over a tonne. The wings were tilt wing, so when the Thumpr was flying normally it benefitted from the aerodynamic lift of the wings and had a faster top speed. However, when it wanted to land the wings and motors would tilt vertically, and a pair of landing skids would deploy, allowing the Thumpr to land like a VTOL aircraft such as the Harrier.

The Thumpr was powered by two hydrogen fuel cells that allowed it to have a far better range than any battery powered drone. The Thumpr was still undergoing trials, but Mike knew they had already seen ranges of over 200 miles and speeds of 180 mph.

It was designed to carry up to two tonnes of equipment, it was almost whisper quiet, automated and thanks to the Radio Beacon that had been sent earlier, it knew exactly where to land. Aurora had designed and developed the Thumpr for military use, for such a task just as tonight and Mike had to admit, he'd never in his wildest imagination have thought that one day he'd be the one benefitting from it. Without wanting to waste any time, Mike ran up to the side of the fuselage, locating the keypad, lifting the cover and punching in the six-digit code he'd received at the end of Peter's message.

"355250" he silently said to himself as he pressed the enter button.

A quick beep and the keypad flashed green. Then standing back, he waited for the Thumpr to do its thing. Had he keyed in the wrong code three times then the keypad would have flashed red, the Thumpr would have taken off and simply flown back to its base. As it flashed green, he knew the code had been accepted. The motor's started up again, the noise sounding more like a small household fan than a one tonne flying machine as the Thumpr took to the sky, leaving behind it on the ground, a large box on tracks, twice the size of any wooden pallet. Mike watched the dark shape disappear into the sky as he quickly looked over the box, his hands settling on the controls. To aide with unloading the Thumpr, its cargo bay had been designed to detach and be left on the ground as the Thumpr remained airborne, flying close by for when the cargo truck had been emptied, after which the Thumpr would come back in and pick up the cargo pallet, and with it all trace of it ever being there. The cargo bay was on tracks controlled by two electric motors, all they had to do was use the controls to manoeuvre the pallet into the woods out of sight, quickly dump off the gear and return the cargo bay. Mike had another quick look around; satisfied no one was there, he manoeuvred the cargo bay into the woods amongst the trees.

Shadows leapt up all around him as the group began to quickly pull off the heavy boxes.

Spider's blackened face appeared next to Mike whispering excitedly, "I don't fucking believe it, I've never seen anything like this before. Fucking amazing!"

Mike said nothing but kept looking around him, expecting at any moment lights to come on illuminating them and the Russians to be standing there. He could understand Spider's excitement, the first time he'd seen it working properly he'd been the same.

Everyone worked hard to clear the pallet of the boxes and within two minutes it was empty.

Mike looked around whispering, "Okay four to go, remember be very careful with this stuff, some of it's explosive and some of it's fragile."

He left Patty to organise the work party as they all began to carry the items back to the centre of the vehicles. He turned, checking the cargo bay was clear of the trees as he drove it back out to the clearing, once he had it set in position, he pressed the recall button on the pallets controls and stood back. Within seconds the black mass was back and settling onto its cargo bay, using LIDAR (Light Detection and Ranging) to line itself up. No sooner had it landed than the Thumpr took off again, the cargo bay now attached, as it disappeared into the sky and leaving Mike waiting for the next drop. He wasn't waiting long, within two minutes the RF beacon was vibrating, the second Thumpr was coming in.

In total five Thumprs landed and every time the procedure was repeated. Mike keyed in the code, waited for the Thumpr to detach its cargo bay, it took off, and then he drove the cargo bay into the woods where they unloaded the pallets out of sight. once unloaded the trucks were picked up by the Thumpr and flown away. The fourth Thumprs cargo truck was different to the others, as everyone came forward to unload it, Mike waved them away, parking it away from the others. Ignoring the curious gazes he went back to the clearing, already the final Thumpr was coming into land. He quickly retrieved the cargo truck and brought it into the woods. When it had been unloaded, he pointed over to where Reaper and Sid were waiting with the two POW's. Both men shepherded the prisoners over to the cargo truck, sitting them cross legged, with their hands resting on their laps and their back resting against an empty box. They were still hooded and gagged, and Mike could see their breathing was heavy and their heads darting about under the hoods trying to make sense of what was going on as he removed the ear defenders from them. Rachel was not far behind, ready to translate as Mike began whispering.

"Tell them that they're going to be loaded onto this cargo pallet and lifted up by a helicopter. The cargo pallet is not that big and that they're not to move about. If they do and it swings to much then the pilot is under orders to cut them loose. The fall will kill them."

As Rachel told them, Mike could see them stiffen at the news. Good, he thought, hopefully they'd remain as they were, too scared to move. The Thumpr could easily manage the weight of the men, but it had never been tested to carry passengers. First time for everything Mike mused, as he waited.

Rachel nodded at Mike, indicating they were ready. He quickly got the cargo truck back into position and stepped back, watching the Thumpr come back in. The POW's remained bolt upright, their heads up, trying to work out the noise of the strange helicopter. They were lost from view as the Thumpr settled over the load, like some huge wasp swallowing a beetle it settled quickly and then lifted gracefully away, leaving nothing left of the truck and the men.

Mike watched the last Thumpr fly away, its dark mass disappearing into the night as more sounds drifted over from the enemy. He looked over, hearing the music, the singing and the laughter. Were they drunk, he thought to himself, probably. A seething anger tore through him as he thought of them partying over there and what they had already done to his country and his people. Well, laugh it up boys, he thought to himself, because come dawn tomorrow, we'll be ready to play and now finally we'll get a chance to strike back.

Tumat Embassy London

Samuel watched the quiet London streets pass silently by, as his convoy made their way through night time London. After only a few minutes they were pulling up to the embassy door, his security detail jumping out and already waiting with the door held open.

He nodded in thanks, ignoring the stares from the Tumat guards, walking inside and up the grand staircase into the lobby.

Inside the embassy there was a hub of activity, various department doors opened, people flashing by carrying reports for the twenty or so signatures they required before filing away. Nobody seemed to notice as he and his security team weaved their way through the mass of workers.

Finally, they came to the door they wanted, the office for the ambassador of Tumat. The security officer leading them in looked less than impressed as having the door closed to the PM was an insult. He showed his displeasure by banging loudly and forcibly on the door. After a few moments he heard the snick of the door unlock, the ambassador's voice inside booming out.

"Come in."

The security detail went in first, quickly checking the room was secure before nodding outside to Samuel.

"Room's clear Sir."

Samuel smiled at them gratefully as he entered, seeing the ambassador behind his huge desk, staring back with curious amusement at the PM's protection detail as they filed in and took up defensive postures nearby.

Samuel saw the ambassador look firstly at his security detail then back to him, his eyebrows raised, and a small grin on his face, clearly hinting their presence was unwanted. As if suddenly realising, Samuel quickly cleared his throat.

"Ahem Geoff, I don't think we need you and your team in here. Why don't you go outside and get yourself a coffee or something. We're amongst friends here."

"I'm sorry Sir, but the Prime Minister is not to be left alone at any time, regardless of where we are." The head of security shot back, shaking his head in response.

Samuel stepped towards the man, clearly irritated.

"Geoff, that wasn't a request. I need to talk privately with the ambassador. We're safe in here. Now, clear the room...Please."

The security officer's eyes flashed over to the ambassador, then back to the PM. This was his boss and if he knew best then so be it.

He smiled disarmingly, admitting defeat as he nodded in acknowledgement.

"Ok Sir, we'll be right outside. You need me, you press the cricket."

Samuel smiled, conscious of the small tracking device attached to his cufflink. If he felt threatened or needed help urgently, he could press it and the detail would come storming back in, guns blazing.

Geoff clicked his fingers, the other two burly security officers following his lead as they left the room, taking up positions outside the door, closing it behind them.

"Taking their jobs seriously I see," the ambassador smiled, leaning back in the chair.

Samuel ignored him, not wishing for small talk as he walked into the centre of the room, ignoring the offer of a seat.

"At least someone bloody is. What the hell is going on? I thought all the bloodshed and killing was to be over by now and your forces were to be here in London. Yet, I'm hearing reports that your troops are still fighting ours on the coast? Why are they still fighting? Why aren't they here yet?"

The ambassador leant forwards, elbows resting on the table, replying,

"That's your department I'm afraid, after all weren't *you* the one who was supposed to have ordered your forces to stand down? If your troops won't surrender and let our troops past, then I'm afraid we will have to continue fighting to get through them."

Samuel banged his fist on the table angrily.

"Dammit Yuri, that's not my fault! You assured me that the cabinet would be taken care of and that I'd be the only legal voice they'd listen to. Now with Jeffery Dickinson still alive, and I might add, the next in line to be PM, I can't order those forces to lay down arms. Not whilst they have another voice to listen to!"

The ambassador looked thoughtfully at Samuel, as out of sight his hand moved under the desk and pressed a button.

Behind him a hidden sliding door opened, and another man entered the room. Samuel recognised Sergei immediately, feeling the dread of past memories of meetings in the cold rainy café. For a second, he thought about the cricket, his hand slowly moving towards it, knowing the protection detail were just outside. He tried to hide the fear crawling up his spine as he smiled and stepped forwards, offering his hand to him out of forced courtesy.

"Sergei, I had no idea you were in the country. I thought you were no longer allowed out of Russia?"

Sergei merely smirked and looked disdainfully down at the outstretched hand, choosing to ignore him and sit down opposite the ambassador, his hands smoothing his jacket as he replied.

"It's amazing what or *who* you can bring in and out of another country via a diplomatic flight from Tumat."

Samuel stood awkwardly, the smile on his face disappearing as he was stood alone in the middle of the room. Finally Sergei looked up irritated.

"Oh, for god's sake Acorn, will you come sit down!"

Samuel was shaken out of his stupor at his agent's name being used. He hadn't heard that name for nearly a year, and with everything going on, with him being the PM, it seemed strange for him to be the one taking orders again. He smiled; the mask of a politician easy to produce on demand, as he sat down looking over at his old handler.

"So *Prime Minister*." Sergei began, the scorn at using his title clear to hear. "I believe you were just telling the ambassador about *your* latest problem?"

"*Our* problem." Samuel corrected. "I was promised that the transition of power would be over in a matter of hours, that aside from the attacks there would be no more bloodshed. Now I'm hearing your troops are killing thousands in their attacks. I'm trying to keep the public from finding out, but with every hour that passes you're galvanising people to fight against you, not help you. When will this end?"

Sergei shared a look with the ambassador before replying slowly.

"Regrettably there have been a few unforeseen problems, this politician who survived being one of them and the resolve of some elements of your military being another. But rest assured, we are taking steps to remedy the situation."

"What kind of steps?" Samuel asked, dreading the answer. He'd only agreed to go along with this if the casualties were kept to a minimum. After the London attacks, and the execution of almost the entire cabinet, he'd almost baulked at the task. He naively assumed by now he would be in charge, and imagined the whole of the UK to have been peacefully occupied, it's army dis-armed. The thought of yet more of his people being slaughtered filled him with a sense of dread and he hoped that somehow, he could find a way out of this for both him and his country.

Sergei stood up and walked over to the drinks cabinet, pouring out three large measures of vodka from the bottle, offering one to each of them, before taking a seat on the edge of the desk, closer to Samuel.

"Before we discuss the next steps, what do you know about where Mr Dickinson is hiding? We already know it's called Wonderland but now need a location. Do you know anything about it?

Samuel sat back, sipping the drink and thinking, before shaking his head.

"No-one knows where it is, but that was the point all along. It was built to house the government in times of crisis, not become a tourist attraction. I only know of it through what I've heard from gossip and rumour, as officially nothing exists and the only people that did know about it are all dead. Well, all except Jeffery."

Sergei nodded in thought, taking a sip of his drink before relenting.

"Very well, we shall continue our endeavours to find Mr Dickinson. Now, you mentioned your problems in London earlier to my colleague, can you repeat them to me."

Samuel's eyes shot over to the ambassador quickly as he thought of the earlier phone call, which was how he'd ended up there now, before replying.

"There's not much to explain, public opinion in London at the moment is divided, some believe the story about the King, others oppose it, but either way, I've only got control at the moment thanks to the Metropolitan Police Force. We control key areas of public influence, certain radio and TV stations and I've ordered the arrests of anyone who we suspect of causing trouble. But London is a tinder box waiting to ignite, the British people aren't stupid. And soon it will take more than the threat of arrest to keep them in check. I was counting on having your troops here soon to help maintain order."

Sergei looked on with a small hint of apology as he replied, "Ahh, unfortunately not even our well-respected military has been able to deliver on its promise, Prime Minister. They'll get to London as we agreed, but not for another seventy-two hours."

"SEVENTY-TWO HOURS?" Samuel shot back, surprised and shocked. "Sergei, I need them here now, not in seventy-two hours. You originally promised to have them here by now! Have you any idea of the questions I'm being asked at the moment behind the scenes by my own officers. I'm expecting any day now to be put under arrest. I need-"

Sergei held up a hand to silence him, keeping his own voice low and controlled.

"I've been sent here to help you maintain control in London."

"Really?" Samuel shot back incredulously, "and how do you propose we do that without your troops?"

Sergei leant forwards on the desk, nodding to the ambassador as he replied.

"Easy, now we move to phase two."

Apprehensively, Samuel watched as the ambassador pulled an envelope from his desk, as the secret door behind them opened again, another figure stepping into the room. The man was hard faced with intense eyes and a lean, fit, tanned, physique. Clearly nothing to do with the political landscape. Samuel looked at him, there was a flash of recognition there, he'd seen him from somewhere before.

As the stranger walked into the room and stood to one side nodding to Sergei in acknowledgement, the ambassador handed Samuel the envelope.

Samuel looked up at the man again, before opening the envelope and scanning the contents, as Sergei talked.

"That envelope contains all the details that we will need from you and the Met Police regarding the anti-monarchy march scheduled for tomorrow."

Looking up from the paper at the new addition in the room and still frustrated at not placing his face, Samuel enquired.

"And who's your new thug here?"

Samuel saw the man flinch, barbed by the tone. So at least he understood English, he thought, as Sergei replied, his tone mocking.

"Prime Minister, why, do you not recognise an old colleague from our glory years?"

Samuel looked again, his eyes searching for something. Suddenly it came to him, the stranger smirking as he saw the flash of recognition. The chef! This man had been the chef back at the truckstop all those years ago. Samuel swallowed nervously remembering what Sergei had said about his speciality dish. 'Truth Stew.'

Ignoring the look of shock on Samuel, Sergei continued.

"Major Laratov will assist us in the implementation of phase two. He and his team will need those details tonight, so I suggest that when we're finished here you contact your Chief of Police and have them sent across promptly."

Samuel ignored the Major's stare as he now began to read some of the details out aloud.

"Police frequencies, callsigns, duty rosters, control point locations, proposed routes of the march, palace duty rosters... Why do you need all of this?" he asked suspiciously, adding, "and why haven't I heard anything about phase two?"

Sergei smiled, leaning forwards.

"I think Prime Minster, that for the greater good, it's probably best that you don't know about phase two."

Samuel stood up, open mouthed.

"Oh god! You're going to kill more people, aren't you?"

All three men looked at him pitifully, as standing up Sergei walked over, looking him in the eyes.

"All wars have casualties, Acorn, I thought that by now you would have learnt that lesson."

Samuels eyes closed for a moment, thinking of all the people that had been killed so far. He knew there would be casualties, he'd expected that, but by now he was supposed to be the PM, the *only* PM. Now, he was being told of more lives having to be sacrificed. Could he do it, he thought to himself, could he keep doing this?

He exhaled, as finally the reality of it hit him. He couldn't stop it, any more than he could stop Jeffery Dickinson. He'd climbed into bed with the devil, now he had to ride it out to the end. He tried to justify it by telling himself that he could build a better country for his family, he could do this. He could believe in what the propaganda machines were already spinning out.

He looked down, nodding in agreement as he picked up the folder.

"Right, whatever Major Laratov needs, I'll see he gets it."

Sergei smiled, holding his hand out to Samuel, who looked down briefly before taking it, pulling him close into an embrace, whispering into his ear.

"You're doing very well Acorn, very well. I promise, it's nearly finished."

They all watched as the Prime Minister left the office, only when the door was closed did the Tumat ambassador look over to "Sergei" an amused expression on his face.

"Dimitry, why the hell did he keep calling you Sergei?

His friend smiled, "Because my friend, that's the game I used to play." Seeing the amused look on the ambassador he raised his arm, urging them all out of the room, ignoring Major Laratov.

"Come Yuri, the night is still young, and I've been away a long time, I want to see what delights London has to offer again..."

24

In From The Cold

Cerne Abbas

Mike walked back in amongst the tree's, the sounds of laughter and music in the distance dying behind him. He walked to the middle of the leaguer, where the boxes had been stacked up ready to be opened. Spider walked up to him, handing him a large envelope.

"This has got your name on it," he whispered.

Mike said nothing as he took the envelope and opened it, pulling out the letter and glancing over the first few lines. It was from Peter.

Seeing everyone waiting, he turned to Spider and said softly, "Right, let's start to get this lot organised now, get Patty to organise a work party, find out what we have and let's start to get it dished out."

"Wouldn't you rather wait for daylight?" Spider warned, "It'll be hard to get all this done by torchlight whilst keeping quiet."

Mike pointed back to where they could still hear the laughter and shouting from the Russians, whispering, "No, so long as they're over there making all the noise, we should be okay, besides if anything kicks off tonight, I want to be able to fight out of here, not skulk out of here with our tails between our legs."

Mike saw Spider nod in agreement as he walked away to organise things, knowing that they now had vehicle ammo had lifted the mood.

Mike went and found himself a spot between the boxes, where he unslung his rifle and placed it on the floor before sitting down and leaning against one of the crates. Pulling out his torch, he checked the red filter was on, before turning it on and opening the envelope to read.

Mike, I'm afraid this letter will be short and to the point, as time is against us and we're trying to get everything packed and arranged for tonight's drop. I must firstly apologise for the 120mm ammunition, the MoD informed me that they could only source the training rounds with the limited time frame they had available. I hope the rest of the ammunition will be sufficient for your use over the coming days.

Training Rounds, Mike thought to himself, why the hell would they send us those? Better than nothing I suppose, he thought, as he continued reading.

I'm not sure of how much you're aware of what's going on around the UK, but from the reports I've seen, it's not looking good. In your area there was an attack on Yeovil which has since been repulsed, however latest intel suggest the enemy are going to attempt again tomorrow, which is where I believe your unit will come in to assist. You'll get further details in your orders.

Now the good news is that the team were able to get you four of the Wasps and two of the Talons ready, plus one of our Hornets. I trust you can remember how all three weapons platforms work, but I've been asked by Kyle to tell you that the Hornet is still in its experimental stage and has yet to be tested in combat. I'll leave it your judgement if you want to use it or not. Please do whatever it takes to keep the kit out of the hands of the enemy, we've sent you some C4 explosives and chainsaws to help you with this purpose if you need them.

Included in the drop is a High Frequency radio, it's already been filled with the necessary codes, and we've included the callsign matrix, so you'll know who to talk to when the time comes. However, be aware that enemy electronic intercept activity in the area is still proving to be problematic, we're hearing reports of units being hunted by their transmissions, so you might be better suited using the satellite phone until you're closer to friendly lines. You're to give the ops room a call on the phone when you're operational. They'll then give you further orders.

One final thing, in case you didn't know already, the Emergency Powers Act has been invoked by our government, meaning all eligible ex-military personnel have now been re-activated, including myself. Given where you are at present and the assets that you now have at your disposal, it's been decided by higher to re-activate you and grant you the temporary rank of Captain. I know how you feel about this, but I'm sorry Mike, the country needs us and we need you. We all must now do our part, remember your oath of allegiance, remember what those words meant. They last your lifetime not just the years you served. I know the kind of man you are and I know you'll find it in your heart and head to do the right thing.

Best of luck Captain Faulkes and with a bit of luck and some well-placed firepower I hope to see you again soon, in the meantime give them hell for us.

Your Friend,

Brigadier Peter Rawlinson.

Mike re-read the last part of the letter again. Peter had been called up as well. He tried to think but no matter how many times he tried to spin it, or justify turning the appointment down in his head, it always came back to what the Brigadier had written. He'd always been a soldier, and you didn't just turn that off when you felt like it.

He was torn from his thoughts as he saw someone approach him. He looked up to see Spider.

"Sir, Patty's organising the work party now, we should have it all packed away in no time."

Mike pointed to the crates around him, "Tell him to ignore this stuff, I'll need to go through and check this myself."

"Okay," Spider replied. Mike looked up to see him still standing there, something was troubling him.

"Spider, what's on your mind?"

He watched as the NCO took a deep breath, before saying quietly,

"Look I just want to apologise again for earlier, I really fucked up there, you were right, I should have secured the sat phone better. If she hadn't grabbed hold of it-"

Mike stood up, shaking his head and interrupting him, "Look Spider, what's done is done. Besides, I've just found out, whatever happened they were always going to pull me back in. Maybe I was too naïve to think I could just somehow keep out of all this."

He could see the Corporal's shoulders lift slightly and the tension disappear from Spider's face.

Mike put a hand on his shoulder, "Look Spider, in case you hadn't worked it out yet, I'm a lot thicker skinned than you think, so don't you go worrying about shit like this. We're not in some cheesy soap opera that loves drama. If we make mistakes, we learn from them and move on. So don't dwell on the past."

Mike saw him smile slightly and his head lift as he replied, "Okay Sir, and...thank you."

Mike eyebrows raised before replying, "Enough of the sir crap, when we're away from the others it's Mike remember."

"OK...Mike."

Spider's gaze went back to the boxes again, his curiosity getting the better of him as he wondered what other interesting things they contained. He was still buzzing from seeing the Thumpr's earlier, he'd always heard about things like that being developed, but had never thought he'd get to see it for himself. He looked over to Mike again.

"Mike, what is all this stuff? Where did it come from?"

"Remember the retired Brigadier I used to work with back in the day?" he saw Spider nod as he continued, "he owns the company that provided us with all of this."

"They're not military then? Not from our lot?"

"No," Mike smiled, "it's a private company, they develop weapon systems for the military, I work with them, freelance, consultancy work and stuff. I helped them to develop some of this kit."

Sensing the questions to come Mike continued, "Spider I'll tell you all about this lot later with the others, but for now let's get the ammo loaded up?"

The Corporal nodded before replying, "Of course Mike, I'll go and get it all organised now."

Mike watched him walk away, before turning his attention to the boxes, now it was time to see if it all worked.

Everyone was working hard and quietly throughout the night, using what little light they could from the moonlight that filtered through the treeline. It was a full moon and Mike was thankful for that, the natural light made it easier to see. There was an air of energy that seemed to drift over the group, and everyone, including the new arrivals from the truck, had offered to lend a hand. With the prisoners gone, the police officers that had been guarding them were now free to help. Patty was walking through the large pile of equipment, using his red torch and covering the light with his hand to stop any of the light leaking out as he examined and checked off the contents. He whistled softly in appreciation as he recognised the writing on the boxes. Whoever had organised this had done well. With his torch in his mouth, he quickly wrote down on paper the amounts before getting the vehicle crews to silently carry off the loads to the vehicles. He looked over at Mike who was standing by another pile of boxes that had come in on the last drop, all carefully opened and laid out in a line. Mike had moved two of the larger boxes over to the briefing area that he had setup earlier. Patty had no idea what was in them, but they were heavy enough to require six people to help Mike move them there. The smaller boxes were large Pelicases, strong plastic lockable boxes that were used to transport sensitive electronics. He watched as Mike knelt at each one, checking their contents before moving to the next one. He had no idea what was in them, but from the way he could see Mike working in the dim light, he knew they must be important.

He watched as the last of the ammo load was carried away before his curiosity got the better of him.

He approached Mike who turned to acknowledge him before resuming checking the cases.

"What have you got there? new toys?" Patty whispered.

Without looking up Mike whispered back, "These are better than any toy you'd wish for at Christmas, Patty. What we have here are our own personal army and air force."

"What!" Patty hissed, "no fucking way! You serious?"

Mike reached into the case, flicking a switch and watching the digital display come to life, quickly adjusting the brightness so that the bright glow became dull. Patty leant over curiously, watching as the display seemed to show some kind of self-test being run. Everything seemed to flash back green as Mike, satisfied with the test closed the display down. Seeing Patty leaning curiously over him he smiled.

"I'll tell you all about these and what they do later with the others, in the meantime how are we looking on the supply drop?"

Patty looked at the paper, cupping the torch in one hand and the paper in the other.

"We did good, for the Warriors we've got 30mm rounds, both AP (Armoured Piercing) and HE (High Explosive) enough for sixty AP and sixty HE per vehicle and for the tank you've got thirty rounds of 120mm, but there was a problem with them, your loader wants to talk about that with you, he wasn't happy about something."

"Right, I'll speak to him about that later. What about 7.62mm?"

"We've got 10,000 rounds, I've divided it up between the four vehicles, so we've got 2000 rounds per Warrior and the tank's got 4000 rounds, your loader says your RWS takes 7.62mm so figured you'd need more."

"Was there anything else on the load?"

"Yes, we've finally got the mapping, lots of it and we've got more boxes of 9mm, and some 5.56mm so even though we're still light on personal weapons, at least we won't be light on ammo now, and the Engineer Corporal was creaming his pants, one of the boxes contained some C4, detonators and chainsaws. Hope you don't mind but I've given it all to him and his guys to take charge of, he says he's worked with C4 already."

"No doubt he's already imagining blowing up a bridge or two," Mike said quietly, as he finished with the pelicase and walked over to the next before adding, "I'm afraid I'll need that C4 back Patty, it's not for him, but tell him he can keep the chainsaws."

"Okay," Patty said grinning as he watched on as Mike pulled out a long tube containing a missile, recognising it's shape straight away.

"Holy shit, is that a Javelin? They've sent us Javelins?" he whispered excitedly, "how many?"

Mike checked over the antitank missile, checking the seeker head was free of damage before replying, "We've got eight Patty and I'm afraid they're not for you."

"Oh, and one other thing," Mike added before forgetting, "there's a HF radio somewhere in all the gear, can you make sure it gets placed over by my vehicle, hopefully we should be able to get comms with someone on it."

"OK will do," Patty replied, adding, "there's something else."

Mike stopped his inspection and stood up looking at him. "What is it?" he asked softly.

"Jonah's asked if he could have a word with you."

"Me?" Mike hissed back, "what the hell would he have to talk to me about? Besides I've got nothing to say to him."

"I know, but when you were off with Rachel earlier, he spoke to me and Spider."

"You've both talked to him? I thought he was supposed to be under military arrest?" Mike tried not to sound surprised, after all, both knew the soldier well.

"He is," Patty countered, "but we can't just gag him and stop people talking to him."

"Stop people talking to him? Why, who else has been talking to him?" Mike asked suspiciously.

"The journalist Linda, the police Chief, some of the guys, the two civilians from the truck."

Mike had forgotten all about Jonah; He'd been so busy with everything else; he hadn't seen what was going on under his own nose. He began to wish now he'd sent him off with the POW's.

Fucking hell, thought Mike, who *hasn't* spoken to him? There'll be no telling now what bullshit he's told them all. No doubt more attempts to undermine him and his authority. At least now, with his rank, it was official.

Curiously he asked, "Okay, so what did he want?"

Patty drew a deep breath before replying, "He's asked for us to speak to you, to get you to go talk to him. Spider just told him to fuck off, he's still angry about what happened."

"I don't blame Spider, I feel the same, but you how do you feel about it?" Mike enquired.

"I'm....I don't know. It's hard you know, I've worked with him for five years, I've never known him to do something stupid like this. It's hard for me to see him as anything other than Jonah."

"So why speak to me about it?"

"Because now you're the officer in charge, you've got the power to decide what to do with him. Now he's your responsibility. I just thought if you spoke with Jonah, heard what he had to say-"

"Then I could somehow go and speak to Spider," Mike interrupted him, "convince him that Jonah's seen the light and now all is to be forgiven?" Patty could hear the sarcasm in his voice.

"Well, you don't have to convince him Sir, you're the ranking officer now, that's for you to decide." Patty said hopefully.

So now it's back to Sir again, not Mike, he thought to himself amusedly. Funny how other people seemed to want to use his rank more than he did.

"Look I'm not saying forgive him," Patty continued.

Mike interrupted him again. "Patty, there's a lot going on right now and I need you to have your head in the game. You shouldn't be worrying about one person, not when you've got the others' lives to be thinking about."

"I know, you're right, but it just didn't seem right having him, one of our own sat there with those other two fuckers earlier. I mean they're evil, they're the enemy, but him, his crime...it's different."

Mike closed his eyes for a second, clearly Patty wasn't going to let this go. He tried to hide the frustration in his voice as he asked, "Different how?"

"Well, you know, it's not like he raped or murdered anyone, he's not the enemy, this is his home, he's not like them."

"Patty, he was selling drugs, last time I checked that was a crime. Have you forgotten that?"

"But do you know why he was selling the drugs?"

"Patty I don't fucking care." Mike replied cutting him off. He turned and knelt back down checking another of the cases. Ignoring the brush off Patty continued.

"His younger sister has MS, pretty bad from what I remember, spends most of her time either in a wheelchair or a mobility brace. Their dad left home when Jonah was just a lad, mum couldn't hack it on her own, turned to drugs, she died of an overdose when he was seventeen. He was the one who found her the following day. When he turned eighteen, he left home to join the army, he needed the money to pay for his sister's care. Their nan had moved in by this stage to help them at home and the sister should have been eligible for NHS treatment, but after two years they stopped the care. Apparently the drugs she needed were far too expensive for the NHS to pay for, so they offered her end-of-life care. Now he's the only one working and needs to bring home the money to pay for her drugs and the care. Can you imagine how much that costs? And with everything they've gone through, the NHS simply say, hey sorry about your sister, but here's a leaflet on how to deal with grief after she's gone."

Mike was tempted to do what Patty had suggested and use his rank, but not to help Jonah, instead to order Patty to shut up and go. But he also knew to do so would cross the line, respect went up and down the rank structure, and Patty deserved better than that. Ignoring the officer in him, he looked at the Corporal.

"I know it's a lot Patty and everyone has some kind of shit going on in their lives, but that doesn't justify what he did." Mike whispered back slowly.

"I'm not trying to justify it, all I'm saying is it's not like he was spending the money on fast cars, holidays and loose women."

Mike closed his eyes for a moment, damn all this bloody nonsense, he thought. Patty still couldn't see it. Why couldn't it be simple? Why did this have to muddy the waters so much? People were always quick to forgive. Perhaps he should have suggested they let Jonah go. Welfare not warfare kept springing to mind.

Keeping his voice low and his anger hidden, Mike replied, "Patty, his actions, regardless of their greater intentions resulted in people being left behind and killed back at the base, his actions resulted in you losing one of your vehicles. What would you have done if I hadn't turned around and come back for you? You could have all been captured or killed. That was all down to him."

"He didn't know though at the time that's what would happen," Patty countered, "besides if we had left on time, and as planned, then Rachel and her friend would have been left behind instead and you would never have met up with us. You could be out there now, on your own, a corpse sat in a burned-out tank with just a driver for company. It works both ways Mike, cause and effect, perhaps Jonah was meant to do this all along, perhaps that's why we're all here now. Think about it, the truck we hijacked, everyone in the back, they'd all be dead and god knows where we'd all be now. Don't forget Rachel's the reason we've got the ammo tonight, if you hadn't have met her..."

Even in the dark Patty could see the face that Mike pulled as he replied, struggling to keep his voice low. "Cause and effect? Patty, since when the fuck did you suddenly become a philosopher? I thought you were a soldier. This isn't some kind of new age physco babble bullshit. What, you really believe all that, a butterfly flaps its wings in one part of the world and a hurricane blows in another crap? In the real world, when the metal hits the meat, it's over, lights out. No second chances. There's no cause and effect in that. It's simple physics, his mistakes have cost lives, it's that simple. I can't believe you're even trying to justify this."

"Have you never made a mistake then. Ever?"

Mike shook his head slowly, knowing what Patty implying. It had been Mike's idea to come north, little realising the Russians had done the same. Now, instead of being ahead of them, they were behind them, and now because of him they'd spent the day stuck here. That was on him.

Mike looked up at Patty, too tired to try to argue further.

"Look Patty, I've really got a lot still to do here, so have you. Let's leave it for now, and later I'll go and listen to what he has to say, but for now, pretty fucking please, leave me be, I really need to concentrate on this.

Sensing he'd pushed it far enough Patty replied, "Okay, all I'm saying though is please don't label him as a monster, not until you've at least walked in his shoes." Before finally adding, "I'll go find that HF Radio now for you, Sir."

Mike watched him walk off towards the vehicles, his shadow swallowed by the darkness. Shaking his head at the irony of it all, as he thought about the differences in the two Corporal's he had. Spider was moody and sombre, and too serious at times, needing a prod to get a laugh, and now he'd found Patty was quite deep in his thoughts and the way he thought about life. The more he got to know them, the more he understood them and the more he was sure he could work with them. Although sometimes, like now, it drove him nuts, it was good to have the two of them as they were, a fine balance between one line and another. Shaking thoughts of Jonah from his head he turned and carried on working. He hadn't been kidding, there was still lots to do.

Twenty minutes later and he was finished with the checks. Leaving the equipment for now, he decided he'd see how his crew were doing. As he got to the tank, he saw Smudge passing up the heavy rounds to Bill, who was on the side of the hull and leaning into the turret. He could hear Baz talking and suddenly saw his head emerge from the operator's hatch, the faint red glow of the lights illuminating him briefly. He was leaning down signalling that he wanted to chat.

"What's up Baz?" Mike whispered as he leaned against the tank.

He watched as the loader climbed out and softly jumped down to stand next to him.

"Sir, we've got a bit of an issue with our bomb load."

"So, what's the issue?" Mike asked.

Baz knelt down and picked up one of the rounds, Mike could see straight away what the problem was.

Tank rounds were expensive, a HESH (High Explosive Squash Head) round would cost £5,000 and an AP (Armour Piercing) depleted uranium round could cost anywhere up to £25,000 a round. Given that tanks could carry fifty-two of them, it was easy to see how the British Army could soon rack up an eye watering bill when carrying out training, with crews firing upwards of twenty to thirty of these every day. To keep training costs down, and prevent a revolt from the taxpayers, the army had designed its own cheaper version of the tank ammo. To replace the Armoured Piercing rounds, it had developed the DST (Discarding Sabot Trainer) as it handled and fired in the same way, but was smaller and lacked the powerful punch of its more expensive brother. To replace the HESH round they had designed the ShushP (Squash Head Practise) which was the same size dimensions, but instead of being filled with powerful explosive, it was filled with concrete. Both training rounds were great for firing at wooden targets, but not the best for engaging real combat vehicles. Mike could see Baz was holding a DST round.

"Shit," he muttered, suddenly remembered the first part of Peter's letter. *They could only source the training rounds.* He'd been so wrapped up in checking the drones, he'd forgotten to mention the training ammo. "How many did we get?"

"Afraid to say Sir, the whole bomb load, we've got twenty DST rounds and ten ShushP. Not what we were expecting."

Keeping his doubts to himself Mike asked, "Vent tubes, did we get those?"

"We've got them Sir, for some reason they sent a hundred of them."

Vent tubes were small cases of brass, filled with an explosive that was ignited by passing an electrical charge through them, looking similar to a large calibre bullet. Each time the main gun was loaded a vent tube would automatically be loaded into the breech, providing the initial bang that would then ignite the main explosive charge, causing the gun to fire. Mike didn't care that they'd sent too many, rather too many than too little.

Trying to sound positive, he remarked, "Well training rounds or not, we're better off now than we were earlier. Besides, I wouldn't want to be hit by one. They'll still do some damage."

"They will Sir, but will it be enough?" the loader asked apprehensively.

Mike clapped him on the shoulder, "I guess we'll find out soon enough. You nearly done?"

The loader pulled a rag out of his pocket, wiping sweat away from his brow, even though it was the middle of the night, the summer heat lingered.

"Nearly done Sir, perhaps another fifteen minutes then we'll be ready. I've put 600 rounds on the coax and another 600 on the RWS, even with the training rounds we've still got a good sting in the tail."

Mike pointed over to where the boxes lay on the floor whispering, "And you haven't even seen the goodies I've brought to the party yet. That sting might be bigger than you think."

Mike saw the HF radio and its bag lying next to the ammo.

"Baz are you happy how to fit that?"

The Lance Corporal looked to where Mike was pointing, replying cheerfully, "High Frequency Radio? Not a bloody clue! But I'll figure it out, they're all the same anyway ain't they, big expensive boxes that cost us an arm and a leg and never work when you need them to."

Mike chuckled at his response, having Baz around was refreshing and Mike was glad to have someone with his experience and the can-do attitude on the crew. He felt far more confident in leaving the tank to him. He put a hand on his shoulder and replied, "Ok well if you need help, Corporal Nock is a signaller."

"Is she now?" Baz answered before adding, "She's the pretty one you were with earlier."

Mike smiled to himself, not wanting to dampen the mood of the young man. "Yes, that's the one Baz, but she's married."

"The pretty ones usually are." Baz replied in mock regret.

Leaving Baz to it, Mike walked down the line to find Spider's Warrior, he wasn't looking very long, when out of the darkness he saw Spider standing on the turret. He was directing his crew on where he wanted the ammo loaded within the vehicle.

"Spider!" he hissed. He watched the Corporal look about in the darkness, trying to locate the noise. "Down here!" Mike hissed again. The NCO peered down towards him, his eyes adjusting to the low light. "That you, Captain?"

Mike cringed at the word Captain. "Yes, can you spare someone to give me a hand shifting some of this gear? Preferably someone strong."

"Sure, give me a second." He leant into the vehicle and muttered something, Mike heard the faint whir of the motor as the Warrior's back door opened, the red light spilling out quickly extinguished and heard someone walk up to him. He looked up to see the hulking shadow of Changa, smiling.

"Changa, I need someone strong, until they get here, you'll have to do." Mike said softly.

He heard the Fusilier chuckle as he followed him back to the cases. Mike knew the Fijian was the strongest person they had. Mike indicated for him to grab the handles at one end, whilst he grabbed the other and between them, they carefully carried the first case up to Spider's vehicle. Ignoring the curious looks from the crew, they managed to manhandle the case up and onto the back decks. Both climbed up and using a pair of ratchet straps secured the pelicase to the armoured plating, ratcheting them tightly so the box remained in place. Mike pulled some of the cables from out of the box and began attaching them into the vehicle's wiring harness, carefully routing the cables so they wouldn't interfere or get in the way of the crew. Then he checked everything over, giving the box a quick tug to check it was secure, then smiled to himself as he high fived Changa who looked at the box curiously. Sensing the question about to come Mike replied, "Changa, I'll explain all to everyone later. Meantime we've got another four of these to fit."

Forty minutes later and all but three of the boxes were fitted to the vehicles, each Warrior had one of the pelicases mounted on its back decks and the tank had two fitted to the rear of the turret. The two largest cases were still on the ground, Mike was stood looking at them. He'd leave them there for now. Besides, he was still conscious that some of their group were civilians and two were reporters. Even without their phones they could still talk and describe what they'd seen and he had to keep some of the new weapon's capabilities secret, they were prototypes after all. He'd already warned Linda not to take pictures of the crates, and now he was in charge she was forced to listen. Even so she'd tried her best to flirt and coerce information out of Mike, but he'd remained tight lipped.

Speaking of which, they needed to decide what to do with the civilians, and soon. The plan had originally been for the civilians and the police officers to drive out that night, using the darkness to escape in the truck, getting far enough away to ditch it and then make their way back to their homes but seeing the artillery setup on the far ridge had stopped that. To get the truck out now, meant moving the armoured vehicles and that meant lots of noise, noise that they would hear, drunk or not, and they weren't ready yet. The party, or whatever it was that they had going on over there was in full swing, and occasionally someone would fire random shots of small arms into the air. Mike had watched open mouthed as the green tracer rounds had come close to the woodline, and at first feared they'd been discovered; however, the firing became more random and he breathed a sigh of relief as the rounds then went skywards. Clearly, they were all drunk as lords, but he couldn't risk that they didn't have someone still alert over there. For now, the civilians and the truck were stuck with them, like it or not.

Speaking of things that were stuck with them, he looked over to the shadow of Jonah by the truck. At first, they'd had him under the guard of the police, but with him now tied up he wasn't going anywhere. For the past few hours, he'd sat there unguarded watching everyone working around him. Mike knew he'd have to deal with him at some point, and Patty was right, he was now in command, Jonah was his problem.

Around him, the darkened shapes of figures still quietly working told him he had some time to kill until they were all ready. He decided that now was the time to speak to him, one way or another, he'd sort out the problem that was Jonah tonight.

He thanked Changa for the help and watched as the Fijian walked back to his vehicle, then putting his doubts aside as he walked up to truck, kneeling besides the Lance Corporal.

"That you, Sir?"

The words surprised Mike. Not only did he know he was now an officer, but he addressed him as such.

"Yes, it's me Jonah, Corporal Patterson has informed me that you wanted to speak to me?" Mike's voice was low, but Jonah could hear his cold tone. Mike wanted this over and done with quickly.

He saw the figure sit up, shuffling closer to Mike to be heard better. Mike instinctively leaned back slightly, wary of any form of attack. The last time they were this close, Jonah was trying to fight him.

"Sir, I want to firstly apologise for earlier, for trying to attack you. I wasn't thinking clearly, I panicked and...well I just...shit. Look, I'm so sorry."

Mike stared impassively back, his face betraying no emotion as he said nothing.

After a few moments of silence, the young Lance Corporal continued.

"I've been sat all-day, having time to think about my mistakes, and I want to get back into the fight."

"You want to get away is what you mean, you want us to release you so you can get away back to your sister." Mike growled.

He watched as Jonah shifted uncomfortably; he hadn't known Mike was aware of his circumstances back home. So, it was true, Mike thought, he did have a sister.

"How do you know about her?" he asked.

"Patty told me." Mike said. "Is it true she has MS?"

"Does it matter either way?" Jonah replied shrugging his shoulders.

"No, it doesn't," Mike agreed keeping his voice low. "But it would help to explain a few things."

"What do you want me to say?" Jonah replied testily, "Want me to say how sad life is, how I was forced into doing what I did? I wasn't forced into anything. Yes, my sister is ill, yes, we live alone, yes, the experimental drugs and care are expensive, no, we don't get any help and yes, I sold the drugs to pay for that care. I've made that decision, and rightly or wrongly I'm going to have to live with it. I chose one evil to make something good for someone I love. I thought in my head the good would outweigh the bad. I was wrong, I see that now and I've let my mates down." Jonah finished with a sigh, his admission sounding more like a confession..

Surprised by the admission of guilt, Mike asked, "What's changed then? Why have you changed your tune all of a sudden?"

Jonah took a few seconds to compose himself, looking around to see no one was close by to hear.

"Do you know that one of the advantages of sitting here and keeping quiet, is that over time, people forget you're there and then suddenly they don't see you anymore."

Mike nodded, thinking about the times he'd watched people walk past homeless people in the street, without giving them a second glance, as Jonah continued.

"I've been sitting here alone, listening to the people from the truck talking to each other, hearing their stories, what happened to them. That reporter Linda, she's been asking loads of questions, building up a picture of what those bastards out there have been doing. Some of the things..."

"Why do you care?" Mike scoffed, his tone argumentative. "You're a drug dealer, you sell drugs to people with a habit, most of those customers rob, cheat and lie to get their money. Some even turn to prostitution to pay for it. Did you ever stop to think about them Jonah?"

"That's not the same thing Sir, my customers were all working people with jobs and steady homes. I never once sold to kids and I've never once sold to anyone that couldn't afford it."

"Oh, how very noble of you," Mike said with a sneer, "a dealer with a conscience."

Ignoring his tone, Jonah continued, "Look I'm not saying what I did was right and I'm not justifying it. I know I've fucked up, if I could, I'd do things differently, but I can't take it back. I know I've got to be punished and am happy to accept that, I take full responsibility for what I've done Sir."

Mikes frowned at the change of tone from the soldier as he continued speaking.

"Sir look, I can't sit this one out any longer, these are my mates, I've let them down I know, but you can't expect me to sit by and watch you all fight on without me."

"Oh, so now you want to fight?" Mike asked suspiciously.

"I never knew it would be this bad, no-one did, but this is my country too and hearing those people and what the Russians have been doing to them, we can't let them win. What if right now that's happening in my hometown? What if right now there's a soldier like me up there, who could stop those things from happening to my sister? But instead of staying to fight, they run away? What then? What happens to my sister? Or the people counting on us to defend them, I never really understood it before, but now, I've realised for this to work, everyone needs to do their bit. And me being tied up, causing you problems is not what I want to be doing. I don't want to be remembered like this." Jonah held his tied arms up for Mike to see what he meant. As he lowered his voice and continued.

"If I'm not helping to be part of the solution, then I'm part of the problem. And I don't want that. Fuck that."

Mike was surprised at how passionate the young NCO had suddenly become. Two days ago he was doing his darndest to get away, now it was almost as if he was in an interview for a propaganda poster. Even in the dim light Mike could see the fire burning in his eyes.

His doubts came to the surface again though as he asked suspiciously.

"You'll forgive me if I don't quite buy into all this straight away, but when we first met, you weren't exactly welcoming with open arms, were you? Why should I suddenly believe you're going to step into line now and listen to orders? You've almost gone out of your way at every step to undermine me."

"I was an idiot and I was scared."

Mike blinked in surprise at the honesty of the answer. For a soldier to admit he was scared was quite a thing.

"Go on." Mike urged as Jonah continued.

"When it all kicked off, none of us knew what to do, none of us expected it, I didn't think we'd make it out of that camp. My crew were screaming at me for orders, I couldn't think of anything, I panicked and all I thought about was who would look after my sister when I'm gone. But then you showed up and suddenly we had someone calm and cool and telling us what to do over the radio. I was glad to see you, but I also resented you, maybe I was just jealous, I don't know. Either way, when I saw you that night and then found out you were a fucking civvy, I hated you even more, because you reminded me about everything I hate about myself."

Mike nodded in understanding, he'd seen it happen before during his time in the army, promising soldiers in the prime of their careers cut down by resentful, jealous, superiors who feared being shown up for the incompetence that they were. At least on that he could agree with Jonah. Except, in this case, Jonah didn't have the ability to sideline Mikes career. Up until six hours ago there had been no career.

Jonah continued, "I thought that after we'd escaped, that being a civvy you'd ditch us when things got rough and leave us in the lurch, trapped with the vehicles. I tried to get Patty and Spider to get rid of you, to give you the push I thought you needed. Then I could get away myself, leaving the lads to make their own way back home to safety. But you wouldn't go, instead you made them more of a unit and every time I thought you'd fuck up, you didn't. And every hour that went by the guys seemed to like you more and more. I should have seen it for myself, I didn't at the time Sir, and in doing so I fucked up, I made the mistake. Even if my plan had worked and I had got rid of you, what would I have to go back to? Don't you understand? If we fail in stopping this then no one is safe, then what kind of country do we want to live in? Not one run by those fuckers."

Mike knelt there rubbing his chin thoughtfully as he listened to the NCO. He was still doubtful, but he had to admit, it would be easier knowing they had an extra pair of hands to help, besides guarding Jonah would be a problem when the police left them later. He was tempted to get them to take Jonah he was military, and like it or not, he was now Mike's problem to deal with. Seeing him deep in thought, Jonah added.

"Sir, I'm not trying to get out of this, I know what I've done is wrong and I know I've got to be punished for it, I'm not disputing that. All I'm asking is that it waits till we're back in camp. I'll do whatever you want, I'll follow your orders and won't try to escape. You have my word on it, Sir."

He was torn from his thoughts as he became aware of two people walking towards him. He looked up to see it was Patty and Spider

"Ammos all loaded up Sir and your operator's told me to tell you the HF set is now up and running, so I think that means we're all good to go." Patty reported.

Mike stood slowly, looking at them both. "Thank you Patty."

Spider just looked uncomprehendingly as Mike looked back down at Jonah.

"I want your word, now in front of these two, that you're going to fall back in line as a good little soldier-"

"I promise Sir, I will-" Jonah cut in excitedly, as Mike raised his voice slightly to cut him off. "LET me finish, before you get excited, you might not like what I have to say."

Spider's jaw dropped as Mike continued, "I want your word that you will do as I say, without question, without delay, and that there will be no attempts to escape, any attempt at escape will result in you being re-arrested. I hope you understand how serious that could be for you. Do I make myself clear?"

Jonah struggled to his feet, standing next to Mike at attention, his bound hands looking awkward as his head nodded furiously. "Absolutely Sir, I promise 100 percent, no escape attempts and I'm under your orders."

Spider quickly interrupted, "Sir, If I may have a word in private?"

Mike remained looking at Jonah as he answered. "You may not Corporal Webb, I've made my mind up and this man is no longer under arrest. Corporal Patterson, cut his bonds please."

Spider looked surprised as Patty stepped forward, unsheathing a small pocketknife and cutting the bonds on Jonah's hands. He smiled in thanks and stood there, rubbing his hands.

Keeping his voice low Mike continued, "Now, as I see it, you can't simply carry on as we left off, so as of this moment I'm relieving you of your rank. From this moment forwards its Fusilier Jones, you don't deserve to wear the rank, and I won't have you being in a position of power. Do you understand?"

Jonah swallowed hard and nodded as he removed his rank slide. "I understand Sir, but what about my crew? What's going to happen to them?"

"They're not your crew anymore, I can't have you commanding a vehicle, instead Fusilier I'm going to transfer you to the back of Corporal Patterson's wagon, it's shit jobs until he decides you've done enough. Now go get your stuff together and get yourself set up on his wagon."

"Yes Sir, thank you." Jonah nodded and was about to leave when Mike stopped him. Looking at him intently, his tone menacing.

"And Fusilier, don't make me regret this. One wrong move, one back handed comment, one sniff of an insurrection with the troops and I'll cut you loose where the Russians will find you. Understand?"

The Fusilier nodded, glancing across to Patty. "I won't let you down Sir, thank you for giving me another chance."

Mike watched him walk off towards the Warrior as Spider suddenly said, "What the fuck just happened? I thought he was under military arrest?"

"He was," Mike replied flatly, "but I've decided to release him, we can't keep wasting soldiers to guard him, besides, we need everyone to be on our side going forward."

"But what if he tries to escape? Or take some of the guys with him?" Spider questioned, trying to keep his voice low.

"That's why I've demoted him and put him on Patty's wagon. Patty knows him best; he can keep an eye on him."

He looked over at Patty as he continued, "Shit jobs Patty, don't go easy on him just because he's a mate. And for now, he's not to be given any weapons until I feel he can be trusted. If he wants a weapon give him a pick handle."

Patty nodded as he replied, "Sure thing, shit jobs until I feel otherwise. We need someone more suitable to command Two-One-Alpha though, Doc's already been telling me he's struggling with it. In his own words, I'm more use to you all as a damn doctor, not a coffin commander."

Mike chewed his bottom lip as he thought it through. Turning to the other two he remarked, "Come on then, you know your troops best, whose best suited to command next? Who do you think is ready?"

Both men answered at once. "Changa."

"Okay, how much experience has he got with 30mm? Has he commanded a Warrior before?"

Spider nodded his head, "Yeah, he used to be a commander, but last year was demoted for punching one of the officers. You know what some people are like after a few beers."

"Reckon he's up to it?" Mike asked with a hint of doubt.

"Yeah, he's more than capable, just don't put him anywhere near the beer." Spider replied jovially.

"Perhaps this will help give him some motivation," Mike replied, handing the rank slide over to Spider. "Before you hand it over to him though, I want you to tell him that I was doubtful, and you had to convince me."

"Why do that?" Patty asked surprised.

"Because it'll mean more to him knowing he's having to fight to keep it, rather than just be gifted it. I'm hoping he'll bust a gut to impress me. Not out of some sense of vanity for me, just out of necessity." Mike added. "We can't afford any mistakes now."

Spider smiled as he took the rank slide, his own mood lifting. "Right, I'll go give him the good news now."

Both men watched him leave as Patty turned to Mike.

"So, I guess that means we're all good to go now then?"

Mike shook his head, "Not yet, I need to explain what these do. Can you get me all vehicle commanders around these three boxes in twenty minutes time. I think it's about time I showed you what it all does."

"Sure thing, I'm looking forward to seeing it myself."

"Oh, and include the three Engineers and Rachel, I want them to see this as well," he called after Patty quietly.

Whiskey-Three-Zero

Cerne Abbas

Twenty minutes later and Mike was standing with the assembled group in the briefing area, shielded from view by the thermal sheeting he'd put up earlier. Not that it mattered, the Russians were still going strong with loud music blaring out of a loudspeaker, singing and occasionally the night sky was lit up by a searchlight or torch arcing skywards. At least the random firing had finished, perhaps someone in charge had got a grip of them. Whatever they had to celebrate though they were making up for lost time. Mike ignored the sounds, concentrating instead on what was in front of him. His team were stood in a semi-circle with Mike in the middle, the boxes at their feet waiting to be opened. He'd already spoken to the police officers who had managed to shepherd the civilians into the back of the truck, out of earshot and sight of the group. Mike didn't want too many people seeing or listening in to what he was about to reveal. Linda had tried to get a look in, but Mike made sure she was kept away, despite her protests. "You can't keep me out Mike," she had pleaded with him, "We had a deal! I get to report on what's going on."

"No Linda, you made a deal with the Colonel, who's not here right now, but I am, and I'm telling you that you don't get to report on any of this."

Mike saw anger flash across her face as he added, "For reasons of operational secrecy this is not to be reported on. I'm the senior officer here, so I get to have the last word."

He couldn't help but smile as he said the last part. She'd help push for Mike to be an officer, and now he was. The trouble for her was that it now meant Mike was the boss, like it or not and his word was now law.

He watched as red faced, she turned and walked away, the police officer guiding her towards the back of the truck. She stomped off and waved his hand away irritated, as if swatting a fly. He waited until he was sure she was out of earshot before turning back to the others.

"So, these boxes contain those Wasps and things? And these are all things that you've helped design?" Rachel asked, as Mike knelt and began to unclasp the lids.

"Wasps, Talons and a Hornet, and yes I helped with the platform integration." Mike replied.

Spider looked up from the contents of the box, "Platform integration?"

Mike smiled, replying, "A posh word for getting them working on the Warriors and the Challengers, I spent two years helping design and develop the lot."

"So, you know how to use all of this then?" Changa asked.

"I do, and within the hour so will all of you. Before we begin though, I must remind you that what you're about to see is highly classified and that, as serving soldiers, you're all bound by the Official Secrets Act. Therefore, none of you are to discuss or talk about what I show you tonight with anyone outside of the group. I'll tell you all I can, but don't get too upset if I don't answer every question. Agreed?"

There were murmurs of agreement as the group nodded, their curiosity piqued. Satisfied, he finished unclasping the first box, letting the sides fall away on the grass. He could hear the mutters of surprise and see the group move excitedly closer as the box opened to reveal it's secret. "Now everyone," Mike began, "I'd like you all to say a big hello to Talon."

Mike stood up, holding a tablet sized control panel, pressing one of the buttons on the display. With a slight click and a whir of motors, the large box shape began to rise up, taking shape. It stood over seven feet high, resembling something more akin to a sci fi movie than a weapon system. At its highest point sat the seeker head. Dome shaped and similar in shape to a hamburger, with an armoured top and bottom with sensors and cameras positioned in the middle part. When necessary, the robot could lower the upper part of its head to marry up with the bottom part, protecting the sensitive cameras and sensors. The head sat atop a gimbal motor, allowing it a 360 degree view of its environment, similar to the movement of an owl's head. The body of the robot was hinged in three places, allowing the robot to lower itself into a much smaller profile, in case there were limited areas of cover. The base of the robot was located on two large sets of tracks, resembling a miniature tank and each track comprised of a new prototype compound of carbon fibre weaved rubber. Each track had four large running wheels mounted to electric servos, which could lower and raise each wheel individually to change the shape of the track depending on the terrain. Mike knew it was tough enough to survive in some of the most hostile environments, he'd seen it personally tested in the Artic tundra, the deserts of the Middle East and the rocky outcrops of Iceland. On the back of the robot, lying vertically, was the weapons platform, on which were two launch tubes, each holding a Javelin anti-tank missile, and in between the launchers was a Suppressed 5.56mm Minini belt fed machine gun. The weapons were stowed out of the way until needed, as the weapons platform was designed to pivot forward and into the horizontal position when ready to fire. The Minimi wasn't standard issue and had been customised to be able to fire both fully automatic and single shot if required and with its stabilised platform could fire accurately out to over a kilometre.

Mike looked at the shocked faces of the group as he slowly began. "TALON, standing for Tracked Anti-armour Listening and Observation Node. It's a fully combat ready anti-armour platform, fitted with two Javelin missiles, one Minimi light machine gun, holding 1000 rounds and 4kg of C4. On the sensor head we've got four cameras, two daytime, two night time, and a targeting suite consisting of laser range finder, LIDAR, and acoustic detection."

"Acoustic what?" the Engineer Corporal called Fletch asked inquisitively.

"It hears things, like rounds being fired, people talking, vehicles moving, it can hear out to four miles away, but is accurate up to two miles away, identifying what it's hearing and detecting if it's a threat. A bit like an owl can." Seeing the disbelieving looks around him, Mike continued, "If I can just get you all to be quiet for a moment, I'll show you."

Mike tapped away on the control pad as the head began to pan around, over to where the Russian positions were. They couldn't see them, thanks to the woodline, but the Talon could hear them. After a few moments he showed them the control panel, the display now changed to a white spotted visual picture, with small red dots in the middle. He zoomed in on the spots, counting at least fifteen of them. Mike read aloud what the display was telling him.

"So according to Talon, we have seventeen very drunk Russian soldiers sat 1,500 metres away, through those trees, we also have a generator running, probably the command post and the sounds of two people having a conversation away from the group over to the east."

"No fucking way!" Spider hissed, as the group began to chat excitedly amongst themselves. Mike smiled proudly as he continued.

"Would you like to hear what they're talking about?"

"That's impossible," Wrighty, one of the Engineer Sappers replied flatly, shaking his head disbelievingly, as Mike spent a few moments of playing with the controls to filter out the background noises. Suddenly the voices of two soldiers could be heard, distinctly chatting over the tablet's speaker, the volume loud enough for all to hear.

Everyone's jaws dropped, as Rachel cocked her head, and began to translate. "He's talking about his wife back home not knowing where they are. She still thinks his unit's in the east of the country training. He's written her lots of letters, but hasn't been able to send them yet, their military police have forbidden it."

The voice changed as the second soldier now began to chat, Rachel quickly adding. "This one's complaining about another soldier not washing enough, who works on his crew, he's beginning to stink."

Mike lowered the volume, ending the conversation as the others began to share looks of excitement. He had to admit, the effect had been the same for him when he'd first seen the Talon's talents being demonstrated. He waited for the excited chatter to die down, before adding.

"Right everyone, let's get back to it, we've got a lot to cover. Now, as you can see the Talon's a tracked robot, it goes extremely well across country and has a top speed of thirty miles per hour, so can keep up with the vehicles if we need it to."

He stopped to check he hadn't lost anyone, seeing nothing but looks of awe he continued, "Talon has been designed primarily to help us identify enemy positions, think of it as a recce vehicle, it can find, identify, and if necessary, destroy a vehicle or attack a position if we need it to."

Mike stepped closer, showing them all the control pad. On it was a view of what the Talon was watching, they could see themselves on the display and Mike tapped on the face of Patty.

"Patty can you just walk over here please." Mike said pointing to a separate area away from the group.

As Patty walked, they could see the sensor head of the robot track and follow Patty smoothly, Spider chuckled and hissed softly, "Fucking hell mate, it's got you targeted for termination!"

Patty looked at Mike worriedly, who seeing his discomfort quickly replied, "It's okay Patty, the weapons aren't loaded yet, besides it's not targeting you, it's *tracking* you."

Mike showed everyone the display, on it was Patty's face, contained within the targeting box, above the box the word, 'OBSERVE' flashed in green.

Mike continued, "So long as I keep Patty selected, the robot will continue to track him, when he disappears from view, the Talon will move to try to re-acquire him, using whatever cover is around to keep itself concealed."

"How can that bloody great thing keep itself concealed? You'd see it a mile away." Fletch exclaimed.

Mike tapped some more options on the tablet and everyone watched on in awe, as with a small whir of the motors, the Talon sank smoothly back in on itself, now, no taller than a wheelbarrow, only the head protruded from the top, the cameras still watching Patty. The weapons rack had lowered horizontally and was laying cross the top of the body, still clear to fire.

People nodded in genuine respect, as Mike continued. "Talon's body is made up of twenty motors and servos all able to move independently of each other and is hinged in three places allowing it to be very flexible. It can contort itself into a number of different shapes, depending on the mission and the level of cover provided. I'm not going to go through all of them now, but just know that, even though it weighs nearly 300kg, it can hide its bulk as well as any yoga instructor."

Showing them the display again, Mike continued with the demonstration. "So, at the moment it's set to observe. If I now select target, the weapons systems become active."

Everyone watched, as with a low whirring noise, the weapons platform lifted smoothly up and over the shoulders of the Talon, its weapons all now pointing directly at Patty. The display had now changed from green to red, and the word 'TARGET' now flashed at them, as Patty's face was bracketed by the targeting crosshairs. Mike kept his voice low as he continued, "When the display is red, it means your targeting, and the weapons are live, I like to think of the rhyme, green means seen, and red means dead. You can't go wrong then. Now all I have to do is simply select fire and the selected weapon will launch."

"Patty now you're being targeted, can you walk slowly right to left please?"

The Corporal tried to look as relaxed as he could with the weapon trained on him, as he walked over to the left. The weapons platform slowly moved with him, tracking his movements. The effect was not lost on the group, the murmurs of excitement beginning to grow. Mike could see the astonished faces all staring in disbelief. This wasn't a sci fi movie, this was real and it was happening here in front of them. Mike continued to explain as he tapped the tablet display.

"I'm using the tablet to show you what the Talon is seeing, but the system's fully automated, I can simply tap on the map display here, to either ask Talon to go to a location or I can ask it to get ears and eyes on a location. Using its onboard systems, it will then either make its way there or, if I've asked it to get ears and eyes on, it will pick a location from where it can hide and listen and observe or hide and attack."

"Unfuckingbelievable." he heard Spider mutter.

Mike tapped another button on the screen and the display changed back to green, the weapons platform retracting back to its stowage position.

"It's back to observe Patty." Mike said reassuringly, as Patty began to breathe a little easier, with Mike ushering him back to rejoin the group. Mike pressed another button, and the robot began to rise again, back to its original height.

"What's powering it?" Spider asked, stepping forward for a closer look.

Mike shook his head, "I'm afraid that's one of those questions I can't answer Spider."

Spider nodded, "Fair enough, but do you know how long it'll run for? can you at least tell us if it needs refuelling, recharging or what?"

Mike smiled, looking back at him. "It'll run for the next five days, which should be more than enough for what we want it for."

Rachel pointed over to the other similar sized box, "Guessing that's where the second one is, you did say we have two of these things, is that correct?"

"That's right, they're better off working as a pair, allows them to pinpoint more accurately where the enemy are," Mike replied.

She continued pointing to the third smaller box, "Okay, so we know what's in box number two, but what's in box number three?"

He saw everyone's heads turn in unison, looking to where she pointed. He knelt and opened the lid as he spoke.

"You'll notice on all your vehicles I've placed a box similar to this one on the back decks. These are the docking stations for your Wasps. Inside the box you'll find one of these ready to go. Mike looked over to Changa again, motioning him to give him a hand. Between them both they lifted out the heavy drone and placed it onto the grass, hearing the murmurs of surprise again as everyone moved forward to get a better look.

On the grass in front of them sat a large drone, similar to the ones you could buy for home use, except this one measured three feet across and four feet in length. At each end sat a motor housing, with the same rimless motor design that they'd seen earlier on the Thumprs. At the front of the drone sat a triangular head, fitted with optics and sensors, resembling a wasp's head, which was how the drone had found its name. The Wasp's body was wide and at its centre sat a large cargo pod area.

Mike knelt down, pointing with his finger as he explained.

"So, this is W.A.S.P, standing for Weapons Augmented Surveillance Platform, it'll give us eyes in the sky and the ability to check ahead into any dead ground. Mike switched it on and everyone watched as the head began to shake and gyrate as it came to life. Mike picked up another control tablet, showing the group the display, which revealed a clear picture of the ground. He quickly tapped away on the screen, a few clicks and beeps later and the drone came to life, the motors softly whirring as it raised off the ground, hovering five feet above the ground. The sound was no louder than a small handheld fan.

"How come it's so quiet?" Manny, the other Engineer Sapper asked in amazement, before continuing, "I've got a drone at home that I fly, it's way louder than that."

"It's all to do with the rimless motors Manny," Mike explained, remembering quickly the soldier's name as he added. "Usually, drones have rotors that beat through the air, which is how you hear them, but all our air platforms use these new rimless motors, designed by one of Aurora's engineers, as you can hear, they're whisper quiet and allow both the Wasp and Thumpr to fly undetected."

"Rimless motors?" Manny asked curiously.

Mike shook his head slowly, "Sorry, but I can't go into too much detail, just know that they're designed in house with our company. It's classified for now; just know they work."

Changing the subject quickly, Mike manoeuvred the drone to face the group, indicating them the tablet display as he talked.

"It's got two camera systems, a day camera with a x16 digital zoom, allowing us to see out to three kilometres and a thermal camera, for use at night or during the day."

Mike switched between the two systems showing everyone what he was explaining.

"Now Wasp also has a sting in the tail." he knelt down and reached into the box, detaching something from within and stood up holding the object for everyone to see. It was about the size and shape of a small milk bottle.

"This is a 60mm high explosive grenade that's been modified with a small rocket booster in the tail. It's designed to freefall from above with the charge in the tail igniting when the grenade is five metres above its target, it gives the round a little bit more oomph."

"Fucking hell!" Patty muttered.

He passed the grenade around for everyone to see as he continued, reciting the words he'd used before from memory, when briefing visiting guests, as if he was at an Aurora sales conference.

"Each Wasp carries six high explosive and six fragmentation rounds inside its cargo bay, giving the user a good option depending on the target. Fragmentation works best against troops and the high explosive is best against soft skinned vehicles or lightly armoured targets. Now the High explosive can work against heavy armoured targets, but, you've got to get the grenade in the right place. If you see an open hatch on the vehicle or you see ammunition or external fuel tanks stored on the back decks, then go for that, chances are it'll set off a fire which will destroy it. If you bounce it off the armour, all you're going to do is scratch their paintwork."

Rachel was the last person to finish examining the grenade, Mike nodded in thanks as she carefully handed it back as he continued.

"The Wasp has been designed for a top-down attack over a target, you hover over the target, select your payload and press the button. However, doing so can make it vulnerable to incoming fire, therefore it can also conduct a fast attack run, coming in quickly and dropping its ordinance. However it's not as accurate, and our company was still trying to get the software bugs ironed out when I left. I doubt in the time we've had, they've managed to do so, therefore if you use this type of attack, be aware of its limitations."

He saw the nods as he talked, at least they were listening, he mused.

He gently ushered them aside, away from the drone, giving it room to manoeuvre as he tapped the screen. Open mouthed they watched on as the drone slowly and gracefully flew over to the box, lining up perfectly before slowly settling itself down into the docking station.

"I've already mentioned the docking stations fitted to your vehicles, they're armoured up to 7.62mm. Anything bigger that hits it and you can expect it to take some damage. The docking stations are hard wired into your vehicles power supplies and comms equipment, I'll explain how another time, but so long as your engines are running, you're charging the drones. When you launch them, they'll have enough power to remain airborne for three hours, then they'll need to land back at your vehicle and charge up. Charge time takes two hours. So, two hours of charge gives you three hours of flight time, provided your engines are running. If your engines are off, then the Wasp won't charge. Regards the comms range, the docking station uses your own vehicles antennae to send and receive its data. With good line of sight, you should get a decent range of between five and eight miles. If the Wasp loses its signal it's programmed to fly back to where it recorded your last position. So, if you do lose the Wasp and if it's tactically viable, remain where you are and it should come back to you."

Mike waited for the information to sink in as he continued. "Regards docking, when your Wasp is taking off or landing, your vehicle has to be stopped. Any movement to the vehicle and the Wasp will abort what it's doing. If it's taking off it'll stay in the docking station until you stop, if it's trying to land, it'll abort and follow you until you stop. It's important that as vehicle commanders you understand that."

Mike looked around the group, keen to impress how essential the instructions were as they nodded back in response.

"You can see that each Wasp has two control tablets, one is the control tablet, for the operator to use and the other is called the BMDS or Battlefield Management Display System for the vehicle commander. The control tablet is the only thing that can fly and fire the drones, the BMDS is there just to observe. I've already put a BMDS into all of your vehicle turrets, they've got magnetic strips on the back, so when we've finished I recommend all commanders go and check their happy with where I've placed them, if not move them to where you want. Now each BMDS comes with mapping loaded onto it, you can see the location of where both the Wasp and the Talon's are operating from, and what they're seeing, but you can't control them. That's why each Warrior will have a drone operator sat in the back with comms to the commander."

Mike turned to the three Engineers and Rachel. "This is where you four now come in. After we've finished here, I want you to stay behind and I'll run through in detail how to use the Wasp's systems, how to fly them, control them and fire them. Rachel, you'll be in command of the two talons, and you three will be flying the remaining Wasps. The fourth Wasp, I'll fly myself from the tank."

"Mike," Rachel began, quickly remembering his newly acquired rank. "Sorry, *Sir*, I'm not a drone pilot, I can't use this! I'm an intelligence analyst." Rachel argued pointing towards the Talon. Fletch, the Engineer Corporal quickly added, "Sir, she's right, my men and me, we're not qualified to just start dropping bombs on people. What if we fuck this up? What if we accidentally drop on our own people? What you're asking us to do, I'm not happy with."

Mike held up a hand to stop them all. "I understand your doubts guys, but you need to be aware these systems were designed for just this role, to be dropped in on units that need them with no training." Mike looked around the group, keen to emphasise, "We've made sure that even at the lowest level *anyone* should be able to operate them. Remember the phrase fool proof? And that's no disrespect aimed at anyone here."

Mike could see the four of them looking doubtful as to emphasise he continued, addressing them all.

"Look every person on these vehicles will be busy, they've all got a role to do, the only people that are spare, without a role will be you four. I've just changed that. Now you're going to be our eyes in the sky and on the ground. I know you don't like it, but tough, that's how it's got to be."

He showed the control panel to the Engineers, the map displayed on it. "All you do is point and click on the map where you want the Wasp to fly to, it's that simple to begin with. You'll see it's location displayed on the map, and when you want it to fly back home, you tap this part of the screen. I promise you all, within twenty minutes you'll be Chuck Yaeger with these things."

Mike put his hand on the Corporal's shoulder as he stepped closer, "Look, we can't spare anyone else to operate these things, we need your help, I need your help. I know it's not the job you signed up for, but it's the job we need you to do." To emphasise further Mike added, "Remember what they did to you and your men? Surely you'd welcome the chance to pay back in kind how they treated you?"

Fletch's eyes darted across to the two Sappers who both silently nodded in response. Taking their cue, he stared back at Mike, more focussed than before.

"Ok Sir, tell us what you need us to do."

"Good," he looked over to Rachel, "And? Rachel, what's it to be? I promise it's not as hard as you think, give me ten minutes to run through the controls and you'll see for yourself."

She bit her bottom lip as she thought it through. "Look I'm not worried about crashing the damn thing. That's *live* ordnance. What if I accidentally fire it at one of us?"

Mike smiled as he saw Patty and Spider grimace at the thought. Pointing to them both playfully he said, "I said the system's been designed to be operated at the lowest level, so if it's been designed with these two in mind, then you shouldn't have any troubles."

Both feigned mock concern as she grimaced. "Okay, but don't say I didn't warn you."

Patty chuckled as Spider muttered loud enough for her to hear, "From now on, I'm driving with my hatches closed."

Rachel looked at him scornfully, as Mike continued, "Good, that's settled then. Right let's get the vehicle commanders away and then I'll run through how to operate these things in detail with the operators."

Spider turned to leave when Patty asked curiously, "Sir, what about this other thing you mentioned, this...Hornet? What does it do?"

"Ahh," replied Mike thoughtfully, "that's fitted to my vehicle, I'll be operating that if we need it."

"But what does it do?" Patty asked, keen to get an answer.

"Let's just say that's going to be our ace in the hole. If we need it, you'll see then what it does."

Realising Mike wasn't going to go into detail Patty nodded as Spider urged. "Come on mate, let's leave them to it." Then looking at Rachel he added jokingly, "some of them will need all the practise they can get."

She smiled and flicked him the finger in response, Spider nodding his head in thanks at the gesture.

Mike smiled. Good, he thought to himself, morale was higher than before and having the ability to fight back had lifted everyone's spirits. He waited for the others to leave before stepping closer to the four newly recruited drone operators.

"Right, everyone, let's get into the interesting stuff, dropping warheads onto fore-heads!"

An hour later and Mike was back in the commander's seat of the tank, in the dimly lit cupola looking at the satellite phone on his lap. His left leg was lazily hanging over the breech as he glanced over to the loader's station, finally seeing ammunition in the racks made him smile. He'd left the newly recruited drone pilots practising on their tablets, which had all come pre-loaded with a computerised training simulation, simulating what they would see when the drones were operating in combat and allowing them to make simulated attack runs on different targets. After a few trial runs, he felt confident they'd all manage to grasp what the drones could do, and although it wasn't perfect, it was enough.

He shook his head to stave off the tiredness that suddenly came over him, something about being in the warm interior of the tank had lulled him into a state of relaxation. He sat up suddenly, talking to himself as he did so, "Not yet Mike, still too much to do, stay with it for now."

He quickly reached down for the phone, dialling the number he'd been given, time to report in, he thought.

After only two rings it was answered, the gruff voice of Colonel Stephens cutting through.

"Go ahead Captain Faulkes."

Mike realised they'd have his phone number logged, at least when he rang in future, they'd know who it was, saving time on unnecessary security.

"Good morning Colonel, I was told to give you a call when we're ready."

"Good work Captain, I've been told to pass on the message that the prisoners you sent back made it here safely, good work with getting them back to us. Hopefully they should give us some good intel."

Mike was doubtful from what he'd seen of them but didn't want to dampen the Colonel's optimism.

"So, Colonel what's the plan? Do you have orders for us?"

"Have you heard what's going on to the north of you?"

"Yeovil's under attack?" Mike queried.

"That's correct Captain, elements of 146 Brigade, assisted by the towns local militia have been defending the town, they've been putting up a hell of a fight, they've fought the lead elements of a Russian BTG to a standstill on the towns outer edge, using not much more than roadblocks and petrol bombs. They're holding for now, but without any support we think the Russians will break through sometime today. Intelligence is reporting the Russians are redeploying more units up there for further attacks. We think those units include the artillery unit located near to you. Command wants the town to remain in our hands. As long as the Russians are concentrating on fighting there, it's delaying the southern push towards London, and that's buying us critical time. This is where you and your new unit will come in. Your mission, Captain, is to break out and fight through the Russian rearguard positions, head west until you're on the 356 Easting then head north, attempt to break through the enemy front lines and link up with 146 Brigade in Yeovil." Mike looked at the map, quickly identifying the line marking the 356 Easting, about 8 km west of where they were now. He listened in as the Colonel continued,

"Your tasks are to destroy any artillery, air defence, command and control and logistical support units that you come across. But you are to avoid where possible, any direct confrontation with enemy armour. We don't want to lose you early on fighting it out with their armour."

Easier said than done Colonel, Mike thought to himself, writing down the orders as the Colonel continued.

"Once you link up with 146 Brigade in the town, you're to place yourself under the command of a Colonel Young and assist in the defence of the town by any means possible."

"Okay, and when have you set H-Hour, when do you want us to go?"

"H-Hour is set for 07:00 this morning."

Mike checked his watch, it was 02:15 that gave him almost five hours from now.

"You want us to try this in the daytime? Not at night?" Mike replied, "Without air support we'll be pretty vulnerable from the air."

"I've been informed that the enemy are suffering from logistical problems, resulting in limited air power in your area for the moment, plus the bulk of their air force seem to be directing their attacks on Southampton. You should be fine for the next twelve hours at least." the Colonel's words didn't exactly fill Mike with confidence. Thinking of the training ammunition they'd been given, Mike replied.

"This all sounds a bit rushed and thrown together last-minute Colonel, we're not a battlegroup, we're just three Warrior's and one tank. I'm not sure what support we can offer the town even if we do manage to make it through. And why do you want us to push out to the west first? Surely it makes sense to head north immediately. Why go to the trouble and risk of us going out to the 356 Easting?

"What did you expect Captain? A full set of orders and a battlegroup stood ready to help you?" The Colonel's voice barked back angrily. "Of course, it's all bloody been thrown together last minute!" Mike looked at the phone, surprised by the Colonel's sudden outburst, wondering what had caused him to get angry. After a few moments of silence, the Colonel came back on his voice placating, "Look Captain, you must understand, that at the moment the situation on the ground for all our forces is looking grave. The troops in Yeovil are made up of reservists and civilian volunteers with no heavy weapons or armour. You're the only unit we know in that area that has both eyes on the enemy and comms with us. That's the reason we want you to push west, we believe the enemy have several logistical units not far from you, you're ideally placed to strike them, thus hampering the attack on the town. If you can find them, destroy them, and manage to get to Yeovil, well then, it might just buy them half a chance.

"Okay," Mike said flatly as the Colonel asked.

"The artillery unit you reported on earlier, is there any change to its location?"

"No change, they just finished partying about twenty minutes ago, it's all quiet now, but if we're leaving at 07:00 they'll see us leaving and report it up. We'll have to think about what to do with them before we go, I'd like to recommend-"

"Leave that to us Captain, we're organising some support to join you." Colonel Stephens interrupted, "just confirm again the eight-figure grid of their location."

Mike read back the numbers he'd jotted down earlier in his notepad, the military maps he'd received had a grid system printing on them to allow the user to give accurate positions of enemy and friendly units, similar to the latitude and longitude that civilian maps used, except these were called Northings and Eastings. By giving the eight-figure grid to the Colonel, he could now plot on his map in the ops room exactly where the artillery were located.

After a few seconds the Colonel added, "The HF radio, did you get it?"

Mike looked over to the radio as he replied, "All fitted now, do you want us to give Ops a radio check after our phone call?"

"No, stay off it for now, it's not for you to chat to us, I want you to turn it on and monitor it from 06:50, you're to listen out for a callsign called Gunslinger Two-Three. They'll contact you when they're ready. Did you get the callsign matrix?"

"Gunslinger Two-Three?" Mike queried, the Colonel replying almost immediately, pre-empting the question.

"I can't say too much now Captain, but when you chat to them, you'll understand. Now the callsign matrix, have you got it?"

Mike looked down to the paper folded in his notepad. On it was written the callsigns of the units in Yeovil that he'd be working with, provided that was if he made it that far. He'd already noted his own units callsign on the HF radio would now be known as Whiskey Three-Zero.

"I've got it Colonel." he confirmed.

"Ok, right then, I guess that's it, once we've finished, I want you on radio silence until H-Hour. Any change to that artillery position, you're to let us know immediately on the phone, stay *off* the radio until 06:50. Be ready to move for 07:00. Any questions Captain?"

"No, I guess that's it." Mike replied. His head was full of questions, but he knew after the Colonel's outburst he'd not get the answers. The Colonel was probably in the dark as much as he was, Mike was on his own and if he wanted answers, he'd have to come up with them himself.

"In that case Captain I'll leave you to it. Good luck."

"Thank you, Colonel," was all Mike was able to say as the line abruptly cut, leaving him in silence as he sat there reading the notes and looking at the map. After a few minutes he stifled a yawn then realised time was wasting. There were still lots to do, he had to plan their next move, and then the crews would need to be briefed. Firming his jaw and fighting the desire to sleep he climbed out of the tank; it was almost time...

Operations Room Three, Southwest Division, Wonderland Operations Centre (WOC)

Over eighty miles away, in one of the smaller offices two floors below the WOC, Colonel Stephens placed the satellite phone back on the desk, looking up at the maps of Dorset that had been taped to the wall. The office had been turned into a smaller ops room, one of five, each with their own area of responsibility in the UK to look after and report on, feeding the larger operations centre above them. Around him a team of fifteen people all worked tirelessly, collating reports, answering radio calls and constantly updating the maps and white boards around them. It was a far cry from the larger more sophisticated room above them, and although basic, it was working well, with information being fed up to the CDS as, and when, required. On the map, different coloured markers denoted different units, friendlies in blue, hostiles in red. Gloomily, he noted the map was mostly covered in red. In amongst the red markers though sat one blue marker, Whiskey Three-Zero. He stared at it as the Major next to him piped up, reading from a piece of paper. "Army Air Corps say they can only spare us two airframes. What do you think John? Should we go with it and send them in?"

Snapping him from his thoughts at the use of his first name the Colonel's head whipped round, ready to chastise the Major, quickly stopping himself, as he realised it was his long-time friend who was addressing him, rank be dammed, he thought. The tiredness and stress were beginning to take its toll on all of them. The look of anger softened as he nodded slowly as he spoke, "Yes, send them in. Two's better than none. At least we can try to give those poor bastards half a chance."

"Half a chance is better than no chance." the Major replied.

"Yes," the Colonel replied slowly before adding, "Shame to just throw them away though after making it this far."

The CDS had come down to visit the ops room early that evening to brief them both on the plan and what he wanted from Whiskey Three-Zero. It was to be part of the biggest diversion that they could muster; He had other plans, one's he wasn't yet willing to divulge with the Colonel, but that meant he needed the enemy to think that Whiskey Three-Zero was a far larger unit, punching through as a counterattack, threatening the very logistical units that the Colonel had just told Mike to locate and attack. Already the LEWT team upstairs in the WOC were creating fake radio messages to play out over the radio, along with the electronic clutter associated with them. By the time they'd finished, come the morning, the enemy would think an entire Brigade was on the move. But that was also why the Colonel had been angry, he'd just lied to Whiskey Three-Zero's commander, there was no plan for them to get to Yeovil, there never was. Mike and his unit had just become sacrificial pawns, and now the Colonel had helped to cement that. Privately he hoped that somehow, they could make it, but professionally, he knew the likelihood of the small unit making it home were probably in single digits percentage wise. Something about sentencing the unit to be destroyed had rankled him, going against his honour, but then, after all, it was for the greater good, or at least that's how the CDS had sold it to him. That's the reason Captain Faulkes had been sent the training rounds, why waste valuable ammunition on a unit not expected to last more than an hour?

He rubbed his nose and eyes, massaging them as the wave of tiredness and exhaustion crept up on him, shaking his head irritably. There was still so much to do, so much to organise, and sleep would have to wait. He stood up, walking out of the room, now it was time for coffee.

Cerne Abbas

Two hours later and Mike was with his team in the briefing area, the red eyed faces and stifled yawns staring back, showing him they'd only just woken up. He'd spent the first hour after the phone call pouring over the mapping in the back of one of the Warriors, trying to come up with a plan, hastily scribbling down notes or marking points on the map. Normally he'd have an idea of what they were facing, but as things were, the best he could do was make an educated guess. At least they didn't have to worry about the dark anymore as the sun had already started to climb over the hills to the east. He had two of the police officers silently standing there holding the map for the others to see as he began to brief them.

With all eyes on him, he began his briefing, his face set like stone and his voice low and confident. "Right, everyone, the moment we've all been waiting for, it happens today..."

To be continued...

Acknowledgments and Authors notes

At the risk of sounding like a broken record, the people I'd like to thank for helping me with '48' are the very same people that helped me with '24'. Therefore again I'd like to convey my heartfelt thanks to Paddy, Victoria, Natalie, and Tim, for helping me to spot the typo's and for reading the draft for the book and giving me their honest feedback. But the biggest thank you I reserve for my wife Emily, whose help and guidance helped me craft the way these series of books have panned out. Speaking of writing the books, when I wrote them, I knew that I had written too much for one book, and originally had the story as two books. However the more I tried to stop writing and to end the story, the more I wanted to write, to tell more of the story, until eventually I found that instead of two, there were now three books. The problem I now faced was how to end book two. I could have continued telling you how Mike and the unit progress from the woods, but then to do that would meant starting a key part of the story that I would have to suddenly slam shut as the pages ran out. Likewise I didn't want to rush the story along for the sake of finishing book two, which is why I hope that you, the reader, can forgive me for the way in which the book did end. Hopefully you've enjoyed the story so far, again some of it based on real life experiences from my past. For instance the part where Peter pretends to call in an air strike using the grenade launcher, was a trick that I and my small unit had used before. Whilst on operations we found ourselves woefully outnumbered, attempting to withdraw one of our small outposts from an angry village. The villagers were all armed and outnumbered us ten to one, deciding their options were better suited allied with the enemy forces than with the British Army. Thankfully, as with Peter in the story, a few well-placed 40mm grenades into some empty fields and the threat of the airstrike and the villagers saw the error of their ways, allowing us to peacefully leave, thus avoiding further bloodshed.

The attack by the Russians on Yeovil being thwarted by Fergus and the lines of clothing was again based on real life events from my past. When serving overseas we would

435

conduct strike operations into some of the towns and villages on the tanks, suicidal in anything other than an armoured vehicle. We would find much to the annoyance of the locals that when the tanks drove through the lines of washed clothes hung across the streets, they would snag and catch on the sights, forcing the crew to stop, rendering the vehicle immobile as the crews fought to clear the clothing away. You can guess what would happen next, crews, unlike tanks are not bullet proof, and many a commander would have a very lucky escape as someone took a shot at them. Thankfully most of the time they were poor shots...most of the time. Likewise in Poland, when training on the older Soviet tank training areas, long lines of wire, left strewn around the huge area would snag and catch in the tank's tracks and sprockets, wrapping itself up tightly into a huge ball of mess which would eventually jam and clog the sprocket, stopping the tank dead in its tracks. I remember once as a driver spending four painstaking, sweaty, muddy hours cutting the deadly wire out of the tracks using wire cutters. Think about that, a main battle tank, costing three-million pounds, disabled for four hours by a piece of wire that cost a few pence! Tanks are master of the battlefield, well I would say that, but they do have their weaknesses, something that I was only too happy for Fergus to exploit in the book.

So readers, hopefully by now you can understand that what you're reading in a way is not only fiction, but a very tiny piece of my military past thrown in for good measure. But as I've alluded to in the past, the characters you're reading about are not based on any one individual that I know, more perhaps a *collection* of people, their best and worst qualities amalgamated into each character. Hopefully you've enjoyed reading the book, and want to know how it all ends, in which case the third and final book will be available soon to purchase. And if you'd like to tell others how much you've enjoyed reading my books then could I ask please that you use Amazon, or Goodreads. I'm an Indie author, with no huge budget for advertising, relying instead on the stories quality and word of mouth to help promote my books, so any help you could give would be greatly appreciated.

In the meantime, "I'll see you when I see you next..."

Glossary

5.56mm – Standard NATO round – What all NATO assault rifles fire, standardised in size to make logistics easy

7.62mm – Standard Russian Round – Larger than the NATO calibre, able to cause more damage

ADJ – Adjutant – usually a Captain and in charge of a units administration

AGC – Adjutants Generals Corp

AK-12 – Russian Assault Rifle

AN124 – Antonov 124 Russian heavy lift cargo plane

ANPR – Automatic Number Plate Recognition

APFSDS - Armoured Piercing Fin Stabilised Discarding Sabot - Tank main gun Armoured Piercing (**AP**) round. Has an outer casing that breaks away allowing the round to fly at extremely high speed, hitting the target with immense power, equivalent to an Elephant hitting at 200mph.

APU – Auxiliary Power unit

ASACS – Air Surveillance and Control System

ASRAAM – Advanced Short-Range Air to Air Missile

ATC – Air Traffic Control

ATGM – Anti Tank Guided Missile

ATDU – Armoured Trials and Development Unit

Bingo – Codeword used by pilots to describe an aircraft low on fuel

BMP-3 – Russian Armoured Infantry Vehicle – Used to transport troops into combat zones under fire

BV – Boiling Vessel – Square shaped large kettle used on armoured vehicles to heat water and rations

BVRAAM – Beyond Visual Range Air to Air Missile

CAS – Chief of Air Staff – Head of the Royal Air Force

CDI – Chief of Defence Intelligence – Head of UK intelligence agencies

CDS – Chief of the Defence Staff – Head of all Military forces

CGS – Chief of the General Staff – Head of the Army

CNS/1SL – Chief of the Naval Staff/ First Sea Lord - Head of the Royal Navy

Chally 2 – Nickname that crews use to describe the Challenger 2 Tank

CO – Commanding Officer

COBR(A) – Cabinet Office Briefing Room (A) – Emergency response meeting usually chaired by the PM and other senior figures of government

CPO – Close Protection Officer

CPS – Commanders Primary Sight – What the Commander uses to sight and fire the tanks weapons. Also has its own laser to acquire the range to target for the Fire Control Computer

CRARRV – Challenger Armoured Repair and Recovery Vehicle – Used by the REME to assist broken and bogged vehicles

DASS – Defensive Aids Sub System – also called **Praetorian**- provides threat assessments, aircraft protection and support measures to the Typhoon

DST - Discarding Sabot Trainer - Tank main gun training round, smaller and cheaper than the APFSDS

DTT – Driver Training Tank – Turretless Tank used to train new drivers

DZ – Drop Zone

ETA – Estimated Time of Arrival

EW – Electronic Warfare

EWO – Electronic Warfare Officer

F-35 Lightning – RAF's next generation multirole fighter plane

FCC – Fire Control Computer – Calculates the computations required to help the crew to aim the gun

FSB – Russian Federal Security Services

GCE – Gun Control Equipment

GCHQ – Government Communication Headquarters

Glock-17 – Standard British forces 9mm semi-automatic pistol

Gold Commander – Police designation for the overall commander of a situation or emergency at the scene

GPS – Gunners Primary Sight – What the Gunner on a Chally 2 uses to sight and fire the tanks weapons. Also has a laser to acquire the range to target for the Fire Control Computer

GSM – Garrison Sergeant Major

GUE - Generator Unit Engine - small auxiliary engine that is used to power the tank systems when stationary, saving the main engine from being on all the time.

HESH- High Explosive Squash Head - Tank main gun Chemical Energy (**CE**) round. Heavier than the AP round, flies at slower speeds and consists of a high explosive that squashes against the target, exploding upon impact. Resulting shock wave breaks off a 'scab' of armour similar to the size of the round inside the target, ricocheting at speeds of 800 mph.

HF – High Frequency

IFR – Instrument Flight Rules

IL-80 – Iiyushin Il-80 'Maxdome' – Russian Airborne Command Centre, similar to the USAF 'Airforce-One'

Javelin – Portable Anti-Tank Guided Missile System, used by most NATO countries

JNCO – Junior Non-Commissioned Officer

Kaliber 3m-54 – Russian cruise missile – can be launched by sea air and land

Kamaz K-4386 Typhoon – Russian oversized armoured 4x4, air portable with a rapid firing 30mm cannon

Kinzhal – (KH-47M2 Khinzal) Russian hypersonic air launched ballistic missile. Nato designation is 'Killjoy'

L-7 GPMG – General Purpose Machine Gun – Belt fed, rapid firing machine gun

L-22 Carbine – Short barrelled variant of the SA-80-A2 assault rifle issued to armoured crews

L-94 Coax – Coaxially mounted Machine Gun, located next to the Main gun

LIDAR – Light Detection and Ranging – A method of determining ranges and objects using a series of lasers

MBT – Main Battle Tank

MIG-31 – Russian Fighter Bomber

MoD – Ministry of Defence

MP443 Grach – Standard Russian forces 9mm semi-automatic pistol

NATO – North Atlantic Treaty Organisation

NATS – National Air Traffic Services

OC – Officer Commanding

PIRATE – Passive Infra-Red Airborne Track Equipment – allows long range visual identification of a target using cameras, sensors and computer

PSTN – Public Switched Telephone Network – Copper telephone landlines

PM – Prime Minister

QM – Quartermasters Department – Where kit and equipment for vehicles and troops are stored and distributed

QRF – Quick Reaction Force

QRA – Quick Reaction Alert

R-37 Vympel – Russian long range hypersonic air-to-air missile

RAC – Royal Armoured Corp

RAF – Royal Air Force

REME – Royal Electrical and Mechanical Engineers

RMP – Royal Military Police

RSM – Regimental Sergeant Major

RUPERT – Nickname given to officers by junior ranks

RWS – Remote Weapons Station – fitted to tanks that are classed as TES

SA-80-A2 – Standard British Army Assault Rifle

SBS – Special Boat Service

SH(P) - Squash Head Practice - Tank main gun training round, similar to the HESH round but filled with concrete instead of high explosive.

SNCO – Senior Non-Commissioned Officer

Sprut 2S25 – Russian air portable light tank, able to field a 125mm gun

SSM – Squadron Sergeant Major

SU-57 – Russian next gen multirole fighter plane

T-80 – Russian Main Battle Tank

TALON - Tracked Anti-armour Listening and Observation Node - Experimental tracked autonomous weapons platform that had been designed by Aurora Defence Systems. Has cutting edge fusion reactor and uses acoustic and visual sensors to locate, assess and if necessary attack the enemy.

TES – Theatre Entry Specific – designation given to the Challenger 2 'Megatron' that has been heavily modified with add on armour, RWS and forward/rearwards facing cameras and other upgrades

TU-54 Bear – Russian Cold War era turboprop bomber

Typhoon – RAF multi role fighter jet – also known as Eurofighter

UHF – Ultra High Frequency

UN – United Nations

VDV – Vozdushno-Desantnye Voyska – Russian Airborne Forces

VT - Vent Tube - Small brass casing filled with propellant, electrically fired and causes the initial explosion in the tanks main gun to fire the main charge.

VHF – Very High Frequency

VID – Visual Identification

VOIP – Voice Over Internet Protocol – A phone line that is digital and relies on the internet instead of a landline

WASP - Weapons Augmented Surveillance Platform - Experimental flying drone designed by Aurora Defence systems. Allows for airborne surveillance of the battlefield and carries a payload of twelve 40mm modified grenades consisting of six high explosive and six fragmentation.

Wildcat – Upgraded version of the Lynx, fast, lightly armed, multirole helicopter used by the British Army and Royal Navy

Winchester – Codeword used by pilots to describe an aircraft out of ammunition

WO2 – Warrant Officer Class 2 – Sergeant Major rank or equivalent

WO1 – Warrant officer Class 1 – RSM or GSM rank or equivalent

WOC – Wonderland Operations Centre

Rank Structures of the UK Armed Forces

Rank structure of the British Army

Other Ranks

Warrant Officer Class 1/
Regimental Sergeant Major/
Garrison Sergeant Major

|

Warrant Officer Class 2/
Sergeant Major/
Squadron Sergeant Major

|

Staff Sergeant/Colour Sergeant

|

Sergeant/Corporal of Horse

|

Corporal/Bombardier/
Lance Sergeant

|

Lance Corporal/Lance Bombardier

|

Private/Trooper/Fusilier/Rifleman/
Sapper/Guardsman/Gunner/
Craftsman/Signalman

Officers

Field Marshal

|

General

|

Lieutenant General

|

Major General

|

Brigadier

|

Colonel

|

Lieutenant Colonel

|

Major

|

Captain

|

Lieutenant

|

Second Lieutenant

Rank structure of the Royal Air Force

Other Ranks	Non-Commissioned Aircew	Officers
Warrant Officer	RAF Master Aircrew	Marshal Of The Royal Air Force
Flight Sergeant	RAF Flight Sergeant Aircrew	Air Chief Marshal
Chief Technician	RAF Sergeant Aircrew	Air Marshal
Sergeant		Air Vice-Marshal
Corporal		Air Commodore
Lance Corporal RAF Regiment		Group Captain
Air Specialist Class 1 Technician		Wing Commander
Air Specialist Class 1		Squadron Leader
Air Specialist Class 2		Flight Lieutenant
		Flying Officer
		Pilot Officer

Rank structure of the Royal Navy

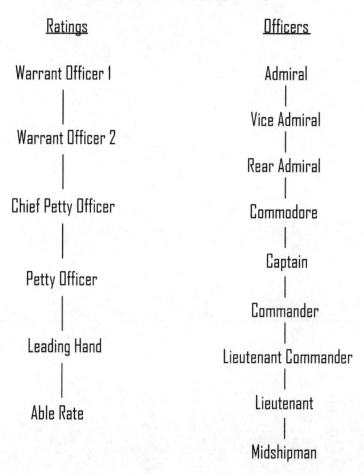

Ratings

Warrant Officer 1

Warrant Officer 2

Chief Petty Officer

Petty Officer

Leading Hand

Able Rate

Officers

Admiral

Vice Admiral

Rear Admiral

Commodore

Captain

Commander

Lieutenant Commander

Lieutenant

Midshipman